William Duguid Geddes

The Problem of the Homeric Poems

William Duguid Geddes

The Problem of the Homeric Poems

ISBN/EAN: 9783337397821

Printed in Europe, USA, Canada, Australia, Japan

Cover: Foto ©Andreas Hilbeck / pixelio.de

More available books at **www.hansebooks.com**

THE
PROBLEM

OF THE

HOMERIC POEMS

BY

WILLIAM D. GEDDES, LL.D.

PROFESSOR OF GREEK IN THE UNIVERSITY OF ABERDEEN

London

MACMILLAN AND CO.

1878

PREFACE.

THE following book contains the results of an extensive investigation into the two great Homeric poems, the object being to determine, if possible, from the internal evidence alone, their mutual relation and connection. How far I may have succeeded in throwing light on the Homeric question, or in solving the problem in all its parts and intricacies, others must determine; but I may claim the credit of having faced the question fairly, and of having contributed materials that may be instrumental towards its ultimate decision.

In such a question, concerning poems of so high antiquity and such remoteness, if not mysteriousness, of origin, the solution must always remain hypothetical[1], but the hypothesis that fits the great facts and explains the largest number of phenomena is the one that possesses the best title to acceptance. The phenomena to which I appeal, many of them now for the first time disclosed, throw considerable light on the question, and whatever may be the fate of my hypothesis, the facts on which it is

---

[1] 'Die Lösung der Homerischen Frage kann immer nur eine hypothetische seyn. Diejenige Hypothese kommt aber der Wahrheit am nächsten, die die meisten Schwierigkeiten beseitigt und die wenigsten Bedenken gegen sich hat.' L. Friedländer, Homerische Kritik, p. 71.

founded will require account to be taken of them in any subsequent criticism of the Homeric Question.

As the result of the investigation, I have been led, by the pure force of the evidence, and not at all in accordance with my own early prepossessions, to accept Mr. Grote's view regarding the composite structure of the Iliad as the only one scientifically tenable. That there is a double authorship in that poem, an Achilleid within the Iliad, forming its kernel, and by a different author from that of the surrounding *integumenta*, I believe the facts not only indicate but demonstrate, and I may claim to have brought out new confirmations of the soundness of Mr. Grote's views and of the acuteness of his critical divination [2].

In pursuing the subject beyond the initial stage at which it was left by Mr. Grote, I have found a close connection to subsist between the Odyssey and the non-Achillean books of the Iliad, and a remarkable convergence of the evidence to associate both of these with the one personal Homer of tradition.

If I have succeeded in my proof, the result is not only that a Homer is revealed to us with his personal surroundings more clearly traced out than has till now

[2] Dr. J. W. Donaldson, in his notes to K. O. Müller's 'History of Greek Literature,' claims the duplex-structure-theory as being properly and originally that of Karl O. Müller, and gives his own adhesion to 'Mr. Grote's modification of the views of Müller' in the following words :—'Müller's distinction between the two parts of the Iliad, namely, an original part referring mainly to Achilles and a superinduced part embracing the exploits of the other heroes and the general conduct of the war, has been enforced and extended by Mr. Grote, in his *History of Greece*, vol. ii. ch. xxi. He has shown that the Iliad was originally an *Achilleis*, built on a narrower plan, and then enlarged; that from the second book to the seventh Achilles is scarcely alluded to; that the Greeks not only do not miss his absence but that Diomedes is exalted to a pitch of glory, in his contests with the gods, which Achilles never obtains, and is even placed above Achilles by the Trojan Helenus; consequently that the primitive *Achilleis* included only Books I. VIII, XI–XXII.'

been possible, but that glimpses are obtained into an earlier period of Poetry, and we can see beyond Homer into a Prehomeric age.

Considerable light has been found to be thrown on critical questions as to disputed readings in the Homeric text. These investigations, however, belong rather to the department of *linguistica*, and will fall to be treated afterwards in a separate work as to the language of the Homeric poems. A considerable amount of confirmatory evidence pointing to the same conclusion is obtainable from this source, such as the remarkable distribution of the Æolic διαπρύσιον, found only in the older area, the Achilleid, and there *seven* times; but the bulk of the notable phenomena under this department must be in the meantime reserved.

The argument, as developed, is of course a cumulative argument. Its force depends not on one or two or several coincidences, which might be set aside as accidents, but upon the united force and weight of those that are far reaching, comprehensive, and decisive. Those that seem to me to carry most weight, and to deserve most attention, are the following :—

1. The dual representation of Ulysses.
2. The dual representation of Hector.
3. The dual representation of Helen.
4. The difference as to hieratic Epithets [3].
5. The contrast as to ' Boasting over the Dead.'
6. The contrast as to Olympus.
7. The contrast as to local mint-marks.

[3] Some of my conclusions, particularly on this head, as acknowledged on p. 148, had been already reached on independent investigation by Mr. Fleay. The basis on which he proceeded was an examination of the treatment of certain epithets such as λευκώλενος, 'Αργυρότοξος, and, though the basis was narrow, his conclusion appears to have been practically on the same lines.

8. The presence of the Ionian local mint-marks
   in one continuous series throughout the non-
   Achillean books, and their limitation to that
   area of the Iliad.

9. The consonance of Ethical purpose discernible
   in the Odyssey, discernible also as a leading
   element in the structure of the non-Achillean
   books of the Iliad.

In some of the statistical enumerations, it is possible
that there may not in every instance be absolute
accuracy of summation, owing perhaps to various
readings or some clerical error on my part of omission
or otherwise. Of such inaccuracies, however, I do not
think the number is large, and although another inves-
tigator might produce some variation in the numerical
detail, I do not believe that, proceeding on the same
general lines, he could produce any alteration in the
general result. The evidence is drawn from too many
and varied sources, and the convergence of proof
advances upon too many lines to admit of any material departure from the belief that a harmonising
theory which promises to explain the most important
facts has been attained.

In making this statement, I by no means wish to
affirm that the proof is always equally strong or even
always, apart from concurring circumstances, sufficient
for a positive verdict. Moreover, if criticism should
hereafter succeed in proving *K* or Book Ten of the
Iliad to be from a later author, and not truly Homeric,
as George Curtius, on philological grounds, seems
inclined to pronounce it, the argument would not
suffer in its main lines, even after such an amputation

of K from the *corpus* of the Iliad, although it might lose some important illustrations.

To prevent misunderstanding, it may be proper to observe that I have used the word Canto or Book to denote such and such sections of the Iliad, merely for convenience. No implication is thereby intended that the poet or poets composed in cantos or mapped out his or their work into sections, much less numerical sections. On the contrary, he or they simply composed poetic narratives more or less extensive of continuous sequence, and the arrangement into Books or Cantos was altogether an affair of the literary and critical time. At the same time the poet or poets have left occasional traces of resting-places or pauses which are adopted by the Grammarians as natural signs of division and mark off the separate Cantos[4].

I have not thought it necessary to enter on an examination of the *Homerica Minora*, such as the Hymns and the sporadic fragments. These lie outside the proper domain of the Homeric question, for it is in an examination of the two Epics themselves that the secret of their origin must be found, if it is found at all.

Among many *subsidia* that I have found useful, I wish to particularise the very valuable Concordance to the Iliad by Mr. Prendergast, a work which, along with old Seber's 'Index Homericus,' has proved of much service in verifying rapidly and surely the various statistical enumerations. It is gratifying to think that, under the liberality of the Clarendon Press,

---

[4] The opening lines of many Books frequently contain a retrospective 'Thus,' and so indicate *continuation* and the resumption of a former thread of narration. Compare the openings of Iliad H, I, M, Π, Σ, Υ, X, Ψ, and in Odyssey, ζ, η, ν.

we may look forward to possessing a similar Concordance to the Odyssey and the Minora, on the same sumptuous scale, by Dr. Henry Dunbar, who has undertaken the laborious but most meritorious task.

Regarding the orthography of Greek proper names, I have not thought it incumbent on me to follow the modern fashion of attempting what by the way it is impossible to effect completely, entire Hellenising of them. I have done so only where historical and scientific accuracy requires it, as, e. g. in Mythological names, where the attributes and associations of Greek Gods might be obscured or inadequately represented by giving them under Roman appellations. In some cases, such as *Zeus* and *Jove*, where the words and ideas are fundamentally the same, this is quite legitimate, as it is certainly often convenient to use *Jove* for *Zeus*; but in the case of such as *Here* compared with *Juno* and of *Athene* compared with *Minerva*, where the names are etymologically distinct, it is better to maintain a distinction. There is also an advantage in retaining the Greek ending in what are Greek Geographical names, such as Samos, unless, like Cyprus, the word has been in its Latin form already naturalised. But as to deserting old familiar names like Ajax or Ulysses to substitute Aias and Odusseus, it appears to me that nothing is to be gained by finical precision of this sort. For in the first place it disturbs old associations, and in the next place the object aimed at cannot be carried out consistently. To write, for example, Klutaimnestra for the old Clytemnestra, is doubtful spelling, for our *u* does not answer precisely to the Greek *v*, and though *ü* may come nearer to it, the Germanising which would thence result would be intolerable, whereas there is no harm in our retaining the *y* of the Romans, which was the vowel with which the Romans, in introducing the heroine first to our acquaintance, thought proper to spell her name. Besides, where is this to end? If we are to say Klutaimnestra, should we not go on to change *mythes* into *muthes*, and, instead of *Hades*, are we to confuse eyes and ears by *Haides* ("Αιδης), and how are we to deal with other 'iotas subscript,' and are we to speak no longer of Homer and Athens, as Shakspere, Milton, Wordsworth, Byron spoke, but only of Homeros and Athenai? As it would be pedantic cruelty to condemn us, when dealing with Italian Literature, to speak only of Firenze, or Venezia, or Roma, instead of Florence, Venice, Rome, so I think it would be a confession that Greek Literature was a mere exotic in our soil, if it were to be severed, as by such a process it would virtually be severed, from the roots which it has already struck deep and abundant in our country's literature.

Acknowledgments are specially due to my friend and former pupil Mr. Robert A. Neil, Fellow of Pembroke College, Cambridge, for the care and courtesy with which he has looked over the sheets while the book was passing through the Press. To the Rev. Professor Wm. Robertson Smith I am also indebted for valuable elucidations and corroborations from the Semitic area of thought. Mr. Henry Stephen, M.A., has likewise rendered important service in drawing up the Index of the book.

INVERNAULD, SUTHERLAND,
   May 7th, 1878.

CONTENTS.

CHAPTER I.

Introductory.

SECTION · · · · · · · · PAGE
1. Statement of Subject 3
2. The two Epics of Greece compared with other Epics . . 4
3. Traditional view as to Origin—Schools of Alexandria and Pergamus 5
4. Separatist School or Ancient Chorizontes 5

CHAPTER II.

The Wolfian Theory.

5. Epoch-making position of Wolf 7
6. Strength of Wolfian Theory 8
7. Reception in Germany 8
8. Services of Wolf to Homerology . . . 9
9. Failure to carry out dissection into Lays . . . 10
10. Dissection attempted by Lachmann . . . 11
11. Reaction under Nitzsch and O. Müller . . 11
12. Attitude of Göthe 12
13. Prevalence of Wolfian Theory in Germany . . 13
14. Discordance of its champions . . . 13
15. Drawn battle between Traditionalists and Wolfians . 14
16. Wolfian Theory in France 15
17. Wolfian Theory in Britain 15
18. Mediating position of Grote 16
19. Chorizontes reappearing in England . . . 17
20. Frederick A. Paley's Theory 18

CHAPTER III.

A 'Via Media.'

21. Present position of the Question . . . 20
22. Bergk's attempt at a 'Via Media' . . . 21
23. His difficulty as to accounting for the Odyssey . 21
24. Weakness of Chorizontic position in the same respect . . 22
25. Asiatic origin of the two Poems, when first historically discernible . 23
26. Peloponnesian or European origin not tenable . . 24
27. Roots of Greek Mythology and Poetry in Thessaly . . . 25
28. Probability of a basis in older poems 26

CHAPTER IV.

The Two Epics compared.

SECTION				PAGE
29.	Anteriority of Iliad in whole or in part to the Odyssey			28
30.	Unity of Odyssey			29
31.	Apparent flaws in its perfect unity			31
32.	Conclusion as to its unity			33
33.	Complexity of Iliad			33
34.	Contrast with Odyssey which acknowledges a single Hero			34
35.	Complexity of Iliad with variety of centre			35
36.	,, ,, from repeated Invocations of the Muse			36
37.	,, ,, beyond the limits of its Proem			36
38.	,, ,, with woes to Trojans superinduced			38
39.	,, ,, with glory to Diomed overpassing Achilles			39
40.	,, ,, through enlargement of ground-plan			41
41.	Consequent difficulty felt by critics as to the plan of the Iliad			42
42.	Mure's statement of its Scheme—Schubarth's Theory			44

CHAPTER V.

Outline of New Grouping.

43.	Double stream or series in the Books of the Iliad			46
44.	Author of one series identical with author of the Odyssey			47
45.	Alcæus's Epigram implies dual subject in Iliad			48
46.	First preliminary objection considered—Importance affirmed of the Odyssey as critical starting-point			49
47.	Second preliminary objection considered—Indication of a safer Chorizontic doctrine than the old one			51

CHAPTER VI.

Failure of old Chorizontic Grouping.

48, 49.	Examples of futility in linguistic arguments of Chorizontes			52
50.	Example of futility in mythologic argument—Charis and Aphrodite			54
51.	Example of futility in mythologic argument—Iris and Hermes			55
52.	Hermes as messenger			56
53.	Iris as messenger			56
54.	Limitation as to Iris who is chiefly visible messenger			58
55.	Employment of Hermes, mainly as invisible messenger			58
56.	Iris and Hermes as allied Powers			59

CHAPTER VII.

Criterion as to Geographical Knowledge.

57.	Cognation of Odyssey with the younger series of the Books of the Iliad.—Characteristics of the Odyssey			61
58.	Geographical horizon of the Odyssey			62
59.	Same geographical horizon in the Ulyssean Cantos			63
60.	Sidon and Egyptian Thebes familiar in both			65
61.	Attitude same to outer nations			66
62.	Aggregation begun in both into Northern and Southern Hellenic groups			67
63.	Narrowness of horizon of Achilleid			69

CHAPTER VIII.

Criterion as to Humour and Pathos.

SECTION   PAGE

64. Plaintiveness and Humour—where diffused . . . 71
65. Localisation of expressions signifying the 'luxury of grief' . 73
66. Humour—Traces of 74
67. Absence of Humour or Pathos in the Achilleid . . 76

CHAPTER IX.

Criterion as to Conjugal Honour and Affection.

68. Elements in Odyssey as to Domestic Affections . 77
69. Parallel elements in Ulyssean Books of Iliad . 78
70. Absence of such elements in Achilleid . . 79
71. Ἑστία—where prominent? 79
72. Conclusion as to *Domestica* 80

CHAPTER X.

Ulysses.

73. Ulysses the type of spirit and intelligence . 81
74. Ulysses in Iliad B 82
75. Ulysses in Iliad Γ 85
76. Ulysses in Iliad Δ 86
77. Ulysses in Iliad E, Z, Π . . . 87
78. Ulysses in Iliad I, K 90
79. Ulysses in Iliad Ψ, Ω . . . 92
80. Ulysses in Iliad Θ (Achillean) . . 93
81. Ulysses in other Achillean Books . . 94

CHAPTER XI.

Latent Sympathies and Antipathies.

82. Latent rivalry between North and South . . 98
83. Pindar's attitude to Ulysses 100
84. Achilles— Double aspect of 101
85. Agamemnon—Double aspect of 103
86. Hector— Double aspect of 104
87. Helen— Double aspect of 108
88. Menestheus and the Athenians—Double aspect of . . 111
89. Ajax the Less—Double aspect of 111
90. Teucer—Double aspect of 113
91. Ajax Telamonius—Double aspect of—General remarks . 113
92. Ajax Telamonius in Achilleid 115
93. Ajax Telamonius in Ulyssean cantos . . . 116
94. Ajax Telamonius—Was he cousin of Achilles? . . 118
95. Ajax Telamonius—Pindar's attitude towards him . . 120
96. Minor Personages. Divergence regarding—(1) Panthoidæ, (2) Polydamas, (3) Helenus, (4) Kebriones, (5) Akamas, (6) Pæonians, (7) Locrians, (8) Mekisteus, (9) Cassandra, (10) Eurybates, (11) Eurymedon, (12) Paris . . . 121

CHAPTER XII.

Archaica.—Religion and Mythology.

SECTION   PAGE

97. General remarks on the subject of *Archaica* 126

98. Fields of investigation for such phenomena 129

99. Oldest Traditions chiefly in Achilleid 129

100-1. Olympian Dynasty under two representations . . . 130

102. Zeus under two aspects—Emergence of ethical adjuncts—Apollo and Artemis under two aspects 134

103. Life of the gods and their worship—Aspects of (a) Blood and Ichor, (β) Athene, (γ) Aphrodite, (δ) Dionysus, (ε) Demeter,—The World of Shades 140

104. Rise of Festivals and Votive Offerings 143

105-6. Hieratic Words and Epithets undergoing Transformation . . 144

CHAPTER XIII.

Archaica.—Psychology and Ethics.

107. Psychology—Divergence in 149

108. Ethical Feeling—Divergence in 152

109. Contrast as to Boasting over the Dead 155

110. Contrast as to Vociferation 157

CHAPTER XIV.

Manners and Customs and Social Appliances.

111. General Remarks—A. Architecture 160

112. B. House Furniture and Dress 163

113. C. General Artistic Advancement. (1) Colour, (2) Material—Ivory 166

114. D. Amusements and Pastimes 170

115. E. Comfort and Diet 170

116. F. Hospitality 172

117. G. Arts and Inventions 174

118. H. Labour and Commerce 183

119. I. Rites and Formalities 185

120. K. Marriage 189

121. L. Modes of Thought and Expression 197

CHAPTER XV.

Personal Idiosyncrasies.—Attitude to the Horse.

122. General remarks as to the Horse in Achilleid . . . 205

123. Minor facts as to Horse in Achilleid 209

124. The Horse in Ulyssean cantos 210

125. The Horse in relation to Ulysses 212

126. The Horse in the Odyssey 214

126*. Ἀγέρωχος—Naming of Steeds 216

CHAPTER XVI.

Personal Idiosyncrasies.—Attitude to the Dog.

127. General remarks as to the Dog 219

128. Aspect of Dog in the Achilleid 220

SECTION		PAGE
129.	Shades on the Dog common to all sections of the Poems	221
130.	Kindly touches as to the Dog in the Odyssey	223
131.	Minor evidences of contrast	225
132.	Ulyssean cantos in same vein with the Odyssey	226

CHAPTER XVII.

Epilogue as to Horse and Dog.

133.	*Minima* as to the Horse	229
134.	*Minima* as to the Dog	232
135.	General conclusion under this branch of inquiry	234

CHAPTER XVIII.

Local Mint-marks.—Achilleid.

136.	Under a dual authorship—Which is the Homer of Tradition ?	236
137.	Local evidence desiderated—Description of the kind of	237
138-9.	Ancient belief as to Homer's locality	239
140.	A Thessalian theory	241
141.	Probable historical nucleus, with Thessalian hero as centre	242
142.	Familiarity shown in Achilleid with Thessaly generally	244
143.	Three special features of Achilleid explicable from Thessalian influence. I. Prominence of the Horse. II. Silvan Scenery. III. Olympus as a mountain	245
144.	Prominence of the Horse in Thessalian Legend	246
145.	Prominence of the Horse in Thessalian History	247
146.	Prominence of the Horse as the symbol of Thessaly on its coins	248
147-8.	Silvan images and scenery	248
149-50.	Epilogue on climatic features and meteorology	252
151.	Mountains and Sea as rival elements in forming Greek character	255
152.	Prominence of Mountains in Achilleid, and especially of Olympus	256
153.	Simile as to Olympus with Mint-mark of Thessaly	258
154.	Confirmatory observations	259
155-6.	Olympus in Achilleid and Olympus in Odyssey—Contrast of	260
157.	Olympus in Ulyssean cantos—General summary as to Olympus	263
158.	Minor Thessalian touches in the Achilleid	264

CHAPTER XIX.

Objections and Difficulties considered.

159.	Objections to a European origin of Achilleid. 1. The Locust-simile	267
160.	2. The similes as to Lions	268
161.	Argument for Achilleid as a separate poem from λῖς (lion)	269
162.	Difficulty as to mention of the ' Heliconian god '	270
163.	Difficulty as to Horses of Diomed	271
164.	Difficulty as to the goddess Dione	273

CHAPTER XX.

Local Mint-marks.—Ulyssean Cantos.

165.	General observations—Robert Wood on Ionian origin of Homer	276
166.	Local Mint-marks in the Ulyssean Books	278
167.	Conclusion from the evidence	288

CHAPTER XXI.

Local Mint-marks—Odyssey.

SECTION		PAGE
168-9.	General remarks	291
170.	Peloponnesian origin or Attic origin less probable	292
171.	Positive indications of origin in Ionia	293
172.	Corroborations	297

CHAPTER XXII.

Glimpses of a Personal Homer.

173.	Theory of Homer as an Æolian	299
174.	Theory of Homer as an Athenian	300
175-6.	Difficulties of the Athenian Theory	300
177-9.	Menestheus and Athenians—Double aspect of	303
180-4.	Æolo-Dorian feeling in Achilleid—Ionian feeling in non-Achilleid and Odyssey	306
185.	The Ionic φρήτρη	312
186.	The Attico-Ionic Oath	312
187.	General result of the evidence	315
188-9.	Ionian Theory explains much otherwise inexplicable	316
190.	Traditions as to *Personalia* of the Poet	318

CHAPTER XXIII.

Symmetry in Ethical Purpose.

191-2.	Achilleid—Probable genesis of—Moralised by the additional Ulyssean cantos	320
193.	How far legitimate to suppose Ethical purpose in Poetical creation	322
194-6.	Ethical purpose manifest in Ulyssean cantos	323

CHAPTER XXIV.

Conclusion.

197-9.	Ethical content and purpose in the Odyssey	328
200.	Elements of grandeur in the Odyssey	331
201.	The greatness of its literary influence	333

APPENDIX.

NOTE A.	On the Antiquity of the Iliad and Odyssey	335
B.	On the σήματα λυγρά	337
C.	Details as to Ἵππος and its Derivatives	341
D.	On the Horse and the Dog in Literature	343
E.	The Story of the Dog Argus	347
F.	On the elements of an Achilleid surviving in Thessaly and Albania	348
	Explanatory Additions	353
INDEX I, Words and Epithets		359
INDEX II, Matters and Authors		364

THE PROBLEM

OF THE

HOMERIC POEMS.

πολλὰ γὰρ πολλᾷ λέλεκται· νεαρὰ δ' ἐξευρόντα δόμεν βασάνῳ

ἐς ἔλεγχον ἅπας κίνδυνος.

THE PROBLEM

OF THE

HOMERIC POEMS.

CHAPTER I.

INTRODUCTORY.

τίς δὲ σύ ἐσσι, φέριστε, καταθνητῶν ἀνθρώπων;

---

1. THE Homeric question, or the problem as to the genesis and mutual relation of the Iliad and Odyssey, is the subject that I propose to deal with in the following pages. It is one that has exercised much and long the foremost scholars in many lands, and, notwithstanding a vast amount of ingenious research and laborious investigation expended upon these poems with a view to determine their authorship, sequence, and veritable connection, it must be confessed that the results have been for the most part unsatisfactory, and the real relation of these poems remains still to be discovered. No consensus of opinion has been attained capable of commanding general assent, and though valuable contributions have from time to time been made towards its determination, the controversy is very far from being settled, and so the struggle over Homer has been, like one of his own battles, a scene of wavering fortune,

πολλὰ δ᾽ ἄρ᾽ ἔνθα καὶ ἔνθ᾽ ἴθυσε μάχη πεδίοιο.

In the course of long-continued Homeric study, the writer has come to the conclusion that there are in these poems important elements yet unobserved, which promise a clue to the solution, phenomena which prove with remarkable clearness different tracts of authorship and enable us to approach the problem with fair hope of a successful elucidation. Before proceeding to unfold the evidence on which the proposed view is built, I premise a brief historical *résumé* of the leading phases of the question.

2. Two great poems have come down to us under the name of the Iliad and Odyssey[1]. They are not only the most valuable and interesting of the literary products of Greece, but they are among the most ancient, if not the most ancient, works of the human spirit in a European tongue. They are what is known as Epic poems, being the perfect type of that species of poem, and they remain still unsurpassed as models of their kind. Each consists of twenty-four Books or Cantos, and constitutes a great and comprehensive and sustained narrative of heroic actions, presenting severally a vast panorama, full of grand and beautiful detail, of a splendid Foretime, brilliant with noble action, sentiment, and adventure, in which the facts of Life and the objects of Nature stand out revealed with the brightness of Painting and the solidity of Sculpture. To any other race than that of Greece, *one* of these poems would have been a great heritage descending from the childhood of its memories, but to possess two such poems is an honour almost unique among the nations of the world[2].

[1] They are not the only poems that appear before us as Homeric, but they are sufficiently differentiated from all others by their vastness of compass and architectonic power to form a group alone and apart, and the nature of our investigation, which is mainly an interrogation of the Epics themselves, forbids an examination of the *minora* professing to be Homeric.

[2] The Mahâbhârata and Râmâyana of Sanskrit Literature are the sole example comparable to the twin Epics of Greece. It is remarkable also that they present the same contrasted relation as to complexity and unity. The Mahâbhârata answers to the Iliad in the multiplicity of its heroes, the Râmâyana to the Odyssey in having only one (cp. M. Williams, Ind. Epic Poetry, pp. 41–2). According to Weber, the Râmâyana is, like the Odyssey, the later poem of the two, but this point is still *sub judice* (Ibid. p. 65). The parallel holds, also, regarding their internal structure. 'Es kann keine Frage seyn, dass wir in Mahâbhârata Stücke aus sehr verschiedenen Zeiten, wie sehr verschieden an Inhalt und Farbe, vor uns haben. Das Râmâyana ist dagegen aus einem Gusse.' Lassen (Ind. Alt. i 584). The chief unlikeness between the Odyssey and the Râmâyana seems to be the greater width of Geographical range in the former, in conformity with the freer and more roaming spirit of the Greek, whereas the Râmâyana is comparatively narrow and confined.

Many nations have no such early inheritance at all, and those that have anything distantly approaching in value and significance, can boast of only one Epic, as the Finns in their 'Kalewala,' and the Germans in their 'Nibelungen Lied.' It is one of the peculiarities of the case that Greece has a *pair* of early Epic poems, a circumstance not sufficiently explained by referring it to the richness of Greek genius, and which appears to us to point to a Dualism in the Greek race whereof these two poems are the joint, yet divergent, expression.

.3. The question then is,·What account can we give of these Forty-Eight Cantos, all and whole, of the Homeric Corpus, as to their authorship and probable connection? For a long period the accepted answer was, They are, one and all, the work of an old Bard, called Homer, but, as to anything further, when he lived, where he was born, or how he composed, there is no knowledge, but only vague and contradictory opinion. This, which may be called the Traditional view, was virtually the answer given to the question by the Greek race itself. For, in the progress of time, these poems came to be regarded with a singular veneration, an intense interest and admiration, by the Greek people generally, and after their own productive energy and artistic faculty in literature had passed away, they began to inquire into these records of their own Past, and great was their energy in commenting upon them, their erudition in expounding them, and their ingenuity in reinterpreting them under the lights of a new age. Foremost among these was the group of erudite and laborious scholars at Alexandria, of whom Aristarchus may be taken as the leading name, and next to these, though far inferior in literary influence, was the rival school of Pergamus, Crates being, in this group, the most distinguished name. All these vied with each other in their critical investigations of the text, laborious discussions of 'various readings,' attempts at reconciliation of discordances and removal of crucial perplexities, and their labours to this day form the basis from which all criticism of the Homeric text proceeds. These critics adopted the Traditional view of the authorship and believed they were dealing in the two poems with the work of a single mind.

4. While adhering to the Traditional view, they had to

defend their opinion against an adverse Theory which arose to dispute the common opinion both of the people and of the Schools. This was the doctrine of the 'Chorizontes,' or *Separatists*, as they were called; a party of critics, who said the two Poems were by different authors and of different ages. The most famous of these were Xenon and Hellanicus. It is remarkable that the ingenuity of these last seems to have been entirely expended in finding and pressing discordances between the two poems, and whatever may be the ultimate value or scientific truth of their proposition, there can be no question that the Chorizontes contributed nothing to the criticism and understanding of the Homeric text at all comparable to the matter furnished by their opponents the orthodox Traditionalists. They cannot be said to have earned a right to be heard on their particular question, and though there was a considerable basis of fact in what they averred, they were virtually silenced, and Antiquity refused to listen to them[a]. In point of fact it is from incidental notices in the notes of their opponents that we come to know that there once existed at all such a school of opinion. That opinion, however, was counted rather a paradox for debate than a sober conclusion, and under the great authority of Aristarchus, it almost disappeared from view, so that in the Greco-Roman period it is hardly ever alluded to except once in a casual way by Seneca, and then only as one of the vagaries of disputation. Thereafter it became entirely dormant and was revived only by the discovery of the Venetian Scholia (1788), a body of ancient annotations upon Homer, out of which so much both of precious and worthless has been, in these latter days, exhumed. Among other things, the existence of the sect of the Chorizontes was discovered, and the doctrine which Aristarchus was thought to have exploded was taken up by some modern Scholars and, fostered by them, revived under new auspices after two thousand years.

---

[a] Hence Suidas (in Ὅμηρος) unites together as 'the undisputed (ἀναμφίλεκτα) poems of Homer,' the Iliad and Odyssey.

CHAPTER II.

THE WOLFIAN THEORY.

τοῖς δὲ πανημερίοις ἔριδος μέγα νεῖκος ὀρώρει.

5. THERE were therefore two theories in the old Greco-Roman world as to the Homeric poems, but one of these was practically extinguished. The Traditional view reigned with unbroken sway through modern times until a comparatively recent period. The next stage in the development of the question[1] brings us to the great name of Friedrich August Wolf, who was the first to subject the poems to the ordeal of a critical examination, and introduces the new era of Homeric investigation. This representative scholar of North Germany, professor at Halle, afterwards at Berlin, first stirred the question, whether one Homer is enough or even two Homers to have given birth to the Homeric poems, whether we do not require a number of Homers to account for poems of such compass in a primitive age. He accordingly put forth the famous doctrine in his Prolegomena (1795) that Homer was not a single poet, as the Traditionalists declared, nor two poets, as the Chorizontes affirmed, but was an 'Eponymous name' for the poetic activity of the early Epic age, and represented a congeries of poets and not an individual[2]. This poetic activity had manifested itself in the

---

[1] I have not thought it necessary to enter into any detail as to prior anticipations of the Wolfian theory, such as Vico's or Bentley's. They were notable as vaticinations, but, as they rested on instinct rather than evidence, may be here passed by as unessential. Bentley's, in particular, was far off from the Wolfian position, as he affirmed not only a personal Homer, but that he *wrote* songs, two propositions which Wolf denied.

[2] The nearest approach in an ancient authority to the Wolfian notion of

creation of a number of lays originally independent or connected only by reference to a common theme, and these lays
had been subsequently gathered together and compacted into
a unity in the time of Pisistratus (about B.C. 560).

6. The strength of this famous Theory consisted in the following facts :—1. It explained or seemed to explain certain discrepancies of the two poems with each other and of each
poem with itself. 2. It supplied an easy explanation of the
phenomenon of long poems in a simple and primitive age
destitute of literary appliances, where poets had to compose
by the aid of memory alone. 3. It professed to bring the
Homeric poems under the analogies of early primitive poetry,
the essence of which is believed to be impersonal, not bound
or attached to any personality, belonging to the tribe or race,
rather than to an individual. These were the main supports
of the theory drawn from internal evidence, and as for external
evidence the great critic rested his case on certain testimonies
of ancient authors, Cicero, Josephus, and others, which went
to affirm that the Homeric poems were not always in the
condition in which they are now found, and that they had
passed through a certain shaping and disposing process which
was referred to the time of Pisistratus[3].

7. This Theory on its first promulgation met with remarkably wide and rapid acceptance in the country of its birth.
It was received with favour not only among the scholars of
Germany, such as Heyne and Niebuhr, but also in the general
circles of Literature, where Herder had prepared the way for
its reception by his views as to popular Poetry and early

'many Homers,' is probably the statement of Proclus (A.D. 412), the commentator
on Hesiod (Gaisf. Poet. Min. Gr. iii. Scholia, p. 6), Ὅμηροι γὰρ πολλοὶ γεγόνασι
ζήλῳ τοῦ πάλαι τὴν κλῆσιν λαμβάνοντες. He wishes to make a wide interval of
time between the *golden* Homer and Hesiod, and supposes it was a Phocian and
later Ὅμηρος that contended with Hesiod in the famous 'Agon' or contest of the
Poets. These 'many Homers' of Proclus were not however conceived by him, like
those of Wolf, as contributing to the Iliad and Odyssey.—Compare also Eustath.
4, ὡς δὲ καὶ πολλοὶ Ὅμηροι, καὶ αὐτὸ ἱστοροῦσιν ἕτεροι.

[3] Lehrs in his Aristarchus makes little of the tradition as to Pisistratus, 'De
Pisistratea opera ne notam quidem his antiquis et Aristarcho videri famam fuisse
ostendam' (p. 334). It is a stumbling-block to the Wolfians to explain how a
concocted Homer would have been accepted emanating from the Athens of B.C. 560,
for the literary influence of Pisistratean Athens is not to be measured by its
ascendancy in the Periclean time (cp. Grote II. i. 458).

primitive Literature. Indeed Herder and Heyne both attempted to claim property in the discovery, a claim that Wolf resented in the case of Heyne with some asperity. The adhesion of Wieland, of the Schlegels, of Fichte, of William von Humboldt, of almost all the young thinkers of that time except Schiller, is an evidence of the immense influence which it exerted on the young mind of Germany. That influence was greatly increased by a number of predisposing causes which rendered the acceptance of the Theory both easy and rapid. It was a time when the French Revolution was in full career, when the air was full of paradox and innovation, and what is of more importance it appeared at a time when a vast interest had been excited by the discovery, in different parts of Europe, of considerable *corpora* of popular poetry, giving evidence of the remarkable vitality of such poetry even under its most anonymous and uncertified character, and that too, as if to exemplify the Wolfian Theory in its main position, with no literary appliances but only oral transmission as its vehicle. The Ossianic controversy, in particular, had opened up large vistas of vague possibility in this direction, and thus in a fortunate hour, by a most dexterous handling of the evidence and a masterly marshalling of the phenomena, Wolf forged the thunderbolt that shattered, in the view of Germany, the unity of the Homeric poems [4].

8. In estimating the work of Wolf, it would, however, be unfair to represent him as simply a destructive critic : the service which he rendered to Homer was immense, and those who differ most widely from his main conclusion cannot fail to acknowledge that he laid bare many phenomena essential to a right theory and initiated the scientific study of the Homeric poems. It was Wolf that first taught us to study those poems, in the only way in which for scientific purposes they should be studied, under the light of the historic conditions in which they were produced, and with a survey of the mode in which they were composed, preserved, and transmitted. To realise the age in which they first appeared, to investigate the social, historical, ethical conditions in which

[4] Wolf mentions Ossian in his forty-ninth chapter and in a note to his twenty-fourth. Heyne on Il. π 53 (Ed. Min.) refers to Ossianic similes as parallel to Homer's.

they were grounded and rooted, to discover what the soil was on which grew flowers of such perennial beauty and significance, to determine the surroundings of the Bard or Bards in his own or their time and their relation to and influence upon subsequent forms of Literature—this was the great Problem [5] put forward by Wolf as an essential preliminary to any right understanding or true scientific appreciation of these Poems. Hence the generally admitted completeness of his victory as to the standard of comparison, that the Homeric poems, though examples of the 'Kunst-Epos,' are to be classed only with the 'Volks-Epos' or Popular Epic, belong therefore to a non-literary age, and are not to be compared or confounded with the Epics of an advanced period of society like the Æneid or the 'Jerusalem Delivered,' where the Poet composes, pen in hand, poems to be read, whereas the Homeric Bard sings or recites in the ear of a simple primitive people.

9. This great service to science is the fruit of Wolf's investigations, and no one will grudge him the *spolia opima* which he has won. At the same time it is worthy of note that the great critic did not carry out his theory to any completeness; for he never exhibited in outline a scheme of the Component Lays out of which according to him the framework of each poem was put together. That he failed or omitted to do so in the course of a tolerably long life [6] in the vigour of his powers, after the publication of the Prolegomena, is a fact which suggests the doubt whether he believed in the possibility of a re-dissection, such as his Theory implied. In all probability he was restrained by the consciousness that the process, if performed, would yield larger aggregates [7], more solid masses of song, than was suitable for his Theory.

---

[5] 'Testes ordine interrogare.' Wolf. Proleg ch. 1.

[6] Nearly thirty years. Prolegomena in 1795. Death in 1824 (Blackie, i. 193).

[7] Cp. Blackie's statement on this point; Homer, i. 246–7. Friedländer (Homerische Kritik von Wolf bis Grote. p. 17) asks regarding Wolf's subsequent silence, 'Sollte nicht vielmehr im spätern Alter die Ueberzeugung sich ihm aufgedrängt haben, dass eine Untersuchung der Gedichte selbst niemals das Resultat ergeben würde, welches er allein für das richtige hielt?'

10. The war, so grandly begun by Wolf, was continued by Godfrey Hermann and William Müller, who carried on a vigorous polemic, more especially against the unity of the Iliad. The former scholar modified so far the Wolfian position by taking up separate ground of his own, in his doctrine of an 'Ur-Ilias' and an 'Ur-Odyssee'—a minor original nucleus to each poem, around which the congeries of lays had been, so to speak, deposited. Substantially, however, he stands on the Wolfian basis. Next to him in importance among the later Wolfians, and, in the opinion of many, the greatest of the Wolfian school after Wolf himself, stands Karl Lachmann, who (in his 'Betrachtungen,' 1843) gave a new direction, as well as a new impetus, to the controversy, and from him the modern Wolfians are often styled 'die Lachmannianer.' His work was especially aimed at carrying out what Wolf left unperformed—the dissection of an Epic into the supposed original Lays; and for this purpose he attempted to break down the somewhat vulnerable corpus of the Iliad, exhibiting the sutures and *callidae juncturae* much in the same way as he operated on the comparatively 'vile corpus' of the 'Nibelungen Lied' with his apprentice hand. Under Lachmann's operation, the Iliad fell asunder into a group of Eighteen primary Lays and the Lachmann view is therefore known as the 'Klein-Lieder-Theorie[8].'

11. Meantime a powerful reaction had arisen against the extreme conclusions of the Wolfians, and, even before the Lachmann period, a school of critics of a more conservative character had made themselves felt by a splendid 'polemik' against the Wolfian Theory. Among these may be named

---

[8] After all, these separate *Lieder* are liable to new dissections on Lachmannian principles. The first of his *Lieder* is not perfectly self-consistent, for Agamemnon said he would go 'himself' and fetch Briseis. He does not, but sends heralds, and yet Achilles speaks of him as having fulfilled his threat 'in person' (αὐτὸς ἀπούρας A 366). Thus the unity of even the first *Lied* would be dissolved. Hypercriticism of this kind would break down any unity. It is worth noting that Agamemnon afterwards speaks of having done the deed 'himself' (T 89), and Thersites, in B 240, so accuses him.—A man does not always act up to his professions, and many a threat in actual life is unfulfilled. Thus Achilles in I 357 threatens to set sail next day, but in the same book (l. 650) admits a supposition entirely inconsistent with his departure. Hence Socrates finds fault with his logical inconsistency (Pl. Hippias Minor, 370 B), but the logical inconsistency of the actors does not prove a plurality of dramatists.

especially Ottfried Müller [9], Welcker, and Gregor W. Nitzsch, who were able, by a more thorough survey of the historical conditions of the case, to reconquer not indeed all, but many, of the apparently lost positions. The first of these did good service by his emphasising the necessity of an organic as against an atomic theory of the poems; the second by his investigation of the Epic Cycle, rendering it certain that poems of great compass, which presupposed the presence of the Iliad and Odyssey, had existed long before the age of Pisistratus; and the last named scholar, by his voluminous and weighty works, dealt very powerful blows at the Wolfians, so that he may well be called 'Malleus Wolfianorum [10].'

12. Besides the powerful diversion effected by this group of scholars, there was an anti-Wolfian breeze which sprang up in the higher regions of Literature. Voss, the great translator of Homer, was an 'Irreconcilable.' Schiller had always opposed the Theory as what he called 'barbaric,' and the great authority of Göthe [11],—upon a question of organic unity, of immense weight—though less uniformly consistent, was on the whole in the anti-Wolfian scale. In a letter to Schiller soon after the appearance of the 'Prolegomena,' he characterized the theory as arbitrary and subjective, and he seemed to resent the intrusion of this 'wild boar' into what he called 'the fairest gardens of the æsthetic world.' Subsequently, however, he seems to have wavered in his opinion, but finally came round to the old belief, as we learn from his interesting little sketch 'Homer noch einmal,' which repre-

---

[9] In his 'Kleine Schriften,' i. 399, O. Müller speaks as if the victory was secure. 'Uns nun den Epigonen jener alten Homerischen Streiter, erscheint diese ganze Aesthetische Ansicht roh, äusserlich, atomistisch; eine andere, die organische Entwickelung, hat im Stillen den Platz erobert.'

[10] Düntzer (Abhandl. 1872, p. 409), although himself a Wolfian, puts a high value on Nitzsch's labours in a scientific point of view, and adds, regarding him, 'Si Pergama dextra defendi possent, etiam hac defensa fuissent.'

[11] In December, 1796, Göthe was under the Wolfian spell, for he proposed a toast to the Man 'der endlich vom Namen Homeros kühn uns befreiend uns auch ruft in die vollere Bahn.' The spell soon vanished. In May 16, 1798, he writes to Schiller regarding the Iliad, 'Ich bin mehr als jemals von der Einheit und Untheilbarkeit des Gedichts überzeugt .... Die Ilias scheint mir so rund und fertig, man mag sagen, was man will, dass nichts dazu noch davon gethan werden kann.' A full account will be found as to the waves of opinion in Germany in Wolf's own time in Volkmann's 'Geschichte und Kritik der Wolfschen Prolegomena' (Leipzig, 1874).

sents his matured opinion, when, at the period of the reaction, he was able to realise a ' Homer once more,' after ' the sundering and dissecting process of the Eighteenth century' was over and the *harmonizing* spirit, as he called it, of the Nineteenth had begun.

13. The vaticinations of Göthe have in this matter not been fully confirmed. The Germany of the Nineteenth century is after all very largely Wolfian, and, notwithstanding the strong reaction a generation ago, the bulk of her scholars in the present day is to be found in the Wolfian camp. According to Nutzhorn[12], the *stream* of opinion is flowing strongly in that direction, and there is a continuation of the school of Lachmann (among whom is included the distinguished name of George Curtius, who may be styled a Wolfian on philologic grounds, founding upon the variety of philologic phenomena in the poems), and these new 'Lachmannianer,' in diverse ways, not always very accordant with either of their great masters or themselves, parcel out the primary lays of the Iliad and even of the Odyssey, with the most confident precision. Foremost among these may be named Arminius Köchly, who is usually looked on as recently the most pronounced exponent of the dominant Wolfian theory. In particular, he has, with more of valour than discretion, put in type a text of the Iliad upon Wolfian principles, in which, by the ejection of the line containing the $\Delta\iota\grave{o}s\ \beta ov\lambda\acute{\eta}$ of the Exordium and by other similar operations, the Iliad falls asunder into sixteen independent lays[13].

14. The influence of this school, we are inclined to think, cannot in the nature of things be permanent. It might have been otherwise if the Köchly doctrine had been confirmatory of the Lachmann, so as to exhibit the same cleavage of strata as prevailing in the structure of the poems; but when each leading champion exhibits sections of his own, and there is no real unanimity in the Wolfian camp (witness the extensive and very effective polemic of the Wolfian Düntzer

---

[12] ' Zwar haben Nitzsch und Bäumlein auch ihre Anhänger, aber *der Strom* geht doch immer in der von Lachmann an gegebenen Richtung.' Nutzhorn (die Entstehungsweise der Homerischen Gedichte, 1869, p. 143).

[13] ' Iliadis Carmina XVI. Restituta edidit Arminius Köchly, Turicensis.' Teubner, 1861.

against both Lachmann and Köchly), it is not likely that the extreme section of the school will be in the end victorious.

15. To any candid mind, however, it must be apparent, from the immense hold which the Wolfian view has obtained of the patient and honest and persevering mind of Germany, that it is no baseless speculation, but one that can produce a large amount of, at all events, *prima facie* evidence in its favour. In point of fact, the difficulties involved in the Homeric Question are about equally great whether one adopts the Traditionalist or the Wolfian supposition[14]. The former credits a single poet with an enormous mass of poetic production, not confined to the Iliad and Odyssey, under what seem to be impossible conditions, antecedent to all literary appliances; the latter supposes a number of poets to have produced, in the exercise of independent activity, separate lays relating to a great action which afterwards combined into an architectonic whole of remarkable symmetry. The former explains unity, but does not account for discrepancies and diversities; the latter explains discrepancies, but it explains nothing else; it cannot account for unity and symmetry[15]. These constitute the Scylla and Charybdis of Homeric speculation between which the critic, who wishes to give a scientific survey of the facts, will have to steer. That survey must be obtained entirely from the poems themselves, and from them alone. Those poems are, in the view of all, the only source of evidence, final and sufficient, upon the question. Unfortunately, they are all but dumb as to themselves and their authorship. Inferences may, no doubt, be drawn, but there is no direct and conscious evidence adducible, and the two Epics appear on the horizon of time so purely *objective* that they seem projected into this visible

---

[14] Nitzsch has left a remarkable confession of his experiences in the whirlpool of Homeric controversy ('Sagenpoesie,' p. 293). After having composed a laborious work, which had for its object to establish the *separate* authorship—a view which has the advantage of lightening the difficulty of accounting for two Epics of such magnitude—he subsequently wrote a refutation of himself and pronounced in favour of the joint authorship of both poems.

[15] 'Lachmann hat auf Incongruenzen und Widersprüche zu viel Gewicht gelegt, und Nitzsch zu wenig.' Friedländer (Hom. Krit. p. 27).

diurnal sphere with hardly a subjective trace adhering to them, and are silent as the stars concerning their own genesis and mutual relation.

Such is the present position, upon German soil, of the Homeric question, and such the leading points in the history of the Wolfian Theory. When applied to the twin stars of the Homeric poems, it has, by a reverse operation from that of the astronomers who resolve nebulæ into stars, converted stars into nebulæ. How has it fared in other countries, and has it affected opinion equally powerfully elsewhere?

16. The Wolfian Theory has not moved, so powerfully as it has in Germany, the learned world either in England or in France. In the latter country the chief fruit which can be traced to it of much scientific value is the Essay of M. Burnouf (Revue des Deux Mondes, 1866), which contains many ingenious, though not always satisfactory, suggestions. Far from adopting Wolf's ultimate conclusions, the Essayist adopts a 'chorizontic' or separatist position, and an attempt is made to differentiate the Iliad from the Odyssey in age and authorship, by classing the former with the *chanson de gestes* of mediæval French literature and the latter with the comparatively more modern *roman d'aventures*. The analogy, though interesting and important, is however insufficient to justify the conclusion or to demand the separation from each other, under different genera, of two poems so cognate in tone and structure, when the differences that exist can be satisfactorily accounted for on a less violent hypothesis [16].

17. Regarding opinion in this country, it cannot be said that the Wolfian Theory has, except in a limited degree [17], modified or materially affected the old traditional belief, that

---

[16] Wolf himself may be claimed as a witness against the 'Chorizontes,' as he strongly emphasises the unity of tone and colouring in both poems. 'Immo congruunt in iis omnia ferme in idem ingenium, in eosdem mores, in eandem formulam *sentiendi* et *loquendi*.' Prolegomena, ch. 50. He elsewhere speaks of this as a '*mirificus* concentus,' though he endeavours to convert it into an argument for his theory of an artificial unity. It is not without reason therefore that Nägelsbach speaks with such contempt of the opinion of Benjamin Constant —'die Chorizontenmanie welche Benjamin Constant verleitet hat zu sagen, dass der Sänger der Odyssee eben so wenig die Ilias habe dichten können, als ein Alexandrinischer Jude die Psalmen oder den Hiob (Tome iii. 435).' Homerische Theologie, p. xvi.

[17] Coleridge, in his 'Table Talk,' seems to have at one time accepted the Wolfian doctrine.

each poem was from the first a unity. British scholarship has been for the most part content to acquiesce in the conservative views of Colonel Mure, whose investigation of the question constitutes the most important exposition in defence of that belief which English scholarship can show. He has endeavoured, not unsuccessfully, to meet the Wolfian positions point by point, and his examination of the question is of importance as it produced, in his own case, a *conversion* from an early belief in the Wolfian doctrine. Mr. Gladstone, who has been so fervent a student of Homer, and who, notwithstanding Düntzer's insinuations as to his 'unscientific' ideas, has added not a little to our *scientific* knowledge of the Homeric poems, disdains to enter upon the question and, with a lofty indifference to such critical inquiries, never allows a Wolfian scruple, just or unjust, to interfere with his homage and veneration. Perhaps he is right. It is better to enjoy the full bloom and aroma of the Eden of Greek song, asking no questions, and accepting in implicit faith, where we may not have the means or power to prove. Very different is the attitude of an equally fervent Homeric scholar, Professor Blackie, inasmuch as he not only discusses the Wolfian question largely, but pronounces the discussion of it to be essential to any right understanding of the Homeric poems as the flower of early popular poetry. With strong Wolfian leanings, and an immense appreciation of Wolf's work and genius, Professor Blackie declares against and substantially sums up adversely to the doctrine that the Iliad and Odyssey are a congeries of lays.

18. The greatest name that can be quoted on the Wolfian side among our English scholars is that of Grote. Not that he is a Wolfian—on the contrary, no one has shown more clearly and incisively the difficulties inherent in the extreme Wolfian position [18]; but he has also shown, in the fairest and most judicial of statements, the difficulties of the traditional view, in so far at least as the Iliad is concerned. The case

[18] Friedländer (Hom. Krit. p. 22), who accepts Grote's mediating position, states this point as follows—'Die Merkmale planmässiger Auflage, auf der die ganze Odyssee und grosse Theile der Ilias beruhen, sind so tief in die Handlung verflochten, dass es unmöglich ist zu glauben, sie seien nachträglich von aussen hinzugethan worden.'

which he has made out in favour of two streams of narrative in that poem, and, in particular, regarding the Books from the second to the seventh as not part of the original current [19], is remarkably complete, and he errs chiefly in this that he performs excision upon some of the most splendid portions of the poem, and assigns these loose gems to no authorship in particular. He has, however, pointed out the path in which the solution of the question seems to lie, and he has done special service in familiarising the English mind with the notion of an 'Achilleid' as the inner kernel of the Iliad and distinct from the Iliad as a whole—a view towards which the whole available evidence seems more and more to converge. Among the scholars of Germany, it is worth noting that Düntzer occupies the same ground as to the Six Books above referred to, and indeed claims to have anticipated Grote in this particular discovery (Abhandl. pp. 46 and 492).

19. While rejecting the Wolfian principle in its most pronounced form, partially regarding the Iliad, entirely regarding the Odyssey, Mr. Grote was disposed, though somewhat doubtfully, to accept the chorizontic doctrine of the separate authorship, a view to which the English 'Left,' if we may so call it, has generally inclined. As early as 1820, Richard Payne Knight, though a decided opponent of the Wolfian principle, pronounced in favour of the chorizontic view, and the arguments which he used produced a certain effect on English opinion. They moved Henry Nelson Coleridge, in his work on Homer, to adopt that position, and constrained Clinton (Fasti Hell. i. p. 381) to express a modified adhesion. More recently, the usual chorizontic arguments have been presented again in a new and expanded form in an article in the Edinburgh Review (April 1871). This article purports to be a review of the treatise of Thiersch ('über das Vaterland Homers') who, though he separated the authorship, held the poems to be of the same age, whereas the Reviewer attempts to make out a great gulf of time between the Iliad and the Odyssey, and against the main probabilities

---

[19] O. Müller had a glimpse of this position, when he admits the existence within the poem of '*a preparatory part*, consisting of the attempts of the other heroes to compensate for the absence of Achilles.' Cp. Grote (II. ii. 256-7), who criticises the statement, and shows that O. Müller did not conceive the true relation clearly or develope it consistently.

of the case, as we hope afterwards to show more at large, assigns only the Iliad to Homer.

20. In this rapid review of the leading phases of English opinion, it would be unfair to omit notice of the peculiar position occupied by one of our greatest living scholars upon the question. I refer to Frederick A. Paley, who has given us an edition of the Iliad, in which he has accumulated a considerable amount of argument to show, among other things, the precarious condition of the Homeric text philologically. The view he has found himself compelled to adopt is to the effect that the Homer that we now have is a comparatively late production [20], that it can be discerned as existing only from about the time of Herodotus, that the Homer of Pindar was a different Homer from ours, with other and more varied legends about the 'Troica,' and that the poems, as we now have them, must have been put into their present shape in or about the Periclean time [21]. The scepticism of Wolf did not proceed to this extremity. He allowed to the Homeric poems a duration in their present shape of at least a century longer, from the time, namely, of Pisistratus [22]. Mr. Paley, however, considers these poems, which belong to the first period of Greek literature, to have been in a molluscous

[20] Dr. Donaldson, in his Cratylus, p. 71, uses similar language without indicating his grounds, but he affirms that 'the Iliad and Odyssey, as we have them, are little more than a *rifacimento* of the original works.'

[21] Yet, in spite of the accidents of time, and after passing through the crucible of Athenian 'editing' and Alexandrian recension, is there any text of any early ballad poet that is in a better state than Homer's? After three thousand years it stands, in the main, as clear and firm as the other after as many hundreds. Hesiod, though generally reputed more recent, and possessing not a tithe of the same bulk, is really in a worse condition (Lehrs' Aristarchus, p. 441). It is singular that the text of Euripides, and perhaps of Sophocles also, is in a firmer state than Shakspere's at this hour. If the Triposes of the future should come to turn upon the Ballad poetry of England instead of Homer, or Shakspere instead of Euripides, the exchange will not be justified by the greater critical security of the ground in such ' pastures new.'

[22] ' Habemus nunc Homerum in manibus, non qui viguit in ore Graecorum suorum, sed inde a Solonis temporibus usque ad haec Alexandrina mutatum varie, interpolatum, castigatum et emendatum,' Wolf, Proleg. ch. 49 ad fin. He adds, however, in ch. 50, the *caveat*, ' Neque vero ita deformata et difficta sunt carmina,' etc.— παρεφθόρη ὑπὸ τῶν μεταχαρακτηρισάντων is a statement of Ven. Schol. on Ξ 241, implying that the ancient critics were aware of the risks to the text involved in and inseparable from the process of adaptation to the new Alphabet. Some further remarks on Mr. Paley's hypothesis will be found in the Appendix, Note A.

condition down to the period when the Athenian Drama, the third great stadium of Greek literature, had already reached its culmination. Linguistically he has, no doubt, a considerable amount if not of evidence to show, at least of difficulties to produce, and great concessions might be made as to the state of the text under such changes as the loss of the Digamma and other metamorphic influences, that must have supervened during the process of adaptation to the new alphabet of B.C. 403. As for the bone and sinew of the poems, considered as an organic structure, a higher antiquity, in respect not only of the subject matter, but of the form, must be assigned, far beyond what Mr. Paley has allowed.

CHAPTER III.

A 'VIA MEDIA' OPENED UP.

ὡς μὲν τῶν ἐπὶ ἶσα μάχη τέτατο πτόλεμός τε.

21. FROM a general survey of the field it therefore appears that the battle of criticism has been a drawn one, and the armies are still in camp, unable to dislodge each other from their entrenchments. On the one hand we behold an array of critics who pronounce for Unity of authorship, discrepancies being only apparent, incidental, easily explicable from the mode of transmission, not therefore of the essence. On the other we behold a rival array of critics equally learned. and acute, in Germany more numerous, who give their verdict for Multiplicity of authorship, each poem being to them a congeries with no original coherence, discrepancies therefore essential, inevitable. Midway between these and under fire from both lies the somewhat straggling line of Chorizontes, who consider each poem singly a unity but by a separate author. The Unigenists, if we may so call them, confront the Wolfian Polygenists, while the Bigenist Chorizontes sustain war from both. The problem therefore is to discover a mode of reconciliation that will unite them all.

It is one of the advantages belonging to the Theory now to be formulated that it prepares the way for such a reconciliation. It acknowledges each of the three contending parties as rightful belligerents and metes out a measure of justice to each by according to each a certain validity, while it supplies an explanation of the facts on which they severally found, so far as the views *are* facts and possessed of a scientific foundation.

22. The discovery of a *Via Media*, such as shall harmonise the conflicting opinions, is therefore now the problem before Homeric scholars, and Theodore Bergk in his recent history of Greek Literature has divined the necessity of such a reconciliation. His own hypothesis, however, cannot be said to be very successful, inasmuch as it proceeds on the supposition that the poet called Homer is the author of the nucleus of the Iliad simply, and that the greatness of his name made him be credited with all the subsequent effusions of the Epic Muse on kindred themes and in similar vein. This is the error into which the Chorizontes both ancient and modern have fallen, and which has largely vitiated their speculations. It proceeds on the assumptions, which cannot be proved, that the Hexameter owes its grandeur, if not its invention, to this remote Homer, that there were no proper ἀοιδοί before Homer, though there might be kings before Agamemnon, assumptions that must be rejected on the evidence of, as I take it, the veritable Homer himself, who makes frequent mention of prior bards towards whom he must have stood in a certain filial relation. The fatal objection, however, is that this view leaves the most notable phenomenon in the whole matter unexplained, which we take to be the unity of the structure of the Odyssey, and so, on Bergk's hypothesis, a Rhapsode or Rhapsodes among the post-Homeric bards, who in this instance are presumed to be imitators working in the Homeric vein, are found to perform a work of constructive skill, in scope of purpose and measured balance of conception, far beyond the art or at least the manifested power of the inspiring Master. This would be an instance of the Epigoni proving themselves, in poetry as in war, 'superior to their sires.' The evidence, however, goes entirely against the hypothesis that the Odyssey can be assigned to any secondary source, and the presumption is entirely the other way.

23. The chorizontic position, virtually adopted by Bergk, that the Odyssey is not to be assigned to *the* Homer, and that the Iliad *is*, involves this improbable consequence : that the poem which is universally considered anterior and further removed from us, whose structure has been the subject of the most serious disputation, is the one about which science is supposed to know most ; whereas the other which is nearer to us, and

comes closer to the dawn of history, about whose structure
there has been scarcely any discussion, is the one about which
we know least, falling to be assigned to some unknown
rhapsodist, on the verge of the time when poems of a kindred
order known as the Cyclic poems, much less remarkable in
power and inferior in interest[1], were confidently assigned each
to a separate author, historically determinable. In fact the
chorizontic doctrine involves the reduction of the Odyssey to
the rank of a Cyclic poem, and, what is more, a cyclic poem
at the extremity of the series of the Cyclus, when the Sagas
were fading away in the approaching dawn of history, and yet
the only cycle of the Trojan series that does not come before
us with a fairly accredited designation of authorship. For if
the Odyssey is not Homer's, whose is it? We know the names
of the authors of the various poems dealing with the 'Troica'
after the death of Achilles. How does it happen that the most
remarkable poem of the subsequent series should be the only
one with no authorship assigned? The presumption, which
we trust to convert into proof, is entirely otherwise, that the
name of Homer as a personality is more likely to belong
specially to the poem which has passed through fewest
changes, is artistically more perfect in its structure and constitutes a unity, than to the other poem, which is on good
grounds considered more remote, has been subjected to
greater changes, bears marks of a less harmonious structure
and contains the complex elements—if complex elements
belong to either poem—in the most pronounced and extensive form.

24. The weakness of the Chorizontic position is seen further in the fact that there is no tradition from ancient times
of a double date having been assigned to Homer. In the long
array of ancient authorities in Clinton's Fasti Hellenici as to
the date of Homer, it is always presumed, notwithstanding the
widest diversity otherwise, that there was but one Homer,
and it is significant that among all the investigators (and they

---

[1] Ὁμήρου μόνου τῶν ἄλλων ῥαψῳδοῦνται τὰ ἔπη, Lycurg. § 209, regarding the
great Panathenæa. Preller (Gr. M. ii. 8) thinks the Trojan war obscured all
other epic remembrances, 'weil seine Erinnerungen die frischesten und die
ergreifendsten waren.' The real reason, however, was not its comparative proximity, but the felicity with which it had been handled in the great pair of Epics.

include such high scientific names as Aristotle and Eratosthenes), there is not one that ventures on a double date, which however ought to be a necessity if the Iliad and the Odyssey are to be separated, as is done in the elaborate article (in Edinburgh Review) to which we have referred, by a period of two or even three generations.

25. Having thus shown reason for rejecting the assumption with which Bergk and others have approached the question and which would exclude the Odyssey as not Homer's, though it might be Homeric or *à la Homer*, I proceed to inquire into the facts presented to us in the structure and relations of these two poems.

It is satisfactorily established that the two Poems come into distinct historic vision first on the Eastern shore of the Egean, either in the islands or in the mainland of Æolis or Ionia. It is there that we find the first sure traces of their having a *habitat*, and without laying much weight on the traditional notices of the poet's *personalia*, it is yet sufficiently remarkable that these connect themselves entirely with Æolis and Ionia. Pindar and Simonides, who furnish our oldest and best testimonies, associate their author with that region, and, according to Plutarch (Lycurg. iv. 4), Lycurgus was believed to have brought from the same quarter to European Greece the poems of Homer[2]. Further, when we take into account (1) the close filiation of the Elegiac branch of poetry to the Epic song of Homer and that that branch is of Ionian growth, (2) the historical fact of a body or guild of men called 'Homerids' having existed in an Ionian island Chios, and that these, on grounds reputed to be more or less valid, claimed actual descent, or, according to others, genuine poetical succession from a poet of the name of Homer; and (3) the internal evidence furnished by the dialect—Ionic with a mixture of Æolian forms,—we find the conclusion irresistible that it was among the islands or shores of Ionia or the borderland of Æolis that the Homeric poems took permanent shape and form[3]. With regard to the Odyssey, in particular, it is

---

[2] Other authorities for this statement are Herakleides, Polit. ii., and Æl., Var. Hist. xiii. 13. They are given at length in La Roche's 'Text Kritik' (pp. 7, 8).

[3] To these grounds might be added the otherwise inexplicable *cultus* of Homer

precisely among the busy maritime communities of the Ionian and Æolian coast that we can discover, during the early ages of the Greek people, that combination in its fullest form of Life in the Agora and Life on the Ocean-wave, which were necessary to form the *nidus* for a romance dealing so largely with maritime adventure.

26. The objections to this view as to the Asiatic origin of the poems are not many nor are they weighty [4]. They consist chiefly in the apparently special familiarity which the author of the Odyssey shows with the Peloponnesus, not greater certainly than the author of the Second Iliad; in the interest which he shows in Sparta and the mountains of the Peloponnesus (Od. ζ 103) [5]; and in the circumstance that according to one interpretation the sun seems to be made to rise in the sea (Od. γ 1) [6], which is certainly favourable to an insular, though not necessarily to a Peloponnesian, origin of the poem. These Peloponnesian touches, if we may so call them, are in keeping with a number of similar phenomena in certain books of the Iliad, regarding which the evidence of Ionian origin is as complete as can be desired, evidence, indeed, such as might be laid before a jury with the utmost confidence as to the precision of the verdict. The full statement on this point must be reserved until that evidence can be presented in detail. Meantime the notion of a Peloponnesian origin to the Poems must be dismissed, and although the arguments of Thiersch on this point have been apparently accepted by Mr. Gladstone as conclusive, they were long ago disposed of by Thirlwall, when dealing with the point in his history of Greece, in the following words (Hist. of Greece, vol. i. p. 276):—

at Smyrna, with a temple dedicated to him and coinage styled after him, as we might speak of ' Napoleons ' or ' Edwards,' or as the ancients spoke of *Darics* and *Philips* (Eckhel, Numism. Vet. in ' Smyrna ').

[4] The circumstance that the Trojan Catalogue in B is much less full and minute in its specifications of localities than the Grecian one is easily accounted for by the patriotic bias of the poet and his greater interest in the heroes of Greece, just as he has left us with a fainter vision of the relative *ages* of the Trojan leaders as compared with those of the captains of the Greek camp (Gl. Homer, iii. 191).

[5] Bergk (Hist. of Gr. Lit.) accounts for some of these features by supposing the Odyssey to have undergone retouching for a Spartan audience.

[6] It is possible that Oceanus is meant by the λίμνη, whence the sun arises (cp. ψ 244), in which case it would no more prove that Homer was a Peloponnesian or European Greek than Mimnermus's ῥοδοδάκτυλος Ἠὼς Ὠκεανὸν προλιποῦσ' would prove that *he* was a European and not an Asiatic of Colophon.

'This is not a case where we have to balance two arguments
of a similar kind against one another; but where we have on
the one side a mass of positive testimony; on the other some
facts, which through our very imperfect knowledge of the poet's
life and times, we are unable to account for. Where this is so,
there can be little doubt which way the principles of sound
criticism require us to decide.'

27. Alongside of this fact must be taken another, that
while the Homeric poems come into historic view first on the
Asiatic shore of Ionia, they presuppose a cradle of legendary
lore which is localised in Europe. The *incunabula* of Greek
mythology is localised to the west of the Egean, and there is
evidence to show that the author or authors of the Homeric
poems 'served themselves heirs' to the traditions and availed
themselves of the imaginative creations of Poets, who had
appeared previously on European soil[7]. The circumstance
that the Olympus of Thessaly is the recognised abode of the
gods, even when their activities are represented as concentrated around the plain of Troy, proves convincingly that
the Homeric poetry had its ultimate roots in Europe. There
can be no question that the Olympus[8] of the Homeric poems,
wherever it is represented as a mountain, is the mountain of
that name overhanging Tempe and the Peneus, and, what is
more remarkable, although we hear of Ida as a seat of one
of the gods, Zeus, even Trojans are represented as sharing
the belief in Olympus as the seat of the conclave of the Immortals; and so Chryses the priest in the first Iliad, and Hector
in the twenty-second, are made by the force of Thessalian
tradition to conform to the Greek belief and speak of the
gods as 'the Olympians.' To prove that the Olympus of the
Iliad is the European mountain and not any Asiatic mountain, not even 'the Olympus high and hoar[9]' which Byron
speaks of as a noble object from Constantinople and the
Golden Horn, it is sufficient to refer to the journey of Heré

---

[7] The Muses are called, in their oldest designation, Olympian. 'I think
this fact might instruct us that we are indebted to the muse-inspired Pierians for
the union of the Olympian gods;' O. Müller, Mythol. p. 159.—As early as Hesiod
(Op. 1) we find the Muses referred to as Pierian in origin, and in Sappho we hear
of βρόδων τῶν ἐκ Πιερίας, as a symbol of poetical immortality (frag. 4).

[8] Cp. Varro on 'Olympus,' L. L., 7. 2. 20.

[9] Μυσῷ ἐν Οὐλύμπῳ, occurs in Callimachus, Hym. Dian. 117.

from it to Ida in the fourteenth Iliad, where the mention of
Athos and Lemnos as intermediate points is quite conclusive.
Further, any indications of prior poets found in the Homeric
poems connect themselves with European localities [10], and all
the cases of ἀοιδοί or Bards of the Epic time (leaving out of
view the case of Demodocus, as depending on the doubtful
localisation of Phæacia) belong to the western side of the
Egean. Phemius in Ithaca, the nameless minstrel at Mycenæ
who had the guardianship of Clytemnestra, and Thamyris,
are clear instances to this effect. The last, in fact, is conclusive, inasmuch as the notice concerning him implies that
Song was already in some form an Art (Preller, ii. p. 341),
and, further, seems to be decidedly realistic and to embody
a nucleus of actual personal history of a pathetic kind [11]. Moreover the *locale* assigned to him is not only European but, in all
probability, Thessalian, the Œchalia, with which his name in
the older traditions is associated, being certainly in Thessaly
(Preller, Gr. M. ii. p. 341, Ven. Schol. B. 596, 730, and Blackie,
Homer, iv. p. 110).

28. The conclusion to which we are conducted by these
facts is confirmed by the following considerations derived
from the poems themselves. These assume a previous acquaintance with the heroes they pourtray. The opening line
of the Iliad, for example, implies that Peleus was already
a familiar hero; Patroclus is first introduced to us by his
patronymic (Α 307), and Achilles has attached to him a series
of epithets which must have been traditional, being no longer

---

[10] The κλέα ἀνδρῶν of Achilles in I 186 are no doubt European, though the
particular instrument was Asiatic.

[11] The name of Thamyris is by Welcker connected with θαμά. If so, he presents an analogy in appellation to Homer himself, whose name cannot be separated
from ὁμοῦ, both words indicating *association*. Accordingly, several of the Wolfian
school, at once sublime them both, in the cremation-furnace of their criticism, into
an *appellativum* or *symbol*, meaning *Aggregation*. Hesychius interprets θάμυρις as
πανήγυρις, σύνοδος ἢ πυκνότης τινῶν, and θαμυρίζει as ἀθροίζει, συνάγει. It does not
follow, however, that Thamyris and Homer were not real individuals, because their
names can be dissected philologically.—Regarding the possible connection of these
two poets, it is not unimportant to note that in the Life of Homer attributed to
Herodotus, in which undoubtedly old traditions are preserved, Thessaly is made
the cradle of his ancestry, for Melanopus, of Magnesia, in Thessaly, is the colonist
of Kyme from whom Homer was traditionally sprung. Compare the descent of
Stesichorus from Hesiod, a parallel case (O. Müller, Lit. ch. 14. 4).—Clemens Al.
(Str. i. 16. 76) makes Thamyris the inventor of the ' Dorian mood or measure.'

easily intelligible from the matter contained in the existing lays [12]. The various epithets designating him as the 'swift-footed,' presuppose a substratum of Thessalian tradition and poetic lore regarding the Thessalian hero, and probably refer to some early Pierian lay as to the youthful feats of the hero in hunting, presumably, under the training of Chiron [13], among the wilds of Pelion (cp. Pind. Nem. iii. 45–52). It may therefore be assumed as scientifically certain that while the poems had their rise on the shore of Asia Minor, they had their roots in the mythology and poetic lore of Thessaly [14].

It will not therefore excite surprise, if the evidence should disclose traces, in one of the poems, of an older kernel which may ultimately be referable in associations, if not in actual origin, to Thessalian soil.

[12] Iliad Υ 189 contains matter to justify the *continuation* of such epithets, not their bestowal.

[13] The nurture of the hero under Chiron rests on Pindaric rather than Homeric tradition in Λ 831. The Scholiast on Il. I 486 actually denies that Homer knew of Chiron as tutor to Achilles.

[14] Heyne thinks 'Herakleiae' had already begun to be formed before the first kernel of the Iliad (cp. his note on Ξ 249). Poetry had therefore spread further south from Olympus and Pieria, as the legends of Herakles belong to a region south of Thessaly, viz. to Thebes and Argolis.

CHAPTER IV.

κρούνω δ' ἵκανον καλλιρρώω ἔνθα τε πηγαί
δοιαὶ ἀναΐσσουσι.

29. IN the previous chapter, we explained the double filiation, in respect of locality, of early Greek song, and showed how Thessaly and Asiatic Ionia, were each, in a certain order, the mother of the Muses. In pursuing our inquiries further, whether there is anything in the two Epics answering to this double stadium of Greek song, we at once raise the question, which is the anterior poem, and whether the anterior poem is a unity.

Regarding the former question, there is not much that needs to be said. The critics, ancient[1] and modern, seem agreed as to this point, that the Iliad is anterior in execution to the Odyssey. Possibly a doubt might be entertained regarding the *Doloneia* or Tenth Book, whose place in the array of cantos is stated to have been an *ex post facto assignment*, after the rest of the poem was in shape (Ven. Schol. K. 1). Yet regarding this book, notwithstanding some philological difficulties that incline George Curtius to give it a later date (cp. Curtius, Griech. Verbum, ii. p. 76), Düntzer has made it probable that it preceded the Odyssey in actual execution (Abhandl. pp. 465–70). Moreover, certain formulæ of expression common to both epics have been shown by Düntzer to have been shaped primarily for the Iliad, before they were utilised in the Odyssey. Thus the precept to Penelope in

---

[1] The author of the Treatise περὶ ὕψους (§ 9), commonly ascribed to Longinus, observes that the Odyssey is the Epilogue (ἐπίλογος) of the Iliad, and assumes familiarity with the heroes celebrated there.—Cp. also Mure, Gr. Lit. ii. p. 134, and Giseke's Hom. Forschungen (p. 33).

α 356-9, and repeated in φ 344 of the latter, is couched in the same terms as the precept to Andromache in Iliad Ζ 490, but the expression, εἰς οἶκον ἰοῦσα, is on the whole more appropriate in the latter, Andromache being then abroad on the public way. This serves to mark the passage in the Iliad, according to Düntzer, as the primary location.

Further, we have only to recall the fact that the whole case of the Chorizontes, ancient and modern, turned upon the recency and subsequence of the Odyssey, and their arguments are not capable of presentation and could never claim a hearing, unless on this postulate of the posteriority of the Odyssey. Without any formal presentation of the evidence we think ourselves entitled to assume to the Iliad anteriority in execution.

30. We now come to consider the question of Unity, regarding which we must enter more into detail. And first, as to the younger poem. That the Odyssey is in its structure remarkably firm and compact, though composed of many parts, yet with each part concurring to constitute a whole that is one and indivisible; that, with all its variety of subject, it is fairly uniform in tone with remarkable continuity of plan, homogeneous purpose, and sustained consistency of conception; that it has come from the mind of its author 'moulded at one projection[2],' are facts, which only extreme scepticism can deny. Wolf himself was forward to confess that the framework of the Odyssey, with its elaborate adjustment of parts and exquisite and complicated preparation for the *dénouement*, was most skilful[3], and he speaks in high

---

[2] The expression is Mr. Grote's, regarding the Odyssey. Like Homer's own σόλος in the Games, it is, as a poem, αὐτοχόωνος, which the Scholiast ad loc. (Ψ 826) well explains, ὁ καθ' ἑαυτὸν κεχωνευμένος, καὶ μηδὲν ἔχων ἐπείσακτον, 'cast in the mould by itself and with no mixture or alloy.'—This however does not exclude the possibility of the mass so moulded having suffered from the rust of time and from tinkering of alien hands (cp. Porson, Orest. 5). Certain insertions seem to have been added to or wedged into it in after time, such as the doubtful portions of the Nekyia in λ, and the after portion subsequent to the *dénouement*, viz. ω, and a part of ψ. In speaking of the Odyssey, hereafter, I do not include in the poem what follows after ψ 296, with which, according to Aristarchus, it comes to a close.

[3] 'Jam vero Odysseam nobis compara. In ea quod abundare, quod deesse videri possit, nihil est; et quod est maximum, quocunque eam loco finieris, multum ad exspectationem legentis, plurimum ad integritatem operis desiderari sentias;' Wolf, Præf. II. p. xxvi. The force of candour can no further go. Again, ' Odysseae admirabilis summa et compages pro praeclarissimo monumento ingenii

praise of the architectonic skill which it displays as 'the most splendid monument of Greek genius [4].' This perfection of structure he endeavours to convert into an argument in his favour, by representing it as an artificial unity superinduced in cultivated times, such as those of Pisistratus. The fact remains, that, if the Odyssey had come down to us alone, the question of unity could not have arisen, and the Wolfian theory would have had no room for existence. The marvellous marshalling of gathered circumstance to bring round the great result at which the poet aims—the hero's restoration to home and kingdom; the skilful arrangement by which the double stream of action, carried on by father and by son, converges to the point of junction when the heroes meet at the hut of Eumæus; the absurdity of supposing that any large section of it (such as the books where Telemachus is the main actor), had any independent existence, except as a part, it might even be an after part, of a great whole,—all unite to render the Odyssey impregnable against disruptive assaults, as they conspire to render it the most perfect and finished story ever told in verse through all the ages of the world [5].

Graeci habenda est;' Wolf, Proleg. ch. 27. How very firm, in general, the texture of the Odyssey is, may be seen in Wolf's remark as to the paucity of ἀθετήσεις. ' In Odyssea quidem, non memini nisi unius versus ab eo (Aristarcho) nominatim ἀθετουμένου (β 137).' Wolf was not aware of such as Od. λ 547. Still the statement is a remarkable one. Compare with this the verdict of Mr. Grote who, in his chapter on the Greek Drama, declares the Odyssey to be equal to the most symmetrical of the plays of Sophocles in architectonic skill.

[4] The following criticism on the artistic unity of the ' Bride of Lammermoor' among Scott's novels applies, *mutatis mutandis*, to the artistic unity of the Odyssey. What the Master of Ravenswood is to the one, Ulysses is to the other. 'No individual in any of the Novels or Poems more completely maintains his pre-eminence as the hero; for the whole action depends upon him and centres in him: his ruling influence is always felt, whether he be present or absent; and of all the passions, whether hatred, love, admiration, hope or fear, which vary and animate the successive scenes, he is the grand ultimate and paramount object.' Adolphus's Letters to Heber, p. 199.—A writer in the *Edinburgh Review*, 1849 (p. 89) challenges the whole world of prose and verse for a Plot to beat that of the Odyssey. ' In the whole range of narrative fiction a Plot more nearly approaching perfection is not to be found.'

[5] The attempt to prove the Telemachia, as it is called, or the preparatory section constituting the first four books to be a separate poem is against all reason. Telemachus is only a *neben-person*, not a central figure, and always implies either the presence, or the expectation of the presence, of a greater. It would be as rational to suppose the arm of a statue when unsocketed an independent member, or to fancy an aisle or rather narthex of a church apart from the building of which it is a portion, as to imagine the Telemachia to exist in independence, disjointed

31. But is there no *per contra?* Is the Odyssey such a perfect chrysolite that no flaw can be found in the members composing its crystallisation? None that will avail to affect materially the evidences of unity. That certain cantos can be *conceived* as separate *ganglia* in formation, that episodes in the Nekyia such as Elpenor's can be dispensed with, that there may be occasional instances of variation such as look to a logical mind contradictions, as, for example, regarding the colour of Ulysses' hair (*dark* in π 176, *blonde* in ν 399, cp. Merry on ζ 231), variation explicable under the variety of characters the hero has to assume,—not to speak of the theurgic conditions rendering these things conceivable—these make up, with one or two chronological difficulties, the sum and substance of what can be advanced against the unity of the Odyssey. The circumstance that Agamemnon's ghost [6] (Od. λ 449) speaks of Telemachus as already among full-grown men when Ulysses has yet before him the seven years with Calypso (η 259), after which the youth comes before us throwing off his minority and taking his place in the assembly of men, is a prophetic anticipation of the future as if actually present remarked on by the ancient scholiast (Od. β 313). The only really formidable difficulty is that as to the chronology of the days within the poem, how the reckoning in the case of the one hero, the son, can be made to square with the reckoning in the case of the other hero, the father,—twenty-eight days, according to Colonel Mure (H. of Gr. Lit. i. 440, 458), unaccounted for in the case of Telemachus [7]. This

from the Odyssey. The story of a young hero searching for his father from land to land is very interesting and graphic, but as it leads to no conclusion except what is found in the poem as a whole, it is a story without a satisfying close, unless in connection with the history of the hero when he reappears, and then it is admirable and appropriate.

[6] Anticlea's utterances in Od. λ 189. do not involve any prolepsis as to time. On the contrary. the use of ἔκηλος implies that the ' siege ' by the Suitors has not yet begun. So Tiresias's words in λ 115 do not imply a state of things as con-temporaneous with the utterance, for κατέδουσι derives a *future* sense from the governing δήεις, being equivalent to the Attic δήεις τοὺς κατέδοντας, ' Thou shalt find men devouring.'

[7] The question is discussed by Mure. as above cited. by Friedländer (p. 24). by Grote (H. ii. 224). The pinch of the difficulty is especially felt in squaring β 374 and δ 588—where a stay of twelve days is looked forward to by Telemachus, and he is anxious not to protract it (δ 594)—with such passages as ε 279. which swallow up that period in the eighteen days' voyage of Ulysses. Telemachus was

difficulty, however, disappears, or at least diminishes greatly, on second considerations. It does appear that, through a certain inadvertence, owing to his handling of numbers in a poetic rather than a mathematical sense, or owing to the infancy of arithmetical calculation (a point on which several illustrations might be given), the poet has allowed a discrepancy to creep in, which, however, is one so subtle that none of the ancient critics appears to have discerned, nine-tenths of his present readers never perceive, and probably none of his auditors in his own time ever observed. A blemish in the workmanship of this nature does not prove a plurality of workmen, and so far from militating against, it rather favours, the genuineness and antiquity of the Odyssey, as belonging to an age when the lynx eye of science had not begun to detect awkward relations as to consistency in numbers, as it certainly would have done if the poem had received shape in the colder and more critical times of Pericles, when such cross-questioners as the Sophists were abroad, or even in the times of Pisistratus, when prose literature with something of positive feeling for reality was beginning to appear. The *diasceuastae* or *rédacteurs* employed by the latter, if with functions so free as to have allowed them to cut and carve and piece together into an ostensibly organic unity, would have been certain to make the arithmetical numbers right [8], but they would have made much else wrong, for we should then have looked in vain for the delightful simplicity and fresh redolence of nature in her morning prime breathing from every part of this pre-eminently

'Speciosa locis morataque recte fabula.'

probably persuaded (cp. ν 423–4) to spend more time at Sparta, in which case there is no discrepancy, though the poet has not inserted the necessary link to harmonise it.—The period during which Telemachus seems to remain inactive at Sparta, might have afforded sufficient time for what would have been an interesting episode, a visit to the court of Idomeneus in Crete, who, we are told, had returned safe home (Od. γ 191). Is it a violent supposition to imagine it possible that such a voyage may have been in the programme, in which case the twenty-eight days would have been fully occupied? It is curious that Zenodotus seems to have had a reading in α 83, κεῖθεν δὲ Κρήτηνδε παρ' Ἰδομενῆα ἄνακτα, as if provision was actually made for such an extension, but it might be hazardous to affirm that such an extension was ever put in actual shape.

[8] There is one arithmetical number that is firmly adhered to through the poem. It is that Ulysses has been twenty years away. Cantos far asunder in position agree in this point, which comes up in the following places, β 175, ρ 327, τ 222, ψ 102, 170.

32 It is not difficult therefore to come to the conclusion that all the exercitations of certain critics such as Rhode and others to find flaws in the Odyssey are labour in vain, and almost equally so the laborious efforts of such as Düntzer to answer them. No human production is proof against hypercriticism. and foregone conclusions will demolish the most adamantine structure[9]. It is enough to justify us in pronouncing a poem a unity, to find, as we do find, the poem, after the subject is propounded, keeping that subject full in view with no superfluous or erratic eccentricity, and with the purpose gradually unfolding and ultimately realised, every important character who has been introduced being disposed of and accounted for. Such is eminently the case with the Odyssey, and I sum up therefore with the verdict of Mr. Grote as one in this matter completely satisfactory: 'If it had happened that the Odyssey had been preserved to us alone without the Iliad, I think the dispute respecting Homeric unity would never have been raised' (H. of Greece, ii. p. 221).

33. If we turn to the Iliad, can the same judgment be formed, and is the same unity discernible? Not in the same sense as the unity of the Odyssey, and for the following reasons.

(1) It is an Epic not so entirely devoted to the fortunes and glory of a single hero as is the Odyssey. The appellations by which the poems are known differentiate them sufficiently in this respect. The Odyssey means the poem in honour of Ulysses, otherwise Odysseus, and his name is imbedded in the structure. The Iliad does not so contain imbedded in it the name of Achilles; it means simply 'the poem of the war at Ilium.' It is in fact an indefinite appellation (as it is, in form, simply a *collective* noun) for what was felt to be a less homogeneous aggregate. Hence the poem in honour of Achilles has to share its lofty honours with the cyclic poem of Lesches, which told of the downfall of Ilium and was known as 'the Little Iliad.' Eustathius, it is true, in the opening sentence of his elephantine commentary, speaks of the Iliad as a σῶμα εὐάρμοστον, 'a well organised body[10],' which is true, but only

---

[9] According to Grote, the Wolfians proceed 'in the case of the Odyssey more on *à priori* rejection of ancient epical unity rather than by any positive evidence in the Odyssey itself' (H. of Greece, ii. 262).

[10] His predecessors, the more ancient critics. had a more just perception of

relatively, and is not true when compared with the Odyssey. The antithesis to this Eustathian doctrine is Paley's view that the Iliad is a composite poem producing the impression of 'a stained glass window that has had a long history, filled up with materials of different ages, some old, some new, and all dove-tailed into a kind of unity of design.' The truth lies between these two extremes. While not so homogeneous as the Odyssey, it is far from being so heterogeneous as Mr. Paley's simile implies, and it will probably be found that a complicity of only two elements will account for the main conditions of the case.

34. It is worthy of remark, as showing the instinct of the ancient mind in this regard, that Aristotle in his Poetics (chap. 8), when dealing with this point of Unity, although he mentions the Iliad, as a matter of form, in the background of his survey, yet draws his actual illustrations from the Odyssey[11]. This he evidently considered as the model Epic, in so far as the great essential of Unity was concerned, inasmuch as it was concentrated around a single person, and moved on with full sweep of complicated and gathered circumstance to a single great and imposing action. On the other hand, when speaking of the *divisibility of parts* in a poem, Aristotle appeals in the first instance to the Iliad and brings in the Odyssey only as an after-thought (Poetics, ch. 27). In like manner the fine instinct of Horace[12], not less true than the sagacious intellect of Aristotle, when he is illustrating his

the state of the case. We find in the Venetian Scholia (Il. A 1) that it had been a question raised and discussed in the schools, why it was that, if the one poem was called an *Odysseia*, the other was not called an *Achilleia*. The answer commonly given was one flattering to the Greek race, that Greece was so rich in heroes with splendid individuality that no single one could be allowed to fill the canvas, and Achilles was only as it were *primus inter pares*. It would thus appear as if the great war poem were premonitory of the fortunes of the Greek race itself, where each branch was to have its turn of ascendancy, but no enduring pre-eminence.—The action of the Iliad is centrifugal; that of the Odyssey, centripetal, being the Return after separation and dispersion.

[11] Compare (besides the fine summary in the end of ch. 17), ch. 8 of the Poetics, where, among other things, he remarks that the Odyssey, though with a single hero, is not a ' Biography' of that hero, and so is unlike such poems as the Herakleis and Theseis.—The *in medias res* principle is really illustrated only by the Odyssey (Wolf, Proleg. ch. 29).

[12] The proem of the Odyssey was evidently a favourite with Horace, for we have two versions of it from his pen.

encomium of *Nil molitur inepte*, turns with the precision of the
magnetic needle to the Odyssey rather than to the Iliad :—

> 'Quanto rectius hic, qui nil molitur inepte ;
> " Die mihi, Musa, virum captae post tempora Trojae,
> Qui mores hominum multorum vidit et urbes."'

The compactness and symmetry of the Odyssey, as well as
the complexity of the Iliad, are therefore, we take it, implied
in the *titles* of the poems, no matter whether we consider
those titles to be as old as the poems themselves, a supposition by no means probable, or to date only from the
time of Herodotus, in whose chapters these names first
emerge to view. The name of the Odyssey is good evidence
as to the conscious feeling of the Greek race that in it they
possessed a poem over which they could inscribe the name of
a single hero, according to its opening line,

> 'Sing to me, O Muse, the Man,'

and that with no appendage or prefix of 'arms' or any other
fulcrum or pedestal whatsoever. What is more notable is the
circumstance that Ulysses is not named in his own Exordium,
as if he were 'the man' pre-eminent, the *vir unicus*, not
needing to be named [13].

35. On the other hand the Iliad, in the shape in which it
has come down to us, consists of a series of pictures taken
from a certain period, and celebrating certain heroes, of the
war around Ilium, and the unity which it possesses is rather
like that of a rich and brilliant historical play of Shakspere,
with many centres of interest, a Cæsar, a Brutus, and an
Antony, or a Henry, a Hotspur, a Glendower, as contrasted
with the unity of his 'Hamlet' or 'King Lear,' where there is
but one protagonist. This complexity, of course, does not

---

[13] This keynote of the Odyssey as to the pre-eminence of Ulysses is well sustained. Apart from ἀνήρ (perhaps *husband*), in α 344, φ 70, we find him simply
κεῖνος in δ 832 and σ 181, and, in the discourse of Eumaeus in ξ, he is referred to
by ἄναξ, κεῖνος, ἐκεῖνος, and other pronouns, before he is named in l. 144. He is
also associated with Athene in a group of θεὰ καὶ καρτερὸς ἀνήρ in υ 393, and a
similar hyperbole occurs in ν 297. There does not appear in the case of Achilles
anything quite equal to this pre-eminence of position ; the nearest approach is
Σ 257, where he is styled οὗτος ἀνήρ without being named. It is also to be noted
that ἀνήρ in Iliad is not so pre-eminent, where all or most at least are ἄνδρες,
while the ἀνήρ of the Odyssey stands out alone, as it were, among ἄνθρωποι, which
last word has an ampler range, and comes much more to the front in the Odyssey
as the ordinary designation of Man.

exclude the possibility of single authorship, but it prepares the way, in the case of a primitive and very early poem like the Iliad, for the entertainment of the supposition of at least a dual origin.

36. (2) So much for the evidence from the *Titles* of the Poems. We come, secondly, to consider the internal structure of each Poem. And here we are met by the curious circumstance, explain it as we may, that in the Iliad we have, besides the opening invocation to the Muse, five others, at different parts throughout the poem, of a more or less formal kind. *The Odyssey knows but one* [14]. These repeated invocations in the Iliad suggest, if they do not imply, different starting points, and favour, to a certain extent, the theory of complex origin [15].

37. Further, we find large sections of the Iliad easily separable, and, what is more, separable without leaving a gap in the plan, not provided for, to all appearance, in the

[14] Minor but still important corroborations of this matter of the 'Invocations' are the following phenomena, showing the homogeneousness of the Odyssey as compared with the Iliad.   1. The figure of speech, *Apostrophe*, where the poet breaks out into an address to some hero, is largely distributed among *various* persons in the Iliad.   In the Odyssey it is never bestowed except on one, Eumæus, and on him frequently (fifteen instances).   Compare Scholiast on Υ 2, who has an interesting enumeration, as to this personal allocution (Mure, ii. p. 61).

Apostrophe in Iliad.	*Apostrophe* in Odyssey.
To Patroclus, frequent (e. g. Π 20)	
— Melanippus, O 582 (sole Trojan)	To Eumæus only (e. g. ξ 55).
— Achilles, Υ 2.	
— Menelaus, N 603, P 679, 702, Δ 127, 146, Π 104, Ψ 600	
— Phoebus, O 365, Υ 152.	

2. The bestowment of the important epithet πτολίπορθος shows similar peculiarity (cp. infra, § 74).   In the Iliad it is bestowed on Achilles oftenest, but it is not limited to him.   In the Odyssey it occurs seven times, and, among all the gods and heroes, it is there given to Ulysses alone.   The occurrences are—

Iliad.		*Odyssey.*	
Achilles .	. 4		
Ulysses	. 2	Ulysses only .	. 7
Ares .	. 1		
Enyo . .	. 1		
Otrynteus	. 1		
Oileus	. 1		
	—		
	10		

[15] It must be remembered, however, that Apollonius Rhodius, after a primary appeal to the Muse, invokes Erato for the special business of his Third Canto, and an unnamed Muse at the opening of his Fourth. Similarly Milton in his longer poem. Compare Conington on partial Invocations in Virg. Georg. iii. 294.

proem of the Poem. The proem proposes as its subject 'the wrath of Achilles and the woes in consequence to the Greeks.' That proem is no doubt amply fulfilled, but a vast deal more than what is actually promised is introduced into the picture. In the *first* place, the 'wrath' is so turned that, after producing woes to the Greeks, it ceases to do so and produces woes to the Trojans and specially to Hector, with whose death it becomes, as it were, extinguished. This, however, is so natural a sequel that the most stringent exactor of Unity must admit that though not in the proem, it follows very naturally upon the events described in the proem. This did not escape the sharp eye of David Hume, who has the following observations upon the point :—

'It is evident that Homer in the course of his narration exceeds the first proposition of his subject, and that the anger of Achilles which caused the death of Hector is not the same with that which produced so many ills to the Greeks. But the strong connection between these two movements, the quick transition from one to the other . . . . and the natural curiosity we have to see Achilles in action, after so long repose; all these causes carry on the reason and produce a sufficient unity in the subject' (Hume, Essay on Association of Ideas).

Against this expansion, up to the death of Hector, there is therefore no critical objection, and if the transference of the wrath to a new object is to be treated as a violation of unity, then the proem of the Odyssey is not immaculate, for, while leading up to the Return or νόστος of the hero, it does not let us into the secret of the events that are the natural sequel of the νόστος, the destruction of the Suitors being only by implication contained in the programme of the Odyssey. There is therefore no exception to be taken to this alteration of the stream, inasmuch as it still flows onward, though its direction is changed and a new course superadded. What excites surprise is the occurrence of a counter stream flowing in a different direction, which forms an important factor in the elements of the Iliad [16]. To this, in the *second* place, we now direct attention.

[16] Mere want of connecting link will not suffice to convict of separate authorship. There must be *disturbance* of purpose in order to a complete proof. Thus in Nonnus's Dionysiaca, according to Dr. Schmitz (Smith's Dict. of Biog.), 'the

38. The Iliad, as it now stands, provides in its proem only for 'woes to the *Greeks.*' Neither the proem nor book I. anticipates woes to the Trojans, but rather woes from them. Soon after the opening, however, when we have passed the first Canto, we come upon a large tract of poetic narrative, in which the Greeks suffer no great woes but inflict many [17], and, instead, we hear mention of woes as being 'determined upon Trojans' (B 15, Z 241) [18]. It is not till the Eighth Book that the misfortunes foretold in the programme as befalling the Greeks make their appearance, and the Books from the second to the seventh inclusive are occupied with various matters, but certainly not with the misfortunes predicted. It is this portion, therefore, that specially appears to be not a continuation of, but an insertion into, or engrafting on, the primary stem. The angry chief has retired to his tents, but instead of misfortunes, as expected, successes in the field and victories in single combats fall to the lot of the Greeks, who seem nowise depressed for want of Achilles, are spoken of by the gods as $\dot{\upsilon}\pi\epsilon\rho\kappa\dot{\upsilon}\delta\alpha\nu\tau\epsilon\varsigma$ (Δ 66), and as *now* daring to fight with gods (E 380), and express no particular regret at the hero's absence. Within Troy there is great consternation. A special supplication to Athene on the part of the Trojan dames is decreed (Z 86) by the Trojan leaders for help in the hour of need. Andromache rushes to the tower because she hears that 'the Trojans are sore pressed and that the great victory belongs to the Greeks' (Z 387), and Hector expresses doubts whether he shall ever again see his home (Z 367), since the battle goes so hard against him. Moreover, the

first six or seven books are so completely devoid of any connecting link that any one of them might by itself be regarded as a separate unit.' Yet no one proposes to break up its authorship on such a ground.

[17] At the very outset of B (l. 4) we hear indeed of mischiefs to the Greeks in the counsels of Zeus, but ere long we hear of the Trojans as combined with them (l. 40, cp. Δ 543, H 70) in the actual experience. The Odyssey (θ 82) states the matter under the same aspect, and agrees with B—H as against the Achillean proem.— It is remarkable that the Ægis, which in Apollo's hands at a later stage brings the promised disasters on the Greeks, is in section B—H rather in Athene's hands, who is *friendly* to the Greeks.

[18] The Ven. Scholiast on Δ 505 is sorely puzzled at the Greeks gaining the day when Zeus wishes them to lose it ($\pi\hat{\omega}\varsigma\ \nu\iota\kappa\hat{\omega}\sigma\iota\nu\ ^{\prime\prime}\mathrm{E}\lambda\lambda\eta\nu\epsilon\varsigma,\ o\hat{\upsilon}\varsigma\ \dot{o}\ Z\epsilon\dot{\upsilon}\varsigma\ \theta\dot{\epsilon}\lambda\epsilon\iota\ \dot{\eta}\tau\tau\hat{\alpha}\sigma\theta\alpha\iota$); and makes vain attempts to solve the puzzle.—The passage in H 478 is ambiguous, as it is not clear to which side the $\kappa\alpha\kappa\dot{\alpha}$ are in this instance aimed. Heyne is in doubt, 'sive Trojanis solis, sive utrique exercitui.'

Trojan dames bewail him as never more to return (Z 501–2).
These incidents do not come under the head of 'misfortunes'
to the Greeks, and we are not surprised therefore to find that
Apollo in the interest of the Trojans proposes a cessation of
war (H 29), and that the result towards the end of the Seventh
Book should be that the Trojans, by Antenor's confession, are
inclined to yield (H 350). Again, the inner machinery and
divine mechanism of the action seem to be arrested or to have
undergone a change. The Zeus of the First Book has made
a certain promise to Thetis that he would bring about the
humbling of the Greeks. The Zeus of the Fourth Book
seems unconscious or even forgetful of this promise; for he
proposes suggestions which, if carried out, would have made
it impossible to fulfil his promise, and would have left
Achilles without honour. It is of course open to say in
reply that he is 'son of Kronos of the crooked counsel' and
knew in the depths of his own mind the purpose he was
planning. The honour of his intellect is saved only by the
compromise of his *morale*, especially when in the Fifth Book
he permits Heré and Athene to chastise Ares for making
havoc among Greeks (E 757), the very thing which he is
himself meditating on a larger scale ere long. It is also
noteworthy that in book II. the same god Zeus is represented
as bestowing special honour on the king (B 478–83) who has
committed the outrage which he recently promised to Thetis to
avenge. There is great difficulty therefore in reconciling the
Zeus of books II, IV, and V, with the Zeus of books I, and VIII.

39. A still more important element of the situation remains.
Not only are the Greeks victorious, but one of their heroes is
represented as so far supplying the absence of Achilles that
he performs feats such as Achilles himself cannot boast of
performing in the climax of his glory. The valiant Diomed
has not only put the Trojans in greater terror even than
Achilles according to their own confession (Z 99), but in the
fervour of the fight he discomfits, with Athene's help, first one
and then another of the gods that come to help the Trojans.
This last achievement is not paralleled by any exploit attributed to Achilles, and the question arises how can such honour
to Diomed be reconciled with the pre-eminence of the chief
hero of the whole poem. Regarding the series of Greek

successes, it may indeed be alleged, that the action is prolonged and the real business of the epic delayed, until the patriotism of the poet has meted out measures of glory to the various Greek chiefs besides Achilles; that this does not constitute a departure from but only a retardation of the primary scheme [19]; and further that in this way the poet was able to vary the episodes of the war and to complete the full gallery of war pictures by scenes that would have otherwise not been portrayed, such as the picture · of the army in assembly, truces, challenges, single combats, all which are splendid embellishments. There is some truth in these views of Nitzsch and other defenders of the unity, but no explanation has yet been devised which entirely meets the difficulty or alleviates the *crux* of the case. how, if it was all the work of one poet, the measure of glory should have been heaped so high for Diomed in the Fifth Book that he is the vanquisher of gods [20], whereas the crowning exploit of the central hero Achilles, in the crisis of the poem, is that he was the vanquisher of a man [21]. The governing reference to Achilles which the proem entitles us to expect has thus manifestly been departed from, and a sort of anticlimax is produced which leads one to conclude either that the author has unconsciously altered his standpoint and enlarged his ground-plan beyond the first conception, or that another poet has been at work who has extended the lines of the primary Programme. To which of these explanations

[19] It is argued by Nitzsch ingeniously that after all Zeus delays only a single day with the execution of his counsel. The point is, however, not the length of time occupied in the occurrences themselves, but the proportion they bear to the whole. When Zeus in the Eleventh Book allows the Greeks to conquer for a hundred lines, in order not utterly to prostrate them, we can understand such a variation. But when five cantos. or nearly a fourth of the poem, are filled with their successes, it matters little that we should discover, when we reach the close of them. that the time occupied has been one day.

[20] In one instance, Diomed produces the impression as if he were himself a god (E 183).

[21] Achilles in Φ 289 is not without ἐπιτάρροθοι among the gods, and in X 20 he wishes he were able to vanquish a certain god, Apollo. This confession of weakness is. however, not to be pressed, since Diomed. though discomfiting Ares and Aphrodite. retires before the same god (E 435). It is, however. remarkable that it is said of Diomed *οὐδὲ θεὸν μέγαν ἅζετο*, 'he dreaded not even the great god,' viz. Apollo (E 434), and that Aphrodite, and even Apollo, say of him. 'he would even fight with Zeus' (E 362 and 457). On the whole, therefore it may be affirmed that Diomed is *more* successful against gods than even Achilles.

the balance of evidence inclines will appear more fully as the investigation proceeds.

40. It is not necessary to enter further in the meantime on the proofs which have been put in so clear and succinct form by Mr. Grote in his great chapter of volume ii. of his History (see esp. pp. 252–3, 257), showing that the original plan of the Iliad has in some form been interfered with and enlarged— proofs that embrace the case not only of Books from the Second to the Seventh, but also that of the Ninth and Tenth Books, which are similarly extrinsic to the primary action. The latter or 'Doloneia,' though expressly said by the ancient critics to be composed 'by Homer,' was yet confidently pronounced to have been a separate composition and an after addition [22] (Ven. Schol. K 1); while the former book or 'the Embassy' is saved by Colonel Mure chiefly by the excision of three lines of a subsequent book (II 84–86), in which Achilles mentions concessions that would conciliate him, which lines are felt to be inconsistent with the prior existence of the Ninth Book, where the terms he asks have been already offered and indeed more than he subsequently claims, and therefore Col. Mure (H. G. L. i. p. 310) pronounces the peccant lines an interpolation [23]. The embassy of the chiefs and the elaborate supplication to the hero to return, form a most impressive and powerful scene, but it is somewhat strange that the action and speech of Achilles for ten books after it imply that no offer of satisfaction has been made.

[22] One of the difficulties attending K as it now stands is the action of the deities Apollo and Athene, who are represented as interfering after the great interdict by Zeus, which stands two books before in opening of Θ. Apollo appears, from K 51 –7, to be in Pergamus, which is his post in the books from Δ to II, whereas in Θ he must be in Olympus at the council (Θ 311 not inconsistent with this), and he is still found there in O 143. The author of K has therefore represented Apollo on the same lines, not with the Apollo of the Achilleid, but with the Apollo of the non-Achilleid, a view that supports our theory, and is inconsistent with any other.

[23] Schoemann has remarked that if the Ninth Book or 'Embassy' was known to the author of the Sixteenth (Π), instead of the strange expression εἰ μοι κρείων Ἀγαμέμνων ἤπια εἰδείη, 'if royal Agamemnon were mollified towards me,' we should rather expect, εἰ ἐγὼν Ἀγαμέμνονι δίῳ ἤπια εἰδείην, 'if I were mollified toward noble Agamemnon;' Nutzhorn, Entstehungslehre. p. 174 5. — A similar argument is derived from Achilles' words in Λ 609, and from Poseidon's recommendation to the Greeks to make atonement (N 116), implying that no attempt had been made to appease the injured chief, and so ignoring the previous Book of the · Embassy.' —The reference in Σ 448 is not to be relied on as proof that the author of the Achilleid knew of the supplication to Achilles.

Are there, now, any other Books, besides those recently named, that seem to be outside the primary plan? None that can be called discordant, but there are two that are extrinsic, viz. the two closing Books, XXIII. and XXIV. (Grote. II. ii. pp. 266–7). The case regarding these is of another kind. They form a most natural sequel[24] and can hardly be said to disturb the original ground-plan, as presented in the Exordium, though they develope and expand it. These two Books are necessary to satisfy the requirement, not perhaps of an Epos, but certainly of a 'Kunst-Epos ;' which could never be complete, as J. S. Mill remarked upon this point (Discussions, ii. p. 321), 'until the two heroes whose successive deaths formed the catastrophe of the poem, had received the accustomed funeral honours.' They are, however, as the Iliad now stands, *outside* the lines of its original projection, and stand in some respects like the Œdipus Coloneus, subjoined to, not contained within, the scope of the Œdipus Rex. The oracle in the latter gives no note of the milder prophecy out of which the second drama has to spring, for the old prophecy has to be remodelled in the second play and altered to admit of the subsequent development (cp. Œd. Rex 789 with Œd. Col. 88 ff.). Moreover, those two closing cantos present so many features in tone and language different from the books immediately preceding them, but accordant with those of books II.–VII, IX, and X, that we are justified in classing them also with the Books not belonging to the primary nucleus of the Poem.

41. We have thus obtained from a survey of the Iliad this result, that certain Books represent the primary structure as described in the proem, others are enlargements and accessions, more or less consistent, but not acknowledged in the primary ground-plan. Before proceeding to deal with these two sections with a view to further comparison, it is proper to advert here to the fact, that a consciousness more or less clear of a peculiar structure in the Iliad has been felt in different ways

---

[24] According to Mr. Grote, the reappearance in Book XXIII. of the two wounded chiefs, lately cripples, viz. Diomed and Ulysses, without any reference to their recovery, implies the hand of a continuator, not the creator of the story. The surprising recuperative powers of the heroes generally may, however, justify the silence, and explain the apparent obliviousness of the poet.

and from different points of view by various observers. Blair, in his Lectures on 'Rhetoric,' gave expression in a mild vague way to the peculiarity if not deficiency of the Iliad in respect of unity. In like manner Blackie admits that the subject of the Iliad is formally double, though he represents it as also intrinsically one. A still more remarkable admission is that made by Colonel Mure, who says that the Iliad, unlike other Epics, contains no great event *within* the poem towards which the whole progression moves [25]. The death of Hector appears to him an inadequate *dénouement* for the previous array of preparation, and he is no doubt constrained to this admission by the extent to which the original plan has been seemingly overweighted. The fall of Troy would no doubt form a catastrophe worthy of being the close of an Epic poem, but it is an event that lies outside and beyond the range of the horizon, however near it may be felt to be, when Hector, the bulwark of the city, falls [26]. Hence Col. Mure has to devise a special theory for the Iliad, which we give as follows in his own words:—

'In the "Odyssey" the restoration of Ulysses to his home and royal authority, in the "Æneid" the establishment of the Trojan dominion in Latium, in the "Jerusalem" the reconquest of the Holy Sepulchre, in the "Paradise Lost" the fall of our first parents, offer each a distinct historical object on which the action is from the first steadily advancing. by however tortuous a course. In the "Iliad" no such object can be discovered. Although the limits of the action are as clearly

---

[25] Jean Paul Richter expressed a wish for a twenty-fifth Canto of the Iliad, as far at least as to the death of Achilles. A similar feeling has produced a Thirteenth Book of the Æneid, and Göthe has given us his Torso of the 'Achilleis,' a sequel to the Iliad. The desideratum which he wished to supply pressed upon him, when a boy, in reading the Prose Translation. 'I found great fault with the work (the Iliad) for affording us no account of the capture of Troy, and breaking off so abruptly with the death of Hector' (Göthe's Autob. i. 29).

[26] Forebodings of the ultimate fall of Troy are found not only in Δ 164, Ζ 448, Ω 243 and 728, but also in the remoter Achilleid. as Ο 71. The sinews of its strength were cut by Achilles' spear, whence Pindar's Τρωΐας ἶνας ἐκταμὼν δορί (Isth. 7. 53), said of Achilles. Yet the actual capture is not by him, and so it is prophesied by Apollo in Π 709. Another posterior event alluded to, but outside the action. is the invitation to Philoctetes, τάχα δὲ μνήσεσθαι ἔμελλον .... Φιλοκτήταο (Β 724).—In the Odyssey, with all its compact concentration, one prophetic announcement is found which is not fulfilled within it (Od. λ 127), and so, though not to such an extent, the Odyssey, like the Iliad, looks out beyond itself.

marked out as in any of the above cases, yet its progress cannot be said to have in view, nor does its conclusion involve, any distinct historical consummation. The fall of Troy, the grand catastrophe of the whole train of events celebrated in the poem, is extraneous to its own narrative. As little does the reconciliation of the chiefs on the death of Hector, form its definitive scope. The selection, therefore, of this particular series of events was owing obviously to its moral rather than its historical importance; to the opportunities it afforded for portraying the great qualities of one extraordinary character with the conception of which the poet's mind was teeming. The genius of the "Iliad," consequently, is superior to that by which those other heroic poems are animated, in so far as the mind of man, in all the depth and variety of its passions and affections, is a more interesting object of study than the vicissitudes of human destiny or worldly adventure' (Mure, Hist. of Gr. Lit. i. p. 293).

42. The above extract will indicate the straits to which able men are reduced in upholding the perfect unity of the Iliad. In order to obtain a satisfactory theory of its plan and purpose, it will be observed that we have here on the part of the critic a strategic movement backward towards high ethical ground, or rather the question has been carried up into the region of the invisible; and so (as with Hecatæus in Herodotus, ii. 23) there can be no 'elenchus,'—no possibility of either proof or disproof. Col. Mure has, however, virtually left the Iliad without an adequate *dénouement*, and one is prepared now to understand, when it is thus 'disboned,' how all manner of paradoxical theories as to the purpose of the Iliad could be put forth with a show of plausibility. Among these the most notable is that of Schubarth (in his 'Ideen über Homer,' Breslau, 1821), that it is not Achilles that is the hero of the Iliad, but Hector [27], with whose obsequies the poem ends (just as some have thought that Satan and not Adam was the hero in Paradise Lost), and, as a corollary, that Homer was a court-

---

[27] It is remarkable that Hector is the only *Trojan* who receives the epithet Διΐφιλος, and that none even among the Greeks receives it more than once, except the two protagonists, Achilles and Ulysses. Achilles receives it five times, Hector four times (cp. also Il 204), Ulysses thrice, Patroclus, Phœnix, Phyleus, each once.

poet at the court of the descendants of Æneas, whose dynasty is prophesied to survive the downfall of Troy (Υ 307), so that the author of the Iliad was a Trojan! If Schubarth had contented himself with the contention that Homer was probably an Asiatic, his position would have been more secure[28].

[28] Schubarth's theory of the Odyssey is that it was the work of an Asiatic, exhibiting the misfortunes that had befallen the invaders of his country. A similar idea seems to have moved Virgil to catalogue the calamities of the Greek heroes after Troy as retributions (Æn. xi. 255–270).

CHAPTER V.

OUTLINE OF NEW GROUPING.

μῦθος δ' ὃς μὲν νῦν ὑγιής, εἰρημένος ἔστω.

43. THE Iliad being thus a poem of complex elements in contrast with the Odyssey, the next step in our investigation is to endeavour to disentangle these elements according to the cantos of primary and those of non-primary character, and, this process once accomplished, to inquire whether any link of connection can be discerned attaching the non-primary cantos to each other, and what affinity these groups thus eliminated severally exhibit. The primary cantos, then, are those detailing the 'Wrath of Achilles' and the working out of the promise of Zeus to Thetis, and the $\Delta\iota\grave{o}s$ $\beta ov\lambda\acute{\eta}$, which is the original kernel of the poem.

They are Books I, VIII, XI—XXII, or (taking their designations in Greek letters, henceforth used for convenience),

Α Θ Λ on to Χ.

These constitute what Mr. Grote calls the 'Achilleis,' and are all that are really necessary to complete the Programme in the opening proem of the Poem. This Achillean stream is one that may be said to flow on continuously from Λ to Χ, but the upper part of its course, to use a happy comparison of Mr. Grote, is now found becalmed in two lakes Α and Θ, lying at some distance apart from each other.

Over against these we have to put the books which (with the exception of one, Ι), are universally admitted not to be provided for in the opening Exordium, to which books the one excepted (*I*) must on other grounds be appended ; viz.

B, Γ, Δ. E, Z, H,   I, K,   Ψ, Ω.

Otherwise, Books II, III, IV, V, VI, VII, IX, X, XXIII, XXIV.

Here a sort of reverse condition of the arrangement occurs, for of this stream the continuous portion comes first, and the gatherings into lakes come later. This is of no moment as an argument, and it is merely put forward to give one a clear conception of the cross mode in which these *duplex* elements in the Iliad are interwoven and interplaited with each other[1].

It is especially the Books of the Iliad in this last group which have long attracted attention—we may even say excited suspicion—as having little direct coherence organically with the main structure. They have been in fact the quarry from which the weapons of the Wolfians have been mainly drawn ; in connection with them the διαφωνίαι πολλαί ascribed to Homer by Josephus, and the *hiantes commissurae et juncturae parum callidae.* on which Wolf founded, are chiefly to be found. In particular, they contain few, if any. clear references to the Διὸς βουλή, so prominent in the Exordium, and distinctly referred to in the Achillean area (Ν 347, Ο 593, Π 103). The explanation of this phenomenon will appear in the subsequent reasoning.

44. The proposition which I now mean to advance and lead evidence to prove, regarding these two groups, is the following : that the primary cantos or Achilleid are by a more ancient author, being what may be called palæozoic ; that the other group of cantos is on a different projection, and by a less ancient author, containing elements more neozoic, and

---

[1] The above division will form a sufficiently good provisional line of demarcation It does not follow, however. that every portion in the books named as Achillean is as ancient as the main portion. and in particular there is reason to believe that this applies to the long discourse of Nestor in (Λ) the Eleventh Book, the portion of X subsequent to the Death of Hector. and the episode of the Shield in Σ or the Eighteenth ; the latter especially in its language and tone suggesting the stiller life and artistic calm of the Odyssey rather than the 'Sturm und Drang' characteristic of the Achilleid (cp. Grote, ii. 255. on 'the Shield' episode, and Gladstone, Hom. Synchr. p. 54, on the kindred artistic feeling of Od. τ 226).— Besides these parts. which are probably of high authorship, there remain portions of the Achilleid. which are of very questionable origin. especially the second Theomachy in Φ, and occasional minor interpolations.

further that this last group manifests special kinship and affinity with the Odyssey and has proceeded from the same author in the same age. Apart from interpolations and in general terms it may be said that the Homeric Corpus of Iliad and Odyssey falls asunder into two great sections, on the one hand the Achilleid, and, on the other, the non-Achilleid, *plus* the Odyssey, and the theory which I have to put forth is that a poet, who is also the author of the Odyssey, has engrafted on a more ancient poem, the Achilleid, splendid and vigorous saplings of his own, transforming and enlarging it into an Iliad, but an Iliad in which the engrafting is not absolutely complete, where the 'sutures' are still visible [2].

45. In the Epigram on Homer by Alcæus the Messenian (Anth. Pal. vii. 1), there occurs a grouping of his works which suits as a point of departure, and is convenient for making clear the exact orientation, so to speak, of the scene. Homer is there celebrated,

$$\text{ὅττι Θέτιν κύδηνε καὶ υἱέα καὶ μόθον ἄλλων}$$
$$\text{ἡρώων, Ἰθάκου τ' ἔργματα Λαρτιάδου.}$$

'As having glorified Thetis and her son, *and the struggles of other heroes*, and the exploits of the Ithacan son of Laertes.'

Here we have the contents of the two Epics in happy and just delineation. The Odyssey is of course manifest, but, as for the Iliad, it receives a twofold description and falls into two groups,—one Achillean, the other non-Achillean, concerned with the *struggles of other heroes* than Achilles. It is regarding this portion, answering to the μόθος ἄλλων ἡρώων, that I propose to show that it belongs to the author of the Odyssey and is not from the author of the Achilleid. It will be incumbent on me to adduce evidence on the one hand separating and differentiating the Achilleid, and, on the other, evidence associating the non-Achilleid with the Odyssey. The proof will not be complete unless the

---

[2] It will be observed that I have not retained in my hypothesis the alternative that the enlargement of the Achilleid into an Iliad may be due to a later alteration or expansion by the *same* author. The evidence about to be adduced contains so many and striking divergences that we must exclude this supposition, and it is one so little compatible with the phenomena that I need not retain it for sustained consideration.

negative arm of the Elenchus as well as the positive be equally plied. It may not follow that in all the area to be traversed the proof will be equally strong, and in certain obscurities we may not always be able to trace the lines clearly all through ; but for the most part it will become clear where they trend, and their general direction is entirely unmistakable.

46. And here may be considered one or two possible preliminary objections.

It may in the first place be thought that this theory reverses our usual conceptions of the relation of the Homeric poems and involves a *hysteron proteron,* inasmuch as it gives the critical precedence to what is sometimes assumed to be the less important and inferior poem. A few remarks are therefore due regarding this point of precedence with a view to putting the matter in a light more accordant with the facts than the common opinion implies. So far from being a *hysteron proteron* procedure, it is the only procedure that is scientifically safe ; viz. to begin with the known and proceed towards the unknown or the less known, and, this being so, the Odyssey, which is the poem nearer to us in point of time and is simpler in structure, becomes the point of departure, and a standing ground is obtained from which we feel our way back into the obscurities of the prior poetry. In adopting this course we are following the counsel of Mr. Grote, whose sagacious eye perceived that the Odyssey ought to be the critical starting-point in Homeric study. But further, it is not only scientifically safe, but it is also æsthetically just, to give the younger poem this precedence. It is a common impression that the Iliad is superior to the Odyssey, and Mr. Gladstone has expressed himself in its favour as the poem of vaster scope and profounder genius ; but there are not a few considerations that move me to call for a different verdict, if assent to that proposition involves a belief that the Iliad is the greater poem. It may be freely admitted that the Iliad has unrivalled *passages,* and the theory propounded in this book supplies a clue to understand the genesis of many of the most notable of them ; yet it remains true that the Odyssey is the greater *poem,* as being, first, the more finished work of art ; and, secondly, the poem of the Greek race, *par excellence*, in its best and most typical characteristics[3]. If we inquire what it is that distinguishes Greece in the annals of the world, any reply will be inadequate unless it embrace two things—that she is the mother of that inquiring intelligence which has given the world Science ; and that she is, further, the fountain of Art. Looked at from this point of view across the ages of history, which of the two poems is the one that possesses the most significance ? We can hardly doubt that the verdict would be in favour of the Odyssey, whose hero is the incarnation of that spirit of eager inquiry that Greece awakened on the earth, and which, in its structure, so sharp and clear of outline, and yet so broad and grand, is itself a prefiguration of that Art, whose inspiration and glory were bestowed on the people of Greece. For, however great may be the character of Achilles—and we cannot be blind to the glory with which he is invested, as gaining the victory not only over foes and friends, over Greeks and Trojans together, but finally over himself and his own impetuous passion—it yet remains true that Achilles is *not* the representative of the Greek race as a whole ; Achilles is not πολύτροπος as was the Greek people, and as their typical hero Ulysses was[4] ; for to accept Achilles in that character would involve our looking to Sparta instead of Athens as the glory of Greece, and would install Alexander over Pericles in the temple of Greek fame. That would be an entire inversion of the justice of the case, and would involve a *hysteron proteron*, from which not only the critical judgment but the historical conscience must recoil.

[3] 'In keinem (der Helden) wiederspiegelt sich der griechische National-character so treu wie in ihm (Odysseus)' Preller, Gr. M. (ii. 284).

[4] Not only in his virtues but in his faults, Ulysses exhibits a type of the Greek people in their special weakness. To be πολύτροπος was akin to εὐτράπελος, and many an unscrupulous Themistocles as well as inquiring Socrates lay hid in germ in this great character of the Epic time. A range of epithets belongs to him far beyond any other hero. He shares the epithet πολύφρων with Hephaestus alone, is coupled by Athene along with herself in μῆτις or counsel (Od. v 296), and is credited with a variety of accomplishments to the number of sixteen (cp. list in the Venetian Scholiast, Il. Θ 93). He is the only one, except Nestor, that bears the appellation 'great glory of the Achaeans' (μέγα κῦδος 'Αχαιῶν), an appellation not bestowed upon Achilles himself. Hence it may be remarked, Nero knew very well what he was about when he selected from among the Greek heroes the statue of Ulysses to carry off to Rome (Pausanias, v. 25. 8-9). He could have chosen none more significant as the symbol of 'Graecia capta.'

47. A second preliminary objection is of the following kind. It may be said, ' In this new theory which you propound, you give us a Dual authorship, and in so doing introduce a new χωρισμός. In what respect is your view better than that of any of the ancient or modern (Χωρίζοντες) Separatists? Why not fall back on that theory as the best explanation of the phenomena?' The answer to this is a simple one. The doctrine of the Separatists, in the crude way of simply disjoining the Iliad from the Odyssey, is insufficient to explain the phenomena. The two poems cannot be made to part asunder in this easy way, large sections of the Iliad being cognate in tone, language, sentiment and ethical views with the Odyssey, and hence, under any candid investigation, the theory of the Chorizontes uniformly breaks down, point after point, for it is possible to produce from certain parts of the Iliad (always keeping away, however, from the Achilleid), evidences of recency, improvement in manners, of higher social feeling, in almost every case parallel to those producible from the Odyssey. Most of the proofs on which the Chorizontes relied are either worthless or, where relevant, favour an entirely different theory. Yet these separatist critics have this merit that they attained to a certain dim discernment of the phenomena. They had an instinct that a valid or scientific differentiation was in some form possible, but they set about the finding of it in a rough superficial way, and hence the cleavage which they proposed was manifestly false, for in separating the *whole* Iliad from the Odyssey, they laid themselves open to a flank fire with weapons drawn from the neozoic books of the Iliad which are cognate with those of the Odyssey, in both of which areas we find entirely parallel phenomena, such as the same range of geographical knowledge, the same artistic products, similar social usages, kindred views of human life and, generally, the same ethical undertones characteristic of an individual author.

CHAPTER VI.

FAILURE OF CHORIZONTIC GROUPING.

ἐν πεδίῳ ἵσταντο, διαρραῖσαι μεμαῶτες.

48. IT is not our intention to enter into any formal refutation of the Chorizontic doctrine, which will be sufficiently proved, in our after investigation, to proceed upon an inadequate view of the facts, but it is proper to give one or two illustrations of our meaning as to the general futility of the Chorizontic weapons. These weapons were drawn partly from linguistic, partly from ethical and social, partly from mythological phenomena. A specimen of the first and third class may here be introduced; the second will come up for illustration, more conveniently, at an after stage.

Among the linguistic arguments of the ancient Separatists (Ven. Schol. K 476) was that turning on the word προπάροιθεν. It was alleged that it was used of *place* or local position in the Iliad, but of *time* in the Odyssey, and the argument was that, since the progression of language is from outward *space* first and then secondarily to *time*, the Iliad represents an older condition of speech, the Odyssey a more advanced, and consequently the Iliad must be considerably older than the Odyssey, and so by a different author. The reasoning is specious and would be good if the facts were well established. Though long ago refuted by a critic (Ven. Schol. ut supra), supposed to be no less a person than Aristarchus, it has been revived by the recent expositor of the Chorizontic doctrine in Ed. Review 1871 (p. 360–1), and therefore demands careful examination. But when we look into the matter, what do we find? Not that the word is *always*, as we are led to infer from the way in which the statement is put, possessed of the secondary *temporal* sense in the Odyssey. On the contrary the *local* sense is there still the normal one, largely predominant (e. g. δ 225, ρ 277, etc.), and, in fact, while only one indubitable instance of a temporal application is producible from the Odyssey (viz. λ 483), fifteen (or, with a var. lect., sixteen) are producible from it in the local sense. The argument thus refutes itself, for it would not be strange, if, among many, there should emerge *one*, occasional and exceptional, instance of the temporal sense, the case of the transition being seen in our English word *before*, which has passed through exactly the same stages. This application to the temporal sense is manifestly not the rule in the Odyssey, but the exception, and the data in the case will simply warrant this conclusion that the Odyssey contains a very ancient form of speech, in which the objective notions of space predominate over the more abstract subjective notions of time. The Chorizontes were, however, too precipitate. Not only were they wrong regarding the Odyssey, but they were in error regarding the Iliad. The temporal sense of προπάροιθεν *is* found even in the Iliad [1]. One instance is in K 476, and is so acknowledged, as early as Apollonius, to relate to *time* (ἐπὶ χρόνον in v. πάροιθεν, Lex. of Apollonius). But K is one of the books which on other grounds can be shown to be cognate with the Odyssey. Thus their argument not only falls to the ground, but is converted to serve a new and more exact division, whereby a portion of the Iliad comes out as cognate with the Odyssey.

49. Again, the occurrence of θύρη (door) in the singular in the Odyssey, instead of the plural, was appealed to by the Edinburgh Reviewer as a peculiarity either of language or of

---

[1] Lehrs in his 'Aristarchus' (p. 115) states the matter thus: 'Προπάροιθε in Iliade etiam invenitur de tempore, non tantum in Odyssea, ut Chorizontes volunt.' He refers to three passages, that mentioned above in K 476, also Λ 734, X 197. With deference to Lehrs, however, this appears to be an overstatement. The last, viz. X 197, will not stand the test, for the ancient critics allowed that it *could* be understood τοπικῶς, i. e. of *place*, and Fäsi admits that view. The other, in Λ 734, occurs in the long speech of Nestor, which is believed not to be so old as the main texture of the book where it is found. This last occurrence, therefore, will not serve the Chorizontes.—The simple πάροιθεν has already a *temporal* sense even in the Achilleid, as O 227, and in Ψ 20, 180, as well as in the Odyssey.

simpler social appliance differentiating the Odyssey from the
Iliad. His induction, however, was incomplete. He failed to
note its occurrence twice in the singular in Ω 317, 483, once of
a $\theta\acute{a}\lambda a\mu os$, again of an $a\mathring{v}\lambda\acute{\eta}$. This book, however, is one
of those marked out as cognate with the Odyssey. So,
regarding $\pi\acute{v}\lambda a\iota$, which is so often plural, the nearest approach to a singular is that found in E 397, $\mathring{\epsilon}v\ \pi\acute{v}\lambda\psi$, which
Aristarchus took to mean 'at the Gate,' viz. of Hades.
But Book E belongs to the same group as Ω and the
Odyssey.

These arguments of the Chorizontes are no doubt trivial,
turning upon mere incidents, not to say accidents, of phrase,
and such also, it may be thought, is their refutation. Their
arguments from mythology may be thought more weighty,
but it is not difficult to show that they share the same fate.
The most famous of these are the apparent discrepancies
between the poems as to the wife of Hephæstus and the
office of messenger to the Gods.

50. In the Iliad *Charis* is the name given to the spouse of
Hephæstus (Σ 383): in the Odyssey, according to a certain
portion of it, it is *Aphrodite*[2]. Moreover *Charis* seems in the
latter poem to have multiplied into *Charites* (known also to
the Iliad, Ξ 267), and these have further subsided into
handmaids to *Aphrodite* (Od. θ 564 and σ 194). It would
therefore appear that Hephæstus in the Iliad had married
one who was the *handmaid* to his Odyssean wife, and the
Chorizontes thought the relation was an awkward one[3]. It is
upon the lay of Demodocus in book eighth of the Odyssey

[2] The Ven. Schol. on Φ 416 endeavoured to remove the difficulty by suppos-
ing that different times of conjugal relation were referred to ($\lambda\acute{\epsilon}\gamma\epsilon\iota\nu\ \delta\grave{\epsilon}\ \delta\epsilon\hat{\iota}\ \ddot{o}\tau\iota$
$o\mathring{v}\chi\ o\acute{\iota}\ a\mathring{v}\tau o\grave{\iota}\ \chi\rho\acute{o}\nu o\iota\ \mathring{\eta}\sigma a\nu\ \tau\hat{\eta}s\ \sigma v\mu\beta\iota\acute{\omega}\sigma\epsilon\omega s$). Mr. Gladstone (Homer, ii. 258) says
Hephæstus may have been like Zeus, with more wives than one, and he has
endeavoured further (Juv. Mundi, p. 213) to get over the difficulty by restricting
the sense of $\ddot{\omega}\pi v\iota\epsilon$ in Σ 383 to *betrothment*, which leaves the matter where it was,
Charis being evidently already *housekeeper* to Hephæstus, cp. $\mathring{\eta}\mu\acute{\epsilon}\tau\epsilon\rho o\nu\ \delta\hat{\omega}$ in 424.

[3] The Chorizontes, with their usual precipitateness, did not perceive that, if
the Iliad had represented Aphrodite as his wife, the relation might have been more
awkward, for husband and spouse would in that case have been on opposite sides
of the combat, Aphrodite being on the Trojan side, Hephæstus on the Grecian
(Υ 36 40 and 73). The Ulyssean Book E (563, 883) coincides with the eighth of
the Odyssey in representing Ares and Aphrodite as mutually interested in each
other.

that the opinion rests as to Aphrodite being spouse of Hephæstus, and it is well known that doubts have been entertained regarding this lay; but supposing it accepted as genuine, the discrepancy is in the case of a Deity, who is the subject of various traditions, being credited with a variety of spouses, much as Zeus is in the Theogony of Hesiod. In the Theogony (945) it is Aglaie, one of the Charites, who is mated with Hephæstus; in the Roman mythology the goddess Maia is so associated; and both Charis and Aglaie and Aphrodite represent the same Spirit of Beauty wedded to Art, personified in Hephæstus.

51. A much more formidable *crux* is the alleged discrepancy as to the office of Messenger to the Gods. It has been argued, both by ancient and by modern Chorizontes, that the Iliad and Odyssey must be from different authors, because in the Iliad Iris discharges that function, in the Odyssey Hermes.

Regarding this point, the first remark that I may make is that, while the premises are in a loose and general way correct, the conclusion is somewhat precipitate, inasmuch as not only would the Iliad and Odyssey be thereby severed, but the undoubted unity of a much smaller poem would, on that principle, be in danger of disruption. The hymn to Demeter (315 and 336) brings before us Iris and Hermes both as Messengers, the latter with the significant addition ($\epsilon\dot{\iota}s$ $\H{E}\rho\epsilon\beta os$), the reason of which will afterwards appear. No one, however, would seriously propose to attribute this hymn to a pair of authors on this account. This is a case in point, and therefore the statement of the Chorizontes must be looked to more narrowly, for, although in a general way correct, it does not embrace all the facts of the case, which are much more multiform. It is not correct to say that either of these deities is the invariable Messenger. Other beings also act in that capacity on certain occasions, as e. g. Athene in Λ 715, 'Rumour' in B 94, 'Sleep' in Ξ 356 [1], Thetis ($\Delta\iota\acute{o}\theta\epsilon\nu$ $\mathring{a}\gamma\gamma\epsilon\lambda os$) in Ω 561; and Zeus in Ω 74 seems to specify no deity in particular ($\epsilon\check{\iota}$ $\tau\iota s$ $\kappa\alpha\lambda\acute{\epsilon}\sigma\epsilon\iota\epsilon$ $\theta\epsilon\hat{\omega}\nu$). We confine ourselves, however, to the cases of Iris and Hermes.

[1] Also, Themis is the summoner of the ἀγορά of the gods in Τ 4, on which Heyne remarks, 'Notabile autem quod Themis nunc deos convocat; non Iris aut Mercurius.' Again, Thetis (P 409) ἀπαγγέλλεσκε Διὸς νόημα.

52. And first, of the Odyssey. The occurrences of Hermes as messenger in this poem amount to only two, viz. a 38 and ε 29, with which last the *proposal* in a 85 is identical. The former concerns the story of Agamemnon's death, and therefore, though *narrated* in the Odyssey, is incidental, no necessary part of its machinery. The other is a very different case, being the mission to Calypso's far-away isle, and the hinge of Ulysses' movements. There is also the apparition of Hermes to Ulysses to present him with the Moly-root (κ 307); but this is not a case in point, as Hermes seems to be acting of his own accord, and is not said to be deputed or spoken of as a messenger. Thus the instances in the Odyssey practically reduce themselves to *one*[5]. Now it so happens that just the same number is producible from the Iliad. It is the instance in Ω 333–5, where the night journey of Priam is performed under the escort of Hermes, who there acts as the messenger of Zeus[6]. Some of the modern Separatists have felt the force of this fact and have endeavoured to get rid of it by denying Ω to form a part of the Iliad. It is not a part of the Achilleid, certainly; but it is one of those books that help to make the Iliad ; only it is one of the neozoic cantos and so is cognate with the Odyssey. The weapon is thus wrested from the hands of the Chorizontes, and made to serve in building up a different theory.

53. The point remains as to the employment of Iris. And first as to the Odyssey. No example of her actual employment is producible, but there is an allusion which shows that her function of ἄγγελος was not unknown, viz. in the line as to Irus the beggar, of whom it is said that he got his appellation of Irus (Od. σ 7), οὕνεκ᾽ ἀπαγγέλλεσκε κιών, 'because he went and delivered messages,' i.e. Iris-like (cp. Gladstone, H. ii. 241). If, however, her rival Hermes appears so comparatively seldom in the Odyssey in the capacity in question,—practically, as we have seen, in only one instance,

---

[5] The case of Lampetie as ἄγγελος to the sun, in μ 375, though she acts spontaneously, is valid to show that Hermes is not, as the Chorizontes affirm, sole ἄγγελος in the Odyssey. Cp. θ 270.

[6] A second example is virtually producible from Ω 24 in the unrealised mission of Hermes there proposed.—It is not improbable that there is one latent in B 104, where the displacement of the Perseidae by the Pelopidae—a work of craft, and therefore appropriate to Hermes—seems darkly indicated.

—it is not just to assume a discrepancy, as the Chorizontes do, on the strength of a single occurrence, since there is evidence that the function in the case of Iris is in the Odyssey virtually acknowledged. We now turn to the Iliad. The occasions in which Iris is there represented as messenger are frequent, and are, on the whole, more frequent in the Achilleid, than in the non-Achilleid. In the latter, the number of instances is not great, after we have deducted such as those in Γ 129 and Ψ 196, where Iris is not spoken of as acting under direction, but seems to proceed spontaneously. The great question, however, is: What account can be given of the fact which is admitted, and which the Chorizontes press upon us, that in the battlefield at Troy and generally in the scenes of the Iliad, we have Iris and not Hermes as messenger? It might be suggested that Hermes, as his after-symbol of the *Caduceus* signified (cp. θεῶν κῆρυξ of Hermes in Hesiod, Op. et Di. 80), was the Messenger of Peace, and therefore was not well suited to the scenes of warfare. This opinion, joining Iris and ἔρις, finds support in the passage in Hesiod, Theog. 780, and comes up clearly in Servius on Æneid (ix. 2), where the commentator, no doubt following Zenodotus, who we know (Ven. Schol. Λ 27) confounded Ἔρις and Ἶρις, states that Iris indicates Strife: 'Iris quasi ἔρις dicta est, nunquam enim ad conciliationem mittitur sed ad disturbationem.' Another view has been suggested, that Iris delivers messages and announcements, whereas Hermes being the διάκτορος, or, as he is called in the Anthology, θεῶν ὑπηρέτης (Anth. xi. 176), transacts business and executes orders[7]. These explanations, though ingenious, do not cover all the facts, and the key to the phenomenon must be sought for in the following considerations.

[7] This is the view pressed by Mr. Gladstone in endeavouring to grapple with the Chorizontes. It is true that the epithet διάκτωρ or διάκτορος (*pursuivant*), is never found applied to Iris, but nevertheless she is more than the mere message bearer, for ἡγεῖτ' is used of her in Ω 96, and, in O 200, she gives advice over and above the verbal tenor of her message.—It is worth noting also how peculiarly the occurrences of this διάκτορος are distributed. It comes up in the Odyssey nine times; in Ω of the Iliad six times; in B of the Iliad, once. The only instance of it in the Achilleid is that in Φ 497, in the peculiar and doubtful section known as the Second *Theomachia.* The occurrences therefore are

Achilleid,	non-Achilleid,	Odyssey,
1 (?)	7	9

which is in favour of the affinity we presume to exist between the non-Achilleid and the Odyssey.

54. Iris is the ordinary celestial messenger, but with a limitation. This limitation is due to the nature of her visible representation—the Rainbow. The Bow in the cloud, as the most brilliant of all aerial phenomena, was early regarded as the descent of a celestial messenger, and the same name ἶρις is given, even in the oldest part of the Iliad, sometimes to the . personified Messenger, sometimes, as in P 547, to the simple visual sign. Iris, then, is a being associated with the Rainbow, and it is remarkable that we find the association closer the further we ascend, for it is in the Achilleid that we find her epithets reflecting most clearly her *physical* symbol[8].

55. A similar affirmation holds regarding the deity of whom she is most frequently the messenger. The physical and atmospheric associations attaching to Zeus, as will be shown at a later stage, accumulate similarly as we ascend, and in the palæozoic portion of the Iliad the conception of that god will be found to be closely associated with the Firmament, as doming over all earthly things.

If, then, Zeus is primarily the Firmament and Iris the Rainbow personified, what may we expect as to the occasions for the manifestations of Iris? The Rainbow is a diurnal, not a nocturnal, phenomenon, and we may be sure that a poet who thought of Iris as the rainbow would not commit the physical solecism of sending her on night errands. The lunar rainbow is too rare a phenomenon to count upon for this purpose[9]. In the course of a pretty long life a man may perhaps see *one*, many have never seen one at all, and we may therefore assume that when the early poets spoke of Iris, they had in view only the diurnal phenomenon[10]. Accordingly, in what may be called the daylight of common life, Iris is the

---

[8] The epithets ποδήνεμος and ἀελλόπος suggestive of her physical attributes are equally distributed, occurring *seven* times in Achilleid, in the non-Achilleid also *seven* times. Her most characteristic epithet of χρυσόπτερος, *golden-winged*, evidently allusive to the hue of the rainbow, is found twice and (apart from an instance in the hymn to Demeter) only in the Achilleid (Θ 398, Λ 185).

[9] The subtlest of modern poets, Robert Browning, in his 'Christmas Eve' (§ vi.), has ventured on the introduction of a Lunar rainbow.—The Aurora Borealis does duty as a celestial 'Nuntius' in Dryden's 'Hind and Panther' (Part II.).

[10] Hesiod shows less perception of the fundamental character of Iris when he tells of Zeus making her fetch from beneath the world a flagon of water from the Styx (Theog. 780, etc.), a river which flows 'in dark night.' This may be reckoned one of the indications that Hesiod was later than Homer.

ordinary messenger, but in the night-time [11], when 'the ways are dark,' it is some other god, such as Hermes, as in the night-journey of Priam to the tent of Achilles, or Athene, who is ἄγγελος .... ἔννυχος in Il. Λ 716, 'messenger by *night.*' Even in the day-time, when Athene is the goddess actually sent, upon an occasion where Zeus has to interfere more actively than by a mere visual spectacle, the simile, in which Athene's descent is described, is drawn from the rainbow, as in P 547, and is therefore suggestive of Iris. Moreover distant or dangerous expeditions are regarded as in the same category with night-journeys, and hence it is Hermes that is sent to the distant Ogygian isle of Calypso—both names suggestive of mystery and darkness—to release the hero of the Odyssey.

That this view of Hermes as the undertaker of dangerous and difficult expeditions is the correct one (witness his naive complaint about the discomforts of his salt-sea journey to Ogygia in Od. ε 100), is further borne out by the evidence of Il. E 390, where he rescues Ares from prison, and the word employed (ἐξέκλεψεν) suggests a task of hazard. Hence he is thought of by certain gods to steal away the body of Hector (Ω 24, κλέψαι). So also, in the case of Herakles going down for the 'Dog of Hades,' we hear not only of Athene but of Hermes as helping him (Od. λ 626); but as the passage occurs in a doubtful part of the Nekyia, less weight is to be attached to it. Enough has been advanced to prove that, in the old Epic poetry, Iris and Hermes are, *both* of them, messengers of the Gods, but under different circumstances; and there is, therefore, no ground for differentiating the whole Iliad from the whole Odyssey in this regard.

56. Thus disappears the once formidable difficulty as to Iris and Hermes. Into the more recondite relations of these two deities I do not enter farther than to observe in corroboration (1) how the office of ψυχοπομπός or conductor of the Shades (which is post-Homeric though coming up in

---

[11] That Iris is not suitable to act as an *invisible* messenger is clear from the fundamental conception, and is borne out by Il. Ω 337, where Zeus requires Hermes to conduct Priam *invisibly*, so as not to be *seen* or noticed on the way (ὡς μήτ' ἄρ τις ἴδῃ μήτ' ἄρ τε νοήσῃ). To the χρυσόπτερος Ἶρις such a command would have been awkwardly inappropriate.

Od. ω 1) was only a natural extension of his duties as
Messenger and διάκτορος in dark and dangerous circumstances, such as he has to encounter in the rescue of Ares
(in E 390) and the release of Ulysses in Od. ε [12]; (2) how
a common root may be found uniting the mythological
representations of these two deities, Iris and Hermes, in the
following considerations.   Iris is, in Hesiod (Theog. 266),
of the same parentage as the Wind-deities, 'the Harpyies,'
being in fact their sister; and, though the Homeric poems
give no special parentage, her affinities are, as we have seen,
atmospheric, and the epithets ἀελλόπος and ποδήνεμος are
suitable to one who may be called sister of the Winds and
who in one instance is represented as acting at the suit of
a mortal as Messenger to fetch the Winds (Ψ 199).   Now there
is a great deal of evidence to show that Hermes, in one of his
aspects, was also a 'Wind-deity [13],' representing the Wind in its
quaint and playful tricksomeness, as in the hymn to Hermes.
He is therefore the deity that undertakes far distant journeys
(cp. 'far-wandered wind,' or ἄνεμος πολύπλαγκτος of Λ 308),
and in those expeditions he moves over sea and land, ἅμα
πνοιῆς ἀνέμοιο (Ω 342 and Od. ε 46), 'along with the breezes
of the wind,' just as Iris's sisters in Hesiod, the Harpyies, are
said 'to follow the breezes of the winds,' ἀνέμων πνοιῇσι
καὶ οἰωνοῖς ἅμ' ἕπονται (Hes. Theog. 268).   There is, therefore, good ground for supposing that both Iris and Hermes
have come from the same tap-root in mythological conception,
the one as a visible, the other the invisible messenger of the
Gods.

---

[12] A ludicrous view of the subject would be, that Hermes, being the god of
language, was naturally a useful deity in foreign expeditions!

[13] Cp. the interesting and important article by Mr. Keary in Contemporary Review,
July '75 (p. 289), on 'Wind-myths.' On the whole Hermes-and-Iris-question,
consult Mure, H. G. L. ii. 179, App. B. 3, and Gladstone, Homer, ii. 239-41 ; also
Fäsi's note on Il. Ω 333, in which last we have a succinct *résumé* of the facts, but
in making *Klugheit* or shrewdness the reason for the employment of Hermes, he
misses the main point of the case.—We hear of θεοί as πομπῆες (γ 376) and again
of οὖροι as πομπῆες νηῶν (δ 362), which was natural enough, if Hermes was originally in any form a wind-deity.

CHAPTER VII.

πολλῶν δ' ἀνθρώπων ἴδεν ἄστεα καὶ νόον ἔγνω.

57. THE above investigations, which might be largely extended, will suffice in the meantime to show that the Chorizontic doctrine is inadequate and therefore untenable, that a new grouping is required in the interests of scientific inquiry, and that the facts to which the Chorizontes appealed, point, when rightly interpreted, to an entirely different cleavage in the poems from what they proposed. I now proceed to lead evidence corroborative of my recent proposition, viz. that the non-Achilleid is cognate in origin with the Odyssey, and that the Achilleid stands in origin apart and alone. In indicating the lines on which the proof of such a proposition must move, I first appeal—in conformity with the principle of proceeding from the known or the admitted to the unknown or problematical—to certain broad and universally recognised characteristics of the Odyssey, which characteristics we shall find to be shared in much the same measure and degree by the books of the Iliad constituting the non-Achilleid and *by no others.* These books I shall indicate provisionally, and, for the sake of brevity. by what is a convenient integral designation, as the ULYSSEAN books of the Iliad, thus in so far anticipating the evidence I shall have to produce regarding the position occupied by Ulysses in these cantos.

Among the characteristics of the Odyssey are—

(1) A large outlook to and acquaintance with the outside world, beyond the properly Grecian area, and a considerable familiarity with the shores of the Eastern Mediterranean, including Egypt and Phœnicia.

(2) Pathos and humour in large measure; the humour in the case of the Gods falling occasionally into the burlesque.

(3) High appreciation of conjugal honour and affection.

(4) Lofty estimate of Ulysses as the highest impersonation of Spirit and Intelligence.

These characteristics I take in order, and after indicating the chief proofs of each in the Odyssey, proceed to show their presence in the non-Achilleid or Ulyssean books, their absence in the Achilleid.

Geographical Horizon.

58. The author of the Odyssey has obtained a tolerably extensive and fairly accurate knowledge of the eastern Mediterranean. Within the Greek domain he knows of Delphi and Delos as well as the older oracle of the Greek race Dodona. The two former are, however, only as it were emerging above the horizon, for Delos is named only once, and Delphi is known only under its primitive name of 'Pytho.' The Dorians, who emerge to historic view at a period comparatively recent, appear to be named as an element in the population in connection with Crete.

Outside the Greek domain, he knows in Asia Minor not only Lycia, but the Solymi, who seem to lie further away than Lycia, and besides Cyprus, he makes familiar mention of Phœnicia and Egypt. The mother-city of the former, Sidon, is known by the frequent reference to its people the Sidonians; the then capital of the latter, Thebes, is spoken of as a city of surpassing treasures. The products of the former country, in textile and metallic fabrics, pass current, and the 'Zeus-descended river' of the other with its 'very fair fields' (Od. ξ 263) is spoken of in a way that implies some knowledge, more or less direct, of the peculiar agriculture by irrigation under the ancient Egyptian civilisation. The Pharos-island is vaguely spoken of, and though its position is inaccurately described, the inaccuracy is probably only as much as an ordinary modern mariner might be allowed in describing, on the impression of a single visit, the entrance to a far away port like Nagasaki or Tahiti. The voyage between Crete and Egypt is one of five days (Od. ξ 257); the unknown 'Beggar' speaks freely of an expedition to

Egypt and subsequent deportation to Cyprus (Od. ρ 443)[1]; and the familiarity with Egypt is such that a man of the name of Αἰγύπτιος, 'the Egyptian,' is a speaker in the *agora* at Ithaca (Od. β 15)[2]. Further, the author of the Odyssey has some knowledge of the West and South, he knows of Libya, which he twice names, and has heard of a delicious country, which must be placed in its neighbourhood, where life is under easy and charming conditions, and men can live on 'flowery food' in the land of the Lotus-eaters. He tells us of the *Sikels* in the West, and, although Niebuhr would find a place for them in Epirus, the most natural interpretation is that of Strabo, that they belong to Italy or Sicily. Finally, along with his knowledge of those outer lands, he has acquired a certain sense of the variety of the human race, of the complexity of human speech, and a disposition to criticise or estimate its quality, according as it was pleasing or otherwise.

59. Precisely the same extent and kind of geographical vision may be predicated as appearing in those books of the Iliad which have already, on other grounds, been set apart for examination. With the exception of the Sicilian area, which, however, is of no moment, as on any view it lies outside the scope of the *action* of the Iliad, the mental horizon is on every side at every point, in both cases. concentric and extends to the same circumference. Delphi is still known under its ancient name of Pytho, and its occurrences are two, as is the case, apparently, in the Odyssey (B 519, and I 405; Od. θ 80, and λ 581 [?]). Delos happens not to occur, and a certain priority might be allowed to the Iliad on this ground, but the interval is not capable of measurement in the face of other considerations. Though the Dorians are not named, the name Dorium (in B 594) may perhaps be taken to indicate

---

[1] The stories of the 'Beggar' are capable of being used as evidence, being in a very different category of verisimilitude from the 'speciosa miracula' told to the Phaeacians.

[2] Mr. Gladstone in his 'Homeric Synchronism' has a chapter in which he follows Lauth, and discovers a strong Egyptian element in Homer. It is doubtful whether, with the evidence as yet produced, any other verdict can be given than 'not proven,' although the proper name Rhadamanthys seems to be most easily explained from Egyptian analogies.

a certain acquaintance with them; and if the 'Dorian irruption,' which led to the driving out of Ionians and other races, was known to him, he maintains an obstinate silence regarding it, just as does the Singer of the Odyssey, and as we should expect a presumably Ionian ministrel to do, who would probably be willing to ignore an episode in the history of his own race for which he had no favour[3]. Thus there is a remarkable correspondence regarding the knowledge of the interior of the Hellenic world.

As to the circumference, point after point revolves and comes into view exactly in the same way. This is the more remarkable, because it was not necessary for the subject of the Iliad that these geographical allusions to the outer world should have been introduced at all, but they emerge in the two areas we are comparing, almost equally, showing that the same horizon was before the author's mind. The Solymi come up in Z 204. Libya, though unnamed, is implied in Γ 4, where the cranes are described as winging their way from the showery lands to the ' land of the Pygmies,' which is probably a semi-mythical designation for a part of the interior of Africa[4]. As for Phœnicia and Egypt, both appear under much the same aspects; the former is familiar from the products of Sidonian skill in forge and loom, the evidence appearing in the Ulyssean books Z and Ψ, and the latter is known (in Book I, Ulyssean)[5], as possessing the most

---

[3] Pindar's silence as to the *Medising* of his own countrymen at the time of Salamis is not so much in point as Shakspere's silence is regarding the Norman Conquest. A cursory reader of his plays would hardly imagine that there had been a time when France, or rather a province of France, conquered England.— The supposed allusion to the Dorian irruption and the Heracleid conquest in the mouth of Heré (Δ 53), though accepted by Clinton (Fasti, i. 362, cp. Strabo, x. p. 457) as proof of the poet's knowledge of the facts, is somewhat vague to found upon, and the impression conveyed by the sceptre passage of B (186) is rather against it, since the epithet of 'imperishable ever' is an awkward compliment regarding Pelops' sceptre, if the poet had fully in his view the Dorian ascendancy, which obliterated the rule of the Pelopidæ. Cp. Mure, ii. 207-9.

[4] The late Italian traveller Miani is believed to have found a race of dwarfs in the heart of Africa, which goes far to yield an historical nucleus for the story of ' the small infantry warred on by cranes.' Cp. Schweinfurth, Heart of Africa, ii. 138, 144.

[5] Prof. Blackie, Homer, iv. 153, has a statement that the Phœnicians in the Iliad are artistic and admired, whereas in the Odyssey ' they are cunning and detested.' This would be an additional arrow to the Chorizontic quiver, if the Odyssey, with its wider experience, did not enable us to understand how the Phœnicians and

splendid and brilliant civilisation and stores of accumulated wealth in its then capital of Thebes.

60. At this point it is interesting to note that the allusions to Egypt and Phœnicia are determinable as lying within a certain chronological area, and mark a period, which must be considered recent in the history of the one country, ancient on the scale of the history of the other. The Odyssey and the cognate books of the Iliad may be said to be locked off chronologically into a period antecedent to the ascendancy of Tyre in the one country and subsequent to that of Memphis in the other[6]. Thebes has obliterated the earlier glory of Memphis, and Egypt seems therefore in her second stadium; whereas Phœnicia is in her first stadium, when Sidon holds the precedence, as it does also in the books of the Pentateuch. The hegemony of Sidon, according to Movers (Phoen. Alterth. vol. iii. p. 21), extends from B.C. 1600 to 1100; and without assuming that the Homeric poems can bear so high a date as to be prior to 1100, inasmuch as poetical fame and the halo of antiquity might preserve the name *Sidonian* in currency for a considerable period after Tyre had come to acquire the ascendancy (just as the name *Median* for 'Persian' survived familiarly in Greece down to the days of Aristophanes, long after the true relations subsisting between Medes and Persians had become known to the Greek people), yet the absence of all mention of the rival city Tyre is in favour of an early date to even the youngest of the Homeric poems.

Along with the mention of Sidonians may be coupled, as indicating oriental influence, the notices of Cadmeans and Cadmus. The most feasible explanation yet given of the name Cadmus is that connecting it with the Hebrew Kedem, 'the East'[7]; in which case *Cadmus* would be a Grecised form meaning simply the 'Easterling' or 'man from the East.' It is remarkable that these *Cadmeans* and *Cadmus* should be found coming up solely in the Odyssey and in those books of

Greeks had begun to feel jealous of each other as rivals upon one domain, a struggle which did not come within the scope of the action of the Iliad.

[6] Compare Gladstone in his 'Homeric Synchronism,' pp. 148, 162, etc.

[7] Preller (Gr. Mythol. ii. 18), while preferring for Cadmus the sense of 'the Ancient' (der Alte, der Ursprüngliche), accepts the oriental origin of the name.— Compare our word *Sterling*, said to be developed out of 'Easterling' from the influence of merchants *East from* England.

the Iliad which have been pronounced Ulyssean (Δ 385, E 804, K 288, Ψ 680). In connection with this undoubted instance of Phœnician influence, it is proper to advert to what would be, if established, a still more remarkable instance of that influence—the near proximity of a passage which appears to indicate some knowledge of the pre-eminently Phœnician art, that of *writing*. In Book Z, where the Sidonians are mentioned for their cunning works (Z 290, and which cannot be separated in authorship from books Δ and E, where the *Cadmeans* with their Phœnician associations appear), is found the famous passage as to the σήματα λυγρά or 'baleful signs,' described as a means of communication between persons at a distance. How far it can be treated as substantially implying a knowledge of the art of writing, may, to some, be doubtful[8]; all that is here argued is simply that, if it is regarded as an instance of the art of writing, it occurs in remarkable proximity to the mention of the races from whom the art emanated, viz. the Sidonians and Cadmeans, the former the reputed inventors, the latter the recognised transmitters of the invention into the Hellenic world.

61. The only other points remaining to be considered under this head concern the poet's attitude to the outer nations and to the Hellenic race. A vague feeling of the complexity of human speech possesses the author of the Odyssey[9], when he speaks of mingling ἐπ' ἀλλοθρόους ἀνθρώπους ('among men of other tongues'). The statement as to the variety of tongues spoken in Crete (Od. τ 175) is paralleled by similar statements in the Iliad, but, as we might expect, the parts are Ulyssean (B 804, Δ 438, K 420). Also, if the author of the Trojan catalogue in B is offended by the quality of the speech of the Carians, who are to him βαρβαρόφωνοι, we find in the Odyssey a similar aversion to that of the Sintians, who are there ἀγριόφωνοι. This brings us to the evidence of the latent feeling of Hellenic nationality as beginning to

---

[8] A discussion of the point, which is not directly material to our main argument, will be found in an Appendix, Note B.

[9] The Achillean poet acknowledges diversity of speech, but it is mainly diversity between the language of Gods and that of men, not the diversity of speech among the different races of mankind. Μέροπες, which is diffused in all parts of the Homeric poems, seems to differentiate the speech of man from the cries of animals.

appear, of a differentiation commencing, such as afterwards produced the sharp distinction in the historic time between Greeks and Barbarians. Thucydides, it is true, has given it as his judgment that in Homer's time the line is not yet formally drawn between them [10], and probably his observation is correct if applied to the Achilleid, but his judgment on this point as well as his picture of the social condition of early Greece which is drawn in too dark colours, must be appealed against, and that mainly on the evidence of the Odyssey and the Ulyssean books of the Iliad, which concur in this regard.

The specially Greek feeling for κόσμος in order and beauty, and that in a region above that of the warrior, has already begun to show itself. It discountenances the ἄκοσμον in speech and thought (B 213), and commends μορφή in the use of ἔπη (Od. λ 367), while the utterance of the Cyclop is pronounced to be *harsh* (φθόγγος βαρύς Od. ι 257). So even in military details, the sense of order is seen on the Greek side in I 66, compared with the loose arrangements of the Trojans in K 417 (cp. Doederlein *ad loc.*), and there is no mistaking the pulse of the poet's own feeling in Γ as distinctly national, when he describes the Trojans as coming on 'with a whoop and a scream like cranes,' while the Greeks he portrays as marching 'in silence breathing forth energy.' The full illustration of this point will come up after, under the more barbarian characteristics of the Achilleid.

62. Under these circumstances we are justified in looking out for more formal indications of the feeling of nationality in the neozoic area. Such we think we discover in the appearance of aggregations like Πανέλληνες (B 530) and especially Παναχαιοί. The latter appears about eleven times in Iliad and Odyssey, and with one doubtful exception they are uniformly Ulyssean [11]. Conformably with this view, we

---

[10] Thucydides might with more truth have added that the notion of opposing continents, a Europe and an Asia, has not yet been formulated in Homer. Archilochus, however, mentions Asia, much as we now do, in opposition to Europe.

[11] The occurrences of Παναχαιοί therefore are

	Achilleid	Ulyssean	Odyssey
	1 (?)	7	2

viz. Il. B 404, H 73, 159. 327, I 301, K 1, T 193 (?), Ψ 236 (also 272 as var. lect. Ven. Schol.); and in Od. α 239, and ξ 369 (besides ω 32). That in T belongs to a part of the poem which has generally been the subject of dubitation. It happens to be in a speech addressed to Ulysses.

are prepared for symptoms of a widening of the name ' Hellas,' so that it should no longer be restricted to its original area— a corner of Thessaly—but be seen to extend its domain. It is still far removed from the extension which it attains as early as Theognis (247) and Pindar (Nem. vi. 27) to embrace the Peloponnesus, and even, in the latter author, Magna Græcia (Pind. Pyth. i. 75), yet it is evidently on the march to that extension. Accordingly most critics, including Bergk, Ebeling, Gladstone, Blackie (Il. iv. 106), and Doederlein (on B 530) follow Strabo (viii. 370 and xiv. 661) in holding that Ἑλλάς in the Odyssey has obtained a more extended application, and that it there embraces Northern Greece as far as to the Gulf of Corinth. The range of a hero's fame is spoken of as extending καθ' Ἑλλάδα καὶ μέσον Ἄργος (Od. a 344 and υ 80) equivalent to saying 'over Northern Greece and the Peloponnesus,' that is, ' famous on either side of the gulf,' as we might say, 'on either side of the Tweed [12].' Is the same tendency to extension exemplified in the Iliad? Such an instance occurs in I 447, where ' Hellas ' is spoken of as *outside* the dominion of Peleus, within whose domain we know the primitive Hellas was contained [13]. Also, in the Catalogue (B 530) we find as a universalising expression Πανέλληνας καὶ Ἀχαιούς, for which reason the line was doubted in ancient times. Fäsi, however, justly remarks that here we have a distribution of people parallel to that of the territory in καθ' Ἑλλάδα καὶ μέσον Ἄργος, and both Fäsi and La Roche retain the line *unbracketed*, notwithstanding the scruples of the ancient Alexandrians [14].

Thus there is a remarkable convergence on various lines of evidence to show an identity of mental horizon between the author of the Odyssey and the author of the non-Achil-

---

[12] Fäsi is inclined to give the same comprehensive interpretation to Ἄργος καὶ Ἀχαιΐδα in Γ 75, as meaning Greece both South and North.—Ι 363 is proof that more than Argolis was included under Argos, the abduction of Helen being properly from Sparta.

[13] If we can assume Amyntor in I 448 and K 266 to be one person, as Mr. Gladstone does (Gl. Homer, i. 269), we have then a further proof that Hellas has begun to include Bœotia, Eleon being certainly in Bœotia (B 500).

[14] Πανέλληνες is manifestly national and not tribal in Hesiod, Op. 526, opposed to the Κυάνεοι, i. e. Ethiopians. It is found also, in fragment of Hesiod in Strabo, regarding the suitors for the Proetides—an ante-Trojan legend. Cp. also Πανέλ-ληνες as early as Archilochus, fr. 47. Hellas in wide sense in Hesiod, Op. 651.

leid. Let us now turn to the books of the Achilleid and endeavour to understand the horizon of their surroundings.

63. The range of the Achillean poet's vision is found to be much more circumscribed. Far from being co-extensive or concentric with that of the poet of the Odyssey or of the Ulyssean books, it is narrow and confined, though in one quarter very precise, and its main region is concentrated round the Northern Ægean.

Dodona is the only oracle of the Greek race to which he refers, from which we may infer that Delphi and Delos were yet in obscurity. Cyprus is the most distant locality known to him, if we may rely on Λ 21, and Lycia in the South of Asia Minor seems the boundary, practically, of his vision to the East. The Æthiopians and the 'Ocean' belong rather to mythology than to geography, and even Egypt seems not to be within his ken. Phœnicia and Sidon are not named, but the mention of κασσίτερος, if it means *tin*, points to knowledge of Phœnician commerce, although the occurrence of φοίνικι φαεινός in Ο 538 [15] does not necessarily imply *trading* with Phœnicia. If, however, his acquaintance with the South and East is greatly inferior, on the Northern frontier, and especially in what may be called the Thracian or afterwards the Scythian area, his acquaintance is close and minute (Ν 5, 301, Ξ 225). He names the *Hippemolgi*, or 'mare-milkers,' evidently a tribe of Scythian Nomads, and speaks of the *Ephyri* with the *Phlegyes*, tribes whose *habitat* was placed near the northern frontier, and on the soil of what was afterwards Thessaly. In one or two points he seems to be more precise, if not more accurate, than the more recent poet. In particular it may be mentioned that he recognises the Achelous as the king of rivers (Φ 194), which would be natural for a Northern Greek, as we take the first shaper of the Achilleid to have been, much as Virgil's compliment of 'Fluviorum rex Eridanus' was natural homage to the Po from a native of

---

[15] A Schol. *ad loc.* takes it to mean 'red with blood-colour' as if from φόνος, interpreting as βεβαμμένος ἐρυθρῷ τῷ αἵματι. Compare φοινικοστερόπας of Pindar, an epithet of Zeus, which does not imply any reference to Phœnicians. In Hesiod (Scut. 194) we have αἵματι φοινικόεις.—The Cyprian Kinyras of Λ 20 is probably a name of Phœnician origin (Preller, Gr. M. i. 320), and Assaracus of Υ 232 is said by Ernst Curtius (II. i. 79) to be found on Assyrian monuments, but *proper* names do not imply knowledge of the countries to which they may philologically belong.

Cisalpine Gaul. What renders the fact more notable is that the poet of the Ulyssean book Ω speaks of an Achelous in an entirely different quarter, near Mount Sipylus, which must indicate an Asiatic locality, and seems to ignore by his silence the great river of Epirus. It may be hazardous to affirm that the poet of the Odyssey has not the same familiarity with Pieria which the Achillean poet shows (Ξ 225-30), but it is doubtful whether the former did not consider Pieria to be bounded by sea to the North, when he makes, or seems to make, Hermes drop into the deep (Od. ε 50) in setting out from Olympus. This argument is not in itself of much weight, but it derives strength from what we shall find to be the case when we come to compare their divergent representations of Mount Olympus, which belongs geographically to this region of Pieria, and with which the Achillean poet shows a fuller familiarity.

Except on the Northern frontier of Greece, the Achilleid shows inferior range and clearness of geographical vision. On the other hand the Ulyssean cantos and the Odyssey exhibit a radius of vision mutually identical and in directions different from the vision of the Achilleid.

CHAPTER VIII.

CRITERION AS TO HUMOUR AND PATHOS.

δακρυόεν γελάσασα.

64. THE next criterion which we proposed to apply was that drawn from the allied qualities of Humour and Pathos, which are marked characteristics of the Odyssey. Are the two sections of the Iliad upon an equality in this respect, or can we trace in the one more than in the other a closer relation of kinship to the Odyssey? The kinship is not difficult to discover, for it is in the Ulyssean books of the Iliad that we find those elements in the same pleasing and attractive form as we find them in the Odyssey. There is this difference, however, that, in conformity with the pervading tone of each poem, the pathos is more marked in the Ulyssean cantos of the Iliad, the humour in the Odyssey itself. As examples of tender pathos, we have only to name the parting of Hector and Andromache and the supplication of Priam for the dead body of his son[1]. These are the masterpieces of the Iliad in pathetic tenderness. They occur in Ulyssean books, viz. Z and Ω. It is difficult, in the face of the internal evidence, to separate the authorship of these two books, and, if Ω on the linguistic evidence is closely connected with the Odyssey, it follows that the kindred book Z must be so

---

[1] According to Col. Mure (H. of Gr. Lit. i. p. 358), the funeral lamentation in the same book Ω (723 seq.) by the three dames of Troy, is also a masterpiece in oratory as well as tenderness. He considers it worthy of being classed with the debate in Achilles' tent for the felicity with which different veins of oratory are adapted to different speakers. Book Ω would thus resemble Z in pathos, and I in oratorical power.

likewise. In the Odyssey, it is true, there is no pathetic scene on such a scale or so long sustained as those we have named ; but, as miniature sketches, the great simile in Od. θ 523 of the weeping widow over her slain patriot husband, and the picture of the death-scene of the dog Argus, in its tender tone and its touches of glorious power, reveal to the full the same master hand [2].

In dealing with this point of Pathos, it falls to be remarked that the Ulyssean poet has interwoven with at least two of his characters an element of tenderness not present elsewhere in the same characters as portrayed in the Achillean books. This tenderness is conspicuous in the case both of Hector and Achilles, all the *softening* touches belonging to the portrait of each having come from the Ulyssean poet. This will appear more fully afterwards when the treatment of the different heroes comes under review.

In like manner, the gentle plaintiveness with which the bloom and evanescence of the generations of men are touched, in the same book Z, with no inferior power—a plaintiveness which very early drew forth the admiration of the greatest subsequent master of pathos in the ancient world, Simonides —harmonizes with the tones of the Odyssey, where symptoms appear of the rise of that melancholy view of life which culminated afterwards in the doctrine of the $\phi\theta\acute{o}\nu os\ \theta\epsilon\hat{\omega}\nu$, 'the envy of the gods [3].' The lament over the vanity of human life, race succeeding race like the leaves of the forest and fading away, is put appropriately into the mouth of Glaucus, who inherits

[2] Mr. Gladstone is truly eloquent in his fine characterisation of this Argus-scene (Homer, iii. 410). Mr. Ruskin has censured the 'cruelty' of letting the dog die without a caress or counter-recognition, but he has forgotten the tributary tear (ρ 304), which was all that Ulysses, with safe neck, could then bestow.

[3] The occurrence in the Odyssey of $\zeta\eta\lambda\acute{\eta}\mu ov\epsilon s$ (Od. ϵ 118) and $\dot{a}\gamma\acute{a}\sigma a\nu\tau o$ (Od. δ 181, ψ 211, cp. θ 228), as descriptive of the dispensations of the gods, is parallel to the ethical feeling of $\phi\theta\acute{o}\nu os$ on their part, which pervades the story of Bellerophon. In the Achilleid, in the excitement of a battle, we hear of some deity interfering to frustrate ($\dot{a}\gamma\acute{a}\sigma\sigma a\tau o$ $\Phi o\hat{\iota}\beta os$ $\text{'}A\pi\acute{o}\lambda\lambda\omega\nu$ P 71, and $\mu\epsilon\gamma\acute{\eta}\rho as$ in N 563 and O 473), but these are not instances of settled jealousy, and do not colour the view of Life as an ethical whole in the same manner as the expressions referred to in the Odyssey and Ulyssean books of the Iliad. Hence Lehrs in his popular Essays (Popul. Aufsätze, p. 39), when giving his list of proofs as to the 'Neid der Götter' or 'Envy of the Gods' in the Homeric poems, formally excepts these three passages as *not* involving any moral condition or implying any theory of human life. They are all Achillean. Φ 83 is an instance of 'hate' rather than 'envy.'

a touch of the melancholy of his ancestor Bellerophon, the man on whom the blight fell so that he was looked on as 'hated by all the gods.'

Alongside of this plaintiveness of tone there also occurs a touch of the never very distant quality of humour, humour and pathos being twin aspects of the same emotional faculty. The same poet who thrills us with the tender lament of Glaucus over the fading existence of man winds up the description of his adventure with an account of the bad bargain he made in the exchange of arms, giving gold armour for bronze, as if the poet felt an internal glow of satisfaction that the cunning Greek had got the better of the lordly Asiatic. In point of fact, this gleam of quiet humour at the close of the Glaucus episode is one of the features that has drawn against it the arrows of certain Wolfians, and, along with the σήματα λυγρά and the reference to the *cultus* of Dionysus, elsewhere little known to either poem, has caused that exquisite episode to be pronounced an interpolation. It is a magnificent bit of painting, however, mainly in honour of Ulysses' brother-chief, Diomed, and will be found to contain in small compass the pathos, somewhat of the humour and much of the spirit of romantic adventure distinguishing the Epos of the Odyssey.

65. Perhaps the most satisfactory proof under this head is that derived from a remarkable group of expressions significant of indulgence in grief. It is now a familiar phrase to speak of 'the luxury of grief' and of the Ossianic charm of Melancholy—the 'Wonne der Wehmuth'—and philosophers have endeavoured to analyse the conditions under which grief becomes a pleasure (Hamilton, Metaph. ii. p. 482-3). It is singular how this idea should emerge largely in the Odyssey and the later Ulyssean books, and be absent, almost or altogether, from the Achillean area. Colonel Mure dwelt at considerable length on the phraseology referred to as an argument against the Wolfians (H. of G. L. ii. 37-41). and he showed easily that there was a remarkable harmony between the tone of the Odyssey and that of certain books of the Iliad in this regard. A glance at his citations will show that he is entirely indebted for his proofs from the Iliad to certain Ulyssean cantos, in which (Ψ, Ω), at the close of

the poem, the pent up fountain of tears was finally allowed to flow [4]. In the Odyssey the recognition scene between the long lost father and the son is characterised by this outbreak of the ἵμερος γόοιο, by affection that can scarcely 'know itself' from grief. The same master of pathos is also at work in the recognition scene by Eumæus in φ 226, and he describes, in the case of Eurycleia in τ 471, the presence together of ἅμα χάρμα καὶ ἄλγος, a mingled feeling that found vent in tears.

66. Under the head of Humour proper, the Odyssey may be generally cited as containing a strong vein of playfulness and delicious half-conscious *naïveté*, which is among the chief charms of the poem. Colonel Mure has drawn out pretty fully the main lines of proof in this regard. The humour culminates in the scene with Irus in the Eighteenth Odyssey, to which it is difficult to produce a companion picture, unless we take the Thersites scene in the Second Iliad—a Ulyssean canto. Ulysses is the protagonist in both, administering sharp

---

[4] The following gives a view of the chief details :—

		Ach.	Ul.	Od.
τέρπεσθαι	γόοιο, γόῳ, ἄλγεσι	o	3	6
ἆσαι	γόοιο	o	1	o
ἵμερος	γόοιο	o	4	4
ἵμερος	κλαυθμοῦ	o	o	1
ἱμερόεις	γόος	o	o	1
ἔρος	γόου	o	1	o
ἄσεσθε	κλαυθμοῖο	o	1	o
πρῆξις	γόοιο, μυρομένοισιν	o	1	2
κύρος	γόοιο	o	o	1
κορέσσατο	κλαίουσα	o	o	1
		o	11	16

θαλερὸς γόος might have been added from Od. κ 457, but it is balanced by στυγερὸς κλαυθμός in Od. ρ 8. Compare also Χ 427 κορεσσάμεθα κλαίοντε, which is subsequent to Hector's death and to the proper close of the Achilleid. The expression in Ρ 37 ἀρητὸς γόος (used also in Ω 741), is employed only in the sense of *detestabilis*. Thus there is a notable absence of the tender element in the Achilleid, but a large amount of evidence as to the tender sympathies of the author of the Odyssey and the closing books of the Ulyssean series, showing that with him the Muse had opened 'the fount of sympathetic tears.' Other plaintive expressions and formulæ belonging to the vocabulary of Pathos are thus distributed :—

	Ach.	Ul.	Od.
αἴ κ' ἐλεήσῃ (or -ῃς)	o	6	1
εἴ ποτ' ἔην γε	o	2	2
ὀλοφυδνός	o	2	1
πολυπενθής	o	1	2

chastisement, and although there is somewhat of a severer tone in the handling of the Thersites-scene [5]—as befits the general surroundings where it is placed—the same powerful pencil may be detected at work in both pictures. Once, in the Odyssey, the humour overflows into the burlesque in the scene in the Eighth Book—the 'Amour of Ares and Aphrodite.' Stronger exception has been taken to this scene on ethical grounds than to almost any other in either poem, from the freedom with which the gods seem to be treated, and the levity that appears to prevail. It is to be observed, however, that it is not in Ithaca but in the quaint fairy realm of Phæacia, where it is rehearsed, and further it has a certain relevancy to the whole poem, in which it serves as *obverse*, or counterpart to the picture of conjugal faithfulness,—the main subject of the Epos where it is found. The most important point, however, for observation is that it is the same two deities figuring disreputably in the Eighth Odyssey, that are subjected to disgrace from the spear of Diomed in the Ulyssean book E of the Iliad.

Other two portions of the Iliad may be mentioned as characterised by a strong infusion of humour. The one is the scene in Olympus at the end of the first book, where Hephæstus makes mirth as the limping cupbearer. This occurs, no doubt, at the point of junction with a Ulyssean book, yet as the first book must be pronounced in the main Achillean, we are not entitled to claim it as an illustration. It savours more of the somewhat rough and barbaric form in which the mirth of the Achillean poet is found to express itself. The other is the misadventure which befalls Ajax the Less, when in the contest in the footrace (against *Ulysses*, as his fellow competitor), he stumbles and meets with mishap

---

[5] The tradition that Thersites, who was chastised for his insolence by Ulysses, was a kinsman of Diomed, has no warrant in the Homeric poems. The Scholiast (B L. in Ven. Schol. on Il. B 212) argues *against* the kinship and says, 'If he had been in fact a kinsman of Diomed, Ulysses would not have struck him,' a remark which is founded on the close connection subsisting between Diomed and Ulysses. —Thersites is named without any parentage, as if the poet did not wish to affix to any of the Greek tribes the responsibility of his disgrace. The most brutal of the suitors in the Odyssey is the son of one with kindred name to *Thersites*, Ctesippus the son of *Polytherses*, in Bunyan phrase, ' son of Mr. Much-Impudence.' The extreme of rudeness in both poems is indicated by analogous nomenclature.

among 'cowdung,' and the crowd 'laughs merrily o'er him.' This occurs, significantly, in a Ulyssean canto (Ψ 777 [6]).

67. We have now to ask, What is the position of the Achilleid in regard to these elements of Humour and Pathos? The answer is a simple one. There is nothing that can be called Pathos, and the Humour, where it appears, is simply Sarcasm, very grim and barbaric. The few flashes that emerge are dark and *lourd*, not playful and lambent, like the humour prevailing in the Odyssey and the Ulyssean books. To say, as the poet *himself* does, of warriors fallen, that 'vultures would be fonder of them now than their wives would' (Λ 162), or to threaten by the mouth of a warrior, 'that there would be more birds than brides around them' (Λ 395), are specimens of the kind of grim humour that we meet with in the Achilleid [7]. Nothing fairly parallel to these is producible from the Odyssey and the non-Achilleid. The differentiation which we found under the former head is therefore shown to be a valid one, upon this second line of investigation.

[6] In support of this view it is important to note that the attitude of the crowd to Ajax the Less recalls that adopted towards Thersites, ἐπ' αὐτῷ ἡδὺ γέλασσαν. The phrase γελᾶν ἐπί τινι occurs six times in the Homeric poems, equally distributed, three Ulyssean, viz. B 270, Ψ 784 and 840, and three in Odyssey (υ 358, 374, and φ 376). In fact the peculiar vocabulary of 'Humour' seems confined to the Odyssey and the Ulyssean area, as an examination of γελοίϊος, γελοιάω, παίζω, φιλοπαίγμων, and, to a certain extent, καγχαλάω, will show.—The five instances of 'Jocosa' or 'amusing and sportive passages' which O. Müller (Lit. ch. v. 8) culls from the Iliad are all Ulyssean.

[7] Heyne remarks on the first of these passages (Λ 162), 'Nostro sensu redolet tota rei species *atrocitatem* aevi.' Other specimens of the savage humour are Π 747, regarding a warrior tumbling from his car, 'What a capital diver for oysters;' Φ 123, of Lycaon pitched into the Scamander, 'Fine food for fishes;' X 373, of Hector lying dead, 'More easy to meddle with now,' on which last the Schol. remarks σαρκαστικὸς ὁ λόγος.—Regarding the one plaintive scene appearing in the Achilleid, that of Briseis in T 290, it is doubtful if it is as ancient as its context, and Heyne (ed. maj.) calls the scene 'serioris rhapsodi commentum.' It is certainly not in the same tone as the surrounding Achilleid. The simile of the Leaves and the Generations of men appears in the second Theomachy attached to the Achilleid, but without any tenderness, expressed, as Mure remarks (II. p. 45), 'in the *contemptuous* language of Apollo' (Φ 464).—It is remarkable that the Achilleid should thus exhibit a quality of sentiment seemingly indigenous to Thessaly, sarcasm being 'racy of the soil,' as we may infer from Athenæus (i. 11. b) in Θεσσαλὸν σόφισμα.

CHAPTER IX.

οὐ μὲν γὰρ τοῦ γε κρεῖσσον καὶ ἄρειον,
ἢ ὅθ' ὁμοφρονέοντε νοήμασιν οἶκον ἔχητον
ἀνὴρ ἠδὲ γυνή.

---

68. THE third indication of alliance between the Odyssey
and the Ulyssean books of the Iliad is that regarding the bliss
of home and the conjugal relation. Although apparently, at
first sight, of minor moment, it assumes more importance
when we remember how largely this element of the 'Hearth'
prevails in the Odyssey, and how it formed the 'salt' of virtue
to the character of Ulysses, since, the moment *that* was lost
as it was by the Tragedians, the grand ideal of the Hero was
dissolved and he became a cunning trickster, nothing more.
Accordingly, in any cognate poems it may well be required
that we should find an echo to the dominant keynote of that
Epos. The Odyssey may be styled the romance of wedded
love, in marked and emphatic contrast to the modern romance
of pre-nuptial love[1]. In modern times, as has been often
remarked, the 'feverish tie' has usurped to itself the whole
or almost the whole arena of imagination, to the exclusion of
other emotions and affections. It is otherwise with Homer,
at all events with the poet of the Odyssey, who has bent

---

[1] The instance of Hæmon's love for Antigone is not sufficient to constitute an
ancient exception. It is an incident, no doubt, of the play; but as Antigone appears not to reciprocate the feeling, it is entirely secondary. Stesichorus, however, seems to have touched upon the romance of pre-nuptial love (O. Müller's
Gr. Lit. ch. xiv. 6.)—It is singular that two stars among our living poets should
in different ways have crossed the orbit of the Odyssey, Tennyson in his 'Enoch
Arden,' and Longfellow in his 'Evangeline.'

the whole force of his genius to portray the constancy and patience, the endurance and triumph, of a queenly lady faithful to her lord. It is no doubt a one-sided picture, inasmuch as the poet, who is so careful of the honour of Penelope, is not equally careful of the fealty of Ulysses towards her[2]. On this matter we do not touch, but simply note in passing that modern morality has no right to reproach antiquity on the score of a looser rule of honour for the one sex, compared with that exacted of the other. It is enough for our purpose to be able to appeal to the Odyssey as presenting a noble ideal of the female character, and to present such an ideal, fortified by such tremendous contrasts as that of the faithless Clytemnestra, we may presume to have been a ruling motive in the mind of its author.

69. Parallel, however, to the larger portraiture in the Odyssey is the smaller but not less beautiful one in the Iliad, in the character of Andromache. It is in one of those cantos which on other grounds we have found to be cognate to the Odyssey, viz. the book Z of the Iliad. It is not without reason that Colonel Mure (H. of Gr. Lit. i. p. 432) appeals to this similarity as an anti-Wolfian argument, and he calls attention to the fact that the mild rebuke recommending attention to domestic matters and not meddling with the affairs that belong to men, is couched in almost identical terms for both princesses in both poems. There is therefore a certain amount of evidence for the affirmation that, if the hand of Sir Walter Scott might be detected through the frequency with which he has sketched the group of an aged father with an only daughter[3], that of Homer may be similarly known by his double picture of the wife and mother with an only son[4]. Andromache and

---

[2] Homer may be said to agree with Shakspere as to the greater constancy of woman's love—

> 'For, boy, however we do praise ourselves,
> Our fancies are more giddy, and infirm,
> More longing, wavering, sooner lost and worn,
> Than women's are.
>
> Duke in *Twelfth Night.*

It is right to observe, however, that Ulysses is οὐκ ἐθέλων in his relations with Calypso (Od. ε 155).—Mr. Gladstone (Juv. Mundi, p. 406) remarks that the law of England *authorises* remarriage after a shorter period of absence than that assigned to Ulysses.

[3] Compare Adolphus's Letters to Heber, p. 211-3.

[4] A third example may be that of Sarpedon, who seems to be portrayed, along

Astyanax are therefore a companion pair to Penelope and Telemachus, and Hector and Ulysses resemble each other in their conjugal affection, the former thinking the doom of Troy with his parents' and brothers' death *not* the bitterest thing, but the sorrows of his spouse, the latter declining the embraces of goddesses with the proffered gift of immortality that he might return to his own Penelope.

70. Regarding the Achilleid, it would be in vain to expect any analogous feature in the domestic relations. The prevailing character of the Achilleid does not afford scope for the tenderer elements of humanity[5], and one important reason will appear when we come to consider the nature of the Marriage-contract as it is found in the Achillean area.

71. Lastly, under this head, I have to remark as a corroboration of my position generally, and an instructive evidence in this matter, that the word ῾Εστία or ῾Ιστίη, the name denoting the Domestic Hearth, is, with all its derivatives, entirely absent from the Achilleid, and belongs solely to those parts where we find the evidences of Domestic and Conjugal affection, viz. the Odyssey and Ulyssean cantos[6].

---

with Hector and Ulysses, as having an ἄλοχος attended by one infant son, νήπιον υἱόν (E 480, 688). Contrast with this line the counterpart in the Achilleid (P 28), where, however, the ἄλοχος has subjoined to her 'the parents' (τοκῆας), and a similar line occurs in Ξ 502.—Straws show sometimes the direction of the wind, and it is curious to note how Dolon in Κ and Nausicaa in Od. ζ exactly reflect each other, the one *sole* son among *five* sisters, the other *sole* daughter among five brothers. Both are Ulyssean touches.

[5] As suggestive of kindliness in the *domestic* relations, probably κεδνότατος and κήδιστος are among the most significant in the Homeric vocabulary. They are, however, absent from the Achilleid. The occurrences are (I 586, 642, κ 225 (bis), θ 583):—

Ach. Ul. Od.

0   2   3

The word κεδνός occurs once in the Achilleid (P 28), of *parents*; but the occurrences in the other parts are

Ul. Od.

1   8,

not reckoning the phrase κεδνὰ ἰδυῖα: φίλιστος, on the other hand, not being suggestive, necessarily, of *domestic* affection, is more equally diffused.

[6] The occurrences are (ἱστίη, ἀνέστιος, ἐφέστιος, and perhaps ἐπίστιον)—

Ach. Ul. Od.

0   2   6.

It is not denied that the Achillean poet had known the word (ἱστία), which is an ancient Indo-germanic one, older than the separation of the races; all that is averred is that he has not, as a matter of fact, used the word, and apparently felt no attraction toward the associated ideas.

72. It may, however, be replied that it is unfair to ask for such *tableaux* of domestic life from the Achillean area; the scope of the great war poem did not include such scenes, neither did the subject favour their introduction. It is a poem of camp-life, where there could be no proper ἑστία, and therefore there are no *domestica*. To this, in the abstract, I have nothing to object, except to remark, what might otherwise be overlooked, that the Iliadic scenes in other books, now found conjoined with the Achillean poem, deal likewise with war and camp-life, and yet the poet who sketched *these* has found means to introduce us, as it were, to the firesides of the Trojans, and even in *his* war poem to interweave those pictures of Domesticity to which we have alluded. The conclusion seems therefore to be justified that we have in the Iliad two different personalities at work, one of these the non-Achillean, possessing sympathies and idiosyncrasies akin to those manifested in the Odyssey, the other apparently possessing sympathies of an entirely different order.

CHAPTER X.

οὐκ ἂν ἔπειτ' Ὀδυσῆϊ ἐρίσσειε βροτὸς ἄλλος.

73. I PASS now to the fourth characteristic of the Odyssey,
—its high estimate of Ulysses as the impersonation of Spirit
and Intelligence. The abundant presence of parallel phenomena in the Ulyssean books, the comparative absence of
anything similar in the Achillean books, is one of the most
important arguments that I have to adduce, and, indeed, it
was this contrast that first directed my attention forcibly to the
subject. The conclusion was gradually reached that the non-
Achillean books are pervaded by a special vein of admiration
for Ulysses, strongly suggestive of that more pronounced
admiration which has poured itself forth in that most splendid
of poems ever consecrated to a single name—the Odyssey.

We have already seen that the Ulyssean books and the
Odyssey exhibit together an equal range of acquaintance
with the outer world, and one of the great sources of obtaining wisdom in early times was by seeing the manners
and cities of the different tribes of men. Ulysses is therefore as the great traveller, or the 'far wandered' man (Od. a 2),
the impersonation of intelligence, and it is singular that, in
the Iliad, his position appears more prominent in those books
which exhibit the widest outlook on the foreign world. The
reference to Egyptian Thebes (I 383) is probably the most
distant from the Hellenic centre of all the non-mythical and
actual localities which Homer names. It occurs significantly in
a canto in which Ulysses may be said to be the foremost figure.

As regards the spirit of Intelligence showing itself in the increasing value of Oratory, and in improved Ethical sentiment,

G

the proof will come more appropriately afterwards, when we deal with the more neozoic features in Life and Manners, of the Homeric poems. These we shall find to be on the whole more abundant in the Ulyssean books and Odyssey than in the older Achilleid.

We turn, then, to test the Ulyssean books as to their attitude towards Ulysses.

74. And first regarding the mass of continuous cantos, viz. B to Ι. In the first of these we find him at once placed as it were in a focus of splendour, and he figures as the mainstay of the Greek Host at a critical time. The old Saga appears to have represented him as the *last* of the chiefs who found his way home, and accordingly the Νόστος or Return, so much desired. was cared for by him only if obtained with duty and honour. He is, accordingly, although more than most with his heart in Home, the determined opponent of any dishonourable Νόστος[1], and in book B, where Agamemnon pretends to propose such a measure, and the army drifts into accepting it, Ulysses steps into the breach at the critical moment and arrests the carrying out of it. Hence. through the greater part of this scene, Ulysses is the principal figure and obtains for a time the *rôle* of the king of men, being invested with the special insignia of the sceptre—never conferred on any other—belonging to the Pelopidæ, which sceptre is described with extraordinary state and splendour of surroundings. Athene is spoken of as standing by his side ' in the likeness of a herald' (B 280), the same relation as she afterwards sustains towards him in Phæacia (Od. θ 7).

And wherefore should the task of staying the Νόστος and repressing the seditious movements of the Assembly be entrusted to Ulysses? Not merely because of his character for eloquent speech, or because of the possible reflection from the older scene in Ξ 82, where he opposes the notion of a dishonourable Νόστος, but because he was pre-eminently the chosen hero to deal with mutiny and sedition. He is the vindicator of order in Ithaca when he returns, and therefore the Homeric maxim of order—οὐκ ἀγαθὸν πολυκοιρανίη—is placed appropriately in his mouth, while in his

---

[1] The Achilleid knows Ulysses also as the enemy of a dishonourable *νόστος* (Ξ 82).

chastisement of the seditious Thersites we recognise a preparation for his treatment of the mutinous crew of the Suitors. The eminence of his position in B is further marked by the circumstance that he is conjoined with Achilles himself in the hatred of Thersites—ἔχθιστος δ᾽ Ἀχιλῆϊ μάλιστ᾽ ἦν ἠδ᾽ Ὀδυσῆϊ—a line marking out the two heroes as standing apart and alone, yet *together*, the full import of which can only be understood if we appreciate the hand of the author of the Odyssey as at work in this portion of the Iliad. Already we find bestowed on him likewise what is a favourite designation in the Odyssey, viz. πτολίπορθος (B 278), which is notable as the name of dread when he throws off the Outis-mask toward the Cyclop (Od. ι 503), and is one virtually given him in the proem of the Odyssey[2]. He is the only *hero present* at Troy who receives this epithet, *except Achilles,* and he wears it in a loftier sense even than Achilles, as he was the sacker of Troy itself, while Achilles was sacker only of the surrounding towns (cp. Π 709, and Aristarchus in Wolf, ch. 49 n). Other touches of similar significance are Athene's address to him couched in the same words that Heré had addressed to *her* as if Athene and he were convertible personalities, (a point remarked by Scholiast, B 179.), a τὶς judgment ascribing to him 'countless good deeds,' (μυρία ἐσθλά, in 272), the *unique* compliment, as coming from the whole army, μῦθον ἐπαινήσαντες Ὀδυσσῆος θείοιο (335), and the place of honourable mention in the feast of the chiefs in B 407, where, after other chiefs have been massed together in twos and threes, Ulysses closes the list, with a full line to describe him[3]. A fact more notable has

---

[2] Compare as to πτολίπορθος the note on § 36. A similar fact attaches to the localisation of another epithet of Ulysses in B, θεῖος. As attached to Proper names *simply*, without κῆρυξ or any word of *office* subjoined, it belongs practically to the two heroes. For (unlike δῖος which is lavishly bestowed), except to Achilles, who receives it four times, all Achillean, it is given to no *living* hero, but to Ulysses, who receives it as often in the Iliad as the hero himself, but the passages are Ulyssean, viz. B 335, I 218, K 243. and probably Λ 806.

	Ach.	Ul.	Od.		Ach.	Ul.	Od.
θεῖος (of Achilles)	4	0	0	θεῖος (of Ulysses)	0	4	20.

Further, the ascription of 'equality with Zeus in counsel,' frequent in this book B, is assigned to Ulysses four times in the Ulyssean area (B 169. 407. 636. K 137), once to Hector (H 47). In the Achillean area it is bestowed once on Hector (Λ 200), and on none else. The nearest approach is once regarding Patroclus (θεόφι μήστωρ ἀτάλαντος P 477).

[3] The Scholiast on B 407 explains his coming last by the reason of his eminence.

yet to be mentioned. The hero, in speaking of himself, chooses to designate himself by a singular title, and one premonitory of the Odyssey. It is one peculiarly significant of those home affections [1] which form the mainspring of the Odyssey. While other heroes have their titles drawn from their paternal ancestors nearer or more remote, and while there are some traces in the heroic time of designation after a *maternal* ancestor such as Λητοΐδης in Hesiod, and, in the Iliad, the problematical case of the Μολίονε, Ulysses chooses as the title by which *he* would be designated, an appellation neither patronymic [5] nor metronymic, but, if we may so style it, pædonymic, *from his son*, viz. 'the father of Telemachus' (l. 260) [6]. The same 'style and title' is assumed in Il. Δ 354, in a passage full of offended personal dignity, and this is one of the minor links binding cantos B and Δ together and attaching both to the framework of the Odyssey [7]. It is,

[1] A minor touch is that in B 292, where Ulysses acknowledges the charms of home, a passage in which the Ven. Scholiast thinks there is a preparation for the great example of Penelope (*τοῦτο προανακρούεται τὴν Πηνελόπης στοργήν*), and so a premonitory note of the Odyssey.

[5] The subject of Patronymics is a curious one, in connection with Anthropological questions as to descent through father or through mother. Aristarchus denied the existence of metronymics in Homer (Lehrs, p. 176), also Apollonius (Lex. p. 113), cp. Ven. Schol. on Λ 72, Λ 749. Preller admits an instance in the Μολίονε, but Donaldson (Pindar, p. 74) denies it to be a clear case. Apart from this instance, the Greeks and also the Trojans as revealed to us in Homer, count descent only through the father.—A grandfather is also acknowledged, for Αἰακίδης is applied to Achilles (a *papponymic*, Schol. Il. I 191), and even remoter ancestors as. e. g. Δαρδανίδης, which is used of Priam (Γ 103) as well as of Ilus (Λ 166). A *mammonymic* is found in Phœbus, as from a grandmother Phœbe (Paley, Hesiod, 404). Ἀλθαία Μελιαγρίς (Ibyc. fr. 12) is a curious instance of a pædonymic.

[6] A preparation for the Odyssey, in the opinion of the Ven. Schol. on B 260 (*προοικονομεῖ δὲ (ὁ ποιητής) τὰ κατὰ τὴν Ὀδύσσειαν*). Similar remarks are found under B 761 and Δ 354 (*σπέρματα προκαταβάλλει, προτετυπωμένως*).

[7] The recognition scene in the Odyssey justifies this view. Ulysses there announces himself to his son: *οὔτις τοι θεός εἰμι . . . . . ἀλλὰ πατὴρ τεός εἰμι* (π 187).—Again, the *converse* comes up, in exact correspondence, in the 'style and title' of Telemachus, namely, 'loved son of Ulysses the godlike,' *Τηλέμαχος φίλος υἱὸς Ὀδυσσῆος θείοιο* with *five* occurrences (γ 398, ο 553, ρ 3, υ 283, φ 432).—It is singular to find the shade of Achilles, while inquiring about his son, intensely eager to learn about his father, to whom he devotes ten lines as against two about his son. The Æolo-Dorian mind was much concerned about the past and the honour of parents. Ulysses in his reply just reverses the relation, can tell nothing of the father but enlarges on the exploits of Achilles' son (λ 494-507).—The Ulysses of the Achilleid drops out the mention of 'son' in connection with 'father and mother' (Λ 452), but the Ulysses of the Odyssey includes 'son' with 'father and

therefore, singular that the hero who more than any other prefigures the *future* character of the Greek race, and especially of the Athenian, should thus be represented as the only one not seeking his honours in the past but looking down into the vista of the future[8]. Whatever might be the poet's consciousness in this matter as to the distant future, there can be little doubt that his vision comprehended the immediate future, and already there came within its ken the important *rôle* to be played by Telemachus in the coming drama of the Odyssey.

A conjoint view of all these particulars leads to the conclusion that the author of canto B has taken special pains to manifest his interest in the hero of the Odyssey.

75. Regarding the next canto, Γ, the same thing holds good in almost equal measure. In the first place, it is to be noted that Ulysses is singled out as standing alongside of Agamemnon, a sort of 'second' to him, in the ratification of the oaths (l. 268); next, he is conjoined with Hector in measuring the lists, on a footing, as it were, of equality with the prince of Troy, and acting as *lieutenant* to the King of men; and, thirdly and most important, his portrait occupies the largest space in the canvas, in that beautiful scene where Helen points out the Greek chiefs from the Trojan wall. He is one of four so named, and is far the most prominent person in this portrait-gallery of the Teichoskopy; for while Ajax, Idomeneus, and even Agamemnon, are dismissed with a few lines, Ulysses is introduced immediately after Agamemnon, is honoured by a special compliment from a distinguished Trojan, Antenor, who stands as 'second' to Priam in the

spouse' (λ 174), and Elpenor's shade (λ 68) makes the name of Telemachus the crowning argument in supplicating the living Ulysses.

[8] On this point it may suffice for the present to state that the thought of posterity and coming generations is much more frequently before the mind of the non-Achillean bard. The type-expressions indicating this outlook over the coming ages are found especially in the use of ἐσσομένοισι with πυθέσθαι and the like appended, and ὀψίγονοι. The following is the view of the case :—

	Ach.	Ul.	Od.	Ach.	Ul.	Od.
ἐσσομένοισι	1	4	5	X 305	B 119 Ζ 355 Γ 287, 460	γ 204, θ 580 Λ 76, 433, Φ 255
ὀψιγόνων	0	2	2		Γ 353 Η 87	α 302, γ 200

How this peculiarity comes up as a valuable index of character and national affinity will afterwards appear.

oath-scene, and, though expressly said to be smaller in stature and king of only a barren rock, he is yet made to fill the field of vision so fully that out of *seventy* lines appropriated to the description of the Greek chiefs, the little Ithacan occupies *thirty-four*, or about half the space[9]. Further, it is to be remarked that in the tribute to his eloquence the palm is bestowed in so marked a manner that it seems to clash with or endanger the pre-eminence in this respect of Achilles himself. Nothing, however, can be more natural, if we consider the poet of the Odyssey as already indulging an unconscious partiality for the insular hero in whom the genius of the Ionian race, to which he himself probably belonged, is more or less consciously prefigured.

76. Passing to book Δ, we find two important particulars to note in his honour. He is represented as performing an important exploit[10], slaying a son of Priam (Δ 500), a feat which has this effect, that it turns the fortune of the day, and rouses Apollo's indignation so that the god immediately thereafter addresses reproaches to his baffled Trojans, at the same time inciting them by telling them of Achilles' absence. The second is a more subtle and recondite point, but the evidence it presents is of a deep and far-reaching significance. It is drawn from the manner in which he is represented in the great scene of the Ἐπιπώλησις, when Agamemnon passes along, reviewing the different chiefs and bands. He is there placed alongside of one who is leader of Athenians, Menestheus; and Agamemnon couples Ulysses and Menestheus together in addressing to them certain

---

[9] Note also the following peculiarities in Γ regarding Ulysses. 1. He is the only one honoured by a simile, and that one probably indicating a sort of *pet* interest (κτίλος), Γ 196. 2. He is said ἐπιπωλεῖσθαι στίχας ἀνδρῶν (Γ 196), words of honour, signifying something like the inspectorial style of a Field-marshal. It is given to Agamemnon *twice* (Δ 231, 250), and never to any other chief. (Its use in the Achilleid—Α 264 and 540—is different, for, as Heyne remarks on the latter, the use there is 'animo *infesto*, aliter ac Γ 196, Δ 231,' whereas in the Ulyssean books it indicates a *friendly* visiting; οἰχόμενοι δ' ἐπὶ πάντας seems to be the Achillean phrase for the visit of a general on survey, cp. Ξ 381; also ἐποιχόμενος στίχας ἀνδρῶν in Ο 279, while πάντη or πάντοσ' ἐποιχόμενος is diffused.)

[10] The expression ἀνδρὸς ἀκοντίσσαντος (Δ 498), as if Ulysses were the ἀνήρ pre-eminent (cp. § 34 n), as in the opening line of the Odyssey, is worth noting, but seems to be accidental. It occurs again only in Ο 575, of an exploit of Antilochus, where no such lofty sense is *necessarily* intended.

words of censure [11]. The special point to be observed is that
Ulysses, who replies, is made the mouth-piece not only of his
own insular troops but of the Athenians, in answering the
taunts of Agamemnon [12].   And why is this?   Because the
Ionian poet (if we may be allowed to anticipate what will
afterwards be more clearly shown), has chosen to bring
Ulysses into the closest connection with the Athenians, the
reputed heads or ancestors of the Ionian race, and has made
him therefore, with a felicity which the poet did not and could
not fully discern, the representative and spokesman of the
great sea people of the historic time.   The further proof of
this point will be more appropriately given when we come to
deal with the traces of predilections and national sympathies
in the two sections of the Iliad.

77. In the remaining three books of the continuous Ulyssean section, E, Z, and H, the position of Ulysses is not so prominent as in the three preceding.   In E he is, for the time,
overshadowed by Diomed, but the overshadowing is by one
who is remarkably associated with Ulysses not only in the Homeric poems, but in the non-Homeric traditions of the Troica,
as in the capture of the Palladium [13].   The fullest evidence
of this companionship is given in book K, where, however,
they are already at the outset looked on as brothers in arms
(l. 109), and the relation is one acknowledged also in the
Odyssey, where Menelaus couples the two warriors together
in close companionship within the 'Wooden Horse,' αὐτὰρ
ἐγὼ καὶ Τυδείδης καὶ δῖος 'Οδυσσεύς (δ 280)[14].   There is
therefore a *prima facie* case to consider them not as rivals
but as confederates [15], and, in point of fact, they are so
linked together, inasmuch as the special favour of Athene

[11] It is worth noting that. in Xenophon's list of 'hunting heroes,' Menestheus
stands *between* Ulysses and Diomed (Xen. de Ven. ch. i.).

[12] The reply of Ulysses has the effect of calling forth a retractation on the part
of Agamemnon.   To him alone an apology for sharp words is tendered by Agamemnon, a point omitted in the case of Diomed and Sthenelus. who protest
similarly but receive no apology.

[13] Diomed is said to have founded a new Argos in Apulia, and resembles Ulysses
in being one of the Eponymous heroes conjoined with him by the Sagas in Italian
colonisation.   Compare on their conjunction in Italy. Preller, K. Myth. p. 663.

[14] Diomed is mentioned in other two passages of the Odyssey (γ 167 and 181).

[15] Hayman (Od. i. p. 47 of Pref.) almost overstates the point when he says,
'Odysseus in the Iliad has Diomedes as an *alter ego*, his subordinate and executive
half.'

is bestowed on both warriors in book E (cp. l. 519 and 669–676), as it is also again in book Ψ in the adventures of the Games. This throws considerable light upon the point, and shows that the glory of Diomed, which seems in this book to transcend that of Achilles at its highest, diffuses a part of its radiance also on Ulysses [16]. Accordingly Ulysses is similarly raised to a position of rival eminence by performing a parallel exploit to that which is afterwards given to Achilles, but which Achilles, the hero of the whole, does not overpass. He slays in succession seven Lycian warriors in lines that are exactly parallel to the exploit of Achilles in slaying (Φ 211) the seven Pæonians. The position of Lycians in the war pictures of the Iliad is in reality nobler than that of the Pæonians, so that, in this respect, the author of E has brought Ulysses, like Diomed, into close competition with the hero of the whole poem. The manner in which this exploit of Ulysses is introduced is also worthy of attention. It is introduced at the point where the greatest exploit of the Trojans in these early cantos has been performed, viz. after Sarpedon's slaying of Tlepolemus, and it is to Ulysses therefore that the poet here attributes the stroke counterbalancing that achievement. He is further described as τλήμονα θυμὸν ἔχων [17], a notable characteristic, for he is the only single hero who is called τλήμων in the Iliad, K 231

[16] The only instances in which the name of Achilles is introduced in the incidents of the First Battle (Δ –Z) are in connection with exploits, either of Ulysses, or of Diomed (Δ 512 and Z 99).—Also, the only *Priamidæ*, who fall in the First Battle, are given to their spears, and the first falls by Ulysses (Δ 499 ubi Schol., and E 159).

[17] This expression τλήμων θυμός recalls a combination largely developed *except* in the Achilleid. The following gives a view of the facts:—

τετληότι θυμῷ, nine times in Odyssey. Cp. Merry on Od. λ 181.

κραδίη τετληυῖα, once in Odyssey (υ 23).

τλήμων and πολυτλήμων θυμός, twice in Ulyssean (E 670 of Ulysses, II 152).

τλητὸς θυμός, once in Ulyssean (Ω 49).

τολμήεις θυμός, { once in Ulyssean (K 205).
{ once in Odyssey (ρ 284 of Ulysses).

When it is further added that τλήμων and πολυτλήμων (without θυμός) are as personal epithets given especially to Ulysses (viz. in K 231 and 498, and Od. σ 319), we obtain a synthesis which binds together the whole group of expressions (eighteen in all) as bearing the mint of a family likeness. It will be difficult to account for this distribution in special areas on the theory of single authorship.

and 498, in the former of which the explanation is subjoined, marking it out as a specialty of the man, αἰεὶ γάρ οἱ ἐνὶ φρεσὶ θυμὸς ἐτόλμα.

In Z and H there is less of specialty to note regarding Ulysses. The former canto is one closely linked on to the preceding, and was indeed in ancient times cited along with it under a common title (Διομήδους ἀριστεία). One exploit, however, is mentioned, the slaying of Pidytes (Z 30). There is ample evidence, in other parts, of affinity to the Odyssey, although, owing partly to the scene being chiefly within the Trojan walls, there are fewer traces of homage to its hero. Neither is there any special homage to him in H, except that he figures as one of the ' Nine Worthies ' that start forth to accept Hector's challenge to single combat. That he is in the poet's eye a marked personage is manifest from the mode in which his name is introduced, namely, at the close of the list, which is a point of great significance, just as we found in B 407. Ulysses is so important a person that he must stand in some way marked out by himself, and hence he is not lumped in with the rest, but, since he could not head the list, or take precedence of Agamemnon, the next place of honour is assigned to him, so that his name comes last and is therefore the climax or copestone [18] (H 168). That this interpretation of the poet's intention is the correct one, rather than another which might explain his coming last upon prudential principles, is shown by the manner in

[18] The place of honour in a poetic enumeration is generally, as in the position of the Æakids in the Camp at Troy, *at the extremes*, either first or last. Among nine instances of the latter are these four, B 407. H 168, I 169, and K 231. all examples of honour to Ulysses. (In the Achilleid Ulysses is generally thrown in, as it were, in the middle, almost like Nestor's κακοί (Δ 299. κακοὺς δ' ἐς μέσσον ἔλασσεν). Cp. A 145, Ξ 29, T 48, 310). Yet in E 519 he occupies the middle place. He also occupies the middle place in the ship-camp, according to Θ 223 and Λ 6 (Achillean parts). The remaining five instances are these: (5) Zeus is *third* in list of Kronid Brothers in O 192; (6) Diomed is last in list of competitors in Ψ 357, where he is expressly called ὄχ' ἄριστος; (7) Pisistratus last of six Nestoridæ in Od γ 415. as being the most prominent surviving son of Nestor; (8) Euryalus last in list of Phæacians, in Od. θ 115, where Naubolides is his patronymic and not, as some have thought, a new individual, otherwise we should have an anticlimax of an unknown person; (9) Klytoneus last among sons of Alcinous. but victor in foot-race (θ 119, 123). Compare the position of Achilles, named last among twenty-one, in Xenophon's list of ' Hunting Heroes ' (Xen. Ven. ch. 1), and the order of arrangement of the three gods in B 478, where the *middle* place is that of the inferior deity.   .

which the hero elsewhere resents the imputation of 'coming last' as if with a view to safety (Δ 354).

Thus it has been shown that, in the continuous section B to II, which is generally regarded even by those inclined to the Wolfian view as a fairly uniform sequence, the position occupied by Ulysses is in four of them transcendant, and, in the remaining two, which cannot be separated from the others, remarkably prominent.

78. Turning to the next group of non-Achillean cantos, I and K, we find him, if possible, in still greater eminence.

In I he is selected to be the spokesman of the Greek chiefs in the supplicatory embassy to Achilles. He is therefore in a position for the time second only to that of Achilles. The hero of the Odyssey addresses the hero of the Iliad. The latter in his reply addresses himself mainly to Ulysses, whom he names *twice*, and who is the only one of the envoys so addressed in the great speech of denunciation [19]. He leads the way when they enter, is the first to rise when taking leave of Achilles (I 657), and gives in the report on his return. This high position, it may be said, is nowise peculiar; he owed it to the reputation he enjoyed in epic tradition of being an adroit and powerful speaker. It is important to note, however, that his eminence is highest in those cantos that are least firmly attached to the nucleus of the Achilleid, and among such cantos the Ninth or I is generally numbered. The fact is strengthened by the proximity of K, still more decidedly external to the primitive Achilleid, in which canto the prominence assigned to him cannot be accounted for, except on the theory previously advanced. The judicious commentator Fäsi, in his notes on the opening of K, joins together I and K as peculiar in the position they hold in the poem, and mentions as one of what he calls the 'difficulties' attaching to the position of these cantos in the poem of the Achilleid, that Ulysses has in both of them the

---

[19] It is remarkable that the effect of Achilles' speech is described in a formula first applied to the eloquence of the Thunderer in Θ 28. The formula occurs once of Zeus, once of Achilles, and of none else with certainty, unless of Ulysses, who is credited according to some interpreters with a similar compliment in I 696. This last line, however, is doubtful, and it is not clear that, if it were genuine, it expresses the effect of Ulysses' speaking.

Hauptrolle or chief *rôle* [20]. Under the theory we are advancing,
these 'difficulties' disappear. When we examine K, we find
that Ulysses is there drawn with especial care, and, though
he is coupled with Diomed in the night adventure, the real
direction of the enterprise is bestowed upon him as the pivot
of the action, so that we consider Payne Knight (Prolegom.
26, 27) and Mr. Gladstone to be justified in calling this canto
the true ἀριστεία of Ulysses, that is, the canto celebrating
his prowess [21]. The manner in which he is introduced last in
the list of volunteers among the heroes (l. 231), with a special
'addition' appertaining only to himself, and the mode in
which the poet invests him with interest by the long history
of the casque [22], which he dons for the occasion, more ample
than the account given of Diomed's armour in the same
expedition, combine to render him the hero of the hour.
How different the relation in which we find him standing
to Diomed in a canto almost contiguous but not Ulyssean
(viz. Θ), is a crucial difficulty on any other hypothesis than

[20] The fact that in K Ulysses is described as arming himself with the *Bow*,
is an important link uniting this book to the Odyssey, where he is represented
in the supreme moment of the action, when *commencing* the attack on the Suitors,
as so armed. Without this incidental mention in book K, we might have
difficulty in identifying the hero of the Odyssey as the one who figures in the
scenes of the Iliad, and therefore K is an important link to connect the Iliad and
Odyssey.

[21] Apuleius (de Deo Socr. ch. 18), referring to this nocturnal expedition, speaks
of Ulysses as the *mens*, Diomed as the *manus*, of the enterprise. Doederlein on K 349
remarks that Ulysses has only to speak, and Diomed complies.—Contrast also
Nestor's respectful demeanour to Ulysses with the somewhat cavalier style of
wakening Diomed (l. 158).

[22] The history of the Helmet in K 260-71 is a characteristic piece of minute
description, paralleled in the Homeric poems only by the descent of the Sceptre in
Iliad B and the Bow of Eurytus in the Odyssey. The moment chosen by the poet
for introducing his descriptive history of these three *instrumenta*, is, remarkably
enough, the moment when *Ulysses takes them into his hands* to handle them. The
bow of Pandarus in Δ, the armour of Ereuthalion in Η, and the shield of Ajax in
Η 220, are similarly invested with interest, though less sustained than in the former
instances by an array of *gradations* of transmission. They happen to be all in
Ulyssean cantos. Behind these little bits of decorative description, it looks as if
we could almost discern looking out upon us the glance of a keen and loving eye like
that with which his nearest compeer in modern times, Walter Scott, would fasten
on and kindle over some piece of ancient armour that had passed through many a
hand and known many a bloody field.—Against these six examples, greater or
smaller, in the non-Achillean area, it is right to note one approach to a parallel in
the Achilleid, in the θώρηξ of Meges (O 530).

that which concludes in favour of two different strata of authorship in the Iliad.

79. There remain only two presumably non-Achillean cantos, Ψ and Ω. In one of these, viz. Ω, we do not find any special reference or homage to him, and the proofs whereby that book appears to be Ulyssean, though we believe sufficient, are mainly linguistic and ethical. It is as if the poet felt that there was no need to decorate a hero who was so near the horizon and about to appear as the rising sun in a new hemisphere.

In Ψ, the canto of the games, his position is remarkable. In the first place, there is no reference to his recent wound and disablement, our knowledge of that being only from the Achilleid[23]. His most important appearance is in the foot-race. That he is not in the chariot race competing with the grander kings, is in accordance with his humble status in the camp, in so far as pomp and state are concerned, for he is without an equipage. In the footrace, however, he is the popular favourite (l. 766), and he wins the prize[24]. This may not mean much, but when we consider that it is through the special favour of Athene, who limits her favour in these games to Ulysses and Diomed, we discern an analogy to the scene in the Eighth Canto of the Odyssey, when Ulysses astonishes the minds of the Phæacians, through the help of the same goddess. The prize too is one that has come from far, from Sidon, and is the only one in all the bestowments in the games that has a special history (l. 743). It is over Ajax, the *swift* son of Oileus, that the victory is won, under circumstances of great mortification to him, and the success of Ulysses is more marked that his rival was regarded as without a peer in nimbleness (Ξ 521). This last passage, however, is in an Achillean canto. The full significance of

<hr>

[23] The Schol. on Ψ 709, either naively or sarcastically, remarks, that 'perhaps the wounds were healed by Athene.'

[24] He also enters the lists against Ajax the Telamonian in the wrestling match — the little man, as he seems to have been conceived by the poet, against the giant. The battle is a drawn one, but he is evidently the popular favourite (l 728), and according to the Scholiast, (Il. Ψ 736), was really first in the contest (τινές φασιν ὅτι τὸ πρῶτον ἐστὶν Ὀδυσσέως, χαρίζεται δὲ Ἀχιλλεὺς Αἴαντι ὡς συγγενεῖ). Ulysses in these contests is made to equal Diomed in successes, each having one clear victory and a 'tie.' Both are conspicuous in success above the others, and in particular it is *over the Ajaxes* that Ulysses especially triumphs.

these details will appear when we bring under review the
position of both the Ajaxes in the Achillean poem.

ULYSSES IN THE ACHILLEID.

80. The evidence in favour of a special interest in and
attachment to Ulysses in the non-Achillean books has thus
been given with some detail. I have now to ask consideration
of the facts appertaining to his position in the Achilleid
itself.

In the Achillean books of the Iliad, Ulysses is an important
but by no means prominent character, to the extent at least
to which he fills the eye and mind of the poet in the cantos
we have been considering. The treatment which he there
receives, though generally respectful, is by no means in all
instances noble[25], and in more than one case it is difficult to
reconcile that treatment with the just honour of the hero of
the Odyssey. He does not intervene in the great debate
and quarrel of A; in that storm Nestor alone ventures to lift
up his voice. He is mentioned respectfully but incidentally
in A 138 and 145, and, as a famous mariner, naturally has
the important charge of taking Chryseis back by sea to her
home and so appeasing Apollo. The next time when we hear
of him in the Achilleid is in Θ, and the adventure in which
he figures (l. 97) is the most significant index in the case. In
the thick of a battle there has been a portent from Zeus
which scares the Greek chiefs and which is designed so to do.
Among other misadventures, old Nestor is sore bestead, his
equipage has got entangled and he himself falls into serious
danger. Diomed observes the risk the old man runs and
calls out to Ulysses *by name* to come and rescue Nestor. In
spite of his loud appeals to stop and not turn his back *like a
coward*, but to stay and shield the old man's head, Ulysses
is represented as 'rushing away past and pays no heed'
(Θ 97)[26]. Other heroes, such as the Ajaxes, are, it is true,

[25] The noblest is probably the ὅσοι πάρος ἦσαν ἄριστοι (A 825), among whom,
though not specially named, he must be regarded as included ; also Διὶ φίλον
applied to him in A 419. 473

[26] The Scholiasts were sorely puzzled at this incident, as the excuses which they

represented as also giving way, alarmed by the divine portent,
but they do so without being appealed to by Diomed. Nor
does Ulysses emerge from his retreat, during that canto, for
he is not mentioned among the heroes who recover courage
and again sally forth a little later, in the same book, to restore
the fortune of the day (l. 261–6), whereas *all* the others who
are spoken of as having retreated before are mentioned as
returning, *except* Ulysses. The strangest thing remains —
strange indeed, if all these cantos as we now have them are
from the same author, and 'at one projection,' namely, that
this incident is entirely overlooked or forgotten by the same
Diomed on the next occasion when there is a dangerous
enterprise ahead (in Κ). There is not only no recollection
of the awkward conduct of Ulysses two books before, but
there is no apology for or allusion to his behaviour by Ulysses,
no explanation on the part of the poet, for Diomed is represented as bestowing unnecessarily lavish praise on him as
the most trusty of comrades (Κ 240–7), and selects him as
his companion-in-arms out of the whole company of the
chiefs. The whole matter becomes plain, and order is at
once restored under these complicated relations, when we
remember that book Κ is from the Ulyssean bard, and Θ is
a part of the Achilleid, left unaffected by the Ulyssean
singer.

81. Interpreted by the analogy of the Achillean Θ, which
must be looked on as normal and regulative upon the point,
the other books cannot be said to present any very marked

make for Ulysses show.—'Das ist kein ruhmvoller Moment,' says Nutzhorn (p. 211),
in dealing with this incident, and he adds that the words πολύτλας δῖος 'Οδυσσεύς
of Il. Θ 97, sound upon the occasion and in this connection almost like a
parody—a remarkable admission from a defender of the Unity of the Iliad.
Making all allowance for 'the fears of the brave' (cp. Pindar's apology for
Amphiaraus, Nem. ix. 27, and Hector's for himself, P 176), it is difficult to
reconcile the Ulysses of the Eighth Iliad with the Ulysses of the Odyssey, impossible to reconcile him with the Ulysses of the Tenth Iliad.—We follow
Aristarchus's interpretation of οὐδ' ἐσάκουσε, viz. 'gave no heed,' in preference to
the untenable one, which seeks to save his honour, that, perhaps owing to the throng,
'he did not hear.' (*'Noluit obtemperare* hortanti. Hoc maluit Aristarchus, nam mox
cum omnes a navibus redeunt (l. 266), Ulixes non redit, ut judicandum sit, dedita
opera se de pugna subtraxisse,' Lehrs, Aristarchus, p. 147).—The Scholiast on Θ 4,
referring to this case of Ulysses, says it was taken to mean ἀκούσας γὰρ οὐκ ἐπείσθη,
and so the Scholiast takes it, on Θ 266, a note probably from Aristarchus.

acknowledgment of Ulysses' eminence, nothing certainly comparable to what has been adduced from the Ulyssean cantos. He is, no doubt, represented as one in whom Athene is interested, so that she interposes to prevent a wound from penetrating too far (Λ 435), probably the most notable distinction to him in the Achilleid, and he is on that occasion addressed as πολύαινος (Λ 430), usually rendered 'much lauded,' though Buttmann prefers to render it 'of much crafty speech.' The expression is found in the mouth of a Trojan and an enemy, and is possibly to be understood ironically (εἰρωνεύεται, among the explanations of Scholiast *ad loc.*). The curious circumstance is that it has an appendage δόλων ἆτ' ἠδὲ πόνοιο, which is nowhere added to the same epithet πολύαινος, when we pass out of the Achilleid, but a new badge, μέγα κῦδος Ἀχαιῶν, takes its place. Therefore, while the address to Ulysses runs in the Achilleid, ὦ Ὀδυσεῦ πολύαινε, δόλων ἆτ' ἠδὲ πόνοιο, it is singular that there should come up this divergence, whatever it may signify, *everywhere* out of the Achilleid, viz. ὦ πολύαιν' Ὀδυσεῦ, μέγα κῦδος Ἀχαιῶν, occurring in Ι 673, Κ 544, Od. μ 184. Further, the representation given of him in this same context (Λ 401 etc.) cannot be called *specially* noble. He is wounded and disabled, as Diomed in that crisis is also, but he is described, —in an appalling moment no doubt,—as having difficulty in screwing his courage up, and so he lets fall an ὤ μοι ἐγὼ τί πάθω ; which is not rendered with any false *nuance* when it is translated, 'O woe is me, what is to become of me[27] !' This, in the midst of a battle, has a very awkward sound, more so than the same utterance when he is cast ashore naked and famishing on the unknown strand (Od. ε 465), where the words are both natural and honourable, and imply no shade or slur on his courage. There is also this equivocal circumstance that while the unwounded Ulysses is compared honourably enough to a κάπριος or wild boar, and proves a very πῆμα or

---

[27] Other instances of the 'fears of the brave' are, Diomed shuddering at the approach of Hector (Λ 345), also Ajax in P 242, before the same hero. These are tributes to Hector from the Achillean bard. It does not appear that Hector was the immediate object of dread to *Ulysses*. Achilles is once *said* to shudder at meeting Hector, but it is on the lips of Agamemnon and not the judgment of the poet, certainly not the Achillean poet (Η 113).—The ῥῖγος of Diomed in Ε 596 is accounted for by the presence of Ares on the side of Hector.

'Tartar' to the Trojans (l. 413), the wounded Ulysses is likened to an ἔλαφος, or 'stag [28],'—not the most warlike of animals,—surrounded by θῶες, and screams with all his might thrice, so that Menelaus gets Ajax to come to his rescue, and thereafter Ulysses is dismissed without much ceremony. It may be doubted, also, if the Ulyssean poet would have introduced Ajax as the warrior who proved his rescuer and benefactor, but, if our vaticinations are right, this was quite natural in the Achillean poet, as we hope afterwards to show.

In the remaining Achillean books after Λ, Ulysses is not mentioned except in Ξ 29, 380, Π 26, and there, as among the wounded, though still bestirring himself in counsel. It is only in the transactions of Τ at the Reconciliation of the chiefs that he can be said to be prominent ; there is no lamentation or regret in the mouth of Menelaus in Ν or of other hero elsewhere for *his* absence or that of Diomed, and he is entirely unacknowledged in Μ, Ν, Ο, Ρ, Σ, Τ, Φ, Χ, fully one-half of the Achillean cantos, a remarkable contrast to the so-called ten Ulyssean cantos, in all of which except one (Ω) there is important and often frequent prominence given to his name. This exaltation in the one section, comparative depression in the other [29], (shared also by Diomed, who is so often linked with Ulysses), cannot be adequately explained by the quiescence from his wound removing him from the scene. The combined circumstances of the case point to the conclusion that in the Iliad we encounter two different currents of feeling

[28] In this scene the part of the Lion who intervenes to save the wounded Stag from the θῶες is enacted by Ajax. The awkwardness of the stag-simile is felt by Fäsi, who remarks that 'it is to be understood merely of the particular situation of Ulysses, not of his character.' The ἔλαφος is the creature to which Agamemnon is compared by Achilles. 'thou dog in forehead and in heart a deer,' (Α 225), to which the Trojans are likened Ν 102 (φυζακινῆς ἐλάφοισιν), and the ridiculous Dolon is compared, at least, to a species of the tribe (κεμάς Κ 361), at the time, when Ulysses sustains the nobler part of the κύων or λέων (Κ 297 and 360). The associations of the ἔλαφος were therefore not complimentary. There seems something also sinister in the phrase (Λ 462) as to his screaming, ὅσον κεφαλὴ χάδε φωτός, 'as loud as the head of the wight could bawl ;' but this is not an argument to be pressed, as φώς is not *confined* to the sense of 'wight.'

[29] A minor criterion of prominence is found in the ascriptions of the characteristic epithets πολυμήχανος and πολύτλας.

	Ach.	Ul.	Od.
πολυμήχανος	1	6	13
πολύτλας	1	4	29.

with regard to Ulysses, one, in the Ulyssean cantos, warmly appreciative, the other dubiously, if not coldly, indifferent in those of the Achilleid. The light which this throws on the probable affinities, nationally, of the two different sections of the Iliad, is very important, confirmed as it is by the treatment of other personages, especially of Ajax, for there is thus discernible a series of 'Refractions,' severally parallel and coincident, regarding various heroes, a phenomenon which promises to afford valuable evidence on the whole structure of the poems.

CHAPTER XI.

παντοίων ἀνέμων, ὅτ' ἂν ἔνθ' ἢ ἔνθα γένωνται.

----

82. THE treatment of Ulysses in the two different sections of the Iliad has been so marked and peculiar that we are tempted to apply a similar elenchus in the case of other heroes and prominent persons. It will be found that the sympathy and antipathy, if we may so phrase it, bestowed on Ulysses are coincident with similar manifestations as to other heroes in the respective regions of the Iliad.

It is remarkable that along with the admiration for Ulysses there emerges a disposition to make much of the heroes of the South, especially those coming from the Peloponnesus.

The Achilleid, on the other hand, being concerned with the position and fortunes of a Northern hero, who has received insult at the hands of the Southern chief, may be said to regard matters from the Northern point of view, and we can detect the current of its sympathies running, on the whole, in a counter direction. The Iliad turns upon a rupture, between what may be called the Thessalian element represented by Achilles, and the Peloponnesian or Argive element represented by Agamemnon[1]. In the Achilleid, the balance preponderates, from the nature of the story, against the Southern chiefs, and the Ulyssean poet has redressed the balance by interweaving fit activities in which the heroes of the South, and particularly Diomed and Ulysses, take prominent part[2].

[1] Compare, to this effect. Blackie, Iliad. vol. iv. p. 337. and Duncker, Alt. iii. p. 217.

[2] This prominence of the Peloponnesian or Southern heroes, manifest in battle, is

This he has done by ignoring, in so far, or depressing, the Thessalian or Northern element, for in the large section Γ to Η. it is doubtful if apart from Eurypylus, whose position is peculiar[3], a single chief from the land of Thessaly is mentioned, except once, Polypœtes (Z 29). and he as it were incidentally. Out of the nine champions who rise to accept Hector's challenge (Η 167), only one proceeds from Thessaly. The brunt of the battles in B—Η falls therefore on the chiefs from Peloponnesus or from the adjacent islands, and hence the honours appertain to *them* almost exclusively. There is no Thessalian chief named as invited to Agamemnon's banquet in B; none attracts the attention of the poet in the *Teichoskopy* of Γ; not one is mentioned as under review of Agamemnon's eye in Δ. The honours seem to be given by the Ulyssean poet exclusively to non-Thessalian men. He seems likewise to pass the Thessalians entirely over, in the enumerations of heroes in Ι 84, Κ 109, 229, these being cantos under the same influence. Even Agamemnon, as we shall find, is treated more tenderly by the Ulyssean than by the Achillean poet, and there is a distinct and palpable accession of interest in Helen as being a princess of the Peloponnesus, felt throughout the Ulyssean cantos and emerging again in the Odyssey.

All these threads of incident, which are otherwise in inexplicable intertanglement. weave into a web of consistent and harmonious texture by the supposition, warranted on other grounds, that the Achilleid has been shaped by a poet with what may be called Northern or Æolian sympathies,

---

still more manifest in debate. Mr. Gladstone remarks that debate is virtually confined to Agamemnon, Ulysses, Nestor, and Diomed (Homer, ii. 326), for Achilles is, by the nature of the plot, excluded.

[3] Eurypylus, who is mentioned twice in E (76, 79). and once each in Z (36), H (167). seems, though a Thessalian, to be in very friendly relations with the Peloponnesian chiefs. Tradition makes both him and Phœnix grandsons of Ormenus (cp. Ebeling, Lex. Hom. in Εὔρ.), and it would appear that Eurypylus shared with his cousin Phœnix the position of a mutual friend to Thessalians and Argives together.—Another leading link between North and South was Nestor and his house, Thessalian by origin, Peloponnesian by habitation. It is noteworthy that his son Antilochus has a personal attachment to Menelaus as well as to Achilles (cp. E 566 and Schol. on O 568, as also Δ 456, and P 705), and it is through Nestor's diplomacy, that the preparation is made by means of Patroclus for the return of Achilles to join the Argives in the field.

while the Odyssey and the Ulyssean books have been composed by one who is not under Northern sympathies, who has his heart in the South or East of Greece, and who is attracted toward the races that afterwards come up historically as the Ionian and Athenian.

83. When this proposition is established, it will become manifest that we have already present in the Homeric 'corpus' that divergence which makes itself felt in the historic time in the great cleft that marks off the Æolo-Dorian element in Greek life from the Ionic-Attic. That division, as is well recognised, can be traced going deep down into Philosophy, into Poetry, into Politics, and even the Peloponnesian war, which was the bursting out of the animosity between the races, may be said to have been virtually foreshadowed by that early disruption between Northern and Southern Greece revealed to us in the Iliad. The consciousness of this discordance finds distinct expression in the poetry of Pindar, who is for us a most significant and weighty witness upon what may be called the Achillean or Æolo-Dorian side. He expresses a strong sympathy for the Æacidae as against Ulysses, and goes so far as to assert that Ulysses had been put into a position of fame beyond his deserts and to the disparagement of worthier men, all through the genius of him whom *he* calls Homer. The passage is that in 'Nemea,' vii. 21:—

ἐγὼ δὲ πλέον' ἔλπομαι
λόγον 'Οδυσσέος ἢ πάθεν διὰ τὸν ἁδυεπῆ γενέσθ' "Ομηρον,
ἐπεὶ ψεύδεσί οἱ ποτανᾷ τε μηχανᾷ
σεμνὸν ἔπεστι τί.

'For my part I deem Ulysses' fame exceeds his achievements, all because of the sweet-voiced Homer, for in his fictions and aery chariot of song there dwells a majestic spell [4].'

That there is a distinct difference of treatment in the case

[4] 'I think that the legends of Ulysses are drawn out by the mellifluous Homer further than his destinies extended; for a certain dignity dwells in his fictions and winged art, and his genius insensibly deludes the mind with fables.' O. Müller, Introd. to Mythology (E. Tr.).

of Ulysses in the Achilleid as against the non-Achilleid, I
have already endeavoured to show. It will naturally be required that we should show a parallel influence operating in
the case of other heroes. Such a 'refraction' is visible in
the treatment of the following personages: Achilles, Agamemnon, Hector, Helen, Menestheus and the Athenians,
Ajax the Less, Teucer and Ajax the Greater. These are
regarded from one angle of vision in the Ulyssean books,
from another in the Achilleid.

1. ACHILLES.

84. The original portrait of Achilles is that presented us in
the Achilleid, and it is mainly from it that Horace's description is drawn, 'Impiger, iracundus, inexorabilis, acer [5].' He
is there the 'most tremendous of all men,' πάντων ἐκπαγλότατ' ἀνδρῶν—a formula confined to the Achilleid and twice
given to Achilles, only once to another. There is no touch of
ἦθος or feeling for aught beyond himself and his own honour,
and apart from his intense love for his second self Patroclus.
He is therefore like the sun god, to whom he has been compared, inexorably scorching in his fierceness [6]. This tremendous being, who is an object of terror in the Achillean
books, comes to be, in the Ulyssean books, softened and
humanised and made an object of admiring, though not perhaps loving, interest. The touches thus added to the portrait,
while they do not alter the original lines,—for he remains
still the terrible hero—yet subdue their harshness, so that we
can gaze on the picture with no feeling of repulsion [7]. The

[5] Jortin called Achilles a 'brute,' and Apollo in Ω 40–3 would appear to be of
the same opinion. The justification of the description can be found only in the
Achillean books, for such sacrificial acts as the slaughter of the twelve Trojan
youths on the pile, in the Ulyssean Ψ 176, are the fulfilment of the vow ascribed to
him by the Saga, contained in Σ 336, and Φ 28. This act is described in such terms
as suggest, if they do not imply, disapproval on the part of the poet, κακὰ δὲ φρεσὶ
μήδετο ἔργα (Ψ 176), regarding which passage Heyne on Il. Σ 336 remarks,
'Immanitatem (Achillis) ipse poeta incusat, Ψ 175.' Compare, however, similar
words in Φ 19.—In the mouth of Zeus in Ω 157, we find the modified Ulyssean
judgment regarding Achilles.

[6] The nearest approach to humanity in the Achilles of the Achilleid is his claim
to have saved many alive *before* Patroclus's death, Φ 101–3, and his releasing for
ransom two prisoners, not in war, Λ 106.

[7] Preller (Gr. Myth. ii. 284) makes an equation among gods and heroes, that

first softening touch that meets us is the incident in Z 407, where we hear of his having—in the days before 'the Wrath' —shown reverence (σέβας) for the dead, so that he refrained from proceeding to extremities and does not exercise all the rights of the conqueror[8]. This is a preparation-note leading up to the action in the final Book, exhibiting the exercise of similar reverence (σέβας) in the case of his most hated victim, and the generosity of Achilles in giving Eetion interment with full honours is premonitory of his relenting in the case of Hector and releasing at Priam's suit the dead body of his son. This incident in Z 417 is an interesting link of connection with Ω, these being the two books in which the pathos of the Iliad reaches its acme. So in Z 427 we hear of him as accepting ransom for a life which he spares. In the Canto of the Embassy or I, he is found by the envoys in an employment the most refined and ennobling that it is possible to conceive. He is singing ' the lays of heroes,' accompanying them by music on the harp, and thus accomplishments, like the Troubadour's, are superadded to the stern virtues of the warrior[9]. Hardly less beautiful and in full harmony with his Ulyssean image is the aspect in which he appears in Ψ as the President of the Games, courteous as a Knight at Tournament in the times of chivalry, and again in Ω in his reception of the suppliant king Priam—two scenes, as Professor Blackie remarks (Homer, i. p. 214), ' enriching the fierceness of these bloody struggles with the soft halo of love and pity.' These elements are, however, from two different fountains. The fierceness is from the Achillean, the

as Apollo is to Hermes, so is Achilles to Ulysses. If by Apollo we mean the ideal such as in art, the Apollo Belvidere, it is only in the Ulyssean books that we can look for the graceful lines of such an image of Achilles.

[8] Σέβας is recommended to him in the Achilleid (Σ 178), but it is to excite him to save his friend Patroclus from the dogs of Troy, and so implies faithfulness to a friend, not, as in Z, humanity to a foe.

[9] Professor Wilson in his ' Homeric Essays' has remarked upon this scene, ' Had it been put to any spirit the most finely-touched to say how the goddess-born should be found employed, could a nobler simpler picture meet us behind the veil where he has lain retired but not buried?.. The swift-footed implacable is singing ancient lays, with no listener but Patroclus, hero listening to hero.' Compare with this scene Rustum found playing with the falcon, in Mr. Arnold's ' Sohrab and Rustum,' or, in actual history, Sir Philip Sidney, in his exile from Court, where he had been insulted, composing the ' Defence of Poesy.'

love and pity from the Ulyssean, minstrel. The softening touches above enumerated are only in Ulyssean cantos (Z, I, Ψ, Ω)[10], and the same influence is discernible in the treatment of his Shade in the Underworld of the Odyssey. The author of Ω agrees with the author of the Eleventh Odyssey in putting into the lips of Achilles (Ω 525, Od. λ 489) the two deepest utterances of melancholy appearing in ancient Thought.

2. AGAMEMNON.

85. The captain of the host at Troy presents under any view a character, somewhat discordant in its elements, and far more difficult to seize than that of his antagonist Achilles. In the quarrel-scene of A he shows a resolute fierceness worthy of being pitted against that of Achilles, and again, in the opening scenes of book Λ, he is the stately and brilliant king who thinks to sweep everything before him in battle. The touches of honour on that occasion and even the exploits with which he is credited in what is called his ἀριστεία, seem intended to make his fall the more severe. The latent feeling in the Achilleid towards the man who has wronged Achilles is nowise kindly, and the expression of the disguised Poseidon respecting him may be taken as normal in this regard, ἡγεμόνος κακότητι (N 108), marking him out as the cause of mischief to the Greeks. The fierce Agamemnon of A, the over-confident Agamemnon of Λ, pass into the craven Agamemnon of Ξ 65–107, who gives up all for lost, and is represented as seriously wishing to take to his ships and flee. He is only restrained from so doing by the remonstrances of two wounded men. No doubt he is himself wounded and weak, but the kind of *animus* towards him in the Achilleid is thus fairly discernible.

How does he stand in the Ulyssean books? As a Peloponnesian hero he shares in the favour which this poet metes out to the Argives. He is brave enough to be named first among the acceptors of Hector's challenge (H 162) and is popular enough to be willingly named by the host as their

---

[10] Otfried Müller (Gr. Lit. ch. 5. 5) says, 'the character of Achilles needs to be purified and sublimed.' It is in the Achilleid that the need is felt, in the Ulyssean cantos that the want is supplied.

champion (Ι 180); he is an active, if not always wise-speaking, field-marshal in Δ, and he slays his 'man' in each of the two books E and Z, besides, in Z, killing one whom Menelaus wished to spare. This last act looks like a piece of cruelty, but, strange to say, the poet approves (Z 62)[11]. In the field of battle, therefore, he is brave and vigorous, and he is, as it were, complimented by the poet of these Ulyssean cantos on his kingliness (Β 478) and his possession of troops who are styled not only 'most numerous' but also 'the bravest,' which sounds somewhat strange while Achilles is still in camp (Β 577). He is, however, not steady and resolute, nor noble and generous, for he *enjoys* the quarrels between the higher chiefs (cp. Od. θ 77), and, being rash and injudicious, tries experiments (in B) upon the temper of the army, in pretending to wish for an immediate return home. What he only pretends in B, he seriously proposes when the disasters have really come, and accordingly we find him quite broken down in spirit at the opening of I. Yet the Ulyssean poet, though he once censures him as a νήπιος in Β 38, has contrived to represent him as on the whole amiable and good, especially brotherly to Menelaus, for whom Agamemnon's kindly feeling comes up in three Ulyssean cantos, Δ, Η, K (240), in a very marked manner and degree. Likewise, in what must be regarded as the poet's own voice speaking through Helen, he is pronounced to be a 'good king and a valiant warrior[12].' The probability is that the pathos of his after fate, of which it is to be noted the Odyssey is full[13], has contributed to soften the representation of him in the Ulyssean books of the Iliad.

3. HECTOR.

86. The divergence as to the representations of this hero is peculiarly marked, and it is only under the theory of two strata in the Iliad that the phenomena can be adequately explained.

---

[11] The significance of this will afterwards appear.

[12] It seems to indicate a sort of kindly interest in Agamemnon that an adjective has been coined from his name, occurring in K 326, Ψ 295 and 525. and Od. γ 264, none of them Achillean.—Ἐκτόρεος is also only Ulyssean (four times).

[13] Compare α 29, 298, γ 248, δ 512, and λ 385—five rehearsals under varied forms. The citations here are those of Preller (Gr. M. ii. 315.)

This hero is in certain cantos drawn as modest, generous, courteous, prone to melancholy. In certain others he is over-bearing, harsh and blustering. In the former he appears as the valiant ill-starred champion of an undeserving cause, and excites our strongest sympathy; in the latter while he is fiercely patriotic, he is domineering and harsh, awaking our aversion. He is now boastful even to arrogance, and again, as conscious that he is fighting under a cloud of doom, tender and melancholy. This duality in the character of Hector—arrogant in book N 823 seq., pensive and of drooping soul in Z—is at once explained when we discover that the tender and faint-hearted Hector belongs to the Ulyssean, the boastful and loud-tongued Hector to the Achillean, portion of the Iliad [14].

In proof of this position it may be noted from the Achil-leid, (1) that the similes regarding him are indicative of fierceness and pride (Θ 355, Λ 297, Ο 268, 605); (2) that the extraordinary vaunt, aspiring to be in honour like Apollo or Athene, occurs twice, and, as Preller (Gr. M. i. 76) has ob-served, only in Hector's mouth (Θ 540, N 827, both Achillean) [15].

---

[14] This double aspect of Hector struck the ancient critics. Hence the Scholiast on Il. Θ 527 refers to what he calls τὸ παλίμβολον Ἕκτορος. and finds a *contradiction* between that passage and the ἔσσεται ἦμαρ utterance in Z spoken to Andromache. —Twice the annotation by the scholiasts is found regarding him as speaking τυραννικῶς, and both passages are Achillean (Θ 523 and Σ 293).

[15] It is from the Hector of the Achilleid that the impression of him still surviving in our 'hectoring fellow' has been derived. The following epithets applied to him point in the same direction :—

	Ach.	Ul.	Ach.	Ul.
λυσσώδης (et simile)	2	1	Θ 299, N 53	I 305
μέγα φρονέων	1	0	Λ 296	
θρασύς	4	3	Θ 89, M 60, 210, N 725	X 455, Ω 72, 786
σθένεϊ βλεμεαίνων	1	1	Θ 337	I 237

The occurrences in I 237 and 305 are echoes from the Achillean representation, and are rhetorical arguments to move Achilles. The expressions σθένεϊ βλε-μεαίνων or βλεμεαίνει, and μέγα φρονέων, whether of Hector or others, are peculiarly Achillean.

	Ach.	Ul.	Od.
σθένεϊ βλεμεαίνων, or -ει	5	1	0
{ μέγα φρονέων, or -οντες or -οντε	8	0	0
{ ὅσσον φρονέουσιν (P 23)	1	0	0
	14	1	0

As a corollary to this, it is proper to add that the reading ἔλπεται in Ξ 366 has

He actually produces the impression of being, like them, 'a child of Zeus' (N 54)   Accordingly, he is frequently insolent and even truculent to his adviser Polydamas (M 245, and Σ 293–6), on the former of which passages Doederlein remarks, 'Atrocior haec est minitatio (Hectoris),' and Heyne, 'Invidiose dicta et amare.'   What is remarkable is that this harshness should come immediately after his famous utterance, εἷς οἰωνὸς ἄριστος κ.τ.λ., which has become a household word, 'The one best omen is our country's cause.'   It is far from clear, however, that the poet intends it as a sentiment entirely praise-worthy, however it may appear so to the modern mind. On the contrary, it appears to partake of the recklessness of Œdipus jeering at the κλάζοντας ὄρνις (Œd. Rex, 966), and accord-ingly the Scholiast on the passage (M 237) thinks it indicates in Hector a lack of piety, and he goes on, in a remarkable note, to contrast the Hector so speaking with *Ulysses* who no-where utters any such sentiment (cp. also Δ 398, Z 183). The most suspicious point is that the same sentiment towards omens appears in the Odyssey, but it is there in the mouth of one of the impious suitors (β 181), and the inference is that it has really an equally sinister tone in the mouth of Hector in Iliad M. The Ulyssean Hector, on the contrary, is not only modest as to himself (Z 479) but speaks in a religious tone (Z 269). One of the unfavourable impressions we obtain of him from the Achilleid, is that he seems to be, if not a toper, a companion of such (P 577, cp. Schol. ad loc.), but in Z 264 he produces the very opposite impression. Further, the denunciations of the Achillean Hector to others besides Polydamas are not only harsh but brutal in tone (N 831, O 349). On the other hand the Ulyssean injunction in the mouth of Nestor, parallel to O 349, 'not to mind the stripping of the arms,' is firm but comparatively mild in tone (Z 68–70).

The Achillean Hector denounces the coming of the Greeks as being against the will of the gods (O 720), a feeling very different from that perceptible in the pensive warrior of the Ulyssean area. The author of the Achilleid has also given him qualities in great measure such as make him a fit victim for the prowess of Achilles, and, with this view, he speaks of

now been replaced by εὔχεται (boasts), on the ground that the latter is suitable to Hector (καυχημάτίας γὰρ ὁ Ἕκτωρ. Schol. ad loc.).

him as an antagonist even to Poseidon (Ξ 390) and as δέμας καὶ εἶδος ἀγητόν (Χ 370). magnifying Hector in order to magnify the conqueror of Hector. to whom Hector, before his death. is made to concede the pre-eminence (Υ 434)[16].

In sharp contrast with the uniform strain of the Achilleid will be found the prevailing notes in the counter strain of the Ulyssean books regarding this hero. The tenderness which he there shows to Andromache is akin to the brotherliness which he shows even to Paris, whose conduct before and during the war he does not commend (Ζ 521). and to Helenus, complying with his directions in Ζ 102, and similarly in Η 54, two instances in which his conduct contrasts strongly with the behaviour of the Achillean Hector to *his* monitor Polydamas. He is not excepted, it is true, from the censure passed on Priam's sons of being ἄπιστοι and ὑπερφίαλοι, but on the other hand he is not put forward as the exulting victor in the event of Grecian defeat, which is a part assigned to Τρώων τις in Δ 176, and is not specialised to Hector. as we may be sure would have been the case in the Achilleid. The only instance in which the Ulyssean Hector approaches the boastful style of the Achillean is in the challenge given in Η 67–91. but it is no more than Ulysses, upon occasion, is represented as claiming for himself when he says καί μευ κλέος οὐρανὸν ἵκει (Od. ι 20). The circumstances are very peculiar, for we find that the soothsayer Helenus has immediately before promised Hector safety, if not victory, in the coming single combat, and this as 'the voice of the everliving gods,' and Hector is naturally enough stimulated, by such a prophetic encouragement, to give the challenge with a brave heart. *Before* this prophetic announcement, however, he is downhearted and melancholy, as we see in Γ, when he is full of moral indignation at Paris's poltroonery (41–57), and in Ε he seems strangely paralysed. possibly by forebodings of evil resulting from the treachery of Pandarus, until he is roused to action by the reproaches of Sarpedon (471, 493), while in the following book Ζ his

---

[16] The epithet ἀνδροφόνος, which is given to Hector only among warriors at Troy, is peculiarly localised. It is bestowed *seven* times in Achilleid, and on him only, except in the formula ἀνδροφόνους χείρας, of Achilles in Σ 317. It is given to Hector (no doubt as a traditive epithet from the Achilleid). *thrice* in Ulyssean Books, where he has to share it with Ares and Lycurgus. In the Odyssey it does not occur except as an epithet of φάρμακον.

pensive melancholy reappears in the most winning and gracious form [17]. In Ω (772) we hear of his 'gentlemindedness' (ἀγανοφροσύνη), and, except Ulysses, he is the only hero to whom that quality is ascribed in either poem.

4. HELEN.

87. In the Achilleid it is remarkable how seldom this heroine is referred to, and then somewhat disparagingly. Apart from the formal title, ἠΰκομος [18], there is an entire absence of the *special* complimentary epithets of state and dignity which she enjoys abundantly in the non-Achilleid and in the Odyssey, but, what is more significant, there is the occurrence of the only decidedly repulsive epithet which is ever applied to her. Once she is called ῥιγεδανή, i.e. '*gruesome,* horrible, odious,' as if her name could only be mentioned with a shudder. It is found in Τ 326, in the mouth of Achilles, *after* the Reconciliation, and though not coming directly from the Achillean bard himself, must be regarded as indicative of his feeling toward her. Elsewhere we may discern an indifference, at least on the part of the great Thessalian chief, to the recovery of Helen. A northern chief was naturally less interested in the honour and restoration of the southern princess, and less concerned in the quarrel with the Trojans, and there is very early expression given to this comparative indifference, in Α 150–160 (cp. afterwards, § 106, 6). On the other hand, when we pass to the Odyssey and Ulyssean cantos, there comes quite an efflorescence of epithets in her honour, and we seem to pass into an entirely new zone of sentiment regarding her. She is portrayed in the most affecting situations, and under the most agreeable and moving incidents, and the only disparaging epithets she

[17] Compare Schubarth's panegyric on Hector, quoted in Nitzsch (Sagen-poesie, p. 207), and the remark of Dr. Arnold in Hist. of Rome, iii. p. 64.

[18] The description of Paris as 'husband of fair-haired Helen' ('Ελένης πόσις ἠϋκόμοιο) seems a stereotyped formula. It contains the only epithet of praise to Helen, *common* to *both* sections of the Iliad, occurring four times in the Achilleid, and thrice in the non-Achilleid. The word ἠΰκομος has, however, very lofty associations. It is given to Athene, Leto, Thetis, Heré, and in the Odyssey to Calypso, among goddesses; among mortals only to Niobe and Briseis. That ἠϋκόμοιο was a stereotyped phrase applied to Helen appears from its occurrence in Hesiod (Op. et Di. 164).

receives are those employed by herself[19]. What bestows on her especial lustre is the circumstance that she bears in this area the epithet of the 'Lady of Argos,' or the 'Argive,' and this epithet she shares with Heré, the celestial consort of Zeus, and with Heré alone[20]. There are *fourteen* occurrences of this word Ἀργείη, and these only in the Odyssey and Ulyssean cantos. Twice it is given to Heré, the remaining twelve are bestowed on Helen. A fact of this kind is sufficient to show that we are not taking up arbitrary ground, but have pierced through to the core of scientific fact, and that we were justified in predicating, as we did, a special interest in Argos, i.e. the Peloponnesus, in the case of the Ulyssean bard.

The following table exhibits the special epithets of Helen, with their various occurrences :—

	Ach.	Ul.	Od.
Ἀργείη	o	9	3
Διὸς ἐκγεγαυῖα	o	2	2
δῖα γυναικῶν	o	3	2
εὐπατέρεια	o	1	1
καλλίκομος	o	o	1
κούρη Διός	o	1	o
καλλιπάρῃος	o	o	1
λευκώλενος	o	1	1
τανύπεπλος	o	1	2
	o	18	13

Thirty-one occurrences of decorative epithets (without reckoning the var. lect. πολυήρατος in Od. υ 126) can thus be cited, and of these the Achilleid contributes none. Moreover there is not only a singular divergence in the case of the Achilleid, but a remarkable balance of practical equality, and therefore conformity of sentiment, between the Odyssey and the Ulyssean cantos. There is, in truth, a real equality of distribution, for the apparent minority of instances in the

[19] Mr. Grote (H. i. 415) remarks on Homer's chivalry towards Helen, in never allowing reproaches against her except from her own lips; very different from the treatment she receives from Stesichorus and Euripides. The remark is quite justified, provided we eliminate the Achillean evidence as shown in T 326.

[20] In one passage Heré is represented as herself applying her own epithet Ἀργείη to Helen (B 161).

Odyssey is quite in keeping with the circumstances of the poem, in which she performs a much less prominent part, compared with what the Ulyssean cantos, from the nature of their subject, have assigned to her. There is a further inference which we may draw incidentally from the above, bearing on one of the weapons of the Chorizontes. They alleged that the Iliad and Odyssey diverged in regard to Helen's abduction; the Iliad, according to them, implying that she was an unwilling victim, the Odyssey representing her as consenting to the abduction. The passages on which they founded were B 356, repeated again in B 590, where mention is made of Ἑλένης ὁρμήματά τε στοναχάς τε, which they held to mean, not unnaturally, 'the violences to Helen and her groans.' Hence they argued, she is a victim in the Iliad, for she goes to Troy δυσανασχετοῦσα καὶ στένουσα (Schol. on B 356), and ἁρπάξας is the word used of Paris in Γ 444. In the Odyssey we find her using language that implies she went with her will, though misled by Aphrodite (Od. δ 261–3), and the groans to which she confesses were those of repentance, not of reluctant innocence. There is, however, no real inconsistency. In both poems Helen is treated as not entirely innocent, though the guilt lies mainly with Paris, who is made to bear the name of Δύσπαρις, whereas we do not hear of Δυσελένη in Homer at all, and nowhere till it appears in Euripides. She has come under the spell of a fatal attraction to which she has succumbed, but even according to the Iliad, she is, by her own confession (Γ 173), not guiltless. Moreover, we hear of an attendant who appears to have accompanied her from Sparta (Γ 387), so that she was not suddenly snapt away but went deliberately after preparation, for the κτήματα accompanying her must have been taken with her connivance (cp. Heyne on Il. Γ 173). As regards the two passages in B on which the Chorizontes build, they are insufficient to justify *their* conclusion, since they express not the poet's own judgment regarding her, but only the *subjective* expression of Greek feeling, evidently as to what the Greeks wished to believe regarding the abducted one. The one passage occurs in a *speech* of Nestor, the other is made subjective to, and interpretative of, the feelings of Menelaus, who would believe the best about his queen[21]. The evidence therefore from the epithets belonging to Helen suffices to disprove entirely the inference drawn on very insufficient grounds by the Chorizontes.

5. MENESTHEUS AND THE ATHENIANS.

88. The marked duality concerning these is a feature that will come up more appropriately in a later section. when we review the local mint-marks of the Homeric poems.

6. AJAX THE LESS[22].

89. This hero is also the subject of divided fortune. Prominent in the Achilleid, and often abreast of his name-sake in importance, he becomes, in the Ulyssean books and in the Odyssey, not obscured only but degraded, and one might almost come to the conclusion that the Ulyssean poet has a personal antipathy to him. Not so the author of the Achilleid. With him the Oilean Ajax is in the front rank of warriors, is not only rapid of foot but quick of mind (N 66), recognising Poseidon even under his disguise, is sharp of hearing (P 256), and seems on one occasion to surpass the other Ajax in his feats of arms (Ξ 520). He stands abreast of the Telamonian Ajax in the rescue of the dead body of Patroclus (cp. esp. P 256 and 732), and has the honour of being coupled with him in the simile of the pair of oxen of equal spirit (ἶσον θυμὸν ἔχοντε) pulling the plough (N 703). He is one of the nine ἡγεμόνες to whom a feat of arms is ascribed (Π 330), a list in which the minstrel does not include or think it necessary to include the greater Ajax[23]. There is therefore only one impression regarding him in the Achilleid, that he is a warrior of the first rank and most honourable.

[21] I have not entered into the question as to the other and less natural interpretation of B 356, 'struggles and groans (of the Greeks' on account of Helen.' The chorizontic weapon is defeated without resorting to such an interpretation.

[22] The remaining heroes, 6, 7, 8, form a remarkable Triad. 'The two Ajaxes and Teucer formed. in the Sagas of the Hellenic races and their war songs, an undoubtedly closely connected group.' Preller. Gr M. (ii 283).—The conclusions in the text will stand. even if Αἴαντε is taken as a Vedic dual for 'Ajax and his brother Teucer.' without Ajax the Less (Wackernagel in Kuhn, xxiii. p. 303).

[23] Diomed, *besides* the great ἀριστεία of E. has a 'vignette,' over and above, in *his* honour (Z 12).

In the Ulyssean books, except where he happens to be coupled with the greater Ajax, and is so far shielded by the homage given to him, he seems to occupy a very different position, and in fact to be under a cloud. Though included in the list of chiefs by Nestor in K 110, he has no personal prominence when *by himself*. He is not among the ἡγεμόνες to whom the 'vignette' of a feat of arms is assigned in the three series of Δ, E, and Z. In the foot-race of Ψ (754–84), he enters the lists against Ulysses, but is disgraced and made a public laughing stock, under circumstances peculiarly obnoxious. In the chariot race, he is made to act the part of *advocatus diaboli* against Diomed, and speaks in rude abuse of Diomed who gains the prize. It is significant that it is for the claim of the northern chief, the Thessalian Eumelus, as against the southern, the Argive Diomed, that the lesser Ajax lifts his voice, and, since he denounces Diomed [24], who is manifestly a favourite of the Ulyssean poet, it would appear that the lesser Ajax was not regarded with favour. If we turn to the Odyssey, we find him a sort of *bête noire* to the poet still. He is spoken of in a mysterious way as incurring the wrath of Athene, as endangering by that wrath the whole host of the Greeks, and as finally drowned, so that his fate is tragic, described in a line which has been thought to express malediction or sarcasm regarding him,

Ὣς ὁ μὲν ἔνθ' ἀπόλωλεν, ἐπεὶ πίεν ἁλμυρὸν ὕδωρ (Od. δ 511.)

Which has been translated by Hayman in this tone, ' So there was an end of him after a mouthful of salt water.' We found him in his collapse in the foot-race in Ψ of the Iliad getting a mouthful of something else unpleasant (§ 66), but, without importing any such *nuance* or remembrance into the passage in the Odyssey, there is little doubt that he is there dismissed without regret by the poet.

The pulse of two different personalities or the play of two diverse influences may thus be felt in the treatment of the lesser Ajax within the compass of the Iliad.

[24] Heyne has an odd remark on this (Ψ 472), 'Putes te inter homines nostros litteratos versari, truculenter statim a conviciis et contumeliis exordium facit (Ajax).' He afterwards adds that he is puzzled why Ajax should be such a partisan for Eumelus. 'Cur Eumelo tantopere ille studeat, non apparet causa.' The cause is now considerably more apparent than it was in Heyne's time.

90. Again, as with Ajax the less, we find this hero receiving his honours almost entirely in the Achilleid. The companionship of Teucer with the Telamonian Ajax is there emphasised, and he comes forward even prominently, if we consider his comparative obscurity in the Ulyssean cantos. In the great rally of the Greeks in Θ (260–6)[25], Teucer occupies a high position of honour, and indeed throughout the Achilleid, even in O 463, where Zeus protects Hector from his shafts. In its fourteen cantos, the name of Teucer comes up twenty-five times. In the ten Ulyssean ones, it occurs but four times, once incidentally in Z 31, and the other three instances are one occurrence in a single book, Ψ, in connection with the archery prize. Further, in this contest, unlike the position he holds in the Achilleid, he is beaten by the Southern archer, Meriones. The bad luck of his half-brother Ajax seems to attend him in the Ulyssean books, for, just as Ajax loses the prize of Achilles' arms against Ulysses, so Teucer, though pronounced in the Achilleid (N 313) 'best of the Greeks in archery,' and though said to have received his weapon from Apollo (O 441), has, in the Ulyssean canto, to yield the prize in archery to another, a friend of Ulysses. That other is Meriones, the same who places Ulysses under marked obligation by the lending of his bow, on the occasion of the night expedition in K 260, also a Ulyssean canto.

Thus we can trace the same change of attitude toward Teucer which we have found similarly manifested in regard to other heroes. The archer-in-chief of the Achilleid is thrown into the shade in the Ulyssean cantos, and that by one who stands in close and friendly relation with Ulysses.

8. Ajax Telamonius.

91. We now come to consider the position of the greater Ajax in the two sections of the Iliad, and propose to inquire whether any divergence similar to that which we have found

---

[25] The list of warriors is almost the same as in H 162, but instead of Thoas we have Menelaus, and what is more significant, instead of Ulysses, Teucer. Cp. Heyne's note on Θ 266.

in the case of other personages is traceable in the representations of Ajax. As the well-known rival of Ulysses in the contest for Achilles' arms, he may be regarded as likely to be unsympathetic with and antagonistic to that hero, and we might be prepared *a priori* for a certain shade of obscuration falling upon the image of Ajax in a poem or poems where there is special exaltation of his rival Ulysses. It does not follow, however, that homage to Ulysses must produce any direct disparagement of his rival, and we find, from whatever cause, the Telamonian Ajax treated on the whole with great respect, much greater than his namesake receives, in both sections of the Iliad. Two causes may be assigned as operating in this direction: (1) The pathos of his fate, reacting upon the representations of his actions, may have, as in the case of Agamemnon, softened the attitude of the Ulyssean poet (Od. λ 469), as it seems to have softened the attitude of Ulysses himself (Od. λ 550–1). (2) The mythical connection of the hero with Salamis rendered him an object of interest to the Ionic-Attic race, who were anxious to claim him as a hero representing them at Troy, and, therefore, in the Ulyssean poem, which was largely influenced, as we shall afterwards find, by Ionic-Attic feeling, one who was adopted as an Ionic-Attic hero was likely to be treated with a certain measure of admiration. Notwithstanding these modifying influences, the same tendencies to differentiation, which we have noted regarding other heroes, may be discerned at work in relation to Ajax.

In the first place, it may be remarked that, in the Achilleid, the position of prominent, if not favourite, hero after Achilles himself, is assigned to the greater Ajax. In the Ulyssean cantos, on the other hand, it is Ulysses that occupies the most conspicuous position and is, so to speak, the cynosure of the poet's eye. These rival heroes, embodying opposite dispositions, foreshadowing different types of national character — types as different as the stolid forceful Spartan from the nimble elastic Athenian, may be said in a certain sense to be weighed in the balance against each other and to sustain a rise or a fall, according as we pass from the Achillean to the Ulyssean area, and conversely, from the Achillean to the Ulyssean.

92. The greatness of the *rôle* assigned to Ajax in the Achilleid before Achilles reappears, is seen especially in the circumstance that he is, on the Greek side, the *one* unwounded hero in the Great Battle, and forms the centre of resistance, the one fixed point on which the whole movement of the battle turns [26]. He is, no doubt, often hard pressed, as he himself confesses in P 242, and his energy is shown rather in dead resistance and tough persistence than in actual onslaught. Hence the simile comparing him to the stubborn ass, which is utterly impervious to the thumps of boys (Λ 557); but in this comparison there is no disparagement, since he is likened in the same connection to a lion standing at bay (Λ 548). So Idomeneus ventures to match him with Achilles himself in the close tug of fight (Ν 324), though not equal to him in nimbleness of foot. The plot of the Achilleid, which gave the initiative of the Greek aggression first to Patroclus and then to Achilles, prevented the ascription of any *decisive* victory to Ajax ; yet the rescue of the dead body of Patroclus, which is one of his feats in concert with the other Ajax, sufficiently vindicates his high position. He appears also to be a favourite of the Achillean poet by the manner in which he is made to blurt out the prayer for light in order to fight, . 'even though it were but to be killed,' ἐν δὲ φάει καὶ ὄλεσσον, an utterance bearing a family resemblance to that which is put into the mouth of Achilles himself, when he prays 'to be delivered from the water, and then let him suffer whatever may befall' (Φ 274).

There is a remarkable expression regarding Ajax, which, if it is accepted as genuine, proves the point conclusively as to the attitude towards him of the Achillean poet. It is the

---

[26] The Scholiasts detected, in a vague somnolent way, the pulse of a special feeling for Ajax, as may be seen in their remarks on P 234 and especially on Λ 598, where the 'economy' of a large portion of the Iliad is said to be largely directed 'to the praise of Ajax' (εἰς ἔπαινον Αἴαντος). He is not only the most prominent of the Greek warriors before the sallying out of Patroclus, but the poet, says the Scholiast, *returns* to him after the fall of that hero —Among the *netanda* as to his position in Achilleid is the application to him twice, there and there only, of the epithet βοὴν ἀγαθός (O 249 and P 102). The distribution of this epithet is somewhat peculiar. It is the usual prefix of Menelaus and of Diomed, twenty-five times of the former, twenty-one of the latter, in both sections of the poems. It is given once *to a Trojan* in each section, to Hector in N 123, to Polites in Ω 250.—As for βοὴγαιε (N 824), that is an invective of the arrogant Achillean Hector.

line, which, though under the shade of brackets, is admitted into the text in Λ 543 by Fäsi and La Roche, and it runs, Ζεὺς γάρ οἱ νεμεσᾶθ' ὅτ' ἀμείνονι φωτὶ μάχοιτο, referring to Hector's avoidance of a fight with Ajax, and implying that 'Zeus was indignant at his fighting with one who was a better man.' Here the Achillean poet seems to throw off his impersonality or impartiality and allows his feeling to flash forth unmistakably in favour of Ajax. It is, however, a line not to be fully relied on, as it is absent from the MSS. and depends only on citations, probably Homeric, by Aristotle (Rhet. ii. 9.) and Plutarch (de Aud. Poetis, 6. 14). Assuming the line to belong to the Homeric 'corpus,' we find that this Achillean passage is the only place that will give it proper location, and, if so, it is evidence of the lofty position assigned to Ajax in the Achilleid.

It is not necessary, however, to press into the service a challengeable line. There is one equally suitable as evidence of that partiality, viz. P 236, where the Achillean poet allows his sympathy to flow out towards him, so that he styles the Trojans 'fools' (νήπιοι) for hoping to drag the corpse of Patroclus away from Ajax. In the Achillean books there is thus ample evidence that Ajax is the first figure after Achilles in their author's eye, coming first in such enumerations of heroes as Λ 138 and 145, appearing as the lion among the lesser animals (Λ 480, one of the lesser animals standing for Ulysses), and generally sustaining as chief champion the Greek cause in Achilles' absence.

93. If we turn to the Ulyssean cantos, it cannot be said that this great position is maintained. The traditional fame no doubt secures for him a high rank, and he receives even an accession of new titles from the renown acquired in the Achillean area. He is called in I 622 and K 112 ἀντίθεος, an epithet given to him nowhere else, and, what is more remarkable, he is called the ἕρκος 'Αχαιῶν, 'bulwark of the Greeks,' a title which he earns, no doubt, in the Achillean books, but which is not there bestowed on him, but upon Achilles alone (Λ 284). As applied to Ajax, it is found only in Ulyssean cantos (Γ 229. Ζ 5, and Η 211), at a time when, according to the chronology of the action, he has not yet achieved the name. It is an anticipation of the same kind as if

we spoke of the 'victor of Waterloo' as conquering at Assye.
There is also one scene, in which he bears the principal part,
a scene bestowing on him new and positive, not traditional,
honour, viz. in H, the duel with Hector, where he is one of the
favourites of the Greeks and is honoured with special distinction at the close. It is, however, a sort of drawn battle, for it
would have been an error in poetic propriety to have represented another as gaining a clear victory over Hector before
Achilles tried conclusions with him. Notwithstanding the
somewhat doubtful or even sinister simile (sinister when outside the Achilleid)[27], comparing him to Ares (H 208), the
general effect of the duel-scene is decidedly to Ajax's honour.
The relative inferiority of his position in the Ulyssean area
is seen more or less clearly in (1) the parsimony of the single
line describing him in the Catalogue, without reference to
parentage or any detail of glorious circumstance. For this
there is no doubt subsequent compensation in the compliment
in B 768, but the Epilogue where this occurs is very doubtful
and no great stress is to be put upon it. More weight must
be laid upon (2) the comparative poverty of his eulogy in the
Teichoskopy, in contrast with the voluminous outburst regarding his rival, Ulysses. Also (3), the ascription of fear to him
in E 623–6, 'lest he should be surrounded,' in terms that place
him on the same level as Thoas in Δ 535 (cp. P 242); (4) the
application in H 212 of a somewhat sinister term to describe
his looks, βλοσυρός, which occurs only twice elsewhere, neither
of the instances being complimentary, viz. once of Hector
(O 608), and once of the Gorgon (Λ 36), and (5) more especially, the severity and even cruelty with which he is treated
in the whole course of the Games in the Ulyssean book Ψ.
It is singular to find the man who has been the champion in
the great field, now, in the small field, really defeated. He
enters the lists oftener than any single competitor, contending
in three out of the seven contests, and comes off victorious

<hr>

[27] **The reason** for this judgment is that Ares in the Ulyssean area (whatever we
may judge as to Patroclus being Ἶσος Ἄρηι in Λ 603), and also in the Odyssey (as
in the lay of Demodocus), is generally, in some way, discredited. Od. θ 518 seems
an exception. The epithet αἴδηλος is applied to Ares only among the gods (E 880,
897, and Od. θ 309), and among men only to the Suitors, in Od. π 29 and ψ 303,
and to the vile Melanthius (χ 165), all therefore bad associations.

in none of them.   The nature of the personal relations between Ajax and Ulysses, though there is nowhere any rupture, does not appear to be cordial.   Ajax is of course, owing to his inferiority in speaking and debate, second to Ulysses in the conduct of the Embassy, but in one instance, if we may judge from the incident, νεῦσ' Αἴας Φοίνικι (I 223), he seems to regard Phœnix as the chief speaker and head of the embassy rather than Ulysses.

94. These are the chief evidences of our present proposition, viz. that the Achilleid shows high favour, the Ulyssean books a diminution of favour, for the Telamonian Ajax[28]. Now it would be an easy explanation to put forth that the Achilleid naturally shows favour to Achilles' cousin, one who is often styled, like himself, an *Æacid*.   This may possibly be the true explanation, but we cannot accept it without some hesitation, owing to the almost profound silence of the Homeric poems, whether Ulyssean or Achillean, as to any relationship between Ajax and Achilles.   It may sound strange, even to good Homeric scholars, to be told that there is no distinct or absolute warrant in the Iliad or Odyssey to affirm such a relationship.   Yet all the direct notices of their kinship are outside of and posterior to the Homeric poems, and the name *Æacides* is not once given to Ajax in either Epic[29].

On the other hand, there is nothing in the Iliad or Odyssey that can be held to contradict or negative the relationship, and there are some features in the 'economy' of both poems that favour the supposition.   In the first place there is a grand suggestiveness of equality if not of kinship, (1) in the manner in which the Achillean poet matches them as guardians of the two horns of the camp, the one at the Sigeian, the other at the Rhœteian promontory, secondly (2), it is notable that Ajax

---

[28] In a rough enumeration I find mention of both the Ajaxes in the Achilleid to have a considerable preponderance.

	Ach.	Ul.
Αἴας (uterque)	125	65.

The sole instance in which the Telamonian Ajax seems to be other than the first figure in the Achilleid is where Hector in Θ 532 singles out Diomed as the champion of the Greeks.   In T 310 Ajax is not included, probably as being no master of persuasive speech.

	Ach.	Ul.	Od.
[29] The occurrences of Αἰακίδης are, of Peleus	3	1	0
„ „ of Achilles	11	5	2.

takes a sort of *personal* responsibility in a certain crisis as to how Achilles should be communicated with (P 651), which consideration (3) Achilles seems to reciprocate in singling out Ajax as the only warrior whose shield it would suit him to put on (Σ 193). These are from the Achillean area. From the Ulyssean area it is to be noted, further (4), that Ajax, in the Embassy-scene, claims for the envoys that they are κή-διστοι καὶ φίλτατοι to Achilles among all the Greeks (I 642), the former term usually suggesting *kinship*, about which, if the reading had been κήδιστος applicable to Ajax alone, there could have been little doubt[30]. The plurality may be owing to the inclusion in his mind of the closely intimate Phœnix. Moreover, it is to be noted (5), that, in the procession of the Ghosts in the Odyssey, while others, such as Agamemnon, march either singly, or with no followers named, the Ghost of Ajax forms one of the same group with Achilles. It is true that the Ghosts of Antilochus[31] and Patroclus appear in the same society; that, however, is easily explicable from the traditional nearness of their companionship; but, in the case of Ajax, there seems no similar reason of living companionship to account for *his* association with Achilles, unless there was latent in the poet's mind the notion of some relationship by which they were linked together. Further (6), the same companionship is given in the thoughts of Nestor when he is naming over the illustrious heroes, and Ajax and Achilles are combined (γ 109). Again, there seems (7) a family likeness in the μῆνις or wrath characterising each after insult and wrong. The μῆνις of Ajax is in fact more implacable than that of Achilles, is prolonged into the underworld, and seems to make Hades darker by its frown.

The strongest of the presumptions that can be referred to on this head is one (8) derived from the discoveries of Modern Philology. It seems clear that, although we cannot quote an

---

[30] Heyne translates these two words, 'genere et animo conjunctissimi,' adding that the first epithet refers to Ajax himself as Achilles' cousin. 'Prius saltem ad Ajacem, Achillis patruelem, spectat.'

[31] Antilochus comes into Patroclus' room as bosom friend of Achilles and according to the 'Æthiopis' a similar chain of events followed. As Hector slew Patroclus and was slain by Achilles, so Memnon slew Antilochus, and fell on that account by the hand of Achilles.

instance of *Αἴας* being called in Homer *Αἰακίδης* [32], there is yet, as we may infer from the archaic Latin form *Ajax*, *Ajacis*, a philological kinship between *Αἴας* and *Αἰακός*. The Greek system of name-giving often produces community between the names of a grandson and a grandfather, and it is well known how there is often a seesaw of names repeating each other in Greek genealogies in the case of persons standing in that relationship. In this instance the grandson's name is the progenitor of the grandfather's, for *Αἰακός* is the shadow of the name *Αἴας* reflected backward. Hence according to Curtius (Gr. Et. ii. p. 221), the equation is valid :—

$$Αἰακός : Αἴας : : Λάβδακος : Λάιος.$$

The above is all the evidence adducible from the Homeric poems as to their relationship. It cannot be said to amount to more than a strong presumption. In any case it is not essential to my hypothesis as a whole, and I do not assume it as assured. The fact remains, in whatever way it may be explained, whether on the ground of relationship to Achilles or otherwise, that the author of the Achilleid manifests a partiality for the Telamonian Ajax, far beyond that shown in the Ulyssean cantos.

95. It is now proper to introduce the reference which corroborates in the strongest manner the conclusions to which we have come, from the treatment of Ajax, as to a differentiation of the Achilleid from the rest of the Homeric ' corpus.' Notwithstanding the adhesion of Ajax to what may be called the Argive side [33], and the apparent absence of any special tie binding him to Achilles, it is remarkable that he is claimed by a poet of strong Æolo-Dorian sympathies as the representative of Æolo-Dorian tendencies and character in the Epic time. The great Lyric poet Pindar is a most valuable and important index as to how feeling stood on this great question of *Ajax versus Ulysses*. How has *he* held the balance in this weighty matter? If there is truth in our

---

[32] Hesiod in Fragmenta, names *Αἰακίδαι* as types of *ἀλκή*. It is not unlikely that Ajax was included.

[33] Ajax, if we may credit the extra-Homeric genealogies, was related to the Atreids, being half a Pelopid, his mother Periboea being daughter of Alcathous, son of Pelops.

representations, we may predict that Pindar's sympathies will be the same as those of the Achillean poet, and so he will exalt Ajax and depress Ulysses. Accordingly, the Æolo-Dorian poet has given forth no uncertain sound, and his evidence casts an instructive light on the whole course of our investigations. Pindar plants himself in the footsteps of the Achillean bard regarding Ajax, gives his verdict in favour of the character of Ajax over that of Ulysses, and falls foul of Homer himself for exalting what was to him the more questionable character of Ulysses (§ 83). In conformity with his Æolo-Dorian sympathies, he attempts to reverse the relations of the two heroes and so espouses the cause of Ajax and through him the old Æolo-Dorian element in Greek life, against the cause of Ulysses and the young and rising Attic-Ionic spirit of the newer time [34]. He names Ulysses *twice*, not by any means with commendation, while to Ajax he gives meed of praise in large volume, at least ten times in the extant remains [35]. That we are right in claiming for the Achillean poet Northern sympathies, akin to what is known as Æolo-Doric feeling in the historic time, is further evinced by the fact that the other Ajax is in Pindar similarly redeemed from the disgrace attaching to him in the Ulyssean region, and is restored to the high position of respect occupied by him in the Achilleid. We hear of the Oïlean Ajax as being in some form ' canonised ' (Pind. Ol. ix. 120), and as having an altar erected to him—an honour that strikes us as a strange sequel after, if not an actual protest against, the narrative of his exit in the Odyssey (cp. *supra* § 89), but quite in keeping with the honour shown towards him in the Achilleid.

9. Minor Personages.

96. I come now to treat of divergences affecting the minor though still important personages of both sections. It is

---

[31] In the Eighth Nemean, large expression is given to this feeling. In the images of the rival heroes, Pindar seems to behold the types of two antagonist peoples in his own day—Eginetans and Athenians,—and under cover of the mythic and heroic names. glances an arrow of indignation against the city that was following Ulysses' footsteps. Cp Dissen's note in Donaldson's Pindar, p. 253.

[35] Compare Grote's statement as to Pindar's attitude toward the two heroes (H. of Gr. i. 510.)

singular that the *personnel* in both should differ considerably, and that sometimes in a startling manner.

It is not unfrequently the case that we find persons of the same name without any attempt to distinguish them, as, e.g. in one book there is an Ἐρύμας killed by Idomeneus and before one hundred lines have passed another is killed by Patroclus (Π 345, 415), and again we find an Agelaus a Trojan slain by Diomed, and another a Greek, slain by Hector, both in the Achilleid (Θ 257, Λ 302). Instances of this kind among the minor persons of the poem prove nothing, and it is not to these that I mean to allude. The cases to which I refer are well-defined groups or well-marked individuals, that come up in the one area, and are absent or treated very differently in the other [36]. The following are examples :—

(1) The family of the *Panthoidæ*, one of the three greatest on the Trojan side, appears only in the Achillean area. It includes Polydamas (of whom afterwards), Hyperenor and Euphorbus, but their activity is entirely ignored in the Ulyssean area. The Ulyssean poet acknowledges their father Panthous among the Trojan elders in Γ, but he has strangely passed over all the sons in the battles occupying books Δ—H.

				Ach.	Ul.
Πανθοΐδης .	.	.	.	9	0
Πάνθου υἱός	.	.	.	4	0
Πάνθοος .	.	.	.	1	1
				14	1.

(2) Polydamas, one of these Panthoidæ, is a great figure by the side of Hector. His prominence is very remarkable in the great stretch of Achillean cantos from XI. to XXII. or Λ to X. It is a singular fact which has not yet attracted sufficient notice that he should be so largely present there and entirely absent in the Ulyssean cantos [37]. In these cantos, however. Hector has another monitor, viz. Helenus, as in Z 76 and Π 44. Why this should be so, if all the cantos are from one author, seems

---

[36] Single instances of presence or absence prove nothing. Nausicaa is not named at the parting-scene with Ulysses in Od. ν 66, though we might expect her presence; and Eurynome, who is an important person in the Ithacan household towards the close of the Odyssey, is not introduced till ρ 495.

[37] Düntzer (Hom. Abh. p. 268) has drawn attention to this divergence.

inexplicable, but the fact remains that the boastful and arrogant Hector of the Achilleid has for his monitor the severe Polydamas [38], whereas the mild and generous Hector of the Ulyssean books has provided for him a critic less severe in a member of his own family, his brother Helenus. The name Polydamas occurs *twenty-eight* times in the Achilleid, not once in the Ulyssean cantos.

(3) Helenus [39], who heads the list of Priam's sons in Ω 249, is the seer of Ulyssean cantos by the side of Hector, and, apparently, no warrior, but he is, in the Achilleid, a warrior, linked repeatedly with Deiphobus (M 94, N 758, 770–81), and not seemingly a seer.

(4) Kebriones [40], a son of Priam, and charioteer of Hector, figures prominently in the Achillean books (*fourteen* times), but is not mentioned once in Ulyssean area.

(5) Akamas of the Achillean books (Λ, M, Ξ, Π), is a son of Antenor and a leader of the Dardanians. The only Akamas of the Ulyssean books (B, E, Z) is a Thracian and son of Eussorus.

(6) The Pæonians in the Achilleid are warriors of noble armature with chariot and shield. They are thrice styled ἱπποκορυσταί and δολιχεγχέες. In the Ulyssean area they are armed as archers, and are styled ἀγκυλότοξοι in B 848 and K 428. In the historic time, these different kinds of armour were incompatible, but perhaps the Epic time allowed them to be combined, of which we find a trace in Π 140 τόξοισι μαχέσκετο δουρί τε μακρῷ. Still the difference of representation seems valid evidence.

(7) The Locrians have been subjected to the converse change. In the Achilleid (N 713) they have primitive armour, for they figure as slingers and bowmen, and are expressly said *not* to

---

[38] The Panthoidæ seem to be in some special relation to Apollo, and were probably a family of augurs. Cp. Heyne on Il. O 521.

[39] ἄναξ, given frequently to Helenus in Achilleid, is the only evidence pointing to the possibility of his being there a Seer. It is a title once given to Polydamas and frequently to Tiresias, but its application to so many who have no augural connection renders any inference doubtful.

[40] The name Κεβριόνης and Γοργυθίων are both suggestive of certain primitive populations of the Troad, the people of the Dardan *Kebrene* and the Γέργιθες. These archaic names, probably Pelasgian, come up, as we might expect, only in the Achillean area.

have had spears, helmets and shields. Yet in the Ulyssean
books we find them credited with all these, without any
mention of the sling and the bow, for Ajax the Less is said
to excel at the spear (B 530), and, if *Αἴαντε* includes him,
his troops, who can be no other than Locrians, are so armed
(Δ 280-2). The Scholiast on N 713 remarked the divergence.

(8) Mekisteus, son of Echius, is a companion of Teucer, and
so belongs only to the Achilleid, to which Teucer chiefly
appertains. The Mekisteus of the Ulyssean books is a son of
Talaus and father of the Euryalus who is the associate of
Ulysses' friend, Diomed. Though not himself present at
Troy, this latter Mekisteus is mentioned thrice in Ulyssean
books (B 566, Z 28, Ψ 678), and is unacknowledged in the
Achilleid.

(9) Cassandra is 'fairest of Priam's Daughters' in the Achilleid (N 365). Laodike has that honour, being twice pronounced
so, in the Ulyssean area (Γ 124, Z 252). The Ulyssean poet
is aware of Cassandra's beauty (Ω 699), but he is consistent
in twice bestowing the palm of beauty only on Laodike.

(10) Eurybates of the Achilleid is herald to Agamemnon
(A 320). Eurybates of the Ulyssean area is herald to Ulysses
(B 184, I 170), and this is confirmed by the Odyssey, which
mentions one of that name as having been with Ulysses at
Troy (Od. τ 247). It is remarkable that the first Eurybates
is undefined, being, as it were, in possession of the field. The
herald of Ulysses is on *his* first appearance *designed* as Ἰθα-
κήσιος, which may be taken as evidence of the posteriority of
the Ulyssean cantos.

(11) Eurymedon of the Achilleid is charioteer to Nestor
(in Θ and Λ). Another Eurymedon appears in the Ulyssean
canto Δ 228, but he is there the squire of Agamemnon. The
former is undefined by any designation. The latter is designed
by father and grandfather, with some genealogical minuteness.
It is remarkable that, as the Iliad now stands, we should make
the acquaintance of the one with the designation *first*, and
then come afterwards upon another of the same name who is
left without any designation. Manifestly, the Eurymedon of
Θ and Λ is the one in primary possession; the other has been
superinduced upon the scene and was found to need a designation, which he has accordingly received.

(12) The contrast as to Paris is also remarkable. He is a formidable and effective warrior in the Achilleid, a contemptible poltroon in the Ulyssean cantos. In the former, he is credited with a series of the most notable exploits on the Trojan side (Θ 82, Λ 369, 506, 581, Ν 660, Ο 341); in the latter, he performs hardly any exploit (except in Π 8) and is the mere beau without being in any sense an effective warrior.

Other divergences of less importance and of origin more obscure might be here appended, such as the double rescue and patronage of Æneas, saved by Apollo and under his patronage in E, saved by Poseidon and under his patronage in Υ, the double *οἰνοχόος* or cup-bearer of the Gods, Hebe in E, Ganymede in Υ, *διχθάδιαι κῆρες* to Achilles in Ulyssean canto (I 411), but apparently only *one αἶσα* to Achilles in Achilleid (Λ 416, Υ 127), etc. These last divergences coincide with, but can hardly be said to necessitate, the division into Achilleid and non-Achilleid, because they are comparatively isolated facts. The others, on which stress is laid, are *groups* of phenomena.

CHAPTER XII.

ARCHAICA—RELIGION AND MYTHOLOGY.

ἄλλος γάρ τ' ἄλλοισιν ἀνὴρ ἐπιτέρπεται ἔργοις.

---

97. THE next branch of evidence that will come under review is what may be called the *Archaica*, or the traces of a higher antiquity in Thought and Manners belonging to the Achilleid compared with what can be predicated of the Odyssey and the non-Achilleid.

In dealing with this portion of the subject it must be premised that great caution is necessary in determining what are the true *Archaica*, and a careful induction, under the exercise of a wise and cautious historic insight, is required before we can safely pronounce between different usages and habits, that one custom is older or more remote than another. Moreover it will not in every case happen that the most archaic phenomena will uniformly be found only in the most archaic sources, for relics of primitive manners will be found appearing in younger literature, being often adopted to diversify by their picturesqueness, though neglected or passed over in literature with which they were more properly contemporary. Even within the Odyssey we come upon strata of thought and manners which are not only diverse but are intended to be diverse, as e. g. Life in the Cyclop's cave, Life in the patriarchal house of Nestor, where the sons and daughters act as chief servitors (γ 465, and cp. Schol. on l. 412), and Life in the court of Menelaus at Sparta, where Helen is portrayed as surrounded with a retinue of servitors in considerable splendour. The larger scope and wider outlook of the poet of the Odyssey would

enable him to observe and inweave peculiar and diversified phenomena, some of which might be, in an anthropological sense,
the oldest of all. Thus, for example, it is in the Odyssey
that we find mention of *poisoned arrows* (α 264),—perhaps
the darkest trait of manners in either poem—not as used in
the actual story, but belonging to a picturesque narration out
of a primitive time, and, in surgery for wounds, we come upon
the use of incantations as a surgical auxiliary, which may be
said to be more primitive than anything of the same kind in
the Iliad, for that poem seems silent in both its sections as to
the use of charms. So in Η 138 of the Iliad we hear of a man
as having been a club-warrior (κορυνήτης),—a more ancient
style of fighting than is described at Troy—but when we
examine into the matter, he is not a contemporary, but only
a picturesque character whose memory had survived long
after his own time[1]. These are instances of *literary* survival
(very different from actual survival), similar to that of ζειά
as an actual cereal the mention of which is limited to the
Odyssey. This grain, the name of which is identified with
the Sanskrit 'yava,' precisely as ζεύγνυμι is with the Sanskrit
yunajmi and Latin *jungo*, must be regarded as the oldest
cereal known to have belonged to the Aryan race, since it
existed in a name which preceded the separation of the different
Aryan peoples[2]. Yet it would be entirely unsafe and even
false to assume an anteriority to the Odyssey because ζειά
happens to be mentioned there as a familiar grain, for in
the Iliad it is acknowledged in the very ancient and almost

[1] Sometimes the most savage shape of a Saga is the most recent in historical
sequence; as the Herakles of the club (κορυνηφόρος) is known to appear in literature long subsequent to the Herakles of the bow (τοξότης) or of the spear
(αἰχμητής) (O. Müller, Dor. i. 450.) — Even of Ulysses the armature seems more
archaic in the Odyssey than in the Iliad. He is in the slaughter-scene, a bowman
in the Odyssey, but in the Iliad we know of him as so armed only in Κ (260),
which is a Ulyssean canto.—The Amazons are very archaic, but they are known
only in the neozoic area, though not introduced into the actual arena. The women-
warriors of Virgil, Tasso and Spenser, differ from the Homeric Amazons in being
single figures. Except Athene herself, there is none upon the Homeric canvas
answering to the style of Camilla or Britomart.

[2] ' Die Gerste (i. e. ζειά) galt namentlich in Eleusis für das älteste Korn.'
Preller, Gr. M. i. 474.—The acorn period of human food seems to be, even in the
Achilleid, very remote, as bread is known as Demeter's in the oldest parts of the
Iliad, and acorns are in the Odyssey the food only of swine or swine-like men
metamorphosed (Od. κ 242, ν 409).

hieratic compound ζείδωρος ἄρουρα. Arguments of the above
kind are of no real scientific value, though they might be
employed in a sort of Socratic fence, to rebut the absolute
conclusions of the cruder Chorizontes, who insist on the Iliad
being in all respects and in all its parts more archaic than
the Odyssey. If, however, it would be false to deduce the
anteriority of the Odyssey from such arguments, it would be
equally so to conclude its entire posteriority from plausible
incidental arguments that might be used in a contrary
direction. Thus it would be an excellent Chorizontic
argument of the old type to allege that as the Odyssey
shows more signs than the Iliad of advancement in the
domestication of animals, the Iliad must be some ages earlier.
Swine are in the Iliad spoken of as wild, in the Odyssey
under Eumæus they are tame. The goose is in the Iliad
(B 460) wild, in the Odyssey (ο 174) domesticated. Bees are in
the Iliad (B 87 and M 167) wild, in the Odyssey (ν 106) they
seem to be domesticated [3]. Yet, when we examine further,
we find it would be unsafe to trust these arguments, inasmuch
as domestication and a wild condition of animals may be
found coexisting, and any instance in the Odyssey may show,
not that it is a younger poem, but that it is a poem dealing
with domestic life, and so the appliances of a domestic
establishment naturally happen to be more frequently alluded
to. Besides, such arguments could sometimes be refuted from
the text of the Iliad itself, where, though swine are spoken
of as wild [4], we yet hear of παῖδα συφορβόν (Φ 282) and
ἀπαλοτρεφὴς σιαλός in Φ 363, expressions that imply their
inclusion among the ancient stock of a houschold in that age.
Also, regarding the goose, the actual domestication of it,
according to Pictet (Orig. Ar. i. p. 389), must extend much

[3] The passage in Od. ν 105 seems to me to show the reverse. I have allowed
the statement, however, to stand, as Buchholz in his ' Realien ' claims τιθαιβώσσω
as so indicating.—Another argument equally fallacious would be ; vultures wild in
Iliad, but in Odyssey acting as falcons. according to the common view of Od.
χ 302.—The revelations of Philology regarding the life of the Aryan race ages
before the Iliad and Odyssey throw great doubt on what may be called ' snap-
arguments ' of this kind. If domestication of various animals is as old as the time
of Aryan unity. the Greek race had originally partaken in this knowledge, and,
accordingly, we find them both in the Iliad and the Odyssey in possession of a
fair measure of such knowledge.

[4] Even σῦς ἄγριος itself. of Θ 338. implies that there was a σῦς not ἄγριος.

higher than either Iliad or Odyssey, since it is among birds, what the ox is among animals, the oldest domesticated creature[5].

98. Passing from these incidental and fallacious arguments, I come to consider evidences of a more weighty character, from which we may infer a certain difference of age and may predicate anteriority of one poem, posteriority of another. It is generally admitted that the Greek race passed through a certain stadium of thought and opinion, with certain phases of manners and ideas succeeding each other in a determinable sequence, and we can discern their progress along the arc of the evolution-process historically cognisable, for although the commencement of the circle is beyond our view, we can mark the different segments of the arc that are visible, and can distinguish these as posterior and anterior, relatively to each other. This progression is apparent in their Religion and Mythology, in their Ethical Ideas and in their Manners and Customs, and although, owing to various disturbing causes, great care must be exercised in estimating age in such matters, a certain amount of substantial and sound evidence is obtainable, after careful sifting under these heads, to justify a certain differentiation between the Odyssey and the older portion of the Iliad. That differentiation rests, however, more upon evidence that implies diversity of authorship and involves a different ethical point of view rather than any great separation in respect of age.

99. In the first place, though it hardly amounts to proof but only to a presumption, it is in the Achilleid that we find the most notable remembrances of primitive tradition, 'anklänge' out of a remote primeval time, from a period when Aryan and Semite were not yet severed. As echoes of this most ancient time appear (a) the mention of the Rainbow twice spoken of as a 'sign' ($\tau\acute{\epsilon}\rho\alpha\varsigma$) in the cloud ($\Lambda$ 28, P 548), and (β) the association of a 'flood' of waters with the punishment for wickedness (Π 386), expressions that recall, under a certain variation, the oldest traditions of the Book of Genesis, even those pre-Abrahamic. It is singular

---

[5] According to Pictet (ibid.), the name of the goose (which is not onomatopoetic) is shown to extend, beyond the Aryan circle proper, to Japan and the Malay area.

that these remote reminiscences from hoary antiquity should be found only in the Achilleid. Further, (γ) it is to be observed that the Achilleid remains very much on the ancient ethical basis common to the oldest Semitic thought, with its theory of Life complete within the orb of the present world and void of any distinct doctrine of Retribution in a Future life, whereas the Ulyssean cantos and Odyssey present a wider horizon of mental vision and recognise Retribution and a Future, though shadowy, life[6]. I proceed now to adduce more tangible grounds, derived from the Mythology of the Achilleid. This can be shown to be in a very archaic condition, and among the traces of archaism may be specified the following.

100. I. *The Olympian dynasty of Zeus, though in possession of supremacy, is regarded in the Achilleid as having recently acceded to this supremacy and only after a struggle with rebellious and not yet entirely subjugated powers. In the Odyssey and Ulyssean cantos of the Iliad, the dynasty of Zeus is in undisputed possession of the world, and the references to rebellious powers are all but entirely vanished.*

That there is a distinct difference under this head may be indicated from the following considerations. While Zeus is everywhere styled the son of Kronos, it is only in the Achilleid that this Kronos is conceived and felt as a distinct personality. In the Odyssey and Ulyssean cantos the name of Κρονίδης is purely titular, and Kronos has faded into a shadow. There is in these hardly an indication of the comparative recency of the Olympian dynasty, scarcely a suggestion that there had been a time when that dynasty was not. Apart from the solitary and, in the view of some critics, doubtful instance of Οὐρανίωνες in E 898[7], *if* it is taken to mean not Olympians but sons of Uranus, there is no allusion outside the Achilleid to any ante-Olympian dynasty, whereas such allusions are there found in comparative frequency, leading to the belief that the dynasty of Zeus is but a 'parvenu' in the succession of the ages. In so far as the Homeric poems are concerned, the evidence for such a

----

[6] The evidence as to this point will be given in a subsequent section, § 103, ε.

[7] Nägelsbach (Hom. Theol. p 78) denies even this instance, and accepts it here in the sense of Ὀλύμπιοι. If this is so, the argument above becomes all the stronger.

position is entirely confined to the Achilleid. In proof let it be noted, (1) Tartarus is the state-prison of the Olympian dynasty, for the confinement of what may be called their state-enemies. It occurs only in the Achilleid (Θ 13, 481, Ξ 279). It is not once referred to in the Ulyssean books or in the Odyssey, even in situations that might have naturally led to some reference, as in the picture of Hades in the Eleventh Odyssey, where, however, it is strangely absent.

(2) The chief occupants of this state-prison are Iapetos and Kronos. The former is known to us only from the Achilleid (Θ 479); the latter, as an *active* personality[8], appears likewise only in the Achilleid (Θ 479, Ξ 203, 274, O 225).

(3) The symptoms of possible rebellion against Zeus, like the memories of opposition in the past against Zeus, are confined to the Achilleid. In evidence may be mentioned the mythe of Briareus in A[9], the threatened disaffection of Athene in Θ, the secret plotting of Poseidon in N. All these phenomena suppose the resistibility of Zeus, a notion of which it would be difficult to find a trace outside the Achilleid.

(4) The mysterious reference to Oceanus as the father of all, the origin even of Gods (Ξ 201 and 244)[10], also Achillean, implies that the Olympian rule was comparatively young. According to Hesiod in the Theogony, Oceanus comes foremost among the sons of Uranus, among whom Kronos comes last, and to this extent the Achillean poet seems to occupy ground akin to that of the Bœotian poet in this matter of dynastic succession among the elder Gods, nearer certainly than that occupied by the poet of the Odyssey and Ulyssean books[11].

[8] Δ 59 is the nearest approach to a recognition of the personality of Kronos in the Ulyssean area.

[9] 'The age of conflicts among the Gods (as Gods and not as interested in spectacles of earth) has passed away, but here, in the Briareus legend, we have an echo of the element of Titanic wars.' Cox, Mythol. i. 336.

[10] This Achillean passage about Oceanus has mythologically such an archaic look about it that Professor Blackie compares it to a 'knob of primeval granite cropping up in a sandstone country' (II. iv. p. 312).

[11] Not only is there an entire absence of the Kronos and Iapetos mythe, as well as of the Prometheus mythe, with their suggestions of antagonism to Zeus, but various rebellious powers seem, in the Odyssey at least, to wear a milder aspect. Thus Atlas in Hesiod and in Æschylus is represented as suffering his doom from his connection with the Titan-fight (Hes. Th. 514); in the Odyssey there is no

101. II. *The conception of the Olympians in the Achilleid is one full of unrest, with little of the calm quiescence in which they are afterwards portrayed, and, as in all primitive mythologies, hyperbole is made the main expression of the godlike and divine. In the Odyssey and Ulyssean cantos, they are represented under more of a quiescent aspect and with the hyperbolic element comparatively subdued.*

A parallel argument to this has been a favourite weapon of the Chorizontes, as between the Iliad and the Odyssey. They aver, what is true, that Olympus in the Odyssey is a much more serene region than in the Iliad, and that the storms and feuds that once raged in it are now at rest[12]. Those critics forgot, however, to make allowance for the inherent exigencies of each poem, and failed to observe that the unrest of the Iliad is mainly within a certain well-defined area, and that the quiescence of Olympus in the Odyssey is in keeping with the calmer character of its theme.

Under this head it may be noted (1) the 'scenes' as they may be called of domestic strife in Olympus are apparently only Achillean (A 586, Ξ 250, O 18[13]). There does not appear to be elsewhere a repetition of them on the same scale, for the opening of Δ cannot be said to indicate domestic disorder in so pronounced a form, and indeed the aspect of Olympus at the opening of this Ulyssean book is comparatively quiescent. Those Achillean 'scenes' were among the most repulsive and indefensible in an ethical point of view, and from them was drawn in after time many a bitter arrow against the literal upholders of the Greek mythology.

allusion to his Titan fight, and it is by no means clear that his position (in α 52) is one of doom or of pure punishment. So the γίγαντες or Giants of the Odyssey are not identical with the γηγενεῖς or rebellious giants of Hesiodic legend, and the Cyclopes of the Odyssey are entirely different from the Cyclopes of the Hesiodic poem (Preller, Gr. M. i. 388, 9).

[12] There is a considerable basis for H. N. Coleridge's clever statement as to four gradations of Mythology in ancient Epics. 'The gods in the Iliad are never *dii ex machinis*; they are providential and governing. The difference even in the Odyssey is very discernible; in the Æneid the mythology is little else than ornamental, and in the Pharsalia there is none at all' (Col. Introd. p. 188).

[13] The above is Preller's enumeration (Gr. Myth. ii. 105), who refers to them as 'diese furchtbar leidenschaftliche Scenen zwischen Zeus und Heré.' He does not include, apparently, as so marked, the incident in Δ 20, which is from the Ulyssean area.—Ὤχθησαν, applied to the Gods as a whole, occurs twice and only in Achilleid.

(2) The deceptions of Zeus by Heré are only Achillean (Ξ 360, Σ 168, T 97). The last is only narrated and does not belong to the plot of the action. The other two, however, are instances of undoubted deception and in connection with the actual scheme of the Achilleid.

(3) The hyperbolic element, though appearing also in the Odyssey and Ulyssean cantos, abounds in the Achilleid. Thus, as examples of the gigantic in the representations of the Gods [14], we have of Zeus—

1. Olympus shaking with the nodding of his eyebrows and the waving of his locks (A 528).
2. Able to push all the Gods from their seats (A 580).
3. Tossing the Gods around the hall and putting them in mortal terror [15] (Ξ 257, with which compare O 117, 136, 181, 224).
4. Suspending Heré with anvils at her feet (O 19).
5. Hurling Hephæstus over the celestial battlements (A 590).
6. Able to draw Gods and Earth and Sea aloft into the sky (Θ 23).
7. Threatening to inflict wounds on Heré and Athene, such as ten years should not heal (Θ 418).

Of Heré we have these hyperboles—

1. Olympus reeling by the rocking of her chair (Θ 199).
2. Grasping Sea with one hand and Earth with the other in oath to Hypnos (Ξ 272).

Of Poseidon—

1. Roaring like nine or ten thousand men (Ξ 148).
2. Making the sea dash up to ships and tents (Ξ 392).
3. Advancing at four strides from Samothrace, whereat hills and woods tremble (N 17, 21).

About a dozen hyperboles as to the Gods are thus producible, without reckoning in those from the second Theomachy in Φ (cp. l. 407) and the portents of Hephæstus burning up Scamander. These last are among what Grote calls 'the vast

---

[14] Among hyperboles in the human area may be named the gigantic weapon of Ajax (twenty-two cubits long), which belongs to the Achilleid (O 677). That of Hector is of more modest dimensions in Θ 494 as well as Z 319.

[15] These strange incidents, Nos. 3, 4, 5, are only *narrated* from some more ancient legends. Regarding the incident in Ξ 257, Heyne remarks, 'Expressit mores rudium aetatium, in quibus irae intemperantia regnat.'

and fantastic conceptions' of superhuman agency, crowded into the closing scenes of the Achilleid [16].

Against these there can be produced hardly any parallel examples from the Ulyssean books, except the one in E (l. 859) as to the roar of Ares, which is modelled after Ξ 148, that as to the Ægis of Athene (E 744), and that as to the motion of the steeds of Heré (E 770), springing at once as far as a man can gaze across the dim deep.

The conclusion under this branch of the subject will be further strengthened by the after evidence as to the aspects under which the *mountain* Olympus is regarded. In the meantime I need only mention the important fact, bearing on the greater quiescence of Olympus in the Odyssey and the Ulyssean cantos, that the famous expression 'the Gods who live at ease' never occurs but outside the Achilleid [17]. It is found only in Z 138 and in Od. δ 805 and ε 122 [18].

102. III. *The conception of Zeus in the Achilleid is accordingly more primitive, with less of the ethical, more of the violent physical, force. In especial, though recognised as* Πατήρ, *which may mean either Father or Possessor, he is represented more as an atmospheric than a spiritual Being. This view of his character, without being foreign to, is less prominent in, the Odyssey and Ulyssean cantos.*

The considerations stated above in § 100 as to the recency of the rule of Zeus, fit in and harmonise with this primitive conception of him. A dynasty, which is regarded as established by force, is naturally maintained by it, and hence harsh and fierce energies are ascribed to Zeus. How far we can discern in the Achilleid *violent* atmospheric phenomena may afterwards more fully appear. There is no mistaking, however, the elemental *rôle* of Zeus in the Achilleid as pre-eminently an atmospheric God, and the four passages, which Preller in his

---

[16] Grote, Hist. of Gr. ii. p. 264.—'The 'speaking horses' belong only to the Achilleid. Arcion is mentioned only once, viz. in the Ulyssean book Ψ, but he is not there vocal, though sometimes elsewhere, as in Propertius, so represented.

[17] Zenodotus sought to introduce it into Υ 114, but it has not been accepted.— The term ἴκηλοι, applied to their enforced inaction in Λ 75. is noteworthy, but it is only for the special situation, not a *characteristic* epithet like ῥεῖα ζώοντες.

[18] To these might be added, as a fourth example, ἀκηδέες of Ω 526, being an equivalent expression. Μάκαρες is an older epithet belonging to both areas, and meant originally, *big*, or *powerful* (cp. Benfey, Lex.), earlier than *blest*.

'Greek Mythology' (i. p. 77), adduces as marking this primitive conception of the God, are supplied by the Achilleid (M 252, N 795, Π 295, 364)[19]. To these might have been added, as almost equally significant, M 279, N 243, and T 357. Alongside of these *seven* examples of what may be called *Jupiter Pluvius* in the Achilleid, may be mentioned, as existing contemporaneously, though not so fully developed, the idea of Zeus as a righteous governor (cp. Il 387, a passage where the ethical and physical attributes are curiously interwoven), and as protector of sacred social relations, whence we hear of him as Zeus Ξείνιος, as in N 625. What is more remarkable, while often and everywhere spoken of as Ζεὺς πατήρ, he is known as Πατήρ, *simply* and alone, in the Achillean area. This occurs *eight* times and is a peculiar phenomenon, unexampled except in the Achilleid[20].

In the Odyssey, on the other hand, while the atmospheric character of Zeus is still frequently acknowledged, though with less amplitude of form (ι 67, μ 313, 405, 415, ξ 303, ο 297, 475, υ 103), the ethical conception becomes more and more prominent. Hence we hear not only of Ζεὺς ξείνιος (ι 271, ξ 284, 389), but also of Ζεὺς ἱκετήσιος (υ 213), as the protector of suppliants. Although the Ulyssean cantos are without these titles of Zeus, the idea underlying these titles is there virtually present in the extended allegory of the 'Litæ' or Supplications, as daughters of Zeus (I 502).

The extent to which the atmospheric and elemental con-

---

[19] In the Achilleid we have in fact so ancient a representation of Zeus that it may be said Zeus is there the Firmament itself as much as the God of the Firmament, and there is a strong leaning to what may be called the old Pelasgian θεολογία which regarded Elemental Powers rather than Persons. It is significant, that the expression αἰθέρι ναίων, 'dwelling in ether' (cp. K 16), does not appear among his titles in the Achilleid. It occurs only in Odyssey and Ulyssean books.

	Ach.	Ul.	Od.		Ul.		Od.
αἰθέρι ναίων	o	2	1		B 412, Δ 166.		o 523.

It is true that the preparation for this expression has begun in the Achilleid, viz. O 610 (unless the ancient ἀθέτησις of the lines 610 4 be sustained) and especially O 192, and we hear also of Διὸς δῶμα or δώματα (A 222, 533, T 10, etc., much as in E 398), though only in the Odyssey we hear of Διὸς αὐλή (δ 74); (ὡς ὑπέρτατα δώματα ναίε, is in Hesiod (Op. et Di. l. 8), who has also αἰθέρι ναίων ibid. l. 18)).

[20] Od. μ 65 is the nearest approach, but the precedence of Διὶ πατρί a little before makes a peculiarity. So Od. ν 324 is probably '*thy* father,' not 'the father.' The *eight* examples of πατήρ alone = Ζεὺς in the Achilleid are A 579, Θ 69, 245, Λ 80, Ξ 352, Π 250, P 648, X 209, recurring with remarkably broad and equable uniformity.

ception of Zeus prevails in the Achilleid as compared with the ethical and spiritual, and the extent to which out of the Achilleid this relation is either modified or reversed, may be seen in the following groups of phenomena :—

ATMOSPHERIC AND PHYSICAL.

I. *Nature-forces under Zeus.*

	Ach.	Ul.	Od.	Ach.	Ul.	Od.
Διὸς αὐγαί[21] (= οὐρανός Schol.)	1	0	0	N 837		
Διόθεν βέλεμνον	1	0	0	O 489		
Διὸς βροντή	1	0	0	N 796		
Διὸς κεραυνός	4(?)	0	1	Ξ 417, O 117, Φ 198, 401 (?)		ξ 306
Διὸς μάστιξ	1	0	0	N 812		
Διὸς νεφέλαι	0	1	0		B 146	
Διὸς νιφάδες	1	0	0	T 357[22]		
Διὸς ὄμβρος	2	1	2	Λ 493, M 286	E 91	ι 111, 358
Διὸς οὖρος or ἐκ Διός	1	0	2	Ξ 19		ε 176, ο 296
Διὸς πληγή (= lightning, v. l. ῥιπή)	1	0	0	Ξ 414		
Διὸς στεροπή	1	1	0	Λ 66	K 154	
Διιπετής (of rivers)	4	0	3[23]	Π 174, P 263 Φ 268, 326		δ 477, 581, η 284
Διοτρεφής (of the Scamander)	1	0	0	Φ 223		
ὃν τέκετο Ζεύς (of the river Xanthus)	2	1?	0	Ξ 434, Φ 2	[Ω 693?]	
	21	4	8			

[21] In this remarkable expression Zeus is made to include the function of Helios and to be the one comprehensive God. Elsewhere we hear of αὐγή or αὐγαὶ ἠελίοιο, which is also common to Achilleid, as a synonym for οὐρανός.

[22] The regimen of Διὸς by νιφάδες is by some thought doubtful. If it is rejected, the proof as to the atmospheric character of Zeus becomes stronger, since Διὸς ἐκ ποτέονται must then be taken to mean, with Eustathius, ἐξ ἀέρος. Cp. Ebeling's Lexicon in ἐκποτέομαι.

[23] Two of the three instances of Διιπετής in the Odyssey are of the Nile, to which it was entirely appropriate. I have not included ἔνδιος, occurring in the debatable portion of Λ 725 and only elsewhere in δ 450, as also the expression Διὸς ἐνιαυτοί in B 134, which, along with ἤματα ἐκ Διός (in Od. ξ 93) are possibly remnants of atmospheric conceptions. Against these would have to be reckoned the peculiar expression Διὸς αἰγίς, which is more clearly *atmospheric* in the Achilleid than anywhere else (cp. O 308, P 593). It has, however, obtained a hieratic and traditional sense, so that no conclusion can be drawn from its occurrences or from those of αἰγίοχος. Ὑψίζυγος and εὐρύοπα or εὐρύόπα (the latter occurring very frequently in Achilleid) are, likewise, not so distinctly *atmospheric* as to be fairly included in these enumerations.

II. *Physical Epithets of Zeus.*

	Ach.	Ul.	Od.		Ach.	Ul.
ἀστεροπητής . . .	3	1	0		Λ 580, 609, Μ 275	ΙΙ 443
ἀργικέραυνος . . .	2 [24]	0	0		Υ 16, Χ 178	
ἐριβρεμέτης . . .	1	0	0		Ν 624	
ἐρίγδουπος . . .	4	3	3			
κελαινεφής . . .	5	3	3			
νεφεληγερέτης . .	19	8	7			
στεροπηγερέτης . .	1	0	0		ΙΙ 298	
τερπικέραυνος . . .	4	4	6			
ὑψιβρεμέτης . . .	4	0	2			
	43	19	21			
Add above	21	4	8			
	64	23	29			

There is therefore a great preponderance of *atmospheric*
associations attached to the Zeus of the Achilleid[25], and a
remarkable equality in the number furnished by the Ulyssean
cantos to that furnished by the Odyssey. The scale of proportion applied to these areas is one of entire *disparity* as
between Achilleid and the non-Achilleid, but of remarkable
parity as between the Odyssey and the Ulyssean cantos of
the Iliad, in their separate extensions.

ETHICAL ASPECTS OF ZEUS.

Passing over the neutral territory of the *Power* of Zeus, where
we meet with such terms as ἐρισθενής, ὑπερμενής, and come
in contact with his βουλή, νόος, φρήν, and φρένες, expressions in
which there is no strictly *ethical* content, we come to a class
of expressions bearing on his moral relations and providential
ordering.

[24] If T 121 is reckoned in, there are three instances of ἀργικέραυνος.

[25] Among the minor peculiarities of the Achilleid is the occurrence of κυάνεαι
ὀφρύες attributed to Zeus in A 528, P 209, and to Heré, O 102. The expression is
one that might be added to the atmospheric associations of the Achilleid, as it is
in origin meteorological.—Heré is also more distinctly an Elemental power in
Achilleid, sends thunder Λ 45, storms and clouds O 26, Φ 6, these citations being
those given in proof by Preller (Gr. M. i. p. 111). The character of Ares, who
was originally an *elemental* power, the Thracian storm-god, appears likewise most
clearly from the Achilleid (Gr. M. i. p. 203).

I. *Moral Forces or Products.*

	Ach.	Ul.	Od.	Ach.	Ul.	Od.
Διὸς αἶσα	1	1	1	P 321	I 608	ι 52
Διὸς ἐφετμαί	1	2	0	O 593	Ω 570, 586	
Διὸς μῆνις	1	1	1	O 122	E 34	ε 146
Διὸς νοῦσος (madness)	0	0	1			ι 411
Διὸς ὅρκια[26]	0	1	0		Γ 107	
Διὸς μῆτις (in Διὶ μῆτιν ἀτάλαντος) . . .	1	5	0			
	4	10	3			

II. *Ethical Epithets of Zeus.*

	Ach.	Ul.	Od.
ἱκετήσιος	0	0	1
ξένιος	1	0	3
μητίετα	9	7	7
ὕπατος μήστωρ . . .	2	0	0
ἄφθιτα μήδεα εἰδώς . .	0	1	0
Κρόνου παῖς ἀγκυλομήτεω .	4	5	1
	16	13	12.

The evidence under this head does not yield so striking
results, though the preponderance of ethical ideas is found on
the whole not to belong to the Achilleid. The ratio is
affected by the recurrence of the somewhat indefinite μητίετα
as a title of honour; but it is worthy of note that it is chiefly
in the Achilleid where Zeus seems to be *at a loss* for μῆτις,
and we have him there described as hesitating like one *without*
counsel [27], and once as addressed sarcastically, δολομῆτα (Α 540).

Under this head may be added, as a corroboration, that
the words ἀγαθός and κακός obtain an ethical, as apart from
an objective and physical, sense, only in the Odyssey and
Ulyssean cantos. The instances in which the former may
be relied on as bearing this deeper sense are Ζ 162, Ω 173,
Od. α 43. The number of instances in which it has an allied

[26] The appeal to Zeus by oath as the upholder of moral right appears mainly in
Ulyssean cantos, as the following list from Ebeling shows. 'Testis est (Zeus) jurantium
Γ 104, (Τ 197) Η 76, 411, Κ 329, Ψ 43. Od. ξ 158 ;' (Ebeling's Lexicon, in v. Ζεύς).
So σπονδαὶ ἄκρητοι καὶ δεξιαί only in Β and Δ, not occurring, however, in Odyssey,
which is parallel to the non-occurrence of the word ὅρκια in the Odyssey.—Θέμιστες
in connection with Zeus may be said to be equally diffused, θέμιστες πρὸς Διός Α 238,
θέμιστες Διός Od. π 403, with which compare the Ulyssean Β 206.

[27] 'Aliquando dubitat quid faciat, Θ 70, Χ 209 (Π 658), cp. Π 432.' Ebeling's
Lexicon, in v. Zeus.

sense, *good for its purpose, worthy,* σπουδαῖος, increases in these books compared with the number in the Achilleid, e. g. B 273, Γ 179, Ι 341, Ψ 770, Ω 632, and frequently in the Odyssey. As instances of κακός implying *moral* disapprobation may be given B 114, Δ 339, E 650, Ι 21, Ψ 493, and they are frequent in the Odyssey, as ξ 337, λ 384, etc.[28]. The case of ἀγαθός is illustrated by the phenomena in regard to αἴσιμος. It has a primitive sense '*fated*,' from αἶσα, 'fate, destiny,' and a secondary sense '*proper*' (*justus*). The former must be the more ancient, judging from its derivation, and accordingly we find the older sense mainly in the Achilleid, the newer appears elsewhere. The following is an approximate representation of the facts :—

	Primary Sense.			Secondary Sense.		
	Ach.	Ul.	Od.	Ach.	Ul.	Od.
αἴσιμος	6	1	0	1	2	9
ἐναίσιμος	0	1	2	0	4	7.

That is to say, sixty per cent. of the occurrences in the older sense belong to the Achilleid, and less than six per cent. of those of the newer sense.

Further, as if under the influence of the same tendency which afterwards developed legislation by codes of laws instead of θέμιστες, and republics instead of monarchies, the rule of Zeus becomes less absolute in the Ulyssean books and in the Odyssey than it is in the Achilleid. Thus in Δ 17 (where cp. Blackie's note), we find Zeus using the language of what may be called a constitutional king and professing to have regard to what might be 'the pleasure of all' (πᾶσι φίλον καὶ ἡδύ). It is quite in keeping with this that in the Odyssey (α 76) we find him *deferring*, in so far, to another God (Poseidon), and calling on the various Gods (περιφραζώμεθα πάντες) to *deliberate* on a certain scheme, all in a tone of comparative complaisance. There is little or nothing of this complaisance

[28] It is right to note that Mr. Grote denies the existence of any strictly *ethical* sense in these words ἀγαθός and κακός until the Socratic age. Mr. Gladstone enters the lists warmly against this restriction, and demands 'permission to protest against whatever savours of the idea that any Socrates whatever was the patentee of that sentiment of right and wrong, which is the most precious part of the patrimony of mankind.' (Gl. Homer, ii. 420.) His most important, if not his sole evidences (viz. Z 162, I 341), against Mr. Grote, are, however, not produced from the Achilleid. For these he is indebted to the neozoic area.

(X 174 the nearest approach) traceable in the Achilleid[29], where, on the contrary, we find Poseidon under the necessity of acting in the capacity of Equerry to Zeus (Θ 440). A similar toning down from a fiercer primitive conception is seen in the treatment of Apollo and Artemis. In the Achilleid, Apollo is, normally, a dark and gloomy God, the fell minister of Death. Beyond the Achilleid we hear of him as sending 'sudden death,' but with this peculiarity in many instances that it is *now* brought ἀγανοῖς βελέεσσι, 'by *gentle* shafts.' The occurrences are, with ἀγανοῖς inserted, Ω 758, and Od. γ 280, ο 409–10. Compare also Od. η 64, ρ 251, 494, where ἀγανοῖς is omitted. Regarding Artemis, the following instances occur, with ἀγανοῖς inserted, ε 124, λ 173, 198, ο 410, to which have to be added μαλακὸς θάνατος of σ 202 and the supplicated death in υ 62–80. (In Ζ 428, Od. ι 324, ο 475, there is no mention of ἀγανοῖς, while in Ζ 205, χολωσαμένη is a relic of the older notion, cp. Τ 59.) It may therefore be said that *eight* instances (*nine*, if ο 410 is reckoned for each deity singly) can be quoted as evidencing the milder view of their solemn function, but of these not one is producible from the Achilleid.

103. IV. *Regarding the life of the Gods, and their mode of worship, the traces of ancient or palæozoic modes of thought are visible chiefly in the Achilleid. The appearances of what seem to be variations or deflections from antique hieratic usages come into view in the Odyssey and Ulyssean area.*

(a) The Gods of the Achilleid, if we may judge from what is said of the *king* of the Gods, are conceived as not differing from mortals in regard to the constituents of their frame. Thus we hear of *blood*-drops, whether in tears or otherwise, proceeding, in certain moments of regret or pity, from the father of Gods and men (Λ 54, Π 459). In both of these passages, αἷμα, 'blood,' is used, or a compound of that word, to describe the efflux, and Hesiod concurs (Theog. 183) as to '*blood*-drops' from Uranus. It is somewhat singular that, in a portion of the Iliad now standing prior in position, there should occur something very like a contradiction to, or at

---

[29] Mr. Grote remarks that the Zeus of the Achilleid needs only one appeal by Thetis to honour Achilles, while the Zeus of the Odyssey needs two appeals (in a and ε) by a much greater deity, Athene, to protect Ulysses (Hist. of Gr. ii. 226). These appeals seem addressed as much to the whole council as to Zeus (a 82, 85).

least a deflection from, this view, for we are told in a very formal confession of belief that the Gods have as *blood* a fluid called 'ichor' (ἰχώρ), 'whence they are styled *bloodless*' (ἀναίμονες)· It is in a Ulyssean canto (E 340) where this occurs, one that now precedes those Achillean cantos where αἷμα is attributed to Zeus. It would appear, however, that the poet of E did not maintain his own innovation, for we read soon after in the case of the god Ares of ἄμβροτον αἷμα (E 870), without in this case the explanation being subjoined that in a divine person it was 'ichor' and not 'blood' that flows from the wound.

(β) In the functions and character of Athene there appears to be a considerable development of new and important features when we go beyond the Achilleid. In the older poem she is little else than the ὀβριμοπάτρη, and a war-goddess. In the newer section we find her epithets multiply and glimpses of new functions appear.

The following epithets are accessions to the older titles given to her in the Achilleid. She is now known

	Ach.	Ul.	Od.	Ul.				Od.
As πολύβουλος . .	0	1	1	E 260	.	.	.	Od. π 282
As κυδίστη . .	0	1	1	Δ 515	.	.	.	Od. γ 378
As ἠΰκομος or εὐπλόκαμος	0	3	1	Z 92, 273, 303 .	.			Od. η 41.

(γ) Among the deities whose *cultus* can be historically discerned to have passed through successive extensions of area stands Aphrodite. In most of the seats of her worship Phœnician influence is known to have been at work, and if we are correct in affirming that acquaintance with Phœnician life and intercourse with Phœnician civilisation can be predicated only of the Odyssey and Ulyssean books, it follows that we may expect in that area a corresponding accession in the acknowledgments of one who ranks in the main developments of her worship as originally a Phœnician goddess. This oriental connection is especially indicated by the two titles Κύπρις and Κυθέρεια. Cyprus and Cythera being two of the most important stepping-stones by which her *cultus* passed from the Orient to Greece [30].

---

[30] To these might be added the small island Κρανάη, which, wherever it is located, was probably under Phœnician influence and a seat of her worship. It occurs in Γ 445, belonging to the Ulyssean area. The epithet ζάθεος applied to

	Ach.	Ul.	Od.
Κύπρις . . .	0	5	0
Κυθέρεια . . .	0	0	2.

Although the name *Κύπρις* does not occur in the Odyssey, Cyprus is recognised as a special seat of her worship, as we see from Od. θ 363, so that there is a virtual identity of view between the Odyssey and the Ulyssean cantos. The Achillean Aphrodite of Ξ 211 is not said to be either Cyprian or Cytherean, and does not appear to be very warmly Trojan in her sympathies, for she assists Heré in an anti-Trojan scheme.

(δ) The worship of Dionysus is a *cultus* which passed through various stadia in the course of Greek history, and there is reason to believe that it was not recognised as among the most ancient forms of worship belonging to the Greek people. Herodotus regards him as introduced comparatively recently into the Greek Pantheon (ii. 49). It harmonises with this to find that in the Achilleid there is no mention of him except once in a passage otherwise doubtful and peculiarly liable to after interpolation (Ξ 325). In the Odyssey and Ulyssean books he is more distinctly acknowledged, but under circumstances that show his *cultus* to be, from whatever cause, only *struggling* into recognition (Z 132, 135, Od. λ 324).

(ε) Demeter is a goddess in after time closely associated with Dionysus, but having more claim to be regarded as of immemorial antiquity. The worship of the productive power of 'Mother Earth' (*Γῆ μήτηρ*, according to Bopp) is among the most ancient of nature-worships, and accordingly we find in the oldest parts of the Iliad *bread* known as *Demeter's bruised corn* (*Δημήτερος ἀκτή* N 322). At the same time, as being an agricultural deity, she is not a prominent figure of the existing Homeric Pantheon, and it has been ingeniously conjectured that both Demeter and Dionysus were gods of peasant life, figured therefore little among the worships or in the poetry of warrior tribes, and so come to be without prominence in either Iliad or Odyssey. This is Welcker's view, and, though Nägelsbach (Hom. Th. p. 117) endeavours to controvert it, it is one that explains, at all events, in the case of Demeter, many otherwise difficult phenomena. Alongside of and over against

Κύθηρα in O 432 *may,* however, denote the presence of this Phoenician *cultus* as early as the Achilleid.

the upper or Olympian Pantheon there now comes into view
an under-world or 'Chthonian court,' in which a new Zeus and
his consort are supposed to rule, and the Night-side of Nature
begins to attract the thought of men[31]. Demeter and her
daughter Persephone now come into remarkable prominence
in connection with this Chthonian counterpart to, or reflection of, Olympus. It is remarkable that there is no certain trace of Persephone in the Achilleid (Ξ 326 belongs to
a suspicious passage), whereas the moment we pass out of
the Achilleid, this dread 'Chthonian' power of the under-
world comes into distinct relief in about twelve occurrences[32]
(I 457, 565, Od. κ 491–4, 534, 564, λ 47, 212–6–25, 386, 634).
Parallel with the development of the 'Chthonian cultus' of
Persephone was the appearance of certain euphemistic expressions to describe the dead under her sway. The remarkable
expression καμόντες[33] comes up only in this same neozoic
area where Persephone appears.

	Ach.	Ul.	Od.	Ul.	Od.
καμόντες (as = θανόντες)	0	2	1	Γ 278, Ψ 72	λ 476.

104. Along with the development of each 'cultus' we can
trace also an accession of formalities attending such celebra-
tions. Among these may be specified (1) the *festival* and
(2) the *votive offering*, as distinct from sacrificial oblation.

It is precisely what we should expect from the general run
of the evidence that specialties of this kind would not appear
in the remoter poem. Accordingly, whether owing to the
greater concentration of vision on the part of the Achillean
poet, whose intensity did not allow him to notice objects outside his proper theme, though they may have been contemporary with him, or whether, as is more likely, such accessories
of religious worship were then less prominent, we must go

---

[31] Compare, on this point, the Rev. A. M. Fairbairn's 'Studies in Philosophy of
History and Religion,' p. 197, where much valuable matter appears on the subject
of primitive Thought.

[32] An additional instance in a Ulyssean canto is the *dual* form τίνυσθον in
Γ 279, explicable only by reference to the latent though unnamed Persephone.
Contrast τίνυνται, *plural*, of 'Ερινύες in T 260, a passage which has this ancient
feature about it that, unlike the parallel in Γ, it does not allude to Persephone.

[33] In the Attic time κεκμηκότες came to be the form preferred for this
euphemism. It is a sign of the tolerably firm state of the Homeric text that this Attic
variation has nowhere obtruded itself, for κεκμηῶτες is limited to the *natural* sense
of 'weary,' and has no *mystic* meaning in the Homeric poems.

outside the Achilleid to meet the word ἑορτή or sacred *Festival*
(Od. υ 156, φ 258).   Parallel to these two occurrences in the
Odyssey, we have in one Ulyssean canto a festival *named*
(Θαλύσια in I 534), and in another (B 550) a virtual mention
of an anniversary festival.   Regarding *votive offerings*, the
nearest approach [34] is that in H 82–3 and another in K 571
compared with K 463.   In the Odyssey the use of ἀνάθημα
twice as an ornament seems to be a *transference* from a
prior signification of 'votive offering,' and ἄγαλμα is there
regularly used as a dedicated ornament.

The evidence under this head would therefore assume this
form—

	Ach.	Ul.	Od.	Ul.	Od.
Sacred festivals . . .	o	2	2	B 550, I 534	υ 156, φ 258
Votive offerings . . .	o	2	4	H 82, K 571	γ 274, 430 θ 509, μ 347
ἄγαλμα and ἀνάθημα applied to any ornament . . .	o	1	2	Δ 144	α 152, φ 430.
	o	5	8		

105. The only remaining illustration I shall advance under
this head consists of a cluster of remarkable usages in certain
hieratic words, originally stamped with a strictly defined
limitation, but afterwards used with more varied application.   It will be found from an examination of these that the
Achilleid treats them on the limited basis, while the extended
basis is adopted in the Ulyssean cantos and the Odyssey,
which, here as elsewhere, keep each other in countenance.
Whatever be the explanation of the fact, account must be taken
and a rationale offered of this peculiarity that in the Achilleid
various epithets of the gods show strictness and fixity, with no
application to human beings, whereas in the Odyssey and Ulyssean books they show a certain fluidity and flexibility, so that
they become applicable to others than their primary divine
possessors.   As an example may be taken λευκώλενος, originally
appropriated to Heré, and so assigned in the Achilleid ; but the
moment we pass out of the Achilleid, it is found not limited
to her, but bestowed freely on various less lofty personages.

---

[34] In one instance in the Achilleid we seem to have a near approach to a
dedicated offering, viz. the arms of Patroclus (P 131), but these are carried away
to be a glory not to a god, but simply to the captor.

In other words, the hieratic application has been modified, and archaic usage departed from—

	Hieratic.				Non-Hieratic.			
	Ach.	Ul.	Od.		Ach.	Ul.	Od.	
λευκώλενος . .	18	6	0	of Heré	0	1	1	of Helen
					0	3	9	of Andromache, Arete, Nausicaa, etc.
βοῶπις . . .	13	1	0	of Heré	0	2	0	of Clymene and Phylome-dusa
πρέσβα . . .	3[35]	1	0	of Heré	0	0	1	of Eurydice (Od. γ 452)[36]
	34	8	0.		0	6	11.	

Thus, of three epithets given to Heré, it is found that they are confined to that goddess in the Achilleid, and there they are given abundantly (34 times). When we pass to the non-Achillean area, we find that they have not only greatly diminished regarding Heré, but have come to be applied to other, even *human*, beings, and of this deflection we can produce not one or two instances but *seventeen*. Something similar takes place in other hieratic words, although still kept to lofty associations. Thus χρυσόθρονος, in the Achilleid given only to Heré, is elsewhere bestowed also on Artemis and Eôs, and a similar relaxation takes place with κούρη Διὸς αἰγιόχοιο.

	Hieratic.				Less Hieratic.			
	Ach.	Ul.	Od.		Ach.	Ul.	Od.	
χρυσόθρονος . .	3	0	0	of Heré	0	1	1	of Artemis
					0	0	10	of Eôs
κούρη (θυγάτηρ, τέ-kος) Διὸς αἰγιόχοιο	5	7	7	of Pallas	0	1	0	of Helen
					0	2	2	of Nymphs and Muses
	8	7	7		0	4	13	
Add above	34	8	0		0	6	11	
	42	15	7.		0	10	24.	

Thus, these last expressions, fixed in the Achilleid, are, though still hieratic, fluid and flexible outside the Achilleid, and the problem is to explain on any other theory of authorship than that which we have advanced, how forty-two instances of the strict usage should come up in the Achilleid with no instance of the free usage, and how in the non-Achillean area,

[35] In T 91, once besides, to Até.

[36] The instance of πρέσβα in Odyssey has this peculiarity, that it has a genitive plural attached. Apart from this, it is quite parallel.

along with twenty-two instances of the strict usage surviving, there should appear there and there only thirty-four instances of the free usage.

106. Minor indications[37] in the same direction are the following—

(1) Χαλκοβατὲς δῶ, as limited to the house of Zeus, occurs twice in the Achilleid (four times, if the second Theomachy is reckoned in). In the Odyssey, while still used of the house of Zeus, in θ 321, it is transferred to less lofty scenes, and we hear of it in the case of the palace of Alcinous (ν 4).

(2) Ἵλαος, of a God only, in the Achilleid (A 583). In the Ulyssean book (I 635) we read of it in connection with a mortal (ἵλαος ἔνθεο θυμόν, where the Schol. says, θεοποιεῖ, i.e. the poet treats Achilles as a god). Except the doubtful T 178, these are its only occurrences.

(3) Διοτρεφής, originally of the βασιλεύς only, has come to be applied more laxly to larger aggregates of men, other than βασιλῆες. Hence διοτρεφέων αἰζηῶν, in B 660, and (with v. l.) Δ 280, besides a similar expression in E 463, with which compare Od. ε 378 ἀνθρώποισι διοτρεφέεσσι, of the Phæacians. (Διογενής, being nowhere found in the *plural* in Homer, does not supply any parallel illustration.) Cp. Mure, H. G. L. ii. p. 79.

(4) Ἀΐδης, always a person or being in the Achilleid, which it often is also in the Ulyssean cantos and the Odyssey, appears as a *place* or *region* only in the neozoic area, in Ψ 244.

(5) The title Ἄναξ, *simpliciter*, in the *vocative* of address, without appendages or regimen, was used specially of Apollo. It is found so, twice, in the Achilleid (Π 514, 523), but in Ulyssean cantos it is five times given to a hero (B 284, 360, I 33, 276, Ψ 588, apart from T 177), in the Odyssey thrice to a hero (Od. λ 71, 144, 561), and once to another God than Apollo (ε 450). A further departure from hieratic usage is seen in the frequency with which the word is, as it were, secularized to signify *master* or *owner* of *property* (Ψ 417, 446, 517, Ω 734, and in the Odyssey in such as α 397, and many other examples). This coordination is confirmed by the use of ἀνάσσω as applied to *things*, viz. in B 108 (with a general

---

[37] On Δημήτερος ἀκτή in Achilleid and ἀκτή without Δημήτερος elsewhere, see afterwards § 117, γ.

class-name νήσοισι), and in Od. with δώμασιν and κτεάτεσσιν, as in a 117 and δ 93.

(6) Ἡΰκομος seems to have belonged properly to Goddesses. It is given to Athene, Heré, Leto, Thetis, and in the Odyssey to Calypso. These usages may be said to be 'diffused.' Helen is the only *mortal* who is so styled in the Achilleid. Her traditional position, however, is so lofty that, although the author of the Achilleid does not style her anywhere 'a daughter of Jove,' and is not specially rapt into admiration regarding her (cp. § 87), he so far associates her with Goddesses. Mere mortals get the epithet ἠΰκομος only in Ulyssean cantos, as Briseis in B 689, and Niobe in Ω 466.

(7) Ἀμβροσίη [38] in Achilleid is chiefly, if not entirely, an *unguent* used by the celestials. Four, if not five, instances are producible (Π 670, 680, Τ 38, 347, 353). No other clear instance exists of this older sense, except that ἀμβρόσιος as adj. occurs in Ψ 187, to which Od. δ 445 presents an analogy. The newer sense of 'celestial *food*' is found with clearness only in the neozoic portion, viz. E 777 (for Heré's steeds), and Od. ε 93, 199, μ 63. (In E 369 and N 35, the presence of εἶδαρ = 'food,' makes evidence from them doubtful.)

The state of the case appears thus to be :—

	Ach.	Ul.	Od.
ἀμβροσίη as 'odorous unguent'	5	1	1
„ as 'food for celestials'	0	1	3.

(8) The solemn expression ἐπ' ὀφρύσι νεῦσε is confined in the Achilleid to the nod of Zeus. It occurs there twice (A 528, P 209). In the Ulyssean canto (I 616), it is given to Achilles, and, as if to put Ulysses on the same high pedestal as Achilles, once in Od. φ 431 (cp. ι 468). To none else is it given, even to Zeus, except once to Athene (π 164).

(9) Ἀργυρότοξος is nowhere applied but to Apollo. It sometimes stands independent as virtually a Proper name. At other times it is an epithet and has Ἀπόλλων subjoined. It is only in the Ulyssean cantos and Odyssey that it occurs as an epithet, and is divested of its lofty independence.

[38] In Hesiod (Theog. 640) it is defined, along with νέκταρ, as the food of the gods. In the Hymn to Demeter (238), ἀμβροσίη is found in its archaic Achillean sense (χρίεσκ' ἀμβροσίῃ). It is remarkable that 'unguents' are a feature of celestial life in the Vedic mythology.

	Ach.	Ul.	Od.
Ἀργυρότοξος alone, as Proper name	3	2	0
„ with Ἀπόλλων, as Epithet	0	6	3 [38].

(10) Themis, in the Achilleid, is concerned only with the assemblies of Gods (O 87, Υ 4). In the Odyssey, she is concerned with the assemblies of Men (β 68).

As a counterpart against these (in round numbers, seventy-four) instances of deflection in hieratic words, I find no example exactly parallel in the usage of the Achilleid. These are the nearest. The phrase χεῖρες ἄαπτοι, which seems hieratic regarding Zeus (A 567, Θ 450), is also frequently given to *heroes* in Achilleid (Λ 169, N 77, 318, Π 244, P 638, Υ 503). Beyond the Achilleid it is given *only* to heroes, viz. in H 309, Od. λ 502, χ 70, 248. Also the epithet κελαινεφής, given to Zeus, is bestowed on αἷμα, even in the Achilleid, as Ξ 437, Π 667, Φ 167, and this is its sole application in the Ulyssean area (Δ 140, E 798). (Regarding ἐρίγδουπος, see § 122. 5.)

As a corollary confirming the whole argument, it is significant of advancing freedom in the treatment of divine personalities that hardly any *formal* comparisons are instituted between them and individuals in the Achilleid, but these emerge not unfrequently when we pass beyond its zone. Hence, with the exception of Ares in such as N 298 (cp. X 132), and the doubtful instance of Aphrodite in T 282, the gods are not employed to furnish mythologic similes in the Achilleid (δαίμονι ἶσος not being of an individual god), but elsewhere they serve to supply material for comparison. Whether from the commencement of artistic, possibly sculptured, representations of the gods supplying such similes, or from a greater freedom of treatment than was possible under the old unplastic Pelasgian (§ 111. fin.) time of the Greek religion, these comparisons become more frequent in the newer area. In proof may be mentioned B 478, H 208, and Od. ζ 102, perhaps Z 513. Compare also I 386, Ω 699, Od. δ 122, ρ 37, τ 54, all neozoic.

---

[38] The instances when it is an epithet are very broadly distributed, B 766, E 449, 760, II 58, K 515, Ω 758, and Od. η 64, ο 410, ρ 251. It is due to the ingenuity and acuteness of Mr. Fleay, the Shakspere critic, to state, that, by an analysis of the localities of this and other epithets, he had arrived at nearly the same conclusions regarding the Homeric poems, and this by research entirely independent of mine, about the time when my views were first published upon the subject.

CHAPTER XIII.

ARCHAICA—PSYCHOLOGY AND ETHICS.

εἴδομεν ἥν τινα μῆτιν ἐνὶ στήθεσσι κέκευθεν.

THE next branch of the subject brings us to examine the Psychology and Ethics of the Homeric Poems. It is hardly to be supposed that any so marked differentiation is possible in this region as in that of mythology, but the following are the most important cognate phenomena.

107. *In the Achilleid we find a psychology which is mainly corporeal, a conception of Human Life more physical and material, whereas beyond the Achilleid there is an indication of greater freedom in the conception of it, as more exempt from physical and material conditions.*

The keynote to the psychology of the Achilleid is found in the opening Proem, where, among the dire things to flow from the wrath of Achilles, we hear of 'the souls of heroes hurled to Hades, and *themselves* made the prey of dogs and fowls of the air.' It is clear from this that the author of the Achilleid regarded the Body as the Man's self, the proper αὐτός constituting individuality[1]. This view is kept

---

[1] There is no departure from this view, though occasionally αὐτός is taken to mean the body as opposed to its armour, as in P 163.—Whately has referred to this feature of the oldest Homeric psychology as diametrically opposite to the Christian conception. 'We should be apt to say that such a man's body is here, and that *he*, properly the man himself, is departed to the other world; but Homer uses the very opposite language in speaking of the heroes slain before Troy; viz. that their souls were despatched to Hades, and that *they themselves* were left a prey to dogs and birds' (Essay on Peculiarities of Christian Religion). The arc traversed by the human mind between these two conceptions can be best measured by the contrast of Iliad A 3 and the lines of Prudentius on a Christian martyr: 'Sic *corpus; ast ipsum* Dei Sedes receptum continet,' the one utterance at the

up by him throughout and reappears at the close, in X 351, where cp. Doederlein. In the Odyssey and Ulyssean books, on the other hand, while there still remains a certain conformity to the primitive Achillean conception, as in Ψ 65, we find indications appearing that point to a higher psychology and to a feeling that the Mind is the Man, in a nearer stricter sense than the Body. This expresses itself in the magnificent passage to which we shall afterwards have occasion to refer, of the 'Heart' writhing like a hound in the leash and commanded to be under law and self-restraint (Od υ 13, where the 'Heart' must be taken to mean the whole emotional *physical* frame). The man himself, the αὐτός, is spoken of as having this κραδίη, or 'heart,' under control, and though we hear of this αὐτός as ἑλισσόμενος ἔνθα καὶ ἔνθα, we must understand this not so much of physical as of mental condition, as is shown by the poet's own interpretation, μερμηρίζων (υ 28), not to mention that, if a *physical* sense is given to ἑλίσσετο, the behaviour thus imputed to Ulysses might have led to a discovery and to death as the consequence [2]. Again, the remarkable expression in the mouth of Apollo (Ω 54), κωφὴ γαῖα, as applied to the body of Hector, indicates a point of view different from that implied in the αὐτός of the Achilleid.

The exit of the soul or spirit is more than once represented, in the Achilleid, as taking place *through* a wound. The soul flies out at the opening made by the sword, and four examples are quoted by Nägelsbach of this phenomenon, all Achillean (Ξ 518, Π 504, 856, X 362). How far the author of the non-Achillean

opening, the other at the close, of the old Ethnic Literature. Cp. the Sanskrit 'âtman,' *soul*, also *self*, and its exact psychological parallel, the Hebrew *nephesh*.

[2] There is one passage in the present text of the Odyssey which, if we could bring it into evidence, would demonstrate the matter. It is that concerning the εἴδωλον of Heracles dwelling in Hades, whereas the αὐτός is expressly said to be in high estate with the gods (λ 602–3). A mode of thought has thus begun which seems a midway step between the Achillean position and that of Pindar, who contrasts the bodily remains of Heracles with the emancipated αὐτός of the Hero (Nem. i. 100). This passage about Heracles, though it comes in not inappropriately at the close of the entire procession of the Shades—he being the greatest of the heroes—is, however, generally regarded as a later interpolation.—There is some ground for believing that νέκυς, which is usually *corpse*, and always so in the Achilleid, begins to receive elsewhere the sense of 'shade,' and therefore is disembodied, e.g. in Π 409, and frequently in the Odyssey. Even νεκρός undergoes the same transference in Od. κ 526. Compare the parallel as to καμόντες, in § 103 ε.

cantos has attained to a different view may be doubtful. In one instance he speaks of the soul in death as 'quitting the portal of the teeth' (I 409), but this may be understood of a natural death, where there is no wound necessarily involved. Both poets speak of the soul leaving 'the limbs,' N 672, II 607, X 68, 362 parallel to II 131, Ψ 880, Od. λ 201, ο 354, and leaving 'the bones,' M 386 and Π 743, conformably to Od. γ 455, λ 221, etc. Still the circumstance that nowhere do we find in the Ulyssean cantos and the Odyssey the notion of the soul 'flying out at a *wound*,' seems to mark a more hoary antiquity to the Achilleid. The grim remark by Gibbon that Jupiter of the Iliad in his lament for Sarpedon shows an imperfect idea of the happiness of a future state, and a melancholy ignorance of the consolations of Elysium, finds a certain justification in the fact that it is in the Achilleid that the *silence* as to Elysium, and generally as to a future life (cp. § 103, ε), prevails.

It is worthy of note, as to the corporeal character of the Achillean psychology, that the word φρένες is still mainly physical and has scarcely disengaged itself from its primary physical sense. Such a sense it bears manifestly in the expression ἦτορ ἐνὶ φρεσί, occurring only in Θ 413, Π 242, P 111, Τ 169 (?), and in φρένες ἀμφιμέλαιναι, occurring in A 103, P 83, 499, 573, all Achillean[3]. As attached to verbs of knowledge and perception, it is found subjoined to ἔγνω (sc. φρεσὶν ᾗσιν), four times in Achilleid (A 333, Θ 446, Π 530, X 296), whereas ἔγνω elsewhere dispenses with that defining addition[4]. Though the Achilleid has in various passages this verb γιγνώσκω alone, the fact of the adherence of φρεσίν in a manner so marked, is a note of antiquity. The only similar instances of archaic usage outside the Achilleid seem to be ἔλπομαι ἐνὶ φρεσί Od. ι 419 (cp. κατὰ θυμόν in K 355)[5], and σύνθεο (σύνθετο) θυμῷ (in Od. ο 27, τ 268, compare II 44 and Od. α 328), whereas σύνθεο, which already stands

---

[3] Φρεσὶν ἦτορ in Od. ν 320, and φρένες ἀμφιμέλαιναι in Od. δ 661, both break down as examples, being found in obelised passages.

[4] So ἔγνω has added to it κατὰ θυμὸν ἀμύμονα in Π 119.

[5] As balancing this counter-instance in Odyssey (ι 419), may be given the case of τρομέω in Achilleid, with φρεσί attached (O 627). In Ulyssean cantos and Odyssey τρομέω is frequently used, but without any defining addition, except in K 492, where κατὰ θυμόν is appended, and we hear of φρένες τρομέοντο in K 10.

independent in A 76, as well as in Z 334, comes up in Odyssey five times *without* θυμῷ (ο 317, π 259, ρ 153, σ 128, υ 92).

The state of the case regarding φρήν and φρένες is remarkably confirmed by the evidence as to the rival word πραπίδες, which has passed through similar modifications. In its physical, anatomical sense, as a part of the human frame, it is *confined* to the Achilleid, of which use there are three examples, Λ 578, N 412, and P 349. It is found applied in the higher sense (mental or emotional), in the Achilleid, also; but in the Odyssey and Ulyssean cantos it is nowhere physical and occurs *only* in the higher application. Here also the Achilleid exhibits the clearest trace of primitive feature.

Any further arguments on this head are more linguistic than psychological, and must be reserved until another opportunity, when the Homeric vocabulary comes more directly under review.

108. The foregoing observations, however, will have prepared the way for our entering on the evidences of greater antiquity appearing in the ethical feeling of the Achilleid as compared with that of the rest of the Homeric ' corpus.' We have already touched on this point so far in previous sections (§§ 67, 84), when dealing with the character of Achilles and with the humour of the Achilleid. It now remains to follow out the proof in greater detail.

The Achilleid, while characterised by intensity and concentration, is also marked by fierceness and a certain grim revelry in blood and wounds. Though the Ulyssean Cantos and Odyssey are not without traces of the same fierce power, they are mellowed by rays of a tenderer tone which are all but absent from the Achilleid.

The epithet βροτολοιγός is one of the most formidable in the Homeric vocabulary. It is given to Ares and is frequent in both areas, but in the one it is a simple affix describing the character of the god, as in E 909, and under a feeling of repulsion; in the Achilleid it is ' encomiastic,' being used in comparisons for the purpose of bringing out in stronger relief the character of certain heroes, *without* any feeling of repulsion. The expression βροτολοιγῷ ἶσος Ἄρηι is only Achillean; twice of Hector, once of Achilles, and once of Leonteus, two *Thessalian* heroes. To these may be added as parallel similes, Θ 349 of

Hector and N 298 of Idomeneus. We may, therefore, from the treatment of this word alone, be prepared for a greater outburst of the grim and terrible within the region of the Achilleid.

The tenderness which shrinks from scenes of slaughter may be said to be confined to the Ulyssean sections and the Odyssey. It is a remarkable harmony of sentiment that has produced the withdrawal of Penelope by the device of slumber (φ 358) during the slaughter scene of the Odyssey, and makes Priam retire from witnessing the combat in which Paris is to be engaged (Γ 306), because he cannot 'endure to witness it with his eyes.' The Priam of the Achilleid, however, is made to look down, no doubt not without emotion, but still with less sensitivity, upon the final scene in which Hector falls (X 25), a divergence, not to say discrepancy, from the Priam of Γ, which was remarked and commented on by the ancient Scholiasts (Γ 306).

Accordingly, it is in the Achillean books that the delight in the description of blood and wounds is found to culminate. There is a certain anatomical delight in the circumstantials of death which casts a lurid gleam over the Achillean cantos. It is there only that we hear (α) of the sword 'warmed' with blood (Π 333, Υ 476), and the wounded warrior with his 'entrails' lacerated in his dying agony (ἔντερα in N 507, P 314, Ξ 517, Υ 418, 420). So (β) the analogous word ἔγκατα figures mainly in Achillean scenes (Λ 176, 438, P 64), and there as a normal feature. Elsewhere it is introduced as a graver touch only in scenes *abnormally* terrible, as in Od. ι 293, μ 363, and possibly Σ 583. Again, (γ) the convulsive clutching of the ground by dying warriors, whether with teeth or hands, is a comparatively *normal* feature of the Achilleid. The Ulyssean cantos have two instances with ὀδάξ (B 418, Ω 738, cp. E 75, not including Λ 748), against probably two in the Achilleid (X 17 and T 61), whereas the Achilleid has, *besides* these, two *formulæ* all its own, ἕλε γαῖαν ἀγοστῷ occurring five times, and κόνιος δεδραγμένος αἱματοέσσης, occurring twice. Which side does the Odyssey take in this case? It seems carefully to avoid the specially Achillean formulæ and adopts the formula of the Ulyssean cantos with ὀδάξ, which, in conformity with its greater softness of tone, it uses only once, viz. in χ 269. Its affinity is thus clearly manifest.

Also (δ) the slapping of one's thighs in agony ($\pi\epsilon\pi\lambda\dot{\eta}\gamma\epsilon\tau o$ $\mu\dot{\eta}\rho\omega$), which Heyne (on O 113) characterises as 'hominum rudiorum more,' a gesture with which the much less sensitive Romans were offended in the oratory of Caius Gracchus, is almost limited to the Achilleid, occurring four times against one elsewhere (in Od. ν 198). Again, (ε) for the insanity of grief ('insanus dolor,' Heyne) we naturally turn to the Achilleid (Σ 22, where see Heyne). The expression (ζ) $\nu\eta\lambda\epsilon\dot{\epsilon}s$ $\ddot{\eta}\mu\alpha\rho$ seems a favourite with the Achillean poet. He uses it seven times as against two occurrences in the much larger non-Achillean area (Od. θ 525, ι 17). Lastly, incidents (η, θ, ι, κ, λ) of the peculiarly horrible in the battle-field are these from the Achilleid. (1) Playing at bowls, as it were, ($\sigma\phi\alpha\iota\rho\eta\delta\dot{o}\nu$) with the severed head of a foe (N 204), or with the severed trunk, tumbling it like a mortar (Λ 147), or splitting the severed head and holding it up on a pole 'like a poppy-head' (Ξ 499). (2) Using a dead body, as a butcher uses his block (Λ 261, ubi Schol.). (3) Dismembering a fallen warrior by the wheels of a chariot (Υ 394). (4) Inflicting of gratuitous wounds (X 375)[6]. (5) Wanton cruelty in dragging the dead body of a foe at the wheels of one's chariot (X 397)[7]. *All these acts are attributed without scruple to Grecian warriors.* Thus nearly twelve examples of *atrocia*[8] are producible from the Achilleid, some of them unique in cruelty. Against these it would be difficult to put in array anything fairly parallel out of the much larger area of the rest of the poems. The slaughter of the sleeping Thracians at night in K 484 is probably the most repulsive act outside the Achilleid, and the

---

[6] The stabbing of the dead Hector by the other Greeks is the only example of needless wounds in either poem; (Gladst., Juv. Mundi, p. 380 and Blackie, Iliad, i. p. 161).—Falstaff's treatment of the dead Hotspur is a parallel on the English stage.

[7] The Scholiast on X 397 states that this was a Thessalian custom down into the historic time. The occurrence of the same cruelty in Ω 15 is merely the repetition of the same, in conformity with the tradition. It is narrated but not necessarily there approved.

[8] The instances of apparent 'cannibalism,' at least in *metaphorical* language, belong to both sections. The worst, however, is Achillean, viz. X 347. Zeus it is true, in Δ 35, *taunts* Here with cannibal propensities, but the reproach by an adversary is not so damnatory as the uttered threat. As for Hecuba's wild word in Ω 212, it is not to be pressed any more than Beatrice's cannibal-like exclamation in ' Much Ado about Nothing' (iv. sc. 1); 'O that I were a man, I would eat his heart in the market-place,' or Theognis's about his foes, $\tau\hat{\omega}\nu$ $\epsilon\dot{\iota}\eta$ $\mu\dot{\epsilon}\lambda\alpha\nu$ $\alpha\dot{\iota}\mu\alpha$ $\pi\iota\epsilon\hat{\iota}\nu$ (l. 349).

punishment of the scoundrel Melanthius and of the female slaves as well as of the Suitors in the Odyssey is no doubt grim and terrible, but so is every execution of retributive justice[9]. Trampling on the breast of a fallen warrior to extract one's spear is found in E 620 and Z 65, and Ulysses does so to a stag (κ 164), but the same phenomenon occurs thrice in the smaller area of the Achilleid (Ν 618, Η 503. 863). Thus, in cases where the dark feature belongs to both sections, the intensity of the darkness is found concentrated in the Achilleid. The stripping of the slain, for example, as an actual occurrence in the battle-field, is almost confined to the Achilleid. It is forbidden by Nestor in Ζ 71 for strategic rather than humane reasons, and, though in a previous book (Δ 466) Elephenor indulges in the practice *before* Nestor's warning, Diomed does so in a book now standing subsequent, viz. Λ (368–73). The latter, however, is in the Achillean area. So the archaic expression τεύχεα δ' ἐξενάριξε[10], as describing an actual feature of contemporary battle, belongs only to the Achilleid, where it occurs thrice (Ν 619, P 537, Φ 183). In Η 146 it is only in a *narrative* and belongs there to an ante-Trojan scene.

109. Among the evidences of inhumanity is to be included the custom of the victor to shout over the dead or the wounded a yell of triumph. The word for *bluster and imprecation* of this Goliath sort is specially ἀρειή. It occurs thrice, and only in the Achilleid. The state of the case in regard to this whole point is of peculiar interest, because it so happens that we have in the Odyssey an authoritative declaration, expressing what must be taken as the poet's own feeling on the point. In the mouth of the hero, but substantially as from the poet himself, is found the following remarkable utterance :—

οὐχ ὁσίη κταμένοισιν ἐπ' ἀνδράσιν εὐχετάασθαι (Od. χ 412).

' 'Tis an impious thing over men that are slain to utter the vaunt of Pride.'

This is the moral verdict of the Odyssey, where it is sub-

---

[9] The case of Agamemnon's cruelty to Adrastus in Z 37–65 will come under review in a subsequent section.

[10] Τεύχεα συλῆσαι belongs to both areas, and continued into the historic time.— As regards mutilation by cutting off ears or noses, Laomedon in Φ 455 may balance Echetus in Od. σ 86. Both are practically outside the Hellenic area. The word δεικίζω occurs five times in Achilleid, thrice elsewhere, with an appropriate preponderance, therefore, in the Achillean area.

stantially sustained [11], and a criterion or touchstone is thus supplied to us of the utmost value and security. When we turn to the Iliad what do we find? One large tract in which the maxim is maintained, one large tract in which it is abundantly violated [12]. The former is the region of the Ulyssean cantos, the latter, where it is violated, the Achilleid.

In the Achilleid the victor, as a rule, breaks out into a 'loud boast' over his victim (ἐπεύξατο μακρὸν ἀύσας), sometimes into a 'tremendous yell' (ἔκπαγλον ἐπεύξατο). Achilles, e. g. does so at the slaying of Hector.

The instances in the Achilleid of this verb ἐπεύχομαι in this sense amount to *sixteen*, and that too without distinction of race, for Greeks as well as Trojans are so described, and the act is one quite normal in the former (M 391). How many are producible from the Ulyssean cantos? None, in the case of a Greek [13], and only one in the case of a Trojan, who turns out to be the detested Pandarus, represented as ἐπευχό-

[11] There is an exception in the Odyssey (χ 286), but it goes to prove the rule. 1. It is antecedent to the utterance of Ulysses. 2. It is over the most brutal of the Suitors (Ctesippus). 3. It is in the mouth of the rustic herdsman.—Similar remark applies to the case in χ 194.

[12] Mr. Grote (Hist. of Gr. ii. p. 125), remarking on the traces of humane feeling dawning among the Greek people, calls attention to this memorable utterance (Od. χ 412), but adds, ' It is an ethical maxim abundantly violated in the Iliad.' If he had said, ' abundantly violated in the Achilleid,' he would have touched the marrow of the matter and so discerned an important proof of that division of the Iliad, which he may be said to have been the first to divine. The normal feeling of the Achilleid is expressed in the Goliath threat κορέεις κύνας ἠδ' οἰωνούς, of which more in a subsequent section (§ 129). It occurs *thrice* and only in that area.

[13] 'Επευξάμενος in K 367 is not in point, as it is directed not so much against the victim as against a rival claimant of the spoil. The presence of εὐχωλή alongside of οἰμωγή in the general description of a battle (Δ 451) is an ancient form surviving from the Achilleid (Θ 64), and is too vague to form a valid exception to the above argument, which concerns the case of *individual* warriors. Neither is the censure of εὐχωλή in P 19 in point, for when examined, it resolves itself into a general condemnation of excessive boasting and does not stigmatise in the same way as the line in the Odyssey (χ 412) condemns the offensive form of it, that over the dead. Moreover it is in the mouth of Menelaus, who himself indulges in the εὐχωλή, forbidden by the Odyssey, under harsh circumstances to his victim (N 619).—An historical analogy to the εὐχωλή of the Achillean area may be discerned in the conduct of the Thebans. The exaltation (ἐπιχαίρειν) over their victims, of which they make no secret (Thuc. iii. 67) is in conformity with their character as ἀναίσθητοι (Demosth.), and it is in such an Æolo-Dorian and *non*-Ionian region that we expect to find *survivals* of Achillean sentiment in the historic time. Compare the kindred behaviour of Romulus over Remus (' *verbis* quoque increpitans,' Livy), and Queen Tomyris over the head of Cyrus.

μένος (E 119), no doubt to render him more detestable [14]. It is a clear proof that we are on scientific ground in these investigations, to find that we have such a crucial confirmation of our theory, in respect that the idiosyncrasy of feeling expressing itself thus directly and palpably in the Odyssey can be clearly detected in the Ulyssean books of the Iliad and *in none beyond*, so that we may say regarding the union of the Odyssey and Ulyssean cantos—

$$\tau\hat{\omega}\nu\delta' \ \dot{\epsilon}\phi\acute{\eta}\lambda\omega\tau\alpha\iota \ \tau o\rho\hat{\omega}s$$
$$\gamma\acute{o}\mu\phi os \ \delta\iota\alpha\mu\pi\acute{a}\xi, \ \dot{\omega}s \ \mu\acute{\epsilon}\nu\epsilon\iota\nu \ \dot{a}\rho\alpha\rho\acute{o}\tau\omega s.$$

As if to render assurance doubly sure, this maxim of Ulysses in the Odyssey, abundantly violated by other warriors, is violated by Ulysses himself (Λ 449) [15]; but it is the Ulysses of the Achilleid, who appears entirely ignorant of the ethical injunction of the Ulysses of the Odyssey, and so shouts lustily over a fallen foe. The inference seems inevitable that we have in the Iliad two distinct strata of authorship, one conformable to the Odyssey, the other not conformable.

110. Parallel to this fact is another of almost equal significance. The same pathetic feeling which has mitigated and even expelled the inhuman boast over the dead at the close of a combat, has modified the war-whoop indulged in at the opening of a battle. The Achillean poet makes no distinction, or at least no marked distinction, between Greeks and Trojans in this respect. With him, *both* hosts indulge in a huge roar

---

[14] The nature of Pandarus's punishment seems to suggest that he was punished for his boasting as well as for his treachery (γλῶσσαν πρυμνὴν τάμε χαλκὸς ἀτειρής = 'the *tongue to the root* was shorn away by the ruthless bronze,' E 292). The Scholiast on Λ 146 cites it as an instance of *appropriate* retribution. Compare Dante (Inferno, c. 28), where he represents Curio, 'who spake that hardy word' impelling Cæsar to his bold deed, as having his *tongue* cut from his throat.—The case of Pedæus, losing his tongue (in E 74), seems to have no such significance.

[15] The Scholiast, on Od. χ 412, is sorely troubled to obtain consistency between the conduct of the Ulysses in Il. Λ 449 and the Ulysses of Od. χ 412, and tries to twist εὐχετάασθαι to another sense than *boast*, viz. to *offer supplication*!—Hermann is struck by the prevalence of the ἐπεύχομαι utterance in N, and remarks ' Accedit illud in hoc carmine memorabile quod qui aliquem occiderunt fere aliquid gloriandi causa dicunt; quo hoc carmen, a caeteris partibus pugnae cui insertum est, insignite distinguitur' (Opusc. v. p. 66). It cannot be said, however, that *insignite* applies to N in this respect, except as contrasted not with the Achilleid but with the Ulyssean cantos.

as they dash upon each other (N 837). In the Ulyssean cantos, however, we find symptoms of an approach to the Hellenic feeling of aftertime and a consciousness dawning of what was proper for Hellenic *ἁρμονία* as against Barbarian harshness and vociferation. One cannot read the opening of Γ, describing the advance of the Trojans as ‘with shouting and screaming, like flocks of cranes,’ while the Greeks are represented as moving on breathing deliberate valour ‘*in silence*,’ without feeling the pulse of the poet's own sympathy in the contrast. The same divergence nationally comes before us under new imagery in Δ 430. It is worth inquiring whether we have not in these touches of Γ and Δ something premonitory of the normal feeling in the Hellenic time, which, while it allowed *βοή* upon proper occasions, postulated, in general, silence and self-control as among the virtues of the warrior (Thuc. ii. 89).

Accordingly we find in these Ulyssean books a distinct diminution of the vocabulary of vociferation [16]. Nowhere do we

[16] Among the chief facts are the following :—

1. General expressions.

	Ach.	Ul.	Od.	Ach.	Ul.	Od.
βοὴ ἄσβεστος	6	0	0			
βοὴ βριήπυος	1	0	0			
ἤχῃ θεσπεσίῃ	6	1	2		Ψ 213 (winds)	γ 150 (Greeks, a sign of confusion) λ 632 (shades)
ἐνοπή	4	3	1	.	Γ 2, Κ 13, Ω 160 (only of Trojans)	κ 147 (in Circe's isle)
αὐίαχος	1	0	0			
ἀτειρέα φωνήν	3	0	0			
	21	4	3			
2. κεκληγώς, etc.	8	2	3	Λ 168 (Ag.)	Thersites in B 222 Hector in E 591	μ 408, Zephyr ξ 30, dogs μ 256, Scylla's victims
3. αὔω and derivatives.						
ἀῠτέω	4	0	0			
ἀῠτή	17	7	4		2 (?) Greeks	ζ 122, λ 382, ξ 265 ρ 434
αὖε	4	0	0			
ἤῠσε	9	1	0	6 Greeks	E 784 (Heré)	
ἄῠσε…σαν, etc.	22	8	2		4 Trojans 4 Greeks	ζ 117 (in Phaeacia), ι 65 (funereal)
	56	16	6			

In Od. α 369 we find the recommendation *μηδὲ βοητὺς ἔστω*. The above will show that it is an injunction practically observed. Od. θ 305 is nowise normal.

meet with ἰαχή or the like, attributed to a Greek *individual* warrior in battle, and even the Trojans seem in this region less vociferous, except that σμερδαλέα ἰάχων occurs once of Æneas (E 302). The occurrence of Δ 506 is the only exception as to the Greeks occurring on the battle-field. It follows on an exploit of Ulysses, and it is not clear that it is not like the same phrase in B 333 and 394, the expression of praise by way of cheer to Ulysses. In the Greek camp, the ἰαχή is usual as the expression of praise at the close of a speech (I 50), in contrast with the κέλαδος[17] of the Trojans.

This paucity, almost absence, of instances in the Ulyssean books contrasts with the large number in the Achilleid. Without enumerating Trojan instances, thirteen cases may be reckoned up of ἰαχή from a *Greek* warrior. The σμερδαλέα ἰάχων, given in the Ulyssean books to no Greek and only once to a Trojan, is now ascribed to Achilles (Υ 285, 382, 443), and even Ulysses of the Achilleid resorts to the ἰαχή (Λ 463) in crying for help. The whole body of Greeks is spoken of as οὖλον κεκληγῶτες in P 759, as if indulging in a κλαγγή like birds, after a fashion which the Ulyssean poet (Γ 2) confines to the Trojans and denies expressly to the Greeks.

Again, on this line of proof, as on previous lines, we have found the Achilleid presenting barbaric and palæozoic features, the line of demarcation between Greek and barbarian (cp. § 61) being less sharply drawn, whereas in the Ulyssean cantos and in the Odyssey we have found the neozoic and specially Hellenic features emerging simultaneously and concurrently.

---

[17] As in Θ 542 and Σ 310. The Greeks indulge in κέλαδος once at Teucer's feat (Ψ 869). Aristarchus (on N 41) remarked that as a rule the Trojans were represented as more tumultuous (ἑκάστοτε γὰρ θορυβώδεῖς τοὺς Τρῶας παρίστησι). The proof of such a proposition is found almost entirely in the Ulyssean Books, more sparingly in the Achillean Books.—The Athene of the Hesiodic Theogony (926) delights in κέλαδοι, a feature in which, as in many others, the Achillean poet and the Hesiodic go together as against the Ulyssean. Cp. remarks on Athene in § 103.—Regarding Artemis and her epithet κελαδεινή, it is in favour of our position generally on this head, that the epithet emerges only in the Achilleid, where it occurs *thrice*, while the less boisterous non-Achilleid presents no example of it.

CHAPTER XIV.

ARCHAICA—MANNERS AND CUSTOMS AND SOCIAL APPLIANCES.

ἔργα τ' ἐπίστασθαι περικαλλέα καὶ φρένας ἐσθλάς.

111. THE evidence from Manners and Customs will now come under review.

If it can be shown that the Odyssey represents on the whole a newer and later platform of social arrangements, and that the Ulyssean books presuppose the same platform as the Odyssey, while the Achilleid exhibits an older social type, or the same social type at an older stage, further important light will be derived upon the whole question.

In entering upon this part of the subject we light upon some of the favourite arguments of the Chorizontes, who thought they saw signs of greater refinement in social life in the Odyssey and asserted that an interval of some generations was necessary to account for the rudeness and barbaric splendour in the one poem, the luxury and taste in the other. Examples of the rudeness they had no difficulty in producing from the Achilleid; but they ignored or slurred over the signs of luxury and refinement in other parts of the Iliad, and so they never proved their case except in half, which was equivalent to 'not proven.'

112. A.—ARCHITECTURE.

It was argued, for example, that in the Odyssey the palaces of Menelaus at Sparta and of Ulysses at Ithaca are described as possessing considerable pretensions to architectural display. In particular, we find these grander houses possessed of three leading divisions, (1) the court or αὐλή, (2) the hall of the men, (3) the apartments of the women. Hence in Od. χ 494, at the purgation of the whole house, it is described by its three constituents,

$$εὖ\ διεθείωσαν\ μέγαρον\ καὶ\ δῶμα\ καὶ\ αὐλήν,$$

a triple division that partly repeats itself in the palace of Alcinous (θ 57),

$$πλῆντο\ δ'\ ἄρ'\ αἴθουσαί\ τε\ καὶ\ ἔρκεα\ καὶ\ δόμοι\ ἀνδρῶν,$$

where ἔρκεα answers to αὐλή in the former passage, δόμοι to δῶμα, and instead of the μέγαρον of the women, which from the circumstances of the latter case would be inappropriate and is omitted, there appears, as a third balancing member, αἴθουσαι, i.e. the αἴθουσα αὐλῆς and the αἴθουσα δώματος.

Is there any parallel instance of a house of this amplitude in the Iliad? There is, in a Ulyssean book, viz. Z (l. 316), where we find the house of Paris represented as possessing the same component parts there styled,

$$θάλαμον\ καὶ\ δῶμα\ καὶ\ αὐλήν,$$

where δῶμα, according to the Scholiast *ad loc.*, is the hall of the men, and θάλαμος naturally falls to the other sex.

There is nothing of a similar kind fairly producible from the Achilleid. Jove's palace with surrounding θάλαμοι (in Α 76; cp. Α 606), resembles in this particular feature the style of Priam's in Z 242 (as Heyne on Il. Ξ 167 affirms), but we look in vain for the same triple *graduation* of parts in a single building belonging to the Achillean time.

The Achilleid is also sparing in the vocabulary of architectural dignity and ornament. Thus loftiness of structure will be found more frequently referred to without than within the Achilleid. Three examples occur in Achilleid of this feature against eight in the smaller area of the Ulyssean cantos, a proportion which is much augmented in the Odyssey[1]. Then

---

[1] The chief facts on this point are these:—

	Ach.	Ul.	Od.	Ach.	Ul.
ὑψηλός applied to δῶμα or δόμος	2	3	Freq.		
ὑψερεφής ,, ,,	1	2	9	Τ 333	Γ 213
ὑψηρεφής ,, ,,					Ι 578
ὑψόροφος ,, ,,	0	3	6		
	3	8	15 +		

Lord Aberdeen (Essay on Grecian Architecture, p. 112) doubted whether in the times

again, the *Epitheta ornantia*, or terms denoting refinement of material[2] in the construction or fineness of effect are thus distributed, as e. g. :—

	Ach.	Ul.	Od.
κηώεις of a chamber	o	3	1
κέδρινος ,,	o	1	o (κέδρος known in Od. ε 60)
ἀγάκλυτος of δώματα	o	o	4
ἠχήεντα of δώματα	o	o	1
ἐρίδουπος of αἴθουσα	o	1	6
αἰθαλόεν of μέλαθρον	o	1	1
τέγεος[3] of θάλαμος	o	1	o
	o	7	13.

It may be doubted whether the Achillean poet knows of the artistic treatment of stone. He describes well what may be called the Cyclopean style of architecture, apparently without cement and not necessarily *isodomous* (Π 210). It is true he once mentions ξεστός in referring to the αἴθουσαι[3] of Jove's palace (Υ 11), but this is rare compared with the frequency with which this term—usually of timber-work—is elsewhere applied to *stone*-work, viz. four times in Ulyssean parts (Z 243-4-8, Σ 504) and as often in Od. (γ 406, θ 6, κ 211, 253).

In general, however, architectural terms become much more frequent, when we go beyond the Achilleid, as, e. g. :—

	Ach.	Ul.	Od.
αἴθουσα	1	5	12
πρόδομος	o	2	6
ὑπερώιον ⎫ ὑπερῷον ⎭	1	1	19
θριγκός and derivatives	o	o	3
κίων (pillar)	o	o	frequent.

The familiarity with architectural terms is thus· found to increase when once we leave the Achilleid for the Ulyssean cantos. It is true that the Ulyssean cantos do not equal the

---

of the Iliad there were upper stories, and the passages with ὑπερῷον occurring he suspected of interpolation. It occurs *once* in each section of the Iliad (Π 184 and B 514). It is frequent in the Odyssey.

[2] In χαρίεντ' ἐπὶ νηὸν ἔρεψα Λ 39, the probability is that χαρίεντ' is not a descriptive epithet of νηός, but an adverbial adjunct to ἔρεψα.

[3] Although τέγεος as adj. is not found in the Odyssey, there is an equivalent for it of frequent occurrence, viz. τέγεος πύκα ποιητοῖο (Od. α 333 and other four times).—αἰθαλόεν in B 415, is probably not strictly ornamental.

proportion contained in the Odyssey, but there is no real disproportion when we remember that the Ulyssean cantos are only half the area of the Odyssey and that their theme is less concerned with the *domestica*, and consequently gives less scope for such phraseology. On the other hand, it is difficult to understand the rarity of such terms in Achillean cantos, which ought, under a common authorship, to present the same proportion of occurrences as the Ulyssean cantos, since the theme is in both the same.

It has sometimes been doubted whether the Homeric Greeks were acquainted with statues of the gods, and it would certainly be difficult to establish their existence from the Achilleid. As with the Romans in the time of Numa, there seem to have been no statues or images of the gods in the Achillean time, and this finds corroboration in the account Herodotus gives of the old Pelasgian worship (Π 52). Whatever be the truth as to images [4], there is evidence of greater elaboration in the structure of temples when we enter the Ulyssean area, for there we hear not only of placing a votive offering 'on the knees of a goddess,' an expression implying some kind of statue, but we read of a ναός of Apollo where there is a subdivision called an ἄδυτον (E 446 and cp. Η 83), in other words, an inner shrine, such as in later times was regarded as appropriate to oracles and mysteries.

Reviewing the evidence on this head, we come to the conclusion that the Achilleid is not on the same platform of architectural advancement as the Ulyssean cantos and the Odyssey, while these last keep each other in countenance and in the main stand upon an equality.

112*. B.—HOUSE FURNITURE AND DRESS.

That a certain richness of terms describing the furniture of a house and the appliances of a domestic establishment appears in the non-Achillean parts is not difficult to show. While θρόνος and θρῆνυς belong to both areas, it is noticeable how large a number of terms for *chair*,

---

[4] The figures of δράκοντες in Λ 26, if the part is genuine, would imply formative art in some form in the Achillean area.

indicating different varieties, comes up outside the Achillean area.

	Ach.	Ul.	Od.
κλισμός	2	2	11
κλισίη (= chair)	0	0	2[5]
κλιντήρ	0	0	1
δίφρος (= chair	0	3	3.

So in regard to couches and bedsteads, especially with epithets of artistic elaboration.

	Ach.	Ul.	Od.
δέμνια	0	2	12
τρητοῖς λεχέεσσι	0	2	5
λέχει ἀσκητῷ	0	0	1
πύκινον λέχος	0	2	4
δινωτοῖσι[6] λέχεσσι	0	1	0.

Respecting decorative coverlets, etc.

	Ach.	Ul.	Od.
τάπης[7]	1	4	5
ῥήγεα	0	2	14
κῶας	0	1	12
λίνοιο λεπτὸν ἄωτον, } for	0	1	0
οἰὸς ἄωτον } sleeping	0	0	1.

As to articles of dress, apart from the essential χιτών (with its compound χαλκοχίτων, and also στρεπτὸς χιτών), and apart from the archaic ἑανός, which are common to both areas of the Iliad, the vocabulary becomes more largely illustrated when we pass beyond the Achilleid.

	Ach.	Ul.	Od.
χλαῖνα	1	7	51
φᾶρος	2	2	20
παρδαλέη	0	2	0
πέπλος	1	10	5
ἑλκεσίπεπλος	1	2	0
κροκόπεπλος	2	2	0.

---

[5] Κλισίη (= *chair*) in Od. δ 123, τ 55.

[6] Δινωτός is of a *shield* in Achilleid (N 407), and therefore *warlike*. The artistic decoration of the Ulyssean cantos and Odyssey appropriates it to furniture, in the one to a κλισίη or chair for reclining (τ 56), in the other to a bedstead (Γ 391), therefore in both, *domestic*. The kindred artistic term ἀμφιδινέω occurs,

Ach.	Ul.	Od.
0	1	1.

[7] The τάπης of the Achilleid (Π 224) is called οὖλος, ' of thick wool,' i.e. without decoration. Beyond the Achilleid, it begins to receive *decorative* epithets, πορφύρεος being added to it in I 200, and Od. υ 150.

	Ach.	Ul.	Od.
τανύπεπλος	o	1	4
εὔπεπλος	o	5	2
ὀθόναι	o	2	1
σπεῖρον (as robe)	o	o	4
πῖλος	o	1	o.

As to shoes or sandals, besides ὑποδήματα twice in Odyssey, we hear once in the Achilleid of καλὰ πέδιλα, but they belong to Heré. In the Odyssey and Ulyssean cantos (without counting χρυσοπέδιλος of λ 604), the καλὰ πέδιλα are more frequently given to men than to gods.

	Ach.	Ul.	Od.
καλὰ πέδιλα to deities	1	1	2
„ „ to men	o	3	5

Other domestic appliances.

	Ach.	Ul.	Od.
πρόχοος	o	1	7
κρητήρ [8]	3	11	27
λέβης [9]	2	8	14
δάος [10]	o	1	4
δαΐδες	o	1	9
λαμπτήρ	o	o	3
ἀσάμινθος	o	1	9
ποδάνιπτρα	o	o	2
τάλαρος	o	1	2
κάνεον	o	2[11]	11
πείρινς	o	2	2.

A considerable preponderance, therefore, of terms indicating

[8] Achilles in the great libation-ceremony of Π 226 seems to have only a δέπας, but he is credited with a κρητήρ as well as δέπας in the Ulyssean books (Ι 202, Ψ 219). In the libation-ceremony of Γ 295, mention is made both of δέπας and κρητήρ, and we may infer the same in the libation of Κ 578. The κρητήρ with κύπελλα is present in Olympus in Α 598.

[9] Τρίπους belongs to all sections, and so ἄγγος.

[10] The Achilleid knows of δεταί, 'faggots' (Λ 553, Ρ 663), occurring twice, but it is not for domestic use; it is part of *huntsman's* weapons in dealing with wild beasts,—another note of archaic time. So δαλός (torch) is twice *warlike* in Achilleid, twice *domestic* in Odyssey.—A minor argument of a modern Chorizont (Ed. Rev., April 1871, p. 368) was to affirm a knowledge of chimneys in the Odyssey (σ 27), to deny them to the Iliad. Yet it is proper to observe that the fire where Patroclus roasted the food in Ι 212 is lit *coram*, and so implies a smoke-exit of some kind, and that the expression κάπνισσαν κατὰ κλισίας of Β 399 seems to imply that the fires of the camp were not outside the κλισίαι. It is accordingly in two *Ulyssean* books that we meet with those indications of presumable approximation to the social arrangements of the Odyssey.

[11] Omitting the debatable Λ 629.

a variety of domestic resources and appliances appears in the Odyssey, and to a certain extent also in the Ulyssean books; a comparative paucity of such terms is noticeable in the Achilleid. Much of this divergence may, however, be due to the nature of the respective poems and to the subject with which they severally deal [12], and the argument is not one on which much stress could be laid in the absence of more relevant and prevailing ones. At the same time the contrast between the two sections of the Iliad, in regard to richness of domestic appliances, is very marked, and, seeing that these sections deal both with a common subject, it is difficult to explain, on any other theory than that we are expounding, the affinity subsisting between the Ulyssean cantos and the Odyssey, and the disparity of both from the Achilleid.

113. C.—General Artistic Advancement.

I. First, in Colour.

According to the speculations of Drs. Geiger and Magnus, commented on by Mr. Gladstone ('Nineteenth Century,' Oct. 1877), the sense of positive colour is only gradually attained by the races of mankind and the perception of distinctions between the primary colours is slowly acquired. Without presuming to pronounce on the truth or ultimate value of these speculations, we can certainly affirm that there is a richer development or efflorescence of epithets suggestive of positive colour occurring in the neozoic portions of these poems. The Achilleid, while recognising brilliancy and general effects of *light,* as in παμφανόων, σιγαλόεις, and the like, equally with the non-Achillean sections, is almost devoid of terms for the finer specialising of colour, such as come up in the neozoic area. Even where the same artistic term appears in both sections, the range of its application is found greatly widened outside the Achillean area, as e. g. πολυδαίδαλος only of *arms* in Achilleid, in Ulyssean cantos of *arms* and a κλισμός, in Odyssey of θάλαμος, χρυσός, ὅρμος.

---

[12] The Odyssey, from the nature of its subject, contains a good many nautical and also domestic terms peculiar to itself. Among these last are λήκυθος, κάλπις, κισσύβιον, χοῖνιξ, πύελος, κλῖμαξ, ἔντεα δαιτός, etc., but the presence of these is easily intelligible from the subject of the story.

In the Achilleid ships are known almost entirely as *black*, with hardly any other indication of colour. Elsewhere, we meet with traces of decoration, for, alongside of the typical μέλαιναι νῆες, descriptive of the whole hull of the vessel, we read of ships having a part, such as the prow, lit up with positive colour. The contrast is very marked, inasmuch as it is the ships of the same chief (Ulysses) that figure only as *black* in the Achilleid (Θ 222, Λ 5), but appear with features of colour superadded, alike in the Ulyssean area (B 637) and in the Odyssey.

	Ach.	Ul.	Od.
κυανόπρωρος[13] (once -ειος Od. γ 299) .	1	2	10
μιλτοπάρηος	0	1	1
φοινικοπάρηος	0	0	2.

In vestments, and objects of art, the epithets of colour and decoration multiply in the neozoic sections.

	Ach.	Ul.	Od.
πορφύρεος (of *textures*) .	1	3	8
ἁλιπόρφυρος (,,) .	0	0	3
φοινικόεις[14] (,,) . .	0	1	2
ἰοδνεφής (of wool) . . .	0	0	2
ἀνθεμόεις (of scenery and art-objects)	0	3	2
ἀγλαός in ἀγλαὰ ἔργα . .	0	0	5
κλυτά, ἀμύμονα, περικαλλέα ἔργα .	1	3	3.

The effect of *variegation* in colour is expressed by ποικίλος. This belongs, even in metaphorical usages, as ποικιλομήτης,

---

[13] Κυανόπρωρος, though it came to suggest *colour*, probably signified originally the metallic *substance* (κύανος) with which the prows of ships were armed or decorated.

[14] The reading σιγαλόεντα has rightly displaced φοινικόεντα from Il. Θ 116.— A chorizontic argument from this item of colour was recently advanced (Ed. Review, April 1871), that because χλαῖνα has got the epithet πορφύρεος in the Odyssey, there was an artistic advance separating it by a long interval from the Iliad, where there is no such epithet. The conclusion was a rash one, partly because we find other vestments in the Iliad having the epithet (Γ 126), partly because χλαῖνα appears with a *parallel* epithet φοινικόεσσα in a certain canto (K 133), which turns out, however, to be Ulyssean, and is kept in countenance by Od. ξ 500, and φ 118. Like other arguments of the Chorizontes it is wrested from their hands and converted to support a different theory. After all, the argument would not have been a very powerful one, even although φοινικόεσσα with χλαῖνα had not appeared opportunely to show its futility. It would have been more to the purpose to have pressed an argument from the presence of ἁλιπόρφυρος in the Odyssey and its absence in the Iliad, but this too would be quite fallacious, inasmuch as the Odyssey brings us more in contact with maritime life and the sphere of Phœnician commerce, which was famous for the production of rich dyes, and so affords ampler scope for the occurrence of such productions.

both to the Achillean and to the Ulyssean sections. The various *derivatives* of the word, however, implying *elaboration*, so as to produce richness of effect by variegated colour, belong to the neozoic section.

	Ach.	Ul.	Od.
ποικίλλω	0	1	0
ποίκιλμα	0	1	1
παμποίκιλος	0	1	1.

II. Second, in Rare Material.

Gold, silver, bronze, and, under certain conditions, iron, seem to be familiar in both areas. Even tin (or the metal indicated by κασσίτερος), and κύανος, whatever it may be, are also diffused. But there are certain precious substances used in artistic works, which we find come up only in Ulyssean books and the Odyssey, and in these as if contemporaneously and simultaneously. These are—

	Ach.	Ul.	Od.
ἤλεκτρος [15] (metallic)	0	0	1
„ (amber)	0	0	2
ἐλέφας (ivory)	0	2	8.

Along with these, as suggestive of foreign intercourse, may be reckoned

	Ach.	Ul.	Od.
βύβλος in βύβλινα ὅπλα	0	0	1
φοίνιξ (palm-tree, cp. § 117, 8).	0	0	1.

[15] Ἤλεκτρος (which is the more probable form of *nominative* on analogy of other metals, such as χρυσός, etc., which are masculine) as an ornament for walls of houses is identified by Lepsius (Die Metalle, Berlin, 1872) with the *asem* of the hieroglyphics, which was a mixture of gold and silver. The canto where it occurs is full of allusions to intercourse with Egypt. The *plural* use of ἤλεκτρος is, however, generally supposed to denote *amber-beads*. Both meanings of ἤλεκτρος are referable to an external source, the one to Egyptian, the other to Phoenician intercourse.—Some think that *amber* is the sole sense of ἤλεκτρος, and appeal to δ 73, as indicating that gold and amber made a kindred combination in colour parallel to that made by another pair, viz. silver and ivory (Dict. of Ant., p. 450). It is remarkable, however, that in the Hissarlik remains Dr. Schliemann has found a mixture of gold and silver, which is considered to answer to ἤλεκτρος.—Although the Odyssey is neozoic in contrast with the Achilleid, it is still very ancient compared with what the Wolfian and Paley theories would allow. A good argument in this direction is the circumstance that ἤλεκτρος as a mixed metal belongs even in Egypt to the ancient period, for according to Lepsius (ibid. p. 48) it ceases about the time of the Psammetichi, 'Schon in der Zeit der Psammetiche ist est kaum noch nachzuweisen.' So the knowledge and memory of it as a *metal* seem to disappear from Greece at an early time, Soph. Antig. 1038 being among its latest acknowledgments (cp. Blakesley on Herod. i. 50), but the Odyssey must have been in shape long before that disappearance.

As an epilogue under this head, it is especially important to weigh the evidence from the occurrences of ἐλέφας or ivory. It is remarkable that the earliest efforts at artistic decoration by *colour*, within the circle of Greek experience, connect themselves with a *material* procurable only through Phœnician sources. The most elaborate description in Homer of artifice in colour is the operation by ' the Carian or Mæonian woman ' of staining *ivory* with purple dye (Δ 141), and it comes up, naturally, in a Ulyssean canto. It is not at all likely that the Greeks had any supply of fossil ivory from mammoth tusks, and the familiar mention of it must, therefore, be attributed to intercourse with Phœnicians, with whom it was an article of commerce. Taken in conjunction with the whole strain of the evidence, it forms an impregnable argument for the truth of our main position as to a double stratum in the Iliad, that ἐλέφας, which means only *ivory* in the Homeric poems, and was therefore procurable only from without, should appear so familiarly in both the non-Achillean sections, where we have found the horizon to be wide, but not once in the Achillean, where the horizon must be admitted to be confined [16]. Yet the uses to which that substance was put in the Homeric age were very various, as has been well stated by Merry on Od. θ 404, his citations being an interplay of Ulyssean and Odyssean references : ' Ivory is described in Homer as in use for chamber decoration (Od. 4. 73) ; as material for a scabbard (4. 404) ; for a key (21. 7) ; for the ornamentation of reins (Il. 5. 583) : of a couch (Od. 19. 55) ; of a bedstead (Od. 23. 200) ; of the headgear of a horse, dyed or painted red (Il. 4. 141).' Ivory had in fact become so familiar that it could be introduced into an allegorical representation as to Truth and Falsity (τ 564), and, as coming to the Greeks through the hands of a cunning and too clever race, was taken to serve as the symbol of Un-veracity.—The Hesiodic corpus, with its circumscription of view, presents only one occurrence of *ivory* (viz. Scut. Herc. 141).

---

[16] It is not unimportant to note that in the Semitic area a similar progression as to the use of Ivory is discernible. In the oldest Hebrew literature it seems unknown ; after a time it appears first as a rarity, then in profusion. Solomon's ivory *throne* is a marvel ; but Ahab builds an ivory *house*, i. e. adorned with it, and in Amos (8th cent. B.C. . we read of *couches* (vi. 4) and *houses* of ivory (iii. 15) as if now common.

The special expressions for gaming come up mainly in the Ulyssean area, or in that of the Odyssey. The most prominent are—

	Ach.	Ul.	Od.
ἀστράγαλοι (in gaming) . .	0	1	0
πεσσοί	0	0	1
δίσκος	0	2	0
σόλος	0	3	0
σφαῖρα	1	0	1
cp. ἐψιάομαι	0	0	2.

So, in the generic expressions for *sport* in general, there is a large preponderance in the same direction.

	Ach.	Ul.	Od.
ἄθυρμα and ἀθύρω . . .	2	0	2
∫ παίζω	0	0	5
⎨ φιλοπαίγμων	0	0	1.

Also, while mere *tumbling* (κυβιστάω), like ἀτάλλω, is found in both sections, *dancing*, properly so called, belongs mainly to the neozoic area.

	Ach.	Ul.	Od.
ὀρχέομαι and derivatives . .	3	2	12
βητάρμων	0	0	2.

115. E.—Comfort and Diet.

Among the most remarkable traces of antiquity in the Achilleid is the astonishing disregard of all that men now consider personal comfort and even sanitary safety. Plato makes much mirth out of the fine healthy condition of the heroes who when wounded are treated to a bowl of wine without suffering any inflammatory consequences, and among other customs that would make a modern physician stare is the practice of drying themselves, when hot and perspiring, by standing in the wind.

> ‘Their tunics sweat-imbued they ventilated.’—Cowper.

Of this last there are three examples, *all in the Achilleid*, viz. Λ 621, Χ 2, Φ 561. Whether, by the time of the Ulyssean poet, the Greeks had changed their hygiene in this respect does not appear; at all events no such hard usage of the Spartan kind comes up outside the Achilleid.   On the other hand, the appliances for domestic comfort are distinctly multiplied in the neozoic area; the bath, even the warm bath (ϑ 450), comes into prominence (cp. ἀσάμινθος in § 112). and Nestor in K 75, and Phœnix in I 621, 659, both repose 'in a soft couch,' of which we hear nowhere else in the Iliad except in X 504, occurring, however, in the Odyssey, χ 196.

	Ach.	Ul.	Od.
εἰνὴ μαλακή . .	o	3	1.

Hence it is not strange that we should come upon an abstract term equivalent to *luxury*, viz. θαλίη. It is found only in the neozoic area, viz. in I 143 (repeated in I 285), and in a doubtful passage in λ 602. A similar advance is marked by the negative term for *want* of comfort, ἀκομιστίη, in φ 284. Compare with this the remarkable analogy as to the distribution of the epithets of Sleep in a later section (§ 183).

Regarding *diet* there is not much to remark, except that (a) *salt* appears as an article of food only in the neozoic area, (β) that 'accompaniments' to give 'relish' to food there begin to be known as ὄψον,

	Ach.	Ul.	Od.	Ul.	Od.
ἅλς (in eating)	o	1	3	I 214	λ 123, ρ 455, ψ 270
ὄψον [17]	o	1	3	I 485	γ 480, ε 267, ζ 77.

It would appear that fish as an article of diet was not much prized by the Homeric heroes, any more than by the Ossianic, and it was long ago a remark of Eubulus, the comic poet (Athenæus, 25, cp. Plato, Rep. iii. p. 404 B), that the Homeric heroes did not at Troy, at all events, though with the Hellespont near, make fish an article of food. The evidence is not conclusive in favour of the comic poet's negation.   In the Achilleid, although fish eat men (Φ 123), we have no very clear instances of men eating fish, but we find the following traces. (a) It describes a mode of fishing, by line and metal instrument, with some detail, of which more afterwards in § 117 β. (β) It speaks of a 'fish-abounding' river (Υ 392). The Ulyssean

---

[17] The occurrence of ὄψον in Λ 629 is probably to be added to the Ulyssean enumeration.

cantos and Odyssey have, however, more and clearer traces. Capture (α) by a net (probably, though not certainly, a *fishing*-net, rather than a *hunting*-net, E 487) [18] ; (β) fish as food in desperate straits (Od. δ 368, μ 331); (γ) the sea praised as furnishing fish to make a land happy (τ 113), and (ε) capture of fish with a casting-net (χ 384). It would be rash to conclude from these incidental notices anything except simply that the Odyssey seems to show a superiority in appliances for the capture of fish, and in frequency of their use as food. This, however, is in favour of a strong Ionian element in that poem, and, accordingly, E. Curtius, in his History (i. 157), finds a contrast between the maritime or Ionian and the inland Greeks in this matter of food [19]. 'The former,' he remarks, 'fed principally on fish, which the latter disliked : accordingly the Ionian bard never wearies in insisting upon the mighty *meat*-banquets of the Achæans.'

116. F.—HOSPITALITY.

The prominence attaching to the virtue of Hospitality outside the Achillean area is a noticeable feature, and, a fact is thus furnished, which, though insufficient of itself to build a structure, supplies a stone to the building. The wider outlook and larger horizon of the Odyssey prepare us for a considerable development in this direction. What is to be noted is that the Ulyssean cantos quite go along with the Odyssey rather than with the Achilleid in this respect. Though hospitality is exercised in the Achilleid, it has not yet assumed a form so systematic as it did afterwards, when it had a certain code of usages attaching to it, modifying even the exigencies

---

[18] Athenæus (25 c) accepts it of *fishing* only.

[19] I have not made use of a possible argument from the archaic use of *ἱερός* as applied to a fish in Π (407). It was once supposed that because fish were called *ἱεροί*, there was some religious scruple preventing their use as food, and hence was explained their supposed absence from the table in Homeric times. It is true that a very effectual as well as not unusual device forbidding the use of any creature as food has been to assign it a place among sacred animals, but it is doubtful whether this notion can be here sustained. The sense of 'holy' or 'sacred' is now given up in the above passage, and we must give the word a primitive sense, which would make it equivalent to its Sanskrit congener *ishiras* and so signify *fresh, lively, agile*, an archaic sense suitable to the Achillean passage.

of war (ἔγχεα δ' ἀλλήλων ἀλεώμεθα Ζ 226), or when, as in the
Odyssey, the 'hospitable board' is included among the sanc-
tions of an oath (ξ 158, ρ 155, υ 230) and the 'Guest' is spoken
of as standing in the relation of a 'Brother' (ο 546). The commencement of this condition has indeed begun, for we hear of
Ζεὺς Ξείνιος, but we have to go outside the Achilleid for the
development of the rich vocabulary attaching to the hospitable
relationship. Thus the special verb ξενίζω, so frequent in the
Odyssey, comes up thrice in the Iliad, but only in Ulyssean
parts, Γ 207, 232, and Ζ 174[20]. Ξεινοσύνη, φιλόξεινος and
κακόξεινος belong to the richer vocabulary of the Odyssey,
the subject of which naturally brings up such expressions; but
it is to be noted that while Ξεῖνος, like the Latin *Hospes*, has
to do duty in the Achillean part, both as 'host' (O 532), and
as 'guest,' the Odyssey, while retaining traces of this old
usage as θ 166, 208, and ξ 53, has a special and unambiguous
term for the *active* relation of 'host,' viz. ξεινοδόκος, occurring
five times. This specialised term emerges also in the Ulyssean
area, viz. Γ 354, a remarkable confirmation of the soundness of
our general position. The inference is further strengthened
by the parallel circumstance that the expression φιλότητα
παρασχεῖν comes up simultaneously in the Odyssey and
Ulyssean cantos to signify the offering of hospitality. Compare Γ 354 (where Schol. explains φιλότης by ξενία) with
Od. ο 55, 158. Further, ξεῖνος, in the neozoic area, comes to
signify 'foreign folk' simply, as in Ω 202 and Od. ρ 485, for
which ξεῖνος in Δ 387 as 'stranger' is a preparation.

	Ach.	Ul.	Od.
ξενίζω	o	3	6
ξεινοσύνη	o	o	1
φιλόξεινος	o	o	4
κακόξεινος	o	o	1
ξεινοδόκος [21]	o	1	5
φιλότητα παρασχεῖν . .	o	1	2
ξεῖνος as 'stranger,' and ξεῖνοι			
as 'foreign folk' . .	o	2	1
Add θοινηθῆναι (δ 36) . . .	o	o	1.

[20] The less definite φιλέω seems to serve in the Achilleid as the expression for
hospitality, viz. in N 627, an application continued also in the Ulyssean cantos and
Odyssey. In Od. ξ 322 we find ξεινίσαι ἠδὲ φιλῆσαι combined, as in Γ 207.

[21] Ξεινοδόκος also in Hesiod, Op. 183.—Πολύξεινος as proper name in Il. B, and as
epithet in Hesiod, Op. 713, 720.

(a) The Achilleid exhibits, with all its rudeness, a social condition far removed above the savage state. In its camplife, we already hear of *physicians* or ' healers with many drugs ' (Π 28), and something like a commissariat class, *dispensers of food*, as distinct from the warriors (Τ 44). There are also walled towns, fortifications [22] for camps, and rich cities ($\pi i \epsilon \iota \rho a \iota$ $\pi \acute{o} \lambda \epsilon \iota s$ Σ 342); there is metallurgy to a certain extent, and there is agriculture, with the formation of a plough by art ($\pi \eta \kappa \tau \grave{o} \nu$ $\check{a} \rho o \tau \rho o \nu$ Ν 703), and the regular production of cereals by tillage. In one instance we catch a trace of what seems the operation of breaking up and dividing a ' common ' (Μ 422). Irrigation is also known (Φ 257), likewise threshing (by feet of oxen as in Υ 495), winnowing as in Ν 590, but there is no mention of manure except in the Odyssey. So, Art, in the sense of the *artificer's*, is known in the Achilleid, and we hear of $\tau \acute{e} \kappa \tau \omega \nu$, $\kappa \lambda \upsilon \tau o \tau \acute{e} \chi \nu \eta s$, and even, in a metaphorical sense, $\kappa a \kappa \acute{o} \tau \epsilon \chi \nu o s$. The more advanced derivatives of $\tau \acute{e} \kappa \tau \omega \nu$ and $\tau \acute{e} \chi \nu \eta$, however, belong to the Ulyssean area and the Odyssey.

	Ach.	Ul.	Od.
$\tau \epsilon \kappa \tau a \acute{\iota} \nu o \mu a \iota$ $\pi a \rho a \tau \epsilon \kappa \tau a \acute{\iota} \nu o \mu a \iota$	1	2	1
$\tau \epsilon \kappa \tau o \sigma \acute{\iota} \nu \eta$	0	0	1
$\tau \epsilon \chi \nu \acute{a} o \mu a \iota$	0	1	3
$\tau \epsilon \chi \nu \acute{\eta} \epsilon \iota s$	0	0	2
$\tau \epsilon \chi \nu \eta \acute{e} \nu \tau \omega s$	0	0	1.

The hunting and fishing stage of the Savage, the pastoral stage of the Nomad, in so far as these may have formed part of the experience of the Greek people, have therefore both been left behind. A few of the great groups of stars have received names; the Achillean poet knows of Orion and his

[22] It is singular that the most important term in ancient fortification, $\check{e} \pi a \lambda \xi \iota s$ (with its verb $\check{e} \pi a \lambda \acute{e} \xi \omega$, which is found twice), should be confined to the Achilleid, but there it occurs *ten* times. It may be said, however, that the mention of $\check{e} \pi \acute{a} \lambda \xi \epsilon \iota s$ could not come till after the construction of the wall of the Greek camp, which is true, and accounts so far for the phenomenon; but it is strange that the poet of Il. who describes that construction, makes no mention of the $\check{e} \pi \acute{a} \lambda \xi \epsilon \iota s$, so prominent in the Achillean narrative. It is corroborative to find that the cognate $\check{e} \pi a \lambda \acute{e} \xi \omega$ seems confined to the Achilleid, where it occurs, with or without tmesis, at least thrice. The local distribution of this word $\check{e} \pi a \lambda \xi \iota s$ is thus very remarkable.

Dog. The Ulyssean poet *adds* a few names to the astronomical nomenclature; but there is this notable fact that while
the star-names are still mainly associated with hunting, there
is, in the neozoic area, a cluster of *synonyms* or double names
now arising, which are taken not from hunting but from
agriculture. The 'Bear' is now found to have a super-name
the 'Wain; the 'Bearwarden' appears as the 'Ox-driver'
(Boôtes); that is to say, to the hunter's name there has been
added the husbandman's name for the great northern constel-
lation ("Ἄμαξα in Σ 487, ε 272; Boôtes in ε 272). A certain
interval would be required for the rise and spread of this
second series of names, and the Achilleid, in which the agricultural names of the stars are absent, must be held to reflect
the features of an older period.

At this point it may be proper to introduce a singular circumstance in regard to the Reckoning of Time. The Achilleid
seems hardly to know any other term for a 'year' than the
archaic and somewhat indefinite term ἐνιαυτός. In the
Odyssey and Ulyssean cantos, while ἐνιαυτός is still familiar,
there is large use made of the younger and seemingly more
definite ἔτος. This last was the term that ultimately came to
the front and became the Hellenic term for a 'year,' to the
exclusion of its rival, in which last we probably discern a
cousin of the Latin *annus.* The traces of the rivalry are
discernible in the neozoic area, but ἐνιαυτός is dominant,
without a rival, in the palæozoic. The occurrences of ἔτος are—

	Ach.	Ul.	Od.
ἔτος simple	0	3 [23]	14
„ compound	0	4 [24]	15
	0	7	29.

Regarding the divisions of the *diurnal* revolution, it is
worth noting that while the Achilleid exhibits the division of
Day into three parts (Φ 111), the Night seems to be as yet

[23] Including Λ 691.

[24] The occurrence of εἰνάετες in Σ 400 favours the conclusion that the close of
that canto is Ulyssean.—Regarding the displacement of ἐνιαυτός by ἔτος, it might
be worth inquiring whether a rectification or adjustment of the Calendar had not
taken place in Greece similar to what we are traditionally told took place among
the sister race of the old Italians, when the old year of ten months had to be dis-
carded. Compare Hesiod, Theog. 59, where ἐνιαυτός seems to mean no more than
a *ten* month cycle.

undivided.   In the Ulyssean area and in the Odyssey, however, we hear of the division of Night into three sections, or watches (K 253, Od. μ 312).   This is an advance, although the division seems to us an awkward one.   It had the advantage of allowing not indeed a middle point but a *middle section* in the division.   The Orientals had in early time the same division (cp. Old Test., Judges vii. 19 and 'Records of the Past,' i. p. 158).   In after time the division into four watches was found more convenient; and in the Roman time became predominant (New Test., Mark xiii. 35).   The Homeric division of the Night, though in the neozoic area, is, therefore, still archaic.

(β) We have already touched upon the appliances for fishing in § 115.   It is interesting to note that while all modes, rude as well as ingenious, appear in the Odyssey and Ulyssean cantos, only a rude and primitive mode appears in the Achilleid.   Thus, we hear only in the former, of fishing by *hooks* (ἄγκιστρα Od. δ 369, perhaps μ 332), with ingenious contrivance of a horn-sheath to keep the line from being bitten through (κέρας in Ω 80 as in Od. μ 251), and the device of nets seems in ordinary use (χ 384 and probably E 487).   In the Achilleid, whether by accident or otherwise, if we may judge from the singular simile in Π 407, as interpreted by the act of war it shadows forth, the mode of fishing seems to have been by *spear* and line, rather than by *hook* and line, and, if so, was a sort of 'harpooning,' a mode of action which the Odyssey relegates to savage Læstrygonian regions (κ 124)[25].

(γ) Among the inventions which afford a criterion of time, may be reckoned the *preparation* of CORN, according as it is by the use of ὄλμοι (*mortars*) or μύλαι (*millstones*).   Apart from the case of the Μολίονε and the mention of μύλαξ in the somewhat questionable passage (M 161), it is doubtful

---

[25] The Ed. Reviewer (April 1871) founds a Chorizontic argument on Π 407, and adduces the example of the Arowauk Indians, who follow the exact mode described, and stand on crags or boulders to fling prongs or darts with strings attached, at the finny tribe as they swim along.   The argument is a fair one rightly used, but it is capable of serving another division than that of the Chorizontes.— The stress is to be laid less upon the fact itself than the circumstance that it occurs in the portion *otherwise* judged to be archaic.   As a mode of fishing, ἰχθυβολία seems to have survived, even among the Greek race, down into the period of the Anthology, and the Trident of Poseidon seems a relic of the archaic time.

if any clear instance of the use of the *millstone* is discernible
in the Achilleid. The method then seems to have been by
the mortar and pestle, much as in Hesiod, who in this respect
appears on a less advanced platform of the arts[26]. Hence
the occurrence of ὅλμος (Λ 147 = *mortar*), only in the Achilleid.
So the archaic phrase Δημήτερος ἀκτή is found only in that
old area, an expression which belongs to the ὅλμος period
rather than to the μύλη period, though ἀκτή continued long as
a poetic expression down into the later time, often without the
hieratic addition (Δημήτερος) being subjoined. On the other
hand, the indications of grinding by means of stones made
to revolve, i. e. by μύλη, come up frequently, at least in the
Odyssey, while those of the other mode seem to disappear.

Palæozoic mode.

	Ach.	Ul.	Od.
ὅλμος	1	0	0
ὀλοί-τροχος (?)	1	0	0
Δημήτερος ἀκτή	2	0	0
	4	0	0.

Neozoic mode.

	Ach.	Ul.	Od.
μύλη	0	0	4
μυλοειδής	0	1	0
? μύλαξ (M 161)	1	0	0
μυλήφατος	0	0	1
ἀκτή[27] without Δημήτερος	0	0	2
ἀλέω[28] and derivatives	0	0	3
	1	1	10.

Thus the balance of archaism under these heads is decidedly
in favour of the Achilleid. The greater richness of terms in
the Odyssey, compared with the Ulyssean cantos, is explicable
by the nature of its theme, as bringing us more into the
region of *domestica*.

[26] Hence βίος ἀληλεμένος continued, in the Attic time, to signify a *civilised* life.

[27] The occurrence of ἀκτή with ἱερός still attached, in Λ 632, is probably Ulyssean. Cp. occurrence of ὄψον and § 115.

[28] The ἀλετρίς works at the μύλαι (υ 105), and therefore, in the Odyssey, we may
regard ἀλέω and its derivatives as indicating the neozoic mode.—In O. T., Numbers,
ch. xi. 8, mills and mortars are contemporaneous.—There is some difficulty as to
ἀλοιάω and ἀπ-αλοιάω, each of which occurs once in Ulyssean parts, whether the
reference is to grinding or perhaps rather to *threshing*, a view which is favoured
by the ancient occurrence of ἀλωή, a *threshing* floor, where oxen had been used to
tread out the corn. These, therefore, have not been used as evidence.

N

(δ) ARBORICULTURE, in relation to fruit-yielding trees, is distinctly more prominent in the Odyssey. In the Achilleid, though κῆποι and ὄρχατοι are familiar (Φ 258, Ξ 123), the prevailing 'feeling' as to landscape is one of forest wildness, a feature to which I shall afterwards have occasion to refer (§ 148); we need to go elsewhere to find distinct traces of the *training* of fruit-yielding trees. The gardens of Alcinous are rich in trees that are ἀγλαόκαρποι, including pear trees and apple trees, fig trees and vines, pomegranates and olive trees. So likewise, though we do not lay much stress on the fact, it may be considered significant that the *palm tree*, probably of Phœnician origin, comes up once in the Odyssey (ζ 163), and though *wine*, by its name οἶνος, belongs to all parts of the Homeric poems, the name for *vine* (ἄμπελος) is strangely limited to the neozoic area [29]. The Achilleid acknowledges the old Indo-Germanic word οἶνος, but not the new and specially *Hellenic* word ἄμπελος, which last marks a vine-culture peculiar to the Greek race alone. The ἀλωή of Σ and the Odyssey clearly contains vines : it is not so clear that the ἀλωή of the Achilleid contained such [30], at least under the name ἄμπελος.

	Ach.	Ul.	Od.
φοῖνιξ (as *palm-tree*) . .	o	o	1
ἄμπελος and ἀμπελόεις . .	o	4	2.

Regarding forest trees it is to be noted that while ξύλον belongs to both areas, and is especially of *felled* wood (cp. ἄξυλος ὕλη), ὕλη in the Achilleid is only of wood in its *natural* growth, *forest*, whereas in the Ulyssean area (Ψ 50, 111, Od. ι 234) it has attained, without relinquishing this first signification, a secondary one, *timber* or *felled* wood. Accordingly in the same area we find emerging ὑλοτόμος as 'wood-cutter,' an expression not known to the Achilleid, where the sole term is the more primitive δρυτόμος, from a time when the word δρῦς had not become limited to the species of *oak*, but was generic for *tree* [31]. Δρυτόμος therefore which occurs

[29] It is quite possible that the Achillean word for vine had been, like *vitis*, a cognate of οἶνος. Cp. υἱήν· τὴν ἄμπελον Hesych.

[30] Cp. Ebeling's Lexicon on ἀλωή, who gives the order of meanings —' 1. Area. 2. Fundus, ager consitus plantis, hortus. 3. Ager vitibus consitus, vinea.' The examples which he cites of the last (3) are only from the Odyssey.

[31] So δρυμός and δρύοχος, also δόρυ as an *arbor viva* (ζ 167), are relics of a time

twice in the Achilleid, once only beyond, is a relic from a time when the Hellenic variety of the Indo-Germanic speech was still under process of becoming specialised, and had not yet assumed its own peculiar features.

(ε) In regard to the arts of SEWING, SPINNING, WEAVING, and EMBROIDERY, it is not possible to establish any criterion of 'before' and 'after,' inasmuch as these arts, in something like regular hand-fabrics, seem familiar in the oldest cantos. The Achilleid knows of *sewing* or *stitching*, (ῥάπτειν M 296), and so familiar is the operation that it has passed into a metaphorical sense and become applicable to *plotting*, as in Σ 367. Compare κακορραφίη as early as O 16. This latter usage, begun in the Achilleid, is extended in the Odyssey. In the end of M (433), mention is made, in a simile, of a γυνὴ χερνῆτις, who earns a living for her children painfully by 'woolworking.' The antiquity of the simile has been doubted as suggesting rather the wool-manufactures of Miletus in an after time (Bergk, H. of Gr. Lit. p. 412, and cp. Weissenborn in Buchholz, p. 302). The presence, however, of χλαῖναι and other woollen fabrics in the chest of Achilles in Ω, a part which has all the marks of hoary antiquity, is sufficient voucher for a tolerably advanced condition of such arts, and Hesiod (Op. 600) keeps the Achilleid in countenance, when he recommends his model farmer to employ as a servant a female ἔριθος that has no following of children. If ἔριθος is primarily a *wool-worker*, from ἔριον, as the tradition has it, this Hesiodic passage throws light on the Achillean in M 433, and no employment was more feasible for a θῆσσα in a remote time.

One or two circumstances, however, point to a certain differentiation. In the neozoic portion we hear not only of the concrete product, νῆμα, 'spinning,' but of 'fine spinning.'

---

when δρῦς had the Indo-Germanic sense of *tree*, and these remained not only in the palæozoic and the neozoic sections of Homer. but through all Greek literature without specialisation to the *oak*. It is remarkable that the passages where the *simple* word δρῦς seems to retain the pristine Indo-Germanic sense, generic not specific, are Achillean (N 390. Π 483; cp. Aristarchus in Schol. in Λ 86, = πᾶν δένδρον), whereas in Ψ 328 of the Ulyssean area it has become specific. The emergence of the neozoic ὑλοτόμος only in the Ulyssean area, just as δρῦς begins to be specialised, shows the balance of archaism in favour of the Achilleid.

	Ach.	Ul.	Od.
εὔννητος	o	2	1
νῆμα	o	o	3.

So the traces of figure-weaving and embroidery become
more frequent in the neozoic area. Apart from the θρόνα of
X 441, the most important evidence is that of Helen's figure-
weaving in Γ 126, and while κεστὸς ἱμάς is once mentioned in
Ξ in connection with the cincture of the goddess Aphrodite,
we hear of πολύκεστος ἱμάς in connection with the apparel of
a *mortal* in Γ 371.

Again, the art of 'weaving' has become so familiar that it
is taken as symbolical of all 'craftiness,' often in a sinister
sense. This metaphorical use of the verb ὑφαίνω (='weave
plots') with μήδεα, etc., seems not to be found in the Achilleid. The following gives a view of its usages :—

	Ach.	Ul.	Od.
ὑφαίνω (*weave*), literal . .	o	2	7
„ „ metaphl. .	o	4	6
ὑφαντός, ὕφασμα, ὑφάω, literal	o	o	5.

(ζ) In regard to instruments of MUSIC, the neozoic portion
naturally furnishes the greatest number of examples. The
great *stringed* instrument is the φόρμιγξ, whether in Olympus
or in the homes of the heroes. It is varied by the name
κίθαρις. There are also *wind* instruments, none of which,
however, appear in actual use at Troy, except the αὐλός and
σύριγξ, and these only among the Trojans (K 13)[32]. The
φόρμιγξ in Achilles' tent is a prize from *Asiatic* spoils.

<table>
<tr><td rowspan="5">Stringed Instruments.</td><td></td><td></td><td></td><td></td><td>Ach.</td><td>Ul.</td><td>Od.</td></tr>
<tr><td>φόρμιγξ .</td><td>.</td><td>.</td><td>.</td><td>1</td><td>5</td><td>14</td></tr>
<tr><td>κίθαρις .</td><td>.</td><td>.</td><td>.</td><td>1 [33]</td><td>1</td><td>3</td></tr>
<tr><td>κιθαριστύς .</td><td>.</td><td>.</td><td>.</td><td>o</td><td>1</td><td>o</td></tr>
<tr><td>κιθαρίζω .</td><td>.</td><td>.</td><td>.</td><td>o</td><td>1</td><td>o</td></tr>
<tr><td>φορμίζω .</td><td>.</td><td>.</td><td>.</td><td>o</td><td>o</td><td>3</td></tr>
<tr><td></td><td></td><td></td><td></td><td></td><td>2</td><td>8</td><td>20.</td></tr>
</table>

---

[32] The line where κίθαρις occurs in Achilleid (N 731) is doubtful, and has been
expunged by Bekker and La Roche.

[33] Olympiodorus (on Plato, Phædo, p. 18) interprets the presence of the αὐλός as
a sign of greater barbarism, since it is given to the Trojans only, not to the
Greeks, in the Homeric poems. It is probable, however, that this interpretation is
a transference of the feeling regarding the αὐλός out of the historic time back into
the prehistoric, where it had as yet no proper existence.

		Ach.	Ul.	Od.
	Contd.	2	8	20
Wind Instruments. { σάλπιγξ, σαλπίζω . . .		2	0	0
αὐλός		0	2	0
σύριγξ [34]		0	2	0
		4	12	20.

The σάλπιγξ seems to have been introduced among the
Greeks from the West, and, if we may judge by the epithet of
Τυρσηνικός in the Attic time, through the Etrurians or Τυρ-
σηνοί, its reputed inventors (Athen., 184 A). It is remarkable
that it is only in the Achilleid where it appears in Homer,
in the poem which seems to have proceeded from the region of Greece lying nearest to that people geographically [35].
All other instruments and their arts seem to have entered
Greece from the South and East, e.g. the formative arts
symbolised by Dædalus, who appears in Crete [36], and hence
the Odyssey and Ulyssean cantos are the areas where artistic
influence generally is found most diffused.

(η) Under the head of ARMATURE [37], the following facts may
be observed. Fighting with clubs or maces (κορύναι) is traditionally known to the Ulyssean poet as in H 141, but is not
introduced in either section into the actual battle-field. The
use of the *bow* may be regarded as on the whole archaic : it
is given especially to Trojans, but it is found assigned also to
Greeks, and among others to Ulysses himself in certain
supreme moments of his adventures, as in K of Iliad and the

---

[34] Σύριγξ in Achilleid is not a musical instrument, but a 'spear-case' (T 387).
So αὐλός in the Achilleid (cp. αὐλωπίς) is only military, a ' socket of spearhead'
(P 297), a meaning which it retains in the Odyssey (τ 227; cp. ι 156). It is
right to note that these military applications *may* be held to presuppose the
musical. The argument in the text, therefore, is good to show, not that these
musical terms were unknown in the older poem, but only that they have obtained
a greater diffusion in the newer poems.—As to the somewhat savage class of
musical instruments, those viz. of *Percussion*, the sole trace, besides κροταλίζω, seems
to be that latent in ἀνακυμβαλιάζω (Π 379). Both are Achillean.

[35] Talthybius has been explained by Schwenck as equal to Θαλτύβιος, from τηλοῦ
and τύβη, i.e. *tuba*, like τηλέπορόν τι βύαμα (Welck. Ep. Ky. ii. p. 15).

[36] Preller (Gr. M. ii. 345), ' Die älteste Technik dieser Künste [viz. Sculpture
and Architecture] kam den Griechen gewiss *aus dem Orient.*'

[37] In defensive armature, it is singular that πήληξ (probably *waving* helmet with
plumes, from πάλλω) is almost entirely confined to the Achilleid. It occurs there
nine times, and appears only once in Od. α 256, the paucity in the Odyssey being
in harmony with its entire absence from the Ulyssean area.

slaughter-scene of the Odyssey. Apart from these traditional archaisms, it is in the Achilleid that we meet with the really *rude* armature in actual use. Thus ἀξῖναι[38], or 'battle-axes,' we hear of only in that area, viz. N 612 and O 711; and slings (σφενδόναι) appear only in N 599 and 716–8. So, although πέλεκυς is known in all the sections for felling trees and slaughtering animals, it is used *in battle* only in the Achilleid (O 711), and it is in harmony with this to find that κεάζω (=*cleave*) is always of splitting 'skulls' in Achilleid (four times), whereas in the Ulyssean books it does not occur at all, and in the Odyssey is applied, and that not unfrequently, only to the cleaving of 'timber.' It may be noted among the *archaica* under this head that κῆλα is only of the missiles of Zeus or Apollo, and is limited to the Achilleid, where it is found thrice; οὐρίαχος, the ' end ' of a spear, occurs thrice in Achilleid, but elsewhere we hear of σαυρωτήρ (K 153), as the name for the same part of a spear; and ξυστόν, which is five times in Achilleid, is found only once in a Ulyssean canto, but disappears altogether in the Odyssey.

(*0*) Regarding the traces of the Art of WRITING, it would be false to assert that either poem indicates a familiar use of it or even a distinct acquaintance with it. The evidences that it was practically unknown are very strong. We have entered into some of the leading points regarding the question in an appendix. The chief point to be noted here is, that the verb γράφω, which in the historic time signified to *write*, travelled through two stages to reach that signification. The first was, to wound or 'scratch' for aggressive purposes, the second was, to 'mark' or to affix a sign to anything, and the third was, to indicate by alphabetical characters, that is, to *write*. The first of these senses is the only one known to the Achilleid ; the second comes up only outside the Achilleid, and, for sure evidence of the third, we must wait till a period subsequent to the Homeric Epos.

---

[38] Mr. Gladstone (Hom. Synch. p. 47) is inclined to identify the ἀξῖναι with certain *stone* axes found by Dr. Schliemann at Hissarlik. The epithet εὐχαλκος in N 612 seems adverse.

Palæozoic.

	Ach.	Ul.	Od.
γράφω = *scratch* or *wound* .	1	1	0
ἐπιγράφω = *scratch* or *wound* .	2	1	0
ἐπιγράβδην = *as a scratch* .	1	0	0
	4	2	0.

Neozoic.

	Ach.	Ul.	Od.
γράφω = *mark* or affix a sign .	0	1	0
ἐπιγράφω = *mark* . . .	0	1	0
	0	2	0.

Thus the preponderance of the archaic use is with the Achilleid, while the neozoic use belongs to the Ulyssean area.

118. H.—LABOUR AND COMMERCE.

(*a*) Under this head there is not much evidence that can be called decisive, though there is a certain amount that is corroborative. The antiquity of the two Homeric poems necessarily excludes commerce in our sense of the word, and it would be vain to look for traces of such in either epic, seeing that both poems descend from times when there was no *coined* money, when transactions were by exchange *in kind*, and when, as in the Zendavesta, values were reckoned by the worth of *oxen*. Still a preparation may be discerned for the rise of commerce, and an approach to greater specialisation of crafts, or what is called the division of Labour. If our theory is correct, these should appear mainly in the neozoic area. Accordingly, while the τέκτων and χαλκεύς are everywhere acknowledged, since they belong to the fundamental necessities of society, it will be found that the evidence for the existence of the more specialised arts, such as κεραοξόος, the horn-polisher, κεραμεύς, the potter, ἁρματοπηγός, the chariot-maker (cp. σκυτοτόμος, χρυσοχόος), is chiefly drawn from the Ulyssean cantos and the Odyssey. Thus the citations given by Mr. Grote (H. of G. ii. p. 131, n. 1) illustrating the 'crafts' belonging to the society of the Homeric age, are furnished by the neozoic area, viz. Od. ρ 384, τ 135, and Il. Δ 187, Η 221, in which grouping he has unconsciously supplied an argument in favour of his own differentiation of the Achilleid as a separate poem.

(β) Regarding the *initia* of commerce, we find these chiefly in the neozoic area. The Achilleid recognises transactions of sale (cp. ἀπριάτην, ὦνος, περνάμενα), imposts as penalty (θωή), the burden of a ship (ἄχθος), and stores of accumulated precious metal (cp. πολύχρυσος, πολύχαλκος[39]), as well as κτήματα and κτῆσις, also κειμήλια, possessions and property in kind, *substance.* In the Odyssey we hear for the first time of χρήματα, *goods*, for use and disposal, rather than for acquirement (κτῆσις), and, though the word is not yet in its Attic sense of *money, riches*, it is so far on the way to that abstract sense. It so happens that no example of χρήματα in this intermediate meaning of *goods* is producible from the Iliad, and the Chorizontes have used the circumstance as one of their arguments. It is among the best they have advanced, but it is not clear that there is proper ground for differentiation, seeing that in Ψ 834 we find χρήματα virtually present in χρεώμενος, which there signifies 'having *goods* in use.' This, however, occurs in a Ulyssean canto, and so keeps the Odyssey in countenance.

Further, while a rich man is still known as πολύχρυσος and πολύχαλκος, additional designations now appear, and he comes to be styled as πολυκτήμων and πολυπάμων, both in the Ulyssean area (E 613, Δ 433 ; cp. ἀκτήμων, I 126). Mention is made in the Odyssey of a new word for ' burden,' viz. φόρτος, or *cargo*, also, *wares* for traffic (ὀδαῖα), and the *freighting* of a ship is spoken of familiarly in the Ulyssean canto I (137, 279, 358), while we hear, as a feature no doubt advantageous, of certain cities, that they are situated ' near the sea ' (I 153).

Presents for leave to trade (the germ of our *customs duties*) are incidentally noticed in Ι 467–75, and in η 8–11, an interesting link between the Odyssey and Ulyssean cantos. A similar link is the attempt after an *abstract* standard of price or value, without the intervention of *oxen*, discernible in the phrase πολέος δέ οἱ ἄξιον ἔσται. It occurs in Ψ 562 and Od. θ 405, and a similar phrase is in α 318. Not the least remark-

---

[39] It is remarkable that πολυάργυρος does not occur in any of the sections of the Homeric poems.

able is the emergence of δωτίνη in connection with dues to a
superior, very suggestive of the euphemism 'benevolences' in
the middle ages. It comes up only in the Ulyssean canto I,
and *twice* in the Odyssey.

Apart from the indefinite μισθός, which belongs to all
sections, the nearest approach to what we might call *money-
stipulations* is in the mention of ἐπίβαθρον. 'passenger's fee' or
'passage money' (ο 449), but in the Ulyssean canto (I 156)
we have something parallel in τελέουσι θέμιστας, where certain
stipulations are spoken of, which had to be made good to the
ruler by the people in the currency 'in kind' of the time.

We have thus shown under this head, in a number of particulars, a certain conformity between the Odyssey and
Ulyssean cantos. The conformity is all the more remarkable that the subject of the Odyssey brings us so closely in
contact with navigation, and implies considerable intercourse
between different countries and nations, while that of the
Iliad supplies very few points of contact in this respect. Still,
even in the Odyssey, notwithstanding the occurrence of ἐμπο-
λάομαι, πρηκτήρ in sense of *trader* (Lat. *negotiator*), we can
hardly speak of *commerce* as existing, but only a certain rude
traffic, for ἔμπορος is not yet the *merchant*, but simply a *passenger by sea*, any one who travels in another person's ship,
and the words ἐμπόριον and ἐμπορίη [40], which the Greek race
was to send on the tour of the world, are as yet remote.

119. I.—Rites and Formalities.

It might be hazardous to affirm that the social condition
portrayed in the Achillean cantos displays any marked differences from that appearing in the Odyssey and Ulyssean
cantos in respect of religious ritual or state and ceremonial,
certainly not more than can be accounted for by the nature
of either poem. In so far as *barbaric* splendour is concerned,
one might almost give the precedence to the Achilleid, if only
because of the extent to which the element of charioteering
predominates, a point of some importance to which I must

[40] Ἐμπορίη appears first in Hesiod, Op. 644, in sense of *trade.*

afterwards recur (§ 122), but in general we find the balance of archaism preponderating here also in favour of the Achilleid.

(*a*) In comparing the two sections together, although both give great value to omens from the flight of birds, we find the older part assigns a higher position to the professional *auspex*. Thus Calchas, the Seer, though no fighter, is prominent mainly in the Achilleid, remarkably so in A, and, to a certain extent, in N, where Poseidon assumes his likeness as a disguise. He is no doubt *named*, and a vaticination of his is quoted in B, but he is not himself introduced upon the scene anywhere in the Ulyssean cantos, even on occasions that might seem to call for his presence, as in the Oath-scene of Γ (cp. as to Polydamas, § 96. 2). It is worth noting, in this regard, the occurrences of the word for *auspex* or *augur*.

	Ach.	Ul.	Od.
οἰωνοπόλος	1	1	0
οἰωνιστής	2	1	0.

In the Odyssey and in K 277 Ulysses seems to be his own augur, much as Agamemnon in Γ acts as his own priest. Theoclymenus, indeed, as a μάντις, interprets οἰωνοί, as in o 531, but he is nowhere styled by the special name οἰωνιστής answering to *augur*. The Achillean poem, therefore, seems to occupy a standing-ground not far removed from the original Græco-Italian position, when the augur proper, as was the case in Rome, had great honour; a feature, in fact, of the Pelasgian foretime, when the hieratic and priestly element had more sway (Welcker, Götterl. i. p. 26). The art of the augur, as concerned with *birds*, never attained the same degree of importance in Greece as it did in Rome (Smith's Dict. of Ant. in 'Divinatio'), and we can trace the signs of diminished importance commencing in the neozoic area of the Homeric poems [41].

[41] On the other hand, though the importance of augury proper decreases, the importance of Dreams in divination seems to increase. It is to be noted that while we hear, in the Achilleid, of ὀνειροπόλος and of the ὄναρ being from Zeus (A 64), the 'Dream' is nowhere introduced as a part of the mechanism of that Poem. On the other hand, the machinery of Dreams plays a prominent part in the contrivances of the Poet both in the Ulyssean cantos and in the Odyssey. Compare Mure on this matter (H. G. Lit. i. p. 492), where the illustrations given of this mechanism are B 20, Ψ 68, and, from the Odyssey, δ 803. ζ 21, υ 32 (to these might be added K 496, where ἐπέστη is parallel with ἐφεστήκει in the apparition of Ψ 106). It will be noted that these illustrations are all from the homogeneous area. It is not

In the Achilleid prominence is given to the term θεοπρόπος and its cognates, generally in connection with augury. The occurrences are—

	Ach.	Il.	Od.
θεοπρόπος	2	0	1
θεοπροπέω	1	1	1
θεοπροπίη	5	0	2
θεοπρόπιον	1	1	0
	9	2	4.

In process of time the μάντις and θυοσκόος appear to have gained upon the οἰωνιστής or augur proper[42], according to the following enumeration, and a larger use of the term μαντεύομαι supervened, whereby it could be applied to common foresight, without reference to 'divination' proper.

	Ach.	Il.	Od.
μάντις	6	1	10
μαντήιον	0	0	1
μαντοσύνη	2	1	1
μαντεύομαι	3	1	9
θυοσκόος	0	1	2
	11	4	23.

The systematic giving forth of 'oracles' at particular shrines appears mainly in the neozoic area. In proof may be mentioned the existence of an ἄδυτον in temples, a feature which

improbable that this feature of the neozoic area is Hellenic rather than Pelasgic, for 'the Romans paid little attention to Dreams, and hardly any to inspired prophets [i.e. μάντεις] and seers' (Smith's Dict. of Ant., in 'Augur').—Along with the machinery of Dreams, we find poetic use made of the terrors of distracted sleep, and the wife of Diomed in the Iliad is threatened with those troubled slumbers which are experienced by the wife of Ulysses in the Odyssey. Il. E. 412 is thus in harmony with Od. τ 515, υ 58.

[42] Contemporaneously with the greater prominence of the μάντις as distinguished from the οἰωνοπόλος comes up the more frequent use of 'lots,' which happens, strangely enough, to be resorted to mainly in the neozoic area. In Γ, Π, Ψ, Ω such instances occur, and the frequency of κλῆρος is an indication of the fact.

Ach. Il. Od.

κλῆρος as 'lot' for *decision* . . . 0 12 4.

It is true that κλῆρος in the sense of 'lot' in inheritance belongs to both areas, and the casting of lots by the Kronid brothers (O 191) is a very archaic example referred to in the Achilleid. It is, however, the fact that no occurrence of the formality of 'lots' occurs in the *human* action of the older poem.

is specially suggestive of oracles, and the occurrence of χράω, Epic χρείω, points in the same direction.

	Ach.	Ul.	Od.
ἄδυτον	0	1	0
χρείων (of a god) . . .	0	0	1
χρησόμενος (of one consulting)	0	0	3
	0	1	4.

(β) In the Assemblies there seems to be in the later poem greater precision as to the order of speech and the formalities of debate. But Achilles in A seems to summon the Assembly without consulting Agamemnon, and without the use of a Herald, and there is no mention of a herald delivering a sceptre into the hand of a speaker. On the other hand, in the non-Achillean parts, assemblies seem always called by heralds, and the formula κηρύκεσσι λιγυφθόγγοισι κέλευσεν comes up only in the Ulyssean area and Odyssey, in *five* instances, viz. B 50, 442, I 10, Ψ 39, and Od. β 6. Again, the formality of the herald handing the sceptre to a speaker and so giving him the *parole* for the occasion, seems not to belong to the Achilleid. It is mentioned only in Ψ 567, Σ 505, and Od. β 37, and probably B 185.

(γ) Regarding state and attendance on great persons, it is to be noted that there is an increase of particularity and detail as we advance beyond the Achilleid, and especially in regard to attendance on noble women. Apart from Agamemnon, who is naturally an exception (A 321), it may be doubted if any warrior in the Achilleid is credited with more than one θεράπων. Patroclus seems to be, in that part of the poem, sole θεράπων (Π 653, etc.) in the strict sense to Achilles (Π 272, Ρ 165 are not in point); but, after Patroclus' death, when we pass beyond the Achilleid, we find two 'squires' to Achilles (Ω 574), Automedon and Alkimus. In accordance with this we hear of θεράποντες (plur.) attending on Idomeneus and on Menelaus (E 48, II 123). *Two* is the normal number of ἀμφίπολοι on a dame of high degree, the Ulyssean cantos and the Odyssey each presenting one instance where they are named (Γ 144, Od. σ 182, without including the peculiar one in δ 125), and one instance where they are not named (X 450, a 331). In the Odyssey we hear of θεράποντες no longer in war, but as the attendants on a great house such as that of Menelaus (δ 38, cp. π 326), for which we discern a preparation and an analogy in the θεράποντες of individual warriors above referred to from two Ulyssean cantos.

120. K.—MARRIAGE.

(a) The next point among the *Archaica* is one of some importance, viz. the phenomena regarding Marriage. The Achilleid discloses to us only the ruder form of marriage, that by purchase or conquest. In the Ulyssean parts and the Odyssey we discover, alongside of the older mode, indications of another mode of contracting the relationship, by the mutual troth of betrothal without the coarser preliminaries being exacted of the ruder time. The proof of this proposition will throw an important light on the aspects of Homeric society, as well as materially strengthen the theory which I defend.

In very ancient and rude times, at a certain stage of human society, it is the 'use and wont,' according to the anthropologists, that the bridegroom captures his bride, in which case she is the prize of bravery, or, he purchases her from the father or the family to whom she belongs, in which case she runs the risk of being only a superior chattel. It is in comparatively later and more refined times that the bridegroom woos and wins the bride, and, instead of paying a purchase price, receives with the bride a dowry. The former is the sole mode in the Achilleid. The latter begins to occur when we pass out of the Achilleid into the Ulyssean area.

There are two—so to speak—technical terms that come up in this inquiry [43], both signifying presents that passed, gifts that were bestowed, either as dowry (using dowry in the modern sense of marriage-portion given by the father *with* the bride), or as purchase price. The one of these is μείλια [44], the other ἔδνα [45]. The former is never used except in the

---

[43] The term προίξ does not come up in Homer, though afterwards appropriated to 'dowry.' Neither do we hear of φερνή, though an instance of φερνὴ ἐπὶ τῇ γυναικί out of mythic times is referred to in Æschines, de Falsa Leg., ch. 14.

[44] μείλια, 'munera nuptialia. quae pro dote haberi possunt. quam προῖκα sequiores dixerunt,' Heyne on Il. I 148. The word is by Curtius (Gr. Et., No. 464) interpreted 'Liebesgabe,' and he connects it with a wide-spread root whence has come *meile* in Lithuanian signifying 'love.'

[45] For ἔδνα we also find a by-form ἔεδνα. Curtius divides it ἔ εδ-νο-ν, and takes it

sense of presents given *with* the bride by the father; the latter, though in the lyric and Attic time used to signify gifts to the bride or to the married pair, was properly and anciently applied to the presents given to the father for the daughter—in the language of the anthropologists, the *purchase-price* of the bride. If our view is correct, we ought to find no μείλια in the Achilleid, only ἕδνα, and that in the barbaric sense.

Over and above these two words, we meet with δῶρα on the occasion of marriage. These seem especially to be personal presents to the bride, ornaments offered by the suitor or suitors, and consequently perquisites of the bride. It is remarkable, that, while we hear of only ἕδνα in the Achilleid, we meet with μείλια and δῶρα, alongside of ἕδνα, in the Non-Achilleid, in which case we have this differentiation that in the Achilleid, the rights of the father or the disposing party are alone dominant, and anything bestowed is upon *him*, while, outside the Achilleid, the rights and feelings of the daughter, the bride, are an element in the case, and we hear of things bestowed by the father upon her and the bridegroom.

(β) Regarding μείλια, as to the meaning and destination of which there is no dispute, the case is quite clear. We have one instance in which it occurs in the Iliad, and one, by implication, in the Odyssey. The former is in I 147 (repeated in 289), where the gifts so designated are bestowed by a father on a daughter when married. The passage is in a prominent Ulyssean canto. The other is in Od. β 133, where things bestowed, by a father, i. e. μείλια, are capable of being reclaimed by him, when the daughter leaves the house to which she came as a bride and contracts a new marriage.

(γ) As to δῶρα, the examples are not unfrequent in the Odyssey, viz. ο 18, where they are distinguished from ἕδνα, and especially σ 286, 291, where they are personal presents to the expected bride. In υ 343 ἄσπετα δῶρα δίδωμι, if the reading is correct, the δῶρα, though not from the suitors, are to accompany the bride. There is also the epithet πολύδωρος in certain passages of the Iliad, regarding which hereafter.

(δ) There remains the term ἕδνα, regarding which there is

for ϝέδ-νον it : is probably from the same origin as ἡδύς, which is the same word as Skt. *svādus* and our *sweet*. Kühner (Gr. i. p. 82) prefers to connect ἕδνα with Skt. *vadaniya* =: 'liberal,' 'free-giving.'

more dubitation as to the *direction* of its destination. In so far as the Achilleid is concerned, there is no room for doubt : it is there unmistakably the gifts to the father or the disposing party, and therefore the 'purchase price.'

Two clear instances are producible from the Achilleid, where we hear of a husband having got a wife, ἐπεὶ πόρε μυρία ἔδνα, or as πορὼν ἀπερείσια ἔδνα, that is, as having furnished no end of ἔδνα (gifts), that is, to the father (Π 178, 190). It might, however, be argued that possibly these ἔδνα were gifts of the bridegroom not to the father but to the bride, and therefore, as she would bring them with her to her adopted home, the notion of actual purchase would not apply. This, however, is disproved by the evidence of other passages such as Λ 243, which shows the true nature of the transaction, even though the term ἔδνα happens there not to be named. Of a certain bridegroom it is there said, ' Much he had given ; first he had bestowed a hundred beeves, and then he had promised a thousand[46].' To whom ? Manifestly, to the father or family of the bride. Again, we hear of ἔδνα offered to the father not always in the form of cattle, but of service or the performance of some exploit, after which the bridegroom claims to receive his bride ἀνάεδνος (ἀνέεδνος Cobet N 366)[47], i. e. without the obligation of giving ἔδνα. This, however, implies that it was at one period the normal thing to give ἔδνα for the bride.

(ε) These are four clear examples in Achilleid from which we can infer marriage by ' purchase ' as the normal mode. As to any other usage, none is thence producible, apart from

---

[46] Cowper in his mild benevolence, unable to bear the barbaric notion of purchase, renders this passage (Λ 242), no doubt wrongly, as if the presents were to the bride. Eustathius had led the way to this by defining ἔδνα in two ways, neither of them being ' purchase,' ἔδνα δὲ κυρίως τὰ ἐκ τοῦ ἀνδρὸς διδόμενα τῇ γυναικί .... ἔδνα ἐστιν ὅτε καὶ τὰ τοῖς ἀνδράσι διδόμενα λέγεται, ὡς πολλαχοῦ φανεῖται (Eust. 742, 743).

[47] Heyne suggests an alternative sense, ' without receiving ἔδνα with his bride,' a view which the Scholiast seems to favour by interpreting ἐεδνωταί in the passage as προικοδόται. This is a wrong view, as there is no evidence that ἔδνα *in the Achilleid* was anything but gifts offered to the father by the bridegroom. The Alexandrian critics and most of the scholiasts were entirely wrong as to the primary use of the word ἔδνα, being misled by the examples in post-Homeric authors when it had shifted to mean ' dowry ' in the modern sense. Cobet has proved this satisfactorily in his Misc. Critica, in his recent disquisition on ἔδνα. Pausanias in his version of the story of Pero (iv. 36. 2) has the credit of showing a clear perception, like Aristotle's (cp. § 120, λ), of the real nature of the oldest ἔδνα.

the doubtful epithet πολύδωρος applied to Andromache in X 88, if it is taken to mean 'much-dowered,' i. e. bringing many gifts (to her husband). It is not clear that this is the sense, and the evidence of the proper name Πολυδώρη in Π 175, which seems to signify as interpreted by a subsequent line, 'one who drew forth no end of ἕδνα,' is against that view. Moreover the reading of X 88 is uncertain, inasmuch as another reading, perhaps more probable, is found in one MS., πολύεδνος, which is more in accord with the state of things in the Achilleid. Again, the peculiar word ἐεδνωτής in N 382 may be quoted as an example, for it signifies 'an exacter of ἕδνα,' and Idomeneus in bantering his Trojan victim, who had been flying at high game in marriage, courting a daughter of Priam, offers ironically to let him off cheaper than Priam would in his suit for the hand of a princess. There remains the singular instance of Altes, king of the Leleges, giving gifts to his daughter Laothoë (X 51), who is a subsidiary or secondary wife to Priam. These gifts are not styled either μείλια or ἕδνα, but simply πολλά (many things). The polygamous relations of Priam are so abnormal that it is hardly safe to draw an inference from a solitary case, and there is reason to believe either that there was a *quid pro quo* in the shape of protection and military aid in time of need, or that the nuptial alliance was a form of 'hostage-rendering' to secure good behaviour. Omitting, therefore, these doubtful instances in X, and including the not doubtful one of N 382, we reckon up five clear instances of 'Marriage by purchase' in the Achilleid, and no clear instance of any other mode.

(ζ) In the Ulyssean book I we have already found μείλια occurring, which is evidence that the purchase-mode was in so far departed from, and that something like 'dowry' in our sense could accompany a favourite daughter. The old mode, however, did not at once disappear, and in fact it continued alongside of the more humane and modern mode until it became obliterated in the historic time. A clear instance of this 'survival' is ἀλφεσίβοιαι as an epithet for maidens (Σ 593), which can only mean 'beeve-winning,' i. e. for the father's benefit (ἀλφεῖν meaning *acquirere*, cp. Heyne on Φ 79). No less clear is the instance in Od. θ 318–9, where Hephæstus

wants to get back from the father of his faithless spouse the
ἔδνα ' which he had bestowed on him for the sake of the
wicked-eyed girl.' Among the Gods, naturally, the archaic
style of things would be represented as prevailing. Two
other instances[48] are in Od. o 367 and σ 279, which look
like cases of *recompense*, if not to the father, at least to the
family of the bride. The latter passage runs in Cowper's
version—

> 'Such was not heretofore
> The suitors' customed practice; all who chose
> To engage in competition for a wife
> Well qualified and well-endowed, produced
> From their own herds and fatted flocks, a feast
> *For the Bride's friends* and splendid presents made.'
>
> (Od. σ 279.)

There are various other instances of ἔδνα appearing;
ν 378, o 18, π 391, τ 529, φ 161. According to Cobet these
are all cases of 'purchase price' bestowed on the father or
the family. The ancient critics regarded them as bestowed
upon the bride, and, as she would bring these along with her,
the old ἔδνα would, when so converted, serve as the neozoic
dowry. Under Cobet's view, they are cases of 'survival;'
under the other view, they are instances preparatory for the
more recent state of things.

(η) At this point we may recall the conditions of the case
among the ancient Germans, who form in many respects a
close parallel to the case of the Homeric Greeks. From the
description given by Tacitus (Germ. ch. 18), we can infer that,
in their marriage relations, the offered presents that had come
from the bridegroom, were, at the pleasure of the father and
the friends, returned to accompany the bride, and so became
part of her outfit and dowry. An example of something
similar is in Od. a 277, where, according to the common reading[49], the ἔδνα is now spoken of as provided by the bride's

---

[48] The instances of Chloris and Pero (λ 282, 290) are in the doubtful part of the
Nekyia. They are good evidence as to the *practice* of ' purchase ' in the early epic
time.

[49] Cóbet (Misc. Crit. p. 239), who holds that ἔδνα is always in Homer the ' bride
price,' wishes to expel the line πολλὰ μάλ', ὅσσα ἔοικε φίλης ἐπὶ παιδὸς ἔπεσθαι, occurring in Od. a 278 and β 195. He thinks that this line 278 and not 277 is the
one referred to by the Scholiast as having been wanting ἐν τῇ κατὰ ῾Ριανόν, in
which case the whole complexion of the passage would be changed, and οἱ δέ

household, and is considered among the things that should follow a beloved 'daughter.' Here, according to Nitzsch's careful interpretation, the ἔδνα, whatever it was originally and from whatever source derived, is now converted into a dowry, 'tochar,' or marriage portion to go with the bride [50]. The same expression recurs in Od. β 196, and from the proximity of this last we must probably reckon as a kindred example β 53, where ἐεδνώσαιτο would have the sense of *dotare* (L. and S.), to *portion* one's daughter.

(θ) Further, and more important, as not dependent on any disputed interpretation of a term like ἔδνα, we reach instances of marriage in which the notion of purchase seems to disappear, and becomes eliminated, as, when the disguised Ulysses is made to say,

> 'I married a wife daughter of affluent men
> *Because of my own good worth.*'—Od. ξ 211.

This is confirmed by the terms in which Alcinous offers (η 313) to make Ulysses his son-in-law, if he would only stay in their land, and to 'bestow on him a *house and possessions.*' There is in these instances no mention of ἔδνα either in the archaic or in the newer sense, and there *is* mention, more or less explicit, of an equivalent for dowry in the neozoic sense.

(ι) Again, in Od. β 133, Telemachus complains that among his other troubles, if Penelope marries a second time, he shall have to repay the presents that came with his mother, in other words, her father will reclaim the 'love gifts' (which we take to be the μείλια though not so named), given along with her on her marriage. From this passage we are entitled to infer

would be the suitors, not Icarius and his house. The reasons for withholding assent to Cobet's view are—1. The line seems ancient, for the metre acknowledges a lost consonant in ἔοικε. 2. In the mouth of Eurymachus in β 195 we should expect it to run ἡμεῖς instead of οἱ δέ, *if* it refers to the suitors. 3. It helps to explain the otherwise inexplicable circumstance that Aristarchus and the ancient critics were led to interpret ἔδνα in its later sense of dowry given to the bride.

[50] In Pindar (Ol. ix. 10) the conversion seems complete, for ἔδνον is there employed to mean the *dower* going *with* the bride (Pal.).—The double application of ἔδνα is parallel to the double sense of our 'dowry,' which in the authorised version of the Old Testament signified originally 'purchase price,' as in Genesis xxxiv. 12, 'dowry and gift.'

that Penelope, in the poet's view, was *not* a purchase by the husband from an exacting father of the ancient type making merchandise of his family. This instance in the Odyssey, being a dominant and prominent one, may be said, if not to give the tone to the poem, yet to indicate the newer mode by which the μνηστὴ ἄλοχος was to be won, and we have a key to understand the nature of the affection subsisting between Penelope and Ulysses, which is conceived by the poet as not resting on 'purchase.' If this is the case with Penelope, how stands it with the other model spouse, Andromache? The probability, though not certainty, is that she too was not conceived as a purchase in the mind of the Ulyssean poet. The question depends on the interpretation of the epithet πολύδωρος of Z 394 [51], and though the interpretations of the Scholiasts differ, the analogy of ἠπιόδωρος and ζείδωρος is in favour of an *active* sense, 'bringing many gifts,' i. e. much dowry, to her husband, in which case the poet of the Ulyssean cantos and the poet of the Odyssey coincide in placing the two ladies whom we have found reason otherwise to compare together, viz. Andromache and Penelope, in the same honourable position relatively to their lords.

(κ) The general result of the foregoing, omitting all doubtful or disputed cases, may be presented in the following summation :—

Palæozoic or barbaric mode.

	Ach.	Ul.	Od.
ἕδνα, expressed or implied as purchase-price	5	1 [52]	3.

---

[51] The epithet πολύδωρος, which should probably be πολύεδνος, in Χ 88, has tended to confuse the interpretation of πολύδωρος in Z 394, and the Scholiasts were sadly perplexed to find a rendering which could allow the two seemingly discordant occurrences of the word to stand together in what they considered one poem.— Regarding Χ 472, which is usually taken as if Hector gave the ἕδνα, no sure argument can be drawn from it, for it is ambiguous, and the strain of the passage is rather in favour of Eetion as the bestower, and as giving the rich outfit with which Andromache is provided. In Od. ο 127, Telemachus receives from Helen the δῶρον of a πέπλος to be given ' to his bride to wear.' This is proof that the marriage transactions could allow certain properties to be at the bride's disposal. Accordingly, in Od. ε 28, we hear of a bride as being expected to make presents of garments to those leading her home, i.e. to the bridegroom and his party.

[52] ἀλφεσίβοιαι in Σ 593.

	Ach.	Ul.	Od.
ἔδνα, dispensed with, not exacted from bridegroom .	o	1[53]	1[54]
μείλια, expressed or implied, as given by father .	o	1[55]	1[56]
δῶρα, as personal presents to the bride from suitor or parent	o	1[57]	2[58]
	o	3	4.

There is thus a considerable balance of evidence [50] in favour of the Odyssey and the Ulyssean cantos being neozoic. It is in them that we meet with indications of more auspicious views of the marriage relation, and these indications we find in the μείλια and δῶρα of those sections.

(λ) From a review of the whole subject it is abundantly manifest that Aristotle was justified in his famous observation in the Politics (ii. ch. 8) upon this matter. He there states that many of the ancient customs of the Greeks were highly primitive and barbaric (νόμους λίαν ἁπλοῦς καὶ βαρβαρικούς), for, among other things, '*they bought their wives* from each other.' The full justification of this statement, if taken absolutely, is obtainable only from the Achilleid.

(μ) How widely the wheel of time had rolled round in the Attic period may be seen by a reference to a famous passage in the Medea of Euripides. Unlike the philosophic Aristotle, Euripides is entirely unaware of this feature of society in the old time, and is so entirely possessed with the state of manners in his own time that he makes the heroine complain that she and her sex brought 'no end of wealth' (ὑπερβολὴ χρημάτων Med. 235, the antithesis to the μυρία ἔδνα of the Achilleid) to endow their husbands, *whom they bought* thereby. The 'subjection of women' had therefore assumed a new form, and the Scholiast has the sensible criticism on this sally

---

[50] Viz. ἀνάεδνος in I. That in N 366 is not in point, the ἔδνα being commuted in another form.

[51] Od. η 313.　　　[53] Il. I 147.　　　[56] Od. β 133.

[57] πολύδωρος Z 394.　　　[58] σ 286-91.

[50] These figures might be subjected to a little variation up or down, according to the rigour of the analysis. Thus another case of ἀνάεδνος virtually is that in δ 6, where there is no mention of ἔδνα when Neoptolemus obtains Hermione. Bellerophon in Z is in a sense an instance of one who is ἀνάεδνος, but as he won his prize by special works, though not in 'beeves,' it is fair to exclude it from the enumeration, like the instance in N 366.

of Euripides, that, unfortunately for the historical accuracy of the poet, in the age to which Medea belonged, matters were just the reverse, for, as living *before* the Trojan war, she belonged to an age when the husband bought the lady.

(*v*) The softer and humaner usage appearing in the neozoic area, though it cannot be called the prime cause, yet helps to explain as a concurring circumstance how there should prevail simultaneously in these parts so beautiful and noble a conception of ὁμοφροσύνη in the domestic circle [60]. It is doubtful whether a character like that of Andromache or of Penelope could have been formed or even existed under 'purchase,' and the 'chattel' system which that involved; but, under the honourable and humaner usages of a later time, we obtain glimpses of a social condition which could develope virtues like those of Penelope, affections like those of Andromache.

121. L.—MODES OF THOUGHT AND EXPRESSION.

A very interesting and important branch of investigation yet remains, to trace out any relics of the infancy of Speech and Thought, and to mark out the area to which these belong. Such *archaica* will be found diffused more or less through all the sections, but the mass of them is, as we might expect, concentrated in the Achilleid [61]. A full investigation of this

---

[60] While κουρίδιος is diffused, the tender expression μνηστὴ ἄλοχος seems to become more frequent as the barbaric mode of κτῆσις disappears.

	Ach.	Ul.	Od.
μνηστὴ and πολυμνήστη ἄλοχος	1	3	7
κουρίδιος	5	2	9.

[61] The only counter-phenomena which I think can be fairly noted as seemingly *non-archaic* in the Achilleid are the occurrence of σοφίη once in O 412, λόγοι in sense of 'discourse' in O 393, and ἀλογέω = *to be reckless*, in O 162. It is somewhat strange to find σοφός, which comes up so largely in the Attic time, absent from the Iliad and Odyssey, except in the above instance, where, however, it contains no intellectual suggestions, but is simply with reference to *handicraft*. The word is Indo-Germanic, a congener of the Latin *sapiens*, and it seems to be an accident that it should crop up only *once* distinctly (apart from Σί-συφος and ἀ-σύφ-ηλος) in the Homeric poems. As for λόγοι, the presence of μυθολογεύω in the Odyssey, of λόγοι in Od. α 57 and of λέγω, both act. and mid., in sense of *recount, tell*, tends to account for its occurrence so early as the Achilleid; ἀλογέω is a greater puzzle, inasmuch as it *appears* to come from a time when λόγος not only has the sense of 'discourse' or 'speech' but of 'reason,' of which last sense we have no example in the Homeric poems. In reality, however, ἀλογέω springs from the stem λέγω at an older point than the appropriation to either *ratio* or *oratio*, viz. at

matter would lead too far, landing us in philological discussions more proper for another place and to be in the meantime reserved. The following gleanings of outstanding phenomena may, however, be accepted as evidence that the same discrimination which we have found prevailing between the two sections of the Iliad is valid in this field of investigation also.

(1) The Achillean poet shows less familiarity with Reflective Thought. He uses once a simile derived not from the external world, but from the operations of the Mind, and he handles it in a way that shows how laborious in that ancient time was the process of introspective Reflection. In describing the rapidity of Heré's movements, he likens it to the rapidity of Thought, and after this cumbrous but archaic style (O 80).

'And as when the mind of a man darts rapidly, one who having travelled over much of the earth reflects in his subtle soul, "There I was once, or there," and meditates many a thought, so with rapid eagerness flew the majestic Heré.'

This is a simile from a time when Thought is just awakening to consciousness, when its processes are watched with a certain child-like interest, and arouse a sensation akin to physical emotion [62]. The later poet has the same idea, but expressed with less of involution, as if he was more familiar with the faculty in question, 'rapid as a bird's wing or *as thought*,' ὡσεὶ πτερὸν ἠὲ νόημα (Od. η 36).

It is an important corroboration to the above position to find occurring only in the Achilleid the singular line identifying meditation with soliloquy or 'self-dialogue' (Mure, G. L. ii. p. 28), as if Thought was a colloquy in which the θυμός is an interlocutor [63], and Thought is dramatised, as if it were Action.

the point when it signified *reckon* or *count*, and just as the Latin *neglego* signifies ' to be reckless,' *without* having had to pass through a stage involving either *ratio* or *oratio*, so ἀλογήσει in the Achilleid, which answers in meaning to *negligo*, springs from the same stem at a similarly early stage.

[62] Compare the important phrase ἐσεμάσσατο θυμόν, '*touched* the soul.' It occurs only in the Achilleid, and there twice (P 564, Υ 425).

[63] The θυμός is, in *all* the areas, said to *urge* (ὀτρύνω), to *bid* (ἄνωγα), to *incite* (ἀνίημι), but this is common to all languages and stages of languages, much as we say 'my mind inclines,' or, as Ovid says, ' In nova *fert animus*.' The expression,

> ἀλλὰ τίη μοι ταῦτα φίλος διελέξατο θυμός ;
>
> '*But why does my dear mind thus discourse to me?*'

Very naive and archaic, but not to be found in the neo-zoic area. It occurs *five* times and is well distributed over the body of the Achilleid (Λ 407, Ρ 97, Φ 562, Χ 122, 385).

On the other hand, the *formulated results* of Reflective Thought are for the most part confined to the neozoic area. In particular, the *formal explanations* of phenomena, and the attempts at rendering a reason for certain statements are mainly in the Ulyssean cantos and in the Odyssey. According to Spitzner in his note on Il. E 342, 'Invenies . . . vel rerum vel nominum interpretamenta ab Homero passim subjecta, vid. Il. 4. 477, 9. 562 ; Od. 18. 7.' The examples to which he refers (including E 342) are all four from one area.

(2) Among the more subtle notions, difficult to the simple primitive mind, as it still is to young children, is that of 'Number' in the abstract. It is remarkable, accordingly, that ἀριθμός and its derivatives belong only to the neozoic section, and while single numbers appear in the Achilleid, the idea of 'Number *per se*' does not appear to have been realised, and substantives for the *aggregate* under any number are not found to emerge. Hence—

	Ach.	Ul.	Od.
ἀριθμός, ἀριθμέω, ἐναρίθμιος . . .	0	2	8
δεκάς (an aggregate number) . .	0	2	1.

This constitutes a distinct advance upon the Achillean position. That ten occurrences of the *abstract* word ἀριθμός should be found beyond the Achilleid and none within, is a circumstance that indicates two different stadia of mental progression. It is true that there is still much inability to *handle*

διελέξατο, above referred to, is, however, too peculiar to be classed with these idioms. The following are variations of the same notion, though not confined to the Achilleid, having become formulæ of Epic speech.

	Ach.	Ul.	Od.
ὀχθήσας δ' ἄρα εἶπε πρὸς ὃν μεγαλήτορα θυμόν	7	0	4 (all 4 within book ε)
κινήσας δὲ κάρη πρὸς ὃν μιθήσατο θυμών	2	0	2.

The latter formula is remarkable as being used in the Achilleid only of Zeus, in the Odyssey only of the other Kronid brother, viz. Poseidon. Regarding the former line, it is to be remarked that it sins against the Digamma in its present shape ; εἶπε ϝον or ϝεον without πρός is the probable correction, for εἶπε is found frequently *dispensing with the preposition*, in the sense of 'addressed' or 'bespoke,' and more especially *in the Achilleid*, of which it is a kind of idiom.

number, and μύριοι does not seem to have reached the stage of a *definite* number; yet a near approach to a *ratio* of comparison, expressing 'as 9 is to 100,' is found in Z 236, also neozoic.

A corroboration of this view is obtained in the peculiarity attaching to the first numeral adverb. It is singular to find that while three occurrences appear of ἅπαξ and καθάπαξ in the Odyssey, the expression for *once* is, in the Achilleid, by a compound, ἕνα χρόνον (O 511), 'at one time.' Other numeral adverbs are no doubt known in the Achilleid, especially τρίς, but ἅπαξ happens not to occur.

(3) Very quaint and primitive are the modes of thought and forms of imagery appearing in the Achilleid. It almost looks as if we could discern the human mind imping its young wings for flight and striving to body forth the unseen, and we feel, as it were, 'a motion toiling in the gloom' to express the unexpressed and the obscure. Among the most instructive and peculiar *archaica* of the Achilleid are the following.

The notion of 'deliberation' is conveyed under the image of a balance, and we catch it at the period where the 'Libra' or balance is introduced as the mental machine for determination of solutions. Zeus himself is supposed to act by such an instrument, and hence we have the famous image of the 'weighing' of the Κῆρες or fates of rival heroes or peoples. It is only in the Achilleid that we discover this operation (Θ 69, X 209), in connection with which we hear four times of τάλαντα or Διὸς τάλαντα in the hands of Zeus, solely Achillean (*ibidem*, also Π 658, T 223). It must be owing to his favour for this image that this poet uses ῥέπω and ἐπιρρέπω, (which are terms originally of the *momentum* of the balance,) thrice metaphorically to describe what we may call the descending scale of Fate (Θ 72, X 212, Ξ 99). This cluster of images is entirely homogeneous, unique, and only Achillean.

So likewise we speak still of the 'tug' of war, and the image is both an ancient and expressive one. It is a favourite and characteristic one of the Achilleid, and in more than one instance we hear of a Rope or Chain as being the normal trial of all strength, the instrument for testing a challenge between competitors. The great challenge of Zeus in Θ to all the Gods turns upon this idea. The letting down of the 'golden chain' is for the purpose of a 'tug' of strength [64], and the Achilleid, in which this challenge forms perhaps the most imposing scene, is, accordingly, replete with imagery as to the *strain* of war and the *tension* of struggle [65].

(4) Among the most unequivocal traces of archaism must be classed the remains of what some would call Fetichism [66], others a primitive and poetic mode of Thought, attributing animation to objects in external nature. A remarkable instance of this is found in the combat between Achilles and the River Scamander. The river is there represented as an animated being 'growing wroth in his heart,' 'meditating in his mind' (Φ 136–7), and 'speaking' with a voice 'out of the deep whirlpool' (213) [67]. So rivers are 'valiant' (ἴφθιμοι) in P 749; waves and shores not only resound but *bellow* and *roar* as animated beings (βοάω, Ξ 394, P 265); and what is more remarkable, the sea is spoken of as *sentient*, for it is described as *prescient* of a coming storm (Ξ 17) [68]. Again, there is in the Achilleid a great number of instances in which weapons of war are represented as animated; *thirsting* for blood, *eager* for the fray, and the like. Thus λιλαιόμενα (or -η) χροὸς ἆσαι occurs thrice, and only in Achilleid; αἰχμὴ (or ἐγχείη) ἱεμένη occurs four times with the same limitation of area (cp. Spitzner on Il. M 185). If we except αἰχμὴ μαιμώωσα, which belongs to both sections (O 542, E 661),

---

[64] 'Sehr alterthümlichen Charakter hat eine allegorische Erfindung in der Ilias, die Kette ...... nach dem Vorbild eines Ziehspiels.' Welcker, Götterl. i. p. 85.

[65] Ten examples occur of τείνω, τανύω, etc. in this connection, Λ 336, M 436, N 359, O 413, Ξ 389, Π 662, P 401, 543, 736, Υ 101. The great challenge of the 'golden chain' makes an eleventh, and *all are Achillean*. Beyond the Achilleid, the nearest approach, but with τείνω dropped out, is in the expression πείρατ' ὀλέθρου ἐφῆπται H 402 (occurring also in M 79, and cp. H 102), and Od. χ 33, 41, where the verb ἐφάπτω = *knit*, requiring us to understand πείρατα as 'rope-ends,' seems to recall in so far the favourite Achillean image.

[66] It is somewhat suggestive of Fetichism that ὀλοόφρων in the Achilleid belongs only to *beasts*, in the Ulyssean canto B is similarly applied to ὕδρος, but in the Odyssey is no longer so applied, but is given to *men* or mythical persons conceived as men.

[67] The nearest approach, elsewhere, to this fetichistic view of rivers is in Od. ε 449, where there is a curious mixture of naturalism and personification (σύν τε ῥόον σά τε γούναθ' ἱκάνω). The river in the Odyssey is, however, not represented as 'speaking,' as that in the Achilleid is.

[68] ὀσσόμενον is the word here, on which Fäsi remarks: 'von einem leblosen Gegenstand, wie von einer Person, *ahnend*.'

we shall hardly find, apart from Δ 126 [69], more than one
clear instance of the same outside the Achilleid.   The same
tendency to personification seems to be at work in determining the predominance of the following expressions :—

	Ach.	Ul.	Od.
θρασύς applied to χεῖρες	5	1	1
θοῦρις applied to αἰγίς	1	0	0
θοῦρις applied to ἀσπίς	2	0	0
μαίνομαι of things inanimate [70]	4	0	0
ὄρμενος, of things inanimate	3	0	0
	15	1	1.

(5) The belief in the prophetic power of dying men is a
feature exemplified twice in the Achilleid (Π 851, X 358).
No such power of vaticination is ascribed to them either in
the Ulyssean cantos or in the Odyssey.

(6) Another idiosyncrasy of the Achillean poet, suggestive
of a simple primitive time, is the singular spell exerted over
him by the element of Fire.   It forms one of the favourite
similes of this forceful Bard, and the changes are rung upon
it almost with an exhaustive frequency and certainly with
a wonderful variety.   The power of that element impressed
itself very early on the thoughts and ideas of the human
race, and the mythes as to the discovery of Fire make up
an important part of early legendary lore.

The Achilleid belongs to a time when the element of Fire
exerts a portion of this primitive fascination on the child-like
mind, and it is the symbol to represent any mysterious force
or power.   (a) The hero's eyes, in speech or fight, are often
said to 'flash like Fire [71].'   There is only one very doubtful
instance in the Odyssey, bracketed by the critics (δ 662); all
the rest are Achillean, A 104, M 466, N 474, O 608, T 17, and
possibly T 366.   So '*hands* like fire' in Υ 371.   (β) The expression φλογὶ εἴκελος (including φλογὶ ἶσος in N 39) occurs
seven times.   All the instances are Achillean.   (γ) Two cla-

---

[69] ἀπὸ σπινθῆρες ἵενται in Δ 77 is not necessarily an instance of animation ascribed.

[70] μαίνομαι, so applied, occurs only in Θ 111, O 606, Π 75, 245.   Something
similar takes place regarding the ascription of a kind of personality to χεῖρες.

	Ach.	Ul.	Od.
χεῖρες (διέπουσι, μαιμῶσι)	3	0	0.

[71] The eye of the wild *boar* is in the Odyssey πῦρ δεδορκώς (τ 446).

borate similes from καπνός, 'smoke,' in a conflagration, are found in Σ 207, Ψ 522. (There is a short simile as to καπνός in Ψ 100, balanced by Σ 110). Compare also the pair of elaborate similes as to 'Fire in a forest,' or 'in a city,' P 737, Υ 490, against which is producible only that in B 455. (δ) Certain combinations expressive of the *vehemence* of Fire occur mainly in Achilleid. These are πυρὸς ὁρμή Λ 157 [72], πῦρ ὄρμενον P 738, Ψ 14. Compare θεσπιδαὲς πῦρ which, by a remarkable balance, occurs once in the Odyssey and once in the Ulyssean area, but is found five times (M 177 not included) in the Achilleid. A similar ratio recurs with almost mathematical exactness in ἀκάματον πῦρ. viz. six times in Achilleid, twice in Ulyssean area, twice in Odyssey. Also, κηλέῳ or κηλείῳ, an ancient epithet of fire, appears in Achilleid *five* times, only twice in Odyssey, and not at all in Ulyssean area. (ε) The famous formula, 'Thus they fought like blazing fire,' is, literally, 'with the *body* of' blazing fire [73]. It occurs only in the Achilleid, and there *four* times (Λ 596, N 763, P 366, Σ 1). These groups of phenomena, which are well nigh unique, suffice to show that the Achillean poet has shown a special homage, poetically, to the element of Fire.

(7) Less notable, but still significant, is the kindred feature of his homage to Night and Darkness. The enemies of the Greeks seem to him to advance 'like Night,' and both Apollo who sends the pestilence and Hector who is the manslayer are described in images drawn from the 'Gloom of Night' (Λ 47, M 463). In curious conformity with this, Hector is spoken of as νέφος πολέμοιο (P 244), the 'Cloud of War,' no

---

[72] It is a curious fact that κύματος ὁρμή comes up in Od. ε 320, as if the poet of the Odyssey was under the spell of the rival element of 'water,' a circumstance in harmony with what we shall afterwards find to be his Ionian affinities.

[73] The phrase δέμας πυρός is not only peculiar as being only Achillean, but it is the sole instance in which δέμας (signifying *body*) is taken as an adverb = *instar*. If not fetichistic, it is at all events a very primitive and archaic mode of expression, coming from a time when fire was reckoned a *living* thing, and as such possessed of a *living* frame, which is the strict sense of δέμας in Homer. The Achillean poet speaks once less archaically of πυρὸς μένος (P 565), but this which is the exception in the older area, becomes the rule in the neozoic portion, for it occurs frequently (Z 182. Ψ 177, 238, Ω 792, Od. λ 220)—(καυστειρὰ μάχη is in Δ 342 as well as M 316, and πυρὸς αἰθομένοιο (with and without μένος), occurs in Z 182, K 246, Od. λ 219, τ 39, ν 25, about one-half the occurrences that come up in the much smaller area of the Achilleid).

doubt from the darkness as well as from the ruin which a storm-cloud brings[74]. There are no parallel similes beyond the Achilleid, for that as to Herakles in Od. λ 606 belongs to a passage generally considered non-Homeric. Compare with this circumstance the remarkable lovingness with which 'Sleep,' who may be called the daughter of Night, is regarded in the Odyssey and Ulyssean cantos (see under § 183). It is not in the Achilleid that we hear of 'ambrosial night' as its *typical* appellation. It occurs no doubt in Σ 268, but there it signifies 'through happy intervention of the Gods,' and expresses the rejoicing of Polydamas in the respite obtained by means of Night coming on. On the other hand, ἀμβροσίη occurs as a characteristic, if not normal, epithet of νύξ, in B 57, K 41, 142, Ω 363, and these four Ulyssean instances have five in the Odyssey to keep them in countenance, δ 429, 574, η 283, ι 404, ο 8. We have thus nine instances as against the solitary and special one in the Achillean area, and that without raising the question as to the meaning of νὺξ ἀβρότη of Ξ 78, and νὺξ ἄμβροτος in Od. λ 329. Lastly, it may serve as a buttress to the frame-work of our reasoning to note what happens in the case of the very archaic phrase ἐν νυκτὸς ἀμολγῷ. Philology has now made it plain that this last word is from a root which had all but perished from the speech of Greece, but which still survives in Teutonic speech in the shape of 'murk,' 'murky,' and the Scotch 'mirk,' and it is now demonstrated that ἐν νυκτὸς ἀμολγῷ means simply 'in the murkiest time of Night.' This archaic phrase, of which the Greeks in the historic time had lost the significance, and which Philology has re-interpreted to us, is found chiefly in the most ancient area, viz. the Achilleid, four times against one occurrence elsewhere (Λ 173, O 324, X 28, 317, against Od. δ 841).

The general result of the foregoing analysis is to fortify the conclusion that the kernel of the Iliad, viz. the Achilleid, is an anterior formation, containing vestiges of an earlier poetic creation, and that that poetic creation has proceeded from a distinct and prior personality.

[74] It seems to be part of the Achillean homage to Night that we find ἱερὸν κνέφας occurring only there, which it does *thrice.* As applied to ἦμαρ, ἱερόν is found in Od. ι 56, as well as in Θ 66, Λ 84: φρένες μέλαιναι is also especially Achillean, and νὺξ ὀλοή is found twice in Achilleid (Π 567, X 102), only once beyond (Od. λ 19).

CHAPTER XV.

PERSONAL IDIOSYNCRASIES—PREDILECTIONS AS TO THE HORSE.

ὁ μὲν πεπόνητο καθ' ἵππους.

122. AMONG the most singular phenomena revealed under this investigation is one appearing in the relation borne towards two animals that have been from immemorial time the companions of man. viz. the Horse and the Dog. It is remarkable that the tone adopted toward these animals in one part of these poems is unlike that adopted in the other part, and the feeling with which these animals are treated suggests the presence and the working of more than one personality. The poet of the Achilleid is an admirer of the Horse but is cold and scornful to the Dog. The poet of the Odyssey and the Ulyssean cantos is lukewarm to the Horse, but is warmly appreciative of the Dog. The evidence in support of these two propositions is of considerable variety and cogency, and, when taken in connection with the other marks of differentiation, forms a not unimportant support to the Theory I have propounded.

It is well known that the Iliad as the great war-poem gives great prominence to the war-chariot and consequently to the martial animal which has been in all times, from the days of the Pharaohs downwards, known as the war horse, the ' bellator Equus.' It is not so generally known that it is from the Achilleid, within the Iliad, that almost all the illustrations, and certainly the most brilliant, of the glories of the horse, are drawn. Nowhere in any poem that the world has known does there appear greater admiration of the beauty and finer appreciation of the graceful motions and high intelligence of the 'lordly creature' than is found concentrated in the Achilleid.

In approaching this subject, we cannot do better than quote Mr. Gladstone's admirable statement on the point in his 'Juventus Mundi' (pp. 518–9):—

'Homer had a profound perception of the beauty of animals, at least in the case of the horse, as to colour, form, and especially movement. We trace in him a commencement of the pedigrees of the animal (E 265–73, Υ 221). It is with an intense sympathy that the Poet describes the lordly creature and his motions, which he has idealised up to the highest point by the tears of horses, their speech, and their scouring the expanse of sea and the tips of standing corn. The whole series of passages relating to the horse in the Iliad is noble and emphatic throughout, and in no parts of the Poem can we more distinctly trace, by the slower or quicker movement of his verse, his adaptation of sound to sense.'

When we examine into this matter more particularly, we find it is in the Achilleid that this idealisation is concentrated. Omitting the two instances of the pedigree, which are not material (the fuller and more marvellous one, viz. Υ 221, being, however, Achillean), we discover the hyperboles referred to by Mr. Gladstone to be as follows :—(1) Their dropping tears of sorrow[1]. (2) Becoming vocal for a brief instant, and uttering words of warning. (3) Flying over tips of corn-ears and crests of waves. The three references are all Achillean (P 426, T 404, Υ 226). It does not alter the case that the pedigree of some of these steeds makes them 'divine,' and descended from the Wind-gods. The imagery describing their flight is naturally drawn from the action of the Wind-god their progenitor.

Besides these *three* hyperboles to which Mr. Gladstone gives prominence in his enumeration, there are others more subtle and recondite, but not less real, in glorification of the Horse. (4) A prophetic insight of coming sorrow is ascribed to it

---

[1] It is one of the analogies of the Mahábhárata to the Iliad that horses are in the Indian epic made susceptible of tears (M. Williams, Ind. Ep. Poetry, p. 106). — In Indian literature, generally, the horse seems to meet with much honour: e. g. the horse Kantaka, called the king of steeds, born in the same day as Buddha the prince, received special caresses from the 'soft hand' of Buddha (Beal's Legend of Sakya Muni).

(Σ 224). (5) The same epithet[2] is bestowed on its prancing feet as on the '*thundering* husband of Heré' ($\epsilon\rho\iota\gamma\delta o\upsilon\pi o\varsigma$ in Λ 152. given only to Zeus and to the foot of steeds). (6) An address of condolence to the steeds of Patroclus and bestowment of pity upon them by the son of Kronos. They are the only creatures on earth that Zeus so honours, except Hector and his own son Sarpedon. This is the more marvellous, as it comes from the God who never speaks *to* men but *mediately*[3], and who is nowhere brought into direct human association (cp. Nägelsbach, H. Theol. p. 156). The number of hyperboles, from the Achilleid, has thus been doubled. All are unique and only Achillean. Another, though not so strictly unique, is the (7) bestowment of a long hortatory address upon them by their charioteer (Θ 185). as if they were reason-gifted creatures[4]. This also occurs, though in a less pronounced form, in a Ulyssean canto Ψ, from the mouth of Antilochus, who, however, belonged to a Poseidonian family famed for equestrian sympathies and capabilities. An eighth (8) might be found, if we were not restrained by the nod of Aristarchus who doubted the genuineness of the passage[5].

---

[2] Another honour is that the great epithet of Poseidon, $\kappa\upsilon\alpha\nu o\chi\alpha\iota\tau\eta\varsigma$, is found bestowed upon a steed (Υ 224). In the Hesiodic 'Shield' it is given to the famous steed *Areion.*

[3] P 201 (to Hector) is the nearest approach to an address to a mortal from Zeus. It is, however, really a monologue.—Contrast P 198 with P 441 in evidence of the *empressement* stirred by them, stronger than that by Hector, in the heart of Zeus.

[4] Compare. in the ballad of 'Auld Maitland,' 'Grey, thou maun carry me away, Or my life lies in wad.' This is akin in tone, but far inferior in compass to the exhortation in the Achilleid, in the same proportion as the simple ballad falls short of the noble Epos.

[5] The famous line. $o\tilde{\iota}\nu o\nu$ τ' $\epsilon\gamma\kappa\epsilon\rho\acute{a}\sigma\alpha\sigma\alpha$ $\pi\iota\epsilon\tilde{\iota}\nu$, $\ddot{o}\tau\epsilon$ $\theta\upsilon\mu\grave{o}\varsigma$ $\dot{a}\nu\acute{\omega}\gamma o\iota$, is the one referred to, in which Andromache is described by Hector as pouring wine among their corn and tending them in precedence of their master. Notwithstanding the doubt expressed by Aristarchus. the evidence decidedly preponderates in favour of its genuineness, and though many editors have bracketed it, Buchholz (Realien, ii. p. 174) sees no absurdity in the fact described (cp. Arist. H. An. 8. 21, and Virg. Georg iii 509). and La Roche, the most careful and judicious of recent editors, has relieved the line from the brackets in which it has been in recent days confined. Two reasons seem to have moved Aristarchus, one that it appears to disturb the sequence of the syntax between $\pi\rho o\tau\acute{\epsilon}\rho o\iota\sigma\iota$ and $\ddot{\eta}$ $\dot{\epsilon}\mu o\acute{\iota}$. and the other, that wine seemed a startling kind of drink to be given to horses. The former difficulty is not formidable, much less fatal, and the latter is none at all, though the Alexandrian critics, even the generally judicious Aristarchus, were too often squeamish, after the fashion of Pope and his school, about many of the natural simplicities of the

It is the place where on a high occasion they are regaled with wine (Θ 189). A ninth (9) is the marked acknowledgment of the equestrian glory of Poseidon in the beginning of book N. Nowhere is there such a rejoicing tribute to the king of Steeds as is there bestowed on Poseidon, and it is appropriately found in the Achillean area.

There remains the famous description of the movement of the Horse and—apart from that in the book of Job—the most glowing picture of the creature ever delineated, which forms one of the best known passages in either poem. There is this peculiarity about it, however, that it occurs twice, being found once in the Achilleid (O 263), where it sets forth the gait of Hector, and once in a Ulyssean canto Z (506), where it sets forth the gait of Paris. One of these is no doubt the primary application, and the question is which of the two it is. Critics dispute the point. Düntzer and Fäsi think it more appropriate regarding Paris. Blackie holds that the application to Hector is the primary and appropriate one. The balance of evidence is in favour of the latter view, that the application to Hector is the older and primary one, for, assuming the anteriority of the Achilleid to be otherwise established, we can explain the repetition of the simile in the newer poem, more readily than a transference of it backward into the texture of the older poem, adaptations *from* an older nucleus being more easily effected than insertions *into* it [6]. Moreover, the application to Paris has the

Homeric opens.   Cobet opens his recent 'Homerica,' Miscell. Critica, 1876, with a disquisition on the Alexandrian timidity as to what was counted ἀπρεπές in the old texts, and proves that Aristarchus and his school allowed subjective feeling as to what *they* thought 'decorous' to interfere with criticism. Two of our living poets have, however, bravely followed the old bard in this incident, *against* Aristarchus. Robert Browning, in the grandest equestrian poem in English literature, so regales Roland after the 'Ride to Aix,' and Matthew Arnold, in his glorification of Ruksh, the horse of Rustum, makes his master say,—

> 'The aged Zal himself
> Has often stroked thy neck and given thee food,
> Corn in a golden platter soaked with wine.'

I do not know that any one has observed that Aristarchus's deletion of the line involves a much greater absurdity than offering horses wine, viz. offering Hector corn.   This is strictly and logically the result of the excision.

[6] The internal evidence is decidedly in favour of this view ; δεσμὸν ἀπορρήξας is more appropriate regarding the resuscitated Hector than the skulking Paris. Heyne on O 263 accordingly says, 'Praeclara comparatio Hectoris recreati cum

appearance of a slightly sarcastic suggestion, that he was a showy creature, more distinguished for form than for worth, and, while it is doubtful if the steed-loving author of the Achilleid would have expended the simile on a warrior of the archer type [7], there is reason to believe that the author of the Ulyssean cantos felt no such scruples.

123. These hyperboles on the large scale are supported by the following minor phenomena. The vocabulary of the Achilleid is found to be replete with what we may call, using the word in its widest acceptation, 'equestrian' expressions.

(1) Proper names occur compounded with ἵππος in very large proportion. If my lists are to be trusted, there are *twenty* occurrences in Achilleid to *ten* in the Ulyssean cantos (of which ten, four are of one person, Hippolochus), and *three* in the Odyssey. Of the individual names, while three are common to Achilleid and Ulyssean area, *six* are peculiar to Achilleid, *one* peculiar to Ulyssean area, *one* peculiar to Odyssey [8].

(2) Special familiarity with equine anatomy, as in Θ 83 (ὅθι τε πρῶται τρίχες ἵππων Κρανίῳ ἐμπεφύασι, μάλιστα δὲ καίριόν ἐστιν). So the word ὁπλή = 'hoof' is only Achillean (Λ 536, Τ 501).

(3) To the Achillean poet belongs the use of ἐδωδή [9] as applied to horses (Θ 504) and of κάπη simply as a '*horse-manger*' (Θ 434). The Odyssey *adds* ἵππειος to this last (ἱππείῃσι κάπῃσιν δ 40), as if κάπη required definition. (φάτνη, which may belong also to the 'ox,' seems diffused.)

(4) The πέδη of Achillean poet (N 36) is for binding steeds. The only πέδη elsewhere is *naval*, for binding a *ship*mast (ἱστοπέδη, as in Od. μ 51).

(5) He has the sole trace of a separate *feminine* to ἵππος, viz. ἵππη, in the word Ἱππημολγοί, 'the mare-milkers [10].'

(6) His predilection for the horse shows itself in the frequency with which he speaks of their *'flowing mane'* as ἔθειραι [11], an expression peculiar to himself, one which he uses *five* times, and which is sought for in vain, in the Iliad and Odyssey, beyond the palæozoic area.

(7) In the descriptions of the pomp and circumstance of war, there is especial prominence given to the attitude, bearing, and behaviour of the Horse as a co-partner in the scenes of war. Compare especially Θ 543-4 and 564-5, in which last the behaviour of that animal is made the climax of the description. Similar phenomena in Λ 280-3, 531-8, M 58-9, N 385, Π 384-93, 468-9, P 457, T 485.

124. A considerable array of evidence has thus been produced regarding the equestrian predilections appearing in the Achilleid. It is necessary that we turn to the non-Achillean area and institute a similar examination. The Elenchus, when applied to this area, yields hardly any *hyperboles* in honour of the horse, and few incidents affecting that animal which can be held to indicate any personal interest or predilection. It is, of course, natural, that in any poems dealing with warfare as then conceived, the Horse and the Chariot should possess a high prominence; but this prominence, which they retain in the Ulyssean cantos, is due more to traditional fame or to the associations of certain steed-loving heroes [12] than to the living, rejoicing glory with which the horse is regarded in the Achilleid. We have already referred to the pedigree of the horses of Tros in E 265-73, and to the simile bestowed on Paris in Z, neither of which is fairly adducible as against the primary and older parallels in the Achilleid Nor is the encomium on the Thracian steeds of Rhesus in K ('equal to the Winds in running'), to be mentioned as in any way corresponding to the hyperbole on the

---

and ἵππη existed side by side. The one survived in Latin literature; the sister word died, and its existence might have been denied but for this single trace in our oldest document of Greek *literature*. Kühner (i. 138) is antiquated in his notion that η here is like η in ὀλιγηπελέων.

[11] ἐθειράδες in Od π 176 is a *falsa lectio*, now given up for γενειάδες.—χαίτη is the term for *'mane'* common to *both* sections of the Iliad, and becomes ultimately the prevailing one in Greek literature.

[12] Thus Nestor is still the ἱππότης, and Achilles is made to speak *in character* as a Thessalian chief regarding the equestrian glory of Egyptian Thebes, and regarding ἵππων ξανθὰ κάρηνα (Ι 407) as the climax of human possessions.

steeds of Erichthonius, whose feats are described as actual
performances (Υ 225). The chariot-race in Ψ occupies no
doubt a very prominent position, being painted with the
greatest fulness of detail, and with fine descriptive touches
(Ψ 13, 284, 507) as to the bearing of the horse, and, if we can
trust the doubtful and somewhat awkward epilogue to the
Grecian catalogue, the traditional superiority of the steeds
of Thessaly is acknowledged in B (763), where Eumelus's
steeds are singled out as the finest, next to the divine steeds
of Achilles, in the camp at Troy. They are, certainly, described, with great precision and minuteness, in terms such
as a skilled admirer of horses would employ.

The tradition as to Eumelus seems to have rested on two
grounds: (1) That Apollo, when tending the herds of his
father Admetus, had reared a breed of fine animals (B 767).
(2) That Eumelus was of Poseidonian [13] descent through his
grandfather Pelias (cp. Schol. B 714), and was therefore
favoured by Poseidon with fine steeds The poet of Ψ has
therefore fully obeyed tradition in acknowledging the equestrian capabilities of Eumelus, and yet he has contrived to pay
a compliment, somewhat at Eumelus's expense, to the friend
and companion of Ulysses, viz. Diomed. Those steeds of
Eumelus, pronounced next to those of Achilles in B, are in Ψ
beaten by those of Diomed [14], a hero for whom there is shown
elsewhere, as in E, Z, and K, a partiality second only to that

---

[13] Poseidonian descent had much to do with charioteering. Compare the
frequency with which equestrian associations surround the names of the *Neleidæ*,
Nestor (*ἱππότης*), Antilochus (cp. Ψ 3c7 and Ψ 584), Thrasymedes. and, in the
Odyssey, Pisistratus. Nestor is made to have the keenest ear for the clatter of
approaching steeds (K 532), and the keenest eye for admiration of them (K 545 50),
no doubt as being himself of Poseidonian descent ; he is emphatic as to δεῖπνον for
steeds (B 383), and the evolutions of chariots (Δ 301, cp. Δ 322), and, when he reappears in the Odyssey (Γ), he is engaged in a special *cultus* of Poseidon. He has an
extra horse to his *biga* in Θ 81, does *not* include steeds among the beasts of mere
burden in caring for the dead (H 333), and addresses to Antilochus (Ψ) a long exhortation full of equestrian associations and advices. His son (Thrasymedes) is the only
Greek warrior *present* at Troy (except Diomed) who has the epithet of ἱππόδαμος.
Antilochus, his other son, captures a team of steeds in N 400, and what is more
remarkable, a team in E 589, the only one falling to a Greek in that book except
to Diomed.—Regarding the sons of Nestor, it is singular that the expression
Νέστορος ἀγλαὸς υἱός should appear six times, but not once in the Achilleid. The
instances are K 196, Ψ 302, and δ 21, 303, ο 4, 144, all Ulyssean or in the Odyssey.

[14] The bad luck of Eumelus is shared by Teucer, whom a similar result befalls.
Cp. above § 90. It is singular that Eumelus should be by marriage a kinsman

exhibited to Ulysses. This same hero is the one on whom the epithet ἱππόδαμος has been bestowed more frequently than on any other individual hero, and six out of the seven occurrences of that epithet regarding him come up in that Ulyssean section with which we have found Canto Ψ closely associated, the canto in which the epithet finds its chief verification.

Apart therefore from the peculiar case of Diomed, there is no incident or 'sentiment [15]' regarding the Horse appearing in the Ulyssean area at all comparable in kind or degree to those in the Achilleid ; but besides the diminution of interest regarding that animal, there is an accession of new rivals among the animal creation, viz. the Mule and the Dog, so that in these Ulyssean books we have a distinct approximation to the position of the Odyssey, where the Ship takes the place of the Horse as the usual vehicle, the Mule [16] rivals it as a beast of burden, and the Dog appears as the chief companion and favourite of Man. The diminution of interest in the Horse is further indicated by the decrease in the number of equestrian similes. The Achilleid contains, within its limited area, four formal similes (O 263, 679, X 22, 162). Only two are found in the much larger non-Achillean area, apportioned equally, as if for mutual consistency, viz. one in Ulyssean canto Z (506), and one in Od. ν 81, the latter being intended as an image of the fleetness of Phæacian navigation.

125. It is in connection with the character of Ulysses that this decrease of interest in the equestrian element is especially noticeable, and it is a strong confirmation of our hypothesis that the Ulysses of the Ulyssean cantos is drawn with features that are cognate, if not preparatory, to those attaching to him in the Odyssey. In the first place let it be noted that he always fights on foot as a πεζός, and that, Ajax excepted, he is the

----

of Ulysses, for he has married a sister of Penelope (Od. δ 798), a circumstance which may have something to do with the interest which surrounds him, although a Thessalian and Northern hero, in book Ψ.

[15] It is not necessary to remark that παρέτρεσσαν δέ οἱ ἵπποι. of E 295, means simply, 'his steeds shyed' or 'started to the side,' not, as Mr. Gladstone (II. iii. 414) has interpreted it, 'with a fine feeling trembled by the corpse.'

[16] The occurrences of the mule are (ἡμίονος and οὐρεύς) Ach. 2, Ul. 30, Od. 17. The breeding of mules connects itself in early times especially with Western Asia (Kitto, Bib. Cyc. in 'Ass,' and cp. 'mules from Togarmah,' i. e. Armenia, in Ezek. xxvii. 14).

only Greek hero at Troy of the first rank that is without an
equipage. Hence he takes no part in the chariot race of Ψ,
the honours of which could not therefore fall to him, and
room is thus left for the decoration of Diomed. Even in
the capture of the splendid steeds of Rhesus, though he has
there done his part, he does not fall into any rapt admiration for them (Κ 556) as does the Poseidonian Nestor, whose
high panegyric he rather tones down in colour, and he claims
no share in them when captured but resigns them to his
companion (Κ 568). The explanation of this singularity is
partly due, no doubt, to the circumstance of his being an
islander (Schol. Il. Λ 488), and that too from a small island
with little scope for horsemanship, a fact which applies also
to the Telamonian Ajax. This inference is a fair one from
what occurs in Od. δ 590–609, where Telemachus politely de-
clines the offer of a fine equipage (although acknowledging it to
be an ἄγαλμα), on the ground that rocky Ithaca was no field
for steeds. On that craggy isle the prince of 'ancient mariners'
had as much need of a horse as a merchant prince of Venice
among the lagoons of the Adriatic. Therefore there is much
significance in his appearing at Troy without an equipage.

Further, we discern some peculiar touches in his portraiture,
which go to show that Ulysses was an object of interest sufficiently great to be able to dispense with, perhaps to despise,
such an appendage. On one occasion, when made to feel
keenly the humbleness of his retinue, we find that hero speaking
with a slight tinge of scorn for the arrogance that generally
characterised the ἱππόδαμοι [17]. In Δ 352 we can discern a ripple
of this feeling in the manner in which, in an irritated mood, he
introduces the ἱππόδαμοι Τρῶες *twice* in six lines, as if to em-
phasize, Antony-like, their being thereby surely *honourable*
men, foemen worthy of his steel, but 'for all that and all that'
he would dare to meet them [18]. Accordingly the first of his

---

[17] It would almost appear as if the poet himself shared the feeling about 'horse-
taming,' that is, 'proud-prancing,' warriors. The Trojans he characterises as
ἱππόδαμοι when he comes to bring Ulysses on the stage (Δ 333), and there is a
sting in the epithet as used by Apollo in so addressing them in Δ 509. Pandarus
in Ε 102 seeks to stir them up by calling them 'spurrers of steeds,' as if reminding
them that '*noblesse oblige.*'

[18] The Ulysses of the Achilleid already possesses the germ of this anti-equestrian
feeling (Λ 450 ᾶ Σῶχ', Ἱππάσου υἱὲ δαίφρονες ἱπποδάμοιο), but it is not in any way

after exploits is so contrived as to make good this boast, to the very letter.   It consists in the discomfiture of a *well-mounted* high-born Trojan (Δ 500), and is described in terms which particularise his triumph over a grand 'cavalier' of Troy[11]. Nowhere in the great variety of his Epithets (and he receives more than any other single hero), is that of ἱππόδαμος or ἱππότης or the like applied to him, and in the long roll of his accomplishments, as enumerated by the Scholiast (on Il. Θ 93), amounting to sixteen (cp. also Grote, H. ii. p. 87), including the rival one of κυνηγός, there is no mention of Equestrianism. This throws light on the curious incident regarding him at the removal of the horses of Rhesus (Κ 500).   Though he is careful to make a nice path for them, free from corpses or other stumbling-blocks, he is represented as awkwardly 'forgetting to take the whip from the car' and so, to make them move along, he has to take to 'whacking them with his bow.'   He is not the last mariner that has been so depicted as nowise at his ease in dealing with horses, and we think we can almost discern a sort of smile on the face of the old Bard, when relating this incident, at the expense of his favourite Hero.

126. The comparative humbleness of Ulysses in the externals of his surroundings is therefore a fair inference from the conspicuous absence in his case of any equestrian appendage. The touches in the Odyssey that harmonise with this view are as follows : (1) The paucity of terms in its vocabulary sug-

developed as it is in the non-Achillean area.   He is, certainly, treated as without an equipage, and when wounded, needs to borrow that of Menelaus (in Λ 488), to retire from the field.   This mishap, which would have been an indignity in the Ulyssean cantos, belongs to the Achilleid.   The only other instance in which we hear of Ulysses in a δίφρος or chariot is when a *captive* in Egypt, in his pseudo-narration of Od. ξ 279. where it seems to be the climax of the λυγρά, that he had to supplicate life from a 'king in his car.'

[19] The great ἀριστεία of Diomed in book E is partly for the exaltation of the πεζός element in warfare, as *able* to dispense with the war-chariot (E 13, 19, 255), though he was eminently an ἱππόδαμος.   The consternation of the Trojans in E 27 29 connects itself with the discomfiture of what may be called their 'cavalry arm,' and the blow by Diomed is followed up by two similar feats of Greek warriors (E 39, 46).—It is remarkable that all through his ἀριστεία, until he is joined by the goddess Athene, Diomed dispenses with his chariot, and Hector is made to quit his chariot (Ζ 103) when he pays his visit to Andromache and Troy, and he is therefore a πεζός at the moment when the Ulyssean poet has thrown around him the greatest halo of sympathy.—On the other hand the Achillean poet distinctly condemns the πεζός element when without the immediate backing of a ἅρμα to retreat to (Λ 340).

gestive of such associations (see above, § 123. 1)[20]. The few
that occur, as ἱπποδάσεια and ἵππουρις, belong to the only warlike scene which it contains (χ 111, 124), and are comparatively
secondary and incidental. (2) The kind of chariot that now
appears prominent is the Ship, which, in one passage (δ 708),
recalling the Arabian counterpart as to 'the Camel the ship of
the Desert,' is formally named the 'chariot of the Sea,' and
the courser that Ulysses is most familiar with, is the 'horse of
tree' upon the fields of foam (ε 371). (3) In his farewell to
Penelope, he had given great prominence to the *equestrian*
forces of his Trojan adversaries as rendering the odds severe
against him (σ 263)[21], and (4) in his challenge to Eurymachus
(σ 376) he claims to rank only as a πεζός with no equipment
as a cavalier. (5) It is the god associated with Horsemanship
(Poseidon), that is represented as chief foe to the non-eques-
trian hero. (6) The Kikonians, who inflict a defeat upon
Ulysses, are spoken of as, in part, fighting ἀφ' ἵππων (ι 49),
and therefore formidable foes. (7) The only epithet given in
the Odyssey to Troy (except the traditional ἱρή) is εὔπωλος[22],
and there seems something pathetic in the manner in which
this memory of its haughtiness is thus recalled, perfectly in
keeping with the appellation of Κακοίλιον which it there receives. Lastly (8), there is something sinister and fateful in
the mention of ἵπποισιν καὶ ὄχεσφιν[23] in the hollow show of

---

[20] Equestrian associations in the Odyssey are mainly in connection with the
Poseidonian Nestor and his sons (cp. § 124, n. 13), or with the reference to the
Thessalian Neoptolemus (δ 8). Also for the princess Nausicaa the mule-equipage
in a long journey is recommended as πολὺ κάλλιον ἠὲ πόδεσσιν (ζ 39).

[21] Pandarus was warned of the propriety of bringing a chariot to Troy (E 199),
a fact implying the predominant equestrianism of that city.

[22] The occurrences of Ἴλιον εἰς εὔπωλον are
Ach. Ul. Od.
1 1 3
viz. Π 576, E 551,
and Od. β 18, λ 169, ξ 71. There is no manifest touch of pathos in the mention
of it in the Achillean Π 576, but, in each of the other non-Achillean passages,
there is an under-tone of melancholy remembrance. That in E 551 is deeply
pathetic in its tone, as to Diocles' twin sons who perished at Troy, and it almost
looks as if the poet had a personal interest in the family to which they belonged;
for not only is their fate mournfully told, but, what is rare, the rescue of their
corpses is described with some detail. It is the same Diocles that appears twice
in the Odyssey as the entertainer of Pisistratus and Telemachus at Pheræ, the
halfway halting place between Pylos and Lacedæmon. The interest manifested in
Diocles in E of the Iliad and in γ 488 and ο 186 of Odyssey forms a minor link
of connection between those cognate areas.

[23] σὺν ἵπποισιν καὶ ὄχεσφιν occurs with tragic tone in Σ 237 as to the sending

welcome to Agamemnon, while Ægisthus was all the time 'meditating mischief,' ἀεικέα μερμηρίζων (Od. δ 533), and escorting him to his doom.

The result of the investigation is to show that while the Achilleid shows great favour for the Horse, the Ulyssean cantos and the Odyssey coincide in giving to that animal less prominence, and there is therefore discernible a double idiosyncrasy suggestive of a divided personality in the authorship of the Homeric Epics. As regards the absence of equestrianism in the portrait of Ulysses, the argument gains further in force from the state of the case as to ἀγέρωχος, a word which seems to have combined the two notions of pride and equestrianism, as indicated by the following facts.

In the historic time there is no question that this epithet was one used in a sinister sense, *haughty, arrogant*[24]. In the Homeric poems it is given to Trojans as a people *five* times (Achillean *twice*, Ulyssean *thrice*), to Mysians *once* (K 430), to Rhodians *once* (B 654, in a passage which has been thought an interpolation), but never to an individual hero except Periclymenus, in Od. λ 286. A larger number of derivations has been proposed for the word than for almost any other Homeric expression (cp. Ebeling's Lexicon *in voce*). Among these the most plausible are γέρας and ἔχω, as if γεράοχος, an ancient derivation (Schol. Γ 36, and cp. O. Müller, Dor. iii. 91), and that of Doederlein, ἀγείρω ὄχους, as if 'chariot-gatherer[25].' The evidence goes to favour, on the whole, the latter as the true origin. In the first place (1) the word is applied only to Asiatic races who are elsewhere known as ἱππόδαμοι, no other *race* being so designated[26]. (2) The peculiarity as to Periclymenus

forth of Patroclus, but, in the case of a Thessalian hero, that was the proper accompaniment.

[24] According to Liddell and Scott, it is used in a good sense in Homer and Pindar = *noble*, in a bad sense = *haughty*, in Alcæus and Archilochus.

[25] Doederlein compares 'Agrippa,' which is undoubtedly a word of equestrian associations. The prefixing of the verb is archaic: cp. δακέθυμος, ἑλκεχίτωνες, ἀγέστρατος, and the like. The derivation presents no difficulty except in the lengthening of o of ὄχος, but this is probably due to the Digamma, as it is properly Ϝόχος. answering to the root of our *waggon*, Germ. *Wagen*. Compare the same phenomena of Digamma slipped and vowel lengthened in συνωχαδόν (= *continuo*) Hes. Theog. 690, and in the no doubt Æolic ὑμωχέται θεοί of Thuc. iv. 97. explained as ὁμοϜεχέται, and thus a complete analogy.

[26] The Asiatic races receive the bulk of these equestrian epithets. The Trojans

connects itself with his Neleid descent and therefore Poseidonian origin (cp. § 124, n. 13)[27]. Therefore, in seven out of the eight occurrences[28], the presumption is otherwise justified of an equestrian reference. Regarding the eighth (Rhodians), without raising the question of the genuineness of the passage, there is the difficulty, that they are islanders. It is to be observed, however, that, besides occupying a large island, they are signalised as possessing 'marvellous wealth' (B 670), which is a feature often associated with ancient equestrianism[29].

The contrast which we have found subsisting between the Achilleid and the rest of the Homeric Corpus is borne out by what we find as to the *naming* of Steeds. It is remarkable that we have in the Achilleid two equipages, embracing, according to the common texts and interpretations, Seven Steeds all with individual names—that of Achilles in T 400, and that of Hector in Θ 185. All these are *present* at Troy. Mention is made besides of the steed *Podarge* (Π 150). In the Ulyssean cantos mention is made of a mythical steed, *Arcion*, in connection with the legends of Thebes and Argos, but only two are named as *present* at Troy, viz. *Æthe*, the steed of

and Phrygians are in twenty-four places ἱππόδαμοι, the Mæonians once ἱπποκορυσταί, the Phrygians once αἰολόπωλοι. The Pæonians, who are on the Trojan side, are twice ἱπποκορυσταί, and only the inferior epithet ταχύπωλοι is given to Greek *races*, viz. to the Danai frequently, and to the Myrmidons.

[27] Compare ἀγανώτατος applied to Neleus in Od. λ 229, as if an interpretation of the ἀγέρωχος of his son Periclymenus; ἀγανός is also of his other son, Nestor, Σ 16.—It will be found that ἀγανός is given largely to ἱππόται, whether individual heroes or tribes. In the Iliad it is given to no *races* except the ἱππόδαμοι Τρῶες and the Ἱππημολγοί. In the Odyssey it seems to be set free from *equestrian* associations, for it is there given to no race but Phæacians and Phœnicians. It is once given to Ulysses himself, but it is in the mouth of a Suitor (β 308), and is meant *in malam partem*. As applied to the Suitors, it is undoubtedly of sinister import.

[28] In Π 343, as applied to the *Trojans* coming 'storming on' with their chariots (cp. ἐπιβρίσῃ), it is an epithet peculiarly appropriate.

[29] In the historic time the connection of pride and equestrianism is in the Greek world largely recognised. Cp. ἱππῆς at Athens, the opening scene of the 'Nubes,' the horse as the ἄγαλμα τῆς ὑπερπλούτου χλιδῆς in Æsch. Prom V. 474, the Æschylean use of καθιππάζεσθαι, 'to ride rough-shod over,' in what we might call *cavalier* fashion, and the sneer of Antisthenes against the magnificence of Plato, whom he called a 'snorting steed' (ἵππος φρυακτής, Diog. La. vi. 1. 7). All these illustrate the use of ἱππόδαμος as symbolical of affluence (cp. B 230, Δ 145), and of ὑπέρθυμος as belonging for the most part either to equestrians or to reckless and violent men. Compare εὐηγενής, used only of the ἱππόδαμοι Τρῶες, and the case of the brutal Κτήσιππος, expressly said to be 'proud of his grand possessions' (υ 289).

Agamemnon, and *Podargus* that of Menelaus (Ψ 296)[30]. In the Odyssey no horse is named except the mythical steeds of Eôs, but we find a Dog so honoured, the immortal Argus. Thus in the Achilleid, we meet with (assuming Θ 185 to be admissible) Seven Steeds bearing a name and no Dog: in the non-Achilleid, two Steeds named upon the stage of action, and one Dog, a circumstance which brings us to the second part of this investigation[31].

[30] Pindar, in conformity (cp. note on § 95) with his generally Achillean tendencies, introduces two steeds by *name*, Pherenikus belonging to Hiero and Phrikias, a Thessalian steed, the latter in the tenth Pythian.

[31] Some notices of the Horse and the Dog in Literature, ancient and modern, will be found in Appendix, Note D.

CHAPTER XVI.

PERSONAL IDIOSYNCRASIES.—PREDILECTIONS AS TO THE DOG.

χρύσειοι δ' ἐκάτερθε καὶ ἀργύρεοι κύνες ἦσαν.

127. WE have shown that Ulysses was conceived as not standing in any marked relation to the Horse, as having, in fact, almost every variety of association except equestrian ones. The loss of interest thus arising is, however, remarkably compensated by the near and frequent association, if not always of himself, yet of his household, with an animal in some respects more attractive, though not more noble—the Dog. In the great Epic, where the war element is predominant, it is natural that the great war-animal should be in the ascendant and especially in cantos where the storm rises fiercest and wildest. In the equally great Epic where the charm of *Home* gleams out so pleasingly, it is no less fitting that the guardian of the Hearth should meet with due recognition[1]. The Dog has received many such recognitions in literature. He has even, as was proper in the 'philosophic animal'—so styled by Plato—penetrated into the region of Philosophy, and given name to a respectable, though not very amiable[2], sect of Philosophers. As the only creature that

---

[1] The Romans placed the figure of a dog beside those of the domestic Lares, and so it is found in the denarii of the Gens *Cæsia* (Ov. Fasti, v. 129, where the reason is given for this remarkable honour). The Romans, however, were not always so complaisant to that animal. Their Flamen Dialis was defiled, if touched by a dog, and the goose was thought to have proved a better watch of the capitol (Prell. R. Myth. p. 255).

[2] According to Athenæus (xiii. 611. b.c.) the balance on the score of philosophic

prefers the society of man to the society of its own kind, as an animal which has attained in the service of man to a species of 'worship,' which a modern French philosopher, Comte, has thought worthy of the name 'anthropolatry,' as the most complete and the most useful conquest man has made among the animal creation, and as the instrument which has been of the most signal service in helping him to his other conquests over the animal world, the Dog is by pre-eminence the creature that has come into the most frequent and close relation to Man, rejoicing with him in life and mourning over him in death. This relation we can discern the Dog to have sustained from a time the most remote, before the Aryan races were separated in the depths of the past. Nowhere, however, along the whole page of human story, has this companion of Man obtained more loving recognition than in the cantos of the Odyssey[3].

To put this matter in a proper critical light it will be proper to glance first at a few points of the aspect in which he appears in the Achilleid.

128. The Dog, while well known in the Achilleid, hardly anywhere appears except in a sinister aspect. He comes before us in the very proem of the poem, but it is not in an amiable light, for he is there associated with fowls of the air, (probably vultures), and is represented as having something wild in his nature preying on the bodies of the dead, not so much the friend as an enemy of man[4]. From this opening keynote

amiability is thought to lie rather with the dogs than the Cynics, so that the dogs have more reason to complain than to be proud of the association!—The Scholiast on Il. A 335 has the facetious remark on their philosophic powers being limited, like those of other philosophers, since they often confound the instrument with the cause, and bite the stone instead of the stone-thrower.—Other instances in which the dog is brought *en rapport* with philosophy are the case of the Ephesian Heracleitus, who is made to speak of himself as a 'growler' in this foolish world (ὑλακτῶν, Anth. Pal. vii. 79), and the delightful simile of Plato comparing destructive novices in Dialectics to 'young barkers' that *must* worry and devour (Pl. Rep. vii. 539 B).—Another member of the Socratic school makes a still nobler application of the simile in the case of the young Cyrus (Cyrop. i. 4. 15), when he compares the eager prince to a σκύλαξ, or 'young dog,' in his youthful glee.

[3] It is interesting to find that, according to Diogenes Laertius, Antisthenes, the founder of the Cynic sect, wrote a treatise on the Odyssey. He was probably attracted to the poem by the homage which it shows to his favourite animal the dog.

[4] The dogs under Turkish rule seem to have returned to Achillean fierceness, if

there is no departure, at least no marked departure, within
the Achilleid. The Dog is known as a denizen of the camp
(Λ 50), without apparently any individual associations. He
is known also as assisting shepherds (M 303), more frequently,
as helping the huntsman (Λ 292, 325, 414, Ν 475, Ο 579).
In many of the similes of the Achilleid, the combat is portrayed under hunting images, and it is a curious, if not significant circumstance that, in by far the greater number, it is
the Trojan side that answers to the Dogs (Θ 338, Λ 292, 325,
414, and in part 549, M 147, Ν 198, Ρ 65, 110, 282, 658, 725).
In canto M there is this variation, that in one simile and partly
in another the Greeks stand in that position (M 41, 303)[5],
and in X 189 Achilles in pursuit of Hector is likened to a
hound chasing a fawn.

There is no instance in the Achilleid of the Dog being
admitted to a *Greek* hero's hut or tent, and, although, in the
older and established society of Troy, it tells us of τραπεζῆες
(X 66), 'dogs feeding at the table,' even these are described
as ὠμησταί, an epithet far from complimentary. The passage
is not one that could be cited as proof of loving appreciation
of the Dog. It is the famous one where Priam amid his woes
forebodes that the very dogs he has 'fed at his table' will
devour his dead body, anticipating as well as illustrating that
unloving prophecy, to which Byron once, in a misanthropic
moment, gave expression :—

> 'Perchance my Dog will whine in vain
> Till fed by stranger hands;
> But long ere I come back again,
> He'd tear me where he stands[6].'

129. This, in the Achilleid, may be said to be the climax

---

we may judge from the grim representation of them in Byron's 'Siege of Corinth.'
Compare Macaulay's description of the Irish dogs after the carnage at Aghrim
(Hist. of Eng. iii. 439).

[5] In Ο 272 the Greeks answer to κύνες τε καὶ ἄνδρες together. In Ο 579
Antilochus ἐπόρουσε κύων ὥς, but this is balanced by Ο 587, where the κύων is a foe
of Antilochus.

[6] Theognis is similarly sceptical of the faithfulness of the horse, and almost
seems to hint a contradiction to the Iliad or rather to the Achilleid :—

> οὔτε γὰρ ἵππος
> ἡνίοχον κλαίει κείμενον ἐν κονίῃ,
> ἀλλὰ τὸν ὕστερον κ.τ.λ. (Theog. 1. 1268).

of malediction regarding the canine race, and there is no *per contra* of redeeming association. As to the scornful associations by which the Dog figures as the symbol of impudence and a nickname of contempt[7], these appear deeply ingrained in the whole texture of the poems. The preponderance of examples will, however, be found again to weigh down the scale of the Achilleid. Thus κύον, κυνάμυια and κυνῶπα, in the *vocative* of address, are found about six times in the Achilleid (Α 159, Θ 423, Λ 362, Υ 449, Χ 345, and κύνες in voc. plur. Ν 623, without reckoning Φ 394 and 481). In the Ulyssean cantos, *no* instance of the vocative so occurs. The nearest approach is that of Helen regarding herself (Ζ 344), but self-accusation never has intensity like the taunt of another. In the Odyssey, three instances of this *vocative* of contempt occur[8]; two of κύον (σ 337 and τ 91), both times to the detested Melantho; the other, κύνες (χ 35), to the crew of the Suitors. There is therefore, on the whole, a preponderance of the *scornful* associations in the smaller area of the Achilleid, and a diminution of them alike in the Odyssey and in the Ulyssean area.

Another dark spot upon the character of the Dog is his devouring propensity exercised on the dead. Again, the shadow is darkest in the Achilleid. About twenty-four instances can be reckoned up in which that propensity is referred to as a familiar thing. In the Ulyssean cantos, if the same proportion were to hold, under a common authorship, there ought to be sixteen instances; there are only seven (Β 393, Χ 509, Ψ 183, 185, Ω 211, 409, 411)[9]. In the Odyssey, the diminution is still greater. The references to their devouring

---

[7] Mahommedan and Christian have equally abused the name of the dog, applying it each to the other. 'Il sepolcro di Cristo è in man di *cani*,' Petrarca (Trionfo della Fama, ch. 2). Ἀπέθανε σκυλί (a dog is dead) is the exclamation of a modern Greek when a Turk dies, and *vice versa* (Lord Broughton's Travels, ii 2).

[8] A fourth, practically in address, occurs in the mouth of Melanthius (ρ 248), and Penelope has the offensive term regarding the wicked δμωαί (τ 154). These, however, are balanced by two similar instances in Achilleid, Θ 299, 527.—The derivative κύντερος is, singularly enough, thrice in the Odyssey, as against a single instance in the Achilleid and one of κύντατος in the Ulyssean area.

[9] It is only in the Achilleid that we find γῦπες and κύνες *coupled* in the work of devouring (Σ 271, Χ 42). Yet here also the γῦπες are found alone as in Α 132, Π 836. In the Odyssey and Ulyssean area the γῦπες *always* appear alone *without* κύνες associated in such company (Δ 237 and χ 30).

propensities are about five in number; (1) γ 259 and χ 476, regarding the cases of supreme villains, Ægisthus and Melanthius, and only one of these cases belongs to the *action* of the Odyssey, that of Ægisthus being merely narrated and no part of the plot. (2) Other two are blackguard threats in the mouth of the Suitors (φ 363 and σ 86) and savour more of traditional Epic style, whereas in the Achilleid they are the grim *reality*. (3) A fifth is a dark surmise on the part of Eumæus (ξ 133), lending intensity to the horror as to the apprehended fate of the absent Ulysses. Still more remarkable is the state of the case as to the *savageness* of the terms in which the fact is referred to. It is *only* in the Achilleid that the grim terms occur; for there we hear of '*glutting* the dogs (κορέειν) with flesh,' and of making one's remains a 'tidbit' or 'plaything' to the Dogs (μέλπηθρα or κύρμα); three instances of the former (Θ 379, Ν 831, Ρ 241), four of the latter (Ν 233, Ρ 255, 272, Σ 179). It is in the Achilleid also that the terrible ἀλύσσω is once used regarding them (Χ 70). To balance against these eight *atrocissima* as to the Dog, there is none producible from the Odyssey nor any from the Ulyssean books [10].

In the Achilleid, therefore, the sinister associations regarding the Dog are numerous and dark, and, what is more, they are unrelieved by any kindly reference. When we pass beyond the Achilleid, the sinister references sensibly diminish, and we seem to have passed into a new zone of feeling regarding the Dog. I proceed now to enter upon the remarkable cluster of happy and kindly associations with which the Dog is invested in the non-Achillean area of the Homeric poems.

130. To begin with the Odyssey. In the first place (a), the young prince Telemachus making his *début* in the agora has no personal followers or θεράποντες, but 'two fleet hounds' attend him [11] (Od β 11). The same escort recurs twice

[10] The nearest approach in the Odyssey is ε 474, but the mention of κύων is spared (δείδω μὴ θήρεσσιν ἕλωρ καὶ κύρμα γένωμαι).—It is singular that ἀλύσσω should be found only in the Achilleid and σαίνω only in the Odyssey, both canine terms of the most divergent character, the former a sign of aversion, the latter of affection.

[11] Mr Gladstone remarks on this strange conjunction. 'When we expect to hear of a personal following, lo! it is only two dogs that follow him.' Virgil has once

elsewhere (ρ 62, υ 145). The master of a house (β) gives them 'fat morsels' (μειλίγματα θυμοῦ) 'to soothe their *spirit*' and they fawn around him (κ 217)[12]. (γ) The hut of the swine-herd is enlivened as well as defended by them, for, in their honest faithfulness, they are like to fall foul of the unknown Beggar (ξ 30). (δ) They notice the return of Telemachus and have the sense to fawn upon him *without barking* (π 5). (ε) The creature can be conscious of the presence of a Divinity[13] (π 160), showing a sagacity in which they are equalled with Ulysses, and made superior to Telemachus. They suppress their bark into a whine, in awe at the presence of Athene. (ζ) In the description of the artistic wonders in the palace of Alcinous, the chief place is given to certain figures in gold and silver. They are *figures of Dogs*, so wonderful that they are ascribed to the god Hephæstus (η 91). (η) The favourite 'insigne' of the Hero, worn in the decoration of his person, is a brooch or περονή, in which there is prominent the figure of a Dog (τ 228). This was an ἄγαλμα to which special significance is meant to be attached, for it was given him by Penelope (τ 258)[14]. (θ) A Dog is the only inmate of the palace that recognises his Master on his return, surpassing all but Eumæus in faithfulness, surpassing even Eumæus, Eury-cleia, and his own wife Penelope, in sagacity. The recognition draws from Ulysses the rare tribute of a tear (ρ 304). His name is the immortal Argus[15]. (ι) Lastly, at the death of

a companion picture regarding Evander (Æn. viii. 461, 'gemini custodes'), where Servius mentions '*Syphax inter duas canes* stans' in conference with Scipio.

[12] This is the only instance in the Odyssey in which they are spoken of as possessing θυμός. Another occurs in the Achilleid (X 70). The Achilleid as-cribes θυμός more frequently to the *horse* than to any other animal (Λ 520, Π 468-9, P 451, and Σ 224), next comes *lion* (Λ 555, M 300), *boar* (M 150, P 22) and *wolf* (Π 162, X 263); and once each to *wasps* (Π 266), *lambs* (X 263), *sheep* (Π 355), and the *eagle* (P 678). In the Ulyssean parts, the *horse* has it twice (K 492, Ψ 468), *lion* once (Ω 42), *dove* once (Ψ 880), *lambs* once (Γ 294). In the Odyssey, besides the *dog* in κ 217, I find only *single* instances of the ascription of θυμός, to the *boar* (τ 454), to *fishes* (χ 388), to the *ox* (γ 455), none to the *horse*.

[13] It is said of Scipio Africanus that the dogs in the capitol received him as a superior being *without barking* (Aul. Gell. vii 1).

[14] The Dolphin, as σῆμα of Ulysses, seems post-Homeric. Cp. Bergk, Lyr. Gr., frag. Stesich. 70.—The figure of Ulysses in the Mamilian denarii is known by his proper adjunct, the dog.

[15] To show more fully the importance of the story as evidencing the poet's personal predilection by the minuteness of the description, a version of the tale of Argus is subjoined in the Appendix, Note E.

this faithful dog, the power of 'Moera' or Divine Fate is introduced, just as when a *hero* descends to Hades (ρ 326)[15].

This therefore is a decade of honours to the Dog, some of them hyperboles, comparable in character to the previous series from the Achilleid in honour of the Horse. There remain various minor touches in this regard throughout the Odyssey, some of which may to many appear equally significant.

131. (a) If the ἀγλαΐη, or 'point of pride,' in the Achilleid connects itself especially with the horse (M 114), it appears rather in connection with the dog in the Odyssey, where we hear of his being kept by rich men *'for pride'* (ρ 310). (β) The huntsman, who in the Achilleid is a θηρευτής or θηρητήρ, 'wild-beast-chaser,' comes now in the Odyssey to receive a new title, that of 'dog-leader' (κυνηγετής), a term marking greater honour to his companion in the chase[16]. (γ) Further, it can hardly be called fortuitous that, in the supreme moment of their destinies, the two heroes of the two poems are each likened to the creature bearing the palm of interest in the respective poems. The Achillean poet, in his crowning simile regarding Achilles, conjures up before him the image of his favourite animal, the steed[17], and, again, the Ulyssean poet, when portraying Ulysses at the crisis of his history, indulges with similar delight in the vision of a noble hound. The

[15] Argus is credited with a δέμας, much as a *human* being. Crusius in his Lexicon remarks that it is never applied to *animals* except to the transformed herds of disguised humanity in the halls of Circe.—Regarding Mr. Ruskin's censure as to the poet's treatment of Argus, that there is cruelty in leaving the dog to die without a caress or recognition, there is this to be observed (cp. § 64, n. 2) that Ulysses gave him all he could safely give him—a tear (ρ 304), and further recognition might have been fatal, if we may judge from the sharpness of his subsequent rebuke to Eurycleia to hold her peace (τ 482). The real difficulty is how it came about that Telemachus and Penelope have failed to care for the dog that Ulysses loved, a difficulty for which there is no adequate provision in the story, though the long absence of Telemachus in his journeys and the comparative privacy of Penelope go far to explain the condition of neglect in which the dog is found.

[16] The Ulyssean cantos show a diminution of terms in the vocabulary of hunting, proportionable to the decrease of occurrences in the Odyssey:—

	Ach.	Ul.	Od.
θηρευτής, θηρητήρ and -τωρ	7	3	0
θηρεύων	0	0	1
κυνηγετής	0	0	1.

[17] This poet is haunted, as it were, by the same image, for he returns to the same simile a few lines after (X 162), and the chase of Hector by Achilles is then likened to a race of *two* prizebearing steeds.

hero of the Achilleid is likened 'to a prize-bearing steed, that nimbly stretches away over the plain—so nimbly Achilles swayed his limbs' (X 22). He is then moving to the combat with Hector. So, in what is the supreme moment in the fortunes of Ulysses, in perhaps the grandest passage in either poem, (witness Plato's magnificent application of it in the Phædo, p. 94), when the King has to appear in his own hall 'among the scullions and the kitchen-knaves,' and must behold the indignities there threatening both hearth and queen, he is represented as all the while suppressing his big soul's rage with 'Peace, down, brave Heart,' and we read 'his heart *growled* (ὑλάκτει) within him' (υ 13)[18]. In this conception of the hero we have manifestly the image of a 'hound,' or mastiff, in the leash, pawing to spring, yet subject to control[19]. It can hardly be other than the result of a profound though unconscious idiosyncrasy shaping the diverse conception of each hero, that the imagery, bodying forth the character of each, should thus flash out with such felicity at the *acmé* of his history.

132. The above is the main evidence in support of the assertion that the author of the Achilleid concentrates his sympathies on the Horse, the author of the Odyssey bestows

[18] Patience and self-control are, as formerly indicated § 77, 78, the preeminent ethical qualities of τλήμων 'Οδυσσεύς. Compare with this situation of Od. υ 13 that in which he appears in Iliad E 670. His power is there shown in the same restraining of impatience (τλήμονα θυμὸν ἔχων, μαίμησε δέ οἱ φίλον ἦτορ), a combination like the ἔνδον ὑλάκτει of the Odyssey. These companion pictures from apparently the same author as to the same hero reflect light on each other.

[19] According to Plato's noble interpretation, it is the inferior nature, or, in Platonic phrase, the θυμός rebelling against the λόγος, that is here symbolised by the 'hound' under control. It is true that Ulysses answers not only to the 'hound,' but to the 'hound's master,' and so the image is strictly to be understood. The application of it in the text is, however, sufficiently justified by the whole circumstances of the case.—That there is no feeling of diminished honour to the hero by this comparison, as some might imagine (witness 'Can Grande' in Dante's time), is manifest from the fact that the same Ulysses, who is thus described, is afterwards in the same canto likened to a lion (X 403), and that in fullest majesty. He receives this latter simile not unfrequently (δ 335, ζ 130), an honour which he shares with Achilles himself (Υ 164), and he bears oftener than any other hero the title of θυμολέων or 'Cœur de Lion.' This title is given once to Achilles (Π 228); once to Herakles (E 639, not reckoning the doubtful Od. λ 267), *twice* to Ulysses (δ 724, 814). The occurrences of θυμολέων are therefore $\frac{\text{Ach. Ul. Od.}}{0 \quad 2 \quad 2}$ so that it seems a kind of Ulyssean word.—Aristotle assigns θυμός, in *his* sense, rather to the dog than to the lion: τὰ μὲν (ζῷα) ἐλευθέρια καὶ ἀνδρεῖα καὶ εὐγενῆ, οἷον Λέων .... τὰ δὲ θυμικὰ καὶ φιλητικὰ καὶ θωπευτικά, οἷον Κύων (Ar., H. Anim. i. 2. 32).

his personal interest largely, though not entirely, on the Dog. To which side does the author of the Ulyssean books adhere? If it is found that he takes the side of the Achillean author, the differentiation proposed would be seriously compromised, for it is necessary to the completeness of the argument to show that the Ulyssean books of the Iliad partake of the character of the Odyssey in this feature as in so many others, or, if they do not, to give a satisfactory reason for the divergence. A good part of the proof has been already advanced, for we have formerly found that the Ulyssean books do exhibit, first, a diminution in the Equestrian element (§ 124–5), and, secondly, a mitigation of the darker associations connected with the Dog (§ 129). We have now to ask : Do they further present any *positive* evidence of loving sympathy with the Dog, such as is manifested in the Odyssey, but which is entirely wanting in the Achilleid? If they do, the argument is complete for their association with the Odyssey in authorship, and for their disjunction in authorship from the Achilleid.

They do not fail us in this respect, and the evidence they give is unequivocal and unmistakable. In the first place (α), we hear of dogs as admitted to the table of a *Greek* hero (Ψ 173). In the second place (β), the companionship so formed seems necessary to the hero's happiness in another world. Two [20] out of his nine dogs are sacrificed, along with four horses, on Patroclus' funeral pile, so as to accompany him into Hades [21]. Thirdly (γ), in the muster for the killing of the Calydonian Boar, special prominence is given to the Dogs in concert with the 'hunting men' (I 545). Fourthly

---

[20] This is the proper number to accompany a 'gentleman,' as we find in the case of Telemachus, as well as in that of Johnnie Armstrong, who, 'besides a fat horse and a fair woman,' aspires to ' *Twa* bonny dogs to kill a deer.' So in Σ 578 we find nearly the same proportion, *four* shepherds and *nine* dogs. Eumæus is rich in having *four* shaggy creatures ' like to wild beasts ' (θήρεσσιν ἐοικότες ξ 21).

[21] Yudhishṭhira, of the Mahâbhârata, refuses to enter Swarga, the Vedic heaven, unless a certain dog is admitted also. Indra, the Zeus of the Hindoos, complies. The dog, however, is a mystic one, being the hero's own father in disguise (M. Williams, Ind. Wisd. p. 413–4).—The dog of the Seven Sleepers, Kitmer, is one of *three* animals admitted into the Mahommedan paradise. The other two are the camel of the Prophet in his flight. and Balaam's ass. It is somewhat strange that the *horse* should have been forgotten by an *Arabian* prophet. It was not overlooked by the steed-loving Pindar, who, with Achillean sympathy (cp. note on § 95), introduces ἵπποι among the ' blessed dead ' as affording the first of pleasures in the Elysian plain (frag. 95. 4).

and more especially (δ, ε), we find *two* delicious pictures of canine life in a Ulyssean canto (Κ 183, 360), one of them (183) worthy of Walter Scott and full of the loving attachment recognisable in the Odyssey. These occur in a prominent Ulyssean book, the same in which the Bard, whoever he be, appears to smile at Ulysses' *equestrian* exploits.

CHAPTER XVII.

EPILOGUE AS TO HORSE AND DOG.

παντῇ ἀναστρωφῶν, πειρώμενος ἔνθα καὶ ἔνθα.

133. In the foregoing chapter we have dealt with the more important of the *Equestria* and *Canina* in the Homeric poems. Though the evidences there adduced are not all of equal strength, they yet possess a certain weight and scientific value singly, while, taken together, they give considerable momentum to the balance of probabilities. There remain various others, little hints and touches, which *may* be significant, and, though to many they may look fanciful, yet to Homeric scholars, with whom nothing is too minute to be counted worthless, if it promises to reveal any atom of truth about these stately poems, these touches will not seem valueless, for trifles will reveal *character*, and the maxim of Agathias has truth in it: *καὶ γὰρ ἐπὶ σμικροῖσι νόος διαφαίνεται ἀνδρός.*

MINIMA AS TO HORSE.

I. And first as to the *indicia* regarding the Horse. Among the *minima* may be noted, (1) The bestowing upon steeds equally with warriors of something like moral suasion (cp. ὀτρύνω, in the Achillean Π 167), and by Achilles himself. It is true that I 709 presents a possible parallel, but it is not normal, for in Ψ 111 ὀτρύνω is given to *mules*, and, in Σ 584, to *dogs*, both Ulyssean. (2) παρήοροs and παρηορίαι are equestrian terms in Achilleid, occurring four times. In Ulyssean cantos the same words occur twice, but with no reference to the horse (Η 156, Ψ 603). (3) The arrows of Apollo slay mules and dogs as well as men, according to the Achillean book A (50), but there is no mention of *horses* as falling by the pestilence (cp. § 134. II. 3). (4) While *panting* steeds (φυσιόωντες, πνείοντες) are found in both sections of the Iliad, it is only in the Achilleid that we hear of steeds *snorting* (M 51), and 'pawing the ground' in their eagerness, Π 834. (5) The Myrmidons, as remarked by Mr. Gladstone (Cont. Rev., July 1876), seem 'the only case in which the possession of horses is named with a soldiery generally' (Π 167 and cp. B 775)[1]. They are troops of Achilles. (6) The direfulness of the panic caused by Jove's thunderbolt in Θ is indicated by the disarray befalling Nestor's equipage (l. 86) through Paris' arrow, and by the reins afterwards slipping from Nestor's hands (l. 137), as if even a Poseidonian 'cavalier' could be made to lose his cunning. (7) Λελασμένος ἱπποσυνάων in the fall of the charioteer Kebriones (Π 776) denotes the climax of misery, to be cut off for ever from 'noble horsemanship.' The above are from the Achilleid, and bear out the characteristics of that poem; but when we·find ourselves away from that area, immediately there are felt touches of another kind.

II. (1) The Bellerophon legends of Z are in a form that gives no place to the winged horse, Pegasus. This is at all events a singular silence, for Pegasus is apparently as ancient as Hesiod (Theog. 283). If the silence had occurred in an Achillean book, it would have been doubly strange. It is less strange in a Ulyssean book. (2) The panegyric on the equestrianism of Egyptian Thebes, which is appropriate in the mouth of the steed-loving Achilles, and so finds a place in a Ulyssean canto (I 384), is dropped out and disappears, when that city comes to be spoken of, without reference to Achilles, in the Odyssey (δ 127). (3) In the list of prizes at the games (Ψ 260), the horse, though the first of the living prizes, is not in the prominent position which it would occupy in Thessalian estimation (cp. Achilles' feeling in I 407, where

<hr>

[1] The case of the Pylians in Δ 297 may be quoted against the absoluteness of Mr. Gladstone's statement in the text, but they are an exception that almost proves the rule, since they are under Nestor, who is a hero of *Poseidonian* descent.

the horse is the climax), but is, as it were, lumped in with the general assortment. (4) Equestrian names come up among the *detested suitors* of the Odyssey, *Elatus, Agelaus, Damas*-toridas, perhaps *Eurydamas*, and especially *Ctesippus*, who is the most brutal of the crew. (5) No stud of steeds, even on the mainland, appears on the roll of possessions of Ulysses, and this although Eumaeus's enumeration is intended to produce admiration of his 'unspeakable substance' ($\zeta\omega\grave{\eta}$ $\check{\alpha}\sigma\pi\epsilon\tau\sigma s$ Od. ξ 96). (6) An Ithacan, however, Noemon, possesses a stud, but it is in Elis, one of twelve brood mares, and a complication arose because of them. almost fatal to Telemachus. Their master, who had lent his ship to Telemachus to go to Pylos, finds afterwards that he needs it himself to cross over to Elis to see his stud, and he has the imprudence to betray the matter to the suitors, who plot accordingly to waylay Telemachus. There is thus something sinister about this business of the 'man with the mares.' The main difficulty is how the man is called Noemon and not rather Anoemon. (7) One of the most tragic things recorded in the Odyssey from the olden time is the death of Iphitus, a friend of Ulysses, by the hands of Herakles (ϕ 21–30). He comes by his death when going in search of his 'mares,' which Herakles had in his possession. 'Those mares,' it is said in an ominous tone, 'proved death and fate to him' ($\alpha\grave{\iota}$ $\delta\acute{\eta}$ $o\acute{\iota}$ $\kappa\alpha\grave{\iota}$ $\check{\epsilon}\pi\epsilon\iota\tau\alpha$ $\phi\acute{o}\nu os$ $\kappa\alpha\grave{\iota}$ $\mu o\hat{\iota}\rho\alpha$ $\gamma\acute{\epsilon}\nu o\nu\tau o$). (8) Ulysses speaks of himself as once in a chariot, but it is as a captive in Egypt (ξ 280). (9) The ruin of Troy twice over is brought into connection with 'horses.' Besides the final ruin by the 'wooden horse,' it is curious to note that the first capture of it, that by Herakles, was in connection with 'Laomedon's horses.' This is mentioned in E 640, which is a Ulyssean canto, whereas the sin of Laomedon is not brought into connection with horses in the Achillean area. These[2] are among the most notable of the *minima* as to

<hr>

[2] Against these various *indicia* which are in favour of my thesis, it is fair to note those seeming to run counter to it. Apart from $\pi\lambda\acute{\eta}\mu\nu\eta$, which is a kind of equestrian expression, the *nave* of a wheel, occurring only in E 726 and Ψ 339, I find only two, and those not material. (1) Athene is twice said to give $\mu\acute{\epsilon}\nu os$ and once $\tau\acute{\alpha}\chi os$ to Diomed's steeds (Ψ 390, 400, 407), and Hermes does the same to Priam's (Ω 442). (2) Horses are spoken of in E 272 as 'inspirers of flight' ($\mu\acute{\eta}\sigma\tau\omega\rho\epsilon s$ $\phi\acute{\upsilon}\beta o\iota o$). Neither of these, however, is unique, for the Achilleid introduces Zeus as bestowing similar qualities on horses in P 456, and, if Θ 108 is genuine, the probability is

the Horse. We now proceed to gather up the evidence similarly regarding the Dog.

MINIMA AS TO DOG.

134. Here the associations ought to recur in an order and with a colour the reverse of what appeared in the former instance. Instead of bright associations regarding the Dog in the Achilleid we may expect to find dark ones, but the reverse in the Odyssey and Ulyssean parts.

I. (1) The Dogstar is mentioned as the 'Dog' in the Achilleid, but it is no compliment, rather an opprobrium, for the description of his influence marks it as 'baleful,' and as breeding pestilence to man ($\Chi$ 29)[3]. The same star is spoken of in the Ulyssean canto ($\Epsilon$ 6), with the baleful associations left out, and, strangely, *without* the indignity of calling it the 'Dog.' Yet there can be no doubt that it is the same autumnal star that is spoken of in each place, and, notwithstanding the dropping out of the word κύων in the canto $\Epsilon$, the Scholiast (*ad loc.*) accepts the simile as descriptive of the Dogstar. These two similes, which describe, the one the advent of Achilles, the other the advent of Diomed, are duplicates of each other (cp. Preller, Gr. Myth. i. p. 305), but with a modifying difference, the origin of which we have now

that the complimentary expression 'inspirers of flight' belonged earlier to the Achilleid. Further, it is not certain that this expression in $\Epsilon$ is applied to the horses; it may be rather to the driver, for there is a var. lect. μήστωρι, a reading adopted by Fäsi, which would give the epithet of honour to their master. The favour of Athene for the steeds of Diomed is in keeping with the preeminence that hero has among the southern chieftains as ἱππόδαμος, and we can discern symptoms of a tendency to consider him as a southern Achilles, so as to be to the ἱππόβοτον Ἄργος of the South what Achilles was to the Πελασγικὸν Ἄργος of the North. The Scholiast on I 695 speaks of Diomed as sustaining the character of an ἀντιστασιώτης or rival to Achilles, and the description of him as τὸν ἄριστον Ἀχαιῶν ($\Epsilon$ 414) and κάρτιστος Ἀχαιῶν ($\Zeta$ 98)—apparently without any *caveat* as to Achilles, the latter phrase being in the mouth of Helenus, who has Achilles fully in his mind—goes far to justify the statement. Both are from Ulyssean cantos, and similar expressions, equally remarkable as trenching on the preeminence of Achilles, are found in $\Epsilon$ 839 and $\Kappa$ 539, Ulyssean also. At the same time the superlative is not to be pressed, since θεῶν ἄριστος (T 413) of Apollo and Τρώων τὸν ἄριστον (P 81) of Euphorbus must be understood as nowise compromising the position of Zeus in Olympus or of Hector in Troy.

[3] It is right to note, however, that the baleful 'star' in the Achillean Λ 62 is identified by the Scholiast with the dogstar, but the name κύων is there omitted.

a clue to understand. (2) The Dog of Hades, afterwards called Cerberus, is referred to once in the Achilleid (ι 368). It is not referred to in the Ulyssean cantos, and, as regards the Odyssey, it comes up only in a passage otherwise suspicious (λ 623). Yet the conception, which the Ulyssean poet seems to shrink from, is an ancient one, as it is common to the Hindoos; cp. the Dogs of Yama.

II. I now turn to the Odyssey and remark: (1) There is no trace of Dogs in the cave of the Cyclop. Subsequent poets, as Euripides (Cyc. 130), assigned him that companionship. The author of the Odyssey apparently thought him unworthy of such company[4]. (2) There is a similar absence of dogs in the case of the blackguard Melanthius (Od. ρ 214), probably for a similar reason. (3) In the Circe scene, though the *levée* of the beasts is compared to the gathering of hounds round their master (κ 216), there is no mention of Dogs as among the beasts into which men were transformed. Her retinue is composed of *wolves, lions, swine.* The Dog seems *not* to be included in her power of metamorphosis (cp. § 133. I. 3). (4) In the legend of Scylla, although she is credited with a 'voice like a young whelp's' (μ 86), there is an absence of the later feature familiar to us from the picture in Paradise Lost, where Milton follows Cicero and Virgil in *their* representations of her, that her extremities ended in Dogs. On the contrary, in the Homeric picture of her, though sea-dogs are mentioned, they are spoken of as victims of her devouring propensities, not a part of her person. (5) While καρχαρόδους and ἀργιόδους alike belong to the Dog in Achilleid (Λ 292, Ν 198), only καρχαρόδους is given to him in the Ulyssean area, whereas ἀργιόδους is not given to him in Odyssey and Ulyssean parts, seemingly because appropriated to the *boar* or *pig;* ἀργιόδους is, as it were, carefully assigned to the *pig* in *three* Ulyssean cantos, I, Κ, Ψ, and the Odyssey follows suit *seven* times, as if avoiding the association of the Dog with a less noble animal[5].

---

[4] The ancient grammatical schools used to make it a subject of disputation 'whether the Cyclop had dogs' (εἰ κύνας εἶχε Κύκλωψ). Cp. Epigr. Anthol. xi. 321. The Scholiast on ι 211 thinks the reason of their absence was that their barking would have disconcerted Ulysses!

[5] The conjunction of σύες and κύνες in σ 105 seems to contradict this, but Ulysses is there speaking in his *incognito.*

(6) In the Odyssey the same expression is used of kindness to dogs as to human beings, viz. κομέω. In the Achilleid it is used only of kind treatment to *horses* [6]. (7) In Eumæus's absence the charge is left with the 'Dogs and herdsmen,' the dogs apparently having the precedence (ρ 200) [7]. Against these I find, beyond those formerly (§ 129) adverted to, no counter-entry.

It is interesting, if not corroborative, to observe that a similar characterisation of the Iliad, or more strictly of the Achilleid, marking it off from the Odyssey, was already made in ancient times by the painter Polygnotus. It is not a mere fortuitous incident, that in his two great companion pictures at Delphi, the one mainly founded on the Iliad, the other drawn largely from the Odyssey, he inserted *two* animal figures in the array of forms—for the Iliad, selecting the Horse, for the Odyssey, the Dog. In the minute description by Pausanias, we read that a horse in a plunging attitude was introduced into the one series, and that a hunting dog figures in the other (Pausan. x. 25. 10, 30. 5) [8]. It is remarkable that the instinct of ancient Art should have anticipated what the internal Criticism now reveals.

135. In a former section, we already found prevailing in the Achilleid traces of personal affinities and partialities akin to those that afterwards appear in the historic time with Pindar as their mouthpiece. It is worth inquiring whether any light can be got from that poet as to this point likewise. A short investigation makes it clear that Pindar adopts in this case also the Achillean standpoint [9] (cp. § 95 and § 126, n. 30), showing very

---

[6] Κομιδή, however, is used of attention to horses, in the Ulyssean Ψ 411 as well as in the Achillean Θ 186.

[7] In attack and defence, the dogs are the first to be reckoned with (ξ 531), and have similar precedence.

[8] The dog is not Argus, as we might have expected, but one of Actæon's, the painter having chosen conditions requiring a dog in Hades that was already deceased at the time of Ulysses' visit to the under-world.—In modern art probably the nearest parallel, though in a *single* picture, to this combination by Polygnotus is that of Rubens in the ' Elevation of the Cross.' To the right of the picture, in front of the group of the weeping daughters of Jerusalem, is a dog evidently howling, and to the left is the horse of Pilate, which is turning its head away.

[9] Hesiod, though without any specially equestrian sympathy, shares the Achillean mal-impression as to the dog. Hermes gives to Pandora κύνεόν τε νόον καὶ ἐπίκλοπον ἦθος (Works and Days, 67), but Hesiod, though he knows the value of a ' housedog with sharp teeth' (ibid. 603), is misogynous and *misokynic* together.

pronounced equestrian sympathies. He rings the changes upon ἵππος very loudly, and is almost silent as to κύων. The occurrences of the former (without including compounds) amount to twenty-nine in the Odes, besides six in the fragments; of the latter, two in the Odes, with four in the fragments. Moreover, (as already indicated, § 130) Pindar introduces steeds into the delights of Elysium (frag. 95. 4), a feature which is adopted by Virgil (Æn. vi. 652), and is an honour transcending even the Achillean ideals.

An objection may naturally occur that the sympathy for the two animals may very well coexist in the same individual and may show itself at different times, and so the same author may in the Iliad show affection for the horse and in the Odyssey for the dog. It is admitted that in general the two sympathies may both coexist and coalesce, as in the case of Horace's young noble, 'gaudet equis canibusque,' or the squire in Locksley Hall who counts his wife 'something better than his dog, a little dearer than his horse,' and Xenophon in historic times stands out as a remarkable instance of the combined attachment[10]. The above objection, however, does not touch the main points of the case, inasmuch as it is not a case of sympathies only, but of antipathies also, recurring under a certain law of polarity, and a theory is wanted which will explain how the sympathies for the two animals came to be so singularly distributed, and how the sympathy for the one creature seems in each case to be accompanied by a corresponding shrinking from, if not antipathy to, the other. Any theory assuming unity of authorship will not account for the distribution of the phenomena, and this investigation therefore has yielded a valuable confirmation of a thesis on other grounds sufficiently probable.

[10] Solon acknowledges the *double* attachment :

> ὄλβιος ᾧ παῖδές τε φίλοι καὶ μώνυχες ἵπποι
> καὶ κύνες ἀγρευταὶ καὶ ξένος ἀλλοδαπός.

Cp. also Theognis (l. 1256), who is not always equally appreciative of the horse (cp. note on § 128):

> ὅστις μὴ παῖδάς τε φιλεῖ καὶ μώνυχας ἵππους
> καὶ κύνας, οὔποτε οἱ θυμὸς ἐν εὐφροσύνῃ.

CHAPTER XVIII

LOCAL MINT-MARKS—ACHILLEID.

εἰπὲ δέ μοι γαῖάν τε τεὴν δῆμόν τε πόλιν τε.

136. THE next branch of our investigation brings us to the important question : Assuming the dual authorship to be in so far established, which of these divergent *corpora* of song is the one that we are to associate with the name of Homer? Is the Homer of tradition, so far as he can be historically cognisable, the author of the Achilleid, or is he the author of the Ulyssean cantos and of the Odyssey? In the former case, the more remote poem is the one that should alone bear the honour of his name, and the subsequent singer or singers who followed in a similar vein are to be regarded as obscured under his brightness, and become absorbed without leaving a trace of their individuality. Something akin to this is the supposition of the Chorizontes who attribute the Iliad to Homer and thus leave the Odyssey to an unknown though subsequent and therefore more recent author. I had occasion to touch upon the difficulties of this supposition in a former section (§ 23), but merely incidentally in a preliminary reconnoitring, for, so far as the special investigation has yet gone, there has been nothing to hinder us from attributing the older and more remote poem to Homer and the younger to a more recent bard. The evidence, however, on which we are now to enter, entirely negatives that supposition, and, while materially confirming the theory of the Dual authorship, requires us to ascribe the Achilleid to an author different from the Homer of tradition.

In arranging the evidence upon this point and in endeavouring to track and measure out the traces of locality here and there discoverable, I expect not only to supply a large amount of valuable confirmation to my main thesis, the proof of which is still carried forward and completed by the after investigation, but I hope to make manifest the existence of a personal Homer with certain personal idiosyncrasies, certain human likings and affinities in connection with certain localities, more clearly than has ever yet been either attempted or proposed [1]. The ease and readiness with which the phenomena have grouped themselves with this result, the light which sprang up over the whole field of vision, when once the proper point of view was attained, have been a confirmation of the strongest character that the right scientific basis has been obtained, with a solid foundation of fact as my standpoint.

137. To the student who loves to get near his author and to enter the *penetralia* of a poet's mind, it is intensely interesting to trace out the circumstantial evidence as to his life and environment, to detect in a great work the outcome of the author's personality, the traces of his surroundings and associations, marking him out as belonging to a certain place, and frequently fixing him down to a certain spot of earth and a certain date in time, among the generations and the dwellings of men. There are few, if any, of the greater names of literature that we could not, from internal evidence alone, and though all external evidence had perished, fasten down to a certain locality, and generally the greater the genius, the more easy it is to determine his dwelling-place and define his environment [2]. In the case of dramatic poets, the task might

---

[1] For the most part, among many modern investigators, it has been too often taken for granted that Homer was so entirely impersonal that it is in vain to look for *personalia*. According to H. N. Coleridge (Introd. p. 321), 'Homer is the embodied spirit of the Greek nation; after him, it is no longer the Muse speaking, but some one with idiosyncrasies, national peculiarities, a Theban, an Italian, a Sicilian poet.' We hope to show ground for a modification of this conclusion.

[2] Plato, for example, among prose-writers has left abundant witness of himself as to his personal surroundings. Even Aristotle, the most impersonal of all thinkers, could be proved to have composed his Metaphysics in a place where Ægina formed a common marine excursion (τὸ πλεῦσαι εἰς Αἴγιναν, a supposed case, Ar. Met. iv. 5), and therefore to have written under the shadow of the Acropolis. It is only artificial buckram poets that toss about their descriptive epithets of locality in a careless inconsequent fashion, as Seneca does when in one poem he styles the

be more difficult, to track them among their Protean manifestations, but even Æschylus and Sophocles and Euripides
could be localised from internal evidence. Shakspere, too,
could be shown, on perfectly cogent evidence, to have been
born near the Welsh frontier, to have been localised in or
about Warwickshire, and to have belonged to the West of
England, where the pebbly streams, according to the picture
in one of his earliest plays, do, in a manner unknown to
Eastern England, 'make sweet music with the enamelled
stones.' Of all the poets Dante is the one that has left the
personal impress of his *habitat* carved deepest into his poetry ;
but Horace and Virgil are not far behind him in the exquisite
embroidery with which they have woven into their poetry
remembrances of local scenes, by which, in default of all other
evidence regarding them, we could still refer them to their
native localities. We could tell from internal allusions that
Horace belonged to Southern Italy, for it is all about Apulia
and Baiæ and the Sabine hills that his personal memories
and likings linger, on the sunny side of snowy Soracte, within
the roar of Aufidus and the rustling of the forests of Garganus.
Virgil, too, though more of a learned poet and a painter of
dissolving views, and, occasionally, of artificial landscapes [3], can
be and often is natural, so that we could fix him down as a
native of Northern Italy, where the Eridanus was the 'king
of rivers,' and where Mantua and Cremona lay near Benacus
and Larius and the shadows of the Alps. Among our own
modern poets, if we select such as Wordsworth and Scott,
who were preeminently poets rooted and grounded in certain
localities, the internal evidence would be simply overwhelming,
and Burns has left such deep dints of himself that we could
fearlessly pronounce him the native of a county in Scotland
where Ailsa Craig was the visible symbol of immobility, where
a stream called Ayr 'gurgling kissed his pebbled shore,' and

Ismenus *languidus* and in another *rapidus* (Phoeniss. i. 116 ; Herc. Œt. i. 140).
All genuine poets give tokens of their presence, prints of their footsteps, more or
less determinable. Even Nonnus speaks of ' my native Nile' (Dionys. 26. 237),
and Meleager of Gadara, who had a true vein of poetry, has not left himself
under a mask (Anth. vii. 417).

  [3] Col. Leake (in his Morea, iii. 399, and Athens, p. 71) accuses the Latin poets,
when dealing with Greek scenery, of carelessness as to topographical detail. Cp.
Dean Stanley's observation on the accusation (Class. Mus. i. p. 61).

where the North Wind blew towards him off the shoulders of Benlomond.

It is evidence of this kind, descriptive strokes revealing the poet as an eye-witness, that we now go in search of in the Homeric poems, if peradventure we may be able in so far to attain the same clearness of view and firmness of footing. For, if the localisation of Hesiod and Archilochus is easy from *their* writings, so that we could prove Archilochus to have been a rover among the Egean isles [4], and Hesiod to have been a Bœotian in the neighbourhood of Helicon, there is a presumption that something similar is possible regarding Homer, be he singular or plural, or, as I think, dual, and in this presumption, after a glance at ancient opinion upon the question, we apply the spectroscope again to his poems.

138. In opening this part of the investigation, we may take as our point of departure the epigram by Antipater of Sidon, who flourished about B.C. 100, dealing with this point of Homeric localisation [5], and embodying, along with some poetic flourishes, the current, more or less critical, opinion of the best ancient investigators upon the point. It runs as follows:—

οἱ μέν σευ Κολοφῶνα τιθηνήτειραν, Ὅμηρε,
οἱ δὲ καλὰν Σμύρναν, οἱ δ' ἐνέπουσι Χίον,
οἱ δ' Ἴον, οἱ δ' ἐβόασαν εὔκλαρον Σαλαμῖνα,
οἱ δέ νυ τῶν Λαπιθέων ματέρα Θεσσαλίην,
ἄλλοι δ' ἄλλην γαῖαν ἀνίαχον· εἰ δέ με Φοίβου
χρὴ λέξαι πινυτὰς ἀμφαδὰ μαντοσύνας,
πάτρα σοι τελέθει μέγας Οὐρανός, ἐκ δὲ τεκούσης
οὐ θνατᾶς, ματρὸς δ' ἔπλεο Καλλιόπας.

Homer, some say that Colophon thee bare,
Some Chios and some Smyrna's city fair;
Some claim the blissful Salamis for thee,
Some Thessaly beyond the sounding sea;
Some Ios' isle: but what Apollo told
To me, to all I to declare am bold;
Heaven is thy home, and in bright halls above,
The Muse thy mother and thy father Jove.—BLACKIE.

[4] In the fragments of Archilochus we find Thasos mentioned *thrice*, Paros *once*, Naxos *once*.

[5] Although there was no unanimity as to the place of his birth, there was virtually unanimity as to the place of his death. Ios was the sole claimant of his tomb.

139. In comparing together this and the rival Lists, of which the principal are found subjoined, to the number of twelve[u], we remark this feature, that, while there is little uniformity as to the ending, there is all but complete unanimity as to the names with which the list should *begin.* These enumerations agree absolutely in this that they uniformly *commence* on the Asiatic shore, and with the exception of a slight variation in a few of them, viz. as to Kyme, they concur in placing a certain *Triad of cities* at the head of the list. The order in which Smyrna, Chios, and Colophon are named varies, but there is practical agreement as to these three having between them the precedence. *These three are all Ionian cities.*

[u] The following is the roll of claimants, according to Suidas, οἱ μὲν γὰρ ἔρασαν γενέσθαι Σμυρναῖον, οἱ δὲ Χῖον, οἱ δὲ Κολοφώνιον, οἱ δ' Ἰήτην, οἱ δὲ Κυμαῖον, οἱ δ' ἐκ Τροίας, ἀπὸ χωρίου Κεγχρεῶν, οἱ δὲ Λυδόν, οἱ δ' Ἀθηναῖον, οἱ δ' Ἰθακήσιον, οἱ δὲ Κύπριον, οἱ δὲ Σαλαμίνιον, οἱ δὲ Κνώσσιον, οἱ δὲ Μυκηναῖον, οἱ δὲ Αἰγύπτιον, οἱ δὲ Θετταλόν, οἱ δὲ Ἰταλιώτην, οἱ δὲ Λευκανόν, οἱ δὲ Γρύνιον, οἱ δὲ Ῥωμαῖον, οἱ δὲ Ῥόδιον. A less copious and more reasonable list is that given by Proclus, the grammarian, in his Chrestomathia, οἱ μὲν Κολοφώνιον αὐτὸν ἀνηγόρευσαν, οἱ δὲ Χῖον, οἱ δὲ Σμυρναῖον, οἱ δὲ Ἰήτην, ἄλλοι δὲ Κυμαῖον. Compare with the foregoing the common Latin couplet and the three Greek epigrams subjoined, the last of which (δ) was used by Varro for a bust of Homer (Aul. Gell. iii. 11):—

(α) Smyrna, Chios, Colophon, Salamis, Rhodos, Argos, Athenæ,
Orbis de patria certat, Homere, tua.

(β) ἑπτὰ ἐριδμαίνουσι πόλεις διὰ ῥίζαν Ὁμήρου,
Κύμη, Σμύρνα, Χίος, Κολοφών, Πύλος, Ἄργος, Ἀθῆναι.
(Anth. Plan. iv. 297.)

(γ) ἑπτὰ πόλεις μάρναντο σοφὴν διὰ ῥίζαν Ὁμήρου,
Σμύρνα, Χίος, Κολοφών, Ἰθάκη, Πύλος, Ἄργος, Ἀθῆναι.
(Anth. Plan. iv. 298.)

(δ) ἑπτὰ πόλεις διερίζουσι περὶ ῥίζαν Ὁμήρου,
Σμίρνα, Ῥύδος, Κολοφών, Σαλαμίν, Ἴος, Ἄργος, Ἀθῆναι.

To these we may add, as registering in a burlesque fashion ancient opinion, Lucian (Ver. Histor. ch. 20) οἱ μὲν Χῖον, οἱ δὲ Σμυρναῖον, πολλοὶ δὲ καὶ Κολοφώνιον αὐτὸν νομίζουσιν, κ.τ.λ. Also, in Lucian's Encom. Demosth. § 9, πατρίδα μὲν αὐτῷ διδόντες Ἰωνικὴν Κολοφῶνα, ἢ Κύμην, ἢ Χίον, ἢ Σμύρναν, ἢ Θήβας τὰς Αἰγυπτίας, ἢ μυρίας ἄλλας, κ.τ.λ. 'Homerum Colophonii civem esse dicunt suum, Chii suum vindicant, Salaminii repetunt, Smyrnæi vero suum esse confirmant' (Cicero, Pro Archia, ch. 8).—'Alii Colophonium, alii Smyrnæum, sunt qui Atheniensem, sunt qui Ægyptium dicant fuisse. Aristoteles tradit ex insula Io natum' (Aul. Gel., iii. 11). In the epigram, Anth. Plan. iv. 299, the order of interrogations is, Chios, Smyrna, Kyme, Colophon, Salamis, and similarly in 295 of same work, Smyrna, Colophon, Chios, Egypt, Cyprus, Ithaca, Argos, Mycenæ, Athens. Scylax, in his Periplus (probably as old as the time of Alexander the Great), declares for Smyrna (Σμύρνα ἐν ᾗ Ὅμηρος ἦν (Geogr. Gr. Min. p. 71, ed. Didot)), and Strabo (xii. 554) speaks of Smyrna alone as having most votes in its favour (τὴν ὑπὸ τῶν πλείστων λεγομένην αὐτοῦ πατρίδα).

140. The only other point that I call attention to at present (the claims of Argos and Athens remaining over for subsequent consideration) is the fact that, according to Suidas and the epigram of Antipater (§ 138), there was also a theory among others that Homer belonged to the 'land of the Lapithæ,' viz. to Thessaly. It is true that it was not an opinion that had many followers, for it is not often referred to, but there is no doubt that such a belief was entertained, and we may presume that certain grounds, more or less plausible, were adducible in support of it. In the course of this investigation we shall discover tolerably strong grounds presumably so adducible, upon which Thessaly might, so to speak, put in an appearance, grounds capable of serving as the basis of an argument to localise the singer of certain cantos of the Iliad in Thessaly, viz. the singer of the Achilleid.

In a former section (§ 27) we had occasion to glance at the *incunabula* of Greek poetry, and found the evidence converge to prove that the early lore and traditions of the Hellenic people in their individualised existence, as separate from the other Aryan races, are rooted in Thessaly. Not that the land was then known by that name, for in the days of tribal existence, there were few names of *districts*, but, as in ancient Gaul, many names of *tribes*, and therefore the name Thessaly, being post-Homeric, is here received and employed simply as a convenient expression to mean the country at the foot of Olympus and Othrys, in other words, Northern Greece[7].

That this country had already in very remote times a school of minstrels who sang lays of the Heroes and hymns to the Gods is manifest from the importance of Pieria in the memories of Greek song, in the commanding importance of Olympus as the abode of the Gods and in the circumstance that the Muses are styled *Olympian* in the Iliad and in Hesiod. By this last poet they are so styled in such a way as to indicate that the Bœotian school of song which he represented was an offshoot from the Olympian or Pierian,

---

[7] In calling Achilles a Thessalian, I put myself under the shield of Aristotle, who is taken to be the author of the epigram Θεσσαλὸς οὗτος ἀνὴρ Ἀχιλεύς, κ.τ.λ. (Bergk, Lyr. Gr., Eleg. Arist. No. 29).—The minor Scholiast, remarking on the corpse-dragging scene, styles him so, ὡς Θεσσαλὸν οὖν καὶ τὸν Ἀχιλλέα, πατρίῳ ἔθει καὶ τοῦτο (φησὶ) ποιῆσαι (Sch. on X 398).

transplanted from Thessalian soil (Hes., Theog. 1, 25, and cp. Preller, Gr. Myth. i. 279). The Bœotians, among whom Hesiod lived, were themselves formerly settled in a part of Thessaly (Thuc. i. 12), and the Bœotian migration out of Thessaly accounts for and explains the rise of a Bœotian school of song owning allegiance to the already consecrated muses of the Olympian region. It may be held therefore as a *prima facie* probability that Thessaly was a seat of song both pre-Homeric and pre-Hesiodic, and there is no *a priori* objection to the belief, if any tangible ground can be found to establish it, that a poem in honour of a Thessalian hero should have first assumed shape under a Thessalian poet on Thessalian soil.

141. And here I may observe that, for our present inquiry, I assume, without reference to prior questions, the early Grecian standpoint, and accept the Iliad and Odyssey as poems historically, and not merely poetically, conceived, that is, that they embodied or were conceived to embody a certain substratum of traditional incident believed in as once veritable fact and not 'a past which never was in any sense a present[8].' The evidence supporting this thesis is weightier than is usually believed, for, besides the strong pulse of a national life that is felt beating, we can at different points obtain glimpses of something like an historic consciousness on the part of the poet, so that he restricts himself as to the features and inventions of his own age, (e.g. κέλης and σάλπιγξ), and, while he may and does use them as similes, refrains from introducing them into the *action* of an age prior to his own[9]. There is therefore a certain allegiance in him to external fact and a subordination to historic conditions, and one might concede as probable an actual basis for the Trojan war as

---

[8] The most sceptical utterance in ancient times is probably that of Megakleides, who regarded the whole as a *fiction* (ταῦτα πάντα πλάσματα, Schol. on X 36).

[9] Col. Leake, in the preface to his 'Numismata Hellenica,' waxes warm against the deniers of Troy and the Trojan war, and thinks that if the monumental remains, illustrating the geography and early history of Greece, had been known to the erudite Germans of the last century, some of their most extravagant theories would never have been promulgated. Another fortunate explorer. Ch. T. Newton ('Travels, i. 135), speaks in glowing terms of the illumination which the landscape of the Troad casts upon the Homeric text. It might be premature to venture an opinion how far Dr. Schliemann's discoveries will modify opinion as to the mythical character of the war of Troy, but they will tend decidedly in that direction.

conducted by the Pelopidæ, for beyond it we discern dimly in
the background a prior expedition conducted by their predecessors the Persidæ, when Herakles and Telamon 'with six ships'
laid waste the city of Laomedon [10]. At the same time one must
be prepared to admit that much of the adornment, and many
of the incidents, may have been in origin purely mythical and
imaginative, and that ideas and situations, taken, we shall
say, from Solar or Storm mythes, may have been adopted as
poetic imagery to body forth the struggles and victories of
actual flesh and blood heroes. The Trojan war is, in all
probability, as Welcker expresses it, a mixture of 'Wahrheit
und Dichtung,' Poetry and Fact, (Ep. Ky. ii. p. 21). Whatever
therefore be the ultimate origin of the *materials*, it is clear
that the nucleus of the Iliad or the Achilleid is conceived
by its author as a great transaction enacted on the shore
of the Hellespont, and was so understood by the Greeks
during the whole period in which they are historically known
to us. But while the scene is on the Hellespont, the hero
belongs to Northern Greece, and is represented as sprung
from the land afterwards known as Thessaly [11]. The presumption therefore is that having before us a poem, such as
the Achilleid, in honour of a Thessalian hero, and having
evidence that Thessaly in the times answering to its appearance, not only possessed a certain fame for song, but was the
only country possessing that character, we are justified, in the
absence of any countervailing evidence, in referring the poem to
Thessaly as its probable source. The higher the antiquity of
the Achilleid, the stronger becomes this presumption, whereas
in the case of such aftergrowths as the Achilleid of Statius or
that of Göthe, where there has been a long interval to allow

[10] This older expedition is known to the older author also, the poet of the
Achilleid. Cp. Ξ 251, O 18, as well as E 640.

[11] 'No ancient poet *invents* the locality of his poem, but embellishes with mythological features what is obscurely known.' Von Bohlen on Genesis ii. 29 (Eng.
Tr.).—Compare also the words of Göthe, 'All national poetry must be shallow or
become shallow which does not rest on that which is most universally human—
upon the events of nations and their shepherds, when both stand for one man.
Kings are to be represented in war and danger, where by that very means they
appear as the first, because they determine and share the fate of the very least,
and thus become much more interesting than the Gods themselves, who, when
they have once determined the fates, withdraw from all participation in them'
(Autobiogr. i. 236).

the migration of legend from its primary *habitat*, such a presumption would be futile. The Achilleid of the Iliad has, however, quite the character of indigenous poetry, and precisely as in the case of the Scottish hero Robert Bruce, we might be certain *a priori* that a poem in his honour so near to his own time as Barbour's 'Bruce,' must be the product of Scottish soil, for the simple reason that no other nation or tribe but his own would take the necessary interest in him, either historically or poetically,—a presumption that would not apply so forcibly to a poem so comparatively late as Walter Scott's 'Lord of the Isles,'—in like manner we may presume to look upon the Achilleid as in all likelihood the outgrowth of the land to which Achilles was reputed to belong. The presumption is sufficient to furnish a working hypothesis which I now proceed to develop.

142. In a former section we had occasion to show how the Achillean poet has his vision comparatively confined, but at the same time clear and distinct, regarding the northern shores of the Ægean and specially in the neighbourhood of Thessaly.

The proofs of this latter position consist in the familar mention (1) of the Scythic tribes adjoining Thessaly on the North, such as the *Hippemolgi*, (2) of the tribes *Ephyri* and *Phlegyes*, (3) of Achelous as the 'king of rivers,'—a cluster of kindred associations enlarged upon in a previous section (§ 63). An important corroboration is found in the additional fact that two of the great legends of Thessaly are found alluded to only in the Achillean area, viz. (4) the Titan fight, and (5) the tradition of a Deluge. Regarding the former the evidence is complete. The battle between the Olympians and the Titans is localised in Thessaly[12], and accordingly the only allusions to the Titan struggle (compare § 99 of *Archaica*) are found in what we consider to be primarily a Thessalian poem, viz. the Achilleid. The other legend, that namely of the Deluge, generally associated, in Greek memory, with the name of the

---

[12] Hesiod is clear on this point (Theog. 632), and hence Preller states it thus, 'On Olympus the Kronidæ are encamped, on Othrys the Titans. Thessaly itself is the battlefield' (Gr. Myth. i. 46).—The name Ὀθρυονεύς in N, though borne by a Trojan, is a Pelasgian reminiscence of Othrys, and is, so far, suggestive of Thessaly.

Thessalian patriarch, Deucalion, seems nowhere alluded to except in Π 384, which may probably be taken, although in an indistinct form, as a Thessalian reminiscence.

143. The above circumstances fit in with the great fact, that Thessaly is the only country in Greece that will supply the *nidus* uniting these conditions characterising the Achilleid.

1. Prominence of Equestrianism and homage to the Horse.
2. Familiarity with Silvan Scenery.
3. Prominence of Olympus as a visible and tangible presence in the landscape.

The Achilleid possesses these features in a very marked manner and degree. The only country that will furnish the united conditions is Thessaly. Other countries might, indeed, set up a claim under the characteristics taken singly, but none, under the conditions combined. The ἱππόβοτον Ἄργος [13] might vie with it in the first, though at a long interval, but it would fail utterly under the other two tests, and Arcadia [14] could enter the lists in the second head, but must give way under the remaining two. Bœotia, with its πολυάρματος Θήβη (Soph. Antig. 149), and its κέντορες ἵππων (Δ 391), on the one hand, and its silvan scenery in Helicon and Cithæron on the other, comes nearest to rival Thessaly; but the evidence otherwise will not permit the ascription of the Achilleid to a native of Bœotia. Nor will the evidence allow any country in Asia Minor, whatever claim may thence be advanced as to

[13] It is not clear that the epithet ἱππόβοτον is applied only to the *Peloponnesian* Argos. It is found so applied in Ulyssean parts, as in Z 152 and Od. ο 274, and Pindar so understood it when he speaks of Ἄργος ἵππιον (Isth. vi. 12), referring to the Peloponnesian city (cp. Nem. x. 41). Compare also Horace's *Aptum dicit equis Argos*, where he couples it with Mycenæ. It may be doubted, however, whether Achilles in T 329 does not apply it to Thessaly, and so the Scholiast, remarking on Γ 75, understands the passage. The Ulyssean poet, in conformity with his relaxation of epithets, does not limit ἱππόβοτος to Argos, but extends it to *Elis* and the Thessalian *Tricca*, as in Δ 202 and Od. φ 347.—The origin of the steeds of the Peloponnesian Argos seems to have been mythically referred to the Diomedean steeds of Thrace, brought to Argos by Herakles, a breed thought to have survived down to Alexander the Great (Preller, Gr. M. ii. 141). In the Peloponnesian war, owing perhaps to the neutrality of Argos, the cavalry of Sparta is furnished chiefly by Bœotians (cp. Thuc. ii. 9, and iii. 62 fin.).

[14] Arcadia might vie in scenery with Thessaly, but the absence of equestrian associations is conclusive against any claim to have given birth to the Achilleid. The silence as to the Arcadian God Pan, and the entire absence of the Pelasgian Arcadians from the action of the Achilleid, are unaccountable on any supposable Arcadian theory.

the authorship of other sections, to come into competition with Thessaly in regard to the Achilleid.

144. In former sections (§ 122–3), we have given the proofs of an especial prominence assigned to the Horse in the Achilleid, and have shown that that animal occupies a lofty position in the thoughts of the minstrel and in the machinery of the poem. This position the horse attains especially in connection with the hero himself, and, Thessaly being his home, it is to Thessaly in particular that we must look for this exaltation of the 'lordly animal[15].' And what is the state of the case in the Achilleid? That the most notable hyperboles as to the powers of steeds, the *acmé* of their idealisation, are applied to the horses of Thessalian birth[16]. The singular honours thus bestowed are precisely such as we might expect to find in a poem taking shape and form in a land that was pre-eminently the equestrian field of Greece. The voice of legend and the testimony of history are conclusive as to Thessaly possessing this character. (1) The birth of the Horse and the taming of him are localised in Thessaly (Lucan, Phars. vi. 396–9). (2) The equine legend as to Kronos or Saturn is associated with Pelion (Virg. Georg. iii. 93[17], cp. Ap. Rh. ii. 1236). (3) The legend of the Centaurs ($K\acute{\epsilon}\nu\tau\alpha\nu\rho\omega$) cannot, in its Grecian form, be severed from the Horse, nor can it be dissociated locally from Thessaly[18]. (4) The eminently equestrian house of the *Neleids* (cp. § 124, n.), is, ultimately, of Thessalian descent.

---

[15] Similarly, regarding his *alter ego*, Patroclus, who is $\i\pi\pi o\kappa\acute{\epsilon}\lambda\epsilon\upsilon\theta os$, without an equal in the conduct of steeds (P 476), and seems to give the precedence to the steeds over the charioteer, if we may judge from the peculiar structure of Π 684 ($\Pi\acute{\alpha}\tau\rho o\kappa\lambda os$ δ' $\i\pi\pi o\iota\sigma\iota$ καὶ $A\upsilon\tau o\mu\acute{\epsilon}\delta o\nu\tau\iota$ $\kappa\epsilon\lambda\epsilon\acute{\upsilon}\sigma as$), which is an eminently Thessalian touch. Also, regarding the Myrmidons, compare § 133·5, for evidence of their special equestrianism.—The carrying off of steeds is specially named by Achilles (A 154) as one of the chief forms of calamity which a foe might inflict on his native land of Phthia, i. e. Thessaly.

[16] This holds good notwithstanding the Trojan descent (Π 153) of the *mortal* steed *Pedasus*. The two immortals are Achilles' own, and have come from Thessaly.

[17] Two out of the four equestrian legends, clustered together by Virgil in this passage, are Thessalian.

[18] The Centaurs are in Plato (Phædrus. ch. 7) still more closely associated with the horse, being called $\i\pi\pi o\kappa\acute{\epsilon}\nu\tau\alpha\nu\rho o\iota$. It is difficult to determine what was exactly symbolised by them, whether we are to take them with Preller as the mountain torrents tearing down the sides of Pelion, ' Demons of the mountain-flood'

145. In the historic time Thessaly continues the home of the steed. The Thessalian nobles were mainly a 'Ritterschaft,' admired ἐφ' ἱππικῇ τε καὶ πλούτῳ (Plato, Meno, 70 A), so that it was a proverb, 'cavaliers in Thessaly' (ἱππεῖς ἐν Θετταλίᾳ καὶ Θρᾴκῃ, Gaisford's Parœm. Gr.), and even their serfs, the πενέσται, when taken out to war by their lords, were 'mounted warriors' (Demosth. in Aristocr., p. 687, 1). An oracle was said to have given the palm to 'Thessalian steeds and Lacedæmonian women' (ἵπποι Θεσσαλικοὶ Λακεδαιμόνιαί τε γυναῖκες, cp. Schol. Il. B 763), a combination parallel to the comparison in Theocritus regarding Helen's beauty, ὡς ἅρματι Θεσσαλὸς ἵππος (Theocr. 18. 38). Elsewhere Theocritus speaks of one as ὁ Θεσσαλὸς ἱπποδιώκτας. In the *Thessalian* play of the Alcestis, Euripides has introduced the Thessalian feature of the steeds being made to participate in a general mourning (Alcest. l. 428), a custom natural to the land where, according to Ælian (Nat. Anim. 34), it was part of the marriage ceremony that the bridegroom should present a richly caparisoned war-horse to his bride. In the Anthology (ix. 21), Thessaly is spoken of as πατρὶς πωλοτρόφος[19]. Already, as early as Pindar, the Thessalians are styled ἱππόται λαοί without further definition (Pyth. iv. 150), and in the time of Alexander the 'Thessalian horse' figures in his campaigns as the most effective arm, along with the Macedonian phalanx, against the hosts of Darius.

('gewaltsam dahinströmende Berg und Waldströme,' Preller, Gr. M. i 318, ii. 135-6, perhaps ancestors of the Scotch 'water-kelpie;' cp. Βοάγριος the river of Locris, Blackie, Il. iv. 77), or, with Duncker, as 'predatory inhabitants of the mountains' having a turn for culling simples, or, with most Sanskritologists, as a variation of the 'Gandharvas' of Indian mythology. The musical accomplishments of the 'Gandharva' (Glendoveer of Southey) survive only in Cheiron among the Greek Centaurs. Blackie (Il. iv. 283) declares for their being men, for how else could the invention of medicine be ascribed to them? It is very strange to find an equestrian race, as the Centaurs are generally taken to be, having their haunts *among mountains* like Pelion (Nieb. Lect. on Geog. i. 158-9). Pliny (N. H. vii. 57) in his list of inventions attributes that of fighting on horse-back (pugnare ex equo) to 'Thessalians called Centaurs dwelling along mount Pelion.' One thing is certain that the Centaur-legend was localised in Thessaly, so that Clemens Alex. (Strom. iv. 3. § 9) speaks of it as a 'Thessalian fiction' (Θεσσαλικὸν πλάσμα). In Lucian (adv. Indoct. ch. 5) we find κενταυρίδαι of a crack breed of steeds, which the Scholiast (*ad loc.*) assigns to Thessaly (οἱ ἐκ Λαρίσσης τῆς Θεσσαλίης).

[19] Even the asses of Thessaly partook in the fame of their nobler relations. They are called διάφυροι καὶ ἄριστοι by Scholiast on Il. B 697.

146. This array of proof that Thessaly was preeminently the *equestrian* land of Greece finds a remarkable confirmation in the symbols of its coins. The Horse, or Horseman, is, in these, the prevailing figure. In Leake's 'Numismata Hellenica' (including its Appendix), will be found many curious facts conclusive in this direction. Thus the leading towns of Thessaly are set down as having the Horse as their favourite symbol, and the varieties of coinage, when compared, give the following result —

	Types with Horse.	Types without Horse.
Crannon	6	0
Larissa	40	4
Pharsalus	7	2
Pheræ	4	2
	57[20]	8.

The very frequent occurrence of the Horse upon the Thessalian coins may therefore be looked upon as a proof that it was a kind of national emblem belonging to the region[21].

If therefore we find a poem specially in honour of a Thessalian hero giving marked prominence to the animal which might be called the pride of Thessaly, and when we bear in mind the strongly 'localistic' character of early popular poetry, there appears ground for accepting as a probable presumption[22] the hypothesis of a Thessalian origin to the Achilleid.

147. We now come to the second of the heads advanced, and the argument thence derived is hardly inferior in force to the one we have been considering. It concerns the familiarity

[20] The preponderance is here sevenfold. In a full enumeration of all the evidences from the same *Numismata*, embracing less aristocratic communities than the above, I find the proportion not so remarkable but still notable, viz. ninety-five types with horse, and sixty-two without horse, from which last might fairly be deducted ten of the *Ænianes* and 'Thessaliae κοινόν,' the latter belonging to the Roman time, making the proportion ninety-five to fifty-two, nearly two to one.

[21] In coins of Magnesia *ad Mæandrum*, a horseman appears. On this type Leake remarks (Numism. p. 77), 'The horseman is a type of Thessalia, from whence came the colonists of Magnesia.'—Panormus in Sicily is the only place or country that can vie with Thessaly in the *frequency* of the type upon its coins. It is, there, probably a Libyan or Mauretanian feature.

[22] It may be worth noting, in passing, that the word ἀκοστήσας in the great simile of the prancing steed, on which see § 122, is suggestive of Thessaly, where the grain ἀκοστή (Buttm. Lex. *in voce*) is said to have had its especial *habitat*. The Schol. on O 263 says ἀκοστή was Cyprian for 'barley,' which is not inconsistent with its occurrence on Thessalian soil, as it may have been a 'survival' in Cyprus and so appeared to be specially Cyprian.—A horse 'fed with grain' (what grain?) was among Vedic offerings (Colebrooke, Essays, i. 40).

with *silvan images and scenery;* which I take to be a Thessalian note of some value, and considerable interest.

It may be assumed, as not likely to be disputed, that Thessaly contained in ancient times. as it does still, the noblest woodland scenery that Greece can show [23]. Its wide rolling plains are surrounded by a girdle of lofty mountains where woods and waters mingled combine to form the most wonderful landscapes. If therefore there is evidence of a special familiarity with silvan scenes in the Achilleid, an ancillary argument results for its Thessalian origin.

The special familiarity of the older minstrel with woodland scenery is thus evinced. It is in one of his cantos that we meet with a remarkable mode of indicating the time of day—a sort of primitive chronometer—whose archaic style is as significant as it is beautiful. When wishing to denote the forenoon of the day, this elder poet says, ' It is the time when the woodcutter takes his meal among the mountain glades after he has tired his arms with felling the tall trees ' (Λ 86). Beautifully silvan this,—a touch of unconscious nature—drawn no doubt from some Rothiemurchus among the spurs of Pelion (ἐν νάπαισι Πηλίου πεσεῖν ποτε τμηθεῖσα πεύκη Eur. Med. 3).

In the Odyssey, on the other hand, what is the index of the

---

[23] Ancient testimonies as to the scenery of Thessaly are Callimachus's Πίνδου ἀν' εὐάγκειαν (Hym. Dem. 83), and Theocritus's καλὰ Τέμπεα. The latter occurs in the passage where. in meditating what beautiful woodland scene may have detained the Nymphs from watching over Daphnis, he names, as *typical* of all beauty, Tempe and Pindus, both Thessalian. Compare also Ap. Rh. i. 597 and Eur. Bacchæ 560, where mention is made of ἐν τοῖς πολυδένδρεσσιν 'Ολύμπου θαλάμοις. Modern testimonies are such as that of Niebuhr (Lect. on Il. and Geo. i. 158). ' Mount Pelion is one of the most beautiful mountains in the world ; it is lovely and fertile up to its top; it is covered with chestnut-trees, and it is probably the place from which they have spread over the world, for their nuts are called *Nuces Castaneæ* from the town of Castanea on the Pagasean gulf. ... Among the Greek botanists it is celebrated for its richness in medicinal plants, and for the variety of its trees.' That of Dodwell (Tour in Greece, ii. 126) is sufficiently ample. ' The natural bulwarks, which encircle the rich Thessalian plains, are the mountains and chains of Œta, Pindos, Othrys, Olympos, Ossa, and Pelion, all of which are of grand dimensions and of imposing altitude. They are amply diversified by forests, fountains, and streams; by deep recesses, wild glens, verdant glades, and luxuriant pastures, with all the attractions of the picturesque. ... Many subordinate valleys are formed by the numerous ramifications of the great Thessalian mountains. Innumerable rivers descend from these towering heights.' Similar testimonies in the same author (vol. ii. pp. 81 and 89). Compare also Blackie, Homer's Iliad, vol. iv. 147, on characteristics of Thessaly.

time of day?   It is there indicated by a method less archaic, suggestive of the aggregation of men in social hives, where the strife of the ἀγορά has commenced and the organism of the πόλις has begun to play. The new mode of reckoning is by the time 'when a man rises from the Agora for his afternoon repast when judging the strifes of brisk youths contending at law' (Od. μ 439)[24]. Apart from the natural βουλυτός as a synonym for 'evening,' which is common to both Achilleid and Odyssey, these are the most marked indications of the *time* of day in either poem. The former, that of the Achilleid, suits with and suggests life in Thessaly; the latter, that of the Odyssey, suits with and suggests life in some busy communities such as those of Ionia, being in fact an early anticipation of the mode of reckoning familiar to us in the ἀγορὰ πλήθουσα of the Attic time[25].

148. The extent to which the vocabulary of woodland scenery and wild uncultivated nature enters into the texture of the Achilleid is very notable[26]. Certain of these terms, as

[24] These lines in Od. μ 439-441 may be accepted, though some doubts were raised in ancient times, probably because they seemed to suggest the scenes of the Athenian Dikastery. Strabo accepts them by commenting on them (i. 44), and no modern critic appears to have bracketed them, much less expelled them.—It is worthy of note, as a corroboration to the argument in the text, that the antithesis between πόλις and ἀγρός is distinctly present only in the neozoic area (Ψ 832, Od. α 185, ρ 182). So the antithesis of πόλις and δῆμος (probably *allotted land*, Mangold, in Curt. Stud. vi. 400) comes up in Γ 50, Ω 706, and four times in the Odyssey.

		Ach.	Ul.	Od.
Antithesis of πόλις and ἀγρός	. .	0	1	2
„ „ δῆμος	. .	0	2	4.

[25] The ἀγορά is no doubt familiar in the Achillean time (Π 387), and the archaic θέμιστες are there the ruling power. The ἀγορά of the Odyssey is more neozoic, and is nearer to the period of the νόμοι; and the term νόμος, though the simple word is found first in Hesiod, comes up in the sense of *law* in εὐνομίη of Odyssey (ρ 487), unless perhaps εὐδικίη, which occurs τ 111, be the true reading.

[26] The vocabulary of *Silvestria*, in woods and waters, is distributed as follows:—

	Ach.	Ul.	Od.
ἄξυλος ὕλη	1	0	0
νέμος	1	0	0
ὄρπηξ	1	0	0
νάπη	2	0	0
ξύλοχος βαθεῖα	2	0	0
χῶρος προαλής	1	0	0
πρών	4	0	0
κρημνός	6	0	0
ἔναυλος	3	0	0
αἰπὰ ῥέεθρα	2	0	0.

may be seen from the note subjoined, are either entirely confined to it or largely developed in that poem. So the pictures
and similes more especially redolent of silvan life are found
concentrated in the Achilleid. They are preeminently these:
Λ 155, 493; Μ 132; Ν 178, 389; Ξ 396, 414; Π 482, 633,
765; Ρ 53, 743; Υ 490; Φ 243. One of these (Μ 132) is particularly appropriate in the case of Thessalian warriors, the
sons of the Lapithæ being there likened to 'tall-topped trees
upon the mountains,' and all of these similes (numbering
thirteen) are full of the glory of woods and waters, and indicative of that scenery in which Thessaly excelled. Nothing
parallel, either in number or quality of descriptions, is producible from the Odyssey or Ulyssean cantos. These have
their own glory, but of another kind. The chief touches of
the *silvestria* in them are: Β 555, Δ 482, Ε 560, Ζ 147, Ψ 118,
and Od. ε 240, 478, ι 186, ξ 353 [27]; fewer from a much larger
area, and in general less luxuriantly depicted. This familiarity
with silvan scenes, claimed for the Achilleid, comes out felici-
tously in the language of Achilles when he dashes down his
sceptre on the ground and utters the great Oath framed in
words describing the woodcutting on the mountains. There is
probably no example in Greek Literature of so abundant an
expression of the pomp of forest scenery, as that given in the
Achilleid, until we come to the *Bacchæ* of Euripides. This
example, however, is one that goes far to prove my case. It
is a work, above all others of the Attic time, abounding in
pictures of silvan beauty and magnificence, and the inspiration under which it was composed is known to have been
drawn not from Attica or the Peloponnesus or Ionia, but
from the forest scenery of a country contiguous to Thessaly,

Ξύλοχος occurs (in Ε 162 and thrice in Odyssey) four times *without* βαθεῖα, which
adjective seems a favourite epithet with the Achillean poet. Contrast βαθέ'
ἄγκεα of Υ 490 as against ἄγκεα ποιήεντα of the Odyssey (δ 337, ρ 128). So
ὕλη βαθεῖα is found thrice in Achilleid, once in each of the two remaining sections
(Ε 555, Od. ρ 316); πυκινή and δάσκιος occur with ὕλη equally. ... Σ 320, Ο 273
as against Od. ζ 128, ε 470. It is singular that ἄσπετος ὕλη occurs only in Ulyssean parts, Β 455, Ψ 127, and Ω 784, and also ῥωχμός in Ψ 420.—Thus there is a
great preponderance in the Achilleid of the vocables denoting silvan and romantic
scenery. Ἀκριτόφυλλος and εἰνοσίφυλλος, along with πτόρθος, are the most notable
additions to the *Silvestria* of speech, not appearing in the Achilleid.

[27] The gardens of Alcinous in η 112-6 are an example of *cultivated* nature, not of
the *Silvestria* proper.

namely, Macedon. The visit of Euripides to the court of Archelaus seems to have opened up to him a new world of wild woodland scenery in which his imagination could disport itself, and hence the peculiarity of the play of the Bacchæ. What Macedon was climatically in the historic time, we may be sure Thessaly had been during the early or prehistoric time.

149. As an epilogue on this branch of the subject, it may be well to note the indications of climate and temperature apparent in the Achilleid. These correspond remarkably with the climatic conditions of Thessaly, and derive augmented force from the contrast which the non-Achilleid presents in its local mint-marks and climatic indications.

In the first place the West Wind or Zephyrus has not the same dominance in the *scenery* of the Achilleid as we shall find it has in that of the Odyssey and Ulyssean cantos. This is precisely what we should expect in a poem of Thessalian origin, and hence in the simile of Π 765 the winds named as warring in the woods are *Eurus* and *Notus*, not Zephyrus[29]. The same winds are no doubt described as at work in the simile of B 145, but there is this difference that the one scene is at sea, the other is on land, and the prevalence of winds on land affords a more significant mark of locality than the occurrence of the same winds on the open bosom of the sea. Moreover the simile in B 145, as we shall afterwards find, contains a mint-mark fixing it down, along with many more, to the Asiatic shore (cp. § 166. 1), whereas the simile in Π may be regarded as European in its standpoint, and so fits in with the Thessalian hypothesis.

In the second place the internal evidence is clearly in favour of referring the Achilleid to a colder and more northerly region, the non-Achilleid and Odyssey to a warmer and more southerly. It is true that meteorological investigations founded on ancient poetry are of a very slippery character, and I do not lay much stress on those I am about to adduce. At the

---

[29] Thessaly, as remarked by Lucan, was sheltered from the violence of Zephyrus by the Pindus range. 'Excipit *adversos zephyros* et Iapyga Pindus' (Phars vi. 330). Zephyrus is, however, acknowledged mythologically in connection with the pedigree of Achilles' steeds (Π 150), and is spoken of as a powerful wind in Λ 305, and in T 415, as having the name of 'fleetest,' where the word φασί appears to indicate a phenomenon less germane to the poet's own experience.

same time, whatever evidence they supply is in harmony with the views which on other grounds appear to be the correct ones as to the genesis of these poems.

150. The wardrobe of Achilles, as described in Π 224, appears to be calculated for the climate of Northern Greece. The mention, in that passage, of 'wind-defending' (ἀνεμοσκεπής) garments [30], suggests the inquiry as to winds and atmospheric phenomena generally. If the indications of these preponderate in the Achilleid, and diminish in the non-Achilleid, it is a fair presumption that the author of the former belongs to the Northern part of Greece, and that the author of the latter belongs to a more southern region. Accordingly we find that the more violent combinations of atmospheric phenomena [31], such as ἀνέμοιο θύελλα, ἀνέμοιο δὲ δεινὸς ἀήτης, abound in the one section, and decrease in the other. We may note especially Λ 297, 308, Μ 253, Ν 794, Ξ 17, 254, Ο 383, 620, 626, Π 213, which are in admirable keeping with the character of Thessaly, flanked by what Pindar calls 'the wind-roaring glens of Pelion' (Pyth. ix. 5) and what Callimachus styles 'the fell-blowing skirts of Pindus' (Hym. Del. 139). Against these *ten* may be put, as fairly parallel, only *two* in the Ulyssean cantos, Ζ 346 and, perhaps, Ψ 713. This disproportion [32] can hardly be explained by referring it to the nature of the subject, for in this respect the Achilleid and Ulyssean books are upon a par, both dealing in warlike scenes,

---

[30] The Odyssey has a parallel, though with a different term, χλαῖναν ἀλεξάνεμον (ξ 529).

[31] The action of Wind on the growth of plants and trees is familiar to the Achillean poet. It is thrice referred to by him (Λ 256, Μ 133, Ρ 55), and, seemingly, by him only. Likewise, δυσθαλπής and δυσπέμφελος, terms suggestive of grim weather, occur only in the Achilleid.

[32] A similar diminution of *violent* atmospheric phenomena is noticeable in the Ulyssean books under the following words. The apparent divergence of the Odyssey and Ulyssean cantos is owing to the nature of the subject of the Odyssey.

	Ach.	Ul.	Od.
βροντή and βροντάω	4	0	5
κεραυνός	8	0	9
λαῖλαψ	6	2	4
στεροπή	2	1	0
ἀστεροπή	2	0	0
χάλαζα	2	1	0

A parallel fact occurs regarding the *atmospheric* epithets of Zeus, formerly discussed. Cp. § 102. The instances of στεροπή as *metallic* gleam are not reckoned on either side.

regarding which the storm and tempest of Nature furnish the appropriate metaphors. The Odyssey gives full play to the Storm and Tempest as well as to the element of Calm Weather[33], but that is because it is a poem dealing with romantic *maritime* adventure, extending over various seas.

Perhaps the most important evidence, adducible under this minor head, is the contrast between two landscapes *under snow*, as depicted in the Achilleid and Odyssey respectively[34]. The former occurs in M 280, the latter is found in Od. τ 205. As rendered by the same translator Cowper, they severally run—

> 'As the feathery snows
> Fall frequent, on some wintry day, when Jove
> Hath risen to shed them on the race of man,
> And show his arrowy stores; he lulls the winds,
> Then shakes them down continual, covering thick
> Mountain tops, promontories, flowery meads,
> And cultured valleys rich; the ports and shores
> Receive it also of the hoary Deep,
> But there the waves bound it, while all beside
> Lies whelmed beneath Jove's fast descending shower,
> So thick, etc.'—(Il. M 280.)

> 'And as the snow by Zephyrus diffused,
> Melts on the mountain tops, when Eurus breathes,
> And fills the channels of the running streams,
> So melted she, and down her lovely cheeks
> Poured fast the tears.'—(Od. τ 205.)

In the former it is to be remarked that the snow is described as mantling the whole land to the edge of the sea; in the photograph from the Odyssey, it is found only as it were powdering the mountain tops[35]. The former picture is characteristic of Thessaly[36]; the latter of the milder region of Ionia.

---

[33] Χειμὼν ἔκπαγλος occurs in Od. ξ 522, against which may be balanced γαλήνη, found only in the Odyssey.

[34] The picture of winter in P 549 is one of cold and discomfort, against which might be set that in K 7. Both are neutral as to local indication, and may be left out of view. Neither could one rely on ἀθέσφατος ὄμβρος of Γ 4 as indicating the shrinking of a southern from the rigours of a northern winter. It very probably does so, but, until interpreted by other evidence, it is only a neutral phenomenon capable of facing either way.

[35] Cp. ἐπάλυνεν ἀρούρας, as to snowfall, in the cognate area of K 7.

[36] Compare with the picture in M 280, Dante's fine 'autotype'—

> 'As snow that lies
> Amidst the living rafters on the back
> Of Italy, congealed, when drifted high
> And closely piled by rough Sclavonian blasts.'
>
> (CARY's Dante, p. 339.)

151. We now come to the third and most important of the evidences for the Thessalian origin of the Achilleid. As yet one cannot say that we have got beyond the hazy region of presumptions. Now, however, we advance to phenomena that will justify the claim to be considered as Proof—whether sufficient in the circumstances for a *positive* verdict may be matter of opinion. It is proof derived from the peculiar prominence of Olympus in the poet's thoughts and mental horizon.

Pliny in his Natural History (iv. 15), when describing Thessaly, gives great importance to the Mountains as the dominant feature of Thessalian topography. Now, if there is truth in our association of the Achilleid with the Æolo-Dorian stem, whose pulse we feel beating proudly in Pindar, we may expect in a presumably Thessalian poem considerable prominence to be given to the influences of Mountain scenery. The Æolo-Dorian character is in its ground-lines that of *mountaineers*, as the character of the Ionians in its main features is that of a *sea-people*; and the rivalry of the two races may be said to have been a contest between marine mobility on the one hand, and mountain fixedness and stability on the other. The gloom and intensity of Sparta and Pindar and Pythagoras is already foreshadowed in the οὔρεα σκιόεντα [37] : the flash and play and brilliancy of Athens and Socrates and Sophocles, in the gleam and manifold motion of the θάλασσα ἠχήεσσα. The synthesis of the two elements composes the history of Greece, and possibly to a similar synthesis is due the wonderful combination of elements in the structure of the two greatest monuments of Greek genius, the Iliad and Odyssey.

These remarks are not to be understood to mean that the two rival educative influences of Mountain and Sea excluded each other. They influenced both races, but not equally,

Thessaly seems still to retain the Achillean characteristic. Col. Leake, in crossing from Joannina out of Epirus into Thessaly in November, had to pass through a forest of beeches, on the Thessalian side of the watershed, which were ' loaded with snow, which lies upon the ground four or five feet deep' (Tr. in N. Greece, i. 413).

[37] Perhaps the finest picture of the ' Mountain gloom and glory ' together is the simile of the Dispersing Storm-cloud in the Achillean Π 297, a picture, in the words of Col. Mure (ii. 70) ' of the thunder-cloud clearing off some lofty mountain range and unfolding to the view, in the bright sunbeams as they struggle through the still lurid atmosphere, the grand outline of peaks, and chasms, and projecting ridges.'

and, where the one influence predominated, the other nevertheless made itself felt as a potent element. Hence Pindar, while loving the mountains most, bestows ample homage on the sea, and so likewise with the author of the Achilleid. Both sea and ships are familiar to him, powerful pictures being drawn and similes (as T 375) being taken from both, and the κύματα παφλάζοντα πολυφλοίσβοιο θαλάσσης forms one of the gems adorning his cantos. This familiarity of the Thessalians with the sea is in fact greater in the prehistoric time than in the historic. In the historic time they have no fleet, and Pagasæ seems their sole seaport [38]. In the former time, the expedition of the Argonauts and the fame of the Minyæ, who are both a 'Ritter-volk' and a 'Schiffer-volk,' belong especially to Thessaly.

152. The poet of the Achilleid is in this respect the representative of prehistoric Thessaly. While the Sea is familiar to him, as it was more or less to every Greek, his special love is with the mountains [39], and in particular with the mountain that is king over his country, the regal Olympus.

There is the clearest evidence as to the dominance of Olympus in the landscape of the Achillean bard. It can be shown to have been to him a visible presence under distinct, almost palpable, recognition, as a veritable mountain and that in Thessaly. That his Olympus is the one in Thessaly is demonstrable, partly from the Pierian traditions at the basis of Greek mythology which connect themselves with Olympus as their centre, partly from the indubitable evidence, as formerly adverted to (§ 27), of the Fourteenth Iliad, an Achillean

---

[38] So Niebuhr (Lect. on Anc. Geog. i. 167).

[39] The occurrences of ὅρος and its derivatives and compounds (not *proper* names) are thus distributed :—

	Ach.	Ul.	Od.
Archaic forms from οὖρος	16	5	2
Less archaic forms from ὅρος	36	10	33
	52	15	35.

It so happens that while the oblique cases of ὅρος are well diffused, the form ὅρος itself as nom. or acc. comes up only in the neozoic area, four in Ulyssean cantos (of which three are topographical, being in Catalogue) and eleven in Odyssey. The apparently larger proportion in Odyssey is partly due to the recurrence of certain stereotyped formulæ, as, ὅρος κατειμένον ὕλη, occurring *twice*, and ὅρος πόλει ἀμφικαλύψαι, which happens to occur *five* times.—It is worth noting how the balance of *archaismus*, as seen above, under οὖρος, weighs down the Achillean scale.

canto. Secondly, that it is the real mountain which he has in view is shown by the epithets bestowed upon it. In particular that of ἀγάννιφος, 'exceedingly snowy,' is applied to it *twice*, and we do not discover this epithet assigned to it except in the Achilleid [40]. The poet of the Odyssey, as we shall find, seems to discard this epithet, for he prefers to impart a more sunny and comfortable view of the divine abode, which he represents as '*exempt* from snow' (cp. § 156).

Again, the familiarity with which the ῥίον (*horn* or *peak*) of Olympus is referred to seems to indicate an 'autotype' from the spot [41]. While the *many* κάρηνα of Olympus and of other mountains passed into a typical commonplace, there is never mention of more than *one* ῥίον of Olympus. It occurs at least *thrice* in the Achilleid. The manner in which this ῥίον is referred to in a concrete form shows that it was not only a visible but commanding object in the poet's landscape, so much so that it embarrasses his physical speculations and conceptions of the Cosmos, since it is made the pinnacle on which the world of sea and land is to be suspended by the golden chain (Θ 25). The ῥίον here, however, must be a part of the veritable mountain, not any idealised Olympus. So we may infer it is from the top of the Thessalian Olympus that Hephæstus is supposed to be precipitated when he falls on the not distant Lemnos (Λ 592). Similarly, in the magnificent line, ἀκροτάτῃ κορυφῇ πολυδείραδος Οὐλύμποιο, we may recognise the mint-mark of some Pierian bard in Thessaly. Its proper area is, as we might expect, the Achilleid, where it occurs twice. The only non-Achillean instance is E 754, where it seems traditional. Thessalian influence is also discernible in the line N 523, ἄκρῳ Ὀλύμπῳ [42] ὑπὸ χρυσέοισι νέφεσσι.

The stamp of Thessaly is likewise seen in the iteration of 'Olympian' as the epithet of the Muses. It is remarkable that this should occur thrice in the smaller area, viz. the Achilleid (Λ 218, Ξ 508, Π 112), only once elsewhere (B 484),

---

[40] Νιφόεις, applied to Olympus in Σ 616, is probably an echo of the traditional ἀγάννιφος.

[41] Probably the ridge of Olympus now called 'Semavat Evi,' which is interpreted 'Heavenly House.' Cp. Völcker, Hom. Geog. p. 16.

[42] The only instance of ἄκρος Ὄλυμπος, but we hear twice of Γαργάρῳ ἄκρῳ, all three only Achillean.

and not at all in the Odyssey, where the Muse does not appear to be thought of as Olympian at all. In this way we are led to infer that Olympus as a mountain occupies a vanishing position in the visible landscape—near and clear in the Achilleid, distant and traditional in the non-Achilleid.

Further, it will be difficult upon any other hypothesis to account for the limitation as to the epithet πολύπτυχος. It is an epithet twice used of Olympus and only in the Achilleid (Θ 411 and Υ 5)[43]. This also is an 'autotype' from the spot, and signifies 'with many folds' or 'reaches.' Nothing could be more appropriate to describe the vast extension of a giant mountain. Ida[44] is the only mountain sharing with Olympus the honour of the epithet (Φ 449, X 171). So the cognate πτύχες (apart from one instance in the Odyssey, as to Parnassus, τ 432), occurs only in the Achillean area, and of the whole seven occurrences of this family of words, as applied to mountain scenery, *six* are in the Achilleid and *four* of these six are given to the *mountain* Olympus.

153. The foregoing indications of locality are only strong presumptions, but they become more than presumptions by the evidence now to be adduced. In the great simile of Π 364, forming one of his war-images, the following lines occur :—

'Ὡς δ' ὅτ' ἀπ' Οὐλύμπου νέφος ἔρχεται οὐρανὸν εἴσω
αἰθέρος ἐκ δίης, ὅτε τε Ζεὺς λαίλαπα τείνῃ, κ.τ.λ.

'And as when *from Olympus* a cloud comes forth into the depths of the sky out from the divine Ether, what time Zeus launches forth the tempest, so, etc.'

[43] In the Hesiodic 'corpus' we find in the Theogony, 113, πολύπτυχον ἔσχον Ὄλυμπον.

[44] It is noticeable that only in the Achilleid is Ida spoken of as a *cluster* of mountains. The mention of Ἰδαίων ὁρέων occurs only in the Achilleid, and there *ten* times (including M 19). The name of its peak, Gargarus, comes up twice, and we hear of κορυφαὶ Ἴδης only in the same area. The occurrences, therefore, are—

	Ach.	Ul.	Od.
Ἰδαίων ὁρέων .	10	0	0
Γάργαρος .	2	0	0
Ἴδης κορυφαί .	5	0	0
	17	0	0.

When we contrast with this the peculiar localisation of Πέργαμα as found only in the *non*-Achillean area, and there *six* times, we find ourselves constrained to accept the theory of a double authorship in the structure of the Iliad.

The minstrel is describing the gathering of a cloud as it
forms itself out of the depths of air upon the battlement of
a huge mountain, before it advances to invade the plain below.
If the poet in such a case *names* the mountain, we may be
certain it will be one familiar to himself, familiar also to his
first auditors. For, the more primitive the minstrel, the more
may we rely on his illustrations as 'autotypes' from the spot,
and so autochthonal. His images are not fetched from far
away objects but spring up unbidden from local illustrations,
drawn from his immediate surroundings [45]. Bearing this
principle of primitive poetry in mind, we cannot doubt that
'Olympus,' named under such circumstances, is a veritable
mint-mark of Thessaly, and trustworthy evidence of the
Thessalian origin of the Achilleid. Thus leaps into view one
fact which lights up the whole field of survey.

154. It is hardly necessary to remark that in this instance
(whatever may be the case in other passages about to come
under review) the word Ὄλυμπος cannot be idealised into
'Heaven.' If that were so, the preposition would have been
ἐξ, not ἀπό, but it so happens that the word is clearly distinguished from both οὐρανός and αἰθήρ, and therefore there is no
escape from the conclusion [46] that Olympus is here a mountain,
and that too, regard being had to the character of primitive
poetry as rooted and grounded in *localities*, the great mountain of Thessaly.

The extent to which Ὄλυμπος enters into the vocabulary of
the two sections is, in this point of view, important. Though
recognised in the neozoic area, it is not so pervasively diffused
as we find it to be in the much smaller area of the Achilleid.
The following gives a rough census of the occurrences.

---

[45] A parallel case, quite in point *regarding this same Olympus*, is found in the fragment of Simonides (Bergk, frag. 170), where the poet at a feast calls for a ' morsel of
Olympus' snows to cool the wine,' an impromptu which we may suppose to have been
called forth by the sight of Olympus as seen from the mansion of the Scopadæ, his
entertainers in Thessaly. Accordingly, Schneidewin (fr. 148, Lyrici Græci) infers the
occasion and scene as Thessalian, 'In *Thessalorum* tyrannorum compotatione, conjeci.'

[46] The Scholiast (Ven. Schol. *ad loc.*) discusses the question, and comes to the
same conclusion as the only one possible (καταλείπεται τοίνυν τὸ ὄρος σημαίνεσθαι).
—A kindred simile is found in Π 297, where, though the word Ὄλυμπος does not
appear, ὄρος does, and that with the epithet μεγάλοιο, which adds to the probability
that Olympus is the mountain intended in this latter passage also, for μέγας, as an
epithet of Olympus, is confined to the Achilleid (Λ 530, Θ 443).

	Ach.	Ul.	Od.
Ὄλυμπος . . .	26	16	12
Οὔλυμπος . . .	30	11	3
	56	27	15.

Again, the preponderance of *archaismus* [47], as shown in the form Οὔλυμπος, is notably in favour of the Achilleid.

155. Let us now turn to the occurrences of Olympus in the Odyssey. What do we find to be its position in the thoughts and vision of this minstrel? Does it come before us with the same firmness of topographical detail and configuration, with which we find it etched into the texture of the Achilleid? It cannot be so affirmed. Apart from the otherwise doubtful passage of the Nekyia (λ 313), where it is no doubt a mountain and a Thessalian mountain, there is no indubitable instance of its being conceived as a mountain *with a definite localisation*. On the contrary there is an increasing number of passages in which it seems to fade away into invisibility and be confounded with the blue heaven itself. In the Achilleid, on the other hand, it everywhere preserves its individuality and, though conjoined with οὐρανός, is not confounded with it. This is manifest in Λ 497, Θ 394, Ο 192 [48], Π 364, and Τ 128 [49].

[47] In particular, the distribution of Οὐλυμπόνδε alone is remarkable, as showing at once the mutual conformity of Ulyssean cantos and Odyssey, and the archaism of Achilleid.

	Ach.	Ul.	Od.
Οὐλυμπόνδε . . .	10	1	1.

The expression μακρὸς Ὄλυμπος is found as often in the Achilleid as in the Ulyssean cantos and Odyssey together. The occurrences are

	Ach.	Ul.	Od.
	7	4	3.

The epithet εὐρύς is never found with Ὄλυμπος, but only with οὐρανός, and οὐρανὸς εὐρύς seems to increase in the area where μακρὸς Ὄλυμπος retires into the distance:

	Ach.	Ul.	Od.
οὐρανὸς εὐρύς . . .	7	5	22.

[48] Heyne remarks on this passage, ' Vides οὐρανόν et Ὄλυμπον discerni.'

[49] Aristarchus (Lehrs, § 175) laid it down as a rule that Ὄλυμπος in Homer was always the mountain of that name. The great critic was right, if he had limited his observation to the Achilleid. In Ο 193 there is a clear distinction between it and Οὐρανός, as well as in Π 364, and further the peculiarly Achillean expression, ' made big Olympus reel' (μέγαν δ' ἐλέλιξεν Ὄλυμπον, cp. πελεμίζετ' Ὄλυμπος, Θ 443), is intelligible only on the supposition of Olympus being a mountain. The nearest approach, within the Achilleid, to the neozoic view is Θ 411, where we hear of πύλαι Οὐλύμποιο soon after πύλαι οὐρανοῦ. The epithet πολύπτυχος, occurring there, applicable only to mountains, is a sufficient barrier to prevent the identifica-

156. How marked the differentiation is in this respect may
best be seen in the picture given of Olympus, now merely
a poetic mountain, which we find in a famous passage of the
Odyssey (ζ 42). It is the beautiful passage, where, though
still described as a mountain, it is sublimed out of the region
of the visible, no longer a cloud-wrapt, snow-clad mountain,
but rather a charmed region of the Empyrean, '*unvisited by
rain or any snow*,' (οὔτε χιὼν ἐπιπίλναται)—a startling departure from, if not contradiction to, the representations of
it in the Achilleid as 'exceedingly snowy' (ἀγάννιφος), and
as reposing 'under golden clouds' (ὑπὸ χρυσέοισι νέφεσσι).
The passage has been thus rendered:—

> 'Olympus, where *they say* the blessed gods
> Repose for ever in secure abodes;
> No stormy blasts athwart those summits sweep;
> No showers or snow bedew the sacred steep;
> But cloudless skies serene above are spread,
> And golden radiance plays around its head[50].'

The ancient critics tortured themselves sorely to find an
explanation that would reconcile this representation with the
Ὄλυμπος ἀγάννιφος of the Iliad, and their crude attempts may
be seen in Apollonius' Lexicon (in ἀγάννιφος). It is manifest,
however, that the true explanation is that the mountain in
each case is regarded from a different stand-point of vision.
The Olympus of this passage is no longer a topographical
presence in the landscape, but is a picture in the mind's
eye, and the minstrel who thus sings has come to regard it
as a tradition or inheritance. The introduction of the phrase
(φασι) 'men say' demonstrates this clearly enough. Further,
against the five examples from the Achilleid, quoted above
(§ 155 fin.), of Ὄλυμπος distinguished from οὐρανός, none is

---

tion with οὐρανός. Niebuhr (Lect. on Geo. i. p. 158) condemns Ennius's *maxima
forta Olympi* as a conception 'foreign to the Greeks.' The Aristarchus of Bonn
had overlooked Il. Θ 411, as well as Ap. Rhod. iii. 158, and Anthol. ix. 526, which
speak of πύλαι Οὐλύμποιο. Compare also βηλός, probably of Olympus, in Α 591,
and which may be suggestive of the threshold of a *gate*.

[50] In this picture many will recognise a resemblance, in one feature, not in all,
to Goldsmith's image of the 'mountain,' serene above, but vexed below, with
'eternal sunshine settling on its head.'—It is worth noting how, alongside of this
more *comfortable* representation of Olympus, come up the neozoic expressions as to
the untroubled life of the Gods, viz. ῥεῖα ζώοντες and ἀκηδέες. Cp. above, § 101.

producible from the Odyssey, but several occur in which they are used interchangeably. From this we are inclined to infer that Ὄλυμπος, as a mountain, was not within the visible horizon of the younger poet and was already passing into a synonym for Οὐρανός, so that the two were no longer, as a matter of fact, kept asunder. Most persons will therefore agree with Fäsi when he says in his note on ἀγάννιφος in Il. A 420: 'A different representation [of the mountain] is given in the Odyssey (ζ 42), and one drawn from the Imagination and the Ideal as to an abode of the gods.' The Achillean representation is therefore drawn from the Real.

The same critic in his 'Introduction' to the Odyssey thus touches on the matter: 'The designation of the gods by the formula οἳ οὐρανὸν εὐρὺν ἔχουσιν, which occurs in the Odyssey *fourteen* [? sixteen] times, occurs in the Iliad only *twice* and that in later books (Υ 298, Φ 267). The seat of the gods, Olympus, appears in the Iliad as a *mountain* situated in Pieria, and consequently with epithets which can be given only to a *mountain*. In the Odyssey, the representation of it has become generalised or idealised to the conception of an exalted Divine Region, and approximates near to that of Οὐρανός, "heaven," so that Οὐρανός and Ὄλυμπος interchange synonymously. (Cp. Od. υ 31 compared with 55 and 103 compared with 113).'

The above statement by Fäsi is, on the whole, both full and accurate, and confirms remarkably the view which the internal criticism reveals. It deserves to be noted, however, (1) that the strength of the proof for Olympus being in the Iliad a '*mountain* in Pieria' depends entirely on the Achilleid. (2) There is no just ground for his incidental remark as to οἳ οὐρανὸν εὐρὺν ἔχουσιν occurring only in later books of the Iliad. The phrase οὐρανὸς εὐρύς, though in another connection, comes up in at least two other passages of the Achilleid in earlier books (Θ 74 and Ο 192). (3) An additional example of the fusion of Ὄλυμπος and οὐρανός in the Odyssey is seen in υ 103, where, after αἰγλήεντος Ὀλύμπου, is added ὑψόθεν ἐκ νεφέων, thus identifying it still more with οὐρανός. A similar interchange may be quoted from τ 40 and 43. Four examples of the identification of the two terms are thus producible from the Odyssey.

The whole matter may be summed up in the words of Ihne, (Smith's Dict. of Biog., in 'Homer,' p. 510) who, without discerning the cause, describes fairly the phenomena. 'The gods of the Iliad [Achilleid] live on Mount Olympus; those of the Odyssey are further removed from the earth; they inhabit the wide heaven. There is nothing [in the Odyssey] which obliges us to think of the *Mount* Olympus.'

157. Thus far as to the position of Olympus in the Achilleid and in the Odyssey. It remains to inquire regarding the Ulyssean cantos, to which of these two areas that section is conformable. There is not much evidence on either side, but on the whole it is in favour of our general conclusion. Οὐρανός and Ὄλυμπος are conjoined once in E 750, which, however, may be an echo of the Achillean Θ 394. The clearest evidence upon the point is (1) that of Ω 97 compared with 104, which shows that in one at least of the Ulyssean cantos the position of the Odyssey has been reached, and Οὐρανός and Ὄλυμπος are interchangeable terms[51]. (2) The remarkable expression regarding Zeus, Ἴδηθεν μεδέων, looks as if the Picrian Olympus was not now so essential as the seat of the gods. It occurs *four* times, and only in the Ulyssean cantos. Compare also (3) the remarkable expression αἰθέρι ναίων, (formerly treated of, § 102, n. 19), as if Olympus was not now necessary as a ἕδος to the gods. It is found *thrice*,

[51] In Hesiod the epithet νιφόεις occurs five times and only of Olympus, πολύπτυχος once of it, and of Ida; ἀπ' οὐρανοῦ ἠδ' ἀπ' Ὀλύμπου ἀστράπτων (Theog. 689) implies a distinction, but ἐντὸς Ὀλύμπου of Theog. 37 seems to identify it with οὐρανός. In subsequent literature, as the centre of gravity of the Greek people moved more and more away from Thessaly, the notion of its being a mountain seems to recede still farther into the background. Thus in Solon (l. 21 of his ὑποθῆκαι) we read of θεῶν ἕδος, αἰπὺν Οὐρανόν, not as in Homeric poems, Ὄλυμπον. On Olympus as appearing in Sophocles, Œd. Rex, 866, Professor Campbell remarks: 'Olympus, the seat of the gods, is in Sophocles a sort of unseen heaven: and has almost lost the associations of place.' Oaths are sworn by it in Œd. Rex, 1087, Ant. 758. The associations of *place* are attached to it mainly in the Achilleid, and this can be readily explained, if that poem had a Thessalian origin.—It is noticeable, however, how instinct long prevented it from receiving other epithets than those suited to a mountain. Ἀστερόεις, for example, was felt to be incongruous and was applicable only to οὐρανός. Seneca, however, reveals the artificial character of his poetry in his ' *stelliger* Olympus,' and Nonnus (Dion. 46. 68) treats us to ἀστερόεις Ὄλυμπος, for which a preparation was perhaps made in πολύχρυσος Ὄλυμπος of Bacchylides (fr. 9). The epithet μέγας is the only one, according to Völcker (Hom. Geogr. p. 7), which Olympus and Οὐρανός have in Homer in common.

two being Ulyssean examples, B 412 and Δ 166. The third is Od. o 522. These three occurrences, however, come from one homogeneous area.

Further, the extent to which οὐρανός gained upon its rival Ὄλυμπος in association with the gods is seen in the fading away of Ὀλύμπιος before ἐπουράνιος and other similar expressions, a phenomenon that coincides with the diminution of Thessalian influence. Though Ὀλύμπιος with Ζεύς attached is nearly equally diffused, there is a preponderance in the Achilleid of examples where Ὀλύμπιος stands alone without needing the addition of Ζεύς or θεοί,—

	Ach.	Ul.	Od.	
Ὀλύμπιος, alone, without Ζεύς .	6	5	2	
Ὀλύμπιοι, alone, without θεοί .	2 *	0	0	* Α 399, Υ 47.
	8	5	2.	

The following are the chief facts as to οὐρανός :—

	Ach.	Ul.	Od.	
ἐπουράνιος, always with θεοί .	0	3	1	
οὐρανίωνες, with θεοί . .	2	1	3	
„ „ without θεοί . .	1 †	3	0	† Φ 275 (Φ 509 is
τοὶ οὐρανὸν εὐρὺν ἔχουσιν . .	2	0	16 [51]	not counted).
	5	7	20.	

The general result is that we find the balance of evidence leads us to associate in this as in many other particulars the Ulyssean cantos with the Odyssey, and to dissociate both from the Achilleid.

The above is the main evidence producible in favour of a Thessalian origin to the Achilleid. There remain some lesser touches which favour such a supposition and may be here detailed.

MINORA THESSALICA.

158. Among minor indications suggestive of a Thessalian origin are these : (a) The heroes of the Epic foretime, with whom Nestor claims to have mingled, viz. Pirithous, Kaineus, etc., are mainly Thessalian. This is from an Achillean book, A 263.

---

[51] The divergence of the Ulyssean cantos from the Odyssey in this expression is somewhat peculiar and would be perplexing, if the equivalent ἐπουράνιοι did not appear as a substitute for it mainly in the Ulyssean area.

(β) The frequent invocation of the muse is best explained as a Thessalian feature and a remnant of Pierian influence. It is found (besides A 1), in A 218, Ξ 508 and Ι1 112, all Achillean, about twice as often as in the Ulyssean cantos, where it occurs twice (B 484 and 761, the latter, however, very doubtful). (γ) The *Lapithæ*, though referred to in the Odyssey (φ 297), are mentioned individually only in the Achilleid (M 128, 181). The same heroes (Leonteus and Polypoetes) appear in Ψ 837 and in Catalogue in B 740, but they are not there designated as *Lapithæ*. The Thessalian poet, however in M, has taken care to stamp them as belonging to one of the Thessalian races. (δ) The Spercheus is once called a Διπετὴς ποταμός (Ι1 174). It is the second greatest river of Thessaly. (ε) The Achilleid specifies a Thessalian town not named in the Catalogue in B, viz. Βούδειον (Ι1 572)[53]. (ζ) The wind Νότος has the epithet Ἀργεστής twice, and only in the Achilleid (A 306, Φ 334). If the sense given to Ἀργεστής is 'blowing clear,' from ἀργός, 'white,' we might find an analogy in Horace's 'Albus Notus,' (perhaps from Apulia, in a latitude nearly the same as that of Thessaly), which wind is described as '*detergens* nubila coelo.' There is this difficulty, however, that the wind is spoken of in the Achilleid as collecting clouds rather than dispersing them, and hence some critics, as Merry in Od. μ 290, interpret the word as 'raising a *white* squall.' Whatever view is taken of it, the epithet marks a *peculiarity*, whether referable to Thessaly or not, in the meteorology of the Achilleid. (η) Patroclus, who is properly a Locrian by birth, is assumed as a Myrmidon and therefore a Thessalian (Il. Σ 8, where cp. Heyne). (θ) A warrior, Leonteus, is once styled βροτολοιγῷ ἶσος Ἄρηι (M 130). This honour he alone shares with Achilles, who has it once, and with Hector,

---

[53] Hayman (Od. vol. i. Pref. p. 97) would deny to the author of the Catalogue in B an intimate knowledge of Thessaly. 'It is clear from the Catalogue in B 681 ff. that the poet knew locally but little of Thessaly, as compared with many other regions which furnished his contingents.' It might, however, be rash to accept entirely such a conclusion, although it may be true that his knowledge of the northern frontier of Thessaly was somewhat vague, and the Catalogue in B does show a diminution in the proportion of epithet-bearing towns in Thessaly compared with Southern and Middle Greece. It seems to be an accident that the river Peneus is not mentioned in the Achilleid, but occurs only in the Catalogue in B. Ossa is named nowhere but in a doubtful passage of the Nekyia in the Odyssey (λ 315).

who has it twice. It is a comparison *never found outside the
Achilleid* (cp. § 108). This hero, however, is a *Lapith* from
Thessaly.

(ι) In the northern oracle of Dodona, Zeus was believed
to communicate his will without delegation to Apollo as his
mouthpiece. It is in harmony with this that the epithet
πανόμφαιος, marking him out as the fountain of augury, is
given to Zeus in the Achilleid (Θ 250).

(κ) Patroclus is thrice ἐνηής in Achilleid (P 204, including
670, Φ 96), and he is the *only* one so designated. Elsewhere,
however, the epithet is not thus limited, and is *shared* by
him with Nestor and Ulysses (Ψ 252, 648, θ 200).

Lastly (λ), if the passage is genuine, it is an interesting
Thessalian touch to find the roll of the sons of Zeus by mortal
mothers commence with a Thessalian hero, viz. Pirithous
(Ξ 318)[54].

It is in the Achilleid, therefore, that the traces of Thessalian influence appear in the greatest copiousness and fresh-
ness, and the general strain of evidence is in favour of its
Thessalian origin.

[51] It is remarkable that the elements for a poem like the Achilleid, in character
and sentiment, still exist in several of its features very largely in the Thessaly and
Albania of the present day, more largely than could now be found exemplified in
any other part of Europe. Illustrations of this point will be found in an Appendix.

CHAPTER XIX.

OBJECTIONS AND DIFFICULTIES CONSIDERED.

ἀλλ' ἄγ' ἀνὴρ ἀντ' ἀνδρὸς ἴτω, μεμάτω δὲ μάχεσθαι.

---

159. THERE are one or two objections that might be taken against the Thessalian and indeed against the European origin of the Homeric poems, either in whole or in part, and with these objections we ought now to deal. They are connected with the *Fauna* of the poem, and turn upon certain similes as to animals. I refer to the simile of the Locusts and the multiplied similes of the Lion. If the Achilleid is claimed as Thessalian, it might be regarded as a difficulty, how it has arisen that the Lion appears so frequently and once the Locust, in its poetic imagery? The prominence of the Horse, it may be said, is natural and intelligible, but what account can be rendered of the presence of the Lion? At first sight the objection has a formidable look, but the gravity of it, as also of the other, soon disappears.

In the first place as to the Locusts (Φ 12). It is true that, according to the Scholiast, some who claimed the poet as a Cyprian appealed to that simile, making him in fact more of an Oriental than the evidence will allow. It is not necessary to account for the simile by supposing that the knowledge of the locust may have been sufficiently familiar even beyond its proper habitat to admit of its being used in a simile, neither shall we claim for an old Epic bard such a licence as that used by Lord Byron, who introduced jackals into a European scene and afterwards apologised for the liberty (Works, p. 130). The fact is that locusts are known in European Greece at the present day, and there is evidence

that under the name of πάρνοπες they were often a plague
in the region of Thessaly in ancient times [1].

160. In the second place, as to the Lions. It has been sometimes argued that the familiarity with the lion is an argument
for the Asiatic origin of the poems as a whole, including, of
course, the Achilleid. It would, however, be quite fallacious,
and, unless we can produce better and sounder arguments for
their Asiatic origin, it would be wise to be discreetly silent.
The Asiatic origin of a considerable stratum of these poems
is scientifically certain, but it is made out independently of
any help from the position of the lion. It so happens that
we have the best of evidence, such as has satisfied the most
cautious historical critics, that the lion was not confined to
Asia in the period when these poems were composed, and
that he was found in Thessaly down into the historic time.
Herodotus records (vii. 125–6) that a part of Xerxes' army
in marching through Thessaly (B. C. 480) was attacked by
lions. Nor is this any fiction or mythe, much less a traveller's
tale, for the historian goes on to define, in the most matter of
fact way, the region or area where lions in his day were still
found, and of the region so defined lying between the Nestus
and the Achelous, Thessaly may be said to form the centre [2].

[1] As to ancient authorities, cp. Pausanias (i. 24. 8), regarding a statue of Apollo
as παρνόπιος, 'locust-killer,' and Strabo (xiii. 613), as to the Œtæans honouring Herakles for a similar service by the name of Κορνοπίων, κόρνοπες being the northern and
more antique name for πάρνοπες. The Œtæans are on the south border of Thessaly.—
Regarding modern authorities consult Dodwell (Travels, i. 213, 243), who gives a
bas-relief containing a figure of a man holding out a locust to a dog (copied in
Wordsworth's Greece, p. 42, and referred to in Müller's Ancient Art, § 96. 28).
The same traveller states that ' locusts, not quite so large as the Asiatic ones, are
sufficiently numerous in European Greece to become a plague.' Again, regarding
Libadea in Bœotia, he states, ' This place, and indeed most parts of Greece, is
infested by locusts, the *Gryllus migratorius*, which destroy great part of the produce
of the land.'—A more recent traveller, Professor Blackie, informs us (Homer,
iv. 391) that he had to encounter a snowstorm of vermilion locusts in a walk across
the isthmus of Corinth. The difficulty as to the locusts, whether we call them
ἀκρίδες or πάρνοπες, is thus disposed of without calling in Theocritus (i. 52) to
give evidence as to *Sicilian* locusts (cp. Leake, N. Greece, iv. 565, as to locusts at
Arta in Southern Albania).

[2] Additional evidence on the point, if such were necessary, is furnished by
Xenophon in his *De Venatione* (ch. 11), who states that, besides other localities
such as Pangæus in Macedonia, Λέοντες, παρδάλεις καὶ τοιαῦτα θηρία ἁλίσκεται ἐν
Πίνδῳ. Pindus is the mountain-backbone separating Epirus from Thessaly.—On
the coins of Acanthus we find an ox seized by a lion, possibly a local emblem.—
Also Pausanias (vi. 5. 4), as late as the middle of the second century after Christ,

Aristotle, who belonged by birth to that territory, twice confirms the statement of Herodotus (H. Anim. vi. 31, viii. 28). If the case was so in the historic time, much more may we presume it to have been in the pre-historic, when the fauna of Europe was still in its early uncircumscribed luxuriance. There is, therefore, no ground for doubting the Thessalian origin of the Achilleid on account of the frequency of similes taken from the lion.

161. But we go further and say there is positive evidence in the Achilleid of acquaintance with lions upon European soil. It so happens that there is *one* Homeric proper name commencing with Λέων, viz. *Leonteus,* and *his* nationality ought to throw light upon the question. It may be a surprise to find that he is neither a Trojan nor an Asiatic, but a Thessalian. He is in fact a Lapith from Thessaly (M 130). This circumstance alone is sufficient to demolish the presumption that the lion was familiarly known only in Asia.

And here I may submit, by way of epilogue on this point of the lions, a philological phenomenon which will prove rather a *crux* to any critic who upholds the absolute unity of the Iliad and denies the dualism of its structure. It is a curious circumstance that while the name λέων for 'lion' is diffused in all sections of the Homeric poems, there is a peculiar variation of the name given to him in the Achilleid and occurring nowhere else in either Iliad or Odyssey. I refer to the probably archaic λῖς, which comes up *five* times, but only in Achillean cantos[3]. It is called 'Æolic' by the Scholiast on

speaks of lions as still in Thrace, which is a country in the same zone and contiguous to Thessaly.—The presence of lions in Sicily is assumed by Euripides in the Cyclops, and, what is more remarkable, by Theocritus, i. 72, and the town *Leontini* seems to receive its name from the circumstance; but, like Shakspere's lion in the forest of Arden, these last are probably a mere poetical figment. Pindar, however, in his Education of Achilles, makes no difficulty as to the presence of lions in Thessaly (Nem. iii. 46). *Plura* in Notes and Queries, second Ser. viii. 81-4, ix. 57-9, xi. 310, from the pen of Sir G. C. Lewis.—In dealing with the Fauna of the Homeric poems, it is singular that we nowhere catch sight of the ἀλώπηξ or *Fox*, which, one might have thought, would have been occasionally appropriate to describe the character of Ulysses, at least as he is usually conceived. The poet Archilochus (B.C. 700) mentions the cunning creature, but it is a sign of the antiquity of the structure of the Odyssey, that neither the Fox is the emblem nor Hermes the immediate patron-deity of Ulysses.

[3] This term λῖς for *lion* seems to be unknown not only in the Odyssey, but also in the minor Homeric poems. It occurs in the Hesiodic poem of the 'Shield

P 109, and it is possible that Æolic here may mean Thessalian, Æolis being one of the old names for Thessaly; but, at all events, whatever account be given of λῖς, it supplies a cogent minor argument for the separation of the Achilleid as forming an individual poem within the 'corpus' of the Iliad.

162. There remain three other possible difficulties, which it is right to consider before leaving the proof for the separation of the Achilleid and for its Thessalian origin [4]. These are (1) The simile as to the sacrifice to the 'Heliconian God' in Υ 404. (2) The difficulty as to the Horses of Diomed in Θ being the same as those captured in the Ulyssean book E. (3) The position of Dione as an Olympian goddess.

(1) The simile, now found in the Achilleid, as to the roaring bull offered to the Heliconian God, has by some been taken to indicate an Asiatic origin, because Poseidon is known to have been worshipped under that name among the Ionian communities in Asia Minor. It was an old controversy, as we see from Strabo (viii. p. 589), whether the rite described in Υ 404 was that of the Panionian festival in Asia or from some older festival, of which that was a copy, in European Greece. Further, the supporters of the European origin of the name Ἑλικώνιος were divided as to whether it came from *Helike* in Achaia, or *Helikon* in Bœotia [5], both of which, and especially the former, were in some way seats of the *cultus* of Poseidon [6].

The objection founded upon Ἑλικώνιος, however, is one that cannot be sustained. It may be regarded as proved that the rite as celebrated in Asia was not native but a transference, having first existed in Europe. The Scholiast on the passage

of Herakles' (l. 172), and there it is quite in keeping with the Achillean usage, the story of that poem being localised *in Thessaly* near Pagasæ. It comes up also long after in Theocritus, but is in him an archaism revived. It is hardly necessary to remark that a λίς is found in the Odyssey, but it is there the equivalent of λισσή, and is the epithet of a rock, having no connection with the lion, and almost implying that that appellation had ceased to be familiar regarding the lion.

[4] I have not included the case of the κύμινδις—a name for a bird among the Ἴωνες, as Aristotle observes (H. of Anim. ix. 12. 5), and yet occurring in the Achilleid (Ξ 291)—as it is too obscure for a conclusion either way.

[5] Doederlein (Hom. Gloss., 466) connects all these words with ἑλίκη, *salix*, and would render Ἑλικών as 'willow-hill.' The affinities of the willow with low moist ground may have associated it with places sacred to Poseidon.

[6] It is not improbable that we have an Ionian trace in the sacrifice of *twelve* bulls to Poseidon in ν 182 of Odyssey, that being the number of states in the federation of the Asiatic Ionians.

states this distinctly (cp. Pausanias, vii. 24. 4), that Neleus the son of Codrus, in colonising Miletus, 'founded a temple in honour of Heliconian Poseidon *in imitation of that in Helike* of Achaia' (κατὰ μίμησιν τοῦ ἐν Ἑλίκῃ τῆς Ἀχαίας). A minor difficulty is how, in that case, the form is Ἑλικώνιος and not Ἑλικήιος[7] (cp. Ἰδήιος). The major difficulty, however, is thereby removed, for the *cultus* is thus shown to have been primarily European. It was therefore cognisable by a Thessalian bard such as we suppose the author of the Achilleid to have been.

163. (2) The passage Θ 105–8 is one that contains a statement by Diomed as to the virtues of certain steeds of the Troian breed 'which *once*,' he says, 'I captured from Æneas, inspirers of flight.' There is a scene in E which answers to this description, for there Diomed is represented as capturing the steeds of Æneas, which steeds are said to be of the Troian breed. But E belongs to the Ulyssean cantos, which are younger, and, the Achilleid being older, Θ, which is Achillean, seems to presuppose the occurrence in the Ulyssean canto. The dilemma is critical, and it is a misfortune that Mr. Grote had not directed his attention to it and shown how it could be removed, since it is the most formidable argument that seems capable of being advanced against his doctrine of the severance of the Achilleid. Let us therefore approach the matter carefully and see what is really the position of the case.

Is it so then that there are references in the Achilleid to passages in the Ulyssean cantos? If so, and if there is no doubt as to the genuineness of the passages, the doctrine of an Achilleid separate and prior could not be maintained. It is, however, in the first place, remarkable how few possible references are producible and how self-contained and independent in its unity the Achilleid is. Among these possible references, it might be alleged that Λ 366 contains an allusion to Athene's having aided Diomed, as described in E. The same line, however, occurs in the mouth of Achilles (Υ 453), where there is no specific reference to assistance on any particular occasion. Therefore in Υ 453 the reference is vague and general, which may be and is probably the case with Λ 366. It is not necessary therefore upon such a ground to infer that E was in origin

---

[7] Steph. Byz. on Ἑλίκη says ὁ πολίτης, Ἑλικώνιος.

antecedent to Λ [8]. As to the *crux* regarding the steeds of Diomed, it is to be remarked, (1) That the Tradition or Saga concerning him made him famous as a capturer of steeds from the Trojans. Those of Æneas are not the only ones captured by him: he takes horses from the sons of Dares (E 25), also from certain sons of Priam (E 165), and he is the possessor of Rhesus' steeds after their capture (K 567). (2) If the author of Θ did refer to E, it is somewhat strange that he should not have referred also to the companion book Z, where Diomed becomes the possessor of a suit of golden armour [9]. Yet in Θ he comes forth equipped with apparently the usual armour of a Greek, possessing a $\theta\omega\rho\eta\xi$ (Θ 194), which, though of brilliant character, is not the golden one he had got from Glaucus in Z (O. Müller, Lit. ch. v. 7), and there is no allusion to the suit recently acquired. Neither in Λ do we gather that Diomed had received any but the ordinary armour. Therefore Θ and Λ agree in making no reference to the great acquisition by Diomed in Z. It may, however, be argued that this is a weapon that tells two ways, for there is no reference to the 'golden armour' afterwards, even in the Ulyssean cantos. The answer to this is that there was no proper or necessary occasion for its introduction, since, (except the night expedition of K, where such accoutrements would have been out of place), there is no *warfare* in which he is afterwards engaged. (3) If the reference in Θ 105 is presumed to be to canto E, it is singular to find an event, which in the present chronology of the poem, belongs to the *previous day*, dated not, as we should expect, $\chi\theta\acute{e}s$ (*yesterday*), but $\pi o\tau\acute{e}$ (*whilome* or *once on a time*). It may, no doubt, be answered that $\pi o\tau\acute{e}$ seems to mean *yesterday* in two other places, Ξ 45 and Od. χ 290. In the latter passage, however, $\pi o\tau\acute{e}$ is naturally enough interpreted in its ordinary sense, and in the other,

---

[8] The taunt of Ares to Athene in Φ 396, reproaching her with stirring up Diomed to fight—seemingly a reminiscence of E—is not to be relied on as counter evidence since it belongs to the second Theomachy, a section of the Achilleid peculiarly suspicious. A similar remark applies to Φ 421.—The speech of Diomed in Ξ 109 contains no clear reference to the incident of Δ 402, but I 34, which is Ulyssean, does show a knowledge of Δ.—No argument can be drawn from $\mathring{\eta}\tau o\iota$ $\mathring{e}\phi\eta\nu$ $\gamma\epsilon$ in Π 61 as a reference to I 650, since it is not clear that $\mathring{e}\phi\eta\nu$ here means *dixi*, but rather $\delta\iota\epsilon\nu o\acute{\eta}\theta\eta\nu$, as the Scholiast interprets it (cp. Grote, II. ii. 241).

[9] Nonnus (Dion. 15. 165) does not omit to refer to the dazzling brilliancy of Diomed's *golden* armour.

it may denote a *general* reference to the boastful utterances of the Achillean Hector without being *necessarily* referred back to Θ 178–182. (4) The line, however, in Θ in which ποτέ appears, and upon which the whole case of an objector would rest, is not above question as to genuineness. Aristonicus among ancient critics expunged it, owing to the awkwardness of the apparent allusion to a transaction of the *previous* day. Lehrs, among modern critics (Arist. p. 431), considers it spurious, and holds it to be an after accretion, modelled upon the line in Ψ 291, where ποτέ as a particle of time is quite appropriate. La Roche, however, does not bracket the line, and therefore we cannot, without stronger reasons, adopt the easy plea of spuriousness. (5) The real state of the case seems to be, as indicated in the outset of these remarks, that the allusion [10] in Θ is to the traditional event or exploit, and not to the narration in E. This is the view of Friedländer, who thus treats of the matter.

'We can assume that the poet of the Achilleid has here (i. e. in Θ), interwoven for the nonce an earlier deed of Diomed, without referring to anything in the previous narrative that has preceded, and that the poet of the Iliad (that is, of the cantos B to H)—whether the same or another—has subsequently availed himself of this 'motive' to be the groundwork of a complete narration. In the insertion of the Iliad into the Achilleid, the declaration of Diomed fell on the day *after* the acquisition of the horses, and the word *once-on-a-time* (ποτέ) came not to suit the circumstances. This is a supposition made only to show that the passage does not *compel* us to suppose in the poet of Θ a prior knowledge of E.' (L. Friedländer, Homerische Kritik, p. 34). The general result is that no conclusion can be drawn from this passage in Θ adverse to the independence and separate individuality of the Achilleid.

164. A third (3) objection, that might naturally be made, relates to the position of Dione. If the Achilleid is Thessalian and if the worship of Zeus at Dodona is especially

---

[10] An analogous case would be that in Ξ 71, where reference is made to interpositions of Zeus in behalf of the Greeks, which cannot be explained by the existing Iliad, but by the traditions of the war before the 'Wrath' begins. So in O 721–3 Hector complains of a state of things, for which there is no adequate explanation *within* the existing poem. Similar remark applies to Z 436.

prominent, how comes it that his Pelasgian consort Dione appears, not in the Achillean, but in the Ulyssean, area? This is, also, an important point, and requires careful elucidation.

The only occurrence of Dione in the Iliad and Odyssey is the incident of E 370, in the reception which she gives to her daughter Aphrodite, when returning wounded to Olympus. She is there a personage of high rank, being styled δῖα θεάων. If this is the Dodonean Dione, it is certainly singular that she should figure only in a Ulyssean canto, and not in the part of the poem where Thessalian elements are interfused.

Although it has been usual to identify Dione of E with the Dodonean Dione, there is little doubt that this is a mere assumption, and in fact there are insuperable barriers to that view. In the first place, the Dione of Dodona was identical with Heré [11] (Ἥρη Διώνη (v. l. Διαίνη) παρὰ Δωδωναίοις, Schol. Od. γ 91, and so Strabo, vii. § 329). But the Dione of E is certainly distinct from Heré. Secondly, the Thessalian legends of the Argonautic cycle acknowledged Jove's chief consort by the name of Heré. It is Heré, not Dione, that figures in the story of Jason [12]. Therefore there is no preliminary necessity that a Thessalian poet should style the consort of Zeus by the name of Dione. Hence it is Heré that appears, in Achillean as in Ulyssean cantos, as the consort of Zeus, and there is no mention of Dione among the secondary consorts in the long list of the same (if we may take it as evidence), in Ξ 317. On the contrary, the Achillean poet leaves no room for Dione when he seems to make Heré mother of Aphrodite, if we may infer as much from the φίλον τέκος of Ξ 190. Thirdly, the Dodonean Dione, though the most famous, is not the only Dione. In the very ancient, and, according to Thucydides, Homeric, hymn to Apollo (l. 93) a Dione figures among the goddesses, αἲ ἄρισται ἔσαν, being named first in a list consisting of Rhea, Themis, Amphitrite, and is specially distinguished from Heré. This is in the Delian legend of the birth of Apollo, which legend is entirely Ionic, and has

---

[11] The Italian name *Juno* stands philologically in much the same relation to 'Jupiter' or 'Jovis,' as Διώνη does to Ζεύς. Hence Fäsi speaks of Dione as a 'Neben-gestalt' of Here.—It is singular that Herodotus, in his account of the *cultus* of Dodona (ii. 52-55), makes no mention of Dione.

[12] Ἥρη Πελαυγίς is acknowledged in the Argonautics of Apoll. Rhod. i. 14.

no Dodonean affinities. As for the Dione of Hesiod (Theog. 17),
she is also distinct from Heré. There are no epithets attaching
her to any locality, but since she appears only in the suspected
proem, and is not acknowledged in the body of the Theogony,
where the poet assigns to Aphrodite another origin, there is
no light thence derivable. The name Dione is found, however, on Asiatic soil in the legend of Tantalus, whose children
are Pelops and Niobe, 'born from Dione [13].' This mention of
Dione, though the evidence for it is post-Homeric, is believed
to appertain to the *cultus* of Zeus on Mount Sipylus in
Western Asia, the same mount Sipylus which figures in the
Ulyssean canto Ω and is contiguous to many of the spots
which we shall find studded with personal associations of the
Ulyssean poet. There is therefore evidence to show that the
name Διώνη does *not necessarily* imply Dodonean affinities.
But the daughter of this Dione, namely, Aphrodite, is, as we
had occasion to show in a previous section (§ 103, γ)[14], uniformly, in the Ulyssean cantos and in the Odyssey, in close
connection with Phœnicia and the East. Therefore we must
inquire whether there is any other Dione than the Dodonean
that could account for this apparition. In the mythology of
the Phœnicians, according to Philo of Byblus, there are two
chief deities, Kronos, as he calls him, and Dione. There is
little doubt that these two formed a pair of the same character
as Jupiter and Juno in Italian, and as Zeus with his ordinary
consort Heré, in Greek mythology. Further, in Diodorus
Siculus (i. 13. 4) we find that Egyptian deities answering to
Zeus and Heré, and so styled by him, have, among other
children, Aphrodite. So in Cretan legends, the same author

[13] Preller (Gr. M. ii. 268) has the following regarding Tantalus, 'Seine Kinder
sind Pelops und Niobe, geboren von der Dione, deren Name gleichfalls auf die
nahe Beziehung dieser Sagen zum Zeusdienste vom Sipylos hinweist.'

[14] 'Tochter der Dione ist in der Ilias Aphrodite, die sich verwundet ihr in den
Schooss wirft (Il. v. 370, 428), was Phidias im Westgiebelfelde des Parthenon
nachgeahmt hat. Die Homerische Aphrodite aber ist ein Kind Asiatischen Cults
und der Pierischen Poesie, also nicht nachweislich Pelasgischen Stammes: sie ist
nicht durch inneren Zusammenhang der Bedeutung oder natürliche Entwicklung
Tochter des Zeus und der Dione, sondern durch dichterische Absicht und Ver-
knüpfung.' Welcker, Gr. Götterlehre, i. 355.—Ernst Curtius (Hist. of Gr. i. 105,
E. Tr.) makes the Dione of Dodona 'a transplantation from the distant east,' and
appeals to her symbol the dove, from which her priestesses were called Πελειάδες.
If this is accepted, the whole difficulty as to Dione vanishes at once.

(v. 72), after telling us of the nuptials of Zeus and Heré, says that among the offspring of Zeus was Aphrodite. It will generally be allowed that Heré, when represented as mother to Aphrodite, as in these two passages of Diodorus, answers to the Dione of the Fifth Iliad [15].

Enough has thus been advanced to show that Dione as the mother of Aphrodite is not necessarily to be referred to the Pelasgian *cultus* at Dodona, and that her absence from the Achillean area and presence in the Ulyssean area can be otherwise sufficiently accounted for, through the southern and eastern associations which we have shown to predominate among those of the Ulyssean Bard.

The difficulties and objections have thus been fairly met and disposed of, so that, in so far as they are concerned, the conclusion formerly reached remains untouched.

[15] It is notable that it is Dione that relates, among other things, the legend in E of Otus and Ephialtes. According to the Scholiast on E 385, these were connected with Adonis-worship and Mount Lebanon. She is also the speaker who uses the curious word κέραμος, said to be *Cyprian* for a *prison*, which is appropriate enough, seeing her affinities were Eastern.—According to Strabo (vii. p. 329), in his account of Dodona, the worship of Dione alongside of Zeus as his σύνναος was not from immemorial time. It almost looks as if the Achilleid was antecedent to the association of the cultus of Dione with that of Zeus at Dodona.

CHAPTER XX.

LOCAL MINT-MARKS—ULYSSEAN CANTOS.

εἰπὲ δέ μοι γαῖάν τε τεήν, δῆμόν τε πόλιν τε.

165. THE local mint-marks of the non-Achillean parts of
the Iliad will next engage our attention.

In the two immediately preceding chapters, we have given
a *résumé* of the evidence for a Thessalian origin to the Achilleid, and we have also refuted some objections that might be
made to such an hypothesis. In a poem so remote, and one that
has been subjected to so many shaping, moulding, and varying
influences of time and criticism, the wonder is that there are
distinct traces of origin still remaining, or any determinable
indications yet visible of its probable locality. In groping
one's way in such obscurity, one has the feeling that the
conclusion thus reached as to the Achilleid is, after all, not
proved, but only a strong probability. In the inquiry, however, which I am now to institute, the proof is not only more
abundant but more circumstantial, and the conclusion under
this branch of the investigation is one that may be looked
upon as established on a due measure of satisfactory evidence.

The evidence regarding the local origin of the Ulyssean
cantos will be found to be, in variety, force, and frequency, of
the utmost cogency, so cogent as to be overwhelming. It is
true that Mr. Gladstone, with the vehemence that characterises
him in defence of certain cherished propositions, has lately re-
committed himself to the doctrine that Homer was a native
of European Greece, and he denounces in no measured terms
any other doctrine as untenable and false, and as a blind

'mechanical assent' to a current tradition [1]. When a splendid racer goes wrong, his very virtues lead him farther astray, and it would be an entire perversion of the truth to accept Mr. Gladstone's obstinate asseverations on the point. To insist on Homer being prior to the Ionic migration with a view to square with certain preconceived notions as to the date of the Troica, is to do despotic violence to the whole conditions of the case; for it involves the absurdity of supposing that the in-that-case European poet, living *before* the Ionic migration, and therefore previous to any widespread popular acquaintance with the scenery of the Asiatic coast, drew his favourite illustrations from phenomena that were localised in a then alien region, and that became familiar only after the Ionian migration had obtained a footing on that shore. It is to these illustrations that I now address myself, to gather up and piece together the fragments of evidence as to local origin. They all point to the Asiatic shore.

In entering on this part of the subject I follow in the footsteps of Robert Wood, who, in his elegant and thoughtful Essay 'on the Original Genius of Homer' (1775), with much geographical and historical insight, first presented the evidence in favour of his Ionian origin in a scientific and satisfactory form. That treatise, notwithstanding Mr. Gladstone's slighting remarks, still remains 'classic' upon this question, and nothing could in general be more fair and judicial than its presentation of the various points of evidence [2]. That evidence has received large accessions of strength since the time of Wood, and there ought to be no reasonable doubt to any ordinary mind as to the locality in which the Iliad received its completion—which it did by the accession of the Ulyssean cantos.

166. Let us proceed to examine that series of cantos to ascertain what are the local indications they contain.

(1). The first of the series is canto B or the second book, and there we meet with several notable indications. At line 145

---

[1] 'At the point to which my endeavours to examine the text of the poems have led me, when I confront the opinion that he was an Asiatic Greek born after the Dorian conquest, I can only say to it "aroint thee." I could almost as easily believe him an Englishman or Shakspeare a Frenchman, or Dante an American.' Gladstone (Hom. Synchronism, p. 72).

[2] Professor Blackie (i. 201) does not share Mr. Gladstone's depreciatory opinion of Wood's Essay. A hint in its pages produced the Wolfian Theory.

we read that 'the assembly was moved like the big waves of the sea *in the Icarian deep*, waves which Eurus and Notus have roused, swooping down from the clouds of Father Zeus.' This is in a simile, and a simile is, of course, a condescension or an approximation on the part of the poet to his audience, an attempt to body forth the invisible by something visible, something less known by what is better known. Hence, in a popular poet, such as Homer, the similes are the nearest approach to a throwing off the mask, a sort of familiar '*asides*,' confidential and confessional, and we may rely upon *them* as the genuine expression of the poet's personality.

What then is the deduction from the above simile? The mention of the winds does not help us, as the scene is at sea. Yet it is no vague description, as to the waves of the sea generally, for a portion of the world of waters is clearly defined. The poet names 'the *Icarian* deep.' Where does it lie? It is a part of the Eastern Egean round the islands of Icaria and Samos, and washes the Ionian seaboard [3].

Some one might perhaps imagine that the poet, if an Ionian, would name a sea more remote, and so the *Icarian deep* would be less appropriate to an Ionian bard. Distance may *now* lend enchantment to the view; but, in old Epic song, that which was near was sufficiently real to be poetic, and the objectivity of Greek Epic poetry was and is its most delightful charm. Even poets much more subjective than Homer have left parallel traces of themselves which are quite in keeping with this mention of the 'Icarian deep.' Theognis, the poet of Megara, when speaking allegorically of the ruin of his country drifting like a ship at sea, speaks of the storms (Μηλίου ἐκ πόντου) 'from out the Melian deep.' The 'Melian deep' is the stretch of sea on which his native Megara looked out as part of the Egean. The Sicilian Theocritus speaks of the adjoining Sea as the *Sicilian*, a fact which one might have inferred, without specification, from the scenes of his chief pastorals. So, to take a modern instance. Spenser, in his Fäery Queen, which was composed *in Ireland*, gives note of his actual surroundings in the following parallel :—

---

[3] It is important to note what seems a *neozoic* feature, viz.. a *section* of the sea receiving a special name. Similar examples are B 145, Ψ 230, and (if Μειλανι is read) Ω 79, all Ulyssean, and showing, so to speak, *nautical* familiarity with the whole Egean.

> ' As when two billows *in the Irish soundes,*
> Forcibly driven with contrarie tides,
> Do meet together, each aback rebounds
> With roaring rage.'—F. Queen, iv. 1. 42.

This simile, therefore, as to the 'Icarian deep,' corroborated as it is by a cluster from the same neighbourhood, is one of considerable value and conclusiveness, and we therefore accept Strabo's judgment upon the point: εὐεπιφόρως δὲ ἔχει (Ὅμηρος) πρὸς τὴν ἐγγυτάτην καὶ γνωριμωτάτην ἑαυτῷ θάλατταν, and in proof he quotes this passage about the 'Icarian deep.'

(2). In a subsequent passage of B (l. 147), we have a simile drawn from the violent action of Zephyrus (the West Wind), sweeping over a cornfield and making it wave with all its army of ears. This then is a scene on land, not by sea, and the wind prevailing may thus afford an indication of locality. The inference is that the poet's country was a land where the *West* wind was the formidable one, and this we know to have been the case in Ionia[4]. This will appear more clearly in subsequent instances.

(3). The next glimpse of locality obtainable is from B 461. Mention is made of the 'Asian meadow,' (in another reading, 'meadow of Asias'), round the 'streams of Cayster,' and reference is made to the wild fowls swarming in the marshes, 'geese, cranes, and long-necked swans[5].' Cayster is one of the streams on the Ionian seaboard, near Ephesus, and this is no doubt a photograph from the poet's own personal environment. The passage contains the oldest mention known to us of the name *Asia*, whatever view be taken of the origin or form of the name as there appearing.

(4). A very interesting note of locality is found in B 535.

---

[4] On the other hand *Notus* or the South Wind, when breaking on the coast, is described as exerting its power not on a line of beach, but on a projecting promontory (B 396), a description quite suitable to promontories like *Mimas* in Ionia.

[5] Swans, we know, haunted the Peneus also (Hom. Hym. 20. 1). It is difficult to understand how, if Homer was, as Mr. Gladstone affirms, a European, he should have drawn his local illustrations so persistently from Asia, when they were readily obtainable in Europe. The poet of B speaks of the Cayster when the Peneus might have served, the reason being that the Cayster was known to him neither by hearsay nor by travel, but was native and familiar to his thoughts and eye. Professor Blackie remarks accordingly as to this passage about the swans (Homer, iv. p. 68), 'Here the bard is evidently painting scenes as familiar to his eye as the whirr of the partridge on Tweedside was to the ear of Walter Scott.'

In describing the geographical situation of the Locrians, he speaks of them as 'dwelling *beyond* sacred Eubœa' (ναίουσι πέρην ἱερῆς Εὐβοίης). This was a note of locality to which R. Wood attached special value, as indicating that the poet's stand-point lay *East* of Eubœa, and Heyne followed him with a verdict clear and unwavering, justifying the reasoning [6]. If the above translation is correct, there can be no question that, to an Ionian, the orientation, so to speak, is the most perfect that can be conceived. To one standing on a head-land of Asiatic Ionia, Locris would lie precisely behind and beyond the long isle of Eubœa, and no description could be more suitable.

The leading translators (except Blackie and Newman) have accordingly taken this view[7]: as, for example, the two German translators :—

> 'Lokrer, die *jenseits* wohnen dem heiligen Lande Euboea.'—Voss.
> 'Lokrer, die *jenseits* wohnen der heiligen Insel Euboea.'—Donner.

It is argued, however, or rather asserted, among others, by Mr. Gladstone, that πέρην here means nothing more than 'over against,' or 'opposite[8]' and so conveys no intimation of the speaker's stand-point. If, however, the majority of translators

---

[6] 'Arguunt haec,' says Heyne in his note on the line, 'poetam non in Graecia sed in insulis Ægaei maris vel in ora maritima Asiae degentem, cui trans Euboeam esset Locris.'—So Düntzer (Hom. Abh. p. 146) holds that it is clear from this passage that 'the poet's stand-point was *outside* European Greece.'

[7] Compare Cowper's :—
> 'Next from *beyond* Eubœa's happy isle
> In forty ships conveyed, stood forth well armed
> The Locrians.'

Brandreth's :—
> 'And with him forty sable vessels went
> Of Locrians who *beyond* Eubœa dwell.'

Lord Derby :—
> 'Him from *beyond* Eubœa's sacred isle
> Of Locrians followed forty dark-ribb'd ships.'

Herschel's :—
> 'Locrians these from the coast *beyond* Eubœa the sacred.'

[8] This would require ἀντίον, not πέρην, and hence the lines of Theolytus, an epic poet of uncertain age, regarding this very coast :—
> 'Ανθηδών νυ τίς ἐστιν ἐπὶ πλευρῇσι θαλάσσης
> ἀντίον Εὐβοίης.

Compare also in Geogr. Gr. Minores (p. 219, ed. Didot), ἀπέναντι δ' Εὐβοίας κατοικοῦσιν Λοκροί. 'Αντίον and ἀπέναντι, unlike πέρην, convey no intimation of the standpoint of the speaker.—πέρην and ἀντίον are *contrasted* in Herod: i. 201.

are right in rendering it *beyond*, it *does* convey such intimation, and the question therefore is, in the first place, what is the primary meaning of $\pi\epsilon\rho\eta\nu$? Curtius, in his 'Etymologie,' gives as the etymon of it the Sanskrit *para-m*, which he renders *jenseits*, i. e. 'beyond.' Hesychius rendered it by $\epsilon\pi\epsilon\kappa\epsilon\iota\nu\alpha$, which means '*on the further side*.' Fortunately we are under no dubiety as to this being the sense and the only sense in another passage of Homer, viz. Ω 752 $\pi\epsilon\rho\nu\alpha\sigma\kappa\epsilon$ $\pi\epsilon\rho\eta\nu$ $\alpha\lambda\delta s$, where no ingenuity could extract the sense 'sold *over against* the sea.' People sell slaves *beyond* sea or across the sea, not *opposite* sea [9]. That is one indubitable instance, and it contains an intimation of direction, and of progression from a *terminus a quo* to a *terminus ad quem*. There is only one other instance in Homer of the disputed word, viz. in B 626, regarding the Echinades islands, which are described as lying $\pi\epsilon\rho\eta\nu$ $\alpha\lambda\delta s$, $^{"}H\lambda\iota\delta os$ $\alpha\nu\tau\alpha$. No one could contend for the meaning here being 'opposite the sea,' instead of 'beyond' or 'across sea,' if for no other reason than because the presence of $\alpha\nu\tau\alpha$ is proof that $\pi\epsilon\rho\eta\nu$ had not the sense of *opposite*, for that belongs to $\alpha\nu\tau\alpha$. It may, indeed, be doubtful whether here, and in $\alpha\nu\tau\iota\pi\epsilon\rho\alpha\iota'$ of B 635, the Ionian poet does not fall into what may be called a Peloponnesian mode of speech ; but this is of no consequence, for his point of view and relation toward these islands of the western sea does not differ from the Peloponnesian ; only it is a point of view more distant.

Is there then any reason for deserting the sole sense which $\pi\epsilon\rho\eta\nu$ can be shown to bear in the Homeric poems and introducing a new and unnecessary interpretation? None within the two Homeric poems, and, though Crusius and Ebeling, following Buttmann (Lexil. § 91)[10], both attempt to relegate $\pi\epsilon\rho\eta\nu$ of this passage into the sense of *opposite*, they do so

---

[9] When the Titans are described as dwelling $\pi\epsilon\rho\eta\nu$ $X\acute{a}\epsilon os$ $\zeta o\phi\epsilon\rho o\hat{\imath}o$ (Hes., Theog. 814), it is clear that $X\acute{a}os$ is the gulf between the speaker and the Titans, and therefore here also the sense of $\pi\epsilon\rho\eta\nu$ is *across* or *beyond*, not *opposite*.

[10] The disturbing cause that led Buttmann wrong was a desire to harmonise the interpretation of $\pi\epsilon\rho\eta\nu$ in Homer with that in $X\alpha\lambda\kappa\iota\delta os$ $\pi\epsilon\rho\alpha\nu$ $\epsilon\chi\omega\nu$ (Æsch. Ag. 182), where he thought the interpretation must be 'halting *opposite* Chalcis.' 'Across from Chalcis' is also a possible rendering, but, in either case, it does not follow that an idiom from Æschylus is to overrule the *natural* interpretation of a word in the Homeric poems.—As to $\pi\epsilon\rho\alpha\nu$ $E\dot{\nu}\beta o\acute{\iota}as$ describing the Locrians in Pausanias (x. 8. 5), this does not imply in that author an Asiatic standpoint, but is a quotation of well-known Homeric phraseology.

without justification. For what reason can be assigned why the position of the Locrians should be described by reference to a more distant and out-lying country, *not yet named* in the enumeration, *if* the speaker's stand-point was within European Greece? Mr. Gladstone feels this difficulty, and thinks he gets over it in the following way :—

'Homer probably describes the position of the Locrians by reference to Euboié, either because of the consecrating epithet ['sacred Euboié'], or because the Abantes, its inhabitants, were a particularly martial and distinguished portion of the Greek army' (Hom. Synchronism, p. 83).

These reasons, however, if correct in point of fact, which may be doubted in the case of the Abantes, are insufficient to explain *geographical* position. Not more successful is the view of Buttmann founded on a passage of Strabo (ix. § 426) that this reference to Euboea was a way of indicating the position of the *other* Locrians who are not named.

The real reason, which I have now to mention, was because *Euboea* to an Ionian was the *vanguard of European Greece.* Its long narrow ridge, as any one looking at the map will discern, must have appeared, to one familiar with the Icarian sea, like a screen concealing the mainland of European Hellas [11].

This conclusion, however, it may be said, is only an inference commending itself by the facility of our modern charts. Have we any *proof*, apart from this passage, that Euboea was a landmark in the thoughts and vision of an Ionian?

We have, and, what is remarkable, proof of the clearest kind that has hitherto been strangely overlooked. It comes, however, from the Odyssey, which, if our theory is correct, is of Ionian authorship also, and cognate with these Ulyssean cantos, and although we thereby anticipate the evidence of locality from the Odyssey, it may be most appropriate to introduce it here.

(a). If we read attentively the account of the home-voyage of the Greeks in Od. γ 169–176, we find two things observable : (1) special familiarity with the navigation along the Ionian coast, where two topographical sites are specified, appearing nowhere else in the two Epics (viz. Psyria and Mimas); (2) along

---

[11] Πέρην, like *trans*, or our *beyond*, in Milton's ' Beyond the stormy Hebrides.' is not limited to *water-boundaries*. Cp. πέραν ὁρᾶν in Strabo, infra in note 18, p. 287.

with this notable familiarity with the Ionian coast we find reference to the course which had to be steered from it across the Ægean. There was *direction* given, said to be from a divine omen, to cleave the sea midway, to where? *To Eubœa* (γ. 174), a clear indication that that was the steersman's mark in pushing west from Ionia, where the Greek fleet had just been.

(β). Again, in Od. η 321, Alcinous is represented as saying that Ulysses would be conveyed to his home, 'even though it were very much farther than *Eubœa*, which those of our folk who have seen it say to be most remote.' Why select Eubœa? Because the poet is wishing to convey to his hearers, presumably Ionian, the notion of the extraordinary remoteness of Phæacia, and contrives to represent as a kind of 'ultima Thule' of the Phæacians that land of Eubœa, which lay on the outskirts of their own Ionian horizon [12].

We can now estimate the value of Buttmann's assertion that 'it is not to be supposed that from the distant coast of Asia, from which no eye could reach to Greece, the poet's first thought should be fixed on the island of Eubœa' (Lexil. p. 468). We do find the poet's first thought fixed, in other instances, on the island of Eubœa, so that we can affirm that island to have been a regulative point of direction in Ionian navigation, a conspicuous land-mark within the poet's horizon. There is thus discovered a powerful 'clavus trabalis' or adamantine bolt binding together the framework of the Odyssey and the Ulyssean cantos of the Iliad.

I pass now to resume consideration of other mint-marks in those Ulyssean cantos.

(5). In Γ 189, we find mention made of the *Amazons*. Without entering into the deeper questions as to this mysterious race, it is important to note that any traces of them that appear to rest on some nucleus of fact connect themselves with Asia Minor, and it is only in Ulyssean cantos that they are mentioned. The city of Ephesus in particular had legends as to the Amazons, and in general the Ionic and Æolic colonies in Asia Minor had stories, if not traditions,

---

[12] The reason in the text for this prominence of Eubœa is more satisfactory than Ernst Curtius's notion (Hist. i. 433, which is good to explain Æschylus as quoted in n. 10) that the early commercial eminence of Chalcis had already rendered Eubœa famous, and that that city kept up a lively trade with Phæacia.

connected with them (O. Müller, Dorians, i. p. 405, E. Tr.) [13]. Now, just as the Thessalian mythic tribes of Ephyri and Phlegyes are mentioned only in the Achilleid, so the Asiatic mythic race of Amazons comes up only in the Ulyssean cantos, in an area where otherwise we find frequent indications of Asiatic associations.

(6). In Γ 276 and 320, Zeus is invoked as Ἴδηθεν μεδέων [14], 'ruling from Ida,' without any reference to his associations with Olympus. This is not strange upon Trojan soil, but the peculiarity is that it occurs in the mouth of Greeks, such as Agamemnon, as well as of Trojans. This corresponds with the fact already noticed (§ 157) that Olympus in the Odyssey retires into the background, and so the Ionian poet seems to find a new seat of Zeus within his own visible horizon. The occurrence of Ἴδηθεν μεδέων, *four* times and only in Ulyssean cantos, is a fact concurring with those other phenomena of the presence of αἰθέρι ναίων, and the withdrawal of Olympus out of the visible diurnal sphere, while the whole can be explained only by regarding it as part of a cluster of evidences witnessing to the Asiatic affinities of an Ionian bard [15].

(7). In Δ 142 we come upon another simile, evidently from personal observation, bearing evidence of the same complete and satisfactory character as in the case of the similes relating to the Icarian sea and the swans of Cayster. It is the place where he describes, as an effect in colour, the red blood over the white limbs of the wounded Menelaus, and says, 'As when a woman stains ivory with a purple dye, *Mæonian* maid or *Carian*, to form a cheek-piece for steeds, etc.' The illustration is drawn from the artistic effect produced by colour in the hands of certain colour-loving races. What are these races? They are those adjoining the Ionians, viz. Mæonians and Carians, and the phenomenon thus described is evidently one familiar not only to himself but to his earliest audience. The Greek settler in Smyrna or Colophon became early aware

---

[13] The Attic legend of the invasion of Attica by the Amazons is not in the same category with the wide-spread traditions as to Amazons rooted in Asia.

[14] Ἴδηθεν μεδέων seems to have interfused itself as a various reading also in B 412. See Lehrs, Arist. p. 363.

[15] Mr. Gladstone (i. 493) remarks on this expression about Ida, and finds it difficult to explain how the *Greeks* are represented not as appealing to Zeus of Dodona or of Olympus, but as accepting what he calls 'a Trojan form of invocation.'

of the decorative qualities of colour, for a knowledge of dyes seems to have been indigenous to that part of Asia, Sardis and Thyatira continuing in the historic time famous for their dyes (cp. Sappho, frag. 22, and N. T., Acts xvi. 13).

(8 and 9). Two other similes in Δ may also be appealed to. We have the action of Zephyrus or West Wind twice described under circumstances that suit only the Ionian coast. In the one (Δ 276) we have the picture presented of the driving Zephyrus, as he comes darkening across the deep, and the shepherd drives his flock to shelter. The poet's point of view is evidently that of one looking *West* from some head-land (ἀπὸ σκοπιῆς, l. 275) commanding the Egean [16]. Similarly, the surging billows beating on the strand under the propulsion of the *west wind* (Ζεφύρου ὑποκινήσαντος, Δ 423) is a sketch from the same stand-point, that from which the old Ionian

> 'Beheld the Iliad and the Odyssee
> Rise to the swelling of the voiceful sea.'

(10). In Z 186 we find the minor mint-mark of the Amazons. This has been already adverted to under No. 5.

(11). In Λ 63 another simile of the same evidential value as those in Δ (Nos. 8 and 9) regarding Zephyrus the West Wind in his stormy moods.

(12). Also in Λ 202 recurs Ἴδηθεν μεδέων, and in the mouth of Greeks, already adverted to under No. 6.

(13). In I 5 occurs probably the most important of these topographical indications. The distraction of Agamemnon's mind is thus described :—

'As when two winds stir up the fish-abounding Sea, viz. Boreas and Zephyrus, which blow from Thrace, swooping suddenly down,' etc. [17].

---

[16] The evidence here is the same as Cumberland or Westmoreland could appeal to as being the fatherland of Wordsworth's ' Prelude,' in which the vale of Furness is spoken of:—

> ' To more than inland peace
> Left by the *West Wind* sweeping overhead
> From a *tumultuous* ocean.'—(Prelude, p. 37.)

And their furrowed glens are described as

> ' Long deep channels for the *Atlantic's* voice.'

The geographical situation of Ionia with reference to the sea is similar to that of Palestine. Cp. N. T., Luke xii. 54, where we hear of the rain-cloud as coming, ἀπὸ δυσμῶν, ' out of the *West*,' and, in 1 Kings xviii. 44, the cloud comes ' out of the sea.'

[17] Mr. Gladstone has failed to represent the evidence rightly in this passage.

The picture ends with the tossing of sea-weed on the strand.

Now, it is quite impossible for anyone to suppose the author of this to be on European soil. The blowing of Boreas over the sea from Thrace down upon European Greece is quite possible, and Hesiod (Op. 505) may be quoted in proof, but not the blowing of *Zephyrus* from Thrace[18]. The scene is evidently in Asiatic Ionia, for, as Thrace in the Epic time extended so far west as to include Macedonia (cp. Ξ 227, where Thrace and its snowy hills evidently extend west of Mount Athos), it was quite possible and even natural for an Ionian to regard the West Wind as well as the North as blowing to him over the sea from Thrace[19].

(14). In Ω 308 occurs the fourth instance of Ἴδηθεν μεδέων, on which see No. 6. Cp. Ζεὺς Ἰδαῖος in Ω 291. Both, however, are here less significant, being in the mouth of Trojans.

(15). In Ω 532 occurs the peculiar term βούβρωστις, by some taken for 'savage hunger,' like that of oxen; by others for an 'ox-stinging gadfly.' In one of the Scholiasts it is explained as a δαίμων ἥνπερ κατηρῶντο τοῖς πολεμίοις, εἶναι δὲ αὐτῆς ἱερὸν ἐν Σμύρνῃ. Plutarch (Symp. vi. 8) quoting from Metrodorus's Ἰωνικά, confirms the fact that the Smyrnæans sacrifice to a goddess or 'Erinnys' under this name βούβρωστις. It is an argument for the Asiatic origin of Ω

He treats it as one 'where Boreas and Zephuros blow down from Thrace *upon the sea*,' and adds, 'I am at a loss to see that it bears in any way upon the argument.' Undoubtedly, if it told us merely of winds at sea, but it does more, it tells us of 'sea-weed cast up along the strand,' and the question is, what strand? The author of the simile is not at sea, but on 'terra firma,' which can only be, as in so many other indications, Asiatic Ionia.

[18] Ebeling (Hom. Lexicon in Θρήκηθεν), though not clear as to πέρην Εὐβοίης (No. 4), is constrained by the evidence from this passage (Ι 5) to accept the doctrine of Robert Wood in favour of the Ionian theory: 'Bene, ut videtur, etsi multi recentiorum aliter sentiunt, Wood poetam putat in Ionia commorantem ventos e regione Thraciae spirantes significare.'—Mr. Gladstone (II. iii. 270) supposes Thrace to have extended west to the Hadriatic (for which he adduces no proof), in order to get the semblance of a Thracian Zephyrus visiting *European* Greece. Strabo (i. § 28) had occasion to deal with a precursor of Mr. Gladstone, and denounces this extension of Thrace: πότερον τὴν Θράκην οὐκ οἶδεν (Ὅμηρος) μὴ προπίπτουσαν πέραν τῶν Παιονικῶν καὶ Θετταλικῶν ὀρῶν;

[19] Although not so significant, since it is not in a simile, the passage in Ψ 229 is corroborative. It speaks of Boreas and Zephyrus, after a visit to the Trojan plain, as 'returning *home* over the Thracian deep,' no doubt, to Thrace as their home. This, however, affords no sure indication of the speaker's stand-point, but only of the scene of the *action* he is describing, and so cannot be relied on as evidence.

that this singular expression had its local habitation on the Asiatic shore [20].

(16). In Ω 615-6 mention is made of the Niobe legend as localised at Sipylus, whence flowed the Achelous of that region. Both these names belong to the vicinity of Smyrna in Ionia, and Fäsi accordingly remarks on the passage, 'The Poet shows a close acquaintance with these regions [21].'

167. The above is the 'beadroll' of *localia* indicative, more or less, and some of them in my judgment demonstrative, of the Poet's locality who composed the Ulyssean cantos [22]. They are not all of equal force and some of them are only inferentially of weight; but they constitute a body of evidence

[20] O. Müller (Gr. Lit., ch. v. 3) thinks this indicates Æolis rather than Ionia. The territories overlapped, however, at Smyrna, and Smyrna is the only city of the seven claiming to be Homer's birthplace, whose history can unite the rival claims of Athens and of the Æolian Kyme, both of which stand as grandmothers to Smyrna. Thus the claim of Smyrna explains those of the more important rivals, but not *vice versa*. It is upon the colonisation of Smyrna that the Athenian claim grounds itself according to the Epigram, Anth. xi. 442.—As for Chios, it is to be noted that it did not assume to have given *birth*, but only *residence* and citizenship to Homer (cp. οἰκεῖ in Hom. Hymn. Apoll., 172, and Welcker, Ep. Kyk. p. 164).

[21] According to Bergk (Gr. Lit. p. 468), the influence of Asiatic associations affected the portraiture of Hector, who was drawn more lovingly out of compliment to a king Hector in Chios. Whatever may be thought of this, it is certain that the great position of the *Neleidæ* in the Iliad and Odyssey did not suffer damage or disparagement by the circumstance that Neleid leaders were prominent in Ionian colonisation (Hdt. i. 147, and v. 65).

[22] I have not included, because the evidence is inconclusive, such as ἐν Λακεδαίμονι αὖθι, in Γ 244, where αὖθι *might* be taken as *ibi*, and, if so, indicates that the singer was not in European Greece, but, as it were, cast his eye over the Egean to a spot 'in Lakedæmon *there*,' far away. Fäsi accordingly interprets '*dort* in Lakedæmon,' and the analogy of B 328, I 690, goes far to justify this interpretation. Ebeling however (in αὖθι) gives it here a sense derived from αὐτός, not in the sense of *is*, but *ipse*, and renders ' in Lacedaemone, *ipso* quo antea fuerant loco.' Doederlein (Hom. Gloss. 242) argues for this latter sense, and says the meaning is 'just where they had been,' since they had never, like Helen, left their native land. The former sense, that of Fäsi, does give an indication of the speaker's locality, the latter not. If κεῖθι, as in Γ 402, had been used instead of αὖθι, the passage would bear to be used in evidence, not otherwise.—Another disputable place is that in Ω 544, Λέσβος ἄνω, κ.τ.λ., where ἄνω seems to mean *northwards*. This is very intelligible from an Ionian stand-point, but it is also intelligible without such a supposition, since, Lesbos being south of Troy and the speaker being in the Troad, it is easily understood of ' what Lesbos northwards *from itself* confines.' I have therefore laid no stress on these passages.—Similarly, ὑπεὶρ ἅλα κίδναται ἠώς in Ψ 227 and Ω 13 affords no clue either way, and the passage as to the flight of the cranes (Γ 6), though a feature of Ionia (cp. Lord Broughton's Travels, ii. 53, regarding Smyrna), is too indefinite to be relied on as evidence. κελαδεινός of Zephyrus in Ψ 208 is probably an Ionian touch.

which it will be difficult if not impossible to controvert. *There is no counter evidence*, for all the passages fairly adducible have been enumerated, and we may say they all point in one direction—*vestigia nulla retrorsum*. It will be observed, further, that they are not only confined to the Ulyssean cantos, but well diffused throughout them; out of ten books, there are only three (E, K, and Ψ) that contribute no decided evidence of *localia*. The remarkable circumstance, however, is this, that these *localia* should be limited to one out of the two areas of the Iliad, while the other area not only exhibits no mint-marks of the same character, but *localia* that point to an entirely different region. No corroboration of our theory could be stronger than to find that two extensive series of local mint-marks pointing to two different regions, and these series *mutually exclusive* of each other, pervade *crosswise* the corpus of the Iliad. The divergence is therefore complete between the two sections of that poem, and the same demarcation is discernible under this as under former heads of inquiry; a demarcation explicable only by the hypothesis of separate authors expressing themselves with a certain independent individuality[23].

The question now rises before us, if two authorships are discernible in the Iliad, one Achillean, the other Ulyssean, which of them is the one best entitled to bear the great name of Homer? Is it the seemingly Thessalian poet, or is it the certainly Ionian author, to whom appertains the right to be considered the Epic genius called Homer? We have already seen that there was some show of belief (§ 139), founded, no doubt, on certain phenomena in the Achilleid, that he might have been a Thessalian; but there was no semblance of any body of tradition to that effect, for it remained a mere unsupported supposition. On the other hand, we find a considerable mass of traditions, more or less accredited, agreeing mainly in this, that Homer had his birth, life, and history upon the eastern shore of the Egean, either on the islands, or the mainland, or both. This has generally been regarded as

---

[23] Uschold (Gesch. des Troj. Krieges, Stuttgardt, 1836) seems to have been, in so far, on the right track, since he considered 'the Iliad to be by a *Myrmidon*, the Odyssey to be from a native of Æolis,' which is the district in Asia adjoining Ionia.

traditionally true [24], but it may also be considered scientifically certain from the internal evidence furnished by a large section of the poems themselves,—evidence deeply imbedded in their structure.

[24] Regarding the opinion of Aristarchus, who was in favour of Athens as the birth-city of Homer, it will be proper to enter into that point somewhat later. Apart from him, the evidence as to the testimony of ancient belief, including such names as Pindar, Simonides, Thucydides, Aristotle, Theocritus (vii. 47, xvi. 57, xxii. 128), is remarkably complete in favour of Asiatic Ionia, and hence Heyne says, ' Homerum Ionem fuisse et in Ionia vixisse, constans est antiquitatis fama ' (Il. vol. viii. 826). Wolf virtually makes Ionia his birthplace: he defines Homer (Proleg. ch. 49) as meaning to him, ' antiqua carmina *Ionum*.' So Preller (Gr. M. ii. 344), who says, ' durch die vielen, aber meist auf Kleinasien und die Inseln beschränkten Sagen von seinem Ursprunge, seinem Leben, seiner Kunstübung und der Tradition seiner Gedichte, wird immer bestimmt *auf Kleinasien* gedeutet.'—Some excellent remarks, from a literary point of view, may be found in Landor, ii. 364, 386–8, on Homer as an Asiatic.—I need hardly add that the name *Mæonides* becomes an absurdity and *Melesigenes*—a name probably as old as Asius B.C. 700 (Welcker, Ep. K. p. 136)—unintelligible, unless upon the assumption of the Asiatic origin of Homer. Mr. Gladstone will find it difficult, upon the hypothesis to which he has committed himself, to give any rational account of these two appellations as surnames for Homer. It is hardly necessary to ask whether the assertion is true which he has hazarded (Hom. Synchr. p. 79) that, ' of Asia Minor, except at the extreme north-western corner, the scene of the war, he has *shown very little knowledge* indeed.' One might venture to ask our scholarly statesman to point out a single *simile* in the Iliad, specifying locality or in which *locality can be in any direct way detected* (apart from the Achillean Π 364), that is *not* based on *personal* knowledge of the western coast of Asia Minor.

CHAPTER XXI.

εἰπὲ δέ μοι γαῖάν τε τεήν, δῆμόν τε πόλιν τε.

168. It only remains to apply the same inquiry to the Odyssey, and to investigate its local affinities and associations. To which of the sections of the Iliad does it incline, and can *it* be regarded as in this matter keeping the Ulyssean cantos in countenance or diverging from them?

The question is not one that can be answered authoritatively or offhand. It so happens that the traces of *personalia* in similes and descriptive notices generally are more rare, because the similes themselves are fewer, and owing to the wide extent over which the action of the Odyssey ranges in space, the stand-point of the author is not so easy to determine. The evidence which I have to adduce under this head is by no means equal in value and clearness to that produced from the Ulyssean sections of the Iliad; but, taken in connection with the other internal evidence of cognate origin, is sufficient to justify an affirmative conclusion.

169. The action of the Odyssey, apart from the imaginative sphere of the Wanderings, is mainly in Ithaca and the Peloponnesus, and lies away from Ionia and the Eastern Egean. Hence the local knowledge of the author is more largely and frequently conversant, because of the nature of the subject, with scenes and spots in the south-west of European Greece. The journey of Telemachus from Pylos to Lacedæmon in two stages is described in such a way as to

indicate a topographical and not a mere vague acquaintance with the route pursued ; epithets are bestowed on Sparta and Lacedaemon of special interest (v 412, 414; compare also the list of towns in ϕ 108); and the simile regarding Nausicaa, comparing her to Artemis walking the mountains, shows a familiarity with Taygetus and Erymanthus, mountains of the Peloponnesus (ζ 103). This familiarity, however, is not necessarily one of nativity; in such a poem as the Odyssey, it may be the result of travel and experience : for had the familiarity been one of nativity upon the *western* coast of European Greece, it would have been more complete in that region than it happens in point of fact to be, and a native of Ithaca or Elis would have known more exactly as to the counter-adjacent countries of Italy and Sicily than the author of the Odyssey seems to have done[1]. Ithaca, though within his experience to a certain extent, is not at the centre but at the circumference of that experience. Along with Ithaca, the same author speaks of Delos with marked minuteness, and compares by the mouth of Ulysses the same princess Nausicaa to a famous palm-tree which was to be seen growing there (ζ 162). It is evident, therefore, that the range of his illustrations is far from limited to Ithaca or to the Peloponnesus ; and there are some considerations that make it highly improbable that the Odyssey proceeded from a native of either of these regions.

170. (1) In the first place, it is to be noted that there is, in the Odyssey, a singular silence as to the dominant local deity of the Peloponnesus, Heré. Though known to be interested in Agamemnon (δ 513), she has no part assigned to her in the plot or action of the poem, and she is not once styled by the epithet 'Αργείη, which is in the Odyssey bestowed upon Helen alone. This seems hardly consistent with a Peloponnesian origin to the Odyssey. The Iliad, however, acknowledges 'Αργείη or 'Peloponnesian' as among the titles of Heré, and this, though the Peloponnesus is not the scene of the action ; while, in several of the books of the Odyssey, on the other hand, that country is the actual arena where the thread

---

[1] Völcker (Hom. Geogr. p. 49) denies to the poet intimate knowledge even of the Grecian region north of Ithaca, ' Dass ihm die Westgegenden Griechenlands sehr entfernt waren, und von Akarnanien an aufwärts ziemlich unbekannt, werden wenige leugnen. Es zeugt dafür sein fabelhaftes Corcyra oder Scheria.'

of the story is evolved, and the virtual silence of the Odyssey as to Heré is therefore doubly remarkable.

(2) In the second place, the associations, in which a personal element is discernible, are not *all* in the direction of the Peloponnesus, but partly also towards Athens and Attica[2]. Marathon and Sunium as well as the shrine of Athene on the Acropolis are particularised with something like personal partiality without any urgent poetical necessity. This, however, does not necessitate an Attic origin, any more than the simile in ζ 103 as to Artemis requires a Peloponnesian origin, for it fits in entirely with the Asiatic or Ionian hypothesis.

171. In the third place (3) there are, in the Odyssey, certain positive phenomena, some of which cannot be accounted for at all, and others only vaguely, upon the Peloponnesian hypothesis.

(a) The singular importance attached to Euboea in the indication of topographical relations. This is explicable on the Ionian hypothesis, not on the Peloponnesian. The evidence on this head has been already anticipated. It may be found in § 166, 4.

(β) The remarkable description of the νῆσος Συρίη, if we may assume it to be the ancient Syros or the modern island *Syra*, seems to be from an Ionian standpoint. It occurs in ο 403, where the disguised Ulysses relates to Eumæus some of his tales, and the passage runs—

> νῆσός τις Συρίη κικλήσκεται, εἴ που ἀκούεις,
> Ὀρτυγίης καθύπερθεν, ὅθι τροπαὶ ἠελίοιο.

'There is an island called Syria, if may-hap thou hast heard of it, away above Ortygia, where are the turnings of the Sun.'

'Eines der Meereiland' heisst Syria, wenn du es hörtest,
Ueber Ortygia hin, wo die Sonnenwende gesehn wird.'—(Voss.)

The passage is one of some difficulty, partly from the obscurity of what is meant by the 'turnings of the Sun,' partly by the ambiguity of Ortygia as a local designation, as to whether it answered to an island at Syracuse or to one among

[2] From the Eleventh Book or Nekyia, as we now have it, a case might be made out for a third claimant, viz. Bœotia. The importance of Tiresias, the Theban seer, and the prominence of the legends of Thebes, which is called πολυήρατος in 275, are very notable in the framework of that book (cp. Mure, G. L. ii. p. 217-8).

the Cyclades. If Ortygia is here the Delian and not the Syracusan, everything is clear. The 'Syrian isle' is then the island 'Syros,' one of the Cyclades. The 'turnings of the Sun' must mean either the *diurnal* turning, i.e. setting (for which προτράπηται in λ 18 is an analogy), or the *annual* turning at the solstitial seasons[3]. The former, or the diurnal turning, is too indefinite as a mark of locality. The latter view affords a more definite indication, as marking a *limit* of the Sun's advance or regression, most probably his regression at the *winter* solstice. In this way the island would be pointed out as the point in the horizon where the sun sank at the shortest day, that is, at the cardinal period of the winter solstice. On this supposition, the whole becomes intelligible, the only difficulty being how Ulysses, sitting in the cabin of Eumæus in Ithaca of the western sea, has shaped his story as a sailor's yarn so as to suit the coast of Ionia. The probability is that it was a story transferred into the Odyssey from its native *habitat* in Ionia without any new adaptation to the locality where it is supposed to be uttered.

On any other supposition, grave and almost insuperable difficulties arise. To suppose the Ortygia[4] of the passage to be the Syracusan, would assume the poet's knowledge of Sicily, which many have doubted and Niebuhr denied; but, apart from this, there would be no sure clue to know what was meant by Συρίη, or why that name should have been chosen. Moreover, τροπαὶ ἠελίοιο would become merely the δύσις or region of the sun's disappearance in the West, a meaning which, according to Fäsi and others, it bears, but which, if accepted, by no means excludes or is inconsistent with the Ionian hypothesis[5]. On the whole, the most tenable

---

[3] The τροπαὶ ἠελίοιο in Hesiod. Theog. 477, 661, is clearly one of the *solstices.* The other interpretation 'sunset' would in Hesiod make utter absurdity—ἤματα πεντήκοντα μετὰ τροπὰς ἠελίοιο.

[4] 'Mit recht versteht O. Müller unter diesem Ortygia Delos.' Welcker (G. G. i. 599).

[5] Several modern commentators, including Fäsi and Autenrieth, adopt the notion that the scene is in the furthest west, and that τροπαὶ ἠελίοιο means only 'the change of direction when at evening the sun turns round his car eastward.' Cp. Merry on Od. κ. 81. The chief objection to this is that ὅθι τροπαὶ ἠελίοιο, 'where are the turnings of the sun,' loses its edge and sharpness when it is interpreted into 'where lies the West,' and that which is evidently meant as a distinctive *note of place* becomes poor and bald. When poets give definitions of the

view of the passage is still that of Robert Wood (Essay, pp. 9 and 17), viż. that the description is one from the stand-point of Ionia or 'from the heights of Chios,' where the sun is seen to set at the winter solstice over the Cyclades in the direction of Syros. It was the winter solstice that was looked upon as the τροπή by preeminence, the return of the sun to the larger circuit being watched with special interest and even emotion, so that the different recurrences would be marked as important seasons, and thus the τροπαὶ ἠελίοιο came to form a familiar point in the horizon.

(γ) The vanishing position of Olympus, as no longer a mountain with a definite localisation, is a feature of the Odyssey already remarked upon (§ 155–6). This feature is, in the early time, hardly consistent with a European origin, and, among non-European regions, no other locality can show pretensions equal to those of Ionia.

(δ) The manner in which Delos is spoken of with its altar of Apollo and famous Palm-tree (ζ 162) is in keeping with what we know of it as a special seat of Ionian worship and a meeting place of the Ionian peoples. The very ancient Hymn to Apollo shows that the Delian festival was one flocked to by the *Asiatic* Ionians.

(ε) One of the important indications regarding the Ulyssean cantos of the Iliad we found to be the repeated and frequent characterisation of Zephyrus as the dominant sea-sweeping and especially shore-lashing Wind. The same character

West, they do so with more amplitude of circumstance. As examples we adduce a beautiful pair, one ancient, the other modern.

ὅρον ἀμφὶ μὲν ἀελίου κνεφαίαν
ἱππόστασιν αἰθέρα τὰν Μολοσσῶν τίθεται. Eur. Alc. 594..

This is spoken from the stand-point of Pheræ, and marks out the western boundary of Admetus' rule, as being 'where the sun stables his steeds in the dusk of eve in the Molossian clime.' Again—

'That course she (Luna) journeyed, which the sun then warms
When they of Rome behold him at his set
Betwixt Sardinia and the Corsic isle.'

Dante, Purgatorio, Canto 18 (Cary's Tr.)

Hence the expression τροπαὶ ἠελίοιο must be credited with a more pregnant meaning than that which renders it simply equivalent to the West.—A case in point as to the position of the' sun at the *winter* solstice being taken as a regulative point in indicating *direction*, is that in Herod. i. 193, πρὸς ἥλιον τετραμμένη τὸν χειμερινόν, where it makes no difference that the solstitial *rising* is spoken of and not the setting.

belongs to the West Wind in the Odyssey, and that in a very notable measure and degree[6]. It is true that the West coast of European Greece would supply this climatic experience; but in the absence of any strong evidence associating the birthplace of Homer with the *Western* shore of European Greece[7], we are entitled to refer the climatic phenomena as to Zephyrus in the Odyssey to the same region to which they undoubtedly belong in the Ulyssean cantos of the Iliad. That Ionia is that region is clear from the similes with which those Ulyssean books are studded, and it is a considerable confirmation of our general position to find Zephyrus bearing exactly the same character in the Odyssey. (1) In one simile in τ 206, it is the snow-bringing wind, Eurus being the snow-melting wind, and (2) there are frequent testimonies betokening its prominence in the poet's mind, so that it is credited with a leading share in Ulysses' shipwreck (β 421, δ 402[8], ε 332, κ 25, μ 408). (3) It is further described as 'always rain-bringing,' αἰὲν ἔφυδρος in ξ 458, and (4) in two other instances is spoken of as δυσαής, 'wildly blowing' (ε 295, μ 289). Some of these passages are indecisive as they refer to the action of Zephyrus at sea, but the first example is not liable to that objection, as it refers to its action in a snow shower by land. Taken together, they go far to prove that the author of the Odyssey described the same climatic experience as the author of the

<hr>

[6] Strabo had no doubt about the topographical evidences of Homer's stand-point. He remarks that even in regard to winds at sea, where Zephyrus receives. (as in E 295 which he cites), an epithet singling out that wind as a special acquaint-ance, Homer 'preserves his own stand-point' (ὅταν οὕτω φῇ [Ζέφυρός τε δυσαής], φυλάττει ("Ομηρος) τὴν οἰκείαν αὐτοῦ τάξιν (i. 28).—His introduction of the Kimmerians, who appear only in the Odyssey, Strabo accounts for by the common hatred of the Ionians to that race of barbarians that had once invaded them (iii. 149.)

[7] There is ground for believing that while acquainted with Ithaca, the author of the Odyssey is less accurately acquainted with it than with the Ionian shore. Compare the description of Ithaca in ι 25, and the difficulties attaching to that description, with the clear and minute and accurate specification of localities on the coast of Ionia in the third book (γ 169–172) of the Odyssey.—Among the minor indications in the same direction is the mention of 'Pramneian wine' (κ 235). It occurs once in the Odyssey, and once in Λ 639 of the Iliad, where it may be possibly Ulyssean. The traditions (Plin. xiv. 4. 54) connect this wine only with the Asiatic coast.—The mention of 'windy Mimas,' which is an Ionian mountain, belongs only to the Odyssey (γ 172).

[8] δ 402 is especially notable since the scene is laid in Egypt, but the meteor-ology, judging by Zephyrus, is Ionian.

Ulyssean cantos. It was, of course, in the wintry season that Zephyrus made himself felt in Ionia as boisterous when he had a hold of the north-west and blew from Thrace-ward. At other seasons he brought cool breezes off the sea, such as are still the delight of Smyrna[9], and hence probably the introduction of Zephyrus into the scenes of the Elysian plain (δ 567), and as a pleasant refreshing breeze in Phæacia (η 119).

172. These are the most important local mint-marks discernible in the Odyssey[10]. Not less important, though lying deeper and interpenetrating the mass, not patent on the surface, are the following features which point in the same direction.

I. The spirit of maritime adventure, typified by Ulysses, was developed, chiefly if not entirely, among the Ionic branch of the Greek race, in the age to which the Homeric poems must be referred[11]. The mariners of the cities of Ionia were in those days the chief if not the only rivals of the Phœnicians in navigation, so that eventually Phocæa competed with Carthage for the commerce of the Tyrrhene Sea, and Miletus came to fill very early the shores of the Black Sea with her clustering colonies.

II. The spirit of inquiry and nascent intelligence[12], personi-

---

[9] 'At Smyrna the West wind blows into the gulf for several hours, almost every day during the summer season.... This wind, upon which the health and pleasure of the inhabitants so much depend, is by them called the Inbat.' R. Wood, Essay, p. 25.

[10] Bergk (Lit. p. 742) finds an historical nucleus for the plot of the Odyssey in the story of Cnopus, an ancient king of Erythræ, one of the Ionic cities. This story is told in Athenæ. vi. 259. and if there were any corroborative and collateral facts, it might be accepted as pointing to an Ionian origin for the Odyssey.

[11] Phæacia, 'that charming mirror of Ionian life,' E. Curtius (H. of Gr. ii. 28). Without committing oneself absolutely to this identification, as if Phæacia, with its 'sense-endowed ships' (θ 556) and other marvels, was a semi-satirical picture of Ionia and its easy luxurious living, an ancient anticipation of Dean Swift's caricatures in national portrait painting, we may freely allow that many Ionian traits from the poet's own surroundings may have been introduced into the picture. It is significant that the *cultus* of Athene and of Poseidon, both of which are specially Ionic, should have been prominent in the account given us of Phæacia (ζ 266, 291, η 110, ν 181), and the 'jocund ease' of Phæacia had no nearer realisation than in the land, which Herodotus pronounces to have enjoyed 'the finest sky and sweetest climate' known to him (i. 142). Plato considers it was 'Ionian Life' rather than Laconian that Homer depicted (Legg. iii. 3. § 680, c).

[12] It is a feature of the 'ethic mechanism' in certain books to play off 'experiments' to test character as if for a process of Baconian induction. Col. Mure

fied in Ulysses, and animating the Odyssey, had its dawn
among the Asiatic Ionians.   To them belong, in Philosophy,
and in History, the earliest efforts of Greek genius that are to
us historically discernible [13].   To ascribe to the same soil the
early perfection of Poetry in the ' Kunst-Epos ' or the artistic
Epic is no unwarrantable supposition, but one justified by a
multitude of concurring phenomena.

(ii. 54–6), has given a copious series of examples. They are all Ulyssean (Il. B 73,
Il 235, I 345, K 444, Ω 390, 433) or in the Odyssey (Od. δ 118, ι 281, τ 215, etc.).

[13] Hesiod forms no real exception, since he belongs by descent to the Asiatic
Kyme, and, without raising the question as to whether he ranks under the ' Kunst-
epos ' or not, must have been, more or less, influenced by Asiatic culture.

CHAPTER XXII.

GLIMPSES OF A PERSONAL HOMER.

οὐκ ὄναρ ἀλλ' ὕπαρ ἐσθλόν, ὅ τοι τετελεσμένον ἐστί.

173. TWO rival views remain, regarding which a word is due. One tradition makes Homer an Æolic Greek rather than Ionic; and again, the great authority of Aristarchus leaned towards an Athenian origin. To each of these views, therefore, some attention requires to be directed.

The former supposition rests chiefly on the authority of the Pseudo-Herodotus in his Life of Homer [1]. The evidence thence deducible is by no means conclusive for an Æolic as against an Ionian origin, and the contiguity of the two races on the same seaboard, along with their overlapping and inter-plaiting at Smyrna, which was at an early time Æolic, but subsequently passed into Ionian hands, sufficiently explains the presence of Æolic elements alongside of the Ionic in the language and manners of the Homeric poems. The preponderance of *Ionismus*, however, justifies adherence to the previous conclusion, more especially since any evidence in favour of Æolis is nearly in all instances adducible to tell equally in favour of Ionia, and, although according to the Pseudo-Herodotus Homer was an Æolian Greek by birth, he was represented by the same authority as being, in habitation and the main incidents of his life, a denizen of Ionia. The Æolic and Ionic hypotheses are therefore virtually one [2].

[1] The details may be found in Blackie's Homer, vol. i. 98.

[2] Bentley, under the influence of his discovery of the so-called Æolic Digamma, thought Homer an *Ionising Æolian* (Heyne, Il. vol. vii. 713, Welcker, Ep. Kyk , 147).

174. The Athenian hypothesis is not so easily disposed of. The important grounds in its favour are (1) the presence of Athens in the roll of the seven cities claiming to be Homer's birthplace, and (2) the authority of Aristarchus (supported by Dionysius Thrax), who inclined to the opinion that Homer was an Athenian. That the man who, out of all antiquity, knew most about the Homeric poems, or at least has added more than any other single name of the ancients to our knowledge of them, entertained this view, is a weighty consideration, and his judgment is therefore one not lightly to be put aside. What were the specific grounds on which he based his opinion, and in what terms it was conveyed, is not very clear [3]. We may, however, presume that among his arguments would have been the following : (a) the interweaving (in B and Δ) of the names of Athens and its leader Menestheus under circumstances indicating some peculiar partiality, hardly justified by the tenor of the rest of the poem (cp. § 178); (β) the familiar mention of Athens as the abode of Athene, who is the directress of the action of the Odyssey; and (γ) the important formula of the Attico-Ionic oath, of which hereafter (§ 186). To the second point we formerly adverted in § 170. 2, where we endeavoured to show that it was not a circumstance of weight sufficient, in the face of the counter evidence, to secure a verdict in favour of Athens.

175. In dealing with the whole matter it is important to remember that Athens counted herself and was also accounted the head of the Ionian race, and it therefore happens that arguments from the *Ionismus* of the poems might be claimed as in favour of the city that was the reputed mother of Ionian influence. All the proofs that tell in favour of Athens the mother, apply also in favour of the daughter Ionia ; but the converse does not hold, for many of the arguments, from geographical locality, climatic associations and the like, plead only in favour of Ionia and are inapplicable to Athens [4].

---

[3] 'Aristarchus's opinion was probably qualified with some explanation.' O. Müller, Lit. ch. v. 1.—He may have held that Homer was born in Attica but passed over, while still young, with the Ionian migration from Athens, which would be a good mediating theory.

[4] 'The Zephyrus of the 'Tower of the Winds' at Athens is *not* according to the Homeric description of him. He alone of all the winds has the shoulders undraped, and has a lapful of flowers, on which Vollmer in his 'Wörterbuch der

The claim of Athens over Homer would thus be parallel to that of Norway over Snorro Sturleson, who may be said to belong to Scandinavia, not indeed as a son, but as a grandson. And such is the claim of Athens to the name of Homer[5]. She stands as the grandmother rather than the mother ; but this claim, instead of conflicting with that of the daughter, Ionia, may be said to confirm it (cp. Blackie, Homer, i. p. 106).

It militates against the Athenian hypothesis to find, first, that there is a singular absence of Theseus from any prominent and distinct remembrance on the part of an Attic poet. This seems hardly reconcilable with the Athenian origin of Homer. Not one of the passages in which his name occurs is to be relied on, for they are all more or less suspicious, savouring of interpolation, and at best are neither numerous nor important[6]. The occasional references to Pirithous, whose Lapith sons figure at Troy, supplied an easy link of attachment, if the poet had been disposed to interweave the memory of his great friend, the hero of Attica. Again, secondly, the frequent mention of Orestes in the Odyssey contains only one allusion (γ 305) to his Athenian experiences, and is silent as to the benefits of the purification he there received[7]. Homer *praises* the deed of Orestes (Preller, Gr. M. ii. p. 318–9), and seems not to acknowledge the need of any purgation. Here, however, was an opportunity to an Athenian poet for patriotic encomia that would have been highly appropriate, but no advantage has been taken of the opportunity. Thirdly, the absence of any *clear* link between Athene and her specially Athenian emblems, the owl and the olive[8], is worthy of note. The

Mythologie' remarks, ' Es scheint übrigens, als müsse die Lage des Landes [i. e. Attica] seine Beschaffenheit modificirt haben, da er bei Homer rauh und unfreundlich genannt wird.'

[5] The Epigram in Bekker's Anecd. ii. 768, gives the key to understand the Athenian claim as not primary, but secondary :—

$$\text{ἡμέτερος γὰρ κεῖνος ὁ χρύσεος ἦν πολιήτης}$$
$$\text{εἴπερ 'Αθηναῖοι Σμύρναν ἀπῳκίσαμεν.}$$

[6] Plutarch (Vit. Thes. ch. 9) remarked that there were no legendary associations of Theseus connecting him with Asiatic Ionia (Preller, Gr. M. ii. 189).

[7] Zenodotus wanted to blot out this slight testimony to Orestes' connection with Athens, by reading ἂψ ἀπὸ Φωκήων, which he thought more consistent with tradition (La Roche, Text-kritik, 15).

[8] The grove in Phæacia said to be sacred to Athene is one not of olives, but of *poplars* (αἴγειροι, ζ 292). Yet ἱερὴ ἐλαίη in ν 372 is the tree under which Athene and Ulysses concert their plans.

interpretation of Γλαυκῶπις, as 'owl-eyed,' or 'owl-faced,' is not yet sufficiently established to be relied on as evidence on such a point, and the affinities of Athene in the Iliad would seem to be rather with the vulture (H 58, a passage which Mr. Gladstone takes as proof that the Poet was unaware of any special connection of Athene with the owl), or with the heron (K 274)[9], a bird not found in connection with Athene on coins (Class. Mus. iv. p. 260), and one that is more probably 'Caystrian' in its associations than Athenian. Fourthly, the silence of the poems, as to Eleusis and the worship of Demeter in Attica, is hardly intelligible, upon the Athenian hypothesis.

In reviewing the whole subject, one cannot but come to the conclusion at which Wolf arrived upon this matter, and which he has expressed in the following words :—

'Ausgemacht ist dass er (Homer) nur in Ionien entstehen konnte, und es ist Unkunde, wenn die Athener ihn zu ihrem Landsmanne machen' (F. A. Wolf, Vorlesungen, ii. p. 145).

'It is proved that Homer could have arisen only in Ionia, and the claim of the Athenians to reckon him their country-man is an entire mistake.'

Lastly, the Athenians of the historic time advanced no claim of the sort, for how should we hear of such a statement as that which we meet with in a dialogue of Plato's school, that 'Hipparchus first *brought to Athens* the poems of Homer' (Plato, Hipparch. p. 228 B)? The region whence the poems were so brought was no doubt Ionia, which was in Hippar-chus' time the fountain of literature, from which country he is known to have fetched to Athens the living Anacreon.

176. And here we come upon the historical fact that the Athenians in the historic time felt sore at the scanty recogni-tion which they obtained in the Homeric poems, and notwith-standing all their interest in the poems and services towards their preservation and elucidation, they could not but feel that they had, as a nation, but a very small share in the glories of the Homeric age [10]. The other Greeks accused them, or at least

---

[9] 'The common *night*-heron, with its pencil of white feathers in the crest, is a species not uncommon in the marshes of Western Asia.' Kitto (Bib. Cyc. in 'Bittern').

[10] Preller (Gr. M. ii. 91) says, 'Das Homerische Epos bekümmert sich bekannt-lich von allen Griechischen Ländern *am wenigsten um Attica.*'

suspected them, of having in their *diasceuastic* work interpolated some few lines at different points in honour of Athenian memories (see a list of suspected lines in Merry, Od. λ 565); but they used their opportunity, not to say liberty, very sparingly, and passed by occasions (such as Od. λ 458), when a tribute to Athens would neither have offended nor have been misplaced. At all events these Diasceuasts did not succeed in satisfying the Athenians with the part assigned to them, and Pericles in fact virtually concedes the point, by claiming for Athens that the glories of her present time enable her to dispense with the lustre which he felt to be lacking in the Homeric age. Moreover it is evidence of the comparative honesty of Pisistratus and his associates, that they not only inserted no interpolations or next to none in honour of Athens or its ruler [11], but they did not retrench or modify certain *uncomplimentary* passages of the Achilleid that reflect severely on Athenian honour [12].

177. The evidence as to this point may best be given in Mr. Gladstone's words :—

'The Athenian soldiers are declared in Il. iv. 328 to be valiant, μήστωρες ἀϋτῆς, but the character of their commander is worse than negative. Though of kingly parentage he (Menestheus) nowhere appears among the governing spirits of the army . . . . and on the only occasion when we find him amid the clash of arms—namely, when the brave Lycians are threatening the part of the rampart committed to his charge, he shudders and looks about him for aid (xii. 331). The inferiority extends to the other Athenian chiefs—Pheidas, Stichios, Bias, Iasòs (xiii. 691, xv. 337, etc.), of whom all are undistinguished, and two—Stichios and Iasos—are " food for powder," slain by Hector and Æneas respectively. Here then there seems to have been bravery without qualities for command, and all this tends to exhibit the Athenians as in a

---

[11] The name Pisistratus in the Odyssey afforded a fine handle to ingenious Greeks to insert a compliment to the living namesake and reputed descendant. A prophecy by Theoclymenus at parting from Pylos, after the fashion of ' Tu Marcellus eris,' would have been easily concocted, if currency could have been secured for it, but the Virgil who could have framed it was not contemporary with the Greek Augustus.

[12] Compare Col. Mure's statement as to the inferior position of Athens in the Homeric poems (Travels in Greece, ii. 53. also in H. of G. L. ii. p. 210.)

marked degree Pelasgian at this epoch, stout but passive, without any of the ardour or the κῖκυς of the Hellenic character' (Juv. Mundi, pp. 81–2).

Although the reason thus assigned for the Athenian inferiority is somewhat questionable, as belonging to what the Germans would call 'the subjective criticism,' the *facts* of the case are precisely as represented by Mr. Gladstone, that the Athenians are either ignored or made mere 'food for powder' in such books as M, N, and O, whereas they seem to hold a high position in other books of the poem—viz. in B and Δ [13]. It has always been felt to be a difficulty, and has even raised, though unjustly, a suspicion of Athenian honesty in the treatment of the text, how Athens should have so great apparent prominence in the Catalogue of the Ships in B, and why Menestheus, their commander, should be praised as a good tactician, and as commanding troops who are called 'inspirers of the war-cry,' while yet there is a singular absence of any exploit in justification of these distinctions. The whole matter becomes clear, however, when we come to perceive that the books in which

[13] In N 195 Menestheus and Stichius officiate less as heroes than as benevolent 'ambulance-men' (τινὲς δὲ χλευάζουσιν ὡς νεκροφόρους, Schol. on N 195), a circumstance which moved the mirth of ancient anti-Athenian critics. It is true that the Ajaces are represented (N 201) as bearing aloft the body of Imbrius, but he was a foe to be despoiled, and Meriones and Menelaus are bearers of the body of Patroclus (P 717), while the Ajaces bear the brunt of the attack. The position of ambulance-man is manifestly secondary and inferior, and we are not surprised to find that one of them, viz. Stichius, is not long after despatched by Hector (O 329), and though Menestheus is called ἀρχὸς 'Αθηναίων, and is styled δῖος, he has no place among the nine captains (ἡγεμόνες Δαναῶν) who perform exploits in the part called 'Patroclcia' (Π 307-350). The inferiority of his position is very clearly seen in the desperate straits to which he is reduced in M 331-41, where he puts himself under the protection of Ajax. It would be unfair to press the fact that he is said to have *shuddered* at the approach of the Lycians, and was not even 'good at the war-cry,' since, owing to the din, he has to send a herald to ask Ajax's aid. The notable thing, however, is this, that we have here the relation of the two warriors reversed, from what the Catalogue represents it. In M Menestheus puts himself under Ajax's wing. In the Catalogue in B, if line 558 is genuine, Ajax seems to range himself under the wing of Menestheus and of the Athenians.—Another point to note is that in the Achilleid the Ionians have the epithet ἑλκεχίτωνες (N 685), 'tunic-trailing,' 'with sweeping robes,' probably not as a compliment, but in disparagement for effeminacy, as the kindred ἑλκεσίπεπλος is always of females, and those only Asiatic (Τρῳάδες). The only other occurrence of the word is in the hymn to Apollo, where, however, it is complimentary, but the author of that is himself an Ionian, and according to Thucydides was Homer himself.

the Athenians figure disadvantageously are Achillean, while those in which they have any encomiums bestowed upon them are Ulyssean. In the former we discern the traces of non-Ionian feeling, in the latter the pulsations of the Ionic heart of a poet who has interwoven among the *Troica* remembrances of his Athenian progenitors. Yet he has done so with great moderation by confining his encomiums to description rather than exhibiting them as won in action.

178. The main reason, however, why Menestheus does not receive a greater share of distinction is because Ulysses is practically the representative of *Ionismus*, the typical embodiment of all the qualities that rendered the Eastern Ionians of the early day supreme in eloquence, ingenuity, and love of naval adventure. Hence it happens, that, in the section of the $\epsilon\pi\iota\pi\omega\lambda\eta\sigma\iota$ where Menestheus and his troops figure to advantage, they are associated with Ulysses [14], and Ulysses accordingly becomes the mouth-piece of the Athenians as well as of his own insular warriors in replying to the censures of Agamemnon [15]. How easily under these circumstances Athenians came to be included under the wing of Ulysses, and how naturally therefore the great Athenian goddess appears as the special patroness of this hero, any one can readily perceive. Mr. Gladstone finds it hard to understand how there is no mention of any special protection to Menestheus by Athene, but when we remember that Ulysses is really the representative of the Ionian people,

---

[14] It is singular that the island of Ithaca bears the epithet in Homer, so often given to Attica in the historic time, viz. $\kappa\rho\alpha\nu\acute{a}\eta$, and (apart from the proper name $K\rho\alpha\nu\acute{a}\eta$ in Γ 445) no other place receives it in Homer. Its occurrences are Ulyssean, once (Γ 201) and in Odyssey, four times (α 247, ο 509, π 124, φ 346)—an interesting link between the Odyssey and Ulyssean books.

[15] The whole passage (Δ 327-64) in which Menestheus and Ulysses are grouped together contains so strong indications of Ionismus, that Franke pronounces it an *addition* by some *Attic* poet ('ab Attico quodam additos esse'), cp. Ebeling in v. $\acute{a}\kappa o\nu\acute{a}\zeta\epsilon\sigma\theta o\nu$. The considerations in the text will show that there is no necessity for so violent a supposition, and will give the key to understand what attracted the attention of the Alexandrian critics, viz. the partnership in this instance between Menestheus and Ulysses ($\sigma\upsilon\lambda\lambda\eta\pi\tau\iota\kappa\tilde{\omega}\varsigma$ $\tau\grave{o}$ $\tau\tilde{\wp}$ $'O\delta\upsilon\sigma\sigma\epsilon\tilde{\iota}$ $\sigma\upsilon\mu\beta\epsilon\beta\eta\kappa\grave{o}\varsigma$ $\kappa\alpha\grave{\iota}$ $\epsilon\pi\grave{\iota}$ $\tau o\tilde{\upsilon}$ $M\epsilon\nu\epsilon\sigma\theta\acute{\epsilon}\omega\varsigma$ $\kappa\epsilon\kappa o\iota\nu o\pi o\acute{\iota}\eta\kappa\epsilon\nu$. Schol. Ven. Δ 343). Unless this view is taken, a discrepancy arises between Δ 343 and B 404-7, but, if Ulysses is considered as representing Athens as well as Ithaca, the discrepancy is modified, if not entirely removed.

and that he enjoys in largest measure the aid of the Athenian goddess, the difficulty is entirely removed [16].

179. The duality in the representations of Menestheus and the Athenians is thus satisfactorily accounted for, and a new and important argument has been developed for Duality of authorship in the Iliad, completing and consolidating the former arguments derived from the divergent treatment of the greater Heroes (cp. § 84–96). This Duality has been shown to connect itself with certain national affinities and susceptibilities, so that a clue has been obtained to coordinate phenomena otherwise entirely discordant. If we have found, through the sure index of Pindar, Æolo-Dorian affinities in the Achilleid, we are now able to discern Ionian affinities, with a certain leaning towards Athens, in the non-Achilleid and in the Odyssey. The proofs of the latter fact, which have been as yet adduced, are mainly founded on the character of Ulysses, who certainly prefigures, and in one instance is the actual representative of and spokesman for, the Athenians, partly also on the local mint-marks appearing in the non-Achilleid, which are conclusive as to origin on the Ionian sea-board. These two, however, are not all the branches of proof, and though perhaps the strongest, they are not the only evidences of Ionic origin and associations.

180. It will be generally admitted, even by the most superficial students of Greek History, that there was a duality in the character of the Greek people, according as it partook of Æolo-Dorian affinities on the one hand or Ionian affinities on the other. Sparta and Athens represent the two poles of Hellenic character, the former the representative of Æolo-Dorismus, the latter of Ionismus, with the several virtues and weaknesses of each phase of character, The former element was strong, repellent, and severe, inclining to hardness and rigidity; the latter was yielding, susceptible, and subtle, inclining to softness and luxury. The former indicated the character of Mountaineers or of a people whose lines of thought were formed originally among mountains — immobility;

---

[16] It is only from the Ulyssean or neozoic parts of the Homeric poems that we gather there was any connection between Athens and Athene at all. They are B 547–551 and Od. η 81, possibly, λ 323, all Ulyssean or neozoic.

the latter that of a maritime sea-loving people—flexibility, mobility [17] (cp. § 151).

The differentiation of these elements, so complete and palpable in the historic time, is only latent in the Homeric time. The separation is yet to come, but the signs of its coming are not undiscernible. The force and sternness of Sparta we find already prefigured in the majestic Achilles; the genius and manifold aptitude of Athens, in the all-accomplished Ulysses [18] (§ 125). This is no arbitrary coordination, for it is one supported by a multitude of evidences, and the philosophic eye of Plato discerned its validity and correctness when he directs us, in order to obtain an idea of what the epic hero Achilles had been in the ancient time, to turn to such an historic figure as that of the Spartan Brasidas in the recent time (Plato, Sympos., 221 C.). There is therefore full justification for regarding Achilles as an early type of what we know to have been the Æolo-Dorian character in the historic time [19].

Such also are the characteristics of the Achilleid. It is, like the Dorian character, self-contained and full of tremendous force, for the intensity is like that of Pindar and the self-containedness like that of Hesiod [20]—both of them more or less typical representatives of Æolo-Dorian feeling.

[17] Mr. Gladstone (H. iii. 276) has remarked that Homer is great in *sea-distances*, measured by so many days, but does not give a hint of measure in journeys by land. The examples of sea-distances will be found to be either in the Odyssey or Ulyssean parts (I 363). Compare the nautical simile, evidently from the life, in II 4, the nautical touches in B 293, Δ 76, and note on § 166. 1, as to naming *sections* of the sea.

[18] Welcker (Ep. Kyk. p. 275) remarks on the Ionian partiality for such a character as Ulysses: 'Dem Ionischen Character und dem zunehmenden bürgerlichen Geiste (der auch durch den Namen Demodokos sich verkündigt) ist die Vorliebe für den Odysseus gemäss.' Compare the important remarks of E. Curtius (H. i. 152-3), where he considers the life in the ἀγορά and the spirit of the *Demos* to have first shown themselves in the Ionian seaports, and holds it to be manifest 'that the traditions of the heroic times received their last form among an Ionian population.'

[19] Cp. Preller (Gr. M. ii. 174), 'Die Dorier, die Erben der Hellenischen Myrmidonen.' 'The Dorians, the heirs of the Hellenic Myrmidons' (i. e. of the warriors under Achilles). According to E. Curtius (II. i. 110) the Dorian character was formed not only in a mountain region, but in the region near Olympus, which was at one time their proper home.

[20] Compare the interesting observations of Pausanias (i. 2. 3) contrasting the confined semi-Dorian spirit of Hesiod with the freer Ionian spirit of Homer. There is little doubt that it was to the non-Achillean parts of Homer that he would look for illustrations of the latter.

181. We have already seen that the geographical horizon of the author of the Achilleid is comparatively narrow and confined, in marked contrast with that of the author of the Ulyssean cantos and of the Odyssey. So his mental vision over time seems to share the narrowness of his vision over space, for his eyes seem to be almost entirely in the Present or the Past, and he seldom looks to the Future and then not always hopefully or far. Not so the author of the Odyssey and non-Achilleid, for he is not so deeply absorbed in the Present or the Past, as to lack, at the same time, a distinct outlook to the Future. The indications under these heads have been already given in former sections and need not now be recapitulated (cp. § 74. n. 7, 8). It will be admitted that the contrast is one that applies also to the Æolo-Doric and Ionic races in the historic time.

The Achillean poet shows a certain premonition of Spartan affinities in his estimate of what constitutes the virtues of a man. It is in battle that he finds his proper sphere, and hence strong fighting is more prominent in the thoughts of the Achillean poet than good speaking. No doubt the epithet κυδιάνειρα is found once regarding ἀγορή (A 490), but it is found *four* times regarding μάχη, the same number of occurrences as κυδιάνειρα shows with μάχη in Ulyssean cantos[21], where ἀλκή is also κράτος μέγιστον (I 39). So likewise μῦθοι are acknowledged as a source of honour (Σ 252), also an instrument of craft (X 281), and ἐρίζειν περὶ μύθων is attributed to a hero as an accomplishment (O 284); but oratory cannot be said to have the prominence which it receives in the non-Achillean sections, where it stands as the *climax* of accomplishments (Od. θ 168). On the contrary, in the Achilleid, the λόχος or ambush, rather than λόγος, seems to stand as the test of a man's ἀρετή or worth (N 277). The praise of μῆτις, 'counsel,' is mainly Ulyssean, as in Ψ (315), and the value of persuasive speech is shown in that area by its being put on an *equality* with action and warfare (I 441 and 443). Hence, while ἀρτύνω is in the Achilleid entirely *military*, in association only with μάχη and ὑσμίνη, it has attached to it

---

[21] It is curious, but seemingly accidental, that κυδιάνειρα is not found with ἀγορή, where we should have most expected it, viz. outside the Achilleid. An equivalent is found for the lack of it in the Ulyssean I 441.

in the Ulyssean area (B 55. K 302) βουλή[22], and in the
Odyssey we hear even of ψεύδεα ἀρτύνοντας.

Further, the Achilleid shows a certain narrow and stereotyped form of conception, premonitory of the rigid type familiar
to us in Spartan thought, while the largeness of view and
liberality of thought, which afterwards distinguished the
Athenian and Ionian peoples, are already present in germ
in the Ulyssean area and in the Odyssey.

182. It may be proper to recall here the statements advanced under a previous section (§ 105–6), when we had occasion to show that the Achilleid exhibits a rigid and almost
Spartan fixedness of conservatism regarding certain hieratic
epithets, whereas the moment we pass beyond the zone of
the Achilleid we meet with freedom and even luxuriance of
fancy in the treatment of those epithets. A similar fact holds
regarding the occurrence of other epithets not originally
hieratic, some of which we find strictly confined to a single
application in the Achilleid ; but, whether from enlargement of
view, or greater richness of thought, or comparative recency of
age, or from all these influences concurring, these are widened
and expanded in their applications outside the Achilleid.

Thus the beautiful and solemn word ὁμοίιος, 'all-levelling,'
'unsparing,' belongs to both areas. The Achillean poet,
however, who is mainly concerned with war. confines it to
πόλεμος, on which he bestows it *five* times. The Ulyssean
poet widens the scope of it, as if discerning that there were
things in the world equally 'unsparing' with 'war,' and so,
while using it once of πόλεμος, he bestows it also upon γῆρας.
'old age,' and νεῖκος, 'feud,' and in the Odyssey we find it
applied to θάνατος, 'death,' as well as to πόλεμος.

Therefore, while each poet uses the epithet five times, the
Achillean poet limits it to 'war': the other bard. with larger
outlook, finds various other powers or elements in the world
that receive from him the epithet.

	Ach.	Ul.	Od.
ὁμοίιος, of war . . .	5	1	1
ὁμοίιος, of other powers . .	0	2	1.

The treatment of πεπνυμένος is an example in the same

---

direction.   In the Achilleid it occurs not unfrequently, but is nowhere found except in connection with persons.   In the non-Achilleid and Odyssey, it is an epithet applied not merely to men but to *things.*   Further, the Achillean poet has not ventured beyond the participle, whereas outside the Achilleid we meet with forms like πέπνυσαι, πεπνῦσθαι.

	Ach.	Ul.	Od.
I. πεπνυμένος of persons	↲	7	Frequent
πεπνυμένος of things—			
(α) μήδεα	0	1	1
(β) without subst., absolutely (πεπνυμένα βάζεις)	0	1	1
(γ) other usages	0	0	7
II. πέπνυμαι in other parts than participle	0	2	1.

183. The next illustration which I shall take is a double proof of our proposition, inasmuch as it shows where *Ionismus* is to be looked for in two of its aspects, viz. in its greater freedom and richness of pictorial designations and also in its tendency towards *bonhomie* and easy indulgence rather than to Spartan austerity.   It concerns the treatment of ὕπνος, 'sleep,' as a phenomenon of human life.   Apart from the archaic νήδυμος, there is hardly one epithet attached to it in the Achilleid, that conveys the idea of *delicious* rest. Epithets of this class abound the moment we pass beyond the severe zone of the Achilleid.

Omitting the examples of Ὕπνος as the god of Sleep personified, examples that prove nothing either way, we find the darker associations of Sleep mainly in the Achilleid.   In the first place Sleep is thrice styled 'Brother of Death,' and all the examples are Achillean[23].   So death is once spoken of as χάλκεος ὕπνος (Λ 241).   It is doubtful if there are any associations so gloomy connected with sleep in the sunnier region of the Ionian poet.   The darkest epithet in the Ulyssean cantos of the Iliad is πανδαμάτωρ (Ω 4, occurring also in Od. ι 373), but that is not necessarily one of sinister import.   In the Odyssey the sinister instances are special, not normal, because of some culpability or other, as in κ 68 and μ 372.   But when we look for epithets denoting the 'sweetness' of sleep, we find them few and far between in the Achilleid, abundant elsewhere.

---

[23] The extraordinary sleep of Ulysses on arriving in Ithaca is described as 'like to Death,' but at the same time as ἥδιστος (ν 80). This is the nearest approach to the Achillean representation.

	Ach.	Ul.	Od.
I. Ὕπνος in sinister aspects .	4	1 (?)	2
II. Ὕπνος in pleasing aspects—			
ἀπήμονά τε λιαρόν τε . .	1	0	0
ἀμβρόσιος	0	1	0
γλυκύς	1	2	12
γλυκερός	0	3	4
ἥδιστος	0	0	1
ἡδύς	0	1	6
μελιηδής	0	0	1
μελίφρων	0	1	0
λύων μελεδήματα θυμοῦ . .	0	1	1
μαλακός	0	2	1
ὕπνου δῶρον ἕλοντο . . .	0	2	2
πάννυχον ὕπνον ἀωτεῖν } γλυκὺν ὕπνον ἀωτεῖν } . .	0	1	1
ἀπείρονα ὕπνον . .	0	0	1
κοῖτος ἡδύς . . .	0	0	1
	2	14	31.

There is thus a marked contrast between the Achilleid
and the rest of the Homeric poems, so that we find again the
same demarcation under this aspect as in those preceding,
with the result that the Ulyssean cantos of the Iliad find
their congeners in the cantos of the Odyssey.

184. Other arguments might be adduced, of more or less
value, pointing uniformly to the same issue. I only allude to
such phenomena as the occurrence (α) of δημιοεργός in its Ionic
industrial sense, not in its Dorian application as a civil
magistrate, (β) of the τέττιξ, with its Ionian and old Attic
associations (Preller, Gr. M. i. 300), (γ) of κέραμος and κεραμεύς, pottery being an art especially Attic or old Ionian,
(δ) of the λέσχη, whence came the ἀδολεσχία of the Ionic race
generally, (ε) αἰσυμνητήρ, a term whose historic occurrences are
chiefly in relation to the Asiatic shore, (ζ) βαρβαρόφωνοι, regarding the Carians, involving a touch of Ionic sensitiveness
and jealousy, cp. Strabo, xiv. 661. All these traces of *Ionismus*
are found to emerge only in the Ulyssean cantos or in the
Odyssey, in either or both, and thus by their distribution
constitute important confirmations. Without dwelling on
these, I must particularise with more detail two groups of

phenomena which are of high significance, as showing 'the beat of an Ionic heart' in the breast of Homer.

185. (1) Among the peculiar institutions of the Ionic race, the Ἀπατούρια, we know, occupied a prominent place. 'They are all Ionians,' says Herodotus (i. 147), 'who are sprung from Athenian descent and hold the festival of Apaturia.' In this festival, the family divisions celebrating it were called φρατρίαι and the term φρατρία or φρήτρη was thus in fact an Ionian term for a special group in their social system. It is therefore a technical word of great importance, and the occurrences of it are tests of high significance. It accordingly comes up precisely in the area where we look for *Ionismus*, and only there, for φρήτρη and ἀφρήτωρ appear twice in Ulyssean cantos, viz. in B 363 and I 63. The peculiar institutions of the Ionic race are thus alluded to in such a way as to indicate that those cantos were composed among and for the Ionic people.

186. (2) Another institution, as it may be called, of the Ionic race, was the oath by a certain Triad of Gods, Zeus, Athene and Apollo. The formula, in which this adjuration appears, is one of high interest and importance. Mr. Gladstone has laid great stress upon it in his attempt to show that the Greeks possessed, latent among them and descending from patriarchal times, something answering to the Doctrine of the Trinity. The formula referred to occurs so frequently and is altogether so remarkable that it deserves the closest attention, and indeed it forms the main support of his hypothesis, which otherwise would be a mere airy though beautiful vision. The adjuration or exclamatory ejaculation runs in these words:—

αἰ γάρ, Ζεῦ τε πάτερ καὶ Ἀθηναίη καὶ Ἄπολλον.

'Would that, O father Zeus and Athene and Apollo.'

Without delaying to inquire whether we can find the lofty doctrine which Mr. Gladstone discovers therein contained, we can safely pronounce it a formula of frequent recurrence and of great significance. But it is not the *only* Triad in the Homeric poems. Thus in O 187 we find a Triad of the Kronid Brothers, Zeus, Poseidon, and Hades, and, in T 87, we come upon another Triad, not quite like a Trinity, Zeus, Mœra, and Erinnys. These two last Triads are probably Achillean. A peculiar grouping of three gods is found in B 478, where Zeus, Ares, and Poseidon are combined, and further we have the rebellious Triad of A 400 who conspire against Zeus.

These last mentioned Triads, however, are in a different category, because they occur only once and are not appealed to in *adjuration*[24], whereas the formula we are dealing with is frequent as an adjuration in a certain area and in fact stands unique in the Homeric poems.

The important point to observe is this, that a formula with the same Triad of Gods (cp. Æsch. Eum. 728–30) is known to have been a favourite oath with the original branch of the Ionic race, the Athenian. It was one of those employed in Athenian courts of law, and in the speech of Demosthenes 'against Meidias' (p. 578) there appears the adjuration, μὴ τὸν Δία καὶ τὸν Ἀπόλλω καὶ τὴν Ἀθηνᾶν, where the ancient commentator Ulpian tells us in his annotations, that 'this is the Attic oath[25].'

The conjunction of these deities is the more remarkable that two of them take *opposite* sides in the struggle at Troy, Apollo on the side of the Trojans, Athene on that of the Greeks. Both of them, however, stand out in many respects separate from the other deities, and their exceptional position is seen in this that the Ægis of Zeus is wielded sometimes by the one and sometimes by the other, but by none else of the Olympian Gods[26]. They stand out, therefore, apart from the

---

[24] A kind of Triad in adjuration is that in A 339, showing how common was the *triple* form of appeal. According to Pollux (viii. 142), τρεῖς θεοὺς ὀμνύναι κελεύει Σόλων, ἱκέσιον καθάρσιον ἐξακεστῆρα.

[25] It was not the only Triad in Athenian oaths, for we hear of a Triad used by Draco (Schol. Il. O 36), another in the Heliastic oath, a third proposed by Plato, Legg. xi. 276. A fourth appears in Demosth., p. 1238, and Aristoph. Eq. 941.

[26] The *warlike* appearance of Apollo with the Ægis bestowed for the time by Zeus belongs only to the Achilleid (O 229, 308, 361, Π 704), all referring to one bestowing of the Ægis. In the Ulyssean area, Apollo is not invested with so tremendous a power, but is perched on Pergamus (Δ 508, E 460, Π 21), and seems to leave that post only to rescue Æneas (E 433), or to confer with Athene (H 22), or to counteract her (K 517). In this Ulyssean area his chief agency is by 'shouting' from Pergamus (Δ 508). Once we find him in the Ulyssean area (Ω 20) having the Ægis, but it is for the *peaceful* purpose of protecting Hector's corpse. There seems ground for the affirmation that there is one representation of Apollo in the Achilleid, and another considerably different in the Ulyssean books (cp. also § 102). —Regarding Athene (apart from Σ 204), she seems to have charge of the Ægis chiefly in the Ulyssean area (B 447, E 738), and in this respect the Odysse

general circle of the Olympians, as entitled to be conjoined with the supreme Ægis-bearer.

It is not so clear how this combination of Gods should have been a favourite one with the Ionian stem of the Greek people. Athene, it is true, was the patron goddess of their primal city, and Apollo, under the title of πατρῷος, was claimed as in a special manner associated with Athens. Whatever was the real cause of the conjunction of these deities, there is ground for believing that the conjunction indicated an advance in Hellenic civilization and marked a distinct stadium of progression, whereby the Greek race overleapt the barbaric level and entered on what may be called the Hellenic, as distinguished from the Pelasgian, platform [27]. Hence the observation of Preller (Gr. M. i. p. 4), on this group of deities : ' Zeus, Athena, und Apollon bilden gleichsam einen engeren Ausschuss aus dieser himmlischen Götterwelt, Zeus als Herrscher und Vater aller Götter und Menschen, Athena und Apollo, als seine Lieblingstochter und sein Lieblingssohn.'

What then are the occurrences of this Ionian formula? They are all in the same area where we find the other traces of *Ionismus*, viz. in the Odyssey and Ulyssean cantos. They are as follows :—

Ach.　Ul.　Od.
o[28]　3　　4　| B 371, Δ 288, H 132 | Od. δ 341, η 311, ρ 132, σ 235.

It is worthy of observation that the number of occurrences is

(χ 297) concurs. She seems, however, to take the Ægis *proprio motu*, and she does so especially in the area where *Ionismus* is most apparent.

[27] The formula is assigned to no Trojan, and to no *northern* Greek. Except in the case of Alcinous, it is only in the mouth of southern heroes, Agamemnon (twice), Nestor, Menelaus, Telemachus (twice).—The only point in which there is any obscurity in the proof is the want of clear evidence that it belonged to the eastern as well as to the European Ionians. It so happens that our authorities for it are mainly as to its existence at Athens ; but the antiquity of the *cultus* of Apollo πατρῷος, makes it probable that the formula was old enough to have preceded the Ionic migration, and so have been transferred to the Asiatic shore. E. Curtius (H. i. p. 324) connects the prevalence of the formula at Athens with the influence of Solon. 'The oath holiest to all the Athenians was now sworn by Zeus, Athene, and Apollo, such being an express ordinance ever since the time of Solon.'

[28] The apparent occurrence of the formula in Π 97 is an interpolation condemned by ancient critics, and, though retained by La Roche, is bracketed by Fäsi and Spitzner. No nearer approach to the combination is producible from the Achilleid than that in N 827, which, however, is not a direct adjuration and concerns only two of these deities.—The instance in Od. ω 376 seems post-Homeric.

in fair proportion as between the Odyssey and the Ulyssean
cantos, and that the distribution is spread equably over the
whole area of the Odyssey.

Here we conclude our survey of the local mint-marks of the
Iliad and the Odyssey.

187. On a review of the whole evidence, and judging from
the manner in which the phenomena group themselves in far
reaching ramifications, $\acute{\rho}\acute{\iota}\zeta\eta\sigma\iota\nu$ $\mu\epsilon\gamma\acute{a}\lambda\eta\sigma\iota$ $\delta\iota\eta\nu\epsilon\kappa\acute{\epsilon}\epsilon\sigma\sigma'$ $\acute{a}\rho\alpha\rho\upsilon\hat{\iota}\alpha\iota$,
an impartial mind will have little difficulty in coming to the
conclusion, that the weight of evidence is in favour of a Dual
authorship to the Iliad, that the older or palæozoic portion is
probably of Thessalian origin, and that the younger or neozoic
portion is certainly from Asiatic Ionia. Regarding the Odyssey, the evidence of local origin is less decisive, but the
paucity of its local mint-marks is amply compensated by
the multitude of analogies, idiosyncrasies, affinities, which
attach it to the neozoic area of the Iliad, and authenticate
it under what may be called the sign-manual of the same
genius.

If we are right in affirming these propositions, we can be
in no doubt that this Ionian genius, whose handiwork and
personality we have been tracing out carefully and reverently,
is none other than the Homer whom all ages have conspired
to reverence. We can now discern the great builder of
epics shaping his work and leaving on it an impress of his
own individuality, so that he becomes more to us than a
mere misty *Eidolon*, and has grown a living personality.

That personality speaks to us most clearly in one passage
where he comes nearest to the unveiling of himself—viz. in
the proem of the Odyssey, where the solitary $\mu o\iota$ of $\check{a}\nu\delta\rho\alpha$
$\mu o\iota$ $\check{\epsilon}\nu\nu\epsilon\pi\epsilon$ is a personal and conscious utterance. It is true
that owing to the objective nature of his poetry, we get fewer
glimpses of his countenance than we obtain, for example, of
Hesiod, yet, as it would argue hopeless scepticism to doubt
the personal existence of Hesiod, or to disbelieve that in the
' Works and Days ' we have the utterances of an actual historic
man, so, in the same kind though not in equal measure, we
have the assurance of a genuine historic personality shaping
the architecture of the Odyssey. The other and more distant poet, who sings ' the Wrath of Achilles,' retires further

back into invisibility, for he does not in *his* proem favour us with even a μοι for science or sentiment to fasten on [29].

188. One or two remarks may be required in order to justify the ascription or restriction of the name Homer to the author of the neozoic poems.

In the first place, the name Homer belongs in all probability to the work which is, in a poetic point of view, the largest and most massive phenomenon. It involves less difficulty to suppose that the name of the author of the more distant poem, the Achilleid, has perished than that the name of the author in the case of the larger, and in some respects more notable, poems, should have vanished, especially as these last were from an age lying nearer to the literary period when personal remembrances had a chance of being in some form preserved. There is, from the tradition of antiquity, only one Homer to be accounted for, and, if we have established the Dual authorship, it follows, from the internal evidence, that it is the younger bard that is to be identified with Homer.

(2) The internal evidence of *Ionismus* is manifest in the sections thus ascribed to him, completely manifest in the Iliad in its Ulyssean sections, partially manifest in the Odyssey; and on this basis we can understand the remarkable uniformity with which antiquity referred him to the Asiatic shore of the Egean, and ascribed to him the otherwise inexplicable titles of Mæonides and Melesigenes, names belonging only to the region of Ionia.

189. Under the foregoing supposition as to Ionia we are able to give a satisfactory account of six things which are otherwise difficult to understand. (1) The *initia* of Elegiac poetry, which is a variation of the Heroic Hexameter, are referable to the land and soil where the Epic muse of Homer has previously appeared. Callinus has the best claim to be considered the earliest Elegiac poet, and he belonged to Ephesus, one of the Ionian cities. (2) The best known and most important of the Cyclic poets [30] are referable to the

---

[29] The passage in M 176, where he complains of the hardness of his task, is generally bracketed as spurious. though La Roche retains it unbracketed.

[30] Welcker, after comparing the position of Agias and Eumelus, Cyclic poets though from Doric communities, to that of Herodotus and Hippocrates, who though Dorian in origin came to own the superior power and attractiveness of Ionismus,

same region. Arctinus, who is said to have been μαθητὴς
'Ομήρου, and whose date is as early as 775 B.C., was of Miletus,
Creophylus of Chios or Samos, Cinæthus of Chios, all Ionic
cities of Asia, without reckoning in the less known Diodorus
from Erythræ, or Lesches of Pyrrha in Lesbos, both from the
Asiatic shore. The locality of Stasinus is not known. The
rest of the Cyclics appear in various parts of the Greek world,
but they are more recent, and therefore more remote from
the common centre of origin.

(3) The Ionic-speaking race manifested the greatest interest
in the text of the Poet, as if they considered it their own peculiar patrimony. Four out of the six so-called ' Civic ' editions,
referred to in the critical notes of the Alexandrian scholars,
belong to Ionic cities either in Ionia or of Ionic population,
viz. the Chian, Massilian, Sinopic and Salaminian or Cyprian.
The Argive and Cretan are the only ones non-Ionian. Further,
in the scholia fifty-two citations are found from the four
Ionian editions, as against nine from the non-Ionian (La
Roche, Text-Kritik, p. 18), a fact which may be looked upon
as both an index and a measure of the greater patrimonial
interest in these poems felt and claimed by the Ionians.

(4) The Rhapsode lingers longest on the soil of Ionia, and
the one that figures in Plato is called Ion, as if in allusion to
the land where the rhapsode was especially a native.

(5) The name "Ομηρος is always in an Ionic form. There
appears to be no trace of "Ομαρος.

(6) The *literary* Epic, called Cyclographic, flourishes on
the Asiatic shore where the early epic had first appeared, and
forms a continuation of the same. The most important of
these is Antimachus of Colophon, with whom may be associated Panyasis of Halicarnassus, Peisander of Camirus, Asius
of Samos, Chœrilus of Samos. The epic poetry of Greece may
thus be said to have remained rooted upon the Asiatic shore [31]

goes on to enumerate the localities claiming a share in the Cyclic or post-Homeric
heroic poetry :—' Die betheiligten Orte sind die Æolischen Städte Neonteichos bey
Kyme, Bolissos auf Chios, Mitylene und Pyrrha auf Lesbos; die Ionischen Milet,
Samos, Chios, Ios, Phokæa, Kolophon; dann Halikarnass, die Attische Salamis in
Cypern, Sparta, Trœzen, Korinth und spät Kyrene. Es ergiebt sich von selbst *der
Zug der Poesie von Asien und seinen Inseln* her nach dem Peloponnes' (Epische
Kyklus, i. 39).

[31] Hesiod, being originally of Kyme, is hardly an exception. The statement

down even to the Alexandrian period, when it sought to find
a *habitat* on other shores. Before that period of diffusion,
the successive shoots from the old epic stem, which are
known as first the Cyclic and then the Cyclographic, show
clearly what was the primary locality of the parent stem.

190. The traditions of the poet's *personalia*, although in
themselves of small critical value, are yet found, singularly
enough, so far as they meet with corroboration in the poems,
to associate themselves entirely with the Odyssey and the
Ulyssean sections, apparently never with what is found in the
Achilleid. The 'Life of Homer' by the Pseudo-Herodotus
is the main storehouse of these traditions, and, except the
incidental name Θεστορίδης, there seems to be no name or
tradition preserved regarding him that suggests the Achilleid, but many are preserved that are now imbedded in the
sections that are to be associated with the Ionian bard—viz.
the Odyssey and Ulyssean area.

Among the friends of the reputed Homer we find mention
made of—

    1. Phemius, the schoolmaster.
    2. Mentes, the ship-captain.
    3. Mentor, the Ithacan gentleman.
    4. Tychius, the shoemaker.

Accordingly the *analoga* to these are to be found in—

    1. Phemius, the bard.   (Odyssey.)
    2. Mentes, the mariner.   (Odyssey.)
    3. Mentor, the Ithacan gentleman. (Odyssey.)
    4. Tychius, the leather-maker.   (Ulyssean, II 221).

Again, (5), the blind bard Demodocus was generally regarded in antiquity (Schol. on Od. θ 63, ι 1, and Max. Tyrius,
38. 1) as an image of himself from his own hand. He belongs
to the Odyssey. (6) One Thersites is said to have been his
unfaithful ἐπίτροπος or guardian (Ven. Schol. B 212). Hence
the satire in Book B of the Iliad was accounted for. (7)
Among these *personalia*, it is interesting to include the curious
story as to Glaucus and his Dogs. It was related that in

<hr>

above is well sustained by a reference to the canon of Epic poets as made up by
the Alexandrian critics. It embraced the following five, Homer, Hesiod, Peisander,
Panyasis, Antimachus (Welck. Ep. Kyk., p. 22), the last three being clearly of
Asiatic origin.

his wanderings the blind bard was once in danger from a goatherd's dogs that came barking round him. He cried out for help, whereupon the owner of them, one Glaucus, ran forward nimbly and chased away the dogs. Leading him to his shieling, the goatherd entertained him kindly. The enjoyment of the entertainment was interfered with by the dogs which went on barking, whereupon the bard is said to have uttered some impromptu lines recommending 'friend Glaucus to provide first good entertainment for the dogs at the door of the court-yard. For a dog so fed is the first to get note of any one approaching, be it man or beast, that enters the fences[32].'

The incident of the assault of the dogs is one that resembles

---

[32] The fondness for the dog does not afford any clue to locality, as the attitude toward the horse in the Achillean bard pointed toward Thessaly. On the Ionian shore, no doubt, the worship of the huntress Artemis at Ephesus had close association with the dog, which is very prominent in connection with the ancient figure of the Ephesian Diana, and ample proof could be obtained from the *later* historic time as to *her* patronage of that animal. In the absence of any reference in Homer to the Asiatic *cultus* of Artemis, which seems to have been in its origin rather barbarian than Greek, we must remain ignorant of any special cause of attraction to that domestic animal other than its useful companionship. Regarding his colder attitude, which I think has been established, toward the horse, one can render no adequate reason, but simply appeal to the facts, which *may* point to a condition of things on the Ionian sea-board, in which the Greeks found themselves outshone by their barbarian neighbours in this respect, an inference which we are inclined to draw from the marked association of equestrian epithets with barbarian Asiatics, such as Trojans, Phrygians, Mæonians, and the like (cp. § 126 n.). It is a mere conjecture, but it seems a not improbable one, that Homer, whose name Mæonides implies a connection with that region, derived his ideas of horsemanship, and probably his aversion to it, from the spectacle of the Mæonians, whom he calls ἱπποκορυσταί, and of the Phrygians, who have the unique epithet αἰολόπωλοι (Γ 185). 'Immer werden,' says Preller (Gr. M. ii. 272), 'die Lyder und überhaupt die Asiatischen Völker als φιλιππότατοι geschildert: Herodot. i. 79; Philostrat. i. 17; daher das Sprichwort Λύδιον ἅρμα; Il. 10. 431, *καὶ Φρύγες ἱππόδαμοι καὶ Μῄονες ἱπποκορυσταί.*' It is a curious circumstance that Pelops should receive the somewhat rare epithet πλήξιππος in B, and that extra Homeric tradition connected him with horse-loving Phrygia, to which belonged *Otreus* (Γ 186), bearing a kindred name to the Pelopid *Atreus;* also that *κέντορες ἵππων* is given only to the Trojans, and to the partly oriental Cadmeans of Thebes; and that in the Ionic festival at Delos, there *was originally no horse-race* (Thuc. iii. 104) until introduced later by the Athenians in the time of their ascendancy. In the ancient hymn to the Delian Apollo, ascribed *to Homer himself* by Thucydides, there is no mention, among the different contests, of ἱπποδρομία.—Mr. Grote (H. ii. 623) goes so far as to argue for the Asiatic origin of the poems as a whole, because of the prominence of the chariot-mode of fighting, which he thinks never really prevailed in the Peloponnesus.

the adventure of Ulysses in ξ, when the dogs of Eumæus threaten at first a rough reception to the disguised beggar. The other part of the story, though seeming to embody a little of that aversion to the Dog, which led Macaulay to call it 'a beast to interrupt conversation,' yet, on the whole, shows a kindly spirit to the Dog. It is curious to find such a story prominent among the traditions regarding a poet who appears, on other and independent evidence, to have felt a special attraction towards, and bestowed special attention upon, the Guardian of the Hearth.

CHAPTER XXIII.

οὐκ ὄναρ ἀλλ' ὕπαρ ἐσθλόν, ὅ τοι τετελεσμένον ἔσται.

191. IT now only remains to sum up the general result of the foregoing investigations. We have found reason to come to the conclusion that in the Homeric Epics there lies imbedded an ancient kernel, viz. the Achilleid, at the basis of the Iliad, and this from some bard unknown, though probably Thessalian, and that the expansion of the Achilleid into an Iliad as well as the structure of the Odyssey are the work of another bard, who, according to all the evidences, is the veritable Homer. We thus not only discover more clearly who Homer was, discerning somewhat of his personal feelings and surroundings, but we can see even beyond Homer, obtaining glimpses into a more ancient world, and recognising the *Eidolon* of a Poet older than Homer.

For, as there were kings before Agamemnon, there were, no doubt, poets before Homer; and though Aristotle[1] says he could name none, he adds 'it is probable there were many older Bards.' Cicero, also, in his Brutus (ch. 18), argues in the same strain that the perfection of the Homeric poems implied a long period of antecedent preparation and cultivation of style, a view that is remarkably confirmed by the investigations of modern Philologists, who are able to show that the language and forms of speech in the Homeric poems have had a long history even on Hellenic soil before they

---

[1] Arist. Poet. 4. 9, *εἰκὸς δὲ εἶναι πολλούς.* Herodotus's verdict, apparently negative (ii. 53), as to poets prior to Homer, must be understood not so much regarding poets as regarding poems, then purporting or currently reported to be of pre-Homeric parentage.

became consolidated into the shape in which they now appear.

192. It is no violent supposition, therefore, to believe that a lay in honour of the hero of Thessaly and composed in that land had been wafted over the Egean with the Æolic migration from Thessaly, that this Achillean lay had been for some time recited in Æolis with a certain consistency of form, becoming a favourite from the circumstance that the scene of the hero's exploits was laid in what was now the adopted country of a part of the Æolic people; that it found its way into the neighbouring land of Ionia[2], probably by the Ionian occupation of the Æolian Smyrna, and that an Ionian minstrel[3] widened its scope and enlarged its compass by interweaving those cantos which moralise it and render it an Iliad.

For, it is to be remarked that to this Ionian minstrel is entirely due the ethical purpose which is discernible in the Iliad, but of which there is no trace in the Achilleid. This ethical purpose forms not the least among the many links of connection between the Ulyssean cantos of the Iliad and the preeminently ethical poem, the Odyssey.

193. The main lines of proof in this regard are now to occupy our attention. We have to deal with what may be called the Teleology of the Poems, and, while in all Teleology, whether in philosophy or in literature, great caution is required in tracing the lines of purpose, it is especially necessary in the case of Poems, which have sprung fresh as it were from the bosom of Earth, and seem, in many respects, free products of the soil. We must carefully distinguish in this matter between a natural and unconscious ethical purpose and a didactic and conscious one. The latter has no

---

[2] An analogy to the supposed transition of the Achilleid across the Egean is found in the case of the oldest heroic poem in Teutonic speech, viz. the Anglo-Saxon poem of Beowulf. Benj. Thorpe describes it, in words remarkably applicable to the Achilleid, under our view of its genesis and history, as a 'metrical paraphrase of an heroic Saga composed in the south-west of Sweden, in the old common language of the north, and probably brought to this country [England] during the sway of the Danish dynasty' (Pref. to Beowulf, p. viii.). Compare E. Curtius, H. of Gr. i. 136, on the analogy of Beowulf, generally, to the Homeric Epos.

[3] This we take to be the meaning of the story that Homer was descended from Melanopus, who is a colonist of Kyme in Æolis, but is ultimately referred to Magnesia in Thessaly (Ps. Herod., Vit. Hom., and cp. § 27, n. 11 above, Mure, ii. 195, and Thiersch, Zeitalter, p. 94).

place in either poem (Grote, H. ii. 278). The *story* of the events, the pictorial narrative, is the first thing in the poet's purpose[4]; his moral teaching is in no sense primary, and yet the pulsation of the poet's sympathies and his whole ethical attitude may be perfectly appreciable underneath the garniture with which he clothes himself, and it may be possible to affirm an unconscious ethical purpose showing itself in character and in the fate of character, discernible beneath the structure of the most objective poem[5].

194. In the Achilleid, notwithstanding an occasional reflection (Π 46-7) upon the course of events as bearing some one on to destruction, it cannot be said that any other purpose can be discerned than simply to magnify Achilles. An attempt has indeed been made to construe it as a poem demonstrative of the mischiefs and misery resulting from implacability, Achilles having punished himself by the loss of Patroclus as much as he punished the Greeks; but such a notion errs through over ingenuity. Even Patroclus seems to be secondary in the poet's estimation, and the quarrel with Troy and the offence of Paris[6] do not in his eye bulk large. The glory of Achilles, or what he counted his glory, is his sole end and aim, and there is no other purpose discernible.

It is otherwise with the Ulyssean cantos, and more particularly with the largest group of them, viz. that from B to H inclusive. These are pervaded partly by a patriotic purpose, to exalt the virtues of the Southern Heroes, those namely of the Peloponnesus, partly by an ethical purpose, to exhibit the Greeks as contending against falsehood and perjury as well as

---

[4] 'A good work of art can, and will indeed, have moral consequences, but to require moral ends of the artist is to destroy his profession.' Göthe, Autob. (i. 469).

[5] 'It is Homer's practice to leave the requisite *moral impression* to be made by the simple combination of the events, without adding any comment of his own' (O. Müller, Lit. ch. 4. 7, note).

[6] Menelaus is once represented as styling the Trojans ἀνέρες ὑβρισταί (N 621), but he is left to be the spokesman of his own feelings. for the Achillean bard seems to have no moral feeling against the Trojans except as antagonists to Achilles in grim war, and as proudly presumptuous (μέγα φρονέοντες, ὑπερφίαλοι).—The 'pannus' in Θ 550, is condemned by all the critics from the want of external evidence, not being in the MSS, and only stitched in by Barnes from the Alcib. ii. of the Platonic *corpus;* but it is also condemned by the internal evidence, since it shows a *moral* antagonism to the Trojans, not according to the tone of the Achilleid, in which it happens to be now included.

violence, and the Trojans as hopelessly in the wrong. The result attained by the poet is that the doom of Troy is seen to be prepared and the sentence of retributive justice already virtually pronounced. It is upon the Ulyssean books B to II that this conclusion rests, and, through these and these alone, is an ethical purpose communicated to the Iliad.

195. Regarding the Odyssey, it has always been felt that an ethical purpose adverse to violence and usurpation is there discernible, and it is seen from the first to be the intention of the poet in his plot to represent the Suitors as doomed men for their reckless audacity. So likewise the Trojans, in that group of Books (B—H) in the Iliad, are similarly seen to be, in the poet's intention, doomed men; and this parallelism between the Trojans of B—H and the Suitors in the Odyssey is a powerful mark of congruity and a strong confirmation of the theory we have been maintaining. It is in Γ that this intention of the poet first becomes apparent. The Trojans are there represented as coming under solemn oaths, conducted with all due ceremonial, to abide the issue of a single combat. The single combat goes against them, but they resile from their compact, under circumstances of gross treachery. Pandarus, during truce, shoots an arrow at Menelaus and wounds him, and the Trojans do not protest against but condone his atrocity, and become parties to what was in fact assassination.

196. But it may be asked, is it clear that the Poet himself has any feeling of moral reprobation? May it not be that he simply *narrates*, as matter of fact, objectively without any subjective feeling? It is true that the moral is not obtruded, and there is nothing like moralising even over the fall of traitors. Yet the poet's own feeling is unmistakable, flashing out occasionally in actual *objective* condemnation, even though it is the goddess Athene that figures as the prime mover and temptress of the Trojans in luring them to their doom. The same or a similar function she performs to the Suitors in the drama of the Odyssey (σ 346, and cp. σ 155). (1) The poet's attitude toward the traitorous Pandarus is not indifferent, or after any Göthe-type of ethical equilibrium; Pandarus is pronounced a 'fool' at the time when he does the dastard deed,

$$\tau\hat{\omega}\ \delta\grave{\epsilon}\ \phi\rho\acute{\epsilon}\nu\alpha s\ \mathring{\alpha}\phi\rho o\nu\iota\ \pi\epsilon\hat{\iota}\theta\epsilon\nu\ (\Delta\ 104).$$

This is the poet's own judgment, and there is no doubt that ἄφρων here implies moral condemnation.

(2) The Trojan heroes are represented as having a bad conscience and fearful misgivings as to the future. Æneas so speaks in E 177; Hector utters the famous lines of foreboding over the city (Z 447); and Antenor is similarly touched with fear (Η 351); which last utterance is expressly connected with the falsehood in the oaths of Γ. Moreover the real feeling of the Trojans in the Ulyssean cantos is one of detestation to Paris (Γ 454), and even Hector, though he condones his deeds, condemns the man (Z 282). The Achillean Hector, until his final hour, has no misgivings.

(3) The Greek heroes on the other hand are confident that the disfavour and vengeance of the gods are now to track the Trojans. Agamemnon gives utterance to this confidence in remarkable words in Δ 158–168, when he speaks of Zeus as being about to 'dash his dark Ægis in the Trojans' eyes, *wroth because of this falsehood.*' Again, in Δ 235, he tells his Argives that 'Zeus will never be the helper of *false* men.' Idomeneus in Δ 270 echoes the assurance that the Trojans are doomed men, *because* of their perfidy.

(4) The harshness of Agamemnon (in Z 62) in hewing down the suppliant Adrastus when Menelaus was willing to spare him and take ransom, is a startling phenomenon. It is explicable only by remembrance of the perjury in which the Trojan people was involved, and which even Hector endeavoured to excuse by throwing the blame on Zeus (Η 69). This Adrastus is spoken of as having an equipage, and he is therefore one of the rich but guilty ἱππόδαμοι of Troy. What is more strange, Agamemnon's harsh words are commended by the Poet, who says of him αἴσιμα παρειπών, 'rightly advising,'—a gleam of *personal* indignation thus flashing forth, akin to the feeling of satisfaction with which, as we shall find, he follows the Suitors to their doom.

(5) That the Trojans are in the same ethical position as the Suitors, may be further inferred from the circumstance that two epithets of dark import are shared by them both, and virtually by them alone [7]. (a) The expression, ὑπερηνο-

---

[7] Ὑπερηνορέων, in the singular, is given to Deiphobus in Ν 258, but it seems to imply no more than μέγα φρονέων, of the same Trojan, in Ν 156.

ῥέοντες, so characteristic in the Odyssey, as the special designation of the Suitors (once of the Cyclopes, ζ 5), comes up similarly in the Iliad as the epithet of a *class*, but only in a Ulyssean part (Δ 176), and there it is applied to the Trojans[8]. (β) Probably the worst epithet in the Homeric vocabulary is ἀλείτης (=*scelestus*). It is used twice, and is distributed between the Suitors in the Odyssey (υ 121) and Paris in a Ulyssean canto (Γ 28). Regarding the last instance, although the expression *may* be thought to indicate simply Menelaus's feeling, it can also be interpreted as containing the poet's own condemnation of the faithless Paris. (γ) The epithet ἀγήνορες is given to the Suitors, and to none else, about twelve times in the Odyssey. It has come to have a sinister sense, notwithstanding its use twice by the suitors regarding themselves (σ 43, υ 292). There is only one parallel occurrence of it, as given, namely, to a *class* of persons, in the Iliad. *It is given to the Trojans in the Ulyssean canto* Κ 299[9].

(6) In Η 402, after a message had been received from the Trojans declining to grant the Greek demands, Diomed is represented as saying, 'Even a child might understand that the toils of death are knit for the Trojans.' This can be explained only with reference to the repeated acts of insolent faithlessness.

Now, the remarkable thing is this, that this vaticination of Diomed is not verified, but rather falsified by the success of the Trojans in the Book that now stands next in order (Θ), which book is Achillean, and indeed is not verified within the Iliad as regards the Trojan people, though the fall of Hector prepares the way. The poet's eye, however, who constructed books B—H, glances outside the scope of the Iliad and discerns the vision of the great Retribution that came upon

---

[8] It is a minor 'Anklang' between the Odyssey and the Ulyssean cantos that the appearance of Penelope among the suitors, whereby Athene contrives to tantalise them on the eve of their destruction (σ 160), is parallel, in so far, to the appearance of Helen fluttering the hearts of the Trojan Elders on the towers of the doomed city (Γ 155).

[9] It is worthy of note that ἀγήνωρ is twice given to *individuals*; to Achilles (Ι 699) and to Laomedon (Φ 443), in both instances with touch of *blame*. Ebeling remarks on the peculiarity of the word: '*Homines* hoc adjectivum praedicare Odyssene potissimum est proprium *Iliadisque librorum, quorum sermo* etiam caeteroquin *propior est Odysseae*.' The remark is justified at all events regarding Books Ι and Κ, in which ἀγήνωρ so occurs.

the perjured city. Further, in the Achillean cantos that now
follow these cantos B—H, there is no reference to the oaths
and their violation by the Trojans, and although they are
spoken of as haughty and insolent, it does not appear that
the author of the Achilleid conceived the Trojans as truce-
breakers and oath-violators. This silence is the more remarkable, inasmuch as the clearest subsequent opportunity for referring to such deeds occurs in an Achillean canto (N 620),
where Menelaus has occasion to describe the character of
the Trojans, but seems to have forgotten what would have
been the climax of their offending, the wounding he had
himself received recently from the bow of a perjured truce-
breaker. The faithless character of the *Priamidæ* generally,
except Hector, is a feature common to Γ (106), and to Ω (260,
cp. H 352), where Priam utters the malediction over them as
being 'liars' ($\psi\epsilon\upsilon\sigma\tau\alpha\acute{\iota}$), a probable allusion to the violation of
the oaths in Δ, and, if so, a link between these various
Ulyssean cantos.

There is, therefore, ample ground for the conclusion that
it is by the cantos B—H, forming the largest integer of the
Ulyssean cantos[10], that the Iliad becomes *moralised*. In
other words, a conformity is obtained between the Iliad which
was originally without ethical purpose and the Odyssey, which
is the poem *par excellence* ethical in its tone and purpose.
The conclusion seems irresistible that under evidence, on so
many lines, showing conformity to the Odyssey, disconformity
to the Achilleid, the tract of cantos B—H has proceeded
from the same author as the Odyssey, whose ethical character
we next proceed to consider.

---

[10] In considering B—H as one integer in the formation of the Iliad, one can
appeal to the Wolfian Düntzer regarding the tract Γ—H. ' Buch Γ bis H mit
ausschluss einzelner Interpolationen ursprünglich ein selbständiges Gedicht bildet.
Dagegen sieht Lachmann hier vier verschiedene Lieder' (Düntzer, Hom. Abh.
p. 46). Elsewhere Düntzer appears to include B, for he speaks of ' unser grosses
Gedicht von B—H' (p. 292).

CHAPTER XXIV.

CONCLUSION.

οὗτος μὲν δὴ ἄεθλος ἀάατος ἐκτετέλεσται.

197. THAT the Odyssey is preeminently ethical in its character is clear from the whole contour of its structure. It is richer than any other single poem the world has seen in tales and fantasies that have become the vehicle of allegory, and have furnished the staple texts of the moralist in all after time. The vast burden of Thought with which it comes laden to us is seen in the bare mention of such names as the 'song of the Sirens,' 'the cup of Circe,' 'the den of the Cyclop,' the 'Suitors' who aspire to the queen but grovel with the maids[1], and, although it would be a transcending of the evidence to affirm in the Poet himself a *conscious* purpose in

---

[1] It is unfortunate for the theory that moral instruction was intended *primarily* by these stories, that the hero is not represented as exercising the self-denial we should expect, for in the Siren song he is saved in his own despite, and in the Circe-scene, he owes his safety not to any self-command in the highest sense, but to a previous divine warning and to a special antidote not granted to the rest (cp. Grote, II. ii. 278). In these narrations, according to Lord Bacon (Adv. of Learning), the fable came first and the moral or exposition after, and, if this was so, the poet will get the credit simply of happy instinct in shaping and selection. Some modern critics will not allow him even this credit, but impute to him ignorance of the original sense of the mythes he has preserved to us, especially of the Cyclop story, of which they say he had lost the key, which, however, they have discovered. Notwithstanding the impossibility of proving that the poet wished to represent Ulysses as in *our* sense a moral hero, it remains true that he intended to represent him as a hero in that form of self-restraint, which consists in mastery of the feelings, and is best understood as ' pluck and patience ' combined. The value of this kind of discipline is taught *expressly* in the Odyssey in such passages as δ 282-8, λ 105, ν 307-10, τ 42, 347, and is virtually taught in the changes rung upon the epithets appropriated to the hero, πολύτλας, ταλασίφρων, τλήμων, and in such expressions as ἀλλ' ἐπετόλμησε, φρεσὶ δ' ἔσχετο (ρ 238). This mastery of his

composing the narrations, or any discernment of the rich mine of Instruction he was providing, it remains a matter of historic fact that the Odyssey was the poetic field that moralists in ancient times found most fruitful in ethical suggestions. Socrates in the Memorabilia (i. 3. 7, ii. 6. 11–31), Herakleides (Grote, H. i. p. 567), Horace (Epp. i. 2. 26), and Cicero (de Fin. v. 18), draw from it as the main fountain of illustration.

It is not, however, to these elements in the Odyssey that we make appeal in claiming for it an ethical purpose. That purpose is discerned in the structure of the plot, in the sympathy of the narrator with the exhibition of a great Retribution, carried out upon a great and imposing scale with every 'moving' circumstance and after all hope of redress seemed gone. The care with which the position of the Suitors is marked out as a usurpation, the expedients by which they are exhibited as 'shameless' (α 255, and more objectively spoken, υ 29, 386), as rude and coarse (α 108), yet luxurious (φ 151), reckless and unscrupulous (ψ 65–7), not hesitating to plot murder against the son of her whom they are wooing, the device by which they receive, near the outset of the poem, the fullest warning, first informally (α 380), then formally and openly (β 145), with all the publicity and solemnity of the Agora [2], and, above all, the frequency with which, in no uncertain flickering form, the poet's own feeling flashes forth like a subterranean flame against the evil-doers, are features that at once compose and demonstrate the ethical purpose inseparable from any just theory of the Odyssey. There is, at the outset in α, the preparatory keynote in the Retribution described as befalling the evil-doer Ægisthus, who is named as having been fully warned of *his* iniquity; thereafter comes the actual warning given to the Suitors in β, a canto which is essential to the moral economy of the poem; there is further in γ and δ the anticipation of their fate in the

feelings is seen especially in his interview with his mother's shade, and his reticence and self-control in the presence of his spouse, and during the whole period of the disguise as a beggar. Compare the previous section, § 78, n. on the τλήμων θυμός of Ulysses.

[2] Grote (II. ii. 92–3) points out the importance of this proceeding ethically, and consequently of the book containing it, to the framework of the Odyssey.

mouth of Nestor and then of Menelaus, the vaticination of their doom in λ from the lips of Tiresias in the Under-world, the mantle of mystery thrown around the hero's Return by Athene, for the express purpose *that he might exact* sure vengeance (v 193), and, above all, there are the reiterated expressions of personal reprobation regarding them, such as π 448, ρ 216, v 394, φ 418, *objective* condemnations, on the poet's part, approving of their fate—all these being only dreadful notes of preparation marking the nearer and nearer advance of the thunder-cloud of Doom.

198. It is this idea of justice and vindicated moral order that may be said to pervade the Odyssey and renders it unique among the poems of the ancient world. In this point of view there is ground for the affirmation that the poet of the Odyssey has struck a note in wonderful harmony with the Christian Ideal of the Kingdom of Righteousness and its Triumph of Justice and victory over Oppression[3]. A very frequent, if not the most frequent, image of that kingdom in the New Testament, brings before us a king who had gone into a far country returning to claim his own, to reward the good and to recompense the evil among his subjects[4].

It is a kindred image that is mirrored in the Odyssey, and if it is true that the action of the poem thus moves in an orbit concentric with the movement and progression of the great drama of the world, this epic becomes invested with a dignity and grandeur to which there is no parallel in human literature.

---

[3] One of the deepest utterances of the Odyssey is the wail of one of the twelve women, kept grinding at the mill for the sake of the Suitors (v 105). It is the nearest approach to a ' Quousque Domine.' in ethnic thought, and goes far to show how deeply the Odyssey is pervaded by the idea of retribution, and by the foreboding of a day of account, in which, very remarkably, kindness or benevolence is proclaimed the test (Od. ρ 362).—It may be proper to note that the *special* vocabulary of *retribution* comes up in the Odyssey or Ulyssean area. Thus, while τίνω and τίσις with ἀποτίνω are found diffused, the compounds ἄντιτος and παλίντιτος belong only to the neozoic area. They occur *four* times in the Odyssey, and once in Ω 213 (with a *var. lect.* ἄν τιτός). Compare the remarkable phrase in Od. τ 92 equivalent to παλίντιτος.

[4] The image is occasionally presented to us in words that recall in remarkable felicity the action of the Odyssey. Compare especially St. Matthew xxiv. 48 ad fin., words in which we seem to hear the argument of the Odyssey.

199. It was under a perception both fine and true of the ethical burden of the Odyssey that Alcidamas the rhetorician (420 B.C.) bestowed upon it the famous appellation of the 'Mirror of human life,' an expression which Aristotle (Rhet. iii. 4) strangely censured, not for the idea, but seemingly for some fault in the image by which it was conveyed.

The voyage of Ulysses through snares and dangers, betwixt fears and pleasures, among Cyclopes and Sirens, through enchanted realms of Circe and Calypso, commended itself then, as it commends itself still, as an apt image of the voyage of human life [5]. And, if it shadowed forth the life of the individual, it could also symbolise the life of a Nation in its grandest moments. It was with the finest instinct that Polygnotus, in decorating the temple of Athene at Platææ, chose for the subject of his fresco the slaughter of the Suitors from the Odyssey. The victory at Platææ over Persia appeared to the Greeks a re-enacting of the drama of the Odyssey, the little nation [6] contending against the giant empire, just as the hero of the Odyssey contended with and foiled, almost alone, the huge gang of the Suitors.

200. If the ethical content of the Odyssey is so weighty and the scope of it thus broad and grand in full equality with its admitted perfection of structure and artistic harmony, what shall we say of the judgment of those who regard it as the inferior poem, or of the criticism of the Chorizontes who,

---

[5] So Dionys. Hal., de Rhetorica, p. 398, Reiske, ὥσπερ ἐν θεάτρῳ, τῷ βίῳ διὰ τοῦ βιβλίου πορεύσῃ.

[6] One of the explanations of the name Ὀδυσσεύς, Lat. *Ulixes*, connects it with ὀλίγος, a kind of suggestion that he was in person the *little* man, as he was king of a *little* island. As to the smallness of the island, there can be no doubt; 'a sergeant and seven men,' according to Lord Byron, took over the kingdom of Ithaca when it came under British sway. Whether we are to conceive the hero as correspondingly diminutive may be doubtful, though Tydeus (E 801) will in that case, like many great men who have been 'in person contemptible,' keep him in countenance. 'Er ist von mittelmässigen Wuchse, aber kräftig und gedrungen' (Buchholz, i. 2. 68). In Italic legends he was known as *Nanus*, or the dwarf, i. e. the dwarf that overthrew the giant, and even in the Homeric poems he is spoken of as none of the tallest (Γ 211), though of reverend look (Γ 212), and the Cyclop seems disappointed with the size and aspect of his enemy (ι 513). Through hardships he is spoken of as having a woebegone look (θ 182), and the first impression regarding him was unfavourable, but the second that he was 'like the gods' (ζ 242).

by denying it to Homer, in effect degrade this masterpiece
to the rank of an unacknowledged Cyclic poem? The position
of the latter is scientifically untenable, that of the former is
æsthetically unsound, proceeding, as it does, on an over-
estimate of turmoil and storm as an indication of strength, in
forgetfulness of the profound truth 'embodied in the maxim,—

'The Gods desire the depth and not the tumult of the Soul.'

Just as there are many that prefer the shaggy Esau, the
unchanged and unchangeable son of the desert, to the smooth
and cautious Jacob, who surrounds himself with flocks and
comfortable tents, (much as Lord Byron was drawn to
celebrate Saul instead of David among the Jewish kings,) so
there are not a few who will with Hippias the Sophist
(Plato, Hipp. Min. 363 B.) exalt the short-lived hurricane-
like hero of the 'unapproachable hands' above the longer-
living calmer-natured hero of the sagacious mind and the
inexhaustible counsel. Yet those who so judge must admit
that the future of the Greek people, as of the Hebrew race,
lay entirely with the heroes whom they would depreciate
and disown. The expansive force of the Greek intellect is
represented potentially not by Achilles, but by Ulysses of
'the manifold counsel.'

It is true there is less of the 'Sturm und Drang' of
impetuous passion, more of the calm strength that controls
passion, in the Odyssey than in the Iliad. There is, however,
not less of real animation in the scenes and incidents, and it
may be doubted whether the grandest things in Homer are
not such gems in the Odyssey as the apparition of the ghosts
of Achilles and Ajax, with the sublime silence of the latter
and the august impetuousness of the former, or the weird prophecy of the seer Theoclymenus on the eve of the slaughter,
or the scene, magnificent in its moral grandeur[7], where
Ulysses is described as standing indignant yet patient amid
the disorders and indignities of his hearth and home. But
the crowning proof that the Odyssey was not inferior in the
qualities that give spirit and animation is the fact that
when Plato is in search of an example of a spirit-stirring

---

[7] Already remarked upon in § 131.

scene and examines the *repertoire*[a] of the Rhapsode for the most 'tingling' piece at his command, he lights first upon a scene in the Odyssey—that, namely, where Ulysses rises up bow in hand, and springs upon the threshold, no longer the suppliant Beggar but the Avenger.

201. The considerations above advanced are entirely in harmony with the actual influence on literature which the Odyssey can be shown to have exerted. That influence has been immense in extent and unequalled in kind, not for splendour and richness only, but still more for subtlety, and the fruitfulness which flowed from it in the past seems still unexhausted. Tennyson, if we may judge from his 'Lotus-eaters' and his 'Ulysses,' has found it, among the old classic fields, a favourite hunting-ground of his Muse, and to Göthe the inspiration from the Odyssey during his tour in Sicily, where the vision of Phæacia seemed to him to be realised, resulted in one of the most classic of his poems, the domestic epic of 'Hermann and Dorothea.' Our own Milton owes much to both the Iliad and the Odyssey in his Paradise Lost ; but it is doubtful whether he does not owe more largely to the Odyssey that poem which is at once the most finished and the subtlest work of his genius, the Mask of Comus.

In the splendid succession of its progeny, the greatest has yet to be named. The first six Books of the Æneid are the glory of the Roman Epic muse. They are, properly and strictly, in subject and setting, the counterpart not of the Iliad but of the Odyssey. To one of its cantos, the eleventh, we owe, in particular, the sixth Æneid, and to the sixth Æneid the world owes the first poem of modern literature, first in time and, in the opinion of many, first in power, the Divine Comedy of Dante. The eleventh Odyssey can thus lay claim to the most illustrious line of progeny, in the literature of the world.

---

[a] Compare the instructive passage in Plato's Ion, ch. 6. Landor's judgment (vol. ii. 639) regarding the two 'scenes supreme' in Homer is worth noting. Both of these scenes are outside the Achilleid, viz. in Ω and Od. λ.

> 'Twice is almighty Homer far above
> Troy and her towers, Olympus and his Jove.
> First, when the God-led Priam bends before
> Him, sprung from Thetis, dark with Hector's gore :
> A second time, when both alike have bled,
> And Agamemnon speaks among the dead.'

How it has influenced the romantic literature of all lands, from the Arabian Nights to the Faery Queen of Spenser, belongs more to the archæology of Thought than to the domain of criticism, and therefore lies beyond the limits of our survey. Enough has been said to vindicate the claim of the Odyssey to occupy a place equal to the highest, and to be associated, under a clearer title than any other single poem can show, with the great name and personality of Homer.

APPENDIX.

NOTE A.

ON THE ANTIQUITY OF THE ILIAD AND ODYSSEY.

THE position assumed and the arguments advanced by Mr. Paley have been partly touched upon in the 20th section. The full consideration of them would require a special work to itself, and the following remarks are therefore given only provisionally, as reasons of dissent. They are sufficient, however, to 'sist procedure' in that direction and to lead up to a verdict of 'not proven' in the case as raised and pleaded by Mr. Paley[1].

1. His hypothesis ignores the fact that the Homeric poems had been commented on in written lucubrations *before* the date when according to Mr. Paley they assumed their present shape. Theagenes of Rhegium, who is contemporary with Cambyses (about 500 B.C.), *writes* observations on Homer, which are quoted or referred to by the critics of the Alexandrian age and bear upon passages in *our* Homer. Now it is impossible to suppose a Homer unwritten and nebulous and at the same time written commentaries upon this nebulous Homer coexisting. A written commentary on a work itself unwritten is surely, as Col. Mure remarks, a thing unheard of (i. p. 207). As soon, however, as commentaries are possible, interpolation and designed alteration become impossible, and it is a maxim in Sanskritology that no unprinted literary production is safe from minor alteration *until* it has been commented on (Colebrooke, i. p. 98).

2. The hypothesis in question is untenable if we look to the manner in which Pericles speaks of Homer in his great speech in Thucydides (ii. 41), about the very time when, according to Mr. Paley, the poems are being put into the shape in which we now have them. In his eulogy of Athens, the statesman professes to dispense with any reflected

---

[1] Some excellent remarks, by Mr. D. B. Monro on Mr. Paley's theory will be found in the 'Academy' (May 1, 1873).

glories to the Athenian people from the poetry of Homer, but he does so in a style of regret under a kind of *sour grape* feeling, showing conclusively that the poems were no longer growing, but had long been a rounded orb of song which no hand could reach to tamper with or in a serious way to modify. The Athenians of the historic time felt sore at the poor figure which they made as a warrior people in the Homeric poems, and there is evidence to show that the associates of Pisistratus, and even Solon himself, were accused of attempting in a much earlier age than the Periclean to remedy the deficiency. This they were said to have done by inserting in one or two passages a line or two suggestive of Athenian associations. But they were not accused of doing more than inserting the smallest chips (cp. § 176, 177), and they seem to have shrunk from using largely that liberty, a proof that the function performed by Pisistratus was only ministerial, not the magisterial and architectonic one which the Wolfian theory ascribes to him. Had their service to Homer been of that high constructive or even regulative character, the chirp of the Athenian grasshopper in aftertime over the performance would have been incessant, and the world would never have heard the end of it.

3. The evidence of Herodotus is intelligible only on the supposition that the poems of the Iliad and Odyssey were already traditionally a *corpus* of known consistency. His attempt to fix the distance between himself and their author as an interval of just four centuries is unintelligible unless the poems were already well-recognised and firm deposits among the boulders of a by-gone age. Further, his silence as to the most wonderful achievement ascribed by Wolf to Pisistratus, when he framed the Epics of Homer, becomes an unaccountable omission in his history, seeing that it was devoted to the recording of the ἔργα μεγάλα καὶ θωυμαστά of the Greeks and Barbarians, an omission fatal to the Wolfian theory and *a fortiori* to the Paleyan form of it.

4. The existence of a Teacher or Schoolmaster class, with Homer presumably as Textbook, can be recognised previous to the Periclean or even the Solonian age. Without relying on the story told of Alcibiades, that he once chastised a Schoolmaster because he had not in his possession a complete copy of the Iliad, it is clear that the tradition as to Tyrtæus presupposes instruction, not perhaps in a school but in the houses of the great (like Ennius in the early Roman time in the family of the Scipios), and that, too, instruction in the text of Homer; for, as early as Xenophanes, who flourished about 538 B.C., in what seems a genuine fragment, we find Homer virtually a school-book :

ἐξ ἀρχῆς καθ᾽ Ὅμηρον ἐπεὶ μεμαθήκασι πάντες.

(cp. Welcker, Ep. Ky. i. p. 172.)

5. If the poems had been, in the period of Pericles, still under process of evolution, such as Mr. Paley's view supposes possible, it is difficult or rather impossible to understand how the representative of Homeric song in the Periclean time had so little honour accorded to him [1]. The Rhapsode had, by that time, sunk into a kind of contempt as an effete relic of by-gone time (cp. Xen. Mem. iv. 2. 10, and the banter of Plato's Ion), a treatment from which he ought to have been secure, if a certain halo of creative genius or at least extensive discretionary powers in shaping and reconstructing still belonged, or had lately appertained to him. Among other things we may remark that a Homer 'concocted' at Athens in the Periclean age would have had a stronger flavour of the democratic element, and, in particular, there would have been a toning down, if not an expurgation, of the Thersites-scene. This was a portion of Homer that rather gravelled the democrats of that age, and, much in the same way as the Coriolanus of Shakspere is not particularly acceptable in America, quotations from or allusions to that scene were scarcely popular at Athens in the historic time (Xen. Mem. i. 2. 58–9).

NOTE B.

On the σήματα λυγρά.

The 'baleful signs' in a 'folded tablet' occur in Z 168. They are a means of communication between persons at a distance. What are we to understand by those signs?

The Wolfians deny that they imply a knowledge of the art of writing. The anti-Wolfians affirm they do. The following are the chief facts of the case.

On the one hand, apart from the passage in dispute, there is the silence elsewhere of both Iliad and Odyssey as to the art of writing. There is the silence also of Hesiod, but, since the Bœotian poet represents a more primitive though not necessarily a more ancient condition of things than the author of the Odyssey reveals, who knows of advanced appliances unknown to the Bœotian farmer, such as the *manuring* (Od. ρ 299) of fields and the use of the *mill* for grinding corn instead of the old *mortar* and *pestle*, this silence of

---

[1] Regarding the arguments from the subjects on 'painted Greek vases,' it is important to note that high authorities, who are specialists in the Archæology of Art, dispute the interpretations. According to A. S. Murray in Cont. Rev., 1874, p. 219, 'The evidence brought forward by Mr. Paley . . . . . fails under examination.'

Hesiod, in his narrow and circumscribed sphere, is less significant and important than the reticence, if such it be, of the singer or singers of the Iliad and Odyssey. What renders the reticence more remarkable is the fact that there is no allusion to writing or any cognate kind of memorial in the circumstances that seem most to call for it, such as in the erection of pillars or monuments to mark the resting-places of the dead. These are spoken of as raised to be an undying glory to certain men (H 89–91), but there seems no security taken in connection with the monument itself as to the fidelity of the transmission.

Another negative argument of importance is the fact that the word for *writing* has as yet no proper or clear existence. The term which in the literary period of the Greek tongue denoted the art of writing, viz. γράφω, is familiar enough in the Homeric time, but it belongs not to the Muse but to Mars, and signifies, in the peaceful Odyssey (χ 280), just as much as in the warlike Iliad, to *scratch* or *graze*. Compare the remarks in § 117, θ. This is one of Wolf's strongholds, from which, in fact, he has never been dislodged. It was from this, as a sallying-point, that he directed his assaults against the fabric of the poems, which, therefore, he concluded must have been not only preserved for a long period without the aid of writing, but must have been also—a more formidable difficulty—memorially composed.

Very ingenious and interesting is the attempt of Bergk (Lit. Gesch., p. 202) to carry up the knowledge of writing to a high antiquity by an argument founded on the use of χράω in oracular responses. This use he connects with χραύω=*scratch* and χαράσσω, and he argues that the art of writing in some rude form must have existed before χράω could have signified to 'give an oracle.' It is so used in Od. θ 79. It is doubtful, however, whether the argument is a just one, since the impersonal χρή already exists in the oldest parts of the poems, and this, on Bergk's theory of the connection, would require long familiarity with the art, and we should certainly expect to find in that case clearer traces of its existence. Moreover, if χράω is connected with χραύω, it is not easy to see how the *God* is said χρᾶν, when he is not the transcriber. Bergk's argument would require a reversal of the relation which subsists between the active χράω which is applied to the God and the middle χράομαι which is applied to the consulter or, on his theory, the transcriber.

To attempt to turn Wolf's position by the introduction of *ex post facto* interpretations, such as the ascription of the art of writing to the heroic ages by the Attic Tragedians, is both futile and illegitimate, and the same fate must befall any arguments from apparently ancient cyclic stories, such as that concerning Palamedes, that he communicated to his friends the story of his death by *scratchings* on oars which were tossed overboard to drift ashore (Arist. Thesmoph., 770).

The Wolfians may justly reject all such *ex post facto* inferences and may claim to have the question decided on the ground of their own choosing—the Homeric poems alone—and therefore the view limits itself to the passage about the ' baleful signs.'

The 'signs' are represented as having been 'scratched on a folded tablet' and are then given to a bearer, in whose case they are to be an instrument of intended death. They are carried from a country on one side of the Egean to a country on the other ; and after being exhibited in the new country, they produce this effect that, though at first the bearer was welcomed and feasted, immediately on their presentation he is put in the way of ' being killed.' These 'signs'[1] were therefore intended to be a message or sentence of death ; and the conclusion seems irresistible that here we have a communication made between two parties at a distance by means tantamount to, or identical with, the art of writing. The more candid Wolfians give up the point and say the Episode of Glaucus and Diomed, where the passage is found, is an interpolation of a later date. On Wolfian principles, it is difficult to understand what is an ' interpolation,' if the whole is a mere *congeries* ; but it is unfortunate that this so-called interpolation should be, in execution and tone, one of the most finished portions of the poem. Those Wolfians, however, who perceive that among documents of presumably equal antiquity, they are not entitled on their own principles to presume upon interpolations, boldly face the question and pronounce the signs to be some kind of picture-writing, like the ancient Mexican, or some conventional sign, fixed upon between friends by which, as by a species of freemasonry (cp. Schol. on Eur. Med. 613 on partition of ἀστράγαλοι in separations), a friend could be introduced and treated accordingly. Neither of these suggested analogies will suit the exigencies of the case. What is wanted is a species of freemason sign that will indicate, not a friend, but a foe, or rather that will suddenly *convert* into a foe one received at first as a friend. There is not only information to be conveyed, which is all that either of the above suggested explanations will cover ; there is also a message to *do* this or that, which neither the picture-writing nor the freemason or other conventional sign seems capable of conveying.

The whole description of the affair is mysterious, precisely as we

---

[1] The so-called 'letter' of David to Joab sent by Uriah the Hittite is in some respects an exact parallel.

might expect the first mention of writing to appear to an unlettered people, and there may be some truth in Dr. Hayman's suggestion that the tablet with its 'signs' was supposed to work on the mind of its receiver by some magic power and to possess some talismanic influence akin to poison[2]. It is certainly strange that the 'signs' are not exhibited on arrival, for they are not delivered till asked for, and so they seem to be 'credentials' rather than a 'letter' in our sense. Yet the question recurs, Why is the tablet said to have been *folded*? Is not the reasonable explanation simply this, that it was folded to prevent the bearer from looking into it and getting a notion of its hostile contents, that is, *reading* it[3]? In these circumstances the evidence seems clear that it was a message conveyed by writing, whether in the early and rudimentary stage of hieroglyphics, after the manner of Egypt, or in the more advanced form of alphabetical writing, after the fashion of Phœnicia.

On the whole, therefore, the natural, and, until the time of Wood and Wolf, universal, interpretation of the 'signs' as signifying writing is the most suitable one, and it is remarkable that the passage occurs in a portion of the Iliad where frequent mention is made of that Phœnician race from whom the art of writing is known to have come into the Hellenic world. Book Z, where it occurs, contains a reference to the *cunning* works of the Sidonians (l. 290), and cannot be separated in authorship from books Δ and E, in both of which we hear of the *Cadmeans*[4] who represent a Phœnician element in Greece.

The view which we have taken, becomes irresistible when we take into account the juxtaposition at a very early time of the Phœnician and Egyptian peoples alongside of the Greek race, according to the evidence of both poems. It is easy and even necessary to concede to the Wolfians that it was long before the art of writing became familiar—compare. the timid way, for instance, in which a single initial letter (a *Koppa* on early Corinthian coins or Φ on Phocæans) was edged in upon the Greek coinage—and, that it was an art practically unknown, for ordinary literary purposes, during a

---

[2] Θυμοφθόροι Doederlein (in loco) would interpret into 'mind-corrupting' or 'poisoning,' that is, the mind of the receiver.

[3] Cp. ἀναπτύσσων of Crœsus, when he opens the *secret* missives (Hdt. i. 48); also ἀνασχίζειν of Cyrus, when he opens the strange packet of Harpagus (Hdt. i. 143-4).

[4] Mr. Gladstone (Juventus Mundi, p. 130) suggests that the art of writing may have been an occult possession of a few Phœnician families settled in Greece. The affinities of Proetus, who sends the mysterious 'tablet' to Lycia, seem accordingly to be Eastern. He has married a princess from Lycia, and, according to the post-Homeric genealogies, is himself connected with Egypt by his descent from Danaus, who is brother of Ægyptus.

considerable period after the Homeric poems had been composed.
It is, however, hardly possible to admit that, in the extensive intercourse carried on with Phœnicia and Egypt, the inquisitive and penetrating Greeks should have caught no glimpse of the alphabetic
writing of the one nation or the hieroglyphics of the other. The
mariners who brought from Egypt the drug of 'Nepenthe' (δ 220),
who handled ropes made of the papyrus (φ 391), and who were
able to report of the river of Egypt and its 'very fair fields,' must
have obtained some notion of the art of writing in viewing the monuments on its banks, and may have described the same with a vague
sense of wonder, much as the descendant of Hiawatha would describe the doings of the electric wire [5].

The evidence is not sufficient to justify the conclusion that Homer
himself used the art of writing, but it is sufficient to enable us to affirm
that it was becoming familiar in his time, and that the poems, though
probably memorially composed, were soon committed to writing and
were not long subjected to the accidents of memorial transmission [6].
The famous inscription in Greek characters on the statue at Abou-
simbel in Upper Egypt (Psampolis in Nubia) by the Greek soldiers,
mercenaries under Psammetichus, which has been compared to our
modern inscriptions by wandering tourists on the rocks of the Brocken
or the Rigi, shows that as early as 590 B.C. (Ludwig Ross says, as
early as the *first* Psammetichus, and if so about the middle of the
seventh century B.C.), the art of writing was familiar to the Greek
people even in its least cultured sections (cp. Ludwig Ross as quoted
in Volkmann, p. 220).

The only other observation I shall add is that the two passages in
which γράφω receives the sense of 'affixing a mark' for recognition
and so approximates to its historic sense are contained in the neozoic
books of the Iliad (Z 169, H 187, and cp. § 117 θ).

NOTE C.

DETAILS AS TO ἵππος AND ITS DERIVATIVES, ETC. (cp. p. 209).

THE following are the chief details as to the proper names compounded with or based upon ἵππος, as a prefix :—

---

[5] O. Müller (Dor., i. p. 148) remarks on the early imperfection of writing in
Greece at a time when other Arts were already in even brilliant form.

[6] Colonel Mure (Hist. of Gr. L., i. p. 512) goes beyond the probabilities of the
case when he attributes to Homer not only a knowledge and use of writing, but
acquaintance with the Phœnician, that is, the Hebrew tongue!

Solely Achillean.	Common to Ach. and Ul.	Solely Ulyssean.	Solely in Odyssey.
Hippasus	Hippodameia	1 Hippocoon	1 Hippotades
Hippodamus	Hippothous		
Hippodamas	3 Hippolochus		
Hippomachus			
Hipponous			
6 Hippotion			

The instances of ἵππος forming the *second* member of a compound in a proper name are not so many as those when it is a prefix. Melanippus is the most common, and there are four persons of that name, mentioned seven times in all. The four are all in the Achilleid. Euippus is another, making five persons in the Achilleid so designated. There does not appear to be more than one in each of the other sections, viz. Pheidippus in the Ulyssean area, and Ctesippus in the Odyssey.

As to common words compounded with ἵππος in the second member, the only example seems to be πολύιππος. It is Achillean (N 171).

Regarding common words in which ἵππος is the prefix, we may begin with ἱπποσύνη. In the Achilleid it is ascribed to individual Trojans, viz. Hector, Euphorbus, Kebriones, and occurs thrice. In the Ulyssean cantos it occurs thrice also, being given to Eumelus, Antilochus, and to Nestor's troops, to each once. The associations of these last names with the Horse are deeply rooted in *tradition* (cp. § 124, n. 13), and therefore the equality is easily explicable.

The distribution of ἱππόδαμος is as follows:—

	Ach.	Ul.
1. As national Epithet of Trojans and Phrygians.	11	13
2. As Epithet of Individual Heroes	8	14.

The apparent preponderance in the Ulyssean cantos requires further investigation.

Ἱππόδαμος of Individual Heroes.

I.   Trojan Heroes.

	Ach.	Ul.
Antenor	1	1
Hector	3	2
Hippasus	1	0
Hyperenor	1	0
	6	3.

II.   Greek Heroes.

(α) *Present at Troy.*

	Ach.	Ul.
Diomed	1	6
Thrasymedes	1	0
	2	6.

(β) *Not present at Troy.*	Ach.	Ul.
Atreus	0	2
Tydeus	0	2
Castor	0	1
	0	5.

It is important to note that the *traditional* use, as seen in this last list (β), is in the Ulyssean and not in the Achillean area. This circumstance, taken in connection with the frequency of the application of the term to Diomed, accounts for the apparent preponderance in the Ulyssean area. The Odyssey may be said to know only the *traditional* use, once of the dead Castor, once of the absent Diomed, and once of the almost vanished Nestor, who, as a Poseidon-worshipper, is entitled to the name ἱππόδαμος: ἱππότης and ἱππηλάτης are diffused similarly to ἱππόδαμος under a preponderance of merely traditional associations.

The ordinary compounds of ἵππος are mostly the following :—

	Ach.	Ul.	Od.
ἱπποκέλευθε (of Patroclus only) .	3	0	0
ἱπποδάσεια	4	3	2
ἵππουρις	4	2	1
ἱππόκομος	5	0	0
ἱπποκορυσταί	2	3	0
ἱππιοχαίτης, ἱππιοχάρμης . . .	0	2	0
	18	10	3.

The epithets of ἵππος itself seem to be peculiarly distributed. A good many, it is true, are diffused and belong to both areas, but it is singular that special ones emerge in each area and do not appear in the other. Thus while ποδώκεες, ὠκέες, and some others are common to both, the following are peculiar to the one area or to the other :—

<table>
<tr><td colspan="2">Achillean only.</td><td colspan="2">Ulyssean only.</td></tr>
<tr><td>ἐρυσάρματες</td><td>2 occurrences</td><td>ἀερσίποδες</td><td>2 occurrences</td></tr>
<tr><td>χαλκύποδε</td><td>2   ,,</td><td>ὑψηχέες</td><td>2   ,,</td></tr>
<tr><td>ὠκυπέτα</td><td>2   ,,</td><td>εὔτριχες</td><td>3   ,,</td></tr>
<tr><td>εὔσκαρθμοι</td><td>1 occurrence</td><td></td><td></td></tr>
<tr><td>κυανοχαίτης</td><td>1   ,,</td><td></td><td></td></tr>
</table>

NOTE D.

ON THE HORSE AND THE DOG IN LITERATURE.

THE following are a few gleanings in a rapid and by no means exhaustive survey.

The Horse in the Old Testament is generally regarded with disfavour as the great war-animal associated with and therefore suggestive of Pride and Oppression.   Egypt with her war-chariots had produced the mal-impression with which the mention of the horse is regarded, and it is remarkable that the oldest stage of Hebrew oriental life seems not to acknowledge it (Gen. xii. 16), and, in the Decalogue, it is the ox and the ass that are taken as the types of property, while there is no mention of the horse.   The glory of his haughty motions is magnificently rendered in the picture in the book of Job, but that is the creature of the Arabian [1] desert rather than of the land of Judah. Deuteronomy xvii. 16 may be said to express the normal feeling of the Old Testament as to the Horse, and this feeling is not materially departed from in the New Testament.

As to the Dog in the Old Testament, he is either wild and without masters, or is employed as the friend and helper of man, for his useful qualities to defend and to watch.   In this respect he can occasionally, in poetry at least, sustain a comparison with man in usefulness and energy (Job xxx. 1).   In general, however, the associations are sinister; his name is the symbol of Impudence and of Voracity—'Is thy servant a Dog?' and so forth, and these sinister associations were so deep that they passed into the currency of religious symbolism, so that the Dog became branded as a creature mysteriously unclean.

In the period after the Old Testament canon is closed, we find the Dog in closer and more loving relation to man, as in Tobit [2] (vi. 1, xi. 9) of the Apocrypha.   In the New Testament the Dog is still under the disfavour arising from mal-associations, and he remains the symbol of heathen impurity.   He suffers also from the general neglect and aversion which follow the creature in most countries of the East.   Apart, however, from these 'shades' of evil days, a new light breaks out in the New Testament.   The milder spirit which it enshrines shows itself in their admission to companionship at table, 'to eat of the crumbs,' and in what appears to be the recognition of their kindliness, when, in the absence of all human friends, in the case of the most miserable of men, 'the dogs came and licked his sores.'

In other Oriental literature, such as that of the Hindoos, the Horse is acknowledged with high honour, and is not eclipsed by

---

[1] Among the most curious compositions in literature must have been the Arabian tributes to the Horse, 'when Ben-zaid of Cordova and Abul-Monder of Valencia wrote a serious history of celebrated horses, as did Alasueco, of camels which had risen to distinction' (Sismondi, Lit. of S. of Eur. i. p. 66, E. Tr.)

[2] Possibly this was an influence from the Medes and Persians, the story of Tobit being laid in Media.   The prejudice regarding the Dog does not appear to have prevailed in the Zoroastrian region, for the Dog is in the Zendavesta the special animal of Ormuzd, and is still regarded with peculiar reverence by the Parsees (Rawlinson's Herodotus, i. ch. 141).

the Elephant in the affections of the early Aryan race. This fact has been already alluded to in § 122, n. 1. Compare the story in Herodotus as to the neighing of the horse of Darius Hystaspes as the omen of Empire, and, also on Persian soil, the story of Rustum and his horse Ruksh (§ 122, n. 5).

The Dog is also acknowledged, as adverted to in § 132, n. 21, where the *canonized* animals of the Mahommedan faith are briefly enumerated. It is worth noting also, from a more ancient period, that the 'dog and man' are coupled together as exempt from the sacrificial knife of a Magian priest (Hdt. i. 140).

In ancient Egypt, as we might infer from the Old Testament, the Horse was in high esteem. In one of the Ancient Texts, 'Records of the Past' (vol. ii. p. 91), we have a parallel in one feature to the Argus story; only it is of the Horse, not of the Dog. 'The king went forth to visit the stud of brood-mares and the stables of the young steeds : he saw that they had famished them. Then said he, By my life, so may Rá [the sun-god] love me, I loathe the youth, wretched creatures are they to my heart, who have starved my steeds : (this is) more than any abomination thou (Nimrod) hast done to-gether.'

The 'Latrator Anubis' is the most prominent honour to the Dog in ancient Egyptian mythology. The Dog occurs with Hermes on the coins of Alexandria (Eckhel, Doct. Num. iv. p. 68).

In medieval legends of the Saints we have the dogs of St. Hubert and the dog of St. Roch.

In Gaelic, Norse, and medieval heroic legends, we meet with Bran the dog of Fingal, Sam the dog of Gunnar in Burnt Njal, a grand creature, and Hodain the hound of Sir Tristrem.

In Welsh legends we find the touching story of the dog Gellert, which may be a western version of an eastern tale, but is certainly evidence of a love for the Dog among the Cymric race. According to the Welsh Triads, the three signs of a gentleman are the Horse, the Hawk, and the Hound.

Dante, in his allegory of the three vices of Youth, Mid Age, and Old Age, gives the place of honour over Panther, Lion, and She-wolf, to the *grey*-hound, that is, to the years that bring grey hairs and 'the philosophic mind' (Inferno, c. 1).

In the literature of England, as distinct from that of Scotland, a larger space and a higher place are accorded to the Horse than to the Dog. The English are among all modern races the fondest of horses, and it is natural that we should find great prominence given to the 'bellator equus' in their literature.

Thomas Fuller, in his 'Holy and Profane State,' thus remarks on Horses as characteristic of the gentleman :—

'He delights to see himself and his servants well-mounted; therefore he loveth good horsemanship. . . . It were no harm if in some needless suits of intricate precedency betwixt equal gentlemen, the priority were adjudged to him who keeps a stable of most serviceable horses' (Fuller, H. and P. State, ch. 40). (The Dog, apparently, does not enter into his calculations among the evidences of gentility.)

Shakspere, on the whole, in conformity with his generally 'lordly' associations, stands very much in the position already indicated by the words of Fuller[3]. Saving the dog Crab and the dogs of Theseus, which are 'marvels,' he has hardly any 'canine portraits,' and Crab is not in connection with a *gentleman*, but with a lackey. In his Sonnets (No. 91) he acknowledges the delight in dogs where he speaks of the various passions in which men glory, and among others,

> 'Some in their hawks and hounds, some in their horse.'

A little after, the hounds are dropped out, when he describes a joy

> 'Of more delight than hawks or horses be.'

In his 'Venus and Adonis,' although the Dog comes in for a minor share of the honours, the strength of his painting is given to the Horse, a glorification unequalled since the Achilleid, unless Browning's 'Ride to Aix' in its pre-Raphaelite minuteness dispute the palm.

Among the *Dii Minorum Gentium* the Dog has fared better. We may instance, besides Cowper's 'Beau' and Mrs. Browning's 'Flush :'—

> Chaucer's Prioresse with her 'smale houndes.'
> Spenser's 'Lowder' in 'Shepherd's Calendar' (September).
> Marston's picture of the Spaniel yclept 'Delight.'
> Herrick, in his verses to his Spaniel 'Tracy' (ii. pp. 107, 127).
> Pope, in his letter to H. Cromwell.
> Somerville, in the 'Chase.'
> Southey's 'Theron' in 'Roderick.'
> Wordsworth's (1) Terrier, the great 'Nameless,' Prelude, p. 89.
>   (2) Dog watching his dead master on Helvellyn.
> Byron, Inscription on 'Boatswain.'
> Longfellow, the Dog in Evangeline.

---

[3] The 'lordly' associations and predilections of Shakspere render him no favourite with certain modern Republicans. In America he is, among certain sections, less the poet of the people than Robert Burns. Compare, as formerly alluded to (p. 337), the position of Homer in the eyes of the most thorough-going democrats of Athens in the ancient days (Xen. Memor. i. 2. 58).

It is, however, in the Scottish branch of English Literature that the fullest expression has been given to the 'Delight in the Dog' as the companion of man. Sir David Lindsay long ago nobly led the way. Then comes Burns, with whom the horse is rather the sorry over-wrought slave of the husbandman than the fleet-footed companion of the chase, whereas his dogs are genuine jubilant rejoicing creatures. The Ettrick Shepherd follows at a respectful distance, with his 'Address to the shepherd-dog Hector,' and the living author of the delightful tale of 'Rab' has added another perennial honour to the literature in praise of the Dog.

Above all names, in this respect, since the time of Homer, stands a fifth Scottish name, that of Walter Scott. Homeric to the core he is in this, that, while honouring 'Gustavus' and his race, he has bestowed the might of his affection on the humbler companions of the hearth, on such as 'Bevis' and 'Maida,' 'Pepper and Mustard,' and 'Elfin' in 'Old Mortality,' the nearest approach to the ancient Argus.

NOTE E.

The Story of Argus. Odyssey XVII (ρ 290–327).

Ulysses disguised as the Beggar and Eumæus approach the palace in company. The Swineherd does not as yet recognise his master.

'Twas thus they talked and as they walked, ere long the hall appears.
Meantime a Dog that lay apart pricked up alert his ears,
Old Argus crouching in his lair, once prized o'er all his peers,
A hound the King himself of yore right tenderly had bred,
But never to the chase had seen the goodly creature led,
For ere the Dog was fully grown, the chief had gone to Troy.
Long time the youths had fetched him to the huntsman's wild employ
To chase the mountain goats, to hunt the harts, and hinds, and hares;
But now he lies neglected and for him no creature cares.
There's little luck about the house, when the true goodman's away.
So on the dunghill near the doors the pining Argus lay,
Where cows and mules made litter and the dung was trodden down,
Till Ulysses' hinds should spread it o'er the acres of the town.
There lay the dog, old Argus, to swarms of tiques a prey.
But when his Master neared the place where the noble creature·lay,

At once he knew and wagged his tail, then flapped down both his ears,
But no step nearer to his lord, although his voice he hears,
Could Argus move.   Ulysses saw and deftly turned aside
To brush the rising tear away, from the Swineherd's eye to hide ;
Then turned and asked with eager look, ' My good friend, that's most
    strange !
A hound upon the dunghill, such as o'er the mountains range !
Fine dog he seems in lith and limb, and I should like to know,
If fleet and fell he used to run, as his form would seem to show,
Or was he like the worthless breed that proud men like to feed,
About their tables, more, I ween, for ornament than speed ?'
To this then, good Eumæus, thou good answer mad'st indeed :
' I tell thee, Friend, that gallant dog of the man we see no more,
Were he in limb and doughty deeds what once he was of yore,
In days before Ulysses took his journey from our shore,
To see at once his speed and strength would fill thine eyes with glee,
For never in the forest depths was Argus known to flee,
No, not from aught with hairy skin, whate'er the beast might be :
Once on their track to hunt them out, most deadly scent had he.
But now he's fallen on evil days, for his master's dead and gone,
And now the careless female slaves neglect him sad and lone,
For servants, when their rightful lord no longer bears the sway,
Soon learn to take things easy and make all a holiday,
And when the great wide-thundering Jove brings under slavery's ban,
O then, I trow, he takes away full half his worth from man.'
He spake and slowly paced along to reach the echoing hall,
Right through the court he strode 'mong the suitors proud and tall.
Old Argus then did droop his head beneath Fate's mighty Doom
At a glimpse of his old master after twenty years of gloom.

NOTE F.

On the Elements of an Achilleid surviving in Thessaly and Albania.

In the annotation on p. 266 I have hazarded the assertion that the
elements of an Achilleid exist to this day in the region of Thessaly
and Albania, probably in larger measure than any other part of Europe
could now exemplify. Tenacity of adherence to ancient manners
and customs has always been a feature of character among mountain
peoples, but it may be doubted whether anywhere in Europe there is

a larger body of 'survivals' continued down from the prehistoric into comparatively recent days, equal to what the above-named region can supply.

1. The character of Achilles, as portrayed in the Achilleid, seems in its main features indigenous to the mountain ranges of Northern Greece. Among these features may be specially named (1) a capacity for Friendship strong and intense, and (2) an equal capacity for inextinguishable Revenge. Among the Morlachs (Illyrian Sclavonians) the Abbé Fortis (Travels in Dalmatia, pp. 55–8, quoted by Grote, H. ii. p. 118–9) describes the state of manners as follows :—

'Friendship is lasting among the Morlacchi. They have even made it a kind of religious point, and tie the sacred bond at the foot of the altar. The Sclavonic ritual contains a particular benediction for the solemn union of two male or female friends in presence of the whole congregation. The male friends thus united are called *Pobratimi*, and the females *Posestreme*, which means half-brothers and sisters. The duties of the Pobratimi are, to assist each other in every case of need and danger, to revenge mutual wrongs, etc. ; *their enthusiasm is often carried so far as to risk and even lose their life.* . . . . But as the friendships of the Morlacchi are strong and sacred, so their quarrels are commonly unextinguishable. . . . . A Morlach is implacable if injured or insulted. With him *revenge and justice have exactly the same meaning*, and truly it is the primitive idea, and I have been told that in Albania[1] the effects of revenge are still more atrocious and more lasting.'

Similar evidence as to the passionate attachment of adopted brothers like Patroclus and Achilles may be found in Tozer's Researches, i. p. 309, in his account of the Miridites :—

'The custom of forming fraternal friendships (*pobratim*), is common among the Miridites, as it is also among some of the other races of European Turkey. . . . This relationship, which reminds us of some of the passionate attachments of ancient history, such as those of David and Jonathan, of Achilles and Patroclus, is regarded as of the most sacred and inviolable character.'

This occurs in connection with the manners and customs of an Albanian tribe, and alongside of this singular custom the *Vindetta* prevails as a natural antithesis.

2. In the same region the Horse is prominent as the great companion of the warrior, and portents and hyperboles similar to those in

---

[1] The Arnaouts or Albanian soldiers retain the habits of the ancient Σελλοί of the country as 'sleeping on the ground' (χαμαιεῦναι) (Dodwell, i. p. 139).

the Achilleid emerge in the local legends and traditions regarding that animal.

In Lord Byron's picture of the court of Alý Pacha, the terrible ruler of Albania, the troops of steeds are a striking feature :—

> 'Richly caparisoned, a ready row,
> Of armed horse, and many a warlike store,
> Circled the wide-extending court below ;
> Above, strange groups adorned the corridore ;
> And oft-times through the area's echoing door,
> Some high-capped Tartar spurred his steed away.'
>
> (Childe Harold, ii. st. 57.)

So Hughes, in his Travels in Albania (vol. ii. p. 382), becomes enthusiastic in praise of certain 'cream-coloured chargers' of Alý Pacha :—

'They were the most picturesque animals I ever beheld, and in their broad haunches and chests, thick-curved necks and waving manes, small heads and eyes of fire, finely illustrated that splendid description of the oriental war-horse in the Book of Job.'

Regarding the horses of Thessaly in modern times, Dodwell informs us (i. p. 339) that they retain as a characteristic feature to this day the thick full neck of Bucephalus and of the Phidian chargers in the frieze of the Parthenon.

As to the friendly relations subsisting between the Horse and his Rider, it may be doubted if there is anything nearer the Achillean type of attachment to the horse than the following from the same area. The first is a Romaic ballad, the scene of which is laid in Macedonia. It is thus referred to by Tozer (Researches, ii. p. 259) :—

'When Demos [the dying Kleft or Brigand] is lying outstretched on the plains of the Vardar, it is his Horse that urges him to rise and follow the rest of the company; and when he (Demos) feels his strength is failing, he commits to him as to a faithful friend the ring and other tokens, which are to be borne to his lady-love, and bids him to dig for him a grave on the spot with his silver-plated hoofs[2]. In these and innumerable other instances the marvellous element is introduced with such perfect simplicity, and withdraws the narrative so completely from the course of ordinary occurrences, as to appear perfectly natural, and by no means to outstep the licence of poetic treatment.'

The next is from the lay in honour of the patriot warrior Scan-

---

[2] The sentiment in this ballad, which is remarkably Achillean, contrasts with the disparaging name of the horse in Romaic. viz. ἄλογον, as of the *irrational* animal. No doubt ἵππος remains in use alongside of it, but the emergence of ἄλογον in modern Greek is a singular phenomenon.

derbeg, also in Tozer (Researches, i. p. 217). In reading it we are reminded now of Ossian and Fingal, now of Sophocles and his Ajax parting with Eurysaces, and again we feel in the warrior's affectionate remembrance of his horse a touch entirely Achillean. The lay receives a new interest in these days when the soul of Prince Alexander (Scanderbeg) seems to have revived among the Montenegrins :—

'My trusty warriors, the Turk will conquer all your country, and you will become his slaves. Ducadjin, bring hither my son, my lovely boy, that I may give him my commands. Unprotected flower, flower of my love, take with thee thy mother, and prepare three of thy finest galleys. If the Turk knows it, he will come and lay hands on thee and will insult thy mother. Descend to the shore ; there grows a cypress dark and sad. Fasten the horse to that cypress, and unfold my standard upon my horse to the sea breeze, and from my standard hang my sword. On its edge is the blood of the Turks, and death sleepeth there. The arms of the dreaded champion—say, will they remain dumb beneath the dark tree? When the north wind blows furiously, the horse will neigh, the flag will wave in the wind, the sword will ring again. The Turk will hear it, and trembling, pale, and sad, will retreat, thinking on death.'

3. Among the prominent features of the Achillean character were found to be fierceness and a certain grim revelry in blood and wounds. It is remarkable that the mountain fastnesses of Albania and its neighbourhood should still exemplify these features, for there is certainly more of atrocity, murder, and mutilation, as a familiar normal thing, in that wild region than could be met with in any equal area within Europe. The name of Alý Pacha, the terrible hero of Albania, still preserves a fearful pre-eminence in barbarity, so that Byron's words are not overcharged :—

> 'For crimes that scorn the tender voice of ruth,
> Beseeming all men ill, but most the man
> In years, have marked him with a tiger's tooth ;
> Blood follows blood, and, through their mortal span,
> In bloodier acts conclude those who with blood began.'
>
> (Childe Harold. ii. st. 63.)

It is remarkable that a poem in honour of Alý Pacha and his exploits sprang up even in his lifetime, bearing a certain resemblance to the Achilleid. It was composed in modern Greek by an illiterate Mussulman Albanian who could not write, and, so far as ἦθος is concerned, is replete with Achillean sentiment.

In proof may be adduced the following, quoted from Col. Leake's account of the Poem in his Note 1 to the first volume of his ' Northern Greece : '—

' The people of Khormovo, whom Alý had ordered to submit, send him a message of defiance, upon which he *mounts his horse Beliosi, swifter than a flying bird*, and falls upon Khormovo, sword in hand.'

> Σὰν τὰ σφαχτὰ στὸ χασαπιὸ κόφτουν καὶ πελεκοῦνε,
> ἀκόμι θάρρος ἔχουνε καὶ δὲν τὸν προσκυνοῦνε·
> σὰν κλόσαις μὲ πολλὰ πουλιὰ ποῦ βλέπουν τὸ σαΐνι,
> ἔτζι φωνάζουν οἱ πικροὶ καὶ ῥάϊ δὲν τοὺς ἐδίδει·
> ἐμβῆκε ἀπὸ τὴν μία μεριὰ καὶ ἀπὸ τὴν ἄλλη βγένει,
> ποδοπατάει τὰ κορμιὰ καὶ ἀκόμι δὲν χορταίνει·
> Ἀλῆ Βελῆς βουλήθηκε ψυχὴ νὰ μὴν ἀφήσῃ,
> καὶ χίθηκαν τασκέριτον σὰ μανιωμένοι λύκοι.

' They cut and hew them like sheep in the butchery,
Yet they still have courage, and do not submit;
Like hens with many chickens, who perceive the falcon,
So they bitterly cry out while he gives them no quarter;
He entered on one side and came out at the other:
He treads on the bodies and is not yet satisfied;
(For) Alý Velý resolved to leave not a soul,
His troops poured down *like hungry wolves*[3].'

(Leake's Northern Greece, i. p. 469-70.)

Similiar *atrocia* will be found in the same author on pp. 481-2, and the Achillean ἀρετή over a subjugated or a fallen foe is not absent, as may be seen on p. 480.

In conclusion I subjoin the account which Col. Leake gives of the nature and composition of this Poem, simply remarking that the description is in many respects analogous to what may be supposed to have been, *mutatis mutandis*, the state of things when the Achilleid was similarly composed in honour of Achilles :—

' As poetry in a rude state of society generally precedes prose as a record of events, or of the exploits of individuals, it is not surprising to find among the Albanians, that the actions of their hero Alý, have been committed to writing in verse. This composition, of which I procured a copy in MS, consists of about 4500 στίχοι πολιτικοί, and although as barbarous in versification, phrase, and sentiment, as the manners which it depicts, is probably, as far as it goes, the most authentic memoir of the life of Alý which can be procured. The author was a Mussulman Albanian, acquainted only with the colloquial Greek of Albania and its borders, without the smallest tincture of Greek learning, and not even able to write his own verses.'

---

[3] Compare the great Achillean simile of the Myrmidons as wolves in Π 156.

EXPLANATORY ADDITIONS.

Page 22. With reference to the statement that the Odyssey is before the close yet near to the end of the Epic time, it is important to note that Ulysses is the last of the Heroes in Hellas who is represented as consorting with a Goddess (Mayor's Odyssey, ι 29).

Page 36. Regarding repeated Invocations of the Muse, it may be right to remark that the Paradise Regained has but one Invocation, whereas the Paradise Lost, like the Faery Queen, has at least three (Books I, III, VII, four including Book IX). This does not imply diversity of authorship within the Paradise Lost but, simply, variety of parts, whereas the Paradise Regained, like the Odyssey, is concentrated to a single event and formed upon one projection.

Page 36, n. 14. The peculiar eminence of the epithet πτολίπορθος is further evinced by the circumstance that, except Achilles and Ulysses, no *living* hero receives it in either poem (Mure, H. of G. L. ii. 81), a fact which attaches to θεῖος, as is remarked on p. 83 n.

Page 40. On the Zeus of Book IV, Dr. Ihne remarks ('Homer' in Dict. of Biog. p. 505), 'In an assembly of the Gods the glory of Achilles is no motive' influencing deliberations as to the fate of Troy.

Page 68. Clinton (F. H. i. p. 45) may be added to the authorities who consider that Hellas in the Odyssey is wider than the primitive Hellas.

Page 69. The view stated as to φοίνικι φαεινόν, that it does no necessarily imply intercourse with Phœnicia, is supported by Kenrick's statement on the same point: 'Homer celebrates the bronze and the embroidery of Sidon but says nothing of the dyes. The name φοῖνιξ given by him to purple colour is no proof that the dye of the *Phœnician* "purpura" is meant, as it is a *Greek* word denoting the colour, and given by the Greeks to Phœnicia, *not derived from it.*' (Kenrick's Phœnicia, p. 245.)

Page 72. It is remarkable that the examples of mortals suffering at the hands of the Gods for haughty or rash words are in the same area where the traces of the φθόνος θεῶν appear. They are—Thamyris in Β 595, Niobe in Ω 607, Ajax Minor in Od. δ 504, and Eurytus in Od. θ 225, viz. two in the Ulyssean cantos and two in the Odyssey, as if equally distributed in what seems a homogeneous area.

Page 84. An Achillean touch is the ascending honour reflected back on the *father* Telamon by the *son* Teucer in Θ 283. So Achilles, in conformity to the traditional type, is represented in Ω (486) as in Od. λ, as moved by the remembrance of his *father*.

Page 94 n. Regarding ἐσάκουσεν in Il. Θ, it is worth noting that the Ionic of Herodotus, which preserves largely the influences of Epic style, frequently uses this verb, and apparently always in the sense claimed for it, viz. ' pay heed to.'

Page 106. On Hector's contempt for Augury, see Mure, H. of G. L. i. 496, and on his ferocity and egotism, Id. i. 282, 352. His *prospective* enjoyment of fame is Ulyssean (Id. i. 353). Kinder feeling toward Hector appears in Η 204–5.

Page 112. Traditional affinities of Ajax Oilei are with Thessaly and the Amphictyonic League (Clinton, F. H. i. p. 67).

Page 114. The fame of Ajax Telamonius was common ground between Dorians and Ionians. (Duncker, Gesch. d. Alt., p. 290–1.)

Page 118. Ajax addresses himself respectfully to Ulysses in Ι 624, but this is after Phœnix no longer belongs to the Embassy, being detained by Achilles.

Page 120. The first distinct authority for cousinship between Ajax and Achilles is a fragment of the Alcmæonis (fr. 5 in Didot Edition of the Cyclus). This is a poem reputed of the 8th or 9th century. Compare Duncker, Gesch. d. Alt., p. 289.

Page 150 n. In comparing Hindoo and Greek belief as to the condition of disembodied spirits, Monier Williams (Ind. Wisdom, p. 431) cites the following Homeric passages (Il. Ψ 72, 104; Od. λ 213, 476; ν 353, ω 14). They are all Ulyssean or in the Odyssey.

Page 156. Compare Mure's citations as to boasting over the Dead (i. p. 248).

Page 156. A parallel to the Achillean style of sarcasm is such as Milton uses in Paradise Lost, but only in the mouths of Satan or Belial, as in Book VI. 609–27.

Page 166-8. Regarding Early Greek Art, the Homeric examples cited by A. S. Murray in his interesting and important paper (Cont. Rev. 1874) are these :—

      (1) The figure of Pallas, Ζ 302.
      (2) The maidens of gold, Σ 407.

(3) Dogs of gold and silver in Odyssey.

(4) Figures of torchbearers in Odyssey.

These he considers explicable without supposing Statuary proper, that is Statuary in the round, and he regards them as only figures in relief or very rude images. He further calls attention to the fact that the personal *names* of artists are now mentioned with defined trade or profession. His instances are Τυχίος the leather-cutter, who made the shield for Ajax, and Ἰκμάλιος, maker of the chair for Penelope. The former is in Il. H 222, the latter in Od. τ 57.

His examples of *foreign* Art are Sidonian crater of bronze, Ψ 743, Sidonian robes (Z 290), and Egyptian spinning-basket (Od. δ 125). Λ 20, if genuine, is the only approach to formative Art from the Achilleid. A Sidonian crater is spoken of as a work of Hephæstus (Od. δ 617).

It will be observed that the bulk of these examples, whether of foreign or Hellenic Art, is furnished by the Ulyssean area or by the Odyssey.

Page 172 n. A case of prohibition because of sacredness is that regarding fish in Syria, which were consecrated to Venus, and hence were forbidden to her worshippers. Authorities in Kenrick's Phœnicia, p. 306.

Page 189. As to the 'Bride-price' among savage races, details will be found in such works as McLennan on 'Primitive Marriage.' Compare Schweinfurth's ludicrous account of the Bongo tribe in his 'Heart of Africa,' i. p. 302 :—

'The very poorest must pay a purchase price to the father of the bride in the form of a number of plates of iron: unless a man could provide the premium, he could get only an old woman for a wife.'

Page 194, n. 50. The conversion of ἔδνα from the 'Bride-price' to the 'Dowry' going with the bride, if it can be scientifically made out to be a fact, is an important and interesting phenomenon. It can certainly be shown that the word ἔδνα, at different periods of Greek literature, bears first the one sense and then the other. This conversion of the 'Bride-price,' in whole or in part, which we illustrated on p. 193. from the case of the ancient Germans, is well indicated in the following remarks of Sir H. S. Maine on this institution :—

'Part of the price which was paid by the bridegroom either at the wedding or the day after it, went to the bride's father as compensation for the Patriarchal or Family authority which was transferred to the husband, but *another part went to the bride herself*, and was very generally enjoyed by her separately and kept apart from her husband's property.' H. S. Maine, Hist. of Institutions, p. 324.

To a similar effect Dr. Dasent writes in his account of old Norse family life :—

'The wife came into the house, in the patriarchal state, either stolen or bought from her nearest male relations ; and though *in later times* when the sale took place it was *softened by settling part of the dower and portion on the wife*, we shall do well to bear in mind, that originally dower was only the price paid by the suitor to the father for his good will ; while portion, on the other hand, was the sum paid by the father to persuade a suitor to take a daughter off his hands.' 'Burnt Njal,' p. xxvi.

As an Epilogue on the whole subject of ἔδνα, the following parallel from the Semitic area is remarkable as showing a similar conversion of ' Bride-price ' into ' Dowry ' given *with* the bride.

The Hebrew *mohar* corresponds precisely to ἔδνα in the first stage. It is the price paid to the father by the suitor (Exodus xxii. 17, with which compare, in ver. 16, '*endow* her for his wife,' literally, '*buy* her for his wife.')

In Genesis xxxiv. 12 we hear of 'gifts,' that is, δῶρα, alongside of the *mohar*, the ' gifts ' being to the bride, the *mohar* to the bride's father.

In 1 Sam xviii. 25 David receives Michal without *mohar*, that is, ἀνέεδνος.

In the more advanced period of Hebrew society we find an equivalent to μείλια appearing. In 1 Kings ix. 16, Pharaoh's daughter receives a city as ' dismissal-gift,' answering to μείλια.

In Arabic, which represents the later Semitic stage, the word corresponding to *mohar* has altered its signification. Gesenius (Lex., in *mohar*) after stating it as in Hebrew the ' bride-price,' then adds : ' Different from this is the use of the Arabic word corresponding, i.e. a spousal gift promised to the future wife, and the Latin *dos*, i.e. the gift given by the parents to their daughter who is about to be married.'

Page 211, n. 13. By an inadvertence, the use of the expression δεῖπνον for horses (in B 383) is attributed to Nestor. It occurs, however, in a speech not of Nestor but of Agamemnon.

Page 226. Regarding Ulysses under the figure of a noble mastiff, it is a singular coincidence that Sophocles in the Ajax (8, 19) happens to represent Ulysses as receiving from Athene and as *accepting* the comparison to a Spartan hound.

Page 226 n. On the occurrences of θυμολέων, it is right to remark, as Col. Mure has pointed out, that both instances regarding Ulysses are in the mouth of Penelope, and are therefore not *objective* by the poet himself, but *subjective* in the mind of his spouse. Compare the interesting remarks on this epithet by Mure, ii. p. 82–3.

Page 235. This point as to the prominence of the Horse in the one poem and of the Dog in the other has not escaped the keen eye of Mr. Mahaffy, who in a recent work has virtually anticipated me in this branch of my inquiry. He states the matter thus:—

‘Throughout the whole Iliad [? Achilleid] the poets seem to be full of sympathy with the energy and fire of the war-horses. In the Odyssey the dog Argus takes the place of the horses of Achilles. . . . The wonderful picture of the old broken down hound recognising his master after twenty years and dying of joy on the dunghill where he lay helpless with age and neglect—this affecting trait could never have been drawn except by men who themselves knew and loved dogs and appreciated their intelligence.’ Mahaffy, ‘Rambles and Studies,’ pp. 56–7.

Page 239–40. It has been suggested by Clinton (F. II. i. 363) that one cause of the multiplicity of claimants may have been that ‘Homer was an inhabitant, perhaps a citizen, of several cities.’ In the historical time it is possible to produce instances of persons who belonged to several cities, and one occurs in Boeckh’s Inscr. Gr. (i. 845) of a citizen of seven cities. It might be doubtful, however, whether such variety was possible in the pre-historic age.

Page 240. To these Lists may be added that found in the Ἀγών or ‘Contest of Hesiod and Homer.’ It is remarkable as *specifying* only the three Ionian claimants, Smyrna, Chios, Colophon. This curious composition, in which occurs the name of the Emperor Hadrian, is from the later Roman period and is of no authority, except as a storehouse of traditions. It may be found in Goettling’s Edition of Hesiod.

Page 255. The predominance of the Mountains in the scenery of Thessaly is well illustrated by Apollonius Rhodius’ description of it (iii. 1084) in the line, ἔστι τις αἰπεινοῖσι περίδρομος οὔρεσι γαῖα.

Page 279. Besides the *Sicilian* sea, Theocritus speaks also of the *Sardinian* sea (Idyl. 16. 86).

Page 284. The geographical relation in which Euboea stands to Ionia in the Homeric poems might be further illustrated, (1) from the community of race occupying both in the historic time; (2) from their intimate commercial relations, the Euboic monetary system having proceeded from Asia Minor and Ionia (Dict. of Ant. p. 811).

Page 284–5. The connection of the Amazons with the East is seen in the representations of them in Art. They wear the Phrygian cap, which is always, in Greek art, a sign of the Orient.

Page 305. Ulysses appears genealogically connected with an Athenian stem in Clinton's Fasti (i. p. 40).

Page 322. The close association of the Odyssey with the name of Homer is singularly indicated in Theocritus. In his 16th Idyl (50 and 57), the Iliad is mentioned with other war poems, products of the ἀοιδοί (plural), but when he comes to the Odyssey, he names simply Ἰάων ἀνήρ (the man of Ionia).

Page 332. Regarding the two Heroes, it may be further remarked that Achilles is drawn with lineaments, and credited with an origin, removing him to a distance from the category of humanity. There is much of the θηρίον as well as θεός in his composition. Ulysses, on the other hand, is pre-eminently a man, the ἀνήρ with the common attributes of man and his common affections, yet exerting a spell beyond that of even the goddess-born. His wife and son and slave are devoted to him as under a species of worship, and the animal creation, as represented by the faithful Dog, joins in the homage.

INDEX I.

WORDS AND EPITHETS.

[N.B. The references are to the pages, either to remarks in the Notes or in the Text, or both.]

'Αγαθός, 138-9.
ἀγάκλυτος, 162.
ἄγαλμα, 144.
'Αγαμεμνόνεος, 104.
ἀγάννιφος, 257.
ἀγανοῖς βελέεσσι, 140.
ἀγανοφροσύνη, 108.
ἀγάσαντο, 72.
ἀγαυός, 217.
ἄγγελος, 56.
ἀγέρωχος, 216.
ἀγήνωρ, 326.
ἄγκεα ποιήεντα, 251.
ἄγκιστρα, 176.
ἀγκυλομήτης, 136.
ἀγκυλότοξος, 123.
ἀγλαός, 167.
ἀγορά, 250.
ἀγριόφωνοι, 166.
ἀγρύς, 250.
ἄδυτον, 163, 188.
ἀεικίζω, 155.
ἀελλόπος, 58, 60.
ἀερσίποδες, 343.
'Αθήνη, epithets and appellations of, 141, 145.
ἄθυρμα, ἀθύρω, 170.
Αἰακίδης, 84, 118, 120..
Αἰακός, 120.
Αἴαντε, 111.
Αἴας, epithets and appellations of, 115-120.
αἰγίοχος, 136.
αἰγὶς Διός, 136.
Αἰγύπτιος, 63.
ἀίδηλος, 117.
'Αΐδης, 146.
αἰθαλόεν, 162.
αἰθέρι ναίων, 135, 285.
αἴθουσα, 161-2.
αἷμα and ἰχώρ, 140-1.
αἰολόπωλοι, 217, 319.

αἰπὰ ῥέεθρα, 250.
αἶσα Διός, 138-9.
αἴσιμος, 139.
αἰσυμνητήρ, 311.
αἰχμή, 201.
ἀκάματον πῦρ, 203.
ἀκηδέες, 134.
ἀκομιστίη, 171.
ἄκοσμον, 67.
ἀκοστή, ἀκοστήσας, 248.
ἀκριτόφυλλος, 251.
ἀκτή, Δημήτερος ἀκτή, 142, 177.
ἀλείτης, 326.
ἀλέω, ἀλετρίς, 177.
'Αλθαία Μελεαγρίς, 84.
ἀλιπόρφυρος, 167.
ἅλς (salt), 171.
ἀλύσσω, 223.
ἀλφεσίβοιαι, 192.
ἀλωή, 178.
"Αμαξα (astronomical), 175.
ἀμβροσίη, 147.
ἄμπελος, 178.
ἀμφίπολος, 188.
ἀνάθημα, 144.
ἀνακυμβαλιάζω, 181.
ἄναξ, 123, 146.
ἀνδροφόνος, 107.
ἀνέμοιο θύελλα, δεινὸς ἀήτης, 253.
ἄνεμος πολύπλαγκτος, 60.
ἀνέστιος, 79.
ἀνήρ (of Ulysses), 35, 86.
ἀνθεμόεις, 167.
ἄνθρωποι and ἄνδρες, 35.
ἀντίθεος, 116.
ἄντιτος, 330.
ἆσαι γύοιο, 74.
ἀτάλαντος (μῆτιν), 83.
ἀξῖναι, 182.
ἄξυλος ὕλη, 250.
ἀοιδοί, 26.
ἅπαξ, καθάπαξ, 200.

Ἀπατούρια, 312.
ἀπριάτην, 184.
Ἀργείη, 109, 292.
ἀργεστής, 265.
ἀργικέραυνος, 137.
ἀργιόδους, 233.
ἀργυρότοξος, 147.
ἀρειή, 155.
ἀριθμός, 199.
ἁρματοπηγός, 183.
ἀσάμινθος, 165.
ἄσπετος ὕλη, 251.
ἀστερόεις, 263.
ἀστεροπητής, 137.
ἀστράγαλοι, 170.
ἀτειρέα φωνήν, 158.
αὐγαὶ Διός, 136.
αὐίαχος, 158.
αὐλή, 160-1 ; αὐλὴ Διός, 135.
αὐτύς, 150.
αὐτοχόωνος, 29.
αὔω, 158.
ἄφθιτα μήδεα εἰδώς, 138.
ἄχθος, 184.

βαθέ' ἄγκεα, 251.
βαρβαρόφωνοι, 66, 311.
βέλεμνον Διόθεν, 136.
βητάρμων, 170.
βίος ἀληλεμένος, 177.
βλεμεαίνω, 105.
βλοσυρύς, 117.
βοὴ ἄσβεστος, βριήπυος, 158.
βοὴν ἀγαθός, 115.
βούβρωστις, 287.
βουλὴ Διός, 46-7, 137.
βουλυτός, 250.
βοῶπις, 145.
βροντή, βροντάω, 253.
βροτολοιγός, 152.
βύβλος, 168.

Γάργαρος, 258.
γελᾶν ἐπί τινι, γελοίιος, γελοιάω, 76.
γηγενεῖς, γίγαντες, 132.
γλαυκῶπις, 302.
γόος, 74.
γράφω, 182-3, 338, 341.
γυνὴ χερνῆτις, 179.
γῦπες, 222.

δαλύς, 165.
δάος, δαΐδες, 165.
Δαρδανίδης, 84.
δεκάς, 199.
δέμας πυρός, 203.
δέμνια, 164.
δέπας, 165.
δεταί, 165.
δημιοεργύς, 311.
δῖα γυναικῶν, 109.
διάκτορος, 57, 60.
Διιπετής, 136.

Διίφιλος, 44.
δινωτός, 164.
Διοτρεφής, 136, 146.
δίφρος, 164.
Διώνη, 274-5.
δολιχεγχέες, 123.
δολομῆτα, 138.
δόμος ὑψηλός, ὑψερεφής, ὑψόροφος, 161.
δράκοντες, 163.
δρῦς, δρυμός, δρύοχος, δρυτόμος, 178-9.
Δυσελένη, 110.
δυσθαλπής, 253.
Δύσπαρις, 110.
δυσπέμφελος, 253.
δῶμα Διός, 135.

ἔγκατα, ἔντερα, 153.
ἔδνα, 189-195, 355.
ἐδωδή, 209.
ἐεδνωτής, 192.
ἔθειραι, 210.
εἶδαρ, 209.
εἰνάετες, 175.
εἰνοσίφυλλος, 251.
εἴ ποτ' ἔην γε, 74.
ἐκγεγαυῖα Διός, 109.
ἔκηλος, 31, 134.
ἐκπαγλότατ', 101.
Ἑκτόρεος, 104.
Ἕκτωρ, epithets of, 107.
ἔλαφος, 96.
ἐλεήσῃ in αἴ κ' ἐλεήσῃ, 74.
Ἑλένη, epithets and appellations of, 109, 145.
ἐλέφας, 168-9.
ἑλκεσίπεπλος, 304.
ἑλκεχίτωνες, 304.
Ἑλλάς, 68.
ἔμπορος, 185.
ἐναίσιμος, 139.
ἐνιαυτοὶ Διός, 136.
ἐνιαυτύς, ἔτος, 175.
ἔναυλος, 250.
ἐνηής, 266.
ἑορτή, 144.
ἔπαλξις, ἐπαλέξω, 174.
ἐπεύχομαι, 156-7.
Ἔρεβος, 55.
ἐριβρεμέτης, 137.
ἐρίγδουπος, 137, 162, 207.
ἐρισθενής, 137.
ἔρκεα, 161.
ἕρκος Ἀχαιῶν, 116.
ἔρος γόου, 74.
ἐρυσάρματες, 343.
ἐσάκουσε, 94, 354.
ἐσσομένοισι, 85.
Ἑστία or Ἱστίη, 79-80.
ἔτος, ἐνιαυτύς, 175.
εὐηγενής, 217.
εὐνή, 171.
εὐνομίη, 250.
εὐπατέρεια, 109.

εὔπεπλος, 165.
εὐπλόκαμος, 141.
εὔπωλος, 215.
εὐρύοπα and εὐρυόπα, 136.
εὔσκαρθμοι, 343.
εὔτριχες, 343.
εὐχωλή, 156.
ἐφέστιος, 79.
ἐφετμαὶ Διός, 138.

ζειά, 127.
ζείδωρος ἄρουρα, 128.
Ζεὺς Ἱκετήσιος, Ξείνιος, Πατήρ, 135.
— nature-forces under, 136.
— physical epithets of, 137.
— moral influences of, 138.
— ethical epithets of, 138.
ζηλήμονες, 72.

ἤλεκτρος, 168.
ἡμίονος, 212.
Ἥρη, epithets of, 145.
ἦτορ ἐνὶ φρεσί, 151.
ἠχὴ θεσπεσίη, 158.
ἠχήεντα, 162.
ἠΰκομος, 108, 147.

θάλαμος, 54, 161.
θαλίη, 171.
Θάμυρις, θαμυρίζω, 26.
θεῖος, 83.
θέμιστες Διός, 138.
θεοπρόπος, θεοπροπέω, θεοπροπίη, θεοπρό-
    πιον, 187.
θεράπων, 188.
Θεσσαλὸν σόφισμα, 76.
θεσπιδαὲς πῦρ, 203.
θηρητήρ, 225.
θοινηθῆναι, 173.
θοῦρις, 202.
θρασύς, 105, 202.
θριγκός, 162.
θρόνα, 180.
θρόνος, θρῆνυς, 163.
θυμός, 88, 198, 224, 226.
θυμολέων, 226, 356.
θυμοφθόρος, 340.
θυοσκόος, 187.
θύρη, 53.
θῶες, 96.
θωή, 184.

ἰαχή, ἰάχων, 159.
Ἰδαίων ὀρέων, 258.
Ἴδηθεν μεδέων, 263, 285.
ἱερὸν ἦμαρ, κνέφας, 204.
ἱερός, 172.
ἱκετήσιος, of Zeus, 135, 138.
ἵλαος, 146.
ἵμερος γόοιο, κλαυθμοῦ, 74.
ἰοδνεφής, 167.
ἵππη, ἱππημολγοί, 209.
ἱππόβοτος, 245.

ἱππόδαμος, 211-216, 342-3.
ἵπποισιν καὶ ὄχεσφιν, 215.
ἱπποκέλευθος, 246.
ἱπποκορυσταί, 123, 217.
ἵππος and derivatives, 209, 215, 341-3.
ἱππότης, 211, 214, 343.
Ἶρις, 59, 60.
Ἶσος Ἄρηϊ, 117, 152, 265.
Ἱστίη, 79-80.
ἰχώρ and αἷμα, 141.

καγχαλάω, 76.
κακός, 138-9.
καλὰ πέδιλα, 165.
καλλίκομος, 109.
καλλιπάρῃος, 109.
καλλιπλόκαμος, 109.
καμόντες, κεκμηῶτες, 143.
κάνεον, 165.
κάπη, 209.
καρχαρόδους, 233.
κασσίτερος, 69, 168.
κατέδουσι, 31.
κεάζω, 182.
κεδνότατος, κήδιστος, 79, 119.
κέδρινος, 162.
κεῖνος, ἐκεῖνος, of Ulysses, 35.
κεκληγώς, 158.
κελαδεινή, 159.
κελαινεφής, 137, 148.
κέλης, 242.
κεμάς, 96.
κέντορες ἵππων, 319.
κέραμος and κεραμεύς, 183, 276, 311.
κεραοξόος, 183.
κέρας, 176.
κεραυνὸς Διός, 136, 253.
κεστός, πολύκεστος, ἱμάς, 180.
κῆλα, 182.
κηλέω, κηλείῳ, 203.
κῆρες, 200.
κηώεις, 162.
κίθαρις, κιθαρίζω, κιθαριστύς, 180.
κίων, 162.
κλαίω, κλαυθμύς, 74.
κλέα ἀνδρῶν, 26.
κλῆρος, 187.
κλιντήρ, 164.
κλισίη, 164.
κλισμός, 164, 166.
κομέω, 234.
κομιδή, 234.
κῦρος γόοιο, 74.
κορύναι, 181.
κορυνητής, 127.
κόσμος, 67.
κούρη Διός, 109, 145.
κουρίδιος, 197.
κραδίη, 150.
κραναή, 305.
κρημνύς, 250.
κρητήρ, 165.
κροκόπεπλος, 164.

Κρονίδης, 130.
κροταλίζω, 181.
κτήματα, κτῆσις, 184.
κυάνεαι ὀφρύες, 137.
κυανόπρωρος, 167.
κύανος, 168.
κυανοχαίτης, 207, 343.
κυδιάνειρα, 308.
κυδίστη, 141.
Κυθέρεια, 141-2.
κύμινδις, 270.
κυνηγετής, 225.
κυνηγός, 214.
κύον, κυνάμυια, κυνῶπα, κύντερος, 222.
κύπελλα, 165.
Κύπρις, 141-2.
κῶας, 164.
κωφὴ γαῖα, 150.

λαῖλαψ, 253.
λαμπτήρ, 165.
λέβης, 165.
λελασμένος ἱπποσυνάων, 230.
λέσχη, ἀδολεσχία, 311.
λευκώλενος, of Helen, 109, of Here, 145.
λεχέεσσι τρητοῖς, 164.
λέχει ἀσκητῷ, 164.
λέχεσσι δινωτοῖσι, 164.
λέχος πυκινόν, 164.
Λητοΐδης, 84.
λῖς, 269.
Λιταί, 135.
λίνοιο λεπτὸν ἄωτον, οἰὸς ἄωτον, 164.
λόγοι, ἀλογέω, 197.
λυσσώδης, 105.

μάκαρες, 134.
μάντις, μαντεύομαι, 187.
μάστιξ Διός, 136.
μέγα κῦδος Ἀχαιῶν, 95.
μέγα φρονέων, 105.
μείλια, 189-90, 194, 196.
μέλαιναι νῆες, 167.
μερμηρίζων, 150.
μέροπες, 66.
μῆνις, 119.
μῆνις Διός, 138.
μήστωρ ὕπατος (of Zeus), 138.
μήστωρες φόβοιο, 231.
μητίετα (of Zeus), 138.
μῆτις, 50, 308.
μῆτις Διός, 138.
μιλτοπάρηος, 167.
μισθός, 185.
μνηστὴ ἄλοχος, 155, 197.
Μολίονε, 84, 176.
μορφή, 67.
μῦθοι, 308, μυθολογέω, 197.
μύλαι, μύλαξ, μυλήφατος, μυλοειδής, 176-7.
μύριοι, 200.

νάπη, 250.

νέκυς, 150.
νέμος, 250.
νεφέλαι Διός, 136.
νέφος πολέμοιο, 203.
νηλεὲς ἦμαρ, 154.
νῆμα, εὔννητος, 179, 180.
νιφόεις, 257, 263.
νόμος (law), 250.
νύος Διός, 137.
νοῦσος Διός, 138.
νυκτὸς ἀμολγῷ, 204.
νὺξ ἄμβροτος, ἀμβροσίη, ὀλοή, 204.

ξεῖνος, ξεινοδόκος, 173.
Ξένιος (of Zeus), 138.
ξύλον, 178.
ξύλοχος βαθεῖα, 182.
ξυστόν, 182.

ὀβριμοπάτρη, 141.
ὀδαῖα, 184.
ὀθόναι, 165.
Ὀθρυονεύς, 244.
οἶνος, 178.
οἰωνιστής, οἰωνοπόλος, 186.
ὅλμοι, 176-7.
ὀλοόφρων, 201.
ὀλοφυδνός, 74.
Ὄλυμπος, Οὔλυμπος, Οὐλυμπόνδε, 259-264.
ὄμβρος Διός, 136.
ὀμοῖϊος, 309.
ὁπλή, 209.
ὀπυίω, 54.
ὅρκια Διός, 138.
ὄρμενος, 202.
ὄρος, οὖρος, 256.
ὄρπηξ, 250.
ὀρχέομαι, 170.
ὀτρύνω, 229.
Οὐρανίωνες, 130.
οὐρανός, 260-4.
οὐρίαχος, 182.
οὖροι, 60.
οὖρος Διός, 136.
ὀχθέω, 132.
ὀψίγονοι, 85.
ὄψον, 171.

παίζω, 76, 170.
Παίονες, 123.
παλίντιτος, 330.
παμφανόων, 166.
Παναχαιοί, 67.
Πανέλληνες, 67, 68.
Πάνθοος, Πανθοΐδης, 122.
πανόμφαιος, 266.
παρδαλέη, 164.
παρήορος, παρηορία, 229.
πάροιθεν, 53.
πατήρ, of Zeus, 135.
πέδη, 209.
πεζοί, 212, 214, 215.

πείρινς, 165.
πέλεκυς, 182.
πέπλος, 164.
πεπνυμένος, 310.
Πέργαμα, 258.
πέρην, 281-2.
περνάμενα, 184.
περονή, 224.
πήληξ, 180.
πῖλος, 165.
πληγὴ Διός, 136.
πλήμνη, 231.
πλήξιππος, 319.
ποδάνιπτρα, 165.
ποδήνεμος, 58, 60.
ποικίλλω, ποικίλος, etc., 168.
πύλις, 250.
πολύαινος, 95.
πολύβουλος, 141.
πολυδαίδαλος, 166.
πολύδωρος, 195.
πολυκτήμων, 184.
πολυμήχανος, 96.
πολυπάμων, 184.
πολυπενθής, 74.
πολύπτυχος, πτύχες, 258, 260.
πολύτλας, 96.
πολυτλήμων, 88.
πολύτροπος, 50.
πολύφρων, 50.
πολύχαλκος, 184.
πολύχρυσος, 184.
πομπῆες, 60.
πορφύρεος, 167.
πράπιδες, 152.
πρέσβα, 145.
πρῆξις γόοιο, 74.
πρόδρομος, 162.
προπάροιθεν, 53.
πρόχοος, 165.
πρών, 250.
πτολίπορθος, 83, 353.
πτυκτός, 340.
πτύχες (of a mountain), 258.
πύλαι, ἐν πύλῳ, 54.
πυρὸς μένος, 203.

ῥάπτειν, κακορραφίη, 179.
ῥέπω, ἐπιρρέπω, 200.
ῥεῖα ζώοντες, 134.
ῥήγεα, 164.
ῥιγεδανή, 108.
ῥῖγος, 95.
ῥωχμός, 251.

σάλπιγξ, 181, 242.
σαυρωτήρ, 182.
σέβας, 103.
σήματα λυγρά, 66, 73, 337-341.
σθένεϊ βλεμεαίνων, 105.
σίαλος, 128.
σιγαλόεις, 165.

σύλος, 29.
σοφός, σοφίη, 197.
σπεῖρον, 165.
στεροπή, ἀστεροπή, 136, 253.
στεροπηγερέτης, 137.
σύριγξ, 180-1.
Συρίη νῆσος, 293.
συφορβός, 128.
σφενδόναι, 182.

τάλαντα, 200.
τάλαρος, 165.
Ταλθύβιος, 181.
τανύπεπλος, 109, 165.
τάπης, 164.
ταχύπωλοι, 217.
Τέγεος, 162.
τείνω, τανύω, 201.
τέκτων, τεκταίνομαι, 174.
τέρπεσθαι γόοιο, 74.
τερπικέραυνος, 137.
τέττιξ, 311.
τεύχεα συλῆσαι, ἐξεναρίζειν, 155.
τιθαιβώσσω, 128.
τίνυσθον, 143.
τλήμων, etc., 88.
τραπεζῆες, 221.
τρομέω, 151.
τροπαὶ ἠελίοιο, 294-5.

ὕλη, ὑλοτόμος, 178, 251.
ὕλη βαθεῖα, 251.
ὑπέρθυμος, 217.
ὑπερηνορέων, 326.
ὑπερμενής, 137.
ὑπερῷον, 162.
ὑπερῷον, 162.
ὑπηρετὴς θεῶν, 57.
ὕπνος and epithets, 310-11.
ὑποδήματα, 165.
ὑφαίνω, etc., 180.
ὑψηχέες, 343.
ὑψερεφής, ὑψόροφος, 161.
ὑψηλός, 161.
ὑψιβρεμέτης, 137.
ὑψίζυγος, 136.

φᾶρος, 164.
φθόνος θεῶν, 72.
φιλέω, 173.
φιλοπαίγμων, 76, 170.
φιλότητα παρασχεῖν, 173.
φλογὶ εἴκελος, 202.
φοινικόεις, 167.
φοίνιξ, 168, 178, 353.
φοινικοπάρῃος, 167.
φόρμιγξ, φορμίζω, 180.
φόρτος, 184.
φρένες, 151.
φρήν, φρένες Διός, 137.
φρήτρη, ἀφρήτωρ, 312.
φρονέω with μέγα, etc., 105.
φώς (wight), 96.

χαίτη, 210.
χάλαζα, 253.
χαλκεύς, 183.
χαλκοβατὲς δῶ, 146.
χαλκύποδε, 343.
χεῖρες ἄαπτοι, 148.
χλαῖνα, 164, 167, 179.
χράω, χραύω, χαράσσω, 338.
χρείων, χρησόμενος, 188.
χρήματα, 184.
χρυσόθρονος, 145.

χρυσόπτερος, 58-9.
Χωρίζοντες, 51.
χῶρος προαλής, 250.

ψυχή, 149.
ψυχοπομπός, 59.

ὠκυπέτα, 343.
ὠμησταί, 221.
ὦνος, 184.

MATTERS AND AUTHORS.

Achilleid, 47.
— horizon of, 69, 70.
— absence of pathos in, 74.
— sarcasm of, 76. 354.
— Thessalian feeling of, 99.
— ethical tone of, 105.
— no ethical purpose in, 323.
Achilles, how far typical hero of Greece, 50.
— in what sense πτολίπορθος, 36, 83.
— epithets of, 44, 83, 226.
— character of, 101, 307, 358.
Ægis, 38, 313.
Æneas, 125, 159.
Æolis, connection of with early epic poetry, 23.
— claim of, 299, 322.
Æolo-Dorismus, 84, 100, 121, 255 307-8.
Agamemnon, character of, 103.
— pathos of his fate, 104.
Ajax, the Telamonian, epithets of, 115, 116.
— relationship to Achilles, 118, 354.
Ajax, the Less, 75, 111-12.
Ajaxes, relation of to Ulysses, 92, 112-18.
Amazons, 127, 284. 357.
Andromache, 78, 192. 195.
Aphrodite and Charis as wives of Hephæstus. 54.
Aphrodite and Ares, 54, 75.
Aphrodite, epithets of, 141-2.
Apollo as minister of Death, 140.
— as Ἀργυρότοξος, 147-8.
Apostrophe, in address, 36.
Arboriculture, 178.
Archaica, 126 ff.
Archilochus, 239.
Architecture, 160-2.
Ares, generally discredited, 117, 152.
Argos. see Peloponnesus.
Argus, death of, 72, 347.
Aristarchus, 5, 290 and passim.
Aristotle, 23 and passim.
Armature, 181.
Art, 174-83, 354.
Artemis as minister of Death, 140.
— epithet of, 159.
Asia, beginning of the name, 67, 280.
Astronomy, 177.
Athene, epithets of, 141.

— connection of with Athens, 306.
Athenians, position of, 85, 87, 302-5.
Athens, claim of, 293, 300-2.
Atlas, 131.
Augury, 186.

Barbour's ' Bruce,' 284.
Bentley, 7, 299.
Beowulf, 322.
Bergk, 21 and passim.
Birth-place of Homer, cities contending for honour of, 239-40. 357.
— probably in Asiatic Ionia, 260.
Blackie, Prof., 16 and passim.
Blair, 43.
Boasting, 105, 155-7.
Bœotia, importance of, 242, 245, 293.
Briareus, 131.
Browning, Robert, 58, 208.
Burnouf, 15.
Buttmann, 95, 282-4.

Cannibalism, metaphorical, 154.
Cassandra, 124.
Centaurs, 246-7.
Cerberus, 233.
Charis and Aphrodite as wives of Hephæstus, 54.
Chios, claims of, 240. 288.
Chorizontes or Separatists, 6, 15, 17, 21 sq. and passim.
Chronometer, Primitive, 249-50.
Chthonian Deities, 143.
Climate, indications of, 252-4.
Cobet, 191, 193, 208.
Coleridge, Henry Nelson, 17, 132, 237.
Coleridge, S. T.. 15.
Colophon, claims of. 240.
Colour, decoration by, 166-8, 285-6.
Commerce. Initia of, 184.
Constant, Benjamin, 15.
Crates, 5.
Curtius, George, 13, 28, 189, 282.
Curtius, Ernst, 69 and passim.
Cyclic Poets. 12, 316-18.
Cyclographic Poets, 317.
Cynics, 294.

Dædalus, 181.
Deliberation, early mode of expressing, 200.
Demeter, cultus of, 142-3

Democracy, attitude toward, 337.
Description, minute decorative, 91.
Deucalion, 245.
Diocles, 215.
Diomed, prominence of, 39.
— compared with Achilles, 40, 232.
— association with Ulysses, 87, 91, 96, 211.
— horses of, 270-4.
Dione, question as to, 273-6.
Dionysus, cultus of, 142.
Divination, 186, 202.
Doederlein, 68 and *passim*.
Dog, phenomena as to, 219-28, 232-5, 319, 344, 356-7.
Doloneia, 28, 41.
Domestica, 79, 163-6.
Domestication of animals, 128.
Donaldson, J. W., 18, 84.
Dorian irruption, relation to the, 64.
Dowry, customs regarding, 189-197.
Dreams, 186.
Düntzer, 12 and *passim*.

Egypt, acquaintance with, 63-5.
Electros, 168.
'Envy of the gods,' traces of, 72, 354.
Epics of the world, 4.
Epithets, traditional and already old, 27.
— in Achilleid, 58.
Eratosthenes, 23.
Ethical purpose, how far discernible, 322-30.
Euboea in Homeric geography, 281-4.
Eumelus, 112, 211.
Euripides, 18, 109, 110.
Eurybates, 124.
Eurymedon, 124.
Eurypylus, 99.
Eustathius, 8 and *passim*.

Fairbairn, A. M., 143.
Füsi, 60 and *passim*.
Fauna of the Poems, 267-9.
'Fears of the brave,' 94, 95.
Fetichism, possible traces of, 201.
Fichte, 9.
Fire, imagery from, 202-3.
Fish, as food, etc., 171-2, 176, 355.
Fleay, Mr., 148.
Fox, absence of the, 269.
Friedländer, 10 and *passim*.

Ganymede, 125.
Gibbon, 151.
Gladstone, 16 and *passim*.
Gods 'who live at ease,' 134, 261.
Goethe, 12, 43, 243, 323.
Goose, 128-9.
Greece, with two epics, 4; two heroes, 34.
— dualism in its history, 100, 306.
— instinct for order and decorum, 67.
Grote, 17 and *passim*.

Harpyes, 60.
Hayman, 87 and *passim*.
Hebe, 125.
Hebrew Literature, illustrations from, 129, 150, 169, 176.
Hector, character of, 104-8, 354.
— epithets of, 44, 105, 107.
'Hectoring fellow,' 105.
Helen, epithets of, 108-10.
Heliconian God, 270.
Hellanicus, 6.
Hellas, extension of the name, 68.
Heracles, 27 and *passim*.
Heralds, 188.
Herder, 8.
Heré, epithets of, 109, 145.
Hermann, Godfrey, 11, 157.
Hermes and Iris as messengers, questions as to, 55-60.
Hermes as a Wind-God, 60.
Hesiod, touches in, akin to Achilleid, 131, 140, 159, 177, 207, 234, 242, 244, 263, 269, 307.
Hestia, 79.
Heyne, 8 and *passim*.
Hindoos, analogies from literature of, 4, 127, 147, 150, 206, 233, 247-8, 354.
Historical sense dawning in Homer, 242-3.
Homer, the name contains ὁμοῦ, 20.
— traces of 'many Homers' in ancient authorities, 8.
— Bards before, 26, 321.
Homerids, 23.
Horace, 34, 101, 238.
Horse, phenomena as to, 205-18, 229-30, 245-8, 319, 342-6, 350, 342-6.
Hospitality, 172-3.
Humboldt, 9.
Hume, David, 37.
Hunting, vocabulary of, 165, 174-5, 225.
Hypercriticism dissolves any unity, 11, 33.

Iapetos, 131.
Ida, 258, 263, 285.
Ihne, 263.
Iliad, question as to its unity, 33.
— double structure of, 37-43, 48.
Interpolations, possibility of, 29, 335.
Invocation of Muse, 36, 353.
Ionia, connection of, with early Epic poetry, 23.
— claims of, 240, 278-290.
Ionians, character of, 304, 306-7.
Ionismus, 85, 86, 87, 121, 172, 250, 255, 270, 295-8, 307, 308, 310-15.
Iris and Hermes as messengers, question as to, 55-60.
Iris, epithets of, 58.
Ivory, 169.

Josephus, 8, 47.
Jortin, 101.

Kalewala, 5.
Keary, 60.
Kebriones, 123.
Kinyras, 69.
Knight, R. P., 17, 91.
Köchly, Arminius, 13.
Kronos, 130-1, 246, 275.

Lachmann, Karl, 11, 13, 327.
Laodike, 124.
La Roche, 23 and *passim*.
Lassen, 4.
Lehrs, 8 and *passim*.
Leonteus, 152, 265.
Lepsius, 168.
Leto, 147.
Lion, familiarity with, 267-9.
Locality, from internal evidence, 237-9.
Locrians, in armature, 123.
Locusts, simile as to, 267-8.
Longfellow, 77.
Longinus, 28.
Lots, 187.
Love, element of, in ancient literature, 77.
Lucian, 240.
Lycurgus, 23.

Mæonides, argument from name, 290.
Magnus. Dr., 166.
Mahâbhârata, 4, 227.
Marriage, phenomena regarding, 189-97, 355-6.
Mekisteus, 124.
Melancholy, sentiment of, 73.
Memnon, 119.
Menelaus, 36 and *passim*.
Menestheus, 86, 101, 111, 305.
Meriones, 113.
Merry, 31 and *passim*.
Messengers of the Gods, 55-60.
Metronymics, 84.
Mill, J. S., 42.
Milton, 144, 233, 333.
Mimnermus, 24.
Movers, 65.
Mountain and sea as rival influences, 255.
Mule, 212.
Müller, O., 12 and *passim*.
Müller, W., 11.
Mure. Colonel, 16 and *passim*.
Music, instruments of, 180-1.

Nägelsbach, 15 and *passim*.
Nausicaa, 79, 122, 145, 292.
Nestor, 47 and *passim*.
— equestrian associations of, 211, 217.
Newton, Ch. T., 242.
Niebuhr, 8 and *passim*.
Night, imagery from, 203-4.
Nitzsch, Gregor, 10 and *passim*.

Nonnus, 38, 238.
Number, inability to handle arithmetical, 32, 199.
Nutzhorn, 13, 41, 94.

Oceanus, as father of Gods, 131.
Odyssey, unity of, 29, 30.
— apparent discrepancies in, 31.
— perfection of, 34, 332-4.
— importance of, critically, 49.
— characteristic of the Greek race, 50.
— supposed inferiority of, considered, 49, 331-4.
— local mint-marks of, 291-8.
— Ethical elements of, 328-31.
Œdipus Rex and Col., connection of, 42.
Olympus, 25, 255-64.
Omens, attitude toward, 106.
Oracles, 187.
Order of honour in poetic enumeration, 89.
Ossian, Ossianic controversy, etc., 9, 73, 171, 351.

Pædonymics, 84.
Pæonians, 123.
Paley, Frederick A., 18 and *passim*.
Pan, silence as to, 245.
Panthoidæ, family of, 122.
Paris, 107-8, 110, 125, 153, 208, 326.
Patronymics, 84.
Pausanias, 50 and *passim*.
Pelasgic traces, 123, 135, 148, 163, 244.
Pelopidæ and Perseidæ, 56, 64, 243.
Peloponnesus, connection of with Epic song, 24, 245.
— heroes of, where prominent, 98-9.
— claim of, 292-3.
Penelope, 28 and *passim*.
Pergamus in Troy, 258.
Periclymenus, 216.
Persephone. cultus of, 143.
‘Personalia,’ traditions of, 318.
Personification of natural objects, 201.
Phæacia, 284, 297.
Phœnicia, acquaintance with, 64-6, 69.
Pictet, 128-9.
Pieria, 25, 70. 241.
Pindar, 23 and *passim*.
Pisistratus, 8 and *passim*.
Plato, 170, 226, 237. 307.
Polydamas, 122-3, 204.
Polygnotus, 234, 331.
Porson, 29.
Portents, 134.
Poseidon, 107 and *passim*.
Preller, 22 and *passim*.
Prudentius, 149.
Psychology, Primitive, 149-51, 198.

Râmâyana, 4.
Retribution, idea of, prominent in the Odyssey. 330.

Rhapsodes, decline in fame of, 337.
Rhode, 33.
Richter, Jean Paul, 43.
'Rumour,' 55.
Ruskin, 72, 225.
Rustum, 102, 208.

Salt in food, 171.
Sanskrit, see Hindoo.
Sappho, 25.
Schiller, 12.
Schlegels, 9.
Schliemann, 168, 182, 242.
Schubarth, 44, 108.
Scott, Sir Walter, 30, 78, 91, 347.
Sea and mountain influences, 255.
Sea, naming *sections* of, 279, 307.
Sea-distances, 307.
Seneca, 6.
Shakspere, 18, 35, 78, 238.
Sidney, Sir Philip, 102.
Silence, arguments from, 64.
— single instances of, 122.
Silvan scenery, 249-52.
Simile, an approximation on the poet's
　part to his audience, 279.
Similes, 96, 115, 208, 212, 220-1, 225,
　251.
Simonides, 23.
'Sleep,' epithets of, 310-11.
Smyrna, weight of evidence in favour of,
　240. 288.
Sophocles, 18, 30.
Speech, diversity of, beginning to be
　observed, 66.
Stesichorus, 26, 77, 109.
Strabo, 63 and *passim*.
Suitors, epithets and character of, 117,
　324, 329.
'Survivals,' 127.

Tartarus, 131.
Telemachia, as a separate poem, not
　possible, 30.
Telemachus, 30 and *passim*.
— in relation to Ulysses, 30, 84.
Tennyson, 77, 333.
Teucer, 101, 113, 124.
Text (Homeric), state of, philologically,
　etc., 18, 29.
Thamyris, 26.
Themis, 148.
Theognis, 68, 154, 235, 279.
Thersites, scene with, 74-5.
Theseus, 301.
Thessaly, its importance in early Greek
　mythic lore, 25. 241.
— land of Homer's traditional an-
　cestors, 26, 322.
— traces of in feelings and customs,
　76, 154, 241.

— in Achilleid, 98, 99, 241-69.
Thiersch, 17, 24.
Thirlwall, 24.
Thought. modes of primitive, 198.
Thucydides, 67 and *passim*.
Tiresias, 31, 123, 293.
Titanic wars, 131.
Traditions. primeval. 129.
Triads of deities. 312-3.
Trojan War, how to be regarded, 242-3.
Trojans, character of, 325-7.
'Tug of war,' expressions regarding,
　200-1.

Ulysses, preeminence of in the Odyssey,
　30.
— the 'Man' preeminent. 35, 83, 86, 358.
— how far the typical hero of Greece,
　50, 305.
— epithets of, 36, 50, 83, 95, 96, 226.
— impersonation of intelligence, 80.
— impersonation of spirit and endur-
　ance, 88, 226, 328.
— matched with Achilles (see also
　under epithets of 'Ul.'), 88, 90.
— as a Bowman, 91, 127.
— not with an equipage, 92, 212-4.
— as probably of small stature, 86, 92,
　331.
— in the Achilleid, 93-6, 157.
— in Pindar, 100.
Unity, forms and aspects of, 11, 12, 42.
Unity of the Odyssey, 21, 29.
Uschold, 289.

Vaticination of dying men. 202.
Vedic analogies, see Hindoos.
Vico, 7.
Virgil, 45, 69, 209, 223, 235.
Völcker, 263, 292.
Volkmann, 12.
Voss, 12.

Weber, 4.
Welcker, 12 and *passim*.
Whately, 149.
Wieland, 9.
Williams, M., 4, 354.
Wilson, Prof., 102.
Wolf, F. A., 7-19 and *passim*.
Wood, R., 'Essay' of, 278, 281, 295, 297.
Writing, art of, 182, 337-41.

Xenon, 6.
Xenophon, 87, 89.

Zend, illustration from, 183.
Zenodotus, 32 and *passim*.
Zephyrus, 252, 280, 286-7, 296, 300.
Zeus, epithets of, 135-8.
— hyperboles regarding, 133.